PASCALE'S WAGER

HOMELANDS OF HEAVEN

Anthony W. Bartlett

Pascale's Wager

Published in the United States by Hopetime Press, Syracuse, New York, 13210.

Original cover art by Susannah and Christopher Bartlett. Background cover photo Alaska North Slope from National Oceanic and Atmospheric Administration, by Rear Admiral Harley D. Nygren.

First Edition 2014

ISBN-13: 978-0615974071
ISBN-10: 0615974074
LCCN: 2014903704

1. Science Fiction. 2. Dystopia. 3. Coming of Age.
4. Religion.

To all Pascales, everywhere

With special thanks to Amber Lough, Cathy Gibbons, Susannah Bartlett, Linda Bartlett and Jim Warren for their astute reading, essential editing, and instant belief.

PASCALE'S WAGER

PART ONE

1. Day 97 1
2. Weather 6
3. Holo-cast 10
4. Friend 15
5. Frostbite 21
6. Day 98 24
7. Menace 27
8. God Talk 30
9. Flight Risk 34
10. Search 40
11. The Lie 45
12. Vigil 50
13. Holy Day 54

PART TWO

1. Touch Down 63
2. Ice Camp 71
3. Conspiracies 83
4. Instruction 95
5. Architecture 109
6. Break Out 120
7. On The Run 129
8. Philosophy 139
9. Borderlands 143
10. Doblepoble 161
11. Entry 165
12. Rave 168
13. Welcome 176

PART THREE

1. Surprise Party 186
2. Nocturnal 191
3. Lovers and Mentors 201

4. Dream Time 212
5. Venice 218
6. Poisoned Banquet 229
7. The Canyons 251
8. Star Student 264
9. Sierra Ride 273
10. Cutting Edge Research 278
11. Detective Work 286

PART FOUR

1. Pitching Tent 294
2. Wilderness Camp 302
3. Story Telling 308
4. Brief Encounter 315
5. A God Is Dead 322
6. Heavenly Rite 332
7. Hell's Fires 339
8. Plague Bringer 357
9. Volunteering 366
10. Brothers In Arms 373
11. Sacrificing The Idol 379
12. Changing Places 386

PART FIVE

1. The Plague 394
2. Wedding Day 404
3. Gathering Chaos 422
4. Canyon Thunder 435
5. Rock Bottom 440
6. Riding Alone 448
7. Stavros 451
8. Crossroads 460
9. Heaven's End 466
10. Fire In The Hole 477
11. Masterpiece 482
12. End Of Time 491

And the Sibyl, with raving lips uttering things mirthless, unbedizened, and unperfumed, reaches over a thousand years with her voice, thanks to the god in her.

Heraclitus

Everybody wants to go to heaven, but nobody wants to die.

Proverbial

If the facts don't fit the theory, change the facts.

Albert Einstein

Love counts faster than light. It is the universal constant.

PART ONE

1. DAY 97

The sun rose, an angry red disk over an icecap waste. The frozen Homeland shivered. Nobody inside the Total Energy Pockets wished to wake to face another day. Even in their sleep, they knew the diurnal systems were about to come on: lighting, heating, music, holograms and announcements. Inside their dreams their souls tensed, trying to hold back the moment.

Cal did not dream. She gazed at the harsh light of dawn creeping through the skylight at the top of the sealed hemisphere. She was willing it to reach the middle line of ceiling rivets before the display of Systems Ignition lit up. There was no reason to want this. It was just a game she played in her head. A way to gain a small advantage over her day, waking early to watch the thin band of light bend across the room before the daytime world clicked itself into life.

Someone stirred in the communal bed. She waited for the movement to subside, praying, hoping for this precious time to last just a few minutes more. The bed was warm and soft, sealed in a thermal envelope. The silvered fabric covering her family was filled with thousands of capillaries which distributed heat equally throughout its skin, siphoning it off to storage cells should it get too warm, or boosting it should the temperature drop. Lifting her head she could see her brother, sister and parents. Their heads, like hers, encased in zippered hoods of the same silvered material. They looked like one of the strange sea creatures, recorded from the old world, which she'd seen sometimes in the holograms.

Before the exhausted light of the sun reached the rivets, the Ignition clicked on. A flashing red spot on a display console set in the wall. Cal knew she had fifteen seconds to go.

***

The Word and Image Announcer appeared simultaneously on two walls of the dwelling. The ritual greeting repeating at set intervals in between a continuous soundtrack of music. There was no way to escape its sound and visuals.

"Welcome to day 97 of our current cycle. All residents of the Homeland are invited to begin this day with hope in everlasting life and an attitude of kindness toward each other."

"That damn WIA!" Cal's brother muttered savagely to himself. "Invited, she says. Really what choice have I got? "

Their twelve year old sister woke up to his voice. "First thing I hear Danny's complaining. It's like he believes he's better than the rest, like he was an Immortal or something."

Cal's mother jerked upright in bed. "Don't talk like that, Sam! You do not speak about Immortals that way. It's blasphemy!"

"Me? He started it!"

Danny laughed as he slid from the silver cocoon with the grace of a cat. "They can come get me anytime. I'm ready."

"What did you say, Danny?" Cal's mother, a small olive-skinned woman, swiveled toward him nervously, as she levered out of the bed. Beside her, her husband groaned. He spoke with his eyes half-shut, struggling to prop himself on his elbows.

"Take no notice. He's just doing it to rile you. Come on, everyone, let's begin the day!"

His voice, with its devout religious tone, seemed to hit a switch in each of them. Everyone began to move with well-drilled precision—even the rebellious Danny. Unzipping themselves from the bed they used the bathrooms and food dispensers that were set into the walls and dressed themselves in thermal suits with a seamless movement in which each person did something different in sequence with the others. It was a well-choreographed dance and even attained a strange kind of beauty because of the holograms that streamed among them. White surf and golden beaches flowed around their bodies and seagulls hung in the air between them as they followed each other across the living space. All the while between bursts of music the voice intoned: "Welcome to Day 97..."

The only person out of step was Cal. She turned to watch the others as she pulled on her suit. She gazed at a seagull swooping by her shoulder. Most of all she watched the sputtering display lights as they kept track of all the systems and functions of the Homeland. Bars and indicators showed heating, water, food, tasks for the day, transport status and time to arrival. Cal counted the frantic blinks in the red and amber alerts before the green lights came on. They flashed at manic speed but she kept count. The counting soothed her and was another of her secret games, one she played everywhere she went.

Cal did not have her brother's feline beauty. Sam, although snide, had spoken the truth. He had something about him that was exceptional. Well-formed, with dark eyes and sculpted features he did seem completely out of place in the confined synthetic space of the TEP (the abbreviation always used for Total Energy Pocket). He was like a caged animal waiting to be free. Cal did not stand out in the same way. She was slightly younger, strong but slim, with softly stated feminine curves. She had dark hair and eyes and some of her brother's natural grace. But there was also a distraction in her manner, a wandering gaze during conversation, which blunted the interest of others. It let her see a great deal of the world while deflecting attention from herself.

At this moment her gaze was directed at the flashing light which said a Sector Communication Vehicle was about to arrive. The display was flickering crazily. Cal already knew in her mind the number of pulses before the communications vehicle hit the port to the TEP and was ready to board. Once the amber light came on there were forty five blinks to go.

***

Outside in the frozen dawn, building shapes that had, moments before, been almost indistinguishable from their icy background glimmered suddenly with a million points of light. The port lights of the TEPs shone in an enormous branching fan, an endless series of stretched arms linked by a monorail system. The rail connected each individual dwelling on its arc with a great central grid of much bigger, dome-like structures arranged down the spine of the fan. Shortly after the lights came on, the communication vehicles appeared like a swarm of electronic beetles. They were small mobile capsules moved on the rails by tractor energy, each having independent destinations and typically holding four persons. The energy was relayed by tall pyramid shapes raised at points along the lines. The communication vehicles—or Bubbles as they were known informally—waited trembling outside the TEPs, vibrating in their equalized energy streams.

3

They would wait for seventy five seconds and not a second longer. The TEP dwellers had that amount of time to exit and board. If they missed the ride they had to put a call into Communications Central and be fined heavily for the dispatch of a second vehicle. Hence the necessity of each family unit working like clockwork the moment ignition fired. It was a matter of conserving energy, something of near mystical value in the Homeland. The conservation of energy lay behind the TEPs austere design, and behind the organization of time, parceling out the precise inputs needed to maintain life. These inputs always had to be balanced against the vast amount of energy required in the production of the permanent arctic climate. The demand for energy shaped everything in the Homeland.

"Your Sector Communication Vehicle has arrived."

Cal heard the announcement as the green light for transport flicked on. She and her brother were scheduled for the Training Center, as always.

"Sector Communications Vehicle for Danny and Cal Anders now ready for boarding. You have seventy five seconds."

Both already knew that. It was the same mathematically exact message every day they went to Training: Cal for technical services, Danny for food supply. But Cal knew it in her bones. She had counted down the last ten seconds before the transport arrived, shooting a swift glance over to Danny to make sure he was ready. Without a word the two of them passed through the vacuum-powered seals as they hissed open and closed, first into the port and then into the vehicle. It had sealed itself hermetically to the port's external door, opening directly into the enclosed space. Nevertheless a blast of cold air always hit the Teppers emerging from their cabins. It was sixty degrees below zero outside and the unheated port air immediately registered a shock. But in their therm-suits the effect was momentary. The doors hissed shut, and, at once, the trembling craft rocketed into motion.

Back inside the TEP the Word and Image Announcer intoned: "Five minutes to Sector Communications Vehicle for Luci Anders, destination Food Production Unit 23. Twelve minutes to Sector Communications Vehicle for Benn Anders, destination Worship Center Five."

Cal's mother was employed in one of the standard

greenhouses and hydroponic units which grew the Homeland's food supplies. Her father had much more weighty employment: he was a Sector Worship Leader. Every day he went to work to lead devotional events and conduct private programs for those in need. Benn fulfilled his duties with eager faith, an essential qualification for his job. The Worship Center was an integral part of everyone's life in the Homeland. Almost everyone attended, and there were dozens of Worship Leaders like Benn scattered throughout the zones of the Sector. No one seemed to know where the religious faith of the Homeland came from, but that was never a problem. They lived within a system of religious belief just as they lived within the rigid schedule of the TEPs, and the unquestioning certainty of their Leaders was a central pillar of their world. Benn and his colleagues kept the Homelanders' hopes fastened to an afterlife of endless warmth, good health and happiness.

Benn stood in front of the port door, waiting with pious calm for his Bubble to arrive.

2. WEATHER

"Wait for it! Here comes the smoke-and-mirrors. Here comes the big lie!"

Cal was sat in place for her first class of the day, in a high, brightly-lit, windowless theater. The circular seating looked across to a raised platform where the professor was speaking. It was one of a range of courses providing technical knowledge needed for Homeland existence, from Energy Production and Conservation, through Propulsion Systems, to Genetic Stocks and Synthetic Food Studies. This one was Climatology and the banks of seats were nearly all filled with students.

The derisive voice whispering fiercely on her neck was Poll's, in the seat directly behind. Without a doubt he was the most brilliant student in the Sector training program but he had been held back for two years for his persistent negative questioning. He would harangue the lecturers, continually deriving opposing arguments from their data. He had sat behind Cal on other occasions, talking to her over her shoulder, but she'd always managed to ignore him, and eventually he'd been told to be quiet by students nearby. This morning, however, despite the crowded auditorium the space around them was somehow empty of other students, and his burning string of comments seemed unstoppable.

"Here it comes, the huge gap in his universe!"

Cal turned and hissed "Shut up!" She tried to look like she was focusing on the lecture.

"Our human survival depends on the Global Weather Shield. As you all know, it is the brilliant invention of Samuel G. Tenet, the scientist sent by God so many years ago: the great ring of nuclear-powered refrigeration plants surrounding the Homeland. Powerful enough to reduce surface temperature it creates a stable area of high barometric pressure, keeping out the chaotic storms destroying the rest of the earth. It's what used to be known as a 'Siberian High' a massive pile of cold air blocking cyclonic activity. Outside the borders of the Global Weather Shield there is a constant hurricane. Inside there is calm. Our task today is to derive the air mass per cubic kilometer and the refrigeration coefficient needed to secure the barrier. It is an essential formula to know and keep in mind. Our survival depends on it. But first to

6

underline the point here's the standard demonstration I'm sure you've all seen before, but it never grows old. Here it is one more time, just for the simple joy of it! "

Stepping away from his podium the lecturer strode toward a table. He grabbed a large empty glass and, inverting it, plunged it into a big transparent basin of water.

"If I keep the glass steady no water enters it. The pressure of air in the glass keeps the water out. This is what Tenet foresaw. A stable climate achieved not by a solid glass giving form to the air. Rather it is the density and pressure of a column of air itself which never allows warmer air to create convection and push it away. As I said, this is what was done, the technology that created our Homeland. A place where we sustain human life as we await the promise of Heaven!"

"Yeah, yeah," Poll muttered viciously two inches from Cal's back. "Forget about the heaven crap, what about the data? You can't stabilize a storm system that way. It will break through any barrier you create. There's gotta be something…"

"Poll Sidak, please leave the lecture hall. I will not tolerate your interruptions." The professor's voice broke angrily into Poll's tirade. The security guards at the door snapped to attention. They glanced knowingly at each other. Poll had a reputation as a damaged item, someone who did not fit smoothly into the Homeland's system. His dismissal from lectures was a regular occurrence and the slightest hint of resistance earned him a rough-handling from the guards plus twenty-four hours in the lock-up. But this time he left his seat without protest.

As he gathered his books he brushed one more time by Cal's ear. "See you outside," he breathed, and exited the lecture hall onto the access platform.

The Training Center, like every other main building in the Homeland, was simply a macro version of the TEPs. Their surface was one of the technical miracles of the Homeland. It was composed of millions of tiny cells which communicated the sun's heat inwards. The top layer received radiated heat the moment the sun came up. Because that source was constant they were able to continually filter warmth to the cells below. The result was to build up a thermal blanket that only little by little lost its warmth overnight. Covered in their fine-sponge bio-plastic the Centers rosé like huge gray-white mushrooms over the land. Against the background of the bleached tundra they were easily lost to sight and when the sun was up the entire scene could merge into a dazzling whiteness that hurt the eyes. Any of the few windows were tinted to keep out the glare, but very few people looked out of them anyway. It was only the interior that had interest. The Training Center structure was of great vertical cliffs, of blocks, halls, rooms, and cubicles, hanging together at multiple levels like a chaotic honeycomb. The levels and spaces were connected by a cat's cradle of pulsing transport tubes and moving walkways. Most of the young people looked forward to hanging out there. It was the closest thing to life they knew.

Poll stood on the access deck to the lecture theater with the security guards eying him contemptuously through the doors. Across the deck, the wall joined a transport tube. Every fifteen seconds in a steady mechanical breath the wall swept open onto the interior of a Communications Vehicle. After five seconds more, if no one was passing through, it swept shut and the Bubble pinged away. Poll gazed dully at the convulsing wall, allowing its hypnotic action to block out his thoughts and feelings. He was tall and angular, with tousled unkempt hair. His long limbs were undisciplined, always somehow in advance of their own movement. Yet the intelligence of his eyes held you and their dark fire convinced you of the power of his personality. Poll was respected by the other students but also feared. They kept their distance from him as someone who meant trouble for himself and anyone seen to be close to him. He was, therefore, almost always alone and the fact that he regularly sat behind Cal and volunteered his opinions into her ear singled her out too. She had tried to ignore him, but now without having decided anything she was being drawn into his misfit world.

The doors of the lecture hall burst open and the students streamed out, lining up to catch the Bubbles to the next class. Poll looked out for Cal and blocked her way as she came through the doors.

"Did you hear what I said to you? What do you think? What do you think about the storms?"

Cal tried to sidestep. "Get away from me! When did I ask you to sit next to me? Or talk to me? You're crazy!"

"Listen," Poll spoke through clenched teeth. "I know there's something going on with you. You look like you don't pay attention but your grades are the best, and I've seen you counting the indicators. I'm certain you'll understand the figures if you let me show them to you."

Students standing in line for the Bubbles were now taking an interest in their conversation. Hardly ever did anyone show that kind of intensity, and a couple of them glanced over expectantly at security who, at this point, were looking the wrong way. Cal knew Poll would be grabbed at once if they saw him harassing her.

"OK, OK I'll talk with you. Just back off or you'll be in the lock-up."

Poll turned around at once trying to control his breathing. The crowd looked disappointed. He spoke sidelong "I'll meet you in Dining. Well set up a time there."

He walked abruptly forward, past the first person in line, and stepped into the next Bubble. The door closed and he was gone, with muffled shouts of protest trailing behind. Cal shrugged disinterestedly at some of the students who turned to her, then buried her nose in a book.

3. HOLO-CAST

At Worship Center Five Benn was putting the final touches to the Holo-cast for the twelve o'clock faith and glory service. When he first arrived he spent an hour in prayer and meditation, then accessed the personalized WIA link. People sent him messages about their relationships. About spouses, about siblings, about the various difficulties they endured living and working together in the confined and regulated conditions of the Homeland. His job was to offer each one consolation and encouragement, directing them to let go of anger and frustration, looking always toward the bliss of heaven to come. There were few pleasures to be had in the TEP world. Whatever discretionary income people held was spent at the workplace stores selling a few luxury foods, or perhaps on the slight variations in fashion in the standard-issue thermal suits. Sport was the one major relaxation activity. Here in Sector Three the preferred sport was swimming. Everyone enjoyed the hours they spent in the warmly heated swimming pools where they could finally forget the unrelenting battle with the cold. Best of all were the competitions, between different zones of the Sector, and even sometimes with other Sectors.

These were the occasions that came closest to evoking large-scale passions. There was a kind of aura attached to the biggest sports stars, some of whom were reported to have retired into lives of exceptional privilege. No one was entirely sure of details but all of the Sectors could remember striking athletes who had suddenly reached a pinnacle of status and disappeared. They were only seen afterward in personal message transmissions saying how happy they were, thanking their fans, and encouraging young people to aspire to the same success. Rumors ran wild, sometimes advancing to the level of a heresy which Worship Leaders like Benn had to deal with. These rumors claimed that the greatest sports stars were taken directly by immortal beings to live in heaven without first having to die. The heresy had expanded to include not only sports stars but also particularly beautiful or gifted individuals. It was because he had more than once found himself having to refute these ridiculous beliefs that Benn had one time mentioned them at home. His daughter, Sam, immediately became quite fascinated with the idea. He regretted having said anything; indeed, only this morning she had repeated the same thing. It was a disgrace for the daughter of a Worship Leader to think like this. He would have a serious talk with her as soon as possible. He should play some of the video files of the stars saying how they had moved to a special Sector in celebration of their success and now wanted simply to be left alone. That should settle the matter. He would add that continuing in the faithful pathway of the Homeland brought everyone in due time to true immortality.

Right now Benn was doing the thing he liked most, the part of his job which was the heart and soul of being a Worship Leader. Before him was a long console with ranks of displays, dials, ports and controls. Using computerized programs, controlling sound, hydraulics, air currents, screens and holograms, the bank of switches allowed the Worship Leader to produce a global spiritual environment. He was able to bathe the crowd of congregants in a stream of strong sensations. It was called a Holo-cast, a sacred performance, and it had the power to lift people up in another world. The worshipers were strapped into seating which could be raised and maneuvered about. They floated gently through space, while angels' wingtips brushed them, clouds bathed them and rays of sunshine struck golden shafts upon them. Strings and birdsong serenaded their ears while a voice of velvet read from sacred scriptures, declaring divine truth and the rewards of a faithful life.

Every Holo-cast was custom-made by the Worship Leader. Mountains, seas, stars and skies, blossom in hues of violet and blue, saffron and green, all could be summoned up and shaken out over the worshipers. Often the sweet smell of perfume, jasmine or myrrh, was spread delicately on the air. At the high point of the service the Worship Leader would rise above the people on a crystal pillar and speak holy words of comfort and hope. This was Benn's finest moment, and as he locked in the midday performance he rehearsed the words he would speak.

"How blessed are we, my friends, to be able to call divine illumination into our minds and souls."

In his imagination he made an expansive gesture, drawing down virtual threads of power attached to his fingers, and at the same time hologram twists of golden light would fall among the worshipers.

"Let us surrender now in faith to visions of glory!" he would

11

say, and all the people would answer fervently "Amen!"

What beauty and wonder there was in his work, and how utterly in contrast to the catastrophe of former times. Most of the relatively small area on earth useful for human use had been wiped out either by massive unpredictable storms or drastic shifts in temperature. No one had known what to do. It was Doomsday, with mass panic, millions starving and numerous additionally destructive wars for control of ever-shrinking resources. How much in contrast then, was the God-given rescue of the Homeland. Its amazing order and security, and the indestructible glory of its Holo-casts. It was his privileged task to remind people of the past, to comfort them in the present, and lift their spirits to a heavenly hope.

He was aroused from his reverie by the movement of people filing into the Center and taking their places. He hit the intro music and gently swelling chords flooded through the stadium while white clouds formed in the high spaces under its roof. Today was an average weekday, so the presentation would be fairly basic: some laughing children running through apple orchards and of course the final fire of divine illumination. Nothing too elaborate. The bigger effects were saved for every tenth day which represented the end of the Homeland week and the standard holy day of the Homelanders. On the 99th day a truly awe-inspiring performance was given. This was the Feast of Storm and Fire, an eagerly anticipated holy day and something very few people would want to miss. The day after, the 100th day, was a day of complete rest and enjoyment. The two days together produced a very special occasion, the conclusion of the Homeland's regular time cycle and its greatest feast. Today the Sector was only two days away from the double holiday.

The program was streaming holograms of sun-dappled children racing among the stadium seating, covering the worshipers with laughing faces and healthy warm limbs, while blossom shook from the trees and fell among them. The audio played a guitar arpeggio and the people visibly relaxed and smiled to themselves and to each other. As Benn rose above the scattered worshipers on his crystal pulpit in his robes of cream and vermillion, he was filled with powerful religious emotion.

"O my friends, let us be mindful of the 99th day festival

which is approaching and its special liturgy. We will experience it once more, the awe and the hope of God's salvation. Let us make ready with attentive hearts for this most important day, when everyone must see the divine power to destroy and create, to punish our sins and yet bring us peace."

"So, now, let us give up all desire for false earthly pleasures and let our thoughts and yearning surrender to the fire of illumination. Thus we will receive the blessing of true and perfect light."

At this last formula an acolyte at the console threw a switch. Suddenly all the heavenly clouds resolved into intense darkness relieved only by a single nuclear fire at the far end of the arena, where the seating gave way to an empty ceremonial setting. There was a collective sigh and "Amen." Then from all points shot trembling rivers of flame flowing powerfully to the single blaze. The sound system generated a thunderous note accompanied by a single piccolo. The tones merged and the bass faded until little by little only the sweet high sound was heard. Just as suddenly the rivers of flame were swallowed in the central fire which blazed up, bathing everyone in a luminous glow and then extinguished, while the piccolo phrase dipped and died in soft surrender. The house lights came up while the seating gently spun back to the floor. The worshipers clicked themselves free and returned quietly to work.

Benn made his way back to his office and took off his robes. He handed them to an assistant to replace in the armoire which contained hundreds of other splendid tunics, veils and chasubles for every occasion. He sat down at his computer and hit the keys, typing "Day of Storm and Fire." A long list of files and folders came up. So many that he had never investigated them all. "Exodus of the Homelanders," "Dividing the Waters: The Weather Shield Miracle," "Fire at the Heart of the Ice": he was familiar with these and had used them all before. Scattered randomly among them were others with less exciting names like "Homeland Climatics" and "Geotherm Theory," and some simply with numbers and letters. It was as if science was mixed in with religion, and, really, this made sense to him—hadn't God given the science that created the Homeland? But really Benn never gave it much thought and this time was no exception. Preparing for the solemn feast in two days he went straight to "Exodus of the Homelanders."

4. FRIEND

"The historic isobar of the Homeland is not possible with the physics they give us! Surely you understand that?"

Poll was staring maniacally at Cal. She had never really talked with him before and if she'd imagined the scene at any other time she knew she would have burst out laughing, or simply turned away. But now as she looked at him she could see an underlying honesty. It caught her and stopped her from shutting him down.

"Relax!" she said. "You have to lighten up. You know they're just itching to expel you. If you go round saying these insane things you'll be doing Refrigeration Maintenance, you know, with frostbite and a short life! Your name's Poll, isn't it?"

Cal knew his name. The young people in the Training Center knew almost everyone's name, and there was always some gossip about Poll. She asked him the question simply to get him off his single topic of conversation. Poll looked at her perplexed.

"I'm Poll Sidak, and you're Cal Anders."

Cal shook her head, "You're something, Poll. You might know a lot of stuff, but it's not just what you know...you know!"

Poll was unfazed. "Really, there's a lot that I *don't* know and...I need your help...."

Cal sighed and looked around her. They were in the Center Dining Area. Thousands of students attended classes at the Training Center and it seemed like most of them were now filing past the stainless steel serving counters at the lunch hour, piling their plates with hydroponic vegetables and synthetic meat. They all wore the same therm-suits but had made some attempt at individualism, with patches or trim, or adjustments for a better fit. Still, everyone was following the Homeland's pathway, staying alive in the relentless regulated existence dictated by their arctic world. Poll was someone looking for another pathway. He was a freak and he was dangerous. Yet now something inside her connected to him and was glad to do so. She looked back at him, this time with a hint of new resolve.

"OK," she said. "I'm up for it. Tell me what you have to tell me."

Poll visibly quivered. He looked as though he were about to

15

start yelling, but he checked himself, and bent his head down to a level with Cal's.

"Basically there isn't enough energy in the reactors to keep out a storm system engulfing the rest of the world." He looked round quickly. "I can't show you the figures right now. I'll slip them to you at the next lecture. You know how it works, don't you, I mean the Global Weather Shield?"

"Well, yes..."

Poll didn't wait for a reply. "It's produced by massive ground and air refrigeration. We're all taught that. They teach us the facts but not the truth—apart from rudimentary equations on energy needed to keep the refrigeration powered up. But even with those figures I've been able to prove there isn't enough air pressure to restrain the hurricane winds they described from before the shield was built. There has to be something more going on, something more complex. What do you think it could it be?"

The question was again rhetorical, for as Cal began to say she had no idea he went straight on without drawing breath.

"And here, here's another one. Do we have any concept of the storm forces created in the rest of the world by the Weather Shield itself? To produce refrigeration there has to be heat exchange. But where does all that heat go? Unless it went somewhere over time it would itself produce massive fronts of low pressure, certainly enough to blow away our precious pile of cold air."

Poll's questions poured out. Cal hardly understood them but suddenly it became intensely exciting just hearing him ask them, sensing they were real, that he was on to something, and she was part of it. Students were taught the principles of nuclear power and refrigeration and what centralized maintenance was required. They were told the nuclear fuel cycle was fully automatic and it would provide an endless generating capability. All that was necessary was to manage its output to maintain the massive refrigeration of the Homeland. It was calm inside its ring, but at the borders everything turned to chaos. For the rest there was religion. God had provided the Global Weather Shield for the remnants of humanity, to convince them of his care and lead them on the pathway to heaven. Once this was explained there were no more questions to ask.

16

In fact Cal had always had a problem with this. She had never fully admitted it to herself, but something was always there nagging at the back of her mind. If God loved everyone and intended to bring them all to a good place why should he put them in such a bad place to begin with? Why not bring them to the good place from the get-go? She suspected that the reason why she counted display pulses was to blot out these terrible questions from her mind. Now Poll was asking his own terrible questions, and for the first time she felt, yes, that really was OK. It was sudden and startling but it was almost as if she had been waiting for it to happen. She wasn't sure about any of the things he was saying, but for the first time she felt truly alive.

As she sat listening and thinking and having this amazing feeling she did not hear her companion's voice steadily rising. People around were staring at them and, suddenly, she realized he was shouting.

"How can they expect people to swallow this stuff? People do, just like the sheep in the holograms chewing stupidly on whatever is put before them!"

Cal fought back a wave of panic. There was nowhere to hide and it seemed very difficult to shift Poll's mood or explain what they were talking about. Then, for almost the first time in her years at the Training Center, she was glad to see Danny, her brother. He was sauntering into Dining in the company, as always, of his posse of beautiful people. By definition they always turned heads, and now Cal waved frantically at them to deflect attention away from herself and Poll. Danny looked around casually and saw it was Cal.

"Hey!" he said. "It's Cal. She's with that crazy guy who's always getting thrown out of class. Let's rescue her."

Danny began to make his way through the tables across to where Cal was sitting. He was trailed by a couple of very attractive girls and a tall young man with a dark-skinned face and a therm-suit covered in black and silver patches. Actually, Danny was pleased to be noticed by Cal. Secretly he admired her a great deal and really would have been pleased to have her join his special group. But Cal always held herself aloof. She lived very much inside her own thoughts and would not be drawn into his circle.

"What am I going to say to him?" Cal muttered fiercely to

Poll who by now was also looking over his shoulder. He shrugged his usual disinterest in other people's responses toward him.

"Is this guy bothering you?"

"Don't be stupid," Cal countered brightly. "He's…he's my boyfriend! Poll, this is my brother, Danny."

It was hard to say who looked the most surprised. Poll's face turned a little ashen.

Danny stared blankly first at Cal, then at Poll, then slowly recovered.

"Oh, yeah, right, great… That's great! Well, hey, say hello to my friends!" He gestured first to a short-cropped blonde wearing a tight gold belt accenting a stunning figure, and then to a raven-haired girl who bubbled with enthusiasm every time Danny opened his mouth. Finally he indicated the young man in the eye-catching therm. "This is Liz, and Esh. And, here, this is Wes."

"And here, guys, is my sister, Cal, with her new…uhh…boyfriend."

The surprise was still echoing in his voice as it trailed off. Cal had never gone out with anyone. She was too different and hard to make friends with. Now, out of nowhere, she had declared herself for an obvious loser.

"Whatever," Danny decided. "If you guys are an item then you'll be together at the 100th Day Fest, won't you?"

Cal had not considered this and was slightly dazed herself by the thought. Romantic relationships in the Homeland were highly organized. In the confined spaces of domestic and social life there was hardly ever an opportunity for young people to be alone. Dating was limited to formal occasions put together by the local Worship Center. Community gatherings called "fests" were held on a regular basis at the Centers, often in conjunction with the religious celebrations. The stadium could be morphed into a kind of town square with the holograph of a fountain in the middle and seating along the edges under colonnades decorated with flowers. Families could walk around the square or gather in groups to chat or sing. Dancing was also offered, a combination of line dances and group circles. Young people looked forward to these occasions intensely, as high points of the social calendar. A couple could be together, in each other's exclusive company, at these events, and even get to disappear briefly behind a few discrete colonnades. The next Fest was due the day after the great 99th day celebration, and it had a special tremor of excitement attached to it. There would be good food, lots of dancing, new dates would be announced and most likely some proposals of marriage. For Danny and his cohorts it was an opportunity to show off even more than usual. But right now Cal was unable to cope with the concept so she just nodded dumbly. Poll just stared.

Danny felt he'd made an impression so he drew up a chair and the others did too.

"What's going on, Poll?"

Poll looked at him as if he had two heads. "I was talking about the weather," he said.

Danny thought he was being sarcastic. He pushed himself back on his chair and glanced around at his courtiers with a mocking grin.

"Some date, eh?"

Esh giggled. Liz smirked.

"He means meteorology." Wes spoke flatly, without irony.

Danny was wrong-footed, but he went with it. "I know that! But can't see why. What's there to talk about? The only weather we get are in the Holo-casts, that's why I like my Dad's shows." He flashed his perfect smile.

"That's exactly my point," broke in Poll, seeming energized once more. Cal was again horrified and she grabbed at what Danny had just said, blurting out anything that might stop Poll talking.

"You know," she said, fixing her new boyfriend with a significant look, "Dad's computer has files dating from very early in the history of the Homeland. They're from before anyone alive today can remember and no one looks at them 'cause they're mostly just numbers..."

This was news to Poll and for the second time in the conversation he looked stunned. "In that case..."

"Yes, indeed," interrupted Cal. "They would be of great meteorological interest. And I would like to invite you personally to come observe my father preparing the Holo-cast and perhaps check them out."

She looked around triumphantly at the company which seemed vaguely aware they'd missed something. Before anyone could comment, she carried straight on to a new topic, one she was certain would get everyone off the weather.

"The swimming finals!" she said. "That's another huge event. Everything's happening all at once! It's tomorrow, Dan, right? And you're competing?"

Her brother at once settled into the role he was best at, the guy with the great athletic body. He wasn't one of the Sector's most able swimmers. He was moderately successful, but every competition gave him the chance to grace the poolside, doing hand springs and flips. His every action was accompanied by the barely suppressed sighs of young female fans who came only to watch him. It was his moment of true glory, and there was something in him that really did expect at such times to be carried off by the gods.

"Yes, I'm swimming," he replied serenely.

"Well, we certainly wish you luck, don't we, Poll?"

Poll who was still registering the information on the Worship Center programs barely acknowledged her.

"Well, we have to get to class now. It was great meeting you guys, really. Come on..."

She stood up with her books and waited by Poll expectantly, until he also got up. As they left she glanced over her shoulder and smiled at Wes.

"That's my sister," Danny said admiringly. And after a pause, "But why is she hanging out with that weirdo?"

5. FROSTBITE

Night in the Homeland and the world was deserted. Lights from the TEPs were extinguished. The great domes of the Centers were likewise shrouded in darkness.

Outside in the lethal cold the only light was the stars. A thousand thousand of them, glittering in the canopy of space. On nights of its cycle the moon would rise up in astonished brilliance over the wastelands of ice. Night was the one true natural beauty of the Homeland. Yet it was very rarely appreciated: the razor edge of minus-sixty made sure people gave it the briefest recognition as they glanced through the external ports. For Cal, however, the night held a precious meaning.

She had found comfort in it ever since, as a child, her father had paused in the port of the TEP and, opening the outside door for a moment, had tilted her head upward. He had told her that every twinkling light she saw was an angel in heaven. When she was in bed she would try to position her head so she could see a patch of the sky through the skylight. So long as she could hold one of those high distant beings in view she would go to sleep comforted. Older now, she sometimes borrowed her father's spare jacket with its extended hood to pull on top of her own. With the annihilating air partially blocked she would exit the TEP to look up at the chorus of the stars. Breathing inside the mask of her hood she drank in the shimmering sky and for a brief instant she felt at one with her world.

Tonight she was anxious to finish the evening meal and for the systems to close down, so at last she could experience that same special peace. Her encounter with Poll had left her deeply unsettled. His restless sense of something not right had infected her. His questions had opened a way for her and it was now impossible not to be deeply suspicious of everything around her. She needed desperately to feel the comfort of her secret guardians, the high fires of the arctic night.

She left the port and stood looking up at the heavens, seeking out the familiar beauty that had always been her anchor. Her cheeks burned in the merciless cold and the vapor of her breath formed an instant crust of ice around her mouth and nose. The boots on her feet grated against unyielding ice, the iron pavement of the Homeland. She sensed around her the city of TEPs but she saw only the merest outlines. The wall of night was impenetrable. She gazed above, pleading with the heavens to be her friend, as so often before. She waited and then, all at once, she was not so sure. She was changing even as she tried to feel the same. She looked intently at the stars, probing the sky for the certainty she sought. Suddenly it was like the dark space both flattened and elongated, stretching back without end. She was pitching headlong into that bottomless, thin nothing, the frozen emptiness around her entering her very soul. She sensed with desperate certainty that if she did not do something she might never again climb out of the abyss.

She remembered Poll, seeing his face in her mind. He had done this to her and now she had to choose. Agree with him and accept his questions as the one honest thing in a universe of lies, or cut him off, have nothing to do with him. Either step could be disastrous. Nothing was certain.

Part of her longed to say, "You're right, Poll, you're right! These questions are our lifeline. They're the only thing that makes sense in this whole horrible world!" But Poll was a freak, a weirdo. His questions might be right, but what confidence could she have in them, or him? The Homeland rules were far too powerful to deviate from and not expect to be destroyed.

There had to be something else, another source. But what was there? There was only God. But Cal had not been able to accept the idea of God. Not when she had understood how awful life was. Her father talked endlessly about heaven as the reason for it all. This seemed to her pointless—putting everyone through this misery, in order to bring them eventually to a better place. And there was the whole thing about being good, of measuring up and being found worthy of everlasting happiness. If you didn't, they said, you went to an even worse place than this one. But that made everything more stupid still. Could anything be worse than the Homeland? If all that God could do was create an ever worse sequence of places for humans to be miserable in, then the whole idea of God was a sick joke.

Cal was desperate. The empty black well of the sky mocked her. Its darkness glittered with icy hate. If God was ever going to have a use it was in the void where her soul was sinking now. Only something like God could catch her. Only God could put life in dead space.

"Please," Cal muttered, "I don't know what you are, whether you are me or you are you, but I need your help right at this moment. I don't care about heaven. I want this world to be good, like we see it in the Holo-casts. Like it must have been before we messed it up. And I do care about hell—because I'm in it now!" After a moment she added: "And while you're at it, please help Poll too, because we're down in this hole together." And in a last falling whisper: "Please, please, I beg you..."

With that she was done. She looked again at the sky and it seemed to stop moving. The stars did not go back to where they had been before, in their comforting majesty, but they had reappeared and they were holding the sky together in some sort of order. They were motionless and she was motionless, and everything was dull and lifeless, but it no longer seemed menacing. She was not sure how long she stood there, emptied of feeling, almost not feeling her surroundings, until all at once she realized her nose and cheeks had stopped hurting. She was gripped by another, much more practical fear: the tale-tell signs of frostbite. She turned rapidly and re-entered the port and then the family cabin. She went straight to the bathroom and ran a bowl of warm water from what was left of the day's allowance. She plunged her face in it and soon felt a fierce pain shooting through her cheeks and nose. She knew at once the blood was returning, she was going to be OK.

6. DAY 98

The tumbled line of cloud heaped under a wash of amber gave evidence of the storm-world, a grim chaos held at bay by ingenious technology. The sun's first rising was obscured by the thick layer of cumulus, but then it emerged in sullen crimson and quickly changed to the dazzling lantern that presided, ever without warmth, over the icefields of the Homeland.

Out there beneath that far horizon thousands of powerful refrigeration units condensed and re-vaporized their gasses, pumping them through a vast underground network of heat exchanges, creating the artificial tundra. Wherever the network ran it froze the earth, and then the arctic ring extended its grip inwards until everything was an unbroken platform of ice. Cal gazed through the observation window next to the door and imagined the machines at work maintaining the rigged climate of the Homeland. For the first time she wondered about the true numbers behind it all. How did it all really happen, and what was beyond the horizon?

She had never thought to ask these questions before Poll put them to her, and now they pounded in her brain. No one had ever traveled farther than the refrigeration plants. No one ever thought of doing so. The only people even near the borders were the maintenance crews, and to work in one of them was to be sentenced to a wretched life and, very possibly, a short one. Only criminals went out there, and the security guards in charge were all criminals themselves. They were people who had produced their own hierarchy and who relished opportunities for cruelty. Abandonment on the ice was rumored to be a frequent practice by the guards. For anyone to be out there on their own meant certain death: no one could survive a single night on the permafrost. As for someone actually breaching the border and experiencing the chaos of wind and flood beyond, that was undreamt of. The world outside the Homeland was the story of religion, a place everyone had been saved from, by God's mercy and the Global Weather Shield. To return there voluntarily would be flying in the face of the universe itself. It would be to deny religion, to engage in suicide, and to be an outlaw, all at once. Yet Poll had gone there in his mind, and somehow he had brought her with him.

24

After her experience the previous night she had been unable to find sleep. Every time she dozed off the shocking nothingness of the stars came back to her and brought her awake with a jolt. Now she stood at the observation window where she'd been from the first hint of light. She was very cold, but she didn't care. For the first time in her life she was seeing things as they were. She saw the whole earth out there, not just the country of salvation, the Homeland. She saw the sun rise as if for the first time, and as it cleared its curtain of cloud she felt as if the planet moved under her feet. As the earth pitched forward she fell with it, down into the forbidden zones, the badlands, the nameless world of flood and storm. She fell but she did not die. Instead she found herself flying across the surface of the waters, swooping and soaring again, seeing in her mind's eye the wild immensity of seas covering the face of the earth. Across them, scattered here and there among the waves, were desolate mountain chains and storm-lashed isles. She fell and soared like a great solitary bird, over the unending ocean.

"Cal, Cal" her mother's voice was calling anxiously. "What on earth are you doing out there? Have you gone crazy? What are you looking at?"

In the background the voice of the WIA was also speaking: "Welcome to day 98 of our current cycle. All residents of the Homeland are invited to begin this day with hope in everlasting life and an attitude of kindness toward each other."

She heard these voices as if in a dream. She was plunging deeper and deeper into the world beyond the border. Everything was gray and bleak, with relentless cloud-cover and roiling sea. Suddenly her brain was stabbed by a blinding flash, and she was falling even farther and faster, into an enormous well of light. Her legs buckled beneath her and she fainted, unable to stand the terrible brightness inside her head.

"Oh, my God," her mother screamed. "Benn! Benn!"

Her father had just unzipped his bed covering and saw Cal fall to the floor.

"How long has she been standing there? We've got to get her back to bed at once. Someone turn on the heat servo right away."

They stumbled over each other to get to her, half carrying, half dragging her to the bed.

"Danny, help us," cried her mother. "Switch on the servo."

25

"Yes, and hit the emergency code to Communications," panted his father.

Danny took in the scene open-mouthed. "Whoa! What's up with her?"

"Just help us," yelled his mother. By this time they had threaded and pushed Cal inside the bed. Danny leaned over and flipped the servo switch on the wall and quickly returned to observe his sister. She was just regaining consciousness.

"Where am I?" she whispered.

"Where have you been is more like it," Danny said. "You look really strange."

"Leave her alone, Danny," snapped his father. "And send that code, or shall I?

"OK, OK, I'm on it." Danny sprang out of bed and hit three buttons on the Communications Console. A voice asked for details of the emergency. Danny texted a message back. "Sister half froze, watching sunrise without therm-suit."

7. MENACE

Later that morning Danny told his group about the family drama.

"You would not believe it, unless you'd been there! She was out cold, and I mean cold, I felt her. It was like she'd been on the icefields all night. What was she thinking?"

"Is she going to be OK?" Esh asked with feeling.

"Well, Emergency got there as I was leaving. They'll check her out and everything. But, if you ask me, it can't be a coincidence that it happened just after she got involved with that Poll guy. He's had some sort of bad influence, I swear!"

"And what would that be?" Wes drawled.

"What did you say?"

"He said, that's not cool," interpreted Liz, keeping the peace.

"Yeah, really." Danny looked at Liz, distracted by another thought, trying to remember what it was.

"Wait! Didn't I see you with some strange man earlier? Who was that? He looked kind of different."

Liz reddened a little. "Oh, that was Dante. He came from another Sector. He's cool. He's interested in swimming." Then almost as afterthought, "Oh yes, he wants to meet you, Dan."

"That's unusual. Not that he wants to meet me," he said, grinning shamelessly, "but that he's from another Sector. Those people only come for the inter-sector competitions."

"He said he was observing, something like that," Liz trailed off.

"Well he found you pretty quick. I'll check him out. Don't want anyone moving in on my girl, do I?"

Wes who was leaning back in his chair spoke up. "Look who's coming."

Everyone followed his eyes. Making his way toward them in an ungainly but determined fashion was Poll.

"Oh boy, that's all we need." Danny was openly hostile, staring straight ahead. No one else made eye contact. Poll did not seem to notice.

"Where's Cal?" he asked abruptly, arriving at the table.

No one answered.

"What's the matter with you? I asked you, where's Cal?"

"You messed her up, that's what" Danny shot back.

27

"What? You're not making any sense. Speak plainly!"

"In words of one syllable, genius, she's been acting weird ever since she began hanging out with you. She didn't sleep and almost froze. We had to call Emergency."

Poll looked at Danny, but his look went through him and out the other side. "Where is she? I've got to see her."

"You go anywhere near her and we'll turn Security on you. You're a public menace!"

Poll said, "You don't understand what's going on, do you?" He turned and walked away.

Danny gazed furiously at the retreating figure. "If he goes anywhere near my sister I'll kill him!"

Well, he won't get near her today at least." Esh tried to calm the situation. "She'll probably be on medical supervision at home and he'll never get transport to see her."

"Yeah," Liz joined in. "Don't worry, Danny, it'll all blow over. You've got to concentrate on the competition this afternoon. You know you've a great chance in the 400."

Danny brightened. "You're right, I'm bound at least to place. It's going to be soooo cool!"

***

Poll guessed to some extent what had happened to Cal. He already believed she was different from the rest: that is why he sat behind her and tried to get her attention in the first place. She tried not to show it, looking like she was day-dreaming all the time, but there had to be something special going on with her. Her grades were always good and every now and again if you caught her looking you could see that thing, whatever it was, happening: she saw everything in a way other people didn't. He was powerfully drawn to her, as the only other person anything like him in the Sector. And now he had told her his questions it made sense they would affect her. What kept him going personally was the will to ask questions and to accept the consequences come what may. But that did not stop moments of free-floating anxiety when he had doubted his own mind. Perhaps it was something like this had happened to her. In this sense Danny was probably correct: he was to blame for what happened. At the same time he did not think he had done wrong. He'd seen signs in Cal of the same deep

28

disconnection to everything that he'd experienced. All he'd done was to bring it to the surface, where it could take on real shape and thought. In that way he had helped her be more herself: it was a matter of truth.

As he exited Dining he thought feverishly of what he should do. He wanted urgently to see Cal, both to support her but he also wanted to hear what she had to say. She might have understood something better than he had and have some answers for him. But going to see her in her TEP was out of the question. Private transport around the sector was severely limited. Such visits were always arranged through the Worship Centers and their Leaders for people with known connections. The only people who knew they had any kind of relationship was Danny and his crew, and they saw him as a cause of her problems not the cure.

Thinking of the Worship Center reminded him of Cal's invitation to see her father's files. Tomorrow was the big 99th day and it was certain that her father would be at the Worship Center getting ready. He decided what he could do. Everyone had a right at any time to request counseling with a Worship Leader. He would contact the Center and arrange an immediate visit, and so be able to talk at least with Cal's father. He went straight to a Communications Booth and put in a code for counseling at Worship Center Five. The text came up at once: "Transport for Poll Sidak. Main port, four minutes."

29

8. GOD TALK

Cal had recovered rapidly from her fainting spell, brought on more by the shock of her vision experience than by the cold. Medical Services had placed her on home rest, but she contacted her father on the WIA link and begged him to arrange a transport to the Worship Center. Benn was persuaded she'd come to no harm, and anyway he wanted to question her about what had happened. It was not hard for him to get clearance and by mid-morning she was in the Holo-cast control room.

"Dad, you know you said that some of the files come from very early in the Homeland's history, not just the world before it. Can you show me where they are? Is it possible to see them?"

"Why are you suddenly interested in these matters, Cal? What's happening to you?"

"I know, Dad, I know. It's hard for me to explain. But I met this student. He was asking questions about things."

"What things?"

"Well, the Homeland's weather, the Shield, the rest of the earth, things like that."

"All these questions are answered by our faith, our story of salvation. You know that, Cal." Benn spoke with firm religious conviction.

"But his questions seemed true, and they gave me a kind of hope. Is that wrong?"

"What happened this morning did not seem hopeful. It caused a lot of anxiety. And I don't know about this young man. He sounds more disturbed than you. What's his name?"

"He's called Poll, and I'm sorry, Dad, I am. I can't really explain what happened this morning. It was like one of your Holo-casts except it wasn't a hologram. I thought I was really seeing it."

Benn looked closely at his daughter. A different thought occurred. "Perhaps God gave you a vision. Perhaps he was answering your questions more directly."

Cal seized the chance. She knew her father probably anticipated God's answers in line with everything he already believed, while what she had seen seemed more like fresh questions. But here was the opportunity to put her father's mind at rest, plus get his help.

30

"Yes, perhaps God did. So would you let me look at your Holo-cast files? They might help me understand the things God was showing me."

Benn hesitated. "Only theological students are allowed access to those files…"

"Well, I think I've just become a student of theology," she said.

Benn smiled at his daughter and softened. He wanted to help her. After all that was his job as a Worship Leader, and, who knows, perhaps what she was saying was genuine and this was her path to becoming a Worship Leader herself? All the same he could not hand over the precious tools of his trade without communicating their immense holiness.

"Cal, all these files come from our distant past, from the depths of our Homeland story. They were recorded during the time the world changed. Nothing can match or replace their importance, the story of the people God raised up to preserve the human race and lead it to its destiny. They are God's gift to guide us on the road to heaven, a treasury of divine light. They come from the fire of illumination, the holy mystery itself!"

"I believe that, Dad, perhaps more than you understand. I just want to see that light more clearly, I really do."

***

Down below in the reception area Poll was having his own introduction to the theology of the Worship Center.

"You cannot see the chief Worship Leader. That is by appointment only. There are two other spiritual counselors available. You can see one of them."

The assistant spoke with a flat voice. The rules were inflexible. Poll looked at her with disgust but tried to keep his voice even.

"I am a friend of his daughter who has been ill. He will want to see me."

"Personal appointments are made through an individual's place of work or training. You requested an opportunity for counseling. Please take a seat, and someone will be with you shortly."

Poll stood back from the booth and looked around. It was a

long time since he had been to a Worship Center. Of course he had been many times as a child and had enjoyed the Holo-casts, but once the questions started coming he had stopped. He had preferred the acute boredom of the TEPs to the frustration provoked by the Centers. Now all that frustration welled up inside him. He took another step back and shouted with a harsh, discordant voice.

"I have questions, serious questions, here in this place. I have the right to speak to someone in authority!"

At once he got the receptionist's attention. She was alarmed. There seemed to be no security—evidently this was a place of peace—so Poll pressed his advantage. He got down on his knees and shouted even louder.

"I have a question to ask God, a really important question, and only a person of religious authority can answer. My question is this: where does all the energy go? What happens to it? That's my question and I ask God for an answer. I need God to answer!"

His last words rang out with such force they seemed to make the heavy walls of the dome shake. People in the area were startled, looking around uneasily. The receptionist was already on the intercom reporting to the Worship Leader the presence of a disturbed individual. Benn could hear Poll's voice above that of the receptionist and he was himself shocked. He'd never heard anything quite like this before. Cal heard it too.

"That's him, the student I was telling you about, I recognize his voice, and there's only one person who'd do anything like that, Poll! He's here for your help!"

Benn spoke to the assistant. "Tell him I'll be down at once."

Cal sprang from her chair. "I'm coming too. He's come to see me as well. I know."

Benn didn't argue. He was anxious about the abnormal behavior; it was vital to deal with it promptly. It also seemed a heaven-sent opportunity to evaluate this person's relationship with his daughter, so having her along was a good thing. They entered a transport idling on the access deck outside his office, and in less than a minute they arrived in the reception area. Poll had been informed of the Worship Leader's imminent arrival and had fallen silent, but he was still on his knees in the middle of the concourse.

Benn hurried over to him and grabbed him by the shoulders, half lifting him to his feet. The moment Poll saw the man coming toward him with Cal beside him he relaxed. He allowed himself to be led without ceremony to a counseling room there on the concourse.

"Please sit down, young man," Benn began. And then to Cal: "I need to see this young man alone for a moment. It's a private counseling. Please wait outside until I call you in."

Cal smiled brightly at Poll, nodding meaningfully to him as if she was agreeing with something, while allowing the door to swing shut. All at once Poll felt a glow, a totally new sensation for him. Looking at Cal right now it was as if a cold immobile world had suddenly began to yield. If something had happened to her it was obviously a positive experience, as if she'd gone through something and come out better, stronger. And she seemed to want to communicate something to him, something she knew. He sensed an opening, and she was the key. Somehow she had seen or grasped something important and would now help him unlock the secrets that oppressed him. It was like a light turning on inside his head. He sensed in her, or began to sense, possibilities that went further than all his arguing had ever done.

"Worship Leader Anders, please let your daughter come in with us, I need to speak to her as well."

9. FLIGHT RISK

At the Sector's main Sports Center the crowd was on its feet, cheering madly as the competitors surged to the finish line. It wasn't Danny's best event and he was trailing in fifth place. All the same his passionate tribe of teenage fans was screaming his name as if he were in the lead. Indeed he emerged from the water like a victor, pumping the air with his fist and looking around in broad triumph. The actual winner was confused, checking the times on the digital display to confirm that he really had come in first. He continued to be frustrated, for a cheer went up as each of the names and times were given, but beginning with Danny who got the most fervent cheer of all.

The excitement in the Center was unparalleled. It seemed to make the electronic display and the pool itself brighter. Everything shimmered with a special brilliance, more even than the sacred performances could produce. For Danny it was a totally wild feeling and when his name was announced he did a forward flip on the artificial beach surface. He landed on his knees with his hands spread wide, sending his fans ecstatic. The noise was deafening. He caught sight of Esh and Wes high in the stands waving and shouting. At the other end of the pool he could see Liz warming up, her beauty even more striking in the frenzied atmosphere. Suddenly he saw the stranger to whom she had been talking earlier—Dante—very close to him in the crowd. Now he could see him more clearly he thought his face was somehow different from anyone else's. It did not have the drawn, dull look that everyone who lived in the Homeland took as normal. Danny was instantly attracted to that look. It was something he didn't have, and he immediately wanted it. The man smiled and made a beckoning motion.

High in the bleachers Esh and Wes saw Danny walk over to the stranger, but Liz's race was about to begin and they were distracted. When they looked back Danny and the stranger had disappeared, lost in the frenzy which was erupting all over again. Liz was not only good-looking but she was an excellent athlete. The race was between her and one other girl and they were both way ahead of the field. Danny's partisans were screaming and chanting for Liz and the excitement they generated infected everyone. In the final two lengths Liz relentlessly drew ahead. She came in three strokes ahead of her rival and emerged from the pool looking like a goddess. Everyone was cheering. Down at the pool edge Danny sprinted over to Liz in her moment of glory. He grabbed her by the hand, speaking animatedly. Very shortly the two of them ran, laughing, from the poolside.

***

In answer to Benn's indignant query of why he needed to speak with his daughter, Poll began to explain his issues with the Weather Shield and the numbers. He mixed these with vague metaphysical questions, statements of personal unhappiness, and hints that Cal had helped him where nobody had before. If he was able to talk with her, with her father present, then her father would begin to understand. Benn was irritated with the notion that his daughter might have a better grasp on theological issues than he did. He interrupted Poll. To demand an answer from God was disrespectful, and anyway the Holo-casts held the answers to everything.

"But that's exactly wrong, sir. The Holo-casts never explain the overall energy of storms in the planet, and they never say what happens to all the heat produced by the refrigeration."

"That's verging on the blasphemous, young man. I would advise you to be much more careful."

Poll glanced bleakly at the Worship Leader. His only hope was Cal.

"Look, I know something happened to your daughter, but it's good. She has understood something. You must see that just looking at her. If we can only talk together then I'll have my answer!"

Benn was caught. Talking with Poll was like an abyss opening up under his feet. It could get worse. He'd be obliged to take stern measures, something he was loath to do. He'd already admitted to Cal the possibility she had been granted a vision. Perhaps it was true, and she offered the one best hope of bringing this strange youth to his senses. He got up, went over and opened the door to where Cal was sitting in the reception area.

"Come on, both of you, I want to talk to you in my private office."

The three of them took the Bubble back to the Worship Leader's suite, but the moment they were alone in the transport the two young people could not contain themselves. Benn was helpless to stop them.

"Tell me what happened, Cal. Tell me everything."

"It's hard to describe what happened. Last night I thought I was losing my mind, basically because I started to agree with you. Then this morning I seemed to be flying, out beyond the borders, into the storm world."

"You're kidding! You went beyond the borders! You penetrated the storm! What was there? What did you see?"

"I don't know, Poll, there was a bright light, and warmth, I think. I remember feeling it. Really, I didn't see anything."

"Sure you did, you're special, Cal. You see stuff other people don't!"

By this time they were in Benn's office and there finally he took charge.

"Please sit down, and remember we're here because of you, young man. You were asking for help. This is not about my daughter."

"Yes, sir, that's correct. But I think my question to God was answered by Cal being here. That's what I'm trying to tell you. She has the key to unlock the whole thing."

"What do you mean?"

"Well, you heard her, didn't you? She's had a vision of the storm world, and we will have a lead on what to look for in the Holo-cast files!"

Benn's mouth fell open and then just as quickly snapped shut. But before he could explode Cal rushed to explain.

"Don't get mad, Dad. I already told him about the files and he's only saying what I was saying—if they can help explain my vision they can explain a lot of other things too."

Benn blew between his lips in barely suppressed anger. "This is what I cannot accept—that there is some truth we don't know, something that has been kept concealed. This is what this young man is saying, and it has infected you, Cal."

"That's not it at all, Dad. If there is something in the files, that is our story. Don't you see? It's only that it's been forgotten or ignored."

Boldly she shifted the argument, "Why be afraid that the files can threaten our faith? If you believe in our story you have to believe in the files. So you see, you must allow us to look at them!"

Benn's shoulders slumped. His daughter's logic seemed irresistible. He'd known these files ever since he was these young people's age and everything he'd ever found there had supported his faith. It was true, he'd never researched a fraction of them; no Worship Leader had. There were far too many well beloved well-known resources to go too far afield. If he really did have faith in these records of grace then he had to say yes. It would also dispose of the problem of how to handle Poll. "And who knows," he thought, "maybe I'll discover new material to use in the presentations? I could become the greatest Worship Leader the Sector has ever known."

***

Away beyond the rim of the frozen Homeland, beyond the refrigeration and nuclear power plants, where the climate had already changed to fierce wind gusts and wild squalls of snow, a rocket shuttle stood waiting. Deep inside a metal tunnel at the base of a half-mile incline, it was like a bullet loaded in the chamber of a gun, except this bullet was able to re-enter the barrel of the rifle, guided with pin-point accuracy on a return flight. The shaft was set in a deep quarry in a chain of hills, so the shuttle departing or re-entering the muzzle would be swallowed by clouds at the level of the mouth. If by remote chance someone was observing from the Sectors it would be indistinguishable from a dull flash of lightning.

Service lights gleamed from a string of support buildings on the surface and along a passageway leading inside the great blast-resistant base of the tunnel. A flurry of activity was occurring in one of the buildings, a small office and control hut. Outside the hut a caterpillar tractor stood idling with no one in it. It had just disembarked three passengers who entered the office directly, two of them tripping over each other as they looked about in amazement. Inside the office was a fourth person who at once began a sequence of procedures with the newcomers. Blood samples were taken, tested and recorded. A camera flashed, retina images and finger prints were scanned. All the information was entered into a computer and transmitted in a radio message.

The four individuals stood around chatting, two of them excited and trembling like children at their first party. A return message was received and immediately the two guides clicked out of some computer screens, threw some switches and led the other two back to the tractor. Together they made the short trip to a garage where they parked the tractor and then crossed a compound and entered the passageway. Their feet sounded a tattoo on the metallic surface as they half ran to an elevator at the end. Its door already lay open and they took the car hundreds of feet down to the level of the shuttle. They exited on a heat-discolored steel deck lit by brilliant floodlights. Before them an automated gantry stretched across the empty cavernous space to the cone of the rocket and an open hatch. The guides assisted their nervous charges along the gantry and through the hatch, showing them to two passenger seats and helping them secure the safety harnesses. One of the guides closed the hatch and when both of them were also strapped in they hit some switches. The gantry separated and retracted and a shield closed across the access deck. Almost simultaneously a firing sequence began. Exhaust from ignited fuel hissed and billowed around the base, the shuttle began to tremble and gradually move forward. Then there was a sudden convulsive flash and huge increase in power. A sheet of fire and smoke broke in all directions and the frame of the craft shot forward with exponential speed up the tunnel. The noise was deafening and the sensation terrifying. After what seemed like an eternity of shaking and roaring the shuttle burst from the mouth of the tunnel into the open air.

For the next few seconds its trajectory maintained a shallow angle toward the sky, like a great bird in a long low take-off. Very quickly it penetrated deep into the storm world and was met by the full power of the winds. Their hurricane force caught it like the branch of a tree, whipping it round. But the ship had been designed to veer with the wind and continue to trim around and upward until it cleared the stratosphere. On a return trip, it would come in at a steeper pitch and level out to the angle of the tunnel just past the most powerful winds. On this escape trip the lucky pair, Danny and Liz, were absolutely terrified. They could not believe what they had done and what was happening. They both screamed and groaned, holding onto their seats, knuckles showing white. Their two guides turned to them and flashed their brilliant smiles. Dante, who had spoken to them at the Sports Center, and told them of the unique privilege for which they were being chosen, yelled above the throbbing and shaking.

"Don't worry kids, it's almost over."

His companion whose name was Milton bellowed, "Really, you've no idea. You're going to enjoy every second of the next one thousand years!"

10. SEARCH

Esh and Wes waited at the changing room entrance for the heroes of the hour to come out, but there was no sign of them. Unable to take the waiting any longer they went inside to search; they were nowhere to be seen. Out on the concourse again they looked at each other in bewilderment, and then in irritation.

"They're playing some sort of stupid game," growled Wes. "What are we supposed to do? Wait till they decide to turn up and jump out in front of us and shout 'Boo!'?"

"I don't know," Esh replied. "They looked pretty psyched. It must have something to do with the guy Danny was talking to."

"Well, where could they go? Do you think went back to Training? It's about the only place they could."

They set out on a search of the limited range of public spaces in the Sector, but they continued to draw a blank. In desperation they went finally to the Worship Center. When they arrived the hot topic among some young people standing in the reception area was Poll's freakish action earlier in the day.

"Seems like everyone's cracking up," Wes remarked sourly. "And where's the weirdo now?"

"Oh, Cal's Dad came to stop him, and Cal was with him. They all went off to his private office."

Wes and Esh felt that the drama at the Worship Center was not unconnected to what had happened to Liz and Danny. Disturbances like this occurred so rarely in the Homeland that the two situations surely had to be linked. They decided to wait for Cal and Poll, but they still had more frustration to endure. Poll's crisis interview with the Worship Leader was still going on. Or at least that's what they thought. In reality Cal and her misfit companion were working their way through the labyrinth of files buried in the Worship Center computer. Benn had finally and grudgingly granted them access.

The Worship Leader used a relatively limited range of themes in his presentations. They were gathered conveniently under a few icons, with headings like "Inspiration," "Relaxation," "Consolation," or standard cycles of the Tenth and Hundredth Day festivals. He showed these to Cal and Poll on his monitor, then showed them how to search the resource folders. By typing in certain names like "Mountains" or "Seascape" any number of files would quickly come to view. It was also possible to pull up playlists of countless videos and holographs from the old world, including a vast number of environmental records, either beautiful or catastrophic. Poll and Cal had very little experience accessing information from computers. There were no independent computers in the TEPS, only the WIA feed and its holograms. In Training it was always a matter of clicking on a standard icon or at most typing in a program referenced by an instructor. The opening up of searchable data was something totally new. Poll and Cal felt a surge of excitement.

"Is there a way of looking at the whole thing overall, a catalogue of all the files, so we can find areas we're interested in?" Poll asked.

Benn shrugged his shoulders irritably. "I suppose you could look in the main directories, but I myself never go in there. There's no reason, and I'm not sure if I even know how to."

All the same, he typed a series of letters with stars and slashes and after a quite a few attempts he eventually opened up a directory—a vast list of numbers and acronyms.

"There you are. But I doubt if you'll make any sense of it." He stood up from his chair and sarcastically waved toward it. Be my guest!"

At once both Poll and Cal moved to sit in the chair, then backed off laughing. They leaned in together over the computer, beginning to scroll down the endless page. It did not seem to be in any order. They clicked randomly on the links and got pages and pages of code. It looked like math calculations or equations, scattered with acronyms and names which made no sense. Once or twice they got a fragment of a video, or random images of landscape or animals.

Cal said, "I suppose a lot of this could be source code for the holograms. And some of it may be from the original period of the Homeland. But without knowing how to analyze it, it means nothing."

Benn gave a smug smile, "Exactly! And what you have there is only one of the main directories, there are dozens more."

Poll bit his lip. They desperately needed to find a short-cut. He asked the Worship Leader whether it was possible to list any of the material by date. Benn said he'd seen a date stamp on one or two of the programs, but normally there was nothing. It looked like he was right. Running down the page and opening files they saw very few dates. It was almost as if they'd been systematically omitted. They did, however, notice some of the acronyms and names reoccurring. Cal asked her father whether they meant anything to him, but he had no idea what they were. The only name that any of them recognized was Tenet, from the history of the Global Weather Shield. For lack of any other lead they opened a couple of files with his name. This only led them to further lists of numbers and names. They seemed like locations but, again, without any dates. Scrolling through one of the sub-lists, however, they had a stroke of luck. A line that made perfect sense: "Nuclear Power Plant Building, P. 79. Approved 9.5.2036."

"Yes," Poll cried triumphantly, gesturing fiercely at the screen, "Now we're getting somewhere."

But when they opened the file it was the same jumble of meaningless numbers. Still Poll persisted: "If we can find other names and dates we can begin to build some kind of a picture."

He entered a search for "nuclear plant," then "nuclear power," but the scans took forever and only retrieved one other link. This time there was almost nothing in the file, just a simple number. It almost seemed as if logical search pathways had been deliberately removed.

Cal took over the pursuit. "Wait, what if we put P.79 in the search? We know it exists, so there might be something else on it, right?"

She entered the search and almost immediately the computer produced a video file in the folder "Inspiration" with the simple name of "Building P.79."

"Yessss!" yelled Poll, and Cal clicked on the file.

Slowly there struggled into view what looked like a half-built reactor, with reinforced concrete taking shape as cooling towers and reactor hall. The video was grainy and murky, taken in what seemed to be a violent storm of rain and wind. Pieces of plastic sheeting whipped across the site and the few figures moving in and out of shot were wrapped in oilskins, their heads bent against the elements. A voice-over commentary spoke of the glorious sacrifices of the Homeland pioneers. Poll was deflated.

"Well, that doesn't tell us very much. Just the usual stuff." He stared glumly at the monitor and Cal clicked off the video.

"I told you," declared Benn. "Now will you believe me? There is no other story but the one our faith has always taught us!"

Cal wasn't listening. "I suppose we could try the same thing with that other power plant number we came up with..."

And without waiting she keyed in S.40. But again there were no results.

Poll shut his eyes and tried to think. "What happens when things go wrong, you know, when programs break down? They have to do sometimes. So there has to be some kind of backup directory. One with more of a logical structure."

Benn made a concerted effort at self-control; he had to see this thing through. He clenched his teeth and hit an intercom switch on his desk, calling for his technical assistant. The acolyte came almost at once, a bespectacled young man with an officious manner. "Nat, please tell my guests what happens when a computer program fails to run."

"Well, that's a problem situation. You have to link up to the network, in order to reboot the program."

Poll asked, "You mean there are computers behind this one?"

"Yes, of course, they back each other up."

"Can we get into the network, I mean now?"

Nat looked unbelievingly at Poll and then at Benn who was breathing heavily in frustration. He glared at everyone fiercely but nodded his permission. Nat raised his eyebrows but sat down at the computer and hit a couple of keys then entered a password. The screen lit up in a completely new way.

"Dad, why does he have a password and you don't?"

"I gave Nat the password. I have implicit trust in my acolyte."

Nat glanced at them with a superior look. "I am deeply conscious of the sacred trust Worship Leader Anders has conferred on me."

He began voice-selecting the screen and Poll and Cal were both impressed with this new technique. The network he was exploring had all the icons Cal and Poll had seen before. When they were opened they glimpsed the same material as before. Nat was selecting in and out at speed, really not wanting them to see, but both Cal and Poll glimpsed a new icon. It was titled "Trash."

"Hey, what's that? Can you open that one?"

"What for? There's nothing in it, just corrupt files, that kind of thing."

"It looks interesting. Why don't you open it?"

Reluctantly Nat opened the folder. Benn drew closer, involved now despite himself. Inside the data looked even more random and indecipherable. Benn relaxed again, hardly bothering to hide a smirk.

Cal leaned over and on a whim typed in the second code name, S.40.

There was a pause and then abruptly a video symbol showed, but this time on its own and outside a presentation folder.

"What's this?" Poll hunched forward. Cal hit the icon. Once again moving images appeared on the screen but entirely unlike what they had seen before.

They all stared blankly at the monitor.

"Holy shit!" said Poll. Cal said, "Oh my God!" Benn, completely exasperated, demanded, "What?"

11. THE LIE

On the screen was a bunch of men and women bathed in brilliant golden light. They men were stripped to the waist, the women in tank-tops, all tanned to a walnut brown. They were dirty, dusty and happy, their arms around each other's shoulders, joking and smiling broadly. In the background were the same half-completed buildings and towers. Around the scene, to the side and behind, everything was brown and green. There was no sound commentary this time, just the group posing for the camera. It lasted only about seven seconds then blinked out.

"Don't you see?" cried Poll. "This has to be something else going on. They're building a nuclear reactor and there's no storm, nothing like it. It proves there's more to the world than storms. There has to be some other place, different from the Homeland!"

"Don't be ridiculous," answered Benn, his voice rising in anger. "It proves nothing of the sort. There had to be some good weather during pioneer times."

"But, Dad, look at the color of their skin. How could that happen in a couple of days? And they're so happy! I've never seen pioneers look like that. That's the way Immortals are supposed to look!"

Poll chimed in immediately: "It's proof positive that what you preach is a cover-up!"

"That's enough," exploded Benn, reaching to pick up the phone. "I'm calling Security and having you detained. You will be reported to the Control Council for blasphemy and heresy."

Cal gasped. "And you," he said, turning on his daughter, "Go to the Worship Area and wait for me. You will never speak with this deviant again!" And, into his phone, "Security to my office, now!"

He turned to his acolyte who was looking shocked and ordered him to shut the computer down. Poll knew what was coming. He jumped from the chair and headed out of the room. Cal stared open-mouthed. She had never seen her father react this way before. "Dad, you can't ..." she protested feebly and trailed off.

Two security officials arrived almost at once, dressed in their black drill with gold trim. They had been put on alert by the assistant after the previous incident. But they had missed Poll.

"Sidak has already left," Benn informed them. "He will be picked up later as soon as I cite him to the Council. In the meantime escort my daughter to the Worship Area and keep her under supervision until I leave with her."

Cal found her voice. "Dad, this is crazy. What have we done? We were only looking at files on your computer."

Benn turned to her, his face like thunder. "I said enough! You will not say 'we' with that young man in mind again. And you won't be seeing him again. He's headed for the Icecamps."

Cal did not know her father like this. Normally a mild-mannered man with bursts of irritability he was displaying a ruthlessness she had never known. She went quiet and turned toward the guards. They fell in almost unconsciously on either side of her and half marched and half followed her out of the room.

***

As Poll exited the Center he knew he was in real trouble. There was nowhere to hide. It was only a matter of time before Security picked him up. But he wanted to delay that moment as long as possible. He needed time to think. To think and figure out the full implications of what he had just seen.

"Hey, Poll, where are you going? Where are Danny and Liz?" Wes and Esh's voices rang out across the concourse as Poll headed through. He glanced round.

"Can't stop," he shouted.

"Why? What crazy stuff have you been doing?" Esh yelled back. "Hey, do you know where Danny and Liz are? They've disappeared."

"Huh?" grunted Poll over his shoulder. But already he was ducking inside a Bubble. The doors pinged shut, and he was gone.

The two young people blew up. "What is going on?" Esh demanded.

Wes swore, "That freakin' Poll, what the hell has he done now?"

They cast around, hesitating, sensing something had happened but not knowing what to do. Then very quickly their confusion was resolved. Cal appeared in the Worship Stadium with her escort. Turning round they saw her through the coral-tinted glass screen.

"Thank God," cried Wes. "It's Cal." They pushed through the heavy revolving doors, not really noticing the uniformed officials with her.

"Stop right there. This young woman is in our custody. You are not permitted contact."

"What?"

Cal rounded on the men. "Are you crazy? The only person I'm not allowed to talk to is Sidak. Keep away from me, or I'll report you for exceeding your authority."

The officials had little experience of articulate resistance. They took a couple of steps back.

Wes was at last getting a handle on his day. "Way to go, Cal! But, explain, please? We're absolutely in the dark here."

She didn't need a second invitation. She spilled out the startling discoveries she and Poll had just made, and her father's reactions to them.

"So the Homeland is not the last place on earth. There's somewhere else, and it's much, much better?"

Wes and Esh stared at her. They momentarily forgot their search for Liz and Danny, facing the enormity of her claim. Wes persisted after Cal nodded. "Let me get this straight. You see an old photo and deduce from it there's another, better place on earth, one that's been hidden for hundreds of years?"

"It's not just the photo, Wes. It's what's in it: happy people building the Shield. They should be desperate but they look like they're in heaven, already. And there's something else. You know when I got frozen that time, looking out the window, well I wasn't frozen, I saw something. I think I saw the sunshine world."

Esh said, "Cal, you had a vision. You saw heaven."

"If I saw heaven, it was in this world."

Wes exclaimed, "So you're saying the whole thing's a lie? Everything we've been told, the Global Shield, humanity on the brink, the pioneers? And what about our religion, is that a lie too?"

It was now Cal's turn to look blank. She had been affected by Poll's questions, seeing a concrete problem to be resolved, but not necessarily excluding belief. Faced by Wes' reaction she saw the possible consequences of her discovery.

"I, I'm not sure," she hesitated. "It means everything is not

47

whut wc thought. What's truc, I don't know."

"As sure as heck it means all that stuff at the Worship Center is full of it!" Wes' tone was one of shocked disgust. "If there's a place on the planet where there's sunshine and people are happy, then we don't have to wait around until we go to heaven. Just show me the way!"

"Well, there's the problem," said Cal, glad to get back to practicalities. "I have no idea how you get in touch with this other place, or whether it's possible at all."

The idea of communication, or lack of it, abruptly reminded Esh of the two swimmers. "Oh and there's something else, Cal. We can't find your brother. He's vanished. Liz, too."

Cal tried to focus on what Esh had just said. Something in it struck one more tremor inside her. The series of shocks she had experienced was becoming an earthquake, changing her landscape out of recognition.

"What's that? Danny's missing?"

"Yeah, he's been missing since the finals. We thought you might know something."

When Wes filled in the details, she pressed them for more: "What did the guy look like, the one he was talking to?"

Esh tried to remember. "We couldn't see very well. It was crazy, and he was gone almost at once."

"Anything at all, was he tall, short, well-built, you know?"

"Well, it sounds kind of lame, but I remember thinking, he sure looks healthy!"

Cal felt a pit open up in her stomach, but before she could say anything her father appeared. He strode toward the group, gesturing to the guards.

"You two, come with me. We're going to my home. There's a security detail looking for that madman, but until they pick him up we need to take precautions."

He caught Cal's arm and propelled his daughter out to the reception area, with the two guards following behind.

"And you," he shouted over his shoulder to the young people, "you stay away from my daughter unless you want to end up in a maintenance camp too."

A Bubble appeared at the external port and, while Esh and Wes watched dumbstruck, the Worship Leader and his party entered and were gone. Wes' bravado deserted him.

"That man's serious. Poll's headed for the Icecamps, for sure. That's not going to happen to me."

Esh turned. "You're right, we should go home. None of this makes sense. Tomorrow's Ninety Nine and Danny's bound to turn up."

Wes nodded but without conviction. They made their way out of the Worship Area, out to the external port and the frozen landscape of the Homeland.

12. VIGIL

"You think you're pretty smart, don't you?"

The Sector Security Chief sat at the table flanked by the members of the Discipline and Control Board. Over to one side stood Nat, summonsed to give evidence and looking pleased and pious. Poll had been picked up riding the Bubbles, knowing that anywhere he stopped his entry swipe would immediately give him away. He had gone from the Worship Center to the Training Center to the Sports Center, and each time punched in a new destination to the vehicle command panel. He had managed to elude capture for three hours. Finally Transport Control had identified a single Bubble in continuous movement and Security had intercepted.

"You have been cited for blasphemy by a Sector Worship Leader, corroborated by the first-hand witness of an acolyte, and there are several other notations in your personal file, none of them good. Now that's not too smart! Do you have anything to say for yourself?"

In his three hours of freedom Poll had understood his situation clearly. There was no way he could submit to the Homeland way of life. Not now he'd seen physical proof of the hollowness of its story. Someone somewhere else was benefiting from all the suffering which the Teppers endured: he didn't know who or how but he was certain of it. The thing that had always bothered him theoretically—the excess energy in the system— was plain now, it had to be part of the plan. Somehow the energy was used to serve and maintain another world, a place of wonderful sunshine. The way that teachers, worship leaders and work managers bought into this lie and colluded in their own misery, it made him feel ill. But he also knew that if he did not apologize abjectly and agree to theological retraining he was certain to be condemned to Refrigeration Maintenance, which meant almost certain death.

In the same instant he was convinced that there had to be some means of communication with this other world. Everything here had to have been set up at some point: it had not taken form spontaneously. The people who had overseen the construction of the Homeland, marketed its religion, convinced and put in place its priests and teachers, and transported its first settlers, they had to have had some way of getting out. They also had to have a way to get back in if there was ever a problem needing to be fixed. Therefore, there had to be some mode of transport between the worlds. It was obviously not on the icefields. The only place left where it could possibly be was on the borders, somewhere beyond the Maintenance Camps. If he was ever going to find the physical connection which would be proof positive of his theory, then he should make sure he was sent to this destination. He had made his decision.

"Yeah, well, what if this whole religion thing is a lie, and you know it. Who's the real blasphemer then?"

The Sector Chief blinked in disbelief. He'd never heard anyone say anything like this. The Board made an audible collective intake of breath. They glanced at each other in shock. The Chief struggled to reassert control.

"What more evidence do we need? This man is a deviant of the most dangerous sort. He must be sanctioned and removed at once to Refrigeration Maintenance. Do we even need to discuss this? We've just heard him undermine the collective beliefs and security of the Homeland!"

The Board all nodded gratefully. One of them, reacting at the last moment to the summary justice, meekly asked whether the youth truly understood the gravity of his situation. Did he realize this was tantamount to a death sentence?

The Chief clamped his lips and rolled his eyes. But he didn't have to worry.

"Thanks, but no thanks. This whole thing is rigged. It's you guys who don't understand what's happening. I'll take my chances with the ice crews."

The Chief shook his head and without waiting bent and signed an order that lay before him on the committee table. Only then did he look around at the others. They gazed back in submissive silence, while over to the side Nat cast a prayer of thanksgiving to heaven. The Chief addressed Poll.

"You are hereby sentenced to five years labor in the Refrigeration Plant Maintenance Crews. You will be taken into custody at once and transferred to a work camp under supervision of its personnel. If you survive your sentence there is the possibility of rehabilitation to the Homeland, depending on evidence of remorse. That is all."

He signaled to the officers who were standing behind Poll, then he folded his hands and watched them escort the tall youth out. It was highly unlikely he would ever see him again.

The detail and their prisoner went by Bubble to a place Poll had not seen before, a building unlike the usual, thermally sealed living spaces of the Homeland. It was a big metal-sided hanger, the temperature inside more or less the same as the temperature outside. In the interior on the bare frozen ground were a number of windowless cement block houses. The impression was of a much more primitive style of housing than the TEPs. The moment Poll saw it and was hustled inside one of the cabins he almost cried out in excitement. The cabin was insulated inside by foil-covered layers of fiberglass, broken and patched in many places. It was lit by bare electric bulbs and furnished with wooden bunks and cupboards. Everything about them said another time, another world.

"This is one of the original camps that built the Homeland," Poll thought. "It's a step toward the truth."

His euphoria was short-lived. The harsh reality of what lay before him quickly overtook any intellectual satisfaction he felt. The temperature inside the cabin was not warm enough to replace body heat—the underfloor heating was weak and in some places non-functioning. The guards who took custody of him from the escort wore blankets over their therm-suits and the padding of these was scarred and repaired all-over. These guards were not much older than him, but their skin was gray under ragged hair and their eyes dead, except for the glint of cruelty which flickered as they took possession of the prisoner. Unlike the regular security who were rarely armed, and only with stun-guns, these carried weapons that looked like they could kill.

The moment the escort left one of the guards hit Poll in the stomach and the other clubbed him as he went down.

The first one jumped on his back and stayed there, yelling.

"We know all about you boy-genius! If you're so fucking smart how'd you end up on the floor, eh? Well get this straight, Sidak, one wrong move and you're out on the tundra where you'll be dead quicker 'n it takes to know which way is home. Up there on the borders it snows about all the time, and snow 'n ice tell no tales. No one will even know. And sure as hell no one here is going to come looking for you."

The other guard joined in. "Transport for the borders leaves at sun-up tomorrow and you're on it with us, your new Mum and Dad. So get your ass over to one of those bunks and shut the fuck up or we'll tuck you in again just like this!" He kicked Poll in the ribs for good measure.

Later that night they brought in another poor wretch, an older man who looked terrified, and they did exactly the same thing to him.

Poll lay on his bunk in vicious pain, without a blanket, frozen and unable to sleep. He felt only his pain was keeping him alive. He thought of his real Mum back in the TEP and his Dad who had died when he was a boy. There had been some kind of accident involving a faulty transport. His mother who lived a life of intense religious devotion did not talk about it. She simply repeated that the Bubble had broken down and his father died of hypothermia. Now he felt very close to the experience of his father and it brought him waves of fear. He fought them by thinking of Cal. He tried to keep her face before his mind. It was his one point of hope. He saw her steady, confident eyes, her quick, intuitive movements. He felt somehow she would stick by him. That's how he survived the night.

13. HOLY DAY

Typically Benn would have been bathing in the delicious warmth of approaching glory, but this time he began 99th Day with very different feelings. Yesterday he'd done things he'd never come close to before. He contacted the Sector Security Chief and insisted that Poll Sidak was a most dangerous nonconformist, and there could be no discussion about him being excommunicated to the Borders. At the same time he'd requested an order that his daughter, Cal, be confined to the family TEP until further notice. The Chief had agreed to both his demands without question.

Then there was the small matter of his missing son. Cal had informed him of what her two friends told her at the Worship Center, and he quickly contacted the supervisor at the Sports Center. The supervisor had received a private WIA message a short while before saying that all inquiries regarding Danny Anders and Liz Fleming should be referred to Entertainment and Information Programming. Benn knew immediately something important had happened. The EIP was an obscure body which managed the Word and Image programs. This was mostly standard transmissions, but every now and again there was something new—a story on some little known figure from pioneer times, an announcement of sports events or special food supplies, or very occasionally a piece on a sporting hero who had found such fame he or she had been granted privileged retirement status.

Benn's heart swelled with pride. His firmness with the deviant Poll had straightaway been rewarded. He phoned the number the supervisor gave him and after some delay he was put through to a representative who told him, yes, Danny had indeed been chosen for retirement status, and to expect a public announcement shortly.

He felt a sense of zeal inside him, different from the religious sentiment that normally moved him. It was akin to anger, but more righteous. As if the holiness of the Holo-casts had entered inside him, full of resolve and power. He felt he was closer to God than he'd ever been. He downgraded in his mind the euphoria of the presentations; really it was a very secondary emotion. He would go ahead with Day 99, but with an entirely new revelation of what religion was really about.

Cal was informed of her house arrest directly and in Benn's new-found manner that brooked no dissent. She did not try to argue but sat in silence until the family bed was released from its wall panel. She climbed in at once and zippered her hood. The next morning, during Ignition, Benn told her he would arrange for the Storm and Fire Holo-cast to be transmitted to the TEP, and she could participate in that way. His communication vehicle arrived and he was gone.

She lay in bed listening to her Mom and sister breathing. Neither of them had to get up because there was no work or school that day, only the High Holy Day at the Worship Center. She knew Poll had been arrested and sentenced because she'd heard her father speak with the Security Chief confirming the tribunal proceedings. So there could be no turning back. If Poll was headed for the Icecamps she had to find a way to rescue him. He would, she was sure, seek some way to survive, but the camps had a brutal reputation and Poll was capable of creating lots more trouble for himself. He needed her. She also needed him. Their lives were intertwined, in a way deeper and more urgent than she could explain. It was all part of the huge upheaval that had changed her life unrecognizably in the space of three days.

She felt stunned by everything that had taken place. The fragility of the Homeland's story had been exposed and it would never be put back together again. It was not the real world. Even her father's ferocity somehow proved it. She thought of Danny. It was amazing how he'd been abducted at the very same time as she and Poll had discovered the existence of the other world. For there was no doubt in her mind. She'd seen it all in a flash when Esh had described Danny's contact. She'd pictured the man right there, like one of those smiling and happy people in the Worship Center video, and now he'd come to collect Danny and Liz. The way it had all happened, on the same day as finding the video, it seemed almost like something was guiding her and Poll. None of it was by accident.

She wanted to believe this. It gave her comfort and strength. She remembered the prayer she had made for herself and Poll. It seemed to have worked, but only up to a point. They'd gotten answers, but Poll was in just about as bad trouble as he could be. Yet, still, her deeper feeling said the game wasn't up, that things could still change, that Poll could in fact escape. It was all about belief. Not the kind of cozy belief that her father peddled, the Worship Center feelings that kept everybody happy with their existences. This was something much less visible, and at the same time much stronger and alive. If she could get hold of this, she thought, she could even perhaps set the Homeland free.

She lay there for a long time, not thinking, not doing anything. She let herself go, piece by piece, nerve by nerve. By now her mother was up and ready to depart with Sam for the Worship Center—her mother who had agreed with Benn's decisions because they seemed to keep her daughter safe. But Cal was a million miles away from the plans and wishes of her parents. She heard the WIA announcer say the data stream for those attending the service of Storm and Fire in their homes was about to begin. Almost directly she heard the patter of rain and the worry of wind fill the TEP. She unzipped her hood and got out of bed. She went into the shower and turned on the jet. As the thin stream poured over her body she continued to surrender. She let the water's gentle sweet touch continue to lead her, to teach her what she did not know.

***

In Worship Center Five Benn had thrown the switches that filled the seating arena with flying holograms of dark cloud. The sound system gave off a low rattle of wind with intermittent showers of rain and the grumble of distant thunder.

People were already filing in and a palpable excitement ran through the stadium as the crowd found seats. Benn was accustomed to this feeling and had anticipated it ever since the last festival. But now things were different. He knew today he was going to give the performance of a lifetime. He scrolled through the files looking for something that would do justice to his new sense of holiness and authority. He found a volcano sequence with glowing red streams cascading from the mountain walls, but rejected it. A brush fire racing down a canyon, torching and popping homes like seed pods, he passed over that too. A level five hurricane devastating a delta farming region attracted him.

The snapping trees and flying roofs held him for a moment, but he was still not satisfied. Finally, the title "Collapsing Dam" caught him and he clicked onto it. He saw high water rising, lapping the top of a concrete barrier then beginning to pour over it in a continuous stream. Suddenly cracks appeared in the vast monolith and the whole structure gave way violently under the weight of water. The camera panned to the foot of the huge wall and showed a great valley filled with fields and animals, and in the distance villages and church spires. In an instant the five hundred feet and ten miles of water were falling vertically upon it. Finally the camera was hovering over one of the villages, with people running like rats and an immense gray wave racing inexorably toward them.

"This is it," Benn said to himself. He selected it into the program, ready to go, and typed in the instructions for Nat, the acolyte.

"Get me the black gown with silvered breast and back plates," he ordered. "And the black miter to go with it. Then lay out the special 99th day robes for the great fire of the Holo-cast."

He turned once more to his master program to add one final touch. Something that would leave a lasting impression, one that might even establish him as the greatest Worship Leader in all the Homeland.

The stadium was full. By now the wind was howling so it was impossible to hear someone speak even in the next seat. Lightning flashed and the faces of the congregants were lashed by virtual rain visible at each moment of dazzling illumination. Already people's breath was taken from them. They were pinned to their seats, simultaneously thrilled and terrified. Suddenly the noise stopped. The images of the storm streaming through the arena were gathered up and disappeared in one movement into a screen at the far end. In their place a peaceful moonlight bathed the arena. A tremulous organ chord sounded, and slowly Benn Anders rose on his crystal pulpit above the heads of the many thousands assembled. The people's tension ebbed and they emitted a collective sigh.

"What is the reason we are here?" Benn began. "You will say to yourselves, I'm sure, 'Reverend Anders knows well why we are here; it's Day 99, the day of Storm and Fire!' Of course, that is

57

truc. Today is the day we celebrate the central truth of the Homeland, the creation by grace of a space free from storm where we may work out our eternal salvation. But, still, why *are* we here? And now I know you are repeating that question deep inside, and you do not know the answer, because you do not know the question, the real question. Why ARE we here?"

"The question is about you, about me, about where we stand in this life of hard work and relentless cold. The question is about whether we complain, even just a little, or, worse, actively criticize the world we live in and its divine purpose."

His voice began to rise in power and conviction, and he brought his fist crashing down on the podium in front of him.

"No, I say. This day says 'No' to all complaint and criticism. The Day of Storm and Fire says we are completely united as a society of Teppers. Our task is to remain alive in the harshest of circumstances and so complete God's sacred purpose of salvation. This is why we are here, and this is the meaning of the Holo-casts. We are united under God's fire and against the storm!"

He threw his hands vertically in the air. The stadium lights were suddenly extinguished and a single brilliant spotlight remained on his black-coped figure with its silvered designs.

"God of Storm and Fire, save us from ourselves, save us from disunity, save the Homeland! We pray you!"

At his prayer the spotlight was killed and the arena was filled in an instant with the presence of the immense dam poised above and at an angle to the seating, the waves cresting its edge. Many people screamed involuntarily. The mountainous cathedral visibly bellied at two-thirds of its height and within seconds flew apart, as if mined by a huge bomb. Enormous chunks of concrete jetted into the air and behind them an implacable body of gray water leaped and formed, seemed to hang suspended, then dipped like a giant prehistoric raptor down upon the valley. Now almost everyone was screaming, instinctively ducking in their seats. But even as they cowered from the disaster coming, very quickly they were watching the scene from above. In less than three minutes, as the mass of water hit the ground and boiled and fumed into a wave, the remarkable engineering of the stadium lifted the central seating on jacks and rails and retracted into banked levels revealing a well-space in the middle. The seismic movement had only increased the sense of a world shaking and unhinged, but, in short order, the people were brought to safety while below them the hologram showed the monstrous wave sweeping forward and crashing into the village.

It demolished houses like matchstick, lifting children and grandparents, dogs and cattle in a fury of disappearing heads and bodies, a thrashing of arms amid a tide of tree branches, debris and floating corpses. The camera lifted to a much longer shot, revealing now the entire valley spreading out into a wider V-shape amid scattered foothills. It had become a single plain of mud and desolation. It was the end of the world.

The people stared in shock and horror. Even as they gazed the apocalyptic waste began to fade and the initial hologram of the day re-formed around the walls, a cloud-filled sky and whipping rain. This time there was no sound to the storm. Instead there was an orchestral piece playing, a wistful sound but also heroic, with woodwind and strings interlaced with a stirring beat of brass and drums. The people's spirits were restored by the music and as it continued the stadium seating reverted with a shudder and roll to its original setting. At the same time the ravaged sky around the walls was cut by twelve radiant pillars of golden light. The music continued to build, its rhythm injecting a decisive note of power and life. Then the orchestra muted and Benn's voice spoke.

"Now we can see the salvation that has been worked for us. We celebrate with a single mind the purpose of the Homeland. It is not for nothing that we were brought here! It was not for nothing the Global Weather Shield was built. It saved us from catastrophe!"

From the foot of the pillars of light there spread a slow crystalline sea, a glittering transparent form that covered the bodies of the faithful like a bridal veil. The music shifted to mystical organ and strings and the air in the stadium blew cool with a hint of incense. The backdrop of storm began to clear and was replaced by a deep sapphire sky. As great as the fear and horror had been, there was the sense now of wonder and peace. Everyone was bathed in serenity, but the service was not yet over.

"The Weather Shield has indeed saved us from catastrophe, but it was God who led our forefathers, the pioneers, to do this, God at the heart of the fire which stills the storm! The pioneers sacrificed themselves willingly in order that we might survive. Now, therefore, as we move to the great fire ceremony with which we conclude every Holo-cast we remember those who fulfilled divine destiny by giving their lives."

Instantaneously the shimmering ice field and its guardian pillars disappeared into total darkness. Benn's voice rang out in a thunderous prophetic tone: "We now in our own time will do no less than sacrifice ourselves completely for the Homeland of God and the God of the Homeland."

In the pitch dark the familiar single fire coalesced at the far end of the arena. It grew in intensity with cascading colors and flares. The infra-bass note sounded, pierced by the solitary piccolo, reverberating through the whole stadium. Streams of fire erupted from every part pouring into the one incandescent core. Then, suddenly, something new happened. Suspended over the heart of the fire appeared an image of a group of men and women, smiling, bathed in light, their arms around each other's shoulders. Benn's trilling voice sounded above the music.

"These are the pioneers, the men who gave us their all!"

The fire exploded into a giant ball. The faces and bodies of the pioneers warped and split apart in the nuclear flash. Its monstrous shape burnt in lurid colors, leaping to the walls and roof. At long last it condensed and resolved into a single candle-like flame, smoky at the edges, bluish at the core. It hung there, peaceful and enduring. After a long moment of silence while the house lights began gently to glow, first a handful began to shout and clap and then rapidly the whole stadium erupted in a massive collective roar. Benn stood up from his chair next to his crystal pillar, acknowledging the cheers like an opera star.

The announcements which normally followed a Holo-cast began to scroll on the video screen at the end of the arena. A voice-over spoke the words. No one paid much attention but Benn caught the reference to his son. "Dan Anders and Liz Fleming have been awarded exceptional athlete status. They are granted the privilege of special retirement, transferring to a sector set aside for these fortunate individuals. Their example serves as an inspiration to all Homeland youth. A special broadcast will be offered, including an interview with our two stars, possibly as early as tomorrow."

Benn's heart, already filled to bursting point, filled a little more. His son had been chosen for lifelong privilege. He had become one of the so-called "Immortals," and this had all happened when he had given the greatest Holo-cast of his life. The resolute fervor and conviction he had shown could not be unconnected to this singular blessing given him and his family. Without a doubt, God approved the rigor of his faith, approved his excommunication of Poll and his disciplining of his daughter. And the approval had been demonstrated for all to see and within the space of a few hours. Benn could not contain his emotions. He shot his hands in the air in exultation and glory.

***

In the family TEP Cal experienced the whole of the sacred performance in solitude. Despite the collective feeling of the crowd at the Center, its sighs and screams and cheers, she was alone. She was alone because the religious sentiments of the occasion left her unmoved, and they left her unmoved because she was already alone. As she watched in solitude, the Holo-cast became a lesson in falsehood, a proof of deception. At each step she saw the way in which people's reactions were used to bring them to a place they had not chosen but had been chosen for them. Each dramatic picture, each powerful sensation, each repetition of the story, everything conspired to create a world that seemed full and true but was simply a painting made inside their heads. The bursting of the dam was a nightmare imprinted in their souls so the cruel life of the Teppers would seem preferable. Its terrifying power allowed them to experience in their bodies the horror of a world fallen apart, and then immediately to be saved by the narrative of the Holo-cast leading to the cold beauty of the ice world. What could that do except make the people completely devoted to the Homeland? Worse still, Cal realized, the nightmare of the dam had at some point been absolutely real and was in all likelihood produced by the same forces and persons which created the Homeland. Cal did not know or understand fully all the connections, but inside she was sure of it.

When it came to the fire at the end a shiver of recognition ran through her. The image of the tanned and happy group in a place of bright sunshine had been turned by her father into something

61

different, something truly terrifying. Because her father could not explain them he had destroyed them there in front of the congregation. Their bodies that looked so good had become a blinding nuclear flash. In this way he had turned them from a question into a force that forbade all questioning. Theirs would be the smiles of Immortals prefiguring the heaven they had gone to, rather than actual smiles on this earth, an actual mystery needing an explanation.

And now Danny and Liz had become part of the same thing. It was so ridiculous and transparent, but its very transparency had made everyone blind. Everyone, that is, except Poll.

He had done something for her that no one else could have done. He had brought her to a place of truth. She imagined him now, and she knew he was suffering. It was hard to bear, thinking of him in such conditions, but she did not despair. Her mind was now free and strong, and she could not help believe he would also find that strength. In her soul she willed him to do so. She would find a way and Poll would too.

PART TWO

1. TOUCH DOWN

Golden light; brilliant and soft. It was the first thing that hit Danny and Liz as they gazed stupefied from the shuttle's observation ports. Dante leaned over and unbuckled the seat harnesses, while a lock on the cabin door released and the hatch folded away. The guides gently grasped their charges and helped them to their feet. They took each by the forearm and led them out onto a jet-bridge moved up to the side of the craft. The sensory load for new arrivals could be overwhelming and they might easily fall headlong.

"Take your time. Breathe deeply. Don't ask or think all the questions at once, there's plenty of time... So, here you are, Danny, Liz, our latest additions to Heaven. Welcome!"

The two Homelanders staggered, blinked and took in hardly anything of their new world. The light dripped like honey. They felt an indescribable warmth, abundant, universal, fragrant. They sensed color, especially a broad river of green. And at the bottom of the stairs a sea of faces, garments and bodies, looking up at them, laughing, applauding, beckoning.

"Did we die? Are we dead?"

Milton laughed. "No, no. This is life, lots and lots of it. But come, we all need to get out of these brutal thermals and into something more comfortable. Then we can find you refreshment and we will begin to talk properly."

"Careful now. Take it slow."

The emissaries led the youth down the stairway while the group at the bottom parted to let them through, laughing and admiring.

When Dante had first spoken with Liz and Danny he told them they were being taken to one of the special colonies for successful athletes. They had worked hard for a reward like this and deserved the privilege, and by leaving the Sector they would give others a chance too. Apart from this there had been very few details. But the assurance with which he spoke had been totally convincing for them. Just the idea of getting away from the routine they'd known all their lives was enough to sell them on the idea. Then, shortly after, when they had been whisked away on a snow tractor and boarded the rocket and experienced its ascent and flight, the sheer pounding excitement had driven almost every connected thought from their minds. Now, faced for the first time with the full physical evidence of another, so-beautiful world, they were quite literally out of their senses. The shock of the new, with its symphony of pleasure, dissolved any critical faculty they possessed.

"Here, this way. This is Emmanuelle, Liz. She will be your personal assistant and friend, so long as you need her. And, Danny, this is Gaius. He will be the same for you. You can trust them implicitly. They will take care of all your needs."

Two individuals detached themselves from the crowd of welcomers and fell in step beside them. The pair smiled radiantly and together the whole group made its way down a path toward a portico of rose and honey colored stone flanked on either side by groves of cypress trees.

Emmanuelle was tall and silk-skinned, her ash blonde hair piled in a tumbling coif. She wore a white silk sheath. It opened on the left side to display the whole of a delicately tanned leg and extended over the opposite shoulder fully exposing the other breast. Gaius wore a short Greek dress, also white, that reached halfway down his muscular thighs. Abundant curls framed a sensual aristocratic face. Liz and Danny did not know which one to look at, or where to look. They stumbled into each other, instinctively grabbing the other for support. Emmanuelle gently took Liz's hand. Gaius clapped Danny on the back and then quickly grabbed his arm to stop him falling.

"Look at me," the two assistants spoke almost in unison.

"Just look at our faces," Emmanuelle continued softly. "You are among friends. This is your home. You will be so happy. Just keep looking at us."

She tipped Liz's chin up to look her directly in the eyes, continuing to smile her dazzling smile. By now Gaius had hold of Danny's hand also, firmly leading him forward. Danny looked at him helplessly and Gaius bestowed on him the same beatific smile.

They passed through the portico and entered a wide agora

laid out on smooth stone paths stretching forward and crossing at right angles. The paths were dappled by sunlight filtering through pergolas and a lacing of flowering vines and roses. In the intimate sunlit squares formed by the intersecting paths fountains played, trailing bougainvillea and passionflower covered low walls, and there were stone seats spread with creamy drapes and deep crimson cushions. In some of the squares there were small domed summer-houses with wooden doors half ajar. People were gathered in the squares, in small groups. Some were lounging in casual embraces. Others were talking, with occasional confident smiles and bursts of tuneful laughter. Every now and then they would steal a glance at the curious procession making its way down the central arcade, and once or twice one of them would give an excited little wave.

"There, up ahead, that is where we're going." Emmanuelle gave the information with a sweet low inflection and pointed to what seemed like a large plaza a hundred or so paces in front. It was dominated by a building much bigger than the others, splendid in crystal white and veined marble.

"This is one of the oldest, most treasured baths we have. Here is where you will be welcomed, be refreshed and enter our company fully. And you will be given proper clothing!" Emmanuelle, Gaius, Dante and Milton all looked at each other and at the heavy thermal suits and laughed gently, allowing just a little humor about the clumsy dress. But they quickly smiled encouragingly at Danny and Liz, inviting them also to share the joke.

The group moved across the plaza and ascended the wide formal steps to the colonnade and door. As they climbed a man stepped out from the shadow to greet them, as if he had been waiting. He was dressed in a white toga with gold edging, and seemed older than the others because of the lines around his eyes and on his forehead. But his dark skin was supple and fresh and the hair of his head and beard was black and lustrous. He looked at the group, singling out Liz and Danny with bright eyes.

"Welcome, O welcome to the first great bathhouse established by the pioneers. Welcome to the weary travelers, and most of all welcome to our dear new children, Homelanders from the north, soon to be the newest gods in Heaven! Here you will

65

begin your transformation from mere mortals into divinities! Do not be alarmed, all will become clear and all will be beautiful. I am Pandit the keeper of the Baths and it is my great privilege to greet you. Now, my little ones, to begin your transformation you must abandon all fear, the curse of mere mortals, and surrender without hesitation to the ministry of my assistants. My dear ones, what are your names?"

Gaius winked at Milton and they both struggled to keep a straight face.

"He's a long-winded old fool," Gaius whispered through the side of his mouth to Danny, "But do what he says, he's been inducting newcomers for four hundred years!"

Pandit was still looking expectantly at the pair. "Well?" he said with arched eyebrows.

Danny finally found his voice. "I, we... My name is Dan."

"I...I am Liz."

"Well, we always want to give more beautiful names to those whose appellations are mired with mortality. So Dan, you obviously must become Daniel, and Liz, let me think what we should do about that: how about changing it to Charlize?"

The Northerners continued to gaze witlessly at the Master of Ceremonies. After a brief moment he simply smiled and said, "Splendid, that's settled then. Follow me." He turned away, clapping his hands together as he led them forward into the semi-gloom of the building.

Six or more eye-level walls of golden onyx extended in a straight line from the door into its interior. On their tiled surfaces were set scented oil lamps, leading the eye forward into an endless dark well. Between the walls steps led down to pools whose waters were stirred by rippling currents. A dozen or so attendants appeared and divided themselves between the travelers. Dante and Milton were each led to a side bath. Liz and Danny, accompanied still by Emmanuelle and Gaius, were surrounded by bands of attendants and guided separately to the central pools. The attendants were male and female, semi-naked or fully naked. Their bodies were midnight black to the same light tan as Emmanuelle, and none of them showed any embarrassment or diffidence. Some of them entered the water immediately and cast up vertical sprays with their hands, filling the air with intoxicating droplets from the perfumed waters.

Liz and Danny were trembling. The effect of the flight, the abrupt assault of a new world, and now the heady atmosphere and easy proximity of male and female bodies had all become a cascade. They fell into the low stone seats at the foot of the steps and the brim of the water. Neither of them could resist as the attendants took off their boots, popped the clasps of their suits and unzipped them. As the thermal layer came off and they were stripped to their underclothes Emmanuelle and Gaius stepped forward carrying trays with pitchers and cups. They set the drink beside them and poured glasses for themselves and for the newcomers. The assistants drank first and offered the refreshment to Liz and Danny. They accepted readily, even greedily, as the cup was guided to their mouths. It was a sweetened cordial with a slightly bitter but not unpleasant aftertaste. Then in a few swift moves by the attendants, and without hardly realizing it, they too were naked.

There was another clap and Pandit's voice rang out from somewhere in the dim recesses of the building.

"These are waters of rebirth. They prepare the mind as well as the body. They will begin in you a generative process, which our wonderful scientists have produced for us. This means you will never age. You will live for untold years and will be gods like the rest of us. But first your souls must pass through the river of divinity! It is from the waters at the dawn of time that all life first came. In the era of the storms our beneficent mother became a tyrant. She rose up against us and threatened all human life. But our great scientists also rose to the height of the challenge, and found a way to control water, to dominate and subdue her, and thus we became greater than our goddess mother. She is now our gentle servant and companion, and she acknowledges we are divine like her. Through unity with her, Charlize and Daniel will become divine in their own eyes, in their own minds. So, now! Let the rebirth begin!"

And he clapped one more time.

The waters had a slight peaty bronze color, an effect perhaps of the stonework, or maybe due to some kind of herb or essence. They were both warm and cool to the touch, like a silk scarf drawn across the skin, and deeply scented, a swirl of honeysuckle and musk. The two neophytes were led by the hand, down shallow steps until they were waist-deep. They had been given a drug that was already beginning to take effect. Emmanuelle and Gaius had also taken it and they, now naked too, were always in sight of their charges continuing to gaze at them with the same beatific smile. Danny and Liz had begun to feel wonderfully relaxed. Their previous bewilderment and shock was replaced by enormous well-being and pleasure. They felt deeply attracted to the water and were very willing to sink into it, forgetting all their previous thoughts and worries.

The attendants guided them backward and placed little floats under their shoulders, heads and tailbones. Danny and Liz allowed themselves to sink back, surrendering fully to the intense comfort. The earthy tint of the water seemed like the earth itself, and so perhaps they were the seed of flowers and the scent of the water was their blossoming. Assistants poured oil on their bodies and flowing hands lightly massaged it across their skin. They were submerging in a sea of pleasure without any one point to focus on. Their breathing had become shallow and had slowed to a prolonged interval. They were reaching a point of pseudo-death, and were losing consciousness except for a last residual sense of liquid well-being. Then they were under the water and not breathing. The attendants had gently slipped the pads and pushed down on their torsos until they were eighteen inches below the surface. Something inside their heads said they were dead because they were under water, not breathing. Yet they were happy, at one with the watery womb in which they were enclosed. They seemed to see Emmanuelle and Gaius floating near to them and slowly dissolving away. It felt as if they were calling them into the water itself, to become one with its endless pleasure and beauty. Then they slipped into oblivion.

***

Many hours later Liz and Danny regained consciousness. They were lying in separate rooms, their bodies covered in sweet bay and roses. There was a slight heaviness in their chests, but they hardly noticed it compared to the delight of relaxation that lingered in their limbs and the astonishing memory of all that had just happened. They lay in perfect stillness. The question that Liz had asked when they first arrived reoccurred and this time with more reason: "Am I dead?" But the sensation in their bodies, the flower petals, and the stone walls of the rooms with their high glassless casements looking out on a cloudless sky, all evoked the world they had just met. With its boundless beauty and power this was a more real world than they had ever imagined possible. So, dead or alive did not matter much.

They both continued to lie where they were, overwhelmed. The Master of Ceremonies had said they would be gods. Perhaps this was it, what it felt like to be a god, an Immortal. They thought of life in the Homeland, the icefields and the Centers. The memory was still there, but it seemed distant, remote, as if they had crossed a bridge they could not return on, nor would they ever want to.

Neither of them knew how long they lay there, not worried, not fearful, just feeling this strange, new way, and liking it, wanting it to go on and on. At last it was Liz who stirred. She felt her muscles stiffening a little, so she sat up and dropped her legs over the cushioned bench where she had been lying. Some of the flower petals dropped to the floor and she brushed others away. On a stool nearby she saw a white chiffon robe, the kind she had noticed some of the people wearing as she had come through the Agora. She wrapped it around her, naturally, as if she had been wearing one all her life.

The room was not large. It was covered in marble up to waist height, then stone, leading up to a wooden roof. There was nothing in it except the couch and the stool. An open door led out to a hallway, which was constructed in the same way. On the far side she saw another room with its door open. She went across the hall and entered the doorway, her bare feet slapping slightly on the marble floor. Danny was lying on his back covered in rose petals as she had been. He did not turn his head.

"Hi," she said.

Danny continued to stare at the roof. "Are you a ghost?"

"I don't think so."

He slowly turned his head toward the door.

"How are you? You look divine. What was the name that man gave you?"

"Charlize."

"It suits you. I think we should call you that."

69

"It is kind of pretty. How about you?"

"I think I'll probably stick to Danny."

"Actually I meant how are you?"

"Oh! Well different, for sure. I'm wearing petals."

"There should be a robe here somewhere. Yes, there, at the foot of the couch."

She walked over to the stool and picked it up. Danny did not move.

"Let me brush you off," she said. She went to his couch and started to brush the petals off his chest.

Danny smiled. "I think the right expression you're looking for is deflower!"

She giggled. And Danny reached for her and pulled her to him.

2. ICE CAMP

Poll sat at the back of the ice-tractor, hunched up on his seat with his feet braced against the floor and his hands locked on the rail in front of him. He was warm—the tractor engine was powerful and it cycled a constant blast of hot air through the cabin, but his ribs ached. The pitching of the suspension as the tracks bumped over the broken tundra was exhausting and made it impossible to rest. Initially the ice road had been good, well-marked and with its surface consistently melted and frozen smooth by the alternating sun and frigid night. But in the borderlands the weather was disrupted by cloud and snowfall and the going got progressively worse. The road was always under fresh snow and the ice sheet was broken by crevasses and ice walls. The tractor was always changing gears and revving up to go around or over obstacles. The noise was high-pitched and nerve-wracking, and the swaying and jolting seemed endless.

There were two other prisoners in the main cabin, Miller, the older man who had been brought to the holding place after Poll, and a morose kid called Finn who had come in that morning and didn't look big enough to be sent to the camps. The two guards sat in the driving cab buckled up on upholstered seats and they were having a famous time. The leader of the pair, Nute, the one who had jumped on Poll, was driving. His associate, Dogg, sat beside him, and together they were creased with laughter, checking over their shoulders to see their passengers flung up to the ceiling each time the tractor hit a ridge. Also the trip had already lasted several hours with no stops, and Finn had peed himself, unable to hold on with the jolting. This was part of the guards' game plan, and once they got the scent it became the source of endless remarks on the bladder weakness of Teppers and how much they stank.

After several hours the tractor finally came to a well-kept ice road with tall markers. About twenty minutes later the bumped and bruised passengers saw orange sodium lights on high steel pillars standing out against the snow of the horizon.

"There she is," yelled back Dogg, "Your new vacation home, Camp Conquest. Isn't she beautiful? Aren't you guys glad to be home?"

71

There was no real entrance to the camp, just a sprawl of ugly dwellings on either side of the road as it wound across the frozen steppe. They were of indistinct colors, dirty gray or rusted yellow, and all had the same shape. They were not like the domed TEPs but semi-cylindrical in form, like barrels halved along their length, their roofs reaching to the ground on either side and raised walkways extending along the apex. As the prisoners drove up the central road it was evident what the walkways were for. There was a number of individuals standing on them, clearing snow from the roofs with long shovels and rakes. The impression these figures made was striking. They were covered in great hoods and ragged capes. On their hands they wore enormous gloves, much bigger than the standard thermal mittens used in the Sector. They looked like misshapen insects and they made the scene grim and fearful in a way that not even Nute and Dogg had managed to convey.

Suddenly the tractor swerved from the road, pulling in sharply next to one of the buildings.

"OK, this is where you get out," announced Dogg. "That door there. Knock and it will be opened!"

He pointed to a heavy metal hatch set in the end wall. The exit from the tractor released with a hiss and steps unfolded beneath it. Miller stumbled off first, followed by Finn and Poll. The cold greeted them like steel knives, wind-assisted, something wholly new in their experience. They all instinctively doubled over and half fell, half ran toward the hut. Miller hit the door with the side of his fist and almost immediately it cracked open. A huge gloved paw reached out and grabbed the prisoners one by one, more or less lifting them over the bulkhead and sending them sprawling on the other side.

"Reception," a voice growled.

From that moment Poll truly entered another world. Any sense of connection with the Sector and the Homeland he had known was broken. He became part of what was clearly a more primitive era. Gone were the finely calibrated energy systems of the TEPs, gone were the transports, gone the holograms, gone the ever-present screens and audios. And gone also was the religion of the Homeland, its promise of a better life to come and its sense of collective purpose.

Instead there was a relentless struggle for survival in a world entirely without beauty. The barrack-style huts had doubled metal skins filled with insulation, but through expansion and contraction it had shifted and in places become ineffective. Secondary insulation was applied inside the buildings, but as this was always drooping or falling off it made them look like subterranean caves with formless stalactites hanging from the roofs. As for routine and order, if you did not keep up you could not expect to live long, as simple as that. New arrivals soon discovered that the camp was run by a group of old-hands recruited from the prisoners themselves. They had little hope of getting back to normal life but neither did any of them really care to. For whatever reason— domestic trouble, a ruined reputation, or sheer ill will —they had no motivation to return, plus the little bit of power and opportunity to make others suffer was more than enough compensation. They were a law unto themselves, and as long as they kept the plant machinery serviced the Sector never interfered with what they did. Some had been there for a very long time, longer than anyone remembered, and this inner group of veterans formed a tacit government. They were known as the Icemen, because the long years of exposure to bitter cold had not killed them, only weathered them, so they seemed almost indifferent to the brutal conditions.

The Icemen were not often seen, and no one was entirely sure anyway who was or was not part of the inner circle. Certain individuals simply had the reputation. In the normal course of things it was dangerous young men like Nute and Dogg who acted as their deputies. These thugs were brought on by hints and nods, suggesting they too would one day be accepted into the brotherhood. While they waited they were kept on the leash by the small measure of power they enjoyed and being played off against each other.

Poll and the others of course understood none of this and saw very little of anything as they were upended on the floor. The giant hand that had pulled them inside belonged to one of the lieutenants, a towering hulk who was acting as enforcer for another, less massive figure also there to welcome them. As the new arrivals lay helpless on the ground this other man stepped forward and walked around them looking down. He was wearing a heavy military cloak, impeccably neat. His face was pale, with soulless gray eyes. He spoke quietly.

"I am your god," he said. "Your existence depends entirely on me. If you displease me you will die. You will die anyway, but it is in my power to delay the onset of that final moment considerably." He lingered over the syllables of the last word as he gazed at the creatures in his power.

"You will continue to lie here on the floor until I tell you to get up. In the meantime you can tell me about yourselves so we get acquainted." He looked down at Miller. "You first. Tell me your name and the crime for which you were sentenced to my camp."

The prisoners proceeded to blurt out their names and the pathetic details of their offenses. Miller had trashed his TEP in a fit of unexplained anger. Finn had chronically missed transports and training. When he came to Poll the charge of blasphemy made the man stop and regard the prisoner with greater interest.

"Well, now you've met your god in all truth, and there's nothing more to say, is there?" His lips curled, but without humor. "Tell me, what led you to your...unorthodox views?"

Poll lay on the bone-numbing concrete, looking into the expressionless eyes. He felt a spasm of fear for this man quite unlike anything he had experienced before. He knew he must be on his guard, but he also knew that here was someone of evident power. If he were to survive, let alone escape, he would have to serve this person in some way. For perhaps the first time in his life Poll altered his tone and allowed his fear to show.

"I...I, I like math. I was asking about equations, about the storm system. I like to figure things out, which upset my professors, and the Worship Leader."

"You like to figure things out, eh? Well, now you know. What it all comes down to."

Poll nodded dumbly. The man was contemptuous but continued to observe him, as if weighing something in his own mind. Finally he asked.

"Can you do computers? Make them work?"

"Yes, I think so. I am good at logic."

The man's eyes seemed to be boring through Poll. "There is no logic," he said, slowly. Then, more carelessly, "Try not to be too clever and you may have a chance."

He turned away from the trio of bodies.

"Stand up, all of you. Gord here will supply you coats, gloves and boots. You are assigned to building 9. The squad leader there will give you your duties. That is all."

He swiveled neatly and disappeared into the interior of the hut. As they struggled to their feet and took in their surroundings they saw a cavernous space lined by ceiling-high cupboards up against the walls and across the middle. The single electric bulbs dangling from the roof showed two cramped corridors between the cupboards. It was some kind of equipment store. Gord, the giant, ambled over to one side and flung open a selection of clothes racks.

"Here, get a kit. The bigger, the better."

This bit of free advice at once struck Poll as a hint for survival. While he had rolled on the floor meeting his new god he had been unable to hold out and finally pissed himself. The sense of helplessness and humiliation this brought made him powerfully sensitive to the other note, a code passed on by people flung together in terrible circumstances, and he took it on faith. He chose the biggest hooded overcoat he could find, patched together from thermal material, and he picked out a pair of huge gauntlets extending well up on his forearms.

He saw Miller and Finn watching him and said, "Do what he said. Get the biggest size you can wear."

They fumbled around inside the cupboards until they too were dressed as shapeless trolls. Gord who was now watching them with something approaching professional zeal, went over to the other side and pulled open some more cupboards.

"Boots. Get them big too. We wear extra socks."

They spent some more time stumbling around in their clumsy capes, trying on thermal-lined boots until they thought they had the right ones. When finally they stood ready Gord pointed them back to the door.

"O.K. You're out of here. Turn right. It's the fifth cabin down on the left. Don't hang about."

He unhooked the two levers clamping the hatch and opened it enough to push the newly inducted prisoners out into the elemental cold. The moment they were through he slammed the door shut behind. The wind struck instantaneously, a laser knife, able to slice through any surface, cutting to nil whatever inner warmth their bodies had. They struggled up the road looking for numbers on the buildings. They found a number seven and then eleven. The huts were not in order and the gaps between them were much longer than they imagined. They were terrified they'd missed their way as their huge coats flapped around them and all their extremities turn to lifeless stumps. Suddenly, there ahead was number nine, about fifty yards away. They stumbled on, up to the door, and hammered against it. Again it opened quickly, but this time a hand helped them step over the low wall so they did not fall when they entered.

***

The routine of camp life was not hard to learn. Each hut had duties which it carried out implacably, day after day. There were huts assigned to food production and others to cooking, and still others to maintenance of the huts themselves, of things like water and sanitation. But the main proportion was given over to the crucial task of upkeep of the Homeland refrigeration system, which was in itself a miracle of engineering. Hut 9 had shared responsibility for a turbine and related compressors along with miles and miles of tunnels, with blowers, vents, lines and freezer coils. Almost the moment Poll and the others stepped over the threshold the essential character of camp life was brought home to them. The place was deserted, because most inmates were out on the day's duties, but the way the space was full and bare all at once spoke precisely of survival and work. They first entered a kind of buffer room between the outside and the living area. It was surrounded by scarred metal shelves with pairs of boots neatly positioned. The hand that had helped them in belonged to the doorkeeper for the day. There was little about him of the menace which had greeted them before. He simply did his job of unlatching and slamming the big door. He nodded and spoke. He'd been waiting for them and had the information they needed.

"Just arrived, huh? Take your boots and gloves off and put them on the bottom shelves. That's for new prisoners. Then go through that door. Spare socks and underwear are in boxes by the showers at the end. Beds 25, 34 & 35 are open. They have towels. Sort yourselves out."

He said this matter-of-factly, but Poll heard again the group sense of survival passed on almost automatically. From that moment he knew he had a chance. He sensed there was something in people that was not just following a track laid out for them: they could work together because they needed to. At this point it was only a feeling but it would grow in the weeks and months that he spent at the camp, until he knew it as a creed. Right now it put just a small lift in his spirits as he and the others strained to pry off their boots in the boot room before they entered the second door. Once through they were able to see all the way to the end, the single light bulbs following each other down in bleak procession. Right in front of them were two big parallel tables at right angles to the hut, and beyond that opposite rows of beds. As they picked their way down past the tables to the beds it was Finn who took the lead. He scouted ahead and found the two in sequence.

"Over here, over here" he shouted to Poll. "Take one of these. I can have the one next."

"OK," Poll nodded. He took bed 34.

***

Ten days later and he was completely exhausted. The work was never-ending. Every tenth day or so half the squad had a day off, but the break had not yet come round for him. The squad leader, a man named Cato, enforced the schedule with neutral zeal. Anyone failing to report for muster in the boot room was called in immediately to the camp enforcers and within ten minutes he was taken away. If someone were evidently ill he might be brought to the camp hospital, but otherwise the culprit disappeared for "re-training." Perhaps he ended up some time later in another billet and there were rumors that such people had been seen, but, again, no one knew for sure. Cato was not an enforcer himself. He had come to his role simply as a technique of survival: ensuring that the whole cabin stuck rigidly to its duties was a way to blot out the horror.

The crew rose together at five thirty and were out in the merciless wind by six. At night if a prisoner awoke he heard its bloodless whine around the cabin and knew soon enough he would feel its teeth. Nothing could ever stop it. Nothing, that is, apart from the tunnels, and these were places which added torment of their own. The work of the cabin crew was to keep a constant eye on their allocated area of the system. The goal was to maintain the Homeland's icefield at a steady sixty degrees below freezing, and it was achieved by a refrigeration equivalent of the ancient Wall of China. A vast ring of underground compressors and condensers girdled the territory. It produced the refrigerant that was then cycled along a web of tunnels until it reached the inner ring of evaporators. Huge branched coils in the inner ring released the pressured liquid causing a sustained drop in surface temperature on top. The effect was to create a vast sheet of ice spreading inwards and outwards. The crew of number nine headed out each day to an endless inspection of the various components: the compressors, condensers and fans, the lines that carried the refrigerant, and the enormous freezer coils which sucked all the heat from the ground above.

Poll lay on his bed unable to move his body, every limb paralyzed with strain and weakness. They had just had finished supper, a watery mix of vegetables with artificial protein, and dry oatcakes on the side. It was the same evening meal he had eaten every day since his arrival, and he was fighting to stop himself from retching. But his thoughts were tormenting him more than his stomach. He had witnessed now at first hand the refrigeration process, and he continued to experience amazement at the immense boldness of the project. Back in the TEPs it had all seemed natural, as if it had fallen from the sky. Now he saw the planning, the materials, the possibilities of breakdown and the painstaking fail-safe measures which had been put in place. He understood why the job of maintenance had been given to prisoners. It needed constant attention in the worst of conditions. Going back and forth from the lethal wind to the constant warm air stream of the condenser tunnel—or from there to the inhuman cold of the inner zone, the "Icebox" as the prisoners called it— was acutely painful and dangerous. At first the heated current was a delight, like a warm bath, but quickly it became too hot, and the prisoners had to abandon their huge coats and unzip their therm-suits in order to continue. The warmth of the tunnel created a constant seeping of ground water which formed pools underfoot. Splashing through puddles the prisoners had to be very careful not to let the water into their boots. Emerging from the tunnel it would freeze immediately and cause crippling frostbite. Meanwhile the puddles themselves evaporated, causing the atmosphere to become humid and provoke asthma attacks. The whole thing was almost unbearable. The prisoners knew scores of men who had been unable to withstand the strains and fallen ill and died. In fact Miller, the older man of the recent arrivals, had been overtaken by uncontrollable shaking and been removed to the hospital.

Finn, on the other hand, was thriving. He even seemed to enjoy it, and the men had taken to him because of his upbeat attitude. He had attached himself to Poll, occupying the bed next to him and sticking close to him through the day. In Poll's company he became free and talkative, asking questions and making comments about everything he saw. This way Poll picked up a lot of information without having to ask too much himself. He found out that the camps did not do all the maintenance of the massive electrical turbines that worked the refrigeration process but the Homeland Sectors sent out additional inspection teams. He supposed he would have been chosen for something like this if he had gotten on better in Training. As for the nuclear reactors they seemed maintenance free. Their fuel cycles were hermetically sealed and perpetual. The energy flows were monitored from the Sectors and that was about it. As he continued to get a picture of all the layers which kept the system working he could see how it all appeared to function as if by divine pleasure, but really it was by intense human ingenuity. He reflected again that the people who had done all this were really quite extraordinary; even as he was bitterly angry about them he also felt a grudging respect. His conviction hardened there had to be a bigger meaning to what they had done, something more than he could see. It was all too smart and calculating, and involving such enormous thermal by-products. All the careful planning and the huge amounts of energy meant that something much more far-reaching was at stake. And, along with that, once again he felt certain that these people would not just abandon the frozen wonder they had created. If it was so important to them they would keep actively involved. There would have to be a way for them to come here and fix things if they went wrong.

The memory of Wes and Esh was nagging at his mind. He remembered them shouting as he was leaving the Worship Center.

Something to do with Danny and Liz. Ah, yes, the famous swimming couple had disappeared. What did that mean? He saw the two of them in his mind's eye. Happy, smiling, just like the people in the photograph. And their bodies looked like those of the laughing men. Their clothes too were different, not the therm-suits of the Sector, but freer somehow, open. Now they were running, chasing through green and colors, like in the holograms. So free, so free! His heart felt an enormous pang of jealously and loss.

"Get up, get up," Finn was shaking him. "Reveille was ten minutes ago. The crews are already eating. If you don't get up you'll miss food."

Poll blinked, confused and feeling empty and sick. He'd been dreaming. He'd fallen asleep exhausted on the top of his bed. It was now already morning and he was stiff and cold and trying to wake up. He struggled to his feet and pulled on the overcoat which he'd instinctively drawn over himself in the middle of the night. He stumbled down to the tables and grabbed the last of the boiled oats before it was taken for seconds. He knew it very ill advised to face a day in the tunnels without something in his stomach, and he was kicking himself for not hearing the wake-up. He didn't feel steady on his feet and wasn't sure he had time to get to the bathroom before the tractor arrived. If he stayed behind he'd immediately be reported. He was still wolfing down the bowl of thick oatmeal when the bang came on the door signaling arrival of the transport. He had no choice but to go with the rest. He lurched out the door to cram on his boots, grab his gauntlets and head out through the hatch into the bitter wind. Following the line of men he fell up the steps into the cabin of the tractor and into a seat that Finn was holding for him.

By the time the vehicle had trundled the half mile to the turbine plant and the housing of the shaft-head, his body was shaking and he was fighting to keep his breakfast down. He tried to get a grip on himself, to stop the trembling by sheer force of will. He told Finn to go ahead of him on the metal ladder fixed in the concrete shaft, and asked him to hold his legs to steady him from falling. His friend carefully guided his feet on the rungs above him to the next step below. He was feeling desperately weak and when he got to the bottom he could not help it but staggered and went down on all fours. Finn helped him up.

"Come on, get up. You gotta keep going."

At the bottom of the shaft was a buffer room with sealed doors to stop the warm air of the condenser tunnel from leaking into the icefield. All the men were filing through the entrance. Leaning a hand on Finn Poll followed them. The first door was sealed and the second unlocked. At once a rush of warmth swirled round the crew and the men began to unhook their coats as they passed through the inner door. The change in atmosphere made him feel nauseous all over again, but the shaking lessened and he was able to walk ahead. He pushed back his hood and fumbled at the clasps on his coat and therm-suit.

On either side a tunnel extended, lit by dim storm lamps. This was the outer condenser ring which surrounded the Homeland, the great artery through which the whole refrigeration process pulsed. At intervals on the surface, above its circular journey, were the turbines, and below ground compressor and condenser halls were hollowed in its outer wall. Every so often, splaying from the same outer edge, there was an exhaust shaft, each with its own fan, propelling the warm air out beyond the icefield. On the inner side of the tunnel, at equal spaces between these shafts, a branch at right angles led the big lines of refrigerant inward to the evaporating coils of the freezer zone.

To the side of the buffer room at about thirty yards was a compressor and condenser hall, its heated air forced out into the tunnel through a huge exhaust fan. There was a constant background throb of the fans in the tunnel and the steady fifteen-miles-per-hour current they produced carried a vibration like the moan of a pipe organ. The men made their way along the tunnel toward it, but Poll had hung back. He unzipped his fly and relieved himself against a wall, leaning his body against the rock to rest, if only for a minute. He was hoping desperately he would not be sent on an inspection detail of the freezer area. He would perhaps be able to recover if he was left in the warm air stream. As he forced himself to rejoin the group Cato was dividing the crew up, giving them their duties. Sure enough, one team was doing inspections of the icebox area, another was to carry wire caging and concrete to shore up a crumbling section of tunnel.

Cato pointed to him. "And you, Mr. Sidak, today you're in

81

luck. Or perhaps not. The Icemen want you for special duties."

3. CONSPIRACIES

Cal had spent the first days of her forced inactivity fluctuating between states of mental nothingness and sudden bursts of intense awareness. She had watched the display lights on the wall and mindlessly counted the intervals between the Bubbles passing her house in the morning rush. She replayed WIA videos, including old sequences she hadn't seen since she was a child: sun-dappled mountains, dolphin pods racing in the bluest seas, children picking from blackberry bushes among tall yellow grass with a dog chasing back and forth. She remembered with a jolt that as a little girl she had firmly believed she and Danny were part of that happy band, and the dog had been theirs. She played this sequence endlessly, trying to get to the part that might have made her think she and her brother were among those virtual children. Eventually she gave up and simply tried to recreate the wonderful memory; but that too had become impossible. She remembered instead that Danny was now in the other world, together with Liz, and that very possibly they were walking together in a scene just like one of the holograms, but this time for real.

She could not help wondering what were they to each other, now that they had fields to wander in and seas to swim. No doubt they were together at this moment, and perhaps more together than they had ever been. They were not married like they would have to be in the Homeland, but what difference would that make if you had real fields and warm sunshine? Everything would have to be very different in a land like that.

Tears welled up inside her and she did not want them to stop. She cried for Poll because he was not there and because his not being there was the same as no one at all being there. She cried because she was alone, because the Homeland was so cruel, because there was never any warm sunshine and no one to kiss her and hold her under a kind sky. She cried because she was young, because she knew so very little and because all she saw ahead of her was unrelenting struggle. The sobs pulsed through her body like lumps of hot metal. She let them out from her throat and sucked back the air in great gasps. The noise was a frequency of human sound she had not known existed, and she was amazed at the sound herself. The Word and Image system never showed people experiencing emotions like this· it was as if they were against the very design of the Homeland itself. Then she hurt and wept even more because she was so different. Yet slowly the sound quieted, quelled by its own powerful force of emotion. Little by little, as the sobs subsided, she felt her tears and her weeping were good. It was an astonishing thing but her tears had emptied and opened her heart at the same time, bringing her to a strange peace and clarity. She knew what she had to do. She would find some means of transport to the camps and she would find Poll. What would happen after that was not so clear, but it did not matter. There was now absolutely no question about the task before her or even the certainty of its success. She got up and bathed and dried her face. She switched off all the holograms, dropped the bed from the wall and lay down. She knew she could wait. She did not have to find the path, it would come to her.

***

She did not have to wait long. Within two days Benn came seeking a solution to their stand-off. Although he had permission from the Security Chief to keep her at home it would reflect badly on him to continue to ground her. If he was to achieve fame as a Worship Leader he had to have a model family. He had to show that his daughter could be exemplary too, just as Danny had proven to be. Also he had noticed she did not in fact seem to suffer from the punishment. She remained calm in herself, even remote. The Worship Leader was irritated. He had to find a way out.

"I suppose you'll say that I was too harsh on that young man, and I'm overreacting keeping you at home. But you're far too young to understand how dangerous the game was you were playing. And Sidak, he had a very destructive side to him."

Cal looked up at her father from the small family table where she was sitting.

"It's you who don't understand."

Benn struggled to control himself. He continued.

"Cal, you have to make a choice, and I want you to think carefully about the future. You clearly have more intelligence than required in those courses you were taking. You should adopt a more serious path of study, for one of the leading professions. I know I can put a good word in for you. In Technical Control perhaps, or Transport Management, or even Entertainment and Information! I need you to think about your direction, now you have this time to yourself."

Cal had more or less guessed that her father would make an offer like this. There was little alternative for him if he wanted to break the stalemate between them, and she'd already thought quite a lot about her answer. She had no interest in a profession in the Homeland, but she did want to learn about transport. She needed to understand the transport system if she was to get to Poll.

"If you're offering me a way out, Dad, I'll take it. I would be glad to go to special classes."

"Great! We'll make a new start together, you and me. So which will it be then?"

"I was thinking of Transport. You know, I like numbers and schedules, that kind of thing. I think I'd be good at that."

"That's wonderful," Benn said, obviously relieved. "I'll make some inquiries and you'll be back on the Early Bubble in no time!"

Not long after that she was accepted into the Department of Transport Management. Her classes began early in the day because in addition to all the basic courses she was to take extra studies. Quantum magnetics, power supply, track, computer control and guidance, along with maintenance, personnel, service request and monitoring, all this had to be learned both theoretically and practically. Cal threw herself into the work with an enthusiasm that rapidly got the attention of her superiors. As she shadowed the trained operators in Transport Control they noticed her uncanny ability to count ahead, to predict real time sequences on screen or in a meter reading. She could assimilate data as it appeared and extrapolate from it to make predictions of astonishing accuracy. Just by looking at bar variations for a section of track she could judge how many Bubbles were using it, how long it would take them to move through the section and at what speed. Her overall skill meant she would eventually have the ability to calculate, virtually in her head, the general transporting needs of the Sector on any given day. Her adviser predicted enormous success for her in Management of the fixed rail system. But she also showed interest in engine maintenance and inquired about independent vehicles which could travel outside the Sector.

85

The adviser told her that they would soon be visiting the machine shops where they had ice-tractors, but really this was way below her abilities and she should concentrate on digital systems. Cal said yes, of course, but she counted the days to the field trip.

She was still attending some of her old courses at the Training Center and once or twice she saw Wes and Esh in Dining, but she stayed out of sight. She was sure they were upset about losing Danny and would value the chance to talk. But she hadn't decided how much she should say to them—about her plans to find Poll. They would consider her absolutely insane and try to dissuade her. On the other hand, if she said nothing and one day she too disappeared, they would never understand what had happened to her brother. She felt ultimately they had a right to know. So one lunch time she went up to their table and sat down.

"Cal! What happened to you? The last time we saw you, you were under arrest."

"Yes, but they couldn't hold me. My Dad was embarrassed about having me at home, so he's got me on a new course of studies. How about you guys? How are you?"

"The Hundredth Day Fest was a complete bummer. It was no fun without Danny. How can they just take people away from their friends like that?"

"Who took them away?"

"They said it was a colony for successful athletes, but in any case it doesn't seem right."

"Those places exist, Esh, but they're different from what we imagine. Danny and Liz were taken to the other world, the place where there's warm sunshine."

Wes looked incredulous. "You're still talking about that! We figured it was some crazy stuff Poll cooked up. You still believe it?"

"I don't believe it, I know it."

Wes stopped her, half looking round again. "Now it's you who's getting crazy, and it's seriously dangerous, I suppose you know *that*."

Cal thought, "You have no idea." But she hesitated. It was a moment of choice. Perhaps it was safer on her own. Then again she needed allies. And perhaps the two young people should be brought in simply because the whole thing was bigger than any one person and they should know it for their own sakes.

"Actually I want to talk to you more about the whole thing. Do you really want to find Danny and Liz again? Or do you want to live like Poll, in a prison, except at least *he knows* he's in prison?"

She wasn't sure where the words came from but they seemed to have an impact. Nobody answered. Esh was looking at her with a tunnel stare, scared yet impressed. Wes seemed about to panic. Cal thought her brother's friend had lost his nerve all together. Then she saw he was not actually looking at her. She turned her head and there right behind was a security guard.

"Hi Officer, can we help you?"

"You kids hung out with Danny Anders, didn't you? And you're his sister, if I'm not mistaken. I recognize you from the Worship Centers Bulletin. I just wanted to say congratulations, on his special retirement. You all must be very proud."

Cal smiled affably and stood up.

"Thank you. I'm sure Danny is very happy. And all of us really want the best for him, don't we?"

Danny's two friends nodded stupidly.

"What's your name, Officer?"

"Seb, everyone calls me Seb."

"Well, Seb, thanks for introducing yourself."

Seb colored slightly.

"No problem, Miss. It's a pleasure!" And he quickly turned away.

Wes and Esh were in awe.

"Wow! You had him eating out of your hand."

Esh was grinning, but her tone quickly shifted back. "But you're serious, aren't you? You're up to something."

"Yes, I am serious. Poll's in the camps and I must help him. All this, everything you see around here, it's all lies. Danny and Liz know the truth, but they probably don't care anymore. I do, and I'm not going to just sit in my TEP for the rest of my life and let it ring me in." Gesturing with her finger down through the table she said, "There's another world, right here in this world. And I'm going to find it. And I'm going to start by finding Poll."

Cal knew how extreme and preposterous her words sounded, but she was in no mood to debate them. She stood up from the table and left without giving the two young people the chance to reply.

***

Poll had been told by Cato to walk the remaining distance to the condenser hall and knock loudly on a door next to the fan in the tunnel wall. When he did an enforcer opened the door and led him across a platform and down a zigzag of metal stairs. The steps descended the wall of a pit filled with hundreds of engines and thousands of clustered pipes with banks of rotating fans playing across them. The noise was deafening and the updraft of warm air like the blast of a foundry. When they reached the bottom it was cooler but here at ground level the layers of rock in the walls were seeping moisture. Pools of water gathered underfoot. They splashed along the pit floor until they came to a heavy metal door in the wall.

"Knock," said the guide, and turned away at once.

Poll did as he'd been told and a gray voice sounded, "Enter."

He pushed down on the handle and stepped into the room. The door swung shut behind him and at once it was much quieter. The space inside was warm, with sealed walls and a concrete floor, but the furnishing was sparse, just a couple of desks and some hardback chairs. There was a musty smell. Sitting in the one easy chair, sipping from a metal flask, was the man who had first welcomed him to the camp, the one who had declared himself Poll's god.

"My name is Guest. Please come, sit down." He waved his hand toward a chair next to him. Poll walked over unsteadily and sat down.

"I'm glad to see our camp life is agreeing with you." The Iceman's words carried more than a hint of mockery, but his face remained motionless.

"I have no complaints, sir. I'm doing pretty well."

"Good, good," the Iceman continued. "You are here at my pleasure, but I want you to relax. Nothing is gained if any of us is tense." And after a moment, "Because I need you to help me."

Poll kept his head slightly lowered as he answered.

"How would I be able to help you, sir?"

Guest looked at him with narrowed eyes. "You want to please, yes. I see it. But why? I must continue to think about that, too. Because I believe you really are a smart one, and I should be on my guard. But there, isn't that the reason why I'm talking to you in the first place, that you're smart? So, at least at the moment, there's nothing for it. I must explain myself to you, Sidak. It is Sidak isn't it?"

He continued without a pause, with a tone of quiet contempt. "I have been in the camps for more years than you have lived. This is not a prison for me but a kingdom. I have no way of communicating how immensely I prefer being here to the stupid little clockwork world you come from, the Sector, the place you miss so desperately every night you curl up in your miserable bed. Here I am free, I am my own lord. Indeed I am god, as I said to you before."

His gaze seemed to penetrate the wall and burrow through the solid earth and the field of ice in which it was encased. He sighed and took a small sip from his flask.

"But being god is a problem if there is a limit to one's power. Here in the borderlands there are things I cannot do. I cannot control the flow of electrical power. I cannot switch off a single turbine or compressor or fan. We can tell when they fail, and then the Sector tells us to replace them and throws the switches. But I switch nothing on or off. I cannot control a single circuit breaker or relay. Now, it is not that I have any particular purpose in turning everything off, but it would suit me greatly to know how to do so."

In his characteristic way he drawled the last few words. As he did so he caught Poll's glance and held it. There was a sense of the enormous power he sought.

"I have asked others before you to help me and I have not been angry with them when they failed, but, let's say, their stories were inevitably lost. I have a feeling about you, Sidak. I don't think your story will be lost. What do you say?"

Poll understood this was an offer of conspiracy. Whatever law had put him here for asking awkward questions would certainly not tolerate any interference in the actual mechanics of the Homeland. Not that he cared. He was desperately interested to find out himself. But he could not give that impression to Guest. If Guest suspected a fraction of what he, Poll, suspected, there would be no telling what he might try to do.

"I like to figure out puzzles, sir. I told you. It makes me happy. Do you have plans, drawings?"

Guest laughed, an abrupt cough that ceased as soon as it had begun. "You're quick to the chase, aren't you? Perhaps too quick. But I need someone like you, so just know I'll be watching you. You hide something and it's easy to take a wrong turn down in the ice tunnels. You understand?"

Poll nodded humbly. Guest again held him in his cold stare, his glance like refrigerant all his own. Then he slipped his flask into a pocket and got up from his chair. "Over here."

Against a back wall was a small table, and standing on it was what looked like a box covered by a cloth. Guest led the way, giving the impression he was approaching something he respected and hated all at once. He carefully took off the cloth to reveal a computer, the same basic type as Poll had worked on in Cal's Worship Center. Guest bent to switch it on, then gestured to the screen as it flickered into life.

"There's a whole load of stuff here but I have no idea what it means. I want you to get into it and find out what's there, to see if it can tell us about the controls of the refrigeration system and anything else of interest. This will be your work. You will come here every day with the others but report immediately to this desk. You will stay on it until you figure it all out, or lose your mind trying. I expect results."

With that Poll was alone. Guest seemed to disappear without warning. He was silent as the grave and Poll felt he could walk up behind him anytime to look over his shoulder and he wouldn't know it. In the meantime here he was again in front of a computer screen seeking answers to the enigma of the Homeland. How ironic it was. The computer in the Worship Center had provided information that got him sent to the camp, and now in the camp they had given him another computer which might possibly supply the way out of the entire Homeland system.

For on the screen page was a tangled mass of lines in a bewildering array of colors, one laid on top of the other in fine detail. Scattered through the maze were tiny white dots. Clicking on the white dots pulled in a zoom on that particular area, showing more lines and various added symbols. Hitting the symbols sometimes revealed an entirely new geography with further pathways and what looked like structural forms. As he continued to click and stare Poll understood this was a design plan of the refrigeration plants and tunnels. It couldn't be anything else. The computer had probably been left behind after construction was completed and it was locked on this page. What he was looking at could possibly contain transport routes, including the final all-important exit route, the one that led from here to the world of sunshine: in other words the proof he was looking for. It was hard for him to believe his luck. His sick feeling was swept away on a tide of hope. It was good that Guest had disappeared for he would not have been able to hide his excitement from those iceberg eyes. But Guest would be back, so it was essential to find something to keep him happy. Poll would have to play along, but he would also be on constant lookout for answers to his own quest.

The following days unfolded in a steady, even pleasant rhythm. Instead of the sweating wind of the condenser tunnel or the traumatic cold of the refrigerant lines he had steady warmth to work in, bracketed by the brief pain of the journey back and forth from the hut. His body settled into the routine. While others endured by pure will or succumbed to illness he reached a state approaching good health. Each day he turned on the computer in good spirits believing that would be the day he would get the information he was after.

He began by looking for the great condenser tunnel, thinking that could be an organizing feature. But there was nothing that resembled it, no obvious circular line. It was more like a multi-leveled maze, with any number of routes, starting at one point and arriving at somewhere unrelated. He started looking at the symbols and copying them down. There was a huge number of them. Even when he began noting where the same ones occurred there were so many others it seemed impossible to establish a pattern with any meaning.

He wondered if the map could go live, whether it was linked to the real-time operation of the system. He had checked the wires leading to the computer. There was a power source and a couple of cables dangling loose. He examined the computer itself and there seemed to be no wireless device. When Guest came back a couple of days later and asked how things were going Poll explained what he was looking for— some link between the computer and the live refrigeration system. If he could find that then he could perhaps begin to identify some of the symbols. Guest told him the computer had come from a storeroom right there in the condenser hall. He had plugged it in and turned it on. Beyond that had no idea whether it could connect to the live system.

Poll asked how the work crews knew if something wasn't functioning. Was there a Control Center that gave them up-to-date information? Guest said that the crews normally turned up faulty equipment by hands-on inspection, checking the warning lights directly on machines and valves. Sometimes the Sector informed them, and in every case they needed to contact the Sector to switch off power in that area so the device could be replaced. So, yes, that was the whole thing he wanted to find out, the Sectors' control system.

"Then that's it, sir. That's the key! It means there must be some kind of live link to computers in the Sectors. There could be a way of hooking into it. If you don't mind me asking, sir, how does the camp stay in contact with the Sectors?"

"By radio, of course. Each camp has a radio tower."

"Which means the system has to be on the radio link somehow if they're able to turn it on and off. Could you tell me where your nearest radio connection is, sir? If we could hook the computer to that maybe it would recognize it somehow? It very likely was on some kind of grid when the whole thing was first set up."

Guest looked at him suspiciously but he reached into his coat and took out a flat phone with a cable wrapped around it. He went over to the side of the room where his chair was and found a small panel in the wall. He flicked it open. "Here it is. I plug in here."

Poll followed him over and looked at the wall jacks mounted in the small cupboard. He had seen that Guest's radio had a single connector and there was a small round silver socket for that. But there were also two other, more complex jacks, and he could see the very small tines that made the contacts. There were six of them in each. He went back to the computer and inspected the cables straggling from the back. Each had six narrow insulated wires of different colors. "One of those jacks might do it. We need to bring the computer over there to see if we can figure out how to hook it in?"

Guest was becoming a little excited himself. He quickly helped Poll carry the computer and its table across the room and continued to watch with keen interest. Poll did a quick calculation. The two cables at the back of the computer could be input and output, but there was no knowing which.

"There are hundreds of possible variations for wiring the cables into those jacks. They could all be wrong, but one could be right. It'll take some time."

"Don't worry. We're not going anywhere. What do you need?"

"A small penknife, fairly sharp."

This time Guest did not hesitate. He reached into his coat again, pulling out a pocket knife and handing it over. Poll very carefully skinned the plastic sheath on the end of each wire and twisted the splayed ends. He got a piece of paper and began writing down the various orders of colors for the wires of each cable. But he quickly became frustrated when he realized how long it was going to take. He decided to go directly to one of the cables, experimenting with the first three or four wires to see if they could produce any kind of signal. The task of prodding the wires into the tiny spaces was delicate and painstaking work, placing the wires, checking the computer and then scoring that sequence off the list. He tried both jacks but no matter which order he used the computer screen remained stubbornly lifeless. After about fifty minutes his hands began to shake. He told Guest he had to take a break.

"Go ahead. Take your time."

He spent a few minutes pacing round the room shaking his shoulders and arms. Then he went at it again, shifting directly to the second cable.

After a number of attempts with the same blank results the screen suddenly crackled and jumped as he prodded the next couple of colors in one of the jacks.

"We started with the wrong cable," he muttered. "This has to be input." He focused his energies more intently, writing down the complete sequence of colors and moving through the remaining wires systematically.

After about thirty tries with the computer flashing and then blacking out a light began to flicker on the computer console and a screen lit up and steadied. It read: ACQUIRING SIGNAL. ACCESS CODE REQUIRED.

"Wow," Poll exclaimed as the screen came up. "We did it!"

"Yes!" Guest uncharacteristically burst out. "I knew you were the real deal. Who would have guessed it could be hooked in like that?"

For a moment Poll forgot his humility. "Well, there had to be some sort of system control and it was simply a matter of putting two and two together."

Guest for once was at a disadvantage. "I've never exactly been in front of a live computer until now," he frowned.

"You mean you've never seen the computers in the Sectors…" Poll's voice trailed off.

Guest's face snapped back instantly to its gray mask. "You have no idea what I've seen. And don't be damn smart, Sidak, remember I still own your skinny ass. Besides," he said, pointing to the computer, "you have another problem to solve, that access code."

With the sliver of a smirk returning to his lips he left the room.

4. INSTRUCTION

By the time the day came for the students' field visit to the
machine shop Cal was well aware of its location in the transport
system. Yet this was of no use if she could not find out where Poll
had been taken or how to drive an ice-tractor to get her there. She
was constantly anxious for him, having no way to communicate
or even imagine what kind of conditions he was going through. It
was as if he'd been dropped down a black hole. So that morning
when she arrived at the Training Center she went directly to the
Supervisor and said she hoped there'd be an opportunity to drive
an ice-tractor, because it was important that trainees knew all
aspects of the transport system.

The Supervisor was leery of this young woman who seemed
to want to run the whole show and was rumored to be capable of
doing it. "If there's time, Cal, I'm sure you'll get all the
opportunities you need."

The class of fifteen students arrived at the transport machine
shop, a huge rambling complex including domes and older-
looking rectangular buildings. They went first to the dome where
the track system entered. Hundreds of Bubbles were parked in
sidings all around its edge. An overhead crane moved on tracks to
lift them in the air and carry them to cradles where robotic arms
cleaned and greased them. Service personnel tested their magnetic
coils and guidance systems and replaced broken parts. It was a
scene of impressive activity and the next couple of hours were
taken up with technical description of the components, indications
of the kind of things that could go wrong with them, and numerous
questions by the students. Cal who would normally have been to
the fore said very little. She could hardly wait to get to the free-
moving vehicles. The session ended and there followed another
hour and a half touring a factory where new Bubbles were
assembled. Next it was lunch, and after that guidance system
programming. She couldn't contain herself any longer and went
to the Supervisor, reminding him that she thought it important also
to get to the ice-tractors.

"I really don't understand you, Cal. The independent mobiles
are the least significant part of our system. But if you must insist
there may be time for other options after this segment."

One of her fellow students overheard her request.

"Why would anybody want to drive border tractors?"

Cal had learned that working with ice-tractors was thought to be the bottom of the barrel among Homeland occupations. The drivers were believed to be former convicts, the only ones who would do the harsh work of transport to and from the borders. She replied, "Well I think it's important. We do need these vehicles sometimes, when the power's out, on the monorails."

The student made a "Whatever!" shrug and turned away. The afternoon session dragged on with Cal willing it to end. After what seemed an eternity the demonstrations concluded and the students were offered the choices Cal had been waiting for. They included new designs and testing, and, at long last, independent mobiles. Cal and one other student followed a technician to a Bubble port. The vehicle ferried them quickly to a large rectangular building set at some distance from the rest of the complex. The moment they stepped through the weather lock Cal knew that there was something seriously different here. It had a distinct smell, acrid and dirty. The light was poor: separated arcs of vision with heavy shadowed spaces in between. There was also much less activity, with just a couple of men moving around in a desultory fashion. And it was cold, not the cheerful sixty six degrees of the domes. The whole thing spoke of another time, another way of living. Cal felt at once she was closer to Poll.

The technician went to one of the men and asked him to show the students the tractors. The worker squinted at the strangers. His therm-suit was dirty and he was unshaven. "What exactly do you want to see?" he drawled.

Cal walked up to him. "We're students in transport management. Not many people pay attention to ice-tractors, but I've always been fascinated. They do essential duty for the Homeland. I want to find out everything about them."

The mechanic's mood changed abruptly, as if Cal had thrown a switch inside him. "Well right on! We don't get many like you. Folks normally avoid us. But I think tractors are the best transport going. We get to drive them out on the ice, how cool is that!"

"I would love to drive one myself! But first you have to tell me about them, how many you have and how they work, that kind of thing!"

"No problemo! Class pay attention!" He gestured around theatrically. "You are standing in the tractor depot where the vehicles are kept and maintained. We have a fleet of three sixteen-seaters and one four-seater. They are powered by lithium ion batteries generating two thousand volts of electricity. They keep going for twenty four hours without recharging, and have back-up systems to maintain heat for another twelve or so—pretty important when you're out on the icefields. We service them here and keep a couple at the camps. Follow me—we have two in the shed, including my favorite, the four-seater. She handles far the best!"

He led them through rows of workbenches littered with tools and bits of machinery and brought them to the back of the shed. Here were two of the tractors, one huge one that looked like a building on wheels, and another, considerably smaller, beside it.

"See these caterpillar tracks?" he said, pointing to the monster. "They chew up snowbanks and ice blocks like they're fresh bread. But if it gets stuck in a crevasse it's tough to maneuver and you can burn up the motor. On the other hand, my little baby here, she can climb over most things and back out of any hole."

"Could we drive that one, your baby?"

The mechanic looked dubious. "You have clearance? We'd probably have to get an OK from the bosses."

Cal smiled. "Yes, we have clearance. My Supervisor said so."

He brightened. "Well your guy must outrank my guy. Hell, let's do it! Get in!"

He jumped up on the track and the cabin step and climbed in, beckoning the others to do the same through the passenger doors. Cal made sure she got round the other side in front, clambering up beside him while the others came in behind.

She saw him enter a code on the instrument panel and was able to memorize it. He hit a button and a powerful whine rose from beneath them making the body of the vehicle shake. He put it in gear and it ground forward slowly. He pushed another switch on a box above his head and a wall section of the shed began to roll to the side revealing a weather lock. He steered in front of it and waited, with the tractor vibrating so strongly everyone felt they were buzzing inside. When the opening cleared he moved the tractor forward into the lock. He switched on heating and hit the overhead panel again. The wall section rolled back behind and an outer gate began to lift vertically in front of them. He told everyone to buckle their safety belts and continued to inch the tractor forward even before there was headroom. Immediately there was clearance he rolled forward and they heard something catch and scrape briefly.

"Don't worry, just the antenna," he shouted. It bends!" He laughed and slammed the tractor into second gear, and immediately third. It lunged forward and they were suddenly out, bouncing across the open tundra with the machine buildings disappearing rapidly behind.

"It's a stick shift," the mechanic yelled above the whine to Cal. "It's easy. All you have to do is depress the clutch—see my foot here?—then move the gear lever and let go of the clutch." He popped into fourth, lifted his foot and the tractor surged forward again. "It's soooo fun!" He was looking over at Cal. "You really want to take a spin, don't you? I can tell."

Cal nodded feverishly, hardly able to speak with the rush of nerves and excitement. The technician behind them leaned forward. "What are you saying? I don't think we have permission for students to drive vehicles."

"No one said we couldn't," countered Cal.

The driver's reply was to bring the tractor to a skidding halt. "I won't say anything if you don't," he said over his shoulder.

He flipped out of gear, pulled his hood over his head, opened the door and jumped out, waving to Cal to do the same. They exchanged places bringing a blast of face-scalding air into the compartment.

"Don't worry, the heating's great." And he cranked it up several notches.

"OK, Just push down on that lever with your foot, then put it in gear here with your hand. Up and down for first and second, then to the middle and the right, then up and down for third and fourth. There's a fifth and reverse too but we won't worry about them. Just remember to steer the wheel!"

Cal pushed down on the clutch, gripped the wheel with one hand and the gear lever with the other, thrusting it into first. Then she released her foot. The tractor bounced forward. She put her foot down on the clutch again, pushed the gear into second, but let her foot up too quickly. The tractor shuddered, groaned, and almost came to a full stop, but the engine continued to torque and slowly regained momentum.

"Ha! See what I mean? My baby! She don't quit. Now, like I said, to the middle and to the right for third and fourth."

Cal continued her lesson, crashing the gears and bouncing her passengers painfully, but essentially getting the hang of the shift. She executed a number of big turns in the open icefield, becoming more and more confident. "You're a natural," her instructor beamed, "but we gotta stop now. We won't want to run the battery down and get reamed out."

They exchanged places once more and turned back toward the shed. On the way in Cal asked casually, "How do you find your way out there? It must be difficult on that endless ice?"

"Nah, it's easy. There's basically one road and you can't miss it. And anyway there's a beacon that keeps you heading in the right direction." And he pointed to a small screen set in the dashboard.

"Where does it all lead?

"To the borderlands of course. Refrigeration, the camps. Where else?"

"Oh, of course, silly me! I suppose you make the trip a lot?"

"Now and then, but there are plenty of others. The guys from the camps usually make their own collections. "

Cal bit her tongue. She was dying to ask more but could think of no good way without sounding too interested. She turned to the passengers behind her. "I hope you're not sore at my driving, I had to try."

The technician looked hostile, but said nothing. The student replied, "It was very cool! By the way, my name is Rory."

"Pleased to meet you, Rory."

"Yeah, and my name is Rip Van Winkle," broke in the mechanic, guffawing.

Cal seized her chance. "Well, good to meet you, Rip. You know, I was thinking I'd like to get an idea of how much these vehicles are used. I might write a term paper on them. Do you keep any kind of log? "

"Sure, we keep a log. Each vehicle has one right in there," and he pointed to a box between the seats. "But this time you really will need permission to start poking around in those things."

"Yes, of course. But thanks anyway for the chance to drive your baby. It was a blast!"

The tractor had entered the lock and they were waiting for the wall section to roll back.

"Pleasure's mine, Cal. Maybe they'll send you down here as manager or something. You would sure brighten the place up!"

"You never know," she responded. "I definitely want to come back!"

***

Danny and Charlize were asleep in each other's arms, entwined on the single couch. They awoke slowly and as they began to focus they saw around them a peaceful circle of white-garmented men and women. Some were cradling small oil lamps, some had their eyes closed smiling blissfully, others stared ahead contemplating an invisible greatness. Charlize was the first to come to and she caught one of the attendants' eyes who smiled at her and, half-conscious, she smiled back. Danny focused and then convulsed, falling off the bed. He landed instinctively, half on all fours and half trying to cover himself, looking desperately around for something to wear. The circle of acolytes all laughed, a noise like chiming bells and falling water. One of them retrieved Danny's robe on its stool and handed it to him.

"Is this what you're looking for?"

Another voice spoke.

"Good morning and welcome again. I am Cyrus. We are here to invite you to the orientation program on the daily life of the Heavenly Homeland. Take a little refreshment now and join us outside when you are ready."

The circle melted away, leaving two attendants carrying white alabaster bowls of fresh water with soft towels draped on their arms. Standing slightly behind them were two more attendants with crystal trays of pomegranate, honeyed grain cakes and slender glasses of mango juice. Charlize leaned over to the other side of the couch and picked her gown off the floor where it had fallen. She shrugged it on and stepped over to the attendant with the bowl to bathe her hands and face. Danny just stood staring around him.

"I didn't just dream this, did I? It's all for real! I, you… last night, it happened didn't it?'

"Yes, of course."

"And now we're in a totally crazy world with everyone running around half naked."

"Calm yourself, Danny, and get freshened up. These people are cool. We had fun yesterday, or whenever it was. I'm definitely not complaining."

Danny skipped washing and went to the attendant with the breakfast. He took a honey cake and glass of juice. The attendant smiled at him. Danny looked at him closely.

"You're real, aren't you? How long have you been here?"

"Friend, please wait for the orientation. Everything will become clear. In the meantime relax. We are all here at your pleasure."

Charlize dried her face and moved to the breakfast attendant. She took a bowl of pomegranate with its tiny fork. "I've never had these before. And what's this juice? It smells so fresh and different."

"It's mango with a touch of orange," the attendant said. "They both grow plentifully here."

"What a place," said Charlize. "It's paradise!"

Danny looked at her frowning. "What did you just say?"

Charlize laughed, "What's up with you, I said this was paradise?"

"You said this place was paradise, *this place*. It was like you agree with these people, that heaven, paradise, is this world, here. It's not up in the sky, a world of spirits or whatnot."

"Of course, that's what I meant. What's the problem, preacher's kid?" She laughed again, hearing the sound of her own words.

One of the attendants broke in smiling: "Will that be all? If so, it seems you're ready for orientation."

Charlize nodded and the attendants bowed gracefully and filed out. Danny was still pursuing his thought. "You know what the kids used to say, that people could be captured by Immortals and brought to heaven. Well, what they're saying—what you're saying—is it's real, completely real. The only difference, it's not up in the sky." He paused and then added, "Wow!"

101

"Sure it's real," said Charlize, and kissed him passionately
After a while Charlize broke away and bent down under the couch.
"We gotta go. Look, our shoes!" She retrieved two pairs of thong
sandals, one of which she slid toward him. They slipped them on
and, laughing, tried out the new footwear. Then she grabbed him
by the hand and ran with him from the room.

In the hallway a door stood ajar, a wedge of golden light.
Instinctively they stepped through and found a sandy courtyard
outside surrounded by a stone wall with an open gate. In the
middle was a tamarix tree and beside it stood a vehicle, sky blue
in color and garlanded with flowers along the pillars of its open
sides. Cyrus was seated in front, and standing beside an open door
a single attendant. Cyrus beckoned, inviting them to get in the
vehicle. The attendant shut the door behind them and took the
wheel, backing the vehicle out of the courtyard and onto a broad
paved road. Beyond the road was scrubland dotted with small trees
and bushes. Cyrus leaning round introduced the driver.

"This is Jonas, my personal assistant. If you have any
problems in your period of orientation please let him know. We
are going now on a small tour of the Homeland so that you can get
a sense of its space and meaning here. As we go the larger picture
will unfold progressively, so I would suggest you sit back, enjoy
the ride and save any questions until the end. Is that OK?"

Charlize and Danny nodded in agreement and Cyrus turned
and settled into his seat. Well-toned and about fifty years old, he
had refined, proportioned features and dusky blond hair. His
manner was lofty and imposing: he was the first person they had
met since their arrival who did not seem to smile at the end of
every statement. He spoke in sculpted phrases across his shoulder
as the car motored smoothly along the paved surface.

"The road we are on turns north and will presently join our
great Appian Way, or Sacred Way as we call it. The Way runs
basically west-to-east and takes us to the heart of our city. The
Homeland of Heaven is laid out on this axis because it's along that
line and in this place that our founding scientists were able to
create the greatest climatic stabilization. Which brings us, in short
order, to the matter of history."

"The Homelands, both north and south are four hundred and
twenty eight years old. Their establishment came after the years

of storm and death which brought humanity to the edge of extinction, forcing the world's leaders to adopt an extreme solution. Millions, billions in fact, had died and continued to die because the earth's climate suffered catastrophic disruption. You are already familiar with much of this through the lessons you received on the Global Weather Shield. However, you were not given the full picture."

Cyrus paused for effect, then continued.

"You were not told that the stabilization took place through two artificial meteorological constructs working together, one in the Northern Homeland where you come from, and one here in the Southern Homeland. They both provide areas of constant high pressure but in synergy with each other. If you think about it, the Northern Homeland produces a lot of heat generating a lot of cold, and that heat has to go somewhere. You have become used to seeing the cold as the main point, essential for your survival in a world of storms. In fact it's a trade-off, the by-product of another, more primary effect. The technical details of this do not matter. The main point is that to save human civilization it was essential to construct one place of stable and pleasant climate, free of storm, where all the best things from the history of our species could be preserved. In order to do this, in order to stabilize the chaos, there had to be a constant, high-altitude stream of warm air flowing toward it from another space on earth purpose-built to exchange cold air for warm."

Danny and Charlize were gazing at him blankly.

"I realize how difficult this may be to take in, given what you have experienced and been taught up to now. You are being invited to see things from a kind of upside-down perspective which, in reality is right-side-up. It is important that you do so because without this you will not appreciate the full drama of this wonderful world you have been brought to share. But wait, I've been chattering on with all this boring history and haven't pointed out any of the sights we've been passing. Jonas, my friend, why don't you describe what we are seeing?"

Cyrus' assistant launched smoothly into the role of commentator. He was a good bit younger than Cyrus, probably in his late twenties, brown-haired, well built like everyone in the Heavenly Homeland, his face pleasant and intelligent, his eyes dark-tinged and sometimes slightly preoccupied. The road had been steadily mounting, threading its way upward through dusty rolling hills with bright stretches of trees and vegetation. At a final sharp incline it made a right hand turn onto a broad road paved in flagstones and fringed by elegant tall trees. As they drove, Jonas pointed out the occasional shape of a building between the stands of acacia and pine lining the route. He explained that these walls signaled dwellings called colonies where groups of residents of the Homeland chose to live, in numbers anywhere from a dozen to sixty or more individuals. They had already passed several of these along the hills. Particular to every villa was a different kind of activity or craft, like flower or fruit growing, viniculture, animal husbandry, also technical specializations, plus of course the humanities—painting, poetry, philosophy. Nobody was obligated to participate in these activities but almost everybody did. Usually people lived in a community together with a long-term partner. But if one of them fell in love with someone else, from another colony, then one or other of the new couple would move. Everyone was always very open and flexible.

Danny and Charlize were having serious difficulty processing all this information. First it was the weird meteorology connecting their old Homeland and this one. Then the dwellings and day-to-day living arrangements which didn't seem to involve any real work. As for falling in love and moving in with someone new, they simply did not follow what was being said.

"Is there any actual work people do, you know, like maintenance, production, that kind of thing?" ventured Danny.

Jonas responded. "Well actually Danny, the Homeland of Heaven is pretty lo-tech and very low-maintenance. This car that we're driving is electric and bits and pieces of it very likely go back to the first establishment of the Homeland Cyrus was describing. And there are not many cars. People don't move around much during the day and when they come out in the evening they ride ponies or take the trams which are always plentiful. As for food and crops, because the climate is so stable and benign, and given the water-supply we've organized, it's very easy to grow things. So the short answer to your question is, yes, people have work, but they will spend only one or two days at it every so often. It doesn't dictate our lives."

Danny couldn't help asking, "What happens if someone doesn't do their job?"

Cyrus interjected. "My dear friend, you have to understand, that kind of thing is simply not going to happen. Everyone in the Homeland of Heaven is far too well-adjusted and contented for anything like that. You will find that for yourself too, as you let this place have its effect. Immortal life begins to flow through you and you flow through immortal life, like a bird in the air! Everything becomes easy."

Right then a tram glided by on its rails in the median. It was a large open-sided vehicle, golden and white, shaped and painted with waves on its sides to resemble a boat. It was moving at little more than a human running pace with five or six people inside. All of them were robed in the diaphanous material that seemed to be the dress of choice. Some were conversing, the others gazing ahead with eloquent faces. At that moment they appeared to Danny and Charlize truly to be divine. Cyrus saw the young people's' upturned glances and smiled

"Ah, yes, you see what I mean, don't you? The word I used, "Immortal," seems entirely fitting, doesn't it? Well, let me explain it to you exactly. It holds the second great mystery to which I must introduce you. Really, the greatest achievement of our scientists in the time of storm and death was something which outstripped even the Global Weather Shield. In fact they had come upon this possibility before the theory of the Shield was developed. But the consequences were so extreme—on top of environmental chaos— that governments waged a war of disinformation against it."

"They denied the discovery absolutely, saying the science was flawed. But scientists had discovered a way of stopping the breakdown of cell replication at the root of the aging process: you know, the way your body over time looks and feels older, and becomes vulnerable to illness. Instead, our scientists were actually able to stop people growing older, finally achieving what humanity has always yearned for—a life of immortality. So, yes, because of this discovery no one here is getting older. Including you. The function of never-ending cell replication has already begun in your bodies. You have become gods like us."

Charlize and Danny's mouths were open. Pandit had said more or less the same thing to them in their Initiation but that was

105

all just a blur. Afterward they had in that decided they were in some kind of heaven, but had not seen themselves as fully part of it. They felt more like visitors on some amazing vacation. Now they were being told they themselves were actually immortal. They were now gods among the gods.

Cyrus had a look of benign triumph, and he was not about to let his moment go.

"Let me explain a bit more, to help get your minds around this. In the old science, before the end of the 20th century, people thought in terms of reactions. The word says it all, one thing acts, another reacts, like millions of tiny solid objects knocking into each other in a line, click, click, click. But then people began to think more in terms of information and signaling, especially in biology. An organism will get a chemical signal from its environment or from itself and that won't simply cause a reaction but a whole complex of events adjusting the total organism to a new situation. That's why it's much better to see everything in the body as signals within a system."

Cyrus was now in full flow, relishing the beautiful details of his story.

"One of the key elements in producing signals in the body is something called an enzyme, which is a tiny, complex structure in the body. Enzymes have a fantastic ability to speed up processes like digestion or locomotion, that kind of thing. Some enzymes have the specific job of ensuring the accurate copy of genes at the heart of the cell. They actually check and proof-read DNA as it's reproduced in the body, rejecting bad copies. Biologists working on the treatment of cancer discovered that you could get an artificially produced strand of enzymes to check cells for cancer and then eliminate the cancerous ones. Cancer, the longtime nemesis of human health, was cured at a stroke. It did not take long then to apply that same function to other processes, including aging. This time rather than eliminate the cell itself they were able to provide a fresh set of signals that it should repair itself. Lo and behold, immortality! It was a miracle of biological engineering: a bunch of tiny workshops circulating through the body continually ensuring its perfection. What's more, they were resilient enough to be administered with the water supply. You two have already begun the treatment. From today on you will be forever the beautiful age you now enjoy!"

"Oh my God!"

"Yes, that was basically the reaction of everybody who knew about the discovery. They all wanted it, and why wouldn't they? But, as I said, it was just one more chaotic factor in the end-game of humanity at that time. How could anybody be immortal when the earth was pouring down its own flood drain? But, as the idea of the Global Shield began to emerge, authorities in the know added the enzyme repair-kit into the equation. Suddenly everything fell into place. We could create a place on earth where the best things of humanity would be preserved but without the problems of death, or having children, and all the conflict that flows from them. Immortals in an earthly paradise: it was and is the perfect solution."

He continued on and on, filling in details of the original plan, the construction of the Northern Homeland, the testing of the meteorology, the selection of the territory for Heaven, the arrival of the first immigrants, the joy and glory of their first experiences. Finally he became quiet, totally caught up in the splendor of his own story. The inductees sat in stunned silence, unable fully to process what they had been told. The only thing that could be heard was the hum of the electric motor and the steady lick of the tires on the Sacred Way. After a moment Jonas broke in, looking at Cyrus. "We're getting near the Forum. Perhaps we should say a little about it before we get there?"

Cyrus nodded abstractedly, and his assistant picked up the narrative. "I am sure you have questions about everything Cyrus has told you and you will have the chance to ask them when we take refreshment at one of the restaurants. But first I should tell you that the whole of the Homeland's life is focused on the Forum. It is surrounded on every side by libraries, museums, galleries and exhibitions. All the accumulated treasures of human culture are gathered there, from Qin's Terracotta Warriors to Hirst's skull, from Oedipus Rex to Catcher in the Rye, it's all there. There are people who have been present from the very beginning of the Homeland but they haven't seen everything in the exhibitions, or read a fraction of the books. Look, you can already see the grid system where the collections are housed."

And as they looked Charlize and Danny could see, at right

angles to their road, spacious tree-lined boulevards flanked by imposing stone buildings stretching out in a motionless glow. Jonas' voice pressed on relentlessly.

"This is just the outer shell, the beautiful husk which holds within an exquisite life, the nectar of the city. It must be experienced to be understood. Every night thousands of people gather in the Forum, and every so often at a chosen time tens and tens of thousands come in. We call it Doblepoble, I'm not sure why but somehow the name has stuck. The place is alive with music and light, with sights and sounds and intoxicating scents. On Doblepoble people exchange partners at will but always return to the one they came with, as much in love as when they started. There are chemicals too, that keep us going, giving us energy to dance until the dawn. There's Tremo that allows us to see other dimensions and Soffo that makes us totally relaxed, and we watch everything in an unbelievable state of bliss. And, Danny and Charlize, you know what? It's not long to the next Doblepoble!"

Jonas stopped and looked back at Cyrus. After a moment their chief guide spoke. "We could head straight to the parking plaza, but first I want to show you a breath-taking panorama, probably the greatest in human history, greater than Machu Pichu or the Hollywood Hills, or the Janiculum in Rome. There you will see it all and understand everything."

The car made a left hand turn and began to climb. It navigated a number of hairpin bends and at each one there was a monument with an inscription and above it a heroic sculpture of laboring groups and individuals pointing in a visionary manner toward the east. The car groaned but finally crested the hill, coming out on a graveled esplanade with a low stone wall forming a balcony and belvedere above the city. Cyrus led the way to the edge. There in the late morning sun spread out below like an extraordinary jewel was the heart of the Heavenly Homeland.

5. ARCHITECTURE

Nothing in the Holo-casts came close. Below Danny and Charlize, as far as the eye could see, were sports fields and running tracks, golf courses and swimming pools, surf pools and yachting lakes, rock climbs, polo fields, ski slopes and kayaking streams, everything melting together in a dream of green and earth and water. But this only served as a frame. What drew the eye was a central zone in the same pattern as the Agora, but now on a far grander scale. In the spaces formed by the intersections was a succession of magnificent buildings, palaces, pyramids, pagodas, ziggurats, stupas, towers, Greek temples, Gaudi spires, coliseums, cathedrals, colonnades and cupolas, the architectural triumphs of humanity reproduced on a single canvas. They were covered in many places with ceramic tiling and the glittering colors had the effect of binding them together, an iridescence of purple, jet, gold, opal and crimson. Light cirrus cloud floated in a perfect sky and the unstinted sun seemed itself in awe of everything its light fell upon. The eye was bedazzled and time came to a skidding stop. Cable cars carried tiny figures to the higher structures, their robes fluttering like the wings of mayflies. Along the roads more figures could be seen, in groups and seated at tables where the smoke of small fires suggested open-air cooking. The single vista had the effect of eternity, a pure dreamlike moment of light and happiness and peace.

After the mind had adjusted a little, the attention drifted upward from the temples, across what looked like a great park and equestrian track beyond. It alighted on an enormous globe set in a turquoise lake at the end of the valley. It was this spectacular feature which truly unified everything. The sphere was at least twenty times bigger than any other building, colored blue and white with little rainbow prisms appearing here and there. It seemed somehow to gather all the other structures into itself. It was open at its cusp, like an egg with its top sliced off, and it exercised an intense wonder and attraction. It was like a magnet pulling them in toward itself.

As Cyrus saw their eyes focusing he said, "Ah yes, *Il Font Eterno*, the eternal fountain, the great *mysterium* of our Homeland. It is utterly fascinating, isn't it, there at the heart of the scene? It

109

is unparalleled. But you know, there is something about it that also reminds me of a particular painting I once saw. I am struck by the resemblance now even if I cannot recall the painting to mind!"

Continuing his line of thought he turned to his assistant, "Jonas, you did not mention all the fine art we have in the galleries, from Lascaux to Dali! I have spent days on end wandering those halls and salons. I have always found them so instructive, so illuminating!"

Cyrus paused, looking pensive, and then gathered himself. "Well, anyway, I know you are dying to ask me what that wondrous structure is, but as I said, it is a mystery, and it must remain so for a little while yet, until you are ready. Indeed I think your souls have had all that they can take in and it is time now to minister to the body. Let us tear ourselves away and find a place to eat."

***

It was shortly after midday when they sat down to eat herb-flavored pastries with radicchio salad, followed by fruit compote with fresh cream, while drinking glasses of mint tea. Again the two young people were not used to this kind of food and they ate with dazed relish. They had entered the Forum on foot and found a food vendor below a replica of the Kaiyuan pagoda with blood-colored tiles and branching eaves. People were cooking and eating, some were gently sweeping or putting things in order, all with an attitude of benign good-humor. Charlize and Danny did not feel out of place. The sun beamed down on their near-naked limbs and it felt the whole world permanently afforded the sensations they once enjoyed briefly and poorly in the swimming baths. Their minds were buzzing but the buzz was receding as a quiet pleasure took its place. They felt indeed like gods among the gods. Charlize curled her legs up and smiled. Danny stretched out his hand to hold hers, looking around with a satisfied air. Cyrus pushed his chair back and regarded them with his contemplative demeanor.

"So tell me what questions do you have for me?"

Charlize remembered there was something which had struck her forcefully during Cyrus' explanations. Although, now, it didn't seem quite so urgent. However, it seemed impolite to say nothing.

"I was wondering how you all chose. I mean at the beginning, how did you chose who would be an Immortal, and who would have to live in the cold of the Northern Homeland?"

"Of course," responded Cyrus at once. "The who-gets-a-place-in-the-lifeboat question. Although in this case there are in fact two boats, very different, yes, a luxury liner in a warm sea and a freighter in the arctic, but both lifeboats. It's important to bear that in mind, Charlize. A berth on the freighter is better than a grave in the ocean. For that is what awaited everyone unless something was done."

"There was always a list of "essential people" who should be kept alive, stemming from the threat of all-out nuclear war in the 20th century. They were politicians, soldiers, scientists, engineers, that kind of people. But this time, with the promise of immortality, there were new priorities, things like maintaining a racial mix, plus a greater emphasis on artistic and religious sensibilities. So probably there were many more film-stars, entertainers and gurus, alongside athletes, painters, and musicians. I'm also sure a few individuals who knew the right people had them pull strings, and got themselves put on the list, even though the whole thing was top-secret. So, all in all, we're probably a fairly average mix of humanity. Maybe even more than those in the frozen Homeland—because *your* ancestors, Charlize, had to be *very* carefully selected. They had to be healthy, hard-working, resilient. A strong traditional religiosity was imperative. There was a theological training school or seminary for the original leaders at the same time as the icefields were being constructed. Only those who could believe a religion of earthly discipline for the sake of heavenly salvation were selected."

Danny burst in suddenly with surprising fervor. "You knew you were all going to get the real thing, *this*, *here*, and you palmed the rest of us off with stupid fairy tales!"

Cyrus was slightly taken aback, but he regained his composure quickly. "How do you know they are fairy tales, Danny? Our philosophers still discuss the question with an open mind. Anyway you can't take that approach. We have created an organic system the same as any organic system. The Immortals depend on the mortals the same as the head depends on the feet. And to counter any sense of personal unfairness we regularly

111

bring in people from the North. You, Danny, represent the equaling out of the system. You are now an Immortal and that means basically the system works for everyone: because someone like you from the Northern Homeland has the chance to become a god. It is true we don't take older people, but that is because older folk have a very difficult time adjusting. With a young person like you that shouldn't be a problem at all, should it?" And he gazed meaningfully at Danny.

The swimming star of Sector Three recanted his outburst as quickly as he'd made it. He lowered his eyes and said, "No, no, definitely not." Charlize, however, pursued something that was now actually bothering her.

"We are the ones who show the system works but there are still people we have left behind. We have family and friends in the Northern Homeland. Won't we ever see them again?"

"To be a god, Charlize, you have to be prepared to leave everything. Your existence proves the whole thing works, and, more than that, it becomes an end in itself. You now have the perfect life, perfection itself, and that must override any personal considerations. Your loyalty is to that perfection, above all else. However, I am glad that you did ask this question, because there is one arrangement we do have and that you should both know about. Gods should leave the past behind but they can bring just one bit of it with them! You may perhaps remember, back in the North, when star athletes were given special colony status sometimes they were allowed to have someone with them, a sister or brother, boyfriend or girlfriend. So here's the thing: we allow you each to choose one other person from your old world and we will bring that person here. It can be a friend or a family member, the only exclusion, for the reasons I stated, that person cannot be old."

Danny was remembering. "Yes, Dad say something like that once." Charlize interrupted him.

"You're saying that we can bring a friend here, someone our age?"

"Yes, that's exactly what I'm saying."

"Oh, I so want Esh to come, she'll love it here," said Charlize, clapping her hands at once. "Danny, who would you bring?"

Danny's face broke into an unhesitating smile, "Cal of

course. She's the one who should really be immortal. This place is totally Cal!"

With the sudden excitement of this last revelation, Danny and Charlize abandoned any lingering doubts and gave themselves over to immortal existence. They thanked Cyrus and Jonas for all they had shown them and said they thought they now understood everything very well. Cyrus and Jonas laughed and hugged them, and because it was getting late they told them they would now bring them to their lodgings. They were to stay with the philosopher Zeno and his companion, Xanthippe. The villa where these two lived was one of the most famous in the Homeland. The almost nightly dinner parties there were legendary both for food and conversation. The two of them, Zeno and Xanthippe, were marvelous thinkers and talkers. Thus the newcomers' orientation in the ways of Heaven would be perfected under their care. There would be one final formality to be completed which was a recorded interview to be broadcast back in the North, telling the Teppers of the sports stars' reward of happiness in a special colony. The camera team would come tomorrow to make the recording. It would be conducted only in general terms, with any sensitive details edited out. Meanwhile arrangement would be made to send a rocket transport to the Northern Homeland to bring back Esh and Cal.

They drove back along the Appian Way with the sun going down in front of them, a red ball in a shot-silk sky. Not long after they left the city they turned off on a road that wound gently up into the surrounding hills. Scarlet light bounced off their faces as they navigated the bends. The air gave off a sweet scent of pine. They arrived at the villa in the last glimmer of day. The car drew into a central courtyard surrounded by cottages covered in climbing flowers. Happy Immortals stood in their doorways to applaud their coming. Zeno and Xanthippe came out to the car to greet them, the oldest people Charlize and Danny had seen in this new world, but extraordinarily vibrant. They opened their arms wide to embrace the newcomers.

"Come, come, you beautiful young people. We are so blessed by Lady Fortune to have you in our midst!"

"Are they not Titania and Oberon?" commented Cyrus, leaning out from the car. "Until tomorrow then, when I return with the camera team!"

He sat back, his hands folded contentedly on his lap. Jonas slipped the car into drive and the two guides disappeared into the perfumed dark, while the latest additions to Heaven basked in the approval of gods and goddesses.

***

Poll, sitting in front of his computer screen, had not needed long to figure out the access code. He remembered when they first arrived Dogg had called the prison "Camp Conquest" although none of the prisoners had ever referred to it that way. The phrase had stuck in his head as just the kind of official title a camp would be given. Guest did not return to help him with suggestions, so he set himself to entering permutations on the screen. Both the public nature of the original construction and its extreme conditions encouraged him to think the code would not be that complex. He set about entering variations of the name and after a couple of score of tries he got to "Conquest04." The screen flickered, blanked and flashed up "CODE ACCEPTED."

His problems, however, were only just beginning. He had been granted access to a world much more baffling than the search for a single password. The welcome screen simply read "System Data" and gave an endless list of live links as incomprehensible strings of numbers and letters. There were occasional recognizable terms like "megawatt," "coefficient" and "cycle" but nothing relatable to any hard feature. He wanted to get information on the original design but whenever he returned to it he lost the live connection. When he clicked on the live links he got screeds of data with further protocols he could not grasp. For the first time he felt defeated. He spent his time clicking aimlessly on links, looking for something, anything. The prospect of recording the numbers and letters and trying to guess connections between them struck him as futile. He supposed Guest might recognize some of the data but he wanted to find answers himself without depending on the Iceman more than he absolutely had to. Then again, without knowing where he was in the system none of the information meant anything. The overall map was of no interest to the individual operators in the Sectors. All they did was keep track of the functioning in their own area. And everything had surely been set up that way, so that no one person would have a complete picture. It only reinforced the conviction that there had to be a program with integrated information for the eyes of the other world only, and connected there by a secure radio link. The transmitter was probably in the same place as the exit transport to the other world. But how to find this all-important site?

In the end it was Guest who broke the impasse. He arrived soundlessly as ever.

"I see you got the access code. What else have you found?" He was standing right behind him, looking over his shoulder.

"Uh, yeah, that's right. It wasn't all that hard, but I don't know how to continue. I can't recognize any of this."

Guest peered in closer and held out his hand to stop Poll's random clicking. "Stop! Some of this I know, some of those numbers. Yes, that one, it's a serial number for a condenser fan. And that one there, that's a fan for an exhaust tunnel. I know because those things break down frequently and the numbers come back with the replacements."

Poll straightened up. "That's crucial information, sir. I suppose I guessed some of those numbers were machinery parts, but I had no way of identifying anything."

"Well, now you know, and I can get you a list of other parts too. But..," Guest checked himself. "I would have thought with your smarts you would have figured all this out. You're not going slack, are you? Remember, you're looking for on/off switches, for electrical relays. You need to figure that out and be quick about it. I'm not leaving you down here in the warm forever." And he was gone, exiting like the restless phantom he had become for Poll, haunting the empty spaces of his searching.

Poll tried to think logically. He now knew what a couple of the formulae meant and he could perhaps build a list of others related to them. But without being able to place them in the system he was not much further forward. If he could only connect them with a symbol on the map then he'd have some point of reference. He realized that he had not continued his initial copying of the symbols, distracted as he had been by the live screen. The discovery of the screen had essentially proven that the map was organized in a logical manner. He decided it was just a matter of continuing patiently to figure it out. The next few days he feverishly went through the white dots one by one, documenting the symbols and sub-symbols they led to. Yet once again he could not discover any key ones. They all appeared many times and at all levels of the map. Again he was getting nowhere. If he only knew the meaning of just one symbol!

"Still on that useless map? Get back to the live screen, I've something to show you. This is going to work, I'm sure of it."

Guest was right behind him and Poll had to make a physical effort not jump out of his skin.

"Right, sure, of course. What have you got?"

"There's a fan broken in the perimeter tunnel, one of the ceiling relays, and I know the code for it. I'm willing to bet it's going to show up on one of those screens."

He read out the serial number and Poll began to trawl through the live links looking for it. It didn't take long to find a list with the basic sequence and scrolling down there it was, the exact number, and what's more it was flashing an alert. Poll clicked the link and at the head of the screen with a long list of numbers a message appeared: "Perimeter relay breakdown S.W. 2 k. from Turbine 4."

"And there she is! That's a hard bit of machinery and all those numbers have to be related to it. Find which one is the switch and we'll have a basic code which will appear everywhere!"

Guest was triumphant. The secrets of his fiefdom were falling before him, almost within his grasp.

"That's something, it really is, sir. I suppose any function that stopped flashing with the component itself could be a switch, but then how would you control it?"

"Don't be an idiot," Guest snarled. "If I can get that information I can handle the rest too. Your job is to isolate the component. Tomorrow we'll radio the Sector that we're replacing the fan and they'll cut the power. I can't use this radio link obviously, so I'll be elsewhere. But you'll be sitting here glued to the screen. And you better get that switch number as it comes back on line!"

But Poll was not affected by the Iceman's threat. He was not really listening. He could hardly restrain the excitement he had suddenly begun to feel. He nodded obediently, "Yes, yes, of course, sir," and started writing down the numbers while he waited for Guest to do his standard vanishing trick. After about a minute he looked round and saw no one. Still he got up and checked the room to make sure Guest really had gone. Then he returned to his seat. There was something on the screen beside the breakdown message and he was certain Guest had not noticed it in his moment of triumph. It was the faint image of a small string of symbols which he recognized from his copying, a kind of screen ghost suggesting another program which might even connect the screen to the map. He'd already guessed from the access code that the number four probably stood for the turbine and its related camp. That was now confirmed by the message and with a compass direction added, so here was solid data he could work with. He clicked on the symbols. After a moment another screen appeared and Poll bit his lip. It displayed large letters reading "SYSTEM DISABLED." But right there again was another ghost of an outline, this time a box and table. As he stared at it he thought he could see the trace of a message and word by word he copied it down. "SEGMENT 10, CONDENSER HALL MAIN FAN, TWENTY FOUR RELAYS, EXHAUST MANIFOLD."

"Gotcha!" he whispered. He now had a continuous sequence of symbols covering a segment of tunnel and knowledge of what they meant. It was obvious the "Disabled" sign was superimposed on a fragment screen from the whole program and no one had bothered to erase it. Now with the meaning of the symbols and the map he was sure he had the tools to decipher the geography of the tunnel. There were four hours left before the ice-tractor returned to the hut and he launched himself into his search with the zeal of a hunter on the heels of his prey. He would not be able to do the search tomorrow because he would be glued to the live screen as per Guest's command. Also he needed to get the information he wanted now for he did not trust Guest to allow him back once he had isolated the switch.

He hardly noticed the time passing as he followed the clues, beginning with the succession of symbols and looking for a matching sequence on the map. Now that he knew the sequence he seemed to find it almost at once. Next, as he investigated the collection of further symbols within each feature, he found one that threw him back each time onto the main map, including a small highlight. Using that symbol at every point he could see that he always moved a short distance. Working from one relay fan to the next, through the exhaust manifolds, and to the next condenser hall, he could track his progress on the map in what looked like a circular direction.

It was intensely exhilarating plotting a route around the screen. He had also noticed another recurring symbol halfway along the standard sequence, containing a whole new set of pathways. He decided it had to be the access to the inner freezer zone, the heavy sealed doorway to the deadly refrigerator grid. Another one, with a very complex set of subordinate pathways, was in all probability the turbine. As he continued he was getting a clearer and clearer picture of the whole set up. Between each condenser hall there were three exhaust manifolds and between each manifold site there were almost always twenty four relays. He remembered in his own trips along the perimeter tunnel he had paced almost without thinking the space between ceiling fans. He had figured they were at roughly half a kilometer distance, so he calculated now there were perhaps about fifty kilometers between each condenser hall.

Everything was falling into place but there was still one thing he didn't know, and that was where Turbine 4 came on the map. There was no numbering at any point and it was becoming increasingly frustrating to have come so far but still to lack this last crucial bit of information. The whole map was following a circular path but how was he to orient himself anywhere in it? He was continuing to click with desperation through the map, when, suddenly, as he was almost three quarters of the way around, he saw an anomaly in the sequence, a symbol he had never seen before. The moment his eyes fell on it simultaneously his limbs froze and a pulse of heat shot from his feet to his head. It was unmistakably the shape of some kind of flying craft. He had seen its type in a couple of Holo-casts which simulated trips out among the stars. Here, beyond the shadow of a doubt, was proof of everything he had believed and with it very nearly all the information he was seeking.

"Poll, can't you hear me? Come on, they're all waiting, the tractor's ready to go!" Finn's voice and insistent banging on the door burst into his hypnotic state, dragging him back to reality. He had to leave right now; the crew, always tired and weak, would wait only a couple of minutes before climbing the shaft and taking the transport back to the hut.

At high speed he copied the last bit of sequence and its position on the map and exited the screen. "I'm right here, Finn. Wait, I'm coming." He shoved his notes inside his shirt, grabbed his coat and his gloves and headed out the door. The two of them ran two steps at a time up the metal stairs and out into the tunnel, screaming with what breath they had, "Hold up, don't leave, we're coming!"

6. BREAK OUT

Cal knew exactly what she had to do. It was only a matter of when. She felt a strange thrill as she sat in the dining hall surrounded by hundreds of youthful Teppers laughing and chatting together. What she was planning would seem idiotic to them, foolish in the extreme, beyond pardon. But it was the only thing she could do, the only thing that made sense. To go to the service shed, steal an ice-tractor and head off to the borderlands would, she was certain, change everything, absolutely. How it would work out she had no idea. She had to rescue Poll, that much was clear, and she had some grasp of how to go about it. What came after, well it was fuzzy to say the least. "I suppose," she thought to herself, "I'm relying on Poll to have a plan. But really that's not it either. It's really odd but I just feel this thing. Everything will change. All I have to do is have the guts to go through with it."

"If you sit there staring into space, people will definitely start talking. I hope you're not still thinking all that weird stuff."

It was Wes and Esh settling into the seats opposite her and looking round in a semi-jokey conspiratorial fashion. Wes was picking up directly from their last conversation and trying hard to get things back to normal.

"Hi, I was looking out for you. I'm glad you're here, 'cause I've got a favor to ask. And, yes, it's exactly to do with what I was telling you about last time."

"Sounds like weird is still what she's thinking," Esh grimaced.

Cal leaned in close to her companions. "It's not weird, it's completely real. All this, everything, is going to change. I'm not exactly sure when or how, but I know it will. When it does you'll be among the first to see it, to understand, and it's going to be incredible." She paused and shifted her approach. "In the meantime I also need your help. I learned how to drive an ice-tractor and where to get one, and I'm going to find Poll. But I need supplies for the trip. I need food. Can you get your maximum allowance for the next couple of days and set aside the extra for me?"

Wes gave a low whistle. "Then we're definitely in trouble. You do realize that by helping you we could get sent to the camps too?"

"Wes, Esh you don't have to fear anything. Even if they take you to the camps, I'll get you out again, the same way as I'm going to get Poll out. I'm just asking you to be strong enough for that. And you know what? I think a chance like this only comes along once in a hundred years. It didn't happen for our parents, and it won't be there for our children. So, are you brave enough to grab it with both hands? Or, are you going to let this chance slip by?"

To hear someone speaking this way was utterly new for the two companions. The Worship Leaders whom they had to listen to all the time said more or less the opposite about people's lives. The important thing was to hang on for somewhere else when they died. But now a nerve inside them stirred. Life could be exciting in a totally new way, very different from the sports events and the Hundred Day celebrations. For a moment no one spoke, then Esh reached her hand hesitantly across the table to Cal.

"You're a special person, Cal, and I want to believe you. I'm totally scared even saying this—but I feel we can't let you do this on your own?"

"Ain't that the simple truth," added Wes. "Because whether we believe you or not, if you do this we're involved. They'll come directly for us, and we'll have to have a pretty good story."

Cal smiled thankfully. "I knew you'd come through. You'll see I'm right and you'll be amazed. And yes, Wes, I thought of that. You can just tell them I was saying the same thing as Poll: that the religion of the Homeland is a cover-up and I was complaining all the time. Put the blame totally on me. They've got nothing to pin on either of you."

Wes shook his head, "Let's hope they buy it. I just couldn't handle it if they send me off to maintenance."

Suddenly another student appeared, leaning over the table. They all looked up.

"Hi Cal, it's me, Rory. Sorry for butting in, but I was hoping to see you. There was somebody at Transport, a stranger, he was looking for you."

Danny's two companions glanced at Cal. She gestured, "Oh, hi Rory, these are some friends, Esh and Wes. And, yes, this here is Rory, from Transport Management. What did the stranger want?"

Pascale's Wager

"He didn't say, but he seemed kind of important."

Wes interrupted, "What did he look like?"

"Hard to describe. He didn't look like the usual bosses."

"Could you say he looked, well, healthy?" It was Esh who prompted.

"Yeah, that would be a good way of putting it. He was definitely healthy."

Cal stood up abruptly in front of Rory. "Thanks so much, Rory, I'm glad you came over. Don't you have a class now?

"No, my next is not for another hour."

"Rory, I'm pretty sure you have a class now." And she continued to stand glaring at him until he buckled.

"OK, OK, I better be going. Good to meet you guys. See you, Cal."

The moment he was gone she sat down and blew out of pursed lips.

"What do you think?" said Esh.

"I think it's beginning. That stranger is from the other world, just like the one you saw with Danny and Liz. I'm certain of it."

"You mean Danny has sent for you to come join him?" Wes was joking, but it struck a chord with Cal.

She looked at him sharply, then half stood, bending in close to the two semi-converts to her cause. "I have to leave straight away. I have to reach Poll before anyone finds me. Can you meet me back here in two hours and get extra rations at first servings for dinner? That will have to be enough."

***

Poll lay in bed trying to organize all the information in his head. He now understood the basic layout of the tunnel and the point that connected the tunnel to the rocket. But he had no idea of where his camp was in the system or in relation to that point. On the map the rocket symbol stood at the bottom, at what could be the south, but he couldn't be sure because the map had no compass points. It could just as possibly be oriented from the south at the top.

He thought it possible the pioneers would have started building from where refrigeration created the most immediate impact—that is toward the south. The read-out for the broken fan

122

had given the direction of south west, which could place camp 4 and its and turbine close to that point of the compass. But still the camps could be numbered from the north, and south-west be only the direction of travel, and then everything would be impossible. Judging from the total of symbols he had written down there were about thirty turbine points in the refrigeration ring. If the map was in fact inverted, or the camps were numbered from the north, he could walk hundreds and hundreds of kilometers and still not find the port, and he would collapse long before that anyway.

His mind was literally going round in circles. Tomorrow he would have very little chance to look for further clues, and he realized if he were ever to find the rocket he had to make his move then. It was vital to get away from Guest before he got deeper into the system and snared him further in his plans. Above all he simply needed to set out, to prove to himself and the Homeland the existence of the other world. Right now he was willing to take the chance of walking the tunnel and dying down there rather than wait any longer.

He got up and went silently over to Finn's bed. He put his hand over his mouth and shook him by the shoulder. Finn's eyes opened wide. Poll whispered, "Listen, I can't explain, and the less you know the better, but tomorrow I need you to keep your second helping of food, the dry stuff like scones and anything else you lay your hands on. Wrap it up in a spare shirt and carry it under your coat to the tunnel. Make sure no one sees you. Give it to me there. I'll tell you when. OK?" He took away his hand.

Finn smiled broadly, "Sure, but on one condition."

"What's that?"

"Whenever you get to where you're going you come back to get me."

Poll stared at Finn and then slowly nodded his head, "I think, yes, perhaps I will."

Finn grabbed his hand, "No perhaps, Poll, say it for sure, say you will come back for me."

"Ok Finn, I'll come back for you."

Finn relaxed, turned over and closed his eyes. Poll went back to his own bed and lay down. Unlike Finn he couldn't sleep. On top of the risk he was about to take Finn's words disturbed him in a way he'd not expected. Never had it occurred to him that anyone else might want to go where he was going. He'd been on a solitary quest: it had been him alone against all the lies. Cal of course had been part of it. No, more than a part, she had been an essential key. But the idea now that someone else, anyone, might want to be with him, and to the point of demanding he'd come back, this seemed totally new. And he'd said yes! In face of all the other challenges he'd taken responsibility for someone else, and he'd never done that before.

He drifted into a fitful sleep, punctuated by the faces of Guest and Finn both speaking to him and questioning him about things for which he had no answer. He was trying hard to formulate a response, but failing. At last, in the small hours of the morning it was the thought of Cal that returned to him, of her belief and support, and he fell into an untroubled sleep which rested and restored him before the klaxon's wail began his day.

***

The tractor moaned and crunched along the ice road to the turbine building and the tunnel shaft. Finn gave Poll the thumbs up indicating he had got the food but Poll didn't respond. When they got to the shaft Finn went first as he always did. At the bottom the men crowded into the buffer room, huddled together. No one wasted energy in conversation. When the lock to the tunnel opened they began to file through and the wave of heat met them at once. The men spaced out automatically and began to unhook their coats with noisy grunts and sighs. Poll bent to Finn who was just in front of him and muttered. "Follow me. No one will notice." He led the way down the tunnel to the point between storm lamps where the shadows were thickest. "OK, give me the food, then get back to the group."

Finn dug inside his coat and produced a small bundle. Poll took it but Finn continued to stand there.

"Don't hang around, they'll see you're missing. You've got to go. Now!"

Before Poll could stop him Finn threw his arms round him in a hug and then just as quickly turned and sprinted away. Poll stared at his retreating figure as it disappeared in the gloom. He continued to stand there listening to the thud of footsteps fading away. The drama of his situation returned to him with the force of

124

a roof caving in. He felt a huge desperation. This was a fool's errand and he would very probably die down here. He was fighting a rising tide of panic and struggled against it with all his might, willing his mind to concentrate.

He was twenty steps from the entrance to the condenser hall. There was a risk Guest would check he was at his post before he gave orders to install the replacement part. But there was also a fifty per cent chance the work detail to fix the fan would come this way. If they did and he was down with the computer he would be trapped behind them. Orienting himself from the surface he figured this direction of the tunnel did in fact run generally in a southerly orientation. Along this route he would be moving along the western edge of the ring or even well on his way south. There was also a chance this was entirely the wrong direction, away from the rocket. He had to decide. He could already hear voices coming. His limbs convulsed into action; he shoved Finn's bundle into his pocket along with the few extra things he had taken, gathered up the tails of his coat and began running as stealthily as he could through the tunnel.

***

At the Transport Center Cal checked for security arrangements at the Machine Shop. The Center had a monitoring system covering Bubble transport and there was a huge room filled with screens recording all movement on the lines. Reviewing the system on one of the control computers she could see nothing showing the tractor shed. She guessed, therefore, it would not be monitored that strictly. To be on the safe side she briefly skimmed a camera maintenance program and was sure that if there was a camera at the tractor bay she'd be able to interrupt the live feed. The only thing left then was to collect the supplies she'd asked for from Esh and Wes. She ordered a Bubble and set out back to Dining.

When she got there they were already in line. She collected her own full allowance and then sat down with them. After chatting casually for a couple of minutes she gently pushed their extra protein rolls and energy bars into her school bag. She left shortly after, calling out she'd see them tomorrow. At once she headed for the transport deck, ordering a Bubble with priority codes she'd seen a supervisor use. She arrived at the Machine Shop just at the end of the work day with a number of people waiting for vehicles. She pulled her hood up and dove into the crowd, remembering the separate bay for the transport vehicle connecting to the tractor shed. There was a dedicated Bubble sitting there. She jumped in and hit the start button. Within seconds she was at the shed, and its particular atmosphere of grime and grease was familiar and pleasant to her. Crossing the short deck and through the access lock she glimpsed shapes of a couple of people behind a plastic strip barrier, but they weren't looking her way. She quickly found the rest room and entered a stall, waiting for things to go quiet.

The hours slipped by. One person came in to use the bathroom and left after a couple of minutes. She still had no clear idea in her head of how exactly she would rescue Poll, but she felt calm, even unworried. The pathway she was following was the one meant to be followed, and she had no doubt somehow she would find and save her friend. As she waited silently the whole sequence of events played through her mind, beginning with Poll cornering her after the lecture, then her out-of-body experiences, all the way to Poll's arrest and sentencing to the camps. As she stared at the stall door with its oily metal finish she felt she was right there on a threshold. It was as if her frozen world had already begun to melt and yield to something new. She had to struggle to suppress a rising excitement. She had to take things gently, one step at a time. The digital hour on her therm-suit said it was past eight o'clock. She was almost certain no technician would still be hanging around the machine shop, but she continued to wait.

Finally at about ten she emerged from the stall and carefully pushed open the door of the restroom, listening closely. The corridor outside was poorly lit and she was sure there were no cameras mounted there. She looked both ways. Everything was deserted. One direction led back to the transport deck and opposite it she saw the plastic strip barrier opening on to the workshop. At the other end of the corridor was a door with a dull glow showing through a reinforced window.

She crept along the corridor and looked sideways through the window. There was another passage running at right angles up to some kind of office with its own window. If there was anyone on duty they would be based there. She carefully opened the door and made her way along the corridor, sliding in next to the glass. Very slowly she inched her face around the edge. A man with his back to her was propped up in a swivel chair in front of three video screens. It didn't seem he was looking at them but was watching a small hand-held device. She checked the video screens above the man; one of them covered the Bubble transport deck and the others seemed to show only the glimmer of ice fields surrounding the building. The man shifted in his chair and she dodged back immediately behind the wall. She returned quickly to the corridor with the restroom. She now knew that the inside of the tractor workshop had no camera, so she headed straight to the plastic strips and pushed inside.

She threaded her way through the shop, grabbing a power screwdriver and wire cutters from its littered benches. She found the tractor bay and the fleet of ice-tractors, fully maintained and ready to go. Her heart was pounding. This was it. Her complete break with the Homeland, her father, the whole system. She clambered up on one of the sixteen-seaters, opened the cabin door and found the box with the travel log. She quickly searched the entries looking for Poll but there was nothing there. She jumped across onto the second big tractor, opened the cabin and found the log. This time she located the entry she was looking for: "Day 100, Poll Sidak, Men's Camp, Hut 9." She jumped down onto the four-seater and climbed inside. It felt comfortable, as if it was already hers. She scanned around on the shed walls for an electrical access panel and saw one very close to the big retractable door. She popped it open with the power tool and quickly recognized the wiring colors from the Training Center computer. There were two feeds and she assumed that meant two cameras. It would take her less than a minute to strip the feed wires and splice them into one. But the wires disappeared into the wall and she had no idea where the cameras were, and so which one to cut and which one to save. Simply cutting both would surely send the watchman down to investigate. There was a fifty per cent chance of choosing the one that looked away from the exit lock. She took a wire in each hand, felt them and placed her bet.

She returned to the four-seater, jumped up and entered the code to start the engine. She put the vehicle in reverse scraping a sixteen-seater as she swung round but she made it safely to the exit position in front of the wall. The remote was located up on the driver's window pillar where she remembered it. She hit the button and waited for the wall section to roll back and then she inched the tractor into the lock. She pushed the button again, jumped out and raced over to the panel, cutting, stripping and splicing the wires in seconds, then dashing back to the lock and slipping through the gap just before the section trundled shut. She vaulted into the cabin as the outer gate began to lift, closing the cabin door and at the same time flipping the switch for the heat.

She did the same thing as Rip had done, putting the tractor in gear the moment there was clearance for its roof. Again the antenna scraped, but immediately she was out on the tundra, heading directly away from the building and picking up speed. As she bounced through the gears, plunging forward into the arctic night, she searched around for the beacon device. There was a display screen on the console and she pushed a toggle next to it. It flickered and a message came up, "Set Destination". All she had to do was toggle up once and "Camp (Men)" appeared. She depressed the toggle again and a gently pulsing light showed with a directional arrow. She swung the vehicle about so the arrow was facing the beacon and then she bumped the vehicle into fifth.

There was no way of knowing whether the splicing of the cameras had worked or if even now the watchman was frantically informing Sector Security. But at least for the moment she was well ahead of any pursuer and she felt safe. As she was thinking this she suddenly realized the tractor was churning forward without any lights, traveling in complete darkness apart from the console. She scanned around for headlamps and finally found the switch. A great flower of light bloomed in front of the tractor showing a bright sheet of ice beneath an immense wall of black. It was only a moment later she glimpsed markers passing by on the left at intervals.

7. ON THE RUN

She nearly missed it, with the hypnotic sameness of the road, but after traveling for the best part of two hours she sensed a momentary change, as if the surface had altered its steady grinding note then quickly returned to it. She hit the brake and stopped. After a moment she put the tractor in reverse and slowly backed up. As she gazed at the road in its brilliant pool of light she saw what looked like a set of tracks breaking the straight-line of the roadway, producing a small ridging. The direction of the break seemed to be to her right. She toggled the beacon to see if there was anything leading that way, but it simply showed "Camp-Men" and "Camp-Women" straight ahead and "Base" right behind. The tracks seemed significant. If there was something down there it might prove a place to hide. But even without this incentive the tracks seemed to invite her. She put the ice-tractor in gear and slowly crawled to the right, her eyes glued to the window and the ice ahead. The going became bumpier and at times the ruts seemed to disappear, but the weight of some vehicle had splintered the ice cover fairly recently and it continued to hold just enough impression for her to follow.

She couldn't be sure how long she followed the tracks— it could not have been much more than a few minutes—but suddenly they took her down a small dip, into a saucer-shaped depression. Something about the way the beam of the headlights bounced off the opposite rim and then flashed over the area between made the hairs on the back of her neck stand up. She slowed even more, scanning the darkness intently for what she thought she'd seen. The slight creasing on the ice continued and then all at once it disappeared. Reversing, she swung the tractor to both sides, peering into the gloom. As she turned to the right, she glimpsed the outline of a large mound. Crawling closer she saw what looked like a large tumulus of ice with a flat near-side. Her heart raced as she drew up and stopped the tractor, gazing at the object in the ghostly light. It was unmistakably some kind of construction, a recessed wall under an ice-covered overhang, and tucked in to its side was what looked like a control box. What could it possibly mean to have a building like this so well hidden and in the middle of nowhere?

She zipped up the front of her therm suit and jerked its hood around her head, then pulled down the sleeve extensions which formed emergency mittens, and zipped them up too. She clambered out and hurried in the numbing cold over to the control box, pulling it open and hitting the button inside. There was a brief silence, then the noise of a hum and a crack and the door began to retract. At once she retreated inside the tractor and slipped it in gear, moving into the lock when the door was raised. It wasn't difficult to locate the inside control and the corresponding switch for the inner lock. Scrambling out once more she pushed the switches and retreated back to the tractor. She watched the inner wall section slowly pull to the side. The sharp light from the headlamps projected into the dark interior picking out the shape of an ice-tractor parked at right angles to the lock. Beyond it and lower to the ground was the astonishing sight of a Bubble, a Sector Communications Vehicle. She inched forward and could clearly see there was a rail line beneath the Bubble and, most amazing of all, she could see the rail stretching out and disappearing into the dark oval of a tunnel. Her mouth fell open. She knew the Bubble-track system as well as anybody and there was absolutely no information of a rail tunnel, let alone one out this far. It could only mean one thing. Only one agency would have use for something like this, and have the ability to construct it and conceal it from sight.

She swung the tractor round beside the parked tractor, drawing up beside it as the lock grumbled shut behind her shoulder. The vehicle had to belong to the stranger whom Rory had talked about this morning, the one who had been looking for her. She could almost feel the other world reaching out to meet her and at the very same moment she felt her own power to surprise it. The crucial question that she needed to answer was where had this tractor traveled from to get to here.

The new tractor was exactly the same size and design as hers. She tried the handle of the door and it was unlocked. For a moment she was fearful there'd be a keypad and code to start the motor but there was nothing. She hit the start button directly and the machine broke into the familiar ascending whine. Yes, it was ready to go. There was a screen similar to the one in the first tractor and she pushed the toggle next to it. The blank space lit up and showed the pulsing light of a beacon, but without a name. She toggled left and right but nothing changed. This vehicle only had one destination and it lay at something like forty five degrees to the left of the beacon direction from the tractor she had just left. This was a significant difference and as she gazed at the small yellow spot expanding and shrinking on the screen she understood clearly what it was. Without a doubt here was the transit point between the sunshine world and this one, a place reachable by this ice-tractor and where some further means of transport must await. The stranger who had been looking for her, and very likely a companion too, had arrived from this shining spot, driving from there to here, and then riding their private Bubble to the Sector. All she had to do was to point the tractor back in the direction of the beacon and she would have solved the riddle of the Homeland.

She was transfixed, staring at the beacon, knowing that this was where she had to go, this was where her destiny lay. But, of course—it was a crucial part of everything—first she had to get Poll. She broke herself free, went back to the first tractor and shut it down. She took her school bag with its supplies and returned to the new vehicle. She re-opened the lock and slipped the tractor in reverse, going through the steps to exit the shed and close its doors. Then it was night again out on the icefield. She headed back to the road that led to the camp, calculating it would lie more or less directly across the path of the new beacon. When she got to the markers it was almost one o'clock in the morning. She made a right turn to go in search of Poll. As she did she reached into her bag and dug out some food, a protein cake and one of the energy bars. There was a long journey ahead.

* * *

Poll had been walking for six hours or more, really more running for a minute or so and then slowing down to walk until he had the energy to run again. But his bursts had gotten less and less and he was now just stumbling along. He had passed the relays and three exhaust manifolds in sequence, confirming the pattern he had discovered. He felt terribly weak. The poor diet and the constant assault of the cold had taken their toll. The tunnel of course was warm and he had to carry his greatcoat under his arm, with the gloves and food bundle shoved in a pocket, hampering

131

his movement and causing him to sweat almost as much as if he'd been wearing it.

He did not know how much longer he could keep this up. He had stopped a few times to eat the dry scones in his pocket and scoop up brackish water from the deeper pools. Each time it had been more difficult to will himself back to movement. As he hobbled along he also knew certainly that his nemesis, Guest, could not be far behind. His initial decision had been right, to start out at once, because he'd soon come across the broken relay with its flashing alert along the route. That also meant it would take little more than an hour for the work detail to reach the relay, replace the part and inform Guest on one of the tunnel phones. Guest would radio the Sector to get it switched on then head straight for his lair in the condenser hall to find out if he, Poll, had identified the switch as it went live. When he found nobody at the computer he would immediately suspect something and begin a search. At the most it would be one more hour before he sent someone down the tunnel. Poll could imagine who it would be.

His lungs felt as if someone had sawn them through. Every breath was another cut of the saw. His head was beginning to spin and he wondered how he had ever imagined he could do this. At the closest the rocket port was something like another hundred kilometers. What had he been thinking? He had set out on whim to prove himself right and he had not thought through the fine details, let alone the physical challenge. Right now it would be Nute and Dogg pursuing him, the young, wolfish Icemen who could travel much faster than he could and would be dying to beat him within an inch of his life.

The thought of this and the certain doom of all his hopes spurred him on beyond his body's limits. His rasping breath and his feet clumping against the tunnel floor forced him to strain his ears continually, to catch any sound of pursuit. He wondered briefly whether, if the pursuers gained on him, he would he be able to hide inside the heavy doors leading to the refrigeration coils, of which he'd seen a couple, but he dismissed the thought at once. Just a few minutes in there and his body would freeze and after the exhaustion of the tunnel it would not stand the shock. His only hope was to get to the next shaft to the surface and perhaps elude them there. He continued to count the fans every half a kilometer:

he had passed ten since the last exhaust manifold which meant there were about fourteen more before the next condenser hall and shaft.

Counting distracted his mind from the ever increasing agony of his chest and legs, but he could not avoid the tunnel, a nightmare from which he was unable to awake. The mildewed storm lamps, the hemorrhaging walls, the constant sweating wind in his face, it was like the stories of hell they sometimes told in the Holo-casts. He was fated to push himself round and round this stinking tunnel for all eternity. Suddenly he thought he heard a voice echoing up the walls. Then, yes, there could be no doubting it; he heard his own name being called: "Poll!"

"Hey, Poll, we're after you! You can run but you can't hide."

He almost gagged from terror. But the jolt of fear became adrenaline which allowed him to start running again for real. Did they know he was near? Had they heard him? There was no way he would reach the buffer room before his pursuers saw him but he desperately had to try. He redoubled his effort to run, his legs shaking and weak and his chest feeling as if a huge grinder had worn away his lungs until he must simply stop breathing. He could hear the voices gaining on him and felt sure by now they would hear him too. He thought he could detect Nute's vicious mocking tones. He made a superhuman effort and increased his speed. The voices seemed to fade but now instead he could hear the steady rhythm of a single pair of running feet. He was certain they were Nute's.

About fifty meters ahead he could see a pile of materials used for reinforcing the tunnel walls. Something told him if he could reach that pile he had a chance. He dared not turn his head for fear he would stumble but he knew the running feet were only a few paces behind. It was as if Nute was enjoying the chase, keeping a steady rhythm, confident of his prey. Poll could now see the pile, only fifteen paces away. It contained waterproof cement bags, heavy wire netting, and various lengths of steel rod. Now he was three paces away and suddenly he dropped the coat from his arm in the path of his oncoming pursuer. He heard Nute swear and leap out of the way. At the same moment Poll came level with the pile and without hardly knowing what he was doing he grabbed up one of the rods in his right hand and crashed against the wall with the other, pivoting around and whipping the rod up and back with all his force. Nute had just side-stepped the coat and was unable to swerve in time. Poll's desperate lunge caught him full on the side of his head, felling him like a tree limb.

The Iceman was down and out, with a very surprised look on his face. But Poll had no time to gloat. Another Iceman was about three storm lights away and was coming as fast as he could, grabbing for his gun. Poll dived for his coat and turned to run again. The Iceman got off a shot but it went wide in the poor light. Poll crouched low, weaving as best he could, while the Iceman steadied himself to get a better aim. This time the bullet whistled close above, but Poll was now in the shadows and increasing his distance from the marksman all the time. There was one more shot which thudded into the wall behind and then the Iceman gave up. He was not that keen on the chase and anyway Nute needed help. As for the fugitive, no one ever escaped the tunnels.

Poll continued to run, his body filled with an amazing burst of energy because of the battle, the only one he had ever been in. Soon he could hear nothing more behind. After several minutes, however, his pain and exhaustion returned, and worse than before. He slowed down to a hobbling pace, and he understood he now had another problem. The Iceman who had shot at him would have found one of the tunnel phones and reported the story to Guest. It would no longer be just a problem of camp discipline but a criminal matter, and the other camps would be alerted. Guest would speak to the next camp's top Iceman and the message would be passed on to the squad leaders. They would be out on work duties and it would take time to make contact with them, so he perhaps had a chance. In any case he had to watch out for squads from the next camp working in the tunnel—another thing he hadn't fully thought through.

But this time luck was on his side and as he struggled on, counting down the fan relays, he saw no one. At last he could hear the more powerful thrum of the condenser hall fan and he increased his pace one more time. The gaping hole came into view, the huge fan sweeping round inside it. As he limped by the fan and the condenser hall door next to it he felt the throb of the motors and heard what he thought were voices. He hurried on by and within a few paces there was the familiar sealed entrance of the buffer room with its control box beside it. He stumbled up to it and threw the switch. The door released and he entered the room, hitting the control to return the seal.

He leaned against the wall and struggled to get his coat on. His breath still felt like molten steel in his chest and his body was shaking. He got the coat buttoned and pulled up the hood, but he had lost one of his gloves. As he paused to recover his strength he realized he was still holding on to the steel rod in his ungloved hand. After a moment he opened the door on the far side of the room. Immediately the bone-snapping cold hit him but it also seemed to give him a jolt of life. He found the shaft with its vertical ladder and grabbing the frozen rungs with his gloved hand, he worked his way up.

He emerged into the housing at the top of the shaft and saw no one. He poked his head out the door and at once instinctively ducked back as he felt the deadly bite of the wind. He pulled his hood over to its full extent and stuck his head out once more. He could see the dark bulk of a turbine building but then, parked right next to it, there was an ice-tractor, its engine running. Immediately he had a surge of hope. It seemed to be the end of the work day and someone had been sent up to start the tractor and wait for the squad of men below. He slipped the rod under his coat and held it there with the ungloved hand thrust under the flap. He walked across to the tractor, mounted the step-up onto the track and swung open the driver's hatch. There was a gray-haired man sitting there, half asleep. Poll had pulled out the rod from his coat and he poked the man sharply in the side. The man grunted, blinked to attention and saw the rod leveled in his face.

"What the hell!"

"Get out of the tractor or I'll stick this in your face."

The man stared in disbelief. "Who the fuck are you?"

Poll lowered the rod and jabbed it very hard into the man's chest, leaving a sharp ding in his coat. "I won't be asking again."

The man gulped in pain and dove for the other hatch. Poll got in, closed the hatch behind him and reached across and yanked the other one shut. He had never driven a tractor but in his trips back and forth from the hut to work he had almost automatically got himself into positions where he could watch the tractor drivers and memorize their actions. He'd even once had the chance to sit up

135

front and ask about the controls. Now he did his best to repeat the motions he'd seen. He pushed down on the clutch and maneuvered the gear stick into first. He lifted his foot and the clutch sprang back. The great machine shuddered and labored into motion. He pumped the power and there was a smell of burning pressure plates, but little by little the vehicle picked up speed. He went through the actions again, ramming the lever into second gear and letting the clutch leap up. Again the tractor bucked and nearly stalled, but still it ground forward, and again it gathered speed. He was safe, at least for the moment.

***

Just before sun-up Cal arrived at the men's camp. She was very tired. It felt like there was a gap in the middle of her head where her brain should be and she was unable to think what she should do next. She had followed the road until the going became so rough she lost the markers. But she kept the direction of travel, using the angle to the line of the beacon, figuring she was bound to come across some sign of the camps. She had endured anxious moments but eventually she'd found the perimeter road and knew she had to be close. Judging from the ruts in the ice most of the traffic seemed to turn right so she also followed in that direction. It wasn't long before she caught the unearthly glow of the orange surveillance lights above the rows of discolored huts and the grim existence of the camps hit her squarely. She rolled to a stop as a smudge of skyline was shivering into daybreak.

It was all so strange and different. She was surprised to see the east lay back in the direction she'd come from. The line of dawn, which she had watched so often from her TEP, was way to the other side of the Sector, while the camps were out here to the west. She began to orient herself accurately and there in her first daybreak outside the Sector she felt real and strangely happy. As the ice-tractor hummed quietly and the wind rattled its metal frame it even felt possible to embrace this world. She could perhaps love the circle of storms and the wretched land beneath it.

Suddenly there was a hammering on the passenger window. An unshaven man in a huge hood was shouting to her. She pulled up her own hood and cracked open the door. He leaned in and stuck his nose and mouth close to the space.

"What are you doing here? Is it something to do with the guy from hut nine?"

An alert went off in Cal's head. "Hut nine, yes, which one is it? I'm looking for it."

The man pointed. Then, despite the crippling cold, he held onto the door and yelled another question, "How come they send someone young as you?"

"I'm older than I look."

She yanked the door shut and slipped the tractor into gear, heading to where he'd pointed. Driving slowly she found the hut with a faded number "9" on it, zipped up her hood and pulled on her mittens. The wind hit her the moment she got out, an unrelenting enemy, and she buckled before it. Bent double she made her way to the hatch and banged on it with her fist and forearm. After a moment a shadowy figure opened the door, beckoning her in over the step and slamming the hatch behind her. She was in some kind of boot room and a voice from inside yelled, "Who is it?"

"Dunno."

A man who looked as if he was in charge came through the inner door, harassed and angry. Right behind him, slipping through the space, was another figure, little more than a boy. The man walked up to her.

"What is it?"

"I'm looking for Poll Sidak."

The man was beside himself. "What the fuck! I've told everyone over and over, he's not here, and they've searched twice. Anyway who the hell are you?

Before she had a chance to say anything the boy interrupted, "Are you his friend?"

The man was about to turn on the boy, but she spoke quickly. "Don't worry, sir, I'm from the Sector. We're looking for information." Turning to face the boy, she smiled. "Yes, I'm his friend."

Again before anyone could stop him the boy blurted out, "Me too; the name's Finn. Poll disappeared into the tunnels and then he shot a guy and stole a tractor at the next camp."

Cal was caught off balance. "What?"

The man saw her confusion. "Wait, you don't know that?

137

Where did you say you were from'?"

Cal felt the danger. "Sir, we were not informed of all these incidents. Your superiors probably wanted to sort things out themselves. I am going at once to investigate.

It was the man's turn to appear confused. He swore at the boy. "Finn, get your punk ass back inside, now." Then turning to the visitor, "Look I think you need talk to my boss. He doesn't like things happening he doesn't know about. We'll be going down to his place shortly and you can come with us."

"Sir, I'm sorry, I do not know you're name. I'm Cal."

The man grunted, "It's Cato."

"Cato I would love to meet your boss, but there's a prisoner on the loose who seems desperate. If we can resolve this situation without any more bloodshed then that's in everyone's interest, don't you think? I really should go now."

Cato decided he didn't care. This woman was not his responsibility. He had no procedure, no orders.

"Well, get the hell out then."

Cal unhooked the external door herself and ducked out. It remained open to the merciless wind while Cato stood looking with Finn still behind him. Someone inside was yelling, "Shut the goddam door!" but the two continued to watch as Cal jumped up into the tractor and reversed back down the road, the tracks churning up ice and snow as she weaved dangerously between the buildings. She got to the end and swung the vehicle round to face south: Poll wouldn't have been going anywhere except where her beacon was pointing, the place where there was transport to the other world. She shunted the stick to forward and lurched into motion, racing up through the gears along the highway. Poll had escaped and now he was on the run. She had to find him before anyone else did, and the only escape would be all the way, to the sunshine world. As she went as fast as she could down the ice road she foraged in her bag for the last of the energy bars. Her mind was awake again, but her body desperately needed something to keep going.

8. PHILOSOPHY

It was now several days that Charlize and Danny had been guests at the villa of the philosopher couple, Zeno and Xanthippe. They had fallen into a routine, rising late in the morning when their hosts or a volunteer couple from the neighboring dwellings would come into their room laughing and carrying trays of fresh fruit and cakes. They would then go and wander the beautiful lanes and gardens surrounding the villa. As they strolled they would bump into different people, exchange pleasantries, and little by little they got to know the members of the philosophers' village.

There was Heloise and Abelard, a willowy couple who dressed in medieval costume and discoursed on logic, ancient and modern. In contrast, Friedrich and Hannah were intense and passionate, with expansive chests and big hair. They talked in aphorisms and hinted at things other people didn't or couldn't grasp. Hypatia and Bacchus believed Greek thought was the only thought there was and with infinite patience would quote and explain what its philosophers had actually said. It was here also that they encountered their first gay couples, Andre and Alex, Lara and Colette. Back in the Homeland the possibility of such relationships had been whispered about, but it was a matter of hints and suspicions, and always controlled by the overriding rule of family and children. Here everything was totally different and, after an initial shock, homosexual partners seemed as natural as the food and the weather. Andre and Alex's stock in trade was the constructed nature of truth—much to the annoyance of Heloise and Abelard. Meanwhile Lara and Colette kept up a constant banter about women and men and the latter's very limited understanding of anything.

At one o'clock a long wooden table would be laid in a courtyard shaded by ancient walnut trees. People would gather to snack on focaccia bread, chilled soup and olives, or slivers of grilled chicken and filo pastries of strawberry and brie. The news would be shared of the lectures and seminars to be held that afternoon and after an hour or so beneath the boughs they would disperse to the venues in different villas. Those who didn't attend would spend the time reading classical texts or preparing pieces of their own. In the late afternoon there would be the meditative chanting of ancient hymns or fragments and afterward everyone would return home to dress for that evening's banquet.

Charlize and Danny experienced the giddy whirl of these social occasions. Each night they went to bed their heads were swimming with fine wine and words they couldn't understand. There were several philosophers who took it in turn to host the symposia, depending on interests and personality. It worked well that way, as conversation would run in unique directions, and then people could quote an argument or aphorism from that occasion at a later separate gathering. But always the most glittering event was at Zeno and Xanthippe's and with the newcomers' arrival the invitation had been issued at once. Neophytes in heaven were a unique opportunity. To have their mouths hanging open at table, but not for the food, told the philosophers that their thoughts were truly worth thinking. And Zeno and Xanthippe naturally claimed first blood.

"What a glorious thing is youth!" declared Xanthippe. "Of course we have so much youth here—are we not all forever young!—but there is something truly exquisite about these faces, so recently bloomed from their chromosomal springtime!"

"Oh Xanthippe," retorted Andre, "So easily seduced by the random products of nature. Why is that a true springtime? Why are the results of our science not just as true? Is that not just a prejudice on your part?"

Heloise had her head at an angle, carefully considering the argument, which provoked Friedrich at once to exclaim, gesturing to the Northerners. "Ah, but how can you replicate the perfect cleanness of those faces? That animal veracity? Do you not secretly covet it?

"Of course we are seduced by these nymphs, these fawns. Why not!" It was Abelard waving his hand across the top of his wine glass in only the slightest imitation of Friedrich "But what is it that stirs our blood? Is it the music of the spheres? Or something much more banal, an insatiable desire for the new? What does the predicate "youth" mean among a set of immortals?"

"All things come to be in accordance with the Logos, but most people fail to notice what they do when awake, just as they forget what they do while asleep." Hypatia was intoning and Zeno was roused from his rapture contemplating his guests.

"Aye yes, Heraclitus, the weeping philosopher, that dear man! *There* was one who suffered for his thought. Not like us pampered dilettantes. But wait, let us hear from our new arrivals. What is it that *they* perceive" And turning his luminous gaze he looked at Danny and Charlize.

"What does it seem like to you, sweet friends, to be so newly young and yet also young forever?"

Danny blinked into the candlelight, grinning and trying to think of something, anything, to say. But Charlize responded with poise.

"Well, ladies and gentlemen, we are very grateful to have been chosen as Immortals. As far as being young, most people we have met seem about the same age as ourselves. So I don't think you have anything to worry about. Enjoy the moment!" And she raised her glass.

"Remarkable, truly, there speaks the voice of genuine thought," Zeno rhapsodized, clapping his hands. "Live in the flow of the moment, even though the moment is forever frozen!" And he looked around for approval of his own pithy paradox. Sure enough a cascade of poignant sighs washed over the table.

"But seriously," he continued, "this is not a trivial matter. One of the reasons you have been sent to our little colony is because sooner or later these questions impose themselves on all citizens of Heaven. We want to show you, right from the start, that we are mindful of them. As you can hear, we discuss them all the time, and in the most enlightened fashion.'

"But you should know also that the Heavenly Homeland has not left things simply to the consolation of mere talk. The holy secret of Heaven has yet to be revealed, and when it is you will be brought at once to a place which only long training in philosophy may otherwise provide. Nevertheless, one step at a time!" And he broke off his wordy musing. "My task at the moment is simply to promise you a rare treat. Not too long now, at another dinner just such as this, we will have a very special visitor who will prepare your minds and souls for the wondrous revelation. His name is Sarobindo and he is a legend among us. When you meet Sarobindo, and later experience the epiphany itself, you will finally become united with the soul of immortality. But now, enough already! A toast, a toast! Who will raise a toast to our glorious novices?"

Colette rose to the occasion. She was a lithe, imposing figure with short hair and a warm generous mouth. She flashed a smile around the table and commanded, "Charge your glasses!" There was a busy flutter while people reached for the bottles and topped up their glasses, then they all held them aloft. Colette continued.

"Once a goddess always a goddess. (Who can be sure about the guys? But we're always hoping!) To Charlize and Danny, the newest among the gods! We don't say 'may you live forever' because that's a given. But we do say 'may you *live* forever!' May you never waste a moment of eternity." And she finished her toast with the standard cry, "We all say, 'Forever!'"

And everyone joined in a full-throated chorus, "Forever!"

After that there was no longer a single conversation at table. Sat next to Danny was Friedrich and on the other side of Charlize, Colette and Lara. Friedrich turned to Danny. "Really, Sarobindo is one of the most significant people in the Heavenly Homeland. He is quite extraordinary. We are always thrilled to have him as our guest. You will be astonished at what this man has given us."

Colette was listening from the other side, a twinkle in her eye. "Don't think too hard for them Friedrich. Didn't you hear what Charlize said? Enjoy the moment!"

Bacchus leaned forward from across the table, giving a sensuous pout to his lips, "And yes, there is Doblepoble to look forward to. I hope you'll enjoy that every bit as much as the august Sarobindo! You know the Greeks invented the lifestyle of the body?"

Danny wasn't thinking about the Greeks. He recognized the exotic name of Doblepoble. "Yes, we already heard about that. Do you guys go?"

"Well I and Hypatia certainly attend. Not sure about some of the others, maybe a little too bumpy for their tastes. But Colette and Lara here, I'm pretty sure I've seen them there more than once."

Charlize looked curiously at Colette and Lara. "Do you...attend the Doblepoble?"

Colette grinned at the recent inductee to Heaven. "My dear Charlize, you will have to come and find out, won't you?"

9. BORDERLANDS

As Poll set out in the hijacked ice-tractor he had no clear idea of where he was going. He was struggling to recover both his strength and wits as he steered unsteadily between the huts and then out on a much larger road. There was a horrible pain in his chest, his heart was beating like a hammer, and his limbs felt like putty. He was still crashing gears and making the motor labor badly but he was getting better at it and the tractor was still moving forward. He was trying to think rationally about his situation, but a blank exhausted mood was overtaking him, matching the dark slew of clouds above. He had gained a means of transport but he had lost the route to guide him to his destination. He could see the day was almost gone, the light leaching from the sky. Snow had begun to fall, single flakes bouncing against the windshield in the bullying wind. He was fascinated by their delicate structure, something he had never properly seen before; he wanted to examine them as they flew by. With difficulty he pulled himself back to the present, recalling that the prisoners said there was a road connecting the camps. He thought in all probability this was it. From the glimmer of the setting sun he figured he was heading south, more or less the same direction he'd been taking down in the tunnel. It struck him the road might very well follow the line of the tunnel or the ring of turbines all the way round the Homeland.

It seemed, however, highly improbable that the rocket port would simply be parked somewhere along this road. In a moment the confidence he had felt in the computer map drained from him. That little rocket shape was probably left over from the time of construction and in reality the transport to the other world could be anywhere. At the very least it would be a good way off-road and how on earth would he find it? Moreover the highway would quickly be as dangerous for him as the tunnels. News of his latest crimes would soon reach the local Iceman and they would be gunning for him in addition to Nute and his gang. At the most he had half an hour start on pursuers. He felt like a hunted animal with the hounds closing in, like one of the holo-programs he had seen back in the Sector; and that prompted a thought about how the fox always looked for ways to conceal its trail. He realized the

143

snow was falling more thickly and would quickly hide the marks of the caterpillar tracks. With an impulse born of desperation he abruptly swung the tractor off the road, heading west away from the refrigeration zone. This would be his one chance to dodge the Icemen and not leave a trail. He could perhaps lay low out in the borderlands and then double back to the Sector. They would not be expecting that.

He had managed somehow to get the vehicle up to fourth gear. Once on the icefield it kept moving at more or less the same pace, lumbering across the monotonous landscape. The glow of the day hung on the snow even though the sun had gone down. In the gathering twilight everywhere looked the same, low bare rises followed by a corresponding dip and then another rise. The tops were scraped by the constant wind but the troughs were filled with drifts and ice walls. The tractor's arrow plow in front seemed to carve through the drifts as if nothing could stand in its way. But peering through the gathering gloom Poll realized he could soon be lost and for the first time he checked the console for its navigation equipment. He saw the beacon display and toggled its switch finding the camps and then the tractor's home base. That put his mind at rest: he could always make his way back to the road. There was also a radio, but that was the last thing he was thinking of using. He saw some other dials and for the first time the thought came to him of the tractor's power supply and how much was left. He found a dial that read "Power Unit" and to his sudden horror he saw that it was down beyond its last fifth, a little over four hours left. It had been nowhere near fully charged when he'd stolen it and now there was not enough power to return to his Sector. His options suddenly narrowed considerably, and then, almost at once, they vanished all together.

He was moving along a valley floor, aiming at a point to climb the hill, when a strange hollow sound came from underneath and almost immediately a succession of terrifying cracks and a sensation of falling. The tractor bellied down with a jarring thump and an avalanche of snow came in on top, suddenly making it completely dark. Meanwhile the caterpillar tracks continued to drive angrily forward, skidding and slicing, burrowing the vehicle deeper into a wall of ice and snow. He had hit a crevasse, a place where the ice had formed across the top of a deeper hole. And now he was in it.

Picking himself up from the side of the driver's seat Poll struggled desperately to find the clutch. Finally he reached it and slipped the gear. He put the tractor in reverse and managed to pull away from the wall in front of him. In the light of the console he looked for the wiper switch. When he found it the big blades shuddered and moaned but finally unburdened the windshield of its mountain of snow. He looked for other switches and found the driving lights. He could see that the wall in front of him was above the height of the tractor. He found another switch for a wiper on the rear window and went back to look but he could make out very little. He put the tractor in reverse again and it rumbled backward but he had no practice and it headed straight into a wall. He tried the maneuver again but kept wedging into the walls. He was knocking more snow and ice into his path and there was no plow on the back.

Poll felt panic take hold of him and he tried hard to control himself. He decided he must push his way out to the front, so once more he charged the ice-tractor forward. He cleared the windshield to look but the snow in front appeared just as mountainous as before. Still he repeated the movement, crawling backward and then plowing forward and keeping the engine turning at maximum power, trying to force his way out. He could not see a thing but still kept the power at full throttle, hoping desperately he would break through.

The tracks churned, gripping and slipping, the engine gave a harsh screaming sound and there was a smell of burning. A heat gauge showed the engine nearing the red warning mark, dangerously hot, but still he pushed forward, believing it might need just a few moments more. Then he glanced at the Power dial and he felt sick to his stomach. The needle was almost visibly falling. It read under three hours. He had to stop if he was to have any hope of getting back, at least to the camp. He took the engine out of gear. There was no other way, he had to dig himself out.

Yet how was he to do that? He flipped the wiper switch. The patch at the top of the windshield was now entirely night and covered quickly with falling snow. He was totally exhausted and gazed helplessly at the bank of dials on the console. After a moment, his eyes lit upon one that read "Auxiliary Heat". He cut the power to the engine and hit the switch under the dial. He heard a slight hum, the meter flickered and held steady at twelve hours. In that instant Poll let go. Something inside him refused to worry anymore, about anything. He had twelve hours of warmth and rest left. Nobody was ever going to find him down here in this underworld. He was completely safe. Tomorrow he would face his world's problems again, but not now, not tonight.

He even felt happy. He hauled himself out of the driver's seat, retrieving his coat which he had shrugged off when he first took control of the tractor. He climbed through the connecting hatch to the benches in the back and sat down, digging into the coat pocket for the last of the scones that he and Finn had saved that morning. A thought made him stop and get back up. He returned to the front and rummaged around in the storage compartments there. Sure enough there was an emergency supply of protein and energy bars and a large container of water. He went back to his bench and gorged himself on the cache of food. He even had a perverse feeling of gratitude. To whom or what should he be grateful? To the Homeland? It was far too much to think about. He lay down, wrapping the coat around him. He stared at the dark, now total except for the few monitor lights still on at the front. The darkness and the solitude did not bother him. Very shortly he was asleep.

He dreamed and in his dream he was in a great ocean and there was no land anywhere. Somehow his feet were on the bottom and his head was above the water. The sun was bright and all the waves glittered in its light. Out of his bones and his body—he did not know how—came a kind of coral which continued growing around him until it formed a large island. The white of the coral reflected the sunlight and it was beautiful and peaceful. He woke up and wanted to be on the island forever. He had a feeling there was someone else living there, on the island, but he didn't know who it was. As he tried to imagine who it could be he fell back to sleep.

***

Cal had been traveling south for something like an hour and was desperately fighting the need to curl up and sleep. In the early day the clouds had thinned considerably and the sun now at a higher angle made the ice dazzle with its standard Homeland ferocity. She was shaking her head every few seconds to try and wake up, but the effort to hold her eyes open together with the constant glare made her vision swim. If she'd not found shaded glasses beneath the dashboard she would have been unable to see at all. Squinting into the road ahead it seemed as if the whiteness melted for a moment and then reformed into the shape of a big ice-tractor bearing down on her from the opposite direction. There should have been space to pass but the vehicle was deliberately occupying the whole of the road and either she had to swerve off the highway or slow down to a stop. When she did the latter the sixteen-seater cut her off at an angle and the driver lowered his window slightly and gestured that she lower hers. The man had a hard unpleasant face. A sudden feeling of fear dispelled her tiredness as he spoke into the crack.

"Who are you and state your business."

She did her best to tough it out. "I should ask the same about you."

There was a movement from inside the vehicle and the window lowered further. A pointed gun came through the space and behind it the face of a man with one side of his head covered in bandages. The remaining eye looked at her murderously.

"Don't fool with me lady. Tell us what you're doing or I'll shoot you on the spot, so help me."

Cal lost her nerve. "I didn't mean to anger you. The name is Cal and I'm from Sector Three, looking for Poll Sidak."

The driver spoke. "That's more like it. We heard about you. Our boss is doing a check right now. You are to follow us until we find out more. If you refuse, just like my friend says, we'll hunt you down and shoot you."

The window rolled up and the big tractor backed round and moved off, this time to the south, the direction Cal had been traveling. As it turned she could see there were at least four men inside and their look was as cold as the ice itself. The tractor pulled ahead and she put her own tractor in gear and followed. These men were plainly the killers who ran the camps. And they were out scouring the road looking for Poll, reckoning he could not have gone far from the highway. She did not give much for his chances if they found him. If Poll had any sense he would leave the road all together. She decided she had to lull them into thinking she was obeying them, but there was no way she was going to stay behind. If little by little she fell back she might be able to swerve out across the tundra and get out of range of the gun before they could turn and follow. The problem was whether they would catch up. Their tractor had a bigger engine, but more weight, and she remembered what Rip had said about the bigger tractors easily getting stuck. She would have to take her chances. It was a matter of when.

She began to fall further behind and had put about thirty yards between herself and her captors when suddenly her decision was made for her. Out on the icefield, somewhere in the wilderness distance, a plume of smoke rose to the sky. Something absolutely abnormal—there should be nothing out there to cause a fire. In the same moment she noticed it she saw the tractor in front swerve slightly. The driver had seen it too. In an instant she turned at right angles to the road to get away, and raced as fast as she could across the ice and snow. But then immediately she experienced the difficulty of traveling in the borders. Going along the higher levels was easy enough, but heading down into the dips the tractor had to labor against accumulated drifts and ice ridges. She dreaded the big tractor following her. If it kept in her tracks it could go faster and from the top of one of the hills she would present an easy target struggling through the troughs. But the pursuit never happened. The men evidently thought the fire could only be made by Poll and they were heading directly across the snow and ice toward it, figuring they would catch up with her later.

This meant they were between her and Poll. She swung round savagely to face the wisp of rising smoke. There was nothing for it but an all-in race. All she could do was hope she beat the other tractor to the finish line.

***

When Poll awoke the second time a dim light suffused the cabin. He got to his feet and made his way to the driver's section. Sunlight was coming through the layer of snow at the top of the windshield. It was about seven o'clock and the Auxiliary Heat read at zero. Thankfully the body of the tractor seemed to have retained warmth and he saw that the top of the windshield was actually melting a little. He searched around in the storage box and found a pair of mittens. He put these in his coat pocket and shuffled it on, grabbing a shovel that was attached to the cabin ceiling. Going to the back, he pushed open the emergency door, released the retractable steps and stepped down into the gulley. It was cold but there was no wind. Putting on his mittens he started to shovel the snow behind the tractor. He soon saw that the level behind was getting deeper and there would be no way of getting the tractor out this way. He would simply descend further into the gulley.

He clambered up the back of the gulley, throwing the shovel ahead of him. On top there was still very little wind and he felt a warmth in the rays of the sun that the cold air did not completely kill. It was the first time he'd experienced anything like it. Stumbling his way to the front of the tractor he thought he could make out the general contours of the gulley. He guessed it extended twenty or thirty yards from where he stood. If he could clear the incline directly in front of the tractor then perhaps he could get it to climb up out of the ditch. He jumped down and started shoveling the impacted wall of snow and ice. It was very hard to dislodge and he used up a lot of energy simply breaking the first couple of feet. He was sweating and he had to remove his coat, something he'd thought impossible there on the borderlands. He kept hacking away and then he came to what he knew at once to be the reason the tractor was blocked. He was hitting a solid ridge of ice that stood more or less in the middle of the gulley, formed no doubt by the melting and freezing of snow. He must have landed toward the end of the ditch, with the rest of the ditch behind covered by wind-hardened ledge of snow. He'd smashed right through the top, landing in a perfect trap. Now he was facing a solid buttress of ice. The shovel barely made a dent on it. It would take him days to knock this down.

He put his coat back on and climbed out of the gulley. He sat on the bank overlooking his vehicle and let the sun warm his face. After a while he got back down, found the clips retaining the hood on the motor and sprung it open. He could see the big coils, the oiled engine parts and the huge batteries resting on the chassis. He went back into the cabin and found an emergency flare gun he'd noticed before, together with a handful of cartridges. One more time he clambered up on the bank and retreated a dozen yards from the front of the tractor. He fiddled with the gun until he got it loaded, then he lowered it in front of him, aimed it at the engine and opened fire.

The shot went high, cracked the windshield and bounced off into the bank where it flashed and sputtered for several minutes. Reloading he stepped closer, aiming and shooting deeper into the engine. The charge buried itself in the belly of the motor and spent itself vigorously. The oil caught fire and flames began to lick along the hood. He fired another flare and then simply lobbed the two remaining cartridges into the engine. The engine casing became a furnace. There were a couple of harsh popping sounds and multiple angry whooshes as the cartridges exploded and the battery gasses ignited. He felt the fierce heat on his face and he retired farther up the bank, sitting on a snow crest to observe the bonfire of the Homeland's vehicle and all it stood for. The cabin caught light, the windows burst and soon the body of the tractor was a mass of flames. In the narrow space of the ditch and on its edges the ice and snow rapidly began to melt and for the first time Poll could see actual rock and lifeless peat. Black twists of smoke found each other and spiraled up to form a grim pillar against the blue sky. Gazing at the inferno he had created Poll lost every sense of time and he didn't notice when two vehicles began to make their way up the length of his valley along its opposing ridges.

Cal was on the western ridge and she was trailing the big tractor by a hundred yards, but she seemed to be moving faster than the larger vehicle and was gaining. The Icemen had noticed her behind them but she was out of gunshot range so it had now become a clear race to get to Poll first. The men could see the blackened hulk of the vehicle and the area surrounding but they did not at first grasp the situation—it looked like someone had exploded a bomb. What they could clearly see, however, was Poll sitting up on the hillside on the far side, nearest to the western ridge.

"There he is, the lunatic! What's the bastard done?"

"That bitch could reach him first. Get down there now and we'll scare her off."

The driver slewed the tractor, aiming on a straight line to where Poll was. At full speed it was difficult to hold steady on the slope and the tracks churned to the bottom more quickly than he intended. Once there the tractor slowed down considerably. Immediately the figure of a man with a bandaged head emerged from a window and began firing wildly first at Cal and then Poll.

"Hey, Poll, it's Nute, back from the dead, your worst fucking nightmare. You'll not get away this time."

Cal saw what was happening and felt helpless. She would probably reach Poll just before they did, but would present an easy target for the gun, as would Poll. He had stood up when he'd heard the gunshots but he wasn't moving. He was just staring at the men's tractor. Why wasn't he moving, at least trying to hide? Suddenly she understood why. The big tractor lurched at a crazy angle, one set of tracks almost in the air. The driver was fighting to right the vehicle but he committed himself the wrong way, trying to steer away from the fissure, and the whole thing flipped over on its side. In a flash Cal saw there were crevasses in the valley, the one where Poll's tractor used to be, and another under the men's tractor. The pursuers had fallen straight into a trap. She raced at full speed on the ridge, confident now she could get to a point close to Poll.

Finally he heard her engine behind him and saw her coming. Instinctively he thought it was more Icemen, and this time he did try to hide, ducking behind a drift. Cal got to the top of the ridge above him and came to a halt, jumping out and yelling.

"Poll, Poll, it's me Cal."

Nute was fighting to exit the upended tractor. He had the door open and was hauling himself out, stamping on the face and shoulder of the driver. Poll heard the female voice and cautiously put his head up, and then stood bolt upright, rooted to the spot. Nute, balancing on the side of the cabin, saw his target and got off another impulsive shot, but the round went wild. It was enough, however, to galvanize Poll. He started floundering his way through the snow toward Cal. He sank two or three feet every step, which allowed Nute to get ready. Standing on the top corner of the tractor cabin he leveled both his hands for a steady aim. The bullet spurted up snow just shy of Poll but Nute himself wasn't so lucky. The kick of the barrel upset his fragile balance and he teetered and pitched sideways into the ditch.

Cal came down the last twenty yards and grabbed Poll's hand, dragging him the remaining steps. They hauled themselves up the ridge, onto the treads of the two-seater and into the cabin. Down in the valley two other Icemen were now standing on the side of their stranded tractor but not bothering to draw their weapons. They were probably out of range and anyway they were laughing too hard at Nute who could be heard cursing foully from the ditch. Cal put the tractor into gear and moved off quickly along the line of the ridge. According to the beacon, it was also the direction of the rocket.

***

Poll was slumped in his seat in a kind of daze. He felt perhaps he was still dreaming. One moment he was sitting out on the tundra playing out the end of the Homeland and the next he was safe inside a cabin with Cal.

Cal reached over and gripped his arm. "Poll, you can't believe how glad I am to see you, but right now I need you to keep going. Are you able to drive this thing, I desperately need a rest?"

The tone of Cal's voice and the touch on his arm helped to rouse him. He looked at her.

"Cal, it really, really is you. How in God's name were you able to do this? How did you know to get out here?"

"Poll, I'll tell you everything, but can you drive this tractor? I'm absolutely dead."

"Sure, I can. Stop the tractor, I'll drive. But where are we going?"

Cal had her hand on the door to get out and double round to the passenger side. She turned back in surprise. "Following the beacon, to the transport to the sunny world. Isn't that where you're going?"

Poll was dumbfounded once more. "You mean the rocket...?" But Cal was already heading out the door. Poll got out his side and stood there as she came round, the amazed look on his face continuing his question. She said to him, "If that's what you call it, yes."

In a single moment all the tension and frustration and fear released inside Poll. He felt it physically like the lifting of an illness, like a weight dropping from his shoulders. Cal had not only rescued him, she had found what he'd been looking for ever since he first began to think about anything. He stood in front of her and there in the bone-chilling cold with the cloud and wind blowing again over the ridge he gripped her by the shoulders.

"Cal you did it, you did it!"

Cal clasped on to his arms, almost to support herself, but at the same to return his awkward straight-armed embrace. "Yes, we did, Poll. We did!"

Then he could not help himself but he hugged her, almost putting his head on her shoulder, and amidst that blighted landscape a gargled noise rose up inside him, half a sob of pain, half a cry of triumph, a sound he'd never made before. At once he was terribly embarrassed. He pushed Cal away abruptly. When they got back inside the tractor and he shoved it in gear he muttered, "Sorry about that, I got kind of carried away."

Cal murmured, "Oh, no, really, I feel exactly the same way. And I've cried like that too." Then to cover his embarrassment, "But tell me, who *were* those guys, wanting to kill you so badly?"

Her voice was already trailing off and as Poll thought to explain about Nute he looked round and saw her eyes were closing, her head thrown back against the seat.

She slept for three hours, despite the wild lurching of the ice-tractor and the grinding every time the gears shifted. Poll quickly located the beacon and right there on the console it shouted confirmation there was a destination that had nothing to do with the Sectors. He would have basked in its glow of vindication but he had to concentrate on navigating the frozen terrain, taking care to cross the valleys at right angles and as quickly as he could. As he continued to drive, however, he got more used to it and his mind returned to Cal and what she had done. He thought he could probably guess some of her story. She had used just over eight hours of battery life which meant that very likely she had gotten the tractor sometime around midnight and traveled through the early hours. The tractor and its beacon clearly suggested a live link with the other world itself. But who was traveling from there to the Sector, and how had Cal known about them and their tractor?

Then another thought struck him forcibly. All he had ever wanted was evidence to prove there was somewhere else on earth apart from the Homeland, but Cal seemed to be a step ahead. As he followed the track of the beacon he understood that for her they were heading not just to the rocket port, but to the rocket itself and the other world to which it linked. It made him almost dizzy to think of this. From being just a need to expose a set of lies, the

153

whole thing had morphed into a trip to the world of sun itself.

Up ahead the landscape was suddenly different. He glimpsed a flinty wasteland, its snow and ice broken by naked rocks and bands of dark moraine. Beyond stood a higher range of hills, almost black against the skyline. The beacon seemed to be pointing toward a small spur at the northern end. As the tractor mounted the crest of the final snow ridge before the flats it was shaken by a squall of wind even more powerful than usual. From then on it was buffeted continually by high-velocity gusts, like a ship sailing close to a hurricane. The storm world was announcing itself for real; they were entering its territory. The shaking woke Cal.

"Hey, what was that?"

"Looks like we're losing the effects of the high pressure. This has to be the start of the storm zone."

"Then the rocket's got to be close."

"I reckon so. But, Cal. I've got a question: are you planning a trip?"

"Of course I am. And you're coming too. You started all this in the first place. And, you know, I was so worried about you, Poll, I'm not letting you out of my sight again!"

He grinned and shrugged. "Fact is, I don't have any other place to go, and really I should stick with you for my own good. I'd totally run out of ideas there on the ice. But, wait, tell me, how did you figure all this out? How did you find the connection to the rocket?"

She told him the whole story, about the guy at the swimming pool talking to Danny the day of the competition and Danny's disappearance, and the way Esh had described him convincing her he was from the sunny other world. About specializing in Transport and learning how to drive a tractor in order to rescue him from the camps. And then just a day ago she'd heard someone, with the same look as the first man, had come searching for her, so she had decided it was now or never, she had to make her move.

"So Danny and Liz were taken to the other world, and all that stuff about sports stars going to special colonies, that's basically what it is, they go to the sunshine world?"

"Looks very much like it."

"But then you thought they were coming for you too?"

154

"I don't know, but I had a pretty strong feeling. Maybe Danny had something to do with it. Anyway now we're both going. Won't that be a surprise for them! But, Poll, who was that crazy man who wanted to kill you? They told me at the camp you shot someone. Is that true?"

Poll gave her the full saga, about the Icemen and Guest, the tunnels and the desperate fight with Nute, and finally his own stealing of a tractor and his decision to go out with a bang there on the ice.

"So, it was a fluke I found you. I thought it was some kind of desperate signal you were sending me. But, of course, how could you know I was anywhere near?" She laughed as she added, "I suppose it's all part of my obsessive belief in saving you!"

"Well, I'm glad you believed that. Otherwise I'd be dead on the tundra."

"Seriously. Those guys were after your blood." After a moment she added, "I really hope nobody carries guns in the sunny world."

"Somehow I think they'll have them in that place too. But we have to get there first. Have you thought about how we're going to fly the rocket? It's got to be more complicated than driving an ice-tractor."

"We got this far, didn't we? If it comes to it we'll just wait until the strangers make it back from the Sector. I'm sure they were going to take me anyway, so I'll convince them to take you, too."

The wind was keeping up its barrage, rocking the body of the tractor back and forth. They were now a good way across the plain and the barren range of hills was much closer. The tractor growled over rocky ground, threading between outcrops and patches of snow, steadily approaching the edge of the range. The beacon kept them to the north, skirting the ascent. Suddenly it began to diminish on the screen, then it disappeared altogether. Almost simultaneously they saw a tall mast secured with steel lines on a ridge in front of them, and directly behind a bulldozed track leading up to the left. It was plain this would take them the rest of the way: they turned onto the grade as the wind lashed fiercely at the side of the cabin, lifting it drunkenly on its suspension.

It grew steadily darker and they needed to switch on the

headlamps. They were no longer talking, focusing instead on the narrow track bordered by a yawning precipice to the side, subdued by the ominous atmosphere of the hills. It was now very dark and after traveling like this for some time the road leveled out and the heights on either side rose dramatically, forming a deep ravine. The effect of the wind softened abruptly and everything became calmer as the walls of the chasm closed about them. Then, after following the narrow, oppressive channel there appeared abruptly, right ahead of them, a vast crater. The road turned at ninety degrees, descending rapidly, doubling down hairpin bends into a pit so huge that it could only have been made by a bomb. They struggled to keep their nerve as they negotiated the tortuous bends. It took them over an hour of concentrated driving to get to the bottom.

As they made their way down they were able to make out little by little an astonishing black shape, an enormous long cylinder rising steadily from the bottom of the crater, seeming to widen until its mouth was lost at the top of the hills on the western ridge. It looked like nothing they had ever seen. All they could imagine it to be was a colossal throat stretching upward to cast objects into the sky. They were both very tired but they were carried forward by the shattering discovery they were making. As they came nearer to the bottom they could see a cluster of lights and buildings surrounding the base of the cylinder which appeared as a great bulb-like dome or rotunda.

"Oh my God. *Oh* my God. This has to be a launch for the transport."

"Can you believe it? Finally the lie to the Homeland. Look at it! It's so perfectly designed, to shield a rocket flare. Proof positive of cynical planning!"

They rolled the tractor down among the service buildings and followed the road to the edge of the huge circular structure sitting at the bottom of the launch cylinder. It loomed above them, a great black mass of metal. They scouted its edge until they found an entrance. The door was very heavy with a single recessed handle. Cal pulled it down and they heard catches release. The door swung back on automatic power, to reveal a long semi-lit corridor made out of the same dull metal. The place had an indescribable chemical odor, bitterly pungent in the confined space. They both coughed and put their hands over their mouths as they went as quickly as they could to where the passage ended in a big sealed double door. There was no obvious entry switch but clearly-printed letters above the door read: DANGER. SHUTTLE LAUNCH ONLY. EVACUATE IMMEDIATELY IF NOT BOARDING.

Between coughs Poll said, "Looks like this has only one purpose. We need to get out and find the control station. Maybe we could jumpstart the sequence."

They hurried out and reversed the tractor around, back to the scatter of buildings they had passed on the track. The obvious candidate was one they'd noticed, with a branching array of antennae and dishes on the roof, and lights on inside.

Cal tried the door handle and it opened to the touch. Inside was a long table covered with computers and a jumble of radio equipment. They immediately began to try the computers, looking for an open screen or turning them on as they went. Poll hit a switch on a control next to a large monitor. A screen buzzed into view, showing multiple panels and tables with headings like fuel, cabin pressure, telemetry, navigation. Cal was looking at screens with data of flights past and called out, "Look at this: here's Danny and Liz's flight record. They were accompanied by a couple of people called *emissaries*, 'Dante' and 'Milton'."

Poll was not answering. He had found a panel which read: INITIATE LAUNCH SEQUENCE and had already clicked on it. But directly he ran into a block. The screen read: ENTER COMMAND CODE.

"Uh oh! We need a code to start this thing."

Cal came over. "What?"

"This looks like the launch program, but you need a pass code. I had the same thing back at the camp. But it didn't take long to guess. I don't think their codes are very complicated."

"Where would you start? With words, numbers, or both?"

"The names of the guys, you know, like the ones you said were with Danny and Liz, that could be a place to start. They might like using their names."

"There could be a vehicle log or something in the tractor, with this flight's names and details!"

They both headed back to the vehicle. Neither had bothered to search it before, now they quickly emptied the compartments under the dashboard and between the seats. Cal dug out something from a side pocket.

"Hey, this looks like a possibility, a schedule or notebook of some kind."

She opened the small palm-sized book. It gave the name "Brutus" with the address "Colony of Sports Monitoring." Inside were various other names, with asterisks and little notes scattered at random like "Rolls Royce Engine," "Shuttle Maintenance," "Mustang Sally!" There didn't seem to be a clear calendar, only references to numbered days without any particular order.

"This is all weird. It doesn't help us."

"We could just begin with 'Brutus' and try a series of numbers, see where that gets us."

"Wait!" Cal interrupted, "This could be it, right here."

There was a note reading, "Northern Rendition, Day 8" and then a series of numbers.

"Don't know what that word means—rendition—but it kind of sounds right."

They returned to the hut and entered the numbers on the screen. It paused, then read CODE ACCEPTED.

"Simple as that!" cried Poll.

The screen brought up a check list with SECTOR SECURITY APPROVED, BIOMETRICS TRANSMITTED, RETURN TELEMETRY, ENGINE SYSTEMS READY and several others.

They went through and checked them all off directly. There was a low hum in the building and the screen showed: IGNITION SEQUENCE COMMENCED: TEN MINUTES TO BOARD.

"Let's go!"

They raced from the hut, into the tractor and back down to the door of the launch building. The corridor was now brilliantly lit and the smell was gone: a powerful ventilation system was sucking fresh air into the building. They ran down the passage and the sound of their running feet rang against the surface matching the thumping of their hearts. At the end of the corridor the elevator door stood open with an amber light flashing on the wall inside. They crashed in and Poll hit a red push button next to a sign, DESCEND TO CABIN. The door rolled shut and the elevator moved into a swift descent, fast and deep enough to make their ears pop. It came to a knee-buckling stop and the door swung back, beckoning the young people to step out. Beyond lay a cantilevered bridge stretched over a blackened cavern. The other end abutted the shuttle, a sleek black bird with narrow swept-back wings poised on a slender undercarriage with semi-retracted wheels. It was about thirty yards across the bridge to the cabin door but it seemed like a thousand miles. "This is it," breathed Cal and they made their way across, gripping the rails.

A hatch was open at the side of the rocket and inside was a compartment at the angle of the craft, so the four seats were slightly off the horizontal. They clambered inside, stooping over, and took the two front places. Before them was a pulsing display, with instruction, CABIN DOOR READY FOR SEAL. SIX MINUTES TO INITIATE LAUNCH. Poll got up and fumbled with the door lever until it swung across and sank into position. They heard the bolts engage and the display turned to FASTEN SEAT HARNESS. They fussed with the belts across their chests until they got them plugged in, and then the display changed to CONFIRM FOR TAKE OFF. They stared at the console wondering where to give the command until the word CONFIRM flashing on the screen made them reach out to touch it. Then another message showed THREE MINUTES TO LAUNCH. Through a port window they glimpsed the bridge retracting and a seal roll down in front of the elevator platform. About thirty seconds later there was a flash and a billowing plume of smoke as the firing sequence began.

The shuttle quivered and inched slowly forward. Before they knew it there was a second bigger flash and a brilliant sheet of fire and smoke exploded round them and the rocket leaped forward with terrifying force. The noise was indescribable and the walls of the tunnel at once became a blur. Everything around them, and inside them shook, and at the same time they felt an enormous, breath-squeezing pressure. They really had no idea of what they had done, whether all the flight systems were working, or even where they were going. They were carried forward by an irresistible flow of events and the strange sense that their path was assured, even destined. Whether this was the arrogance of youth or reflected a deep truth, the effect was the same. They were on their way out of the Homeland toward another world. All the same, when the rocket left the tunnel and almost immediately hit the level of the storms it did a sixty degree yaw and they both let out terrified screams and groans. They were plunging head-first into the intense chaos which lay between their own world and the next.

10. DOBLEPOBLE

A million stars lit the blessed night. The air tasted of caramel and peppermint and the great arc of heavenly bodies seemed itself to be alive, exhaling the same delicious flavors. Danny and Charlize walked arm in arm through the broad streets of the Forum, meeting and greeting people at every turn. It was Doblepoble and it felt like the whole race of gods and goddesses had come downtown to celebrate. Booths were set up along the great esplanades--wooden tent frames wrapped in swathes of white cotton, while all the monumental buildings were open and spread around inside with couches of carmine silk and tables filled with glimmering lamps. At the intersections small fires flickered, with merry groups of people roasting nuts and sugared apples. Artisan food colonies offered tapas of fresh bread, olives and chorizo, samosas and tiki, or fresh pancakes with maple syrup and ice cream. In the squares musicians were playing, fiddles and guitars, flutes, clarinets and steel drums, creating a constant stream of sweet sound that mixed and separated insensibly from one space to the next. Barrels at the back of hay-wains provided zesty wines and ales, cider and lemonade. People were dancing, laughing, embracing and throwing admiring glances full of hints of future trysts. Every sensation, sight, sound, taste or smell, seemed marvelously heightened, as if someone had injected an electric liquid into everything. All the spaces between things were filled, making the whole scene a single bite of the most delicious fruit.

Emmanuelle and Gaius found the neophytes and embraced them in a frank and eager way.

"You look fantastic, both of you. You are going to have such an absolutely wonderful time. People know you are new and they won't bother you, not too much anyway! But you must try at least some new experiences, promise you will!"

Emmanuelle was so beautiful and vibrant Charlize couldn't help reply, "Oh for sure, we will, we will!"

Gaius joined in, speaking to Danny in particular, "Remember there's more than enough to go round for all," and to Danny's total surprise he touched him lightly and erotically, and then shimmied away beckoning Emmanuelle after him. She laughed like a peal of bells and followed, turning as she went and opening her hand to reveal a number of little pills.

"And don't avoid these delights either!"

After they disappeared Danny looked at Charlize open-mouthed, "Did you see what he did?"

"Pretty wild. Wouldn't happen up north, would it."

"Well, you never feel anything through those therm-suits, so no point anyway!"

And they both laughed, the only thing they could do at the comparison of their old life to the totally new and crazy one they were in.

"But what about those little pills," continued Charlize, "Are you going to have one?"

"Don't see why not, we're already loaded with their immortality potion, so what difference could it make?"

"None, I'm sure. It's just...I wonder what it will be like."

"Well, there's one way to find out, isn't there? Come on!"

They went into one of the booths which had a big sign posted *Jethro's Soffo, Doblepoble's Preferred Ecstasy*. Inside seated at a table was a small rotund man with glowing features and an unctuous smile. On the table were several items, a small brass weighing scale, a set of test tubes and glass slides and several dispensing jars with pills and powders.

"Come in, come in. The night is young and the young stay young even when it has grown old! There, you're already baffled, but don't worry, you've arrived at the right place for perfect enlightenment!"

He waved his hand at a couple of upholstered chairs, "Do sit down and tell me what you'd like."

"This is our first Doblepoble, sir, so we're not entirely sure."

"Then Lady Fortune has smiled on you, because I am the best possible person to put you on the path to chemical heaven! These pills you see here are produced at my own colony and it's my professional pride to ensure their purest quality, guaranteeing the most exquisite experience. There are many other substances available at Doblepoble but it's my considered opinion that the Soffo I provide is a summit without peers, an Everest of soul satisfaction!"

"So what exactly happens?" Charlize required specifics.

"Oh my dear, you have no idea! So let me explain, we'll start

162

with the brain! The brain, as you know, is the most extraordinary organ. Everything we are depends on it; we can't see, think, feel or know anything without it. I sound like one of your soupy philosophers, don't I, but it's simply the facts. And another simple fact is the brain is made up of chemicals in an enormously complex system. Altering the balance of these chemicals can have truly astonishing effects. Here in the Heavenly Homeland we have overcome death, but we have not plumbed the mysteries of the brain. One of the joys of Doblepoble is that people have the chance to experience these mysteries again and again, and who knows what revelations or epiphanies are still awaiting? Now, there are some providers who want continually to engineer new variants to reach the goal, and there is of course a market for that. But the platform I offer is the unrivaled purity of a classic, one which has made possible the most incandescent moments. People return to it again and again. They know it is the surest path to the mystery."

The two potential customers were impressed, but Danny persisted with Charlize's question, "But what exactly happens?"

"Young man, please forgive me, I didn't introduce myself. I am, as the sign says, Jethro. And you wonderful people are…?"

"The name's Danny, and this is Charlize."

"Danny and Charlize, my sweet friends, I had to ask your names, because the answer to your question is in one way quite personal. What exactly happens depends on your individual brain and I want you to know this. But it does happen within a general range and I can say it includes the following: deep peace and self-acceptance, diminished aggression and jealousy, powerful feelings of empathy, intimacy and love, increased intensity of sound, sight and touch, and strongly funded energy and arousal. You may find yourself at the highest points of these experiences, or somewhere in the middle, but in every case you will be truly blessed."

"I think we'll have some," said Charlize. "How many of the pills do we need?"

"And, yes, the wholly appropriate question. Correct dosage is everything: too little, no effect; too much, counterproductive. I would recommend only half a pill each. You can expect results in a little under an hour. Depending on how you react you might take another dose six or seven hours later. But I would not advise more than two repeats."

He opened a drawer in his table and pulled out a small inlaid pillbox with *Jethro's Soffo* engraved on the side. "I give one of these to all my first-timers." He placed three pills in it and snapped it shut.

"Here you are Charlize. You can be keeper of the Grail. Now, both of you, enjoy your Doblepoble!"

They left the booth, hand in hand. Immediately they were outside the tent Charlize grabbed Danny and kissed him passionately. "I love you so much. Let's take Soffo and we'll find a booth."

They ran over to one of the hay-wains and took glasses of wine, then they went searching for a vacant booth. There was a simple system of placing a bright apricot flag above the entrance flap to indicate the booth was in use. They didn't search long before they found a vacant one, placed the flag and went inside. It was furnished with a small table and a low couch the color of rose. With eager hands Charlize broke one of the tabs, gave a half to Danny and they both swallowed the drug, washing it down with the wine. Charlize pulled Danny to her and embraced him, repeating the intimate gesture made earlier by Gaius.

"I can do this way nicer than Gaius, don't you think?"

"No competition, really, and please don't stop."

Locked in embrace they fell on the couch, laughing insanely.

Outside no one had paid any mind to the behavior of the recent inductees to Doblepoble. So many people were doing the same things themselves they really had no attention to spare. Anyone else was simply drinking in the whole atmosphere without thinking or questioning anything. Being an Immortal had become its own special habit. It meant swimming day by day in a haze of pleasures and experiences, some remembered, some renewed, but never worrying that any of it could fade. The stars above shone with the same everlasting indulgence, and just to be present at Doblepoble was to bathe in a sea of bliss. Every smile, every telltale laugh belonged to each and every person without remainder. For in the end it would all come round to each and every individual again…and again, and again.

11. ENTRY

Somewhere a few hundred miles north of the Forum Cal and Poll's shuttle was re-entering the atmosphere. From the initial angle of ascent it had finally escaped the hurricane winds and attained the quiet of space. Once there it performed a broad parabola, arcing back down to re-enter the southern latitudes at the spot where the Homeland of Heaven was hidden. Many people at Doblepoble heard the sonic boom as the ship entered the air space. A few were slightly confused, as their usual business was to help organize welcome committees and they had not been notified. But it was Doblepoble and the whole point was not to worry about anything, and they didn't.

Cal and Poll were exhausted by their journey in the tractor and then the terror of the flight. They sat strapped in the cabin gripping the arm rests, desperately waiting for this impossible flight to be over. They'd been shot into space through cloud cover and winds which seemed to go on forever, and then all at once there'd been the eerie calm of outer space. At first the experience mimicked the Worship Center Holo-casts, with wild sensations followed by a strange sort of peace. But really it was nothing like the Holo-casts. It was hard and bitter, with the initial banging and bucking of the ship and the cabin oxygen tasting of electricity and making them feel sick and dizzy. Originally beyond the earth it had been the depth of night, but almost at once the dazzling radiance of the sun had broken above the horizon behind. They glimpsed through the portholes the roiling cloud mass below and for the first time began to understood, without any filtering explanation, the cruel condition of their world.

As they sped silently south and west across the long curve of the planet they could see with their own eyes the chaos created by the storms, and with each passing minute they gained a more vivid sense of the disaster that had taken place. This was not a huge natural catastrophe from which they had been miraculously saved. Because they had progressively exposed the lie of the Homeland, and because they were flying above the storms in a sophisticated spaceship, they also sensed the truth of the storms below. Those cumulus mountains and the stratus continents had a horribly human look. Everything down there had a history: it had been humanly produced, just like the Homeland they'd just left and the rocket they were in.

The mood of the young people changed from triumph and excitement to a state they had never really known before. Somewhere between horror and grief, they had no name for it. It silenced them as the rocket continued its glide toward earth and the storm world, and then suddenly, without warning, there appeared the final confirmation of the human character of everything. There beneath they saw an area of the earth's surface not covered by clouds. They realized the morning sun was breaking upon a fabulous land of color. There were hues of green and brown and gold and blue, and small glittering patches which were unmistakably human buildings. The shuttle was piercing directly down into this magical kingdom. It descended lower and lower and they were craning their necks to see through the portholes, understanding they were arriving at the goal of their journey. It was without doubt the other world, the place which had ruled their whole existence, and about which nobody had ever known.

Poll spoke, thunderstruck: "Who can these people be? How did they do this?"

"It really is a sunshine world, so different from everything…." Cal's voiced trailed off.

There was a thump as the shuttle extended its landing gear. Within seconds they glimpsed the shape of real trees lining roads and clustered together in groups like beautiful friends. Then everything was whizzing by just below and very soon they felt a strong bump as the wheels touched the ground and another one as the nose came down. Heavy drogue chutes were released and air brakes applied to slow the shuttle on the runway. They felt them pull and pull until finally the speed reduced to little more than walking pace, then the craft made a turn, then another one, and then stopped altogether. After a moment they heard the locking bolts on the door clunk in release and finally all the noise had ceased except for the hiss of the cabin air and the occasional small cracking sounds as the metal body began to cool. A sign came up on the display "Release Safety Harness. Cabin Door Ready."

They sat there for a few minutes waiting for their hearts to stop racing. Then Poll pressed the central button on his straps and the restraints sprang away. He sank forward slowly on his knees and crawled to the door. Bracing himself against the bulkhead he struggled with the lever until he got it to move and the door swung out and away from the hatchway. There was a fifteen foot drop to the ground below and no steps or bridge. He sat back against the wall and pulled his legs up, hugging his knees. Light and perfumed air flooded into the cabin, once more overwhelming the senses of the two voyagers. For a while they were unable to say anything. Cal was gazing through the open hatch and it was she who finally spoke, "This, this world...I could never have imagined...."

"I know, I know..." Poll said helplessly. After a moment he added, "It's what it was all for, the whole thing, the ice, the refrigeration, the worship."

"And you see why," Cal continued. "It's got to be truly heavenly...for those who have all this. Who could say no to anything in order to have it...?"

They continued to sit there in silence, aware that they had broken out of a world which produced only pain and landed in one which promised simply pleasure. And they had done it without permission from those who had built this other world. In a sense they had stolen heaven and were about to be caught for their crime. They continued to wait there, waiting for something to happen. They were sure it would.

167

12. RAVE

Danny and Charlize giggled uncontrollably, made love, laughed again because they had so much fun laughing earlier, and then they made love again. They felt they could go on forever in this heightened state. After a couple of hours their energy in fact seemed to increase, so that they felt it now impossible to stay in one spot. They had to go and be with other people. One of them said, "Let's go outside," and without hesitation they got up from the couch, replaced their robes and left the booth.

They fell in with the crowd making its way down the Way of Tenochtitlan, following numerous other couples and groups converging on its broad black-stone thoroughfare. They gazed around wide-eyed as people pointed to the Aztec temples bordering the road all lit up by glowing electric lamps and the dancing flames of torches. Then they heard the music.

Unlike anything they had heard before it had very little resemblance to the sweet melodies and folksy rhythms of the crossroad minstrels. It was hard and overpowering and sounded like huge pieces of metal being slammed together, while underneath there was the deepest driving beat which seemed impossible to resist. As they drew nearer the crowd got thicker and they could feel the excitement pulsing through the bodies pressing against them and around them. Suddenly the crowd burst into a great open space and someone shouted "The Temple of the Sun!" Looking up they saw an immense pyramid with broad ascending steps crowned by a massive platform. Brilliant rays of light played across its surface like some amazing hopping insect leaving a liquid trail in colors of magenta, silver, green and gold. On top of the platform was a giant video screen and on it they could see a group of musicians and singers dressed in glittering clothes and playing instruments with intense energy and producing this enormous sound. The moment they burst into the open the people around them started dancing, bouncing their bodies up and down and back and forth in time to the beat. It seemed the easiest and most natural thing to do and within seconds Danny and Charlize were flinging themselves around like the people next to them. It was intensely exhilarating. They felt like they were riding on the sound itself and their stomachs and chests were reaching to the sky. As they looked about them they saw other pyramids too, smaller that the Temple of the Sun, but bathed all in the same streaming rays of light and their tops covered with crowds of people, all dancing. It was the most fantastic scene and absolutely the place for them to pour out their rivers of energy.

Danny grabbed Charlize, "Let's get to the top of one of the temples. How about that one there?"

With that they were off, racing up the temple steps, hoisting their robes around their thighs, clambering in leaps and bounds up the steps, their hearts throbbing like the drums of the music itself. When they got to the top they did not stop but immediately started dancing, this time not imitating others but letting their bodies feel the music and going where it took them. They could not be sure how long they spent like this. The vast ceremonial space was spinning round them like a shimmering galaxy and they were at its center. Time stood still and they were dancing like stars in the heavens, surrounded by stars.

Without quite knowing how, they became linked up with a group of five or six other dancers holding hands and dancing in a vibrating circle, a living constellation floating apart by itself. Nobody seemed to decide but the next moment they had all set out together, jumping down the steps, holding on to each other, smiling and finding out each other's names. The others introduced themselves as Kadaysha, Omar, Eboni, Chen Jin, Artemis, Lucius. Quickly they made their way down the far side of the temple and crossed a large sandy space dotted with fan palms and lit by glimmering golden lamps. Here the music wasn't so loud and the crowd had thinned out. On the other side of the park there was another wide boulevard and beyond that, through the trees, big ornate mansions filled with light and activity of their own. Danny and Charlize allowed themselves to be led along without resisting. Their limbs were aching with the violent activity but at the same time they felt wonderfully relaxed, their minds still spinning in the fabulous universe of temples, music and dancing. As they walked along Omar asked Charlize how many people she'd done it with so far at the Doblepoble.

"I'm sorry, what did you say?"

"You know, how many people have you had sex with?"

Charlize stuttered slightly, "I, I…"

Danny came to her rescue. "This is our first Doblepoble. We're new here."

Omar smiled. "Ah, we thought you might be the newcomers. Well, we have exactly the right experience to get you started."

They crossed to one of the mansions and climbed the spacious formal stairway to the entrance. Stucco of heraldic shields and statues of crouching lions framed the paneled front doors. Passing through the hall they entered a grand salon, deeply carpeted, furnished in richly upholstered chairs and sofas, and lit by a huge diamond candelabra. The group threaded its way past knots of men and women surrounding large tables. Some seemed to be dressed very formally in dark suits and beautiful full dresses. Others were in the familiar voile robes, and yet others were almost naked. The new group found a large brightly colored wheel set in a table and divided in hundreds of segments. It was surrounded by several luxurious chairs and sofas. They all sat down and little round chips were thrust into Danny and Charlize's hands. They followed the example of the others and placed some of their chips on a large board next to the wheel and then the game began. Little by little the Northerners understood the point of the activity.

By spinning the wheel and allowing a small ball to run across its surface and finally drop in one of the segments you either lost or gained chips. If you lost most of your chips you could offer to have sex with someone and get a large pile back. If you ran out completely you had to have sex with whoever was then acting as banker. Chen Jin offered to have sex with Kadaysha and she accepted, right there on her couch. At that point Danny and Charlize began to pay a lot more attention to where they put their chips and how the ball fell. All the same Danny quickly lost everything and Artemis went over to where he was sitting. She sat on his lap and began to kiss him with relish. At first Danny was intensely uncomfortable and squirmed beneath her attentions, but then he looked sideways at Charlize and saw she had a strange, flushed excitement on her face, and he began to relax. Little by little he responded to Artemis and then everything sped up rapidly and quickly it was over.

The game continued and after a few more spins of the wheel Charlize offered to have sex with Omar and he readily accepted. Danny watched, paralyzed. All the others were looking at him, not the couple. Eboni had a little vanity bag and she reached into it, pulling out a small green vial. She pushed it over to Danny.

"Here drink some of this. It takes the edge off. Newcomers almost always have a little bit of a reaction. It's nothing to be ashamed of."

Danny accepted the offer without hesitation. It was a sweet syrup with a heady chemical aftertaste. Within moments he felt a huge peaceful glow and became a great deal more accepting.

Omar and Charlize spent longer at it than Artemis and Danny, and after a while everyone turned back to watch them. When they had finished Omar kissed Charlize lightly on the cheek. He looked up at everyone. "I'd say perhaps the game is over here, what do you think? Shall we split up?"

Everyone was easy about quitting the roulette game and heading in different directions. Most seemed to have other connections they wanted to make, but Eboni and Chen Jin said they wanted to stay with Danny and Charlize.

As the others left, Eboni said, "Let's go listen to some spacey music. It's very relaxing. I think we should all relax a little?" She explained that if they continued on the road of the Mansions they would soon come to a pretty half-timbered house where people went to sing. The singing was really beautiful and it would fill their souls with tranquility.

Charlize put her arm round Danny, "Do you want to go?"

Danny looked at her, "I think I could use something for my soul right now."

She replied, "Cool, and hey, Danny, remember, 'The night is young and the young stay young even when it has grown old!'" She triumphantly rattled in her hand the little pillbox Jethro, the apothecary, had given them. She took out a pill and broke it in two, popping a half in her mouth.

"Want some?"

Danny shook his head, "No, I'm good."

On their way out of the salon Charlize found a water-fountain and washed down the pill. They stepped outside onto the stone entrance and there was a faint glimmer at the edge of the sky.

Eboni pointed, "Oh look, it's almost the second day of Doblepoble. We have to hurry to catch the last hour of singing."

They took off down the road, half running, until they came to a smaller mansion with wooden beams, blue plaster and elaborate carved cornices under the gable and eaves.

Eboni cried out, "There it is, just like I'd imagine a fairy house in the woods!"

Inside her description was even more apt. The hearth fire cast shadows and a cloud of mist floated across the room and hung between the rafters. But it was the sound of a sweet and wistful singing which truly carried people into ethereal space. Over by the fire two women with elfin faces, framed by flaxen hair, sang in close harmony. It was truly an unearthly sound, washing over the audience spread around the floor on rugs and cushions. Danny at once found a space and sank down into a dream with the magical voices becoming shapes and colors floating behind his eyelids. Charlize, Eboni and Chen Jin remained standing by the wall. After a few moments a figure detached itself from the mass of bodies and came over.

She whispered, "Charlize, it is wonderful to see you. Do you remember? It's me, Colette. I'm sure they don't mind if you come over and sit by me. Why don't you?"

She embraced her warmly. Charlize, responding, held out her hand and Colette led her across to the cushions where she was sitting. Eboni and Chen Jin smiled and then looked to see where Danny was. They threaded their way through and squeezed in next to him. As everyone settled back, letting the enchanted singing carry them wherever their hearts wished, the first rays of the sun spread across the Homeland of Heaven. A few moments later a sonic boom rattled the windows of the fairy house, but no one paid it any mind, so swept up were they by a dawn chorus in Heaven.

* * *

Not everyone at the Doblepoble, however, was unconcerned about the sonic boom. Jonas had been seated at an open table most of the night, nursing a tall glass of wine spiced with a white powder which made him feel alert and connected. But he had no great interest in acting on his feelings. When he had first arrived in Heaven he, like everyone else, had plunged into the intense excitement of Doblepoble. Yet now he preferred just to watch, drinking in the strange wonder of everything before him. He had seen Danny and Charlize running hand in hand and had congratulated himself on a job well done. For himself, however, deep down, he felt he was waiting for something or someone, he was not sure what. It was not an unpleasant sensation, but it was a strange one for an Immortal, and he kept it to himself, even as it held him back.

As the night wore to an end and the shapes of the booths and temples showed ghostly in the first light he got up to stretch his legs. He loved this time of day. He set out on a stroll along the great central boulevard. Most of the musicians had stopped playing and the fires hardly raised a spark. Here and there he could see a few individuals and couples still wandering back and forth from temple and booth, but most people were lost to sight in the interiors, folded in chosen pleasures. He loved the quiet and mystery of the moment. It seemed to him that just for a few minutes he could see the small grain of the shadows of the city, almost like the basic particles of the universe, just before they were swallowed up into colors. If you didn't pay close attention you might miss the wonder of that moment.

He also wanted to get to a certain place ahead of the crowd. Soon, when the sun was up and had begun to warm the stones of the city, people would start to emerge and make their way to the huge plaza of the fountains that lay to the north of the Sacred Way. There the carnival atmosphere would begin all over again with splashing and bathing in the flower-scented pools, refreshments and massage, and at midday there would be a great dance which was always hugely popular. He wanted to get to the fountains first in order to watch the play of the light upon the water and then he would sit back and enjoy the people as they arrived. He made his way to the plaza listening for the sound of the waters, and by the time he entered the magnificent space with its hundreds of fountains, sunken pools, waterfalls, baths and grottos the first rays of the sun were striking. They slanted across the space bathing the upper half of the fountains in warm light while the lower sections were still plunged in darkness. He sat by a sheet of falling water, watching the sunlight slice through its surface, and it was then that he heard it: the unmistakable boom and whistle of the shuttle returning from the Northern Homeland.

It took him a moment to figure out why the noise bothered him. It was a pleasant sound, always meaning new and interesting people to meet, but right there was the problem: he had heard nothing about any new inductees. He was not always engaged to accompany Cyrus during orientation, but it was always Cyrus who did it and he had seen him just a few hours ago at the Doblepoble. He had said nothing. More to the point, Heaven's master historian was someone who dived into the chemical side of the festivities with the zeal of a seeker, and he would not be available socially for at least a couple of days. If Cyrus had known he was due to orient newcomers in less than forty eight hours he would never have come downtown. The whole thing seemed very odd.

Jonas puzzled to himself as the sunlight turned the scallops of water golden in the basin of the pool. Who should he inform? There was the colony which monitored the sports activities of the Sectors and which chose the lucky ones to be rendered from the TEPs to Heaven. The colony arranged for emissaries and transport, and then made contact with Cyrus telling him to get ready for his party piece. He could try to reach the people there, but it was probable they were all at Doblepoble. In fact last night he'd seen Emmanuelle and Gaius, who were part of the colony, and the only newcomers they seemed to be interested in were Danny and Charlize.

Perhaps he should try checking the colony via the telephone system which could be accessed from the great buildings of the Forum. But that way of communicating was hardly ever used, its only active purpose being to summon the fire brigade. Consequently he hardly knew where he'd get a list of numbers.

The unpleasant thought crossed his mind that maybe the person to contact would be the shadowy figure of Magus, Heaven's rarely mentioned and even less encountered chief of security. It was not something much talked about, certainly to inductees, but the Homeland of Heaven was not entirely without problems. Very occasional individuals were known to have become incurably anti-social or had been unable to de-tox and normalize after excessive use of chemicals. It was generally understood these people were handed over to the care of Magus. How he got the job and what he did to perform it nobody seemed to know, or want to know, but everyone seemed happy he was there to do it. The rumor was that if you phoned the fire brigade and asked for Magus they would connect you.

Something about that made Jonas uneasy. He had no real information and if someone had slipped up he didn't want to make things worse. The first groups were now arriving in the plaza, shouting happily, stripping off their robes and jumping and splashing in the fountains and pools. Unwillingly and not really knowing why Jonas got up and made his way back to the Sacred Way. He'd catch a tram back to the parking lot where he'd left the car which he shared with others in the History colony. He'd drive out to the Shuttle Port to find out for himself.

13. WELCOME

Cal and Poll had sat in the rocket in a daze, trying to adjust to the incredible things that had happened to them, things which they themselves had instigated. It was a great deal warmer than they were used to, so they quickly unzipped the fronts and cuffs of their therm-suits to try to stay cool. Cal got out of her seat and made her way over to the open hatch, and knelt next to Poll. They could see the line of trees and the shape of the low buildings beyond them.

"You don't see anybody?"

"Weird, isn't it? You'd think someone would have noticed a rocket arriving. It's like the whole place is deserted."

"But it doesn't look uninhabited—too neat, too clean."

"Yeah, really. So where's everyone gone? Perhaps it's like a Tenth Day for us, when nobody works."

"Still you'd think somebody would come. Maybe they're all resting and thinking someone else will get to it."

Together they began yelling and waving their hands out the hatchway. "Helloooo! Is there anybody there? Helloooo!"

They kept this up, off and on for ten minutes, basically because there was nothing else to do. Finally it produced results.

"Look there! There's somebody, between the trees. There!"

Sure enough a figure had emerged just to the side of what looked like an entrance. They waved and beckoned madly until hesitantly it began to make its way across to them. As it approached they could see it was a woman, of indeterminate age, with whitish or light blond hair, and walking in an erratic manner, like a rabbit, moving forward, then stopping, then starting again.

"Someone who got left behind, pretty obviously."

They continued beckoning until the woman was in earshot and they could see her clearly. She was wearing long blue robes, folded round her, and the skin of her face was smooth but her eyes were set deep and creased in a way that made them look very old. She shouted at them.

"Nobody comes here today, not on Doblepoble. Who are you?"

Her statement made little sense, but her question was straightforward. Cal launched into a shouted explanation, saying they had just flown in from the frozen Homeland to the north and they wanted to meet the people who lived here.

"You have to be initiated. Pandit's not here. Nobody's here. You came on the wrong day."

"Yes, we think so. But perhaps you can help us get off the rocket. What is your name?"

"I have no name. What is yours?"

"I am Cal and this is Poll. Why don't you have a name?

"If I explained why I have no name then I would have a name."

Poll interjected, "OK, OK, but can you help us? I mean, to get off this rocket."

The woman considered for a bit. "If I got you off the rocket I would have to initiate you, and I can't do that."

Poll threw his hands up in exasperation. Cal said, "Well where are the people who could initiate us?"

"There's nobody here. I told you."

"So why are you here?"

There was another pause, then the woman threw her arms wide: "I am the one who cannot be counted." And with that she turned and walked away, in the same rabbit fashion as before.

"Damn," said Poll. "If they're all as crazy as she is then we should turn this ship around and go back to where we came from!"

"You know, I'm not sure if she was all that crazy. She gave us important information: there's something going on today which is why people are not here, and if they were they'd be putting us through some kind of initiation. Maybe it's a good thing we arrived when we did. It gives us time to adjust and see things for ourselves."

"Perhaps you're right, but there's not much we're going to see stuck here on this spaceship."

They sat there in the hatch in silence, eventually dangling their legs over the edge, gazing out at the stands of cypress trees, the stone portico and the boundless warm sunshine. The smell of the earth came up to them, something they'd never experienced before, sweet, tangy, alive. The scent and the heat made them drowsy. Poll went back inside to lie down but Cal stayed in the hatch propped up against its frame. She closed her eyes, drinking in the delicious sensations. Her mind flitted back to the Sector, to the rescue of Poll and the trip across the surface of the storm world. It all hardly seemed real now with the warmth soaking on her face and the scent of the land in her nostrils. She wondered vaguely about the woman without a name. Why was she here when no one else was? But then, how nice it would it be just to hang out here in the sunshine and the peace? She could imagine doing that.

She opened her eyes and right there before her was a car coming from somewhere between the trees, trundling across the runway toward them.

"Hey, Poll, wake up, someone's coming."

Poll got up and came to the hatch. "Finally, someone official coming to check."

It was Jonas. He had come south off the Sacred Way onto the road to the Shuttle Port, finally catching sight of the shuttle parked in place in front of the Agora. He had been fighting his anxieties all through the trip, on the tram and in the car, even telling himself he had perhaps imagined the whole thing. But now the evidence was right there in broad daylight and it was strange in the extreme. What could it possibly mean? As he drove across the concrete he could see two people framed in the hatchway. He swung the car to a halt opposite and got out. He walked a few feet toward the shuttle and looked up at the young man and young woman looking down at him. One of them spoke at once.

"Hello, can you get us down from here?"

"Oh, yes, certainly, I will, but tell me please, who are you and how did you get here? Where are your guides? Are they inside?"

The young woman answered: "We had no guides. I'm Cal, this is Poll. We found the rocket ship and took it ourselves, just the two of us, and now we would really like to get down from here."

"For sure, for sure, I will get the stairway at once. But I have to tell you, this is very irregular, in fact unheard of. You really can't have any idea of what you've done." He spoke over his shoulder as he gathered his robe and got back into the car, heading back toward the tree line.

"I think we have more idea than you might guess," countered Poll as he drove off.

"Yes, that's for sure, but did you see how he was dressed? He

178

was practically naked, except for that thin robe. And the woman without a name, she wasn't much different. It makes me think this beautiful place has a very different life from ours. That's perhaps why they think an initiation is necessary."

"Well, I don't want any initiation. I hated the Holo-casts back home and I'm sure I'll hate whatever they have here."

"You can't know that, Poll. What they have here might be so totally different from what we had back in the Sector. We should at least find out."

"Well, I don't trust them. And you shouldn't either. They could soon have us moon crazy just like that woman."

They continued to watch from the hatch. After a few minutes they saw Jonas returning with the mobile stairs in tow behind his car. The woman without a name was following, her walking now much more direct. Jonas maneuvered the stairs in as close as he could and then he, with the woman helping, pushed and bumped them into position. He went to mount the staircase to help the newcomers, remembering they were always a little unsteady on their feet. But Poll and Cal had already started down. Their time in the rocket waiting had acclimatized them and they were desperate to exit the cabin. All the same, as the only official present, it was his duty to offer the formal welcome. He stood back at the bottom of the stairs.

"Welcome to the Homeland of Heaven. Welcome to humanity's triumph, its last and best chance. My name is Jonas. Please accompany me as we proceed to the very first baths founded by the pioneers, the first building of the Immortals."

Poll and Cal looked at him with a mixture of curiosity and suspicion, but they allowed themselves to be led to the car and placed in the back seats. The woman without a name got in the front with Jonas who did not object—she was the closest thing he had to a crowd.

"Where did you say we were going?" Poll demanded.

"I am going to show you the ancient Baths. Unfortunately you will not be initiated there directly, not for some several hours, but at least I will show them to you. Then I'll take you to the rooms normally reserved for the initiates. There really is nowhere else to put you."

Cal leant forward. "We understand this is causing you some

179

trouble, Jonas, but really we are happy to go along with the arrangements you make. We have our own story to tell, and at some point we would like to do that, but we're more than willing to learn yours."

Jonas looked round and caught a glimpse at close quarters of the young woman talking to him. He saw her dark hair framing a wide forehead and features which were finely proportioned yet firm. But it was not her appearance that captured his attention so much as a feeling that he caught from her. He was completely taken by surprise: if he'd had to give it a name it would have been a great upwelling sense of life, but it was only later that he was able to put that term on it. At the moment he was too preoccupied with his need to maintain some order in the situation and the most he could register was a kind of shock. Shock, and a deep, electric attraction.

"I, I am very happy…I mean I am glad to be at your service." And to cover his embarrassment he looked round at both of them, "I have no idea how you both managed to fly that shuttle. You must be very competent persons. I am sure I speak for the Heavenly Homeland: we are fortunate to have you here with us."

The woman without a name suddenly joined the conversation. "You are a foolish person, Jonas, and have no idea of your words. These two flew here on wings of evil: they bring only plague into Heaven."

Jonas was intensely irritated. He barely knew this woman and had actually never been in a conversation with her. He'd brought her along just to make up some sort of a party, yet now she was ruining the little bit of decorum he'd managed to achieve.

"You must excuse our company. This person resides in the Agora of the Baths and normally she bothers no one, but because everyone else is away at the festival suddenly she is important. Pay no heed. In the Homeland of Heaven very few people have these psychological problems, and even if they do they are able to live peacefully among us." And he glared meaningfully at the woman.

She was immediately chastened and lapsed into silence. Poll had only half suppressed a laugh when the woman had spoken her mind, but Cal wanted to put Jonas at his ease and tried to lessen his embarrassment.

180

"Please don't be concerned. We are very glad that you came to get us. And this woman without a name, she helped us. She told us where everybody had gone. We would have had no idea but for her."

With these few words Cal immediately made everything seem pleasant. Jonas' attraction to her washed through his soul and he was astonished. As an Immortal he experienced attraction in a casual, even slightly bored and cynical way. Now he felt a desire to be with this person and it had a freshness he had never known before. Skirting the Agora he drove the car to a space close to the Baths, approaching the ancient site at right angles. From there they continued on foot along a path bordered by ancient vines and low rough-hewn pillars, emerging to the side of the front portico. Arising before them was the dazzling marble facade with its columns and pediment, a place like nothing Cal and Poll had seen before, or even dreamed of. It filled them with a peculiar longing and at the same time a deep unease. There was something here way beyond their experience or comprehension.

"This is one of the most revered spots in the Heavenly Homeland, the first building that we established and the place where the experience of immortality first began. Unfortunately we cannot go inside as that is intended expressly for the event of initiation. You will have to wait until later for that to take place, when I have assembled all the relevant parties. But I want you at least to know of the great privilege that awaits you and to have a sense of the splendor that is now yours in the Homeland of Heaven."

After his little speech he started back to the car and beckoned them to follow. "I must apologize if I seem abrupt but I really have to head back to get the others; without them there is no way of presenting things further."

They returned to the vehicle and he took the road farther along the side of the Baths, swinging around at the other end and entering a small courtyard. They got out of the car and passed through a wooden door into a hall at the end of the building. It was a high marble and stone space with rooms to either side and what looked like a ceremonial entrance about one hundred and fifty paces opposite. He waved to the left and the right.

"Here are your rooms. You will find a shower to the right side

181

of the courtyard outside. You will also find a change of robes and garments in the armoire there." Then he pointed down the hallway to the great doors. "Down there is the other end of the ritual baths, the place where neophytes emerge after Initiation, after their whole world has been changed. This will be the case for you too, so please do not go in there for now. You won't be able to see anything anyway—it is totally dark—and you might easily hurt yourselves.'

Turning to the woman who was still hovering in the background he told her to bring them food from the Agora. "Get some fruit and honey cakes from one of the stalls there, and also something to drink. I hardly need impress on you nothing should be said to disturb our new friends. They will shortly join us as Immortals and if they have an unpleasant experience because of you it cannot be overlooked."

And with that undisguised threat he returned to the car and was gone. The woman left too, perhaps to get the food, perhaps to avoid the risk of opening her mouth again. Cal and Poll were left in the elegant hallway looking at each other, feeling a powerful flux of emotion. Not ten hours ago they had been battling a brutal environment ruled by unquestioning Worship Leaders and murderous Icemen. They were still dressed in the uniform of that world, boots and therm-suits, which now felt stifling and absurd against a background of summer warmth and gleaming marble. At the same time they could not be comfortable about abandoning the badge of an existence in which they had struggled so hard to find the truth—as if, now they had found it, none of the struggle mattered. And that was apart from the awkwardness of having to put on robes the same as Jonas and the woman. Poll could not contain the tensions inside him and he let his feelings explode the moment Jonas was out of earshot, discharging on the one target he had, Cal.

"Fuck that guy! How the hell could you be so cozy with him, Cal? Don't you understand, he's one of the people who did this to us. Look around you! It's a paradise, a total fucking playground, and we've probably seen nothing yet. While the Northerners, the Teppers, people like *us*, what kind of existence did we ever have? Nothing except work and survival. There's no way we can cozy up with these people!"

Cal was taken aback. "Wow, Poll, what's got into you? I was only making the guy feel OK. You just got out of a prison camp. We don't want to end up in another one. Anyway, what *do* you want? Just like you say, there's probably a lot more to see and find out yet, and they won't tell us anything if they don't trust us."

"I said there's more to see, not to find out. You can know for certain they set the whole thing up on the backs of the Teppers. All this perfect weather has to depend on the refrigeration zone. They would never have gone to the trouble otherwise. So, we already know where we stand, and who the enemy is!"

"Poll, you remind me exactly of how you used to be with the professors back in the Training Center, talking back to them and getting thrown out of class. You think because you're so smart you don't have to worry about how people react. Haven't you learned anything? Your experience in the Camp showed you people will kill you without thinking twice, and here there are forces much bigger than those of the Camp, they have to be!"

Now it was Poll's turn to be surprised. Cal had never spoken to him like this before. But it only made him angrier.

"Tell me then, seeing you're so down with all this, what are they hiding inside those precious baths of theirs, eh? When they get you in there tomorrow it will be far too late to ask questions. I can only hope I have the chance to say I told you so!" And he stormed off toward one of the rooms, slamming the door as hard as he could behind him.

Cal headed back out to the courtyard, searching out the showers and the cupboard with fresh clothes. She had decided that despite the problem of the robes anything was preferable to the increasing sweat and itchiness of the therms. She also wanted to experience the shower, one of her greatest consolations back home in the TEP. Only now she would not be in a narrow cubicle with her eyes shut, relying on her imagination and images from the holograms. The world she had imagined back then seemed to have become real all around her. She wanted to know what a shower felt like here in the actual world of golden light and warmth. And after that she badly needed to sleep.

In his room Poll lay on his couch sweating and fuming. He unzipped the top of his therm-suit all the way down but he was still miserably hot. He could only bear it for a couple of minutes and then he swung himself round and crashed his feet to the floor. He pulled the top part of the one-piece suit off and tied the arms around his waist, leaving the synthetic undershirt below. Then he made a decision. He marched out of the room, heading down to the ceremonial doors at the far end of the hall. When he got to them he grasped the double handles and dragged them back against their heavy, close fit. As Jonas had warned it was pitch dark inside but immediately something else struck him, like a slap to the face. He was hit at once by the languid scent of the place as if something huge and of enormous beauty had just kissed him mockingly in the mouth. There was no way he could describe the scent: it was both a bouquet of rare flowers and a hint of bodily sense beyond anything he had imagined and it made his skin shiver. He thought spontaneously of the phrase Jonas had used, "the experience of immortality," and it made him dizzy. He slowly shut the doors and turned around, staring at the hall and the exit door at the end. Cal was right: there were forces here much larger than anything they had encountered so far. His old feeling of grudging awe for what these people had done returned to him, despite his anger. He walked slowly back up and out the building, passing through the courtyard and onto the route by which they'd come. He was still very hot and tired but it was impossible to rest. He was going to make his way back to the Agora and see what he could discover there.

***

Cal had showered for nearly a whole hour and then put on a robe she found in the fitted cupboard next to the showers. She discovered a pair of sandals and adjusted the thongs until they held comfortably. She was so very tired but it was just not possible to sleep. There was a whole world out there and it called to her, just as the stars had called to her back in the Homeland. She had to see and experience at least a part of it, to feel the warm air and sense the earth beneath her feet. She walked from the gate of the courtyard out onto the road which skirted it to the south. Across from it was a vast open space, tanned and white, dotted with bushes and low trees, all shimmering in the heat. What was it that Jonas had called it, the "Homeland of Heaven?" And Poll had said "Paradise!" After all her life spent in the deadly cold whiteness of the North how could these names be anything but true?

She ran across the road out into the open bush, dancing in circles and flinging her arms wide above her head and singing random notes plucked from she knew not where. The air tingled on her skin, the sun caressed it, the scent of the plants around her intoxicated her. She was completely overwhelmed, feeling her body melt into its surroundings and wanting to let it do so. She found a bare patch and lay down on the sand. Her eyes were closed and she felt the generous warmth striking her limbs on all sides and penetrating the thin gauze of her robe. It was as if she'd never been alive before, as if everything before was not an existence at all, just a long dead sleep. Through her lids she could still see the glow of the sky and it was like a giant light was coming not from outside but inside her body. Gone were the hard display lights of the wall panels, the monitors and control banks back in the North, and instead there was only this vast single light infusing everything. There was nothing anymore to count and she let herself drift with the light, to surrender to it fully. After a long moment—she wasn't sure how long—she heard something and opened her eyes. There was a small bird close to her; it had landed on a bush only a few feet away. She looked at the bird and the bird looked at her, and it was absolutely unlike the dead holograms. All at once it was as if some kind of communication passed between them. Something new moved in her and she didn't know what it was. The bird flew off and she followed it until her eyes were dazzled and she could see it no longer.

She got to her feet. She really needed to sleep. That man Jonas said he would be returning soon, for an initiation, whatever that was. Also she'd argued with Poll. She needed to make up with him, but they were both too tired to think clearly. Right now she could not even remember what they'd been arguing about. She retraced her steps to the courtyard and the hall still in the happiest, most pleasant state she had ever experienced. She entered her room, closed the door and fell on her bed, into a deep dreamless sleep.

PART THREE

1. SURPRISE PARTY

Jonas drove as fast as he could in an electric car. The effects of his chemical experience at Doblepoble were now fading rapidly and he was obliged to fight an increasing drowsiness. But if ever a situation was urgent this was it. Two young people had arrived in the Homeland of Heaven unexpected and uninvited. The elaborate preparation which always greeted inductees had been completely missed. It meant they were now gaining experiences not expressly constructed for them, and who knows what thoughts and impressions they were forming. The results could be unpredictable. He badly needed to let others in the Homeland know so they could decide on a way to handle the situation.

The trouble was there was nobody with any expertise in this kind of problem. Everything had been set up hundreds of years ago and had worked with well-oiled efficiency, which meant no one had to think very much about it at all. Cyrus, he knew, would be aghast. Even if he found him with his full faculties Jonas doubted whether he'd respond helpfully. Members of the Sports Stars Selection Colony, people like Gaius and Emmanuelle, would be the angriest, seeing their careful work trashed like this. But probably, for that reason, they'd also be the ones best able to focus on the problem. Jonas decided he really should look for them first.

As he drove at frustratingly slow speed along the Appian Way he found himself thinking in a way he never had before, trying urgently to solve a real problem. This effort, alongside the overwhelming impact Cal had produced in him, made him feel unsettled and unhappy. He wanted to get out and push the car to help it along, so he could get to the Forum more quickly, share the whole thing with other people and return, if possible, to his normal relaxed state.

The sun was at full heat, just past its zenith. He felt hot and sticky under the roof of the car. The architectural wonders of the city were coming into sight and the shadows stood directly beneath the buildings. It was as if momentarily another darker layer had been added to their construction. The place looked surreal, lacking shape and solidity. When he reached the parking plaza in front of the great gate to the Avenue of the Monuments the familiar groups were gathered beneath the trees and on the steps of the palaces and temples. He drew the car to a stop, jumped out and started running. He had to find the key people as quickly as he could.

He was fairly certain Gaius and Emmanuelle would be at the dance plaza. So many people went there on the second day of Doblepoble, and the Sports Monitoring Colony generally liked to be present, getting a chance to check on their protégés. Milton and Dante would be there, as well as colleagues like Kanna, Amala and Ivan, the usual inductee crew. He grabbed a tram and as he got near the end of the Avenue he could already feel the vibrations from the huge crowd clapping and stamping in unison. He jumped off and turned toward the plaza and then for certain he heard them, with the squeal and thump of the amplified music and the roar of the dancers as they came to the end of a set. The numbers of people were growing at every step, all looking a little wasted and disheveled from their twenty four hours of partying. Within a few hours most of them would be heading home to sleep it all off. Only a few hardy souls would stay the extra night to experience a further expansion of soul. Right now he knew it would be a challenge to get people to listen, but he had to try.

The plaza was accessed through corner openings in a great balustrade overlooking it on all sides. The whole arena was surrounded by banks of plane trees and a giant red top on a soaring ring of pylons was stretched over the middle. The atmosphere under the tent was of huge merriment and enthusiasm, with people throwing themselves with abandon into the movement of the dance. Jonas ran along the balustrade, feeling momentarily helpless facing the throng of swaying bodies. There were thousands of people whirling before him and a thin pall of dust hung over the whole scene. He could hardly recognize anyone but he cast around on either side hoping to find someone nearer to hand. A couple of dozen yards along he thought he made out a familiar figure among the crowd of spectators. It was Pandit, sitting on the wall, clapping and wagging his head like a mechanical doll.

"Pandit, Pandit, you have to come with me. Something has

happened. It demands your immediate attention."

Pandit continued to smile and nod in a beatific fashion, as if Jonas had said something deeply inspired. Jonas decided it was useless to press him further. He clambered up on the wall, keenly scanning the great crowd. Another large-scale formation dance had just begun, involving long opposing lines ducking under each other's arms, working their way progressively from one end to the other, accompanied all the while by the skirl of fiddles and beat of drums. His eyes were straining. Suddenly he saw Emmanuelle bending under an archway of arms, her blonde hair tousled and her gown tied up in a knot around her legs. He jumped down off the balustrade and dashed into the plaza. Weaving among bystanders, he ran to the point where he had seen her, scanning all the time the hot press of bodies as it surged back and forth.

"Hey, is that you, Jonas? Get in here! Looks like you're in need of fun!"

It was Dante, directly opposite him, shouting at him and holding out his hand from the line. Jonas didn't hesitate but grasped the offered palm firmly and pulled as hard as he could, toppling Dante out on top of him.

"What the…! Are you crazy?" Dante struggled to his feet. "Did no one ever teach you to dance?"

"I'm not here to dance. I've just driven from the Shuttle Port. A rocket ship arrived this morning with two Northerners and no guides aboard."

Jonas could see Dante working hard to make sense of what he'd heard, against the sweet pulse of pleasure beating in his veins. This was not about having fun at Doblepoble. It was serious.

"What's that you're saying? Makes no sense!"

Just then Emmanuelle came into view about half a dozen dancers down the line. He started waving and beckoning to her furiously. Surprisingly she quickly shook herself loose and gracefully dodged her way along the chain of dancers.

"What's up Jonas? What are you doing to Dante? Looks like he's not enjoying it very much!"

She spoke breathlessly but Jonas was relieved she seemed more or less in her right mind. He repeated his news, adding that he had left the newcomers in the accommodation at the Baths. Emmanuelle let loose with one of her bell-like laughs.

"What are you talking about? You must have taken bad Tremo last night. New inductees are not due for at least a couple of days, and Brutus and Fyodor are their guides. No Northerners could possibly fly the shuttle here by themselves. "

"The fact is they did, and I don't do hallucinates. I heard the sonic boom and went back in the car and found them. There are two Northerners at the Shuttle Port named Poll and Cal and the only initiation they're getting is from the crazy lady at the Agora."

Emmanuelle recognized Cal's name and her jaw dropped.

"Look, I don't know where you're getting this from but you have to stop. You're seriously freaking me out!"

"I know, I know, you have to believe me. I saw the shuttle on the tarmac and I drove the two of them in my car. I can tell you they are both highly unusual people. It's like they're somehow in charge. If we don't get them initiated very soon we won't know how to deal with them at all."

Emmanuelle and Dante finally grasped that Jonas was serious. Something must have happened and whatever it was he not going to stop until they responded. Dante struggled to organize his thoughts.

"OK, OK so we need a plan. What are we going to do?"

Emmanuelle said, "Let's go get Gaius. He should be in on this. I think he's still at the fountains."

No one had a better idea and they all headed out of the dance plaza, along the smooth flag roads lined with Roman pines, to the great plaza of the fountains. They passed among the ornamental marble and the pools of dimpled water, asking people still lounging there if anyone had seen Gaius. It did not take long to locate him stretched out inside a frothing marble extravaganza. It was an allegory with stone naiads, animals and personifications, all encased in an inverted liquid vase. The group shouted urgently through the waterfall and after a couple of attempts Gaius emerged looking displeased.

"What on earth are you yelling about?"

Emmanuelle told him what Jonas had said, adding, "He really doesn't seem to be tripping. If Northerners have arrived without guides we definitely need a response."

Gaius grabbed his robe draped on a wall. "How the hell could that happen? If it's true, and not some ridiculous prank, I'd say it's what used to be called a crime. Like stealing government property. It makes these individuals criminals."

Dante agreed. "Yeah, that crossed my mind too. Perhaps Magus should be in on this."

The mention of the obscure official of Heavenly Security had the effect of making everyone focus sharply. Jonas objected.

"That, I think, is the wrong way. It's jumping to conclusions, and anyway what these two individuals did is quite extraordinary. I would say they are like us, exceptional cases chosen for immortality. Only they just did the choosing themselves. If anything we should go to extra trouble to integrate them, not hand them over to Magus." He glanced at Emmanuelle, "What do you say?"

She furrowed her brow. "I think that involving Magus at this point would have him snooping around the whole induction process, and we certainly don't want that. Besides one of these Northerners is called Cal and that's the name of someone just selected, the sister of Danny, the swimmer. The guides were due to bring her, along with the friend chosen by Charlize. If this Cal is the same person then she already has official status."

Gaius said, "On the other hand she could be an imposter. And that's one more crime to add to the list. We need to get Danny right away, to make a positive ID."

"Of course, but if she *is* the same person then we really could go ahead. She's already been selected and it would be unheard of to initiate without the other person. We always do it in twos."

The solution seemed to pose the least disruption. The group agreed Emmanuelle would look for Danny, while Jonas and Dante grabbed Pandit. Gaius would round up any of the others who were used to helping Pandit with the ritual. They would meet up at the junction of the Sacred Way and be at the Baths by late nightfall.

As they all left Gaius turned to a figure hidden inside the fountain, waving. "Later, Roland. Got to go."

2. NOCTURNAL

Poll had entered the Agora through the gate opposite the baths. He wandered around among the flower-covered pergolas, the satin couches, the food barrows and the mysterious summer houses and pavilions. He found a knife next to a stand with some oranges and a melon. Cutting open an orange he put it to his mouth, tasting the first fresh fruit of his life. He tore away the peel and greedily devoured the segments. He sliced the melon and bit into its cool crispy flesh. Wiping the knife on his sleeve he used it to hack away at the therm-suit hanging from his waist. After some fierce stabbing and slashing he cut most of the top part free and tied the remaining strips off around his middle. He stood there in his undershirt like one of the pioneers he'd first seen in the sunshine photo, wearing their rough working clothes. He felt like a pioneer himself. Everything before him, the incredible beauty, the lavish luxury, it was all the same thing as the ice world, just its hidden face, a sneering far side of the moon. But, at the same time, he understood that Cal was exactly right. He could learn from these people, and that would be his task. If he was going to do something different, if he was going to be his own kind of pioneer, he would have to know all the secrets of this world.

He started to walk back along the road beside the Baths, returning to the end courtyard and his room. He wanted to apologize to Cal and tell her he had come round to seeing things her way. He would explain his idea of a new kind of pioneer and invite her to be one. They had gone through so much together, they should not stop now. Back there on the icefield when she rescued him he had been overwhelmed by awe and love for her. But they had been children then and everything had happened to them as children. This other world here was for grown-ups and was made by grown-ups. They would both have to grow up too, and fast, if they were to make a difference. He would show her the problem, and they'd seek its solution together, just like back in the Sector. He turned into the courtyard, a strip of torn therm-suit trailing behind him, eager to talk to his friend.

When he entered the hallway Poll saw a table just inside set with bread, cheese, olives and a flask of water. He guessed that the woman without a name had gone to the Agora ahead of him and

191

returned with food, somehow not crossing his path. He grabbed a loaf and a round of the cheese and walked directly across the floor to Cal's room. Then he hesitated. Her door was closed, so perhaps she was asleep. It also struck him that she'd probably showered, and might have taken up the offer of robes Jonas had mentioned. Suddenly he lost his conviction. She could be reacting to all this quite differently. If so he didn't want to deal with it now when his own thoughts were just beginning to take form. He turned away disconsolate, his wave of energy ebbing to reveal its undertow of anger and frustration.

He propped the bread under his arm and grabbed the flask, shambled back to his room and closed the door after him. Sitting on his couch he gorged himself on the bread and cheese until it was all gone, washing it down with large gulps of water. After he had finished he stripped off the remainder of his therm-suit and lay back. He stared at the ceiling, at its ancient beams and plaster, wondering vaguely when Jonas would return. He closed his eyes and almost at once he was asleep.

He dreamed he was again in the ice world, inside his TEP. He was lying on his bed and his Mom was sitting at the table, crying. She was saying something about his Dad, which he couldn't figure out. He started kicking with his feet and before he knew it his boots had connected with the big strong thermal wall of the TEP, puncturing a hole right through it. However, instead of the deadly cold air flooding in there were only golden light and a warm soft breeze. Suddenly he was crying too, sobbing from the heart because his father could not experience the warmth of the sun.

And then came a knocking at the door. He awoke in thick darkness with the tears still in his throat.

***

"Poll, please come out into the hallway. It's Jonas. I have returned with the Initiation party and we need to clear up some details before we can proceed."

Poll fought back the terrible feeling inside him. He knew that the moment had come. He had to will himself to surrender to whatever they had planned, in order somehow to bring the warm sunshine to the Teppers, to all like his father who had never known anything like it.

"Hold on, I'm coming."

He swung his legs off the couch. Groping on the floor he found the remnants of his therm-suit. Because of its tattered state and the darkness he couldn't separate one end from another. He gave up and in his undershirt and long johns he groped his way in the direction of Jonas' voice. He got to the door and jerked it open. At once his eyes were met by dancing firelight from numerous oil lamps and a patchwork of faces and bodies he didn't know. Jonas stepped forward and took his hand. "Come," he said, "there is someone here who must be the first to greet both you and Cal."

He was led through the crowd to the middle of the hallway where Cal was standing. She was dressed in the organdie robes that everyone else appeared to be wearing. For a moment he was shocked, not so much by her semi-nakedness but how it seemed she had never dressed any other way. He was taken aback at how the robes showed off her graceful body in a wholly easy fashion. He suddenly felt how stupid he must look in his clumsy underwear. But any thoughts about himself were abruptly interrupted when he saw the person Jonas wanted them to meet. It was Liz who was led forward, also clothed in the familiar robes but rumpled and bundled around her in a disheveled fashion. But more than anything it was her face that riveted Poll. She had somehow become so much older, by an age, he would have said. It was not lines or wrinkles: her face and skin were as smooth as they'd ever been. There was a cast in the eyes, a set to the mouth, which at once marked her off as belonging to something else, something that had been around long before she was born.

"Liz!" cried Cal, starting toward her to embrace her.

At once a man strode out and blocked her. "Please step back and allow us a moment." Then turning to Charlize the man said, "Do you recognize these people and if so could you tell us who they are?"

Charlize looked at the man and at Cal and Poll. She was both puzzled and annoyed. "Yes, Gaius, this is Cal, Danny's sister. We were told she was coming. But the other one is Poll, and it was supposed to be Esh. Why's she not here? I didn't invite him, he was always making…" And her voice trailed off.

Jonas broke in. "So that's settled. This is Cal, an official inductee and the other person, Poll, is her companion. We can go ahead and initiate."

Gaius was not put off that easily. "Wait, she didn't finish. She was going to say something."

Everyone turned back toward Charlize. She had been told very little on the way to the Baths, beyond that there were new arrivals who for some reason needed identifying. Emmanuelle had tracked her down at the Fairy House and asked her where Danny was, but Danny had left with Eboni hours ago and she didn't know where. Charlize had stayed on with Colette and had become progressively intimate with both her and Lara. By the time Emmanuelle found her everything had reached a state of calm and she was ready simply to sleep. But because Danny's trail had gone cold Emmanuelle insisted she come along instead, and it seemed so urgent it was impossible to refuse. Now when faced with Poll she had a good idea why. He was a known trouble-maker and she remembered he had recently got together with Cal. Very likely he had done something to mess up the arrangements and take her friend's place on the shuttle. As this was dawning on her she became more and more angry. At the same time, Cal was looking at her in a perfectly happy way. Danny's sister was clearly OK with Poll being there. So Charlize checked herself, despite her anger. She felt wary about being the one to ruin things; after all, they were all in Heaven now. In the end what she said came out lamely.

"Poll, he's, he's Cal's boyfriend, but he was always making ...objections to what the professors said."

"You mean he's disruptive. And then he stole a ride in the shuttle."

"That's not what she said and you know it, Gaius," Emmanuelle intervened decisively. "It means he's an independent thinker, and we surely have no objection to that, do we?"

She addressed Cal and Poll, "Please excuse me if I consult a moment with my colleagues." Grabbing Gaius and Jonas by the arms she marched them out of earshot. She hissed, "You heard what Charlize said: Poll is Cal's boyfriend. They're an item, so he's a natural for Initiation. The only thing out of place is they hijacked the shuttle, but isn't that what young love is all about? Just because it never happened before doesn't mean we can't be open to it, at least once. Meantime the longer we stand here arguing the less and less integrating the whole experience is bound to be, for them, and for everyone. If there are any loose ends we can deal with them later, but I vote we begin Initiation at once."

At this point it sounded a powerful argument. In the hallowed precincts of the ancient baths it seemed sacrilegious to be even debating the issue. Gaius felt the pressure of the moment and grudgingly relented. "OK, but I don't trust that Poll guy. I'll be watching him like a hawk!"

"Fine, fine. Plenty of time for that. Right now I'll tell Pandit."

Emmanuelle turned back to the crowd of Immortals standing around Cal and Poll, all looking toward her for the next move. They had been rounded up by Gaius and driven here in various cars, knowing only that their services were required at short notice. The guttering light from the lamps showed their faces bleary and dazed, arriving from Doblepoble for an unprecedented eleventh-hour Initiation. Pandit stood in their midst, trying to retain his beatific smile here in the temple where he was high priest. He struggled to clear his mind. As Emmanuelle called out, "Pandit, let the Initiation begin!" he blinked at her. Then he thrust his head back a couple of times and clapped his hands.

"Assistants, please prepare the baths to receive our Initiates. Enter here at these doors and make everything ready to receive them. And, now, who will be the sponsors for our beautiful neophytes?"

Emmanuelle pulled Jonas with her, "We are the sponsors."

"Very well. Bring the candidates and come with me to the ceremonial entrance."

Then turning to Cal and Poll, "My young friends, you have traveled far, but now you begin the truly epic journey of your lives!"

The assistants scattered toward the doors at the far end of the hallway while Pandit, Emmanuelle and Jonas escorted their charges out to the courtyard and the car, driving with them to the front entrance to the baths. Somehow Emmanuelle fell in at Poll's side while Jonas found himself next to Cal. The great formal steps of the building were illuminated by a single torch set in a bracket on a pillar. They ascended the steps as a group, following behind Pandit. When he arrived at the platform of the colonnade he faced around and made his speech about the sacred character of the place

195

and how they were now entering the astonishing experience of immortality. He asked the couple their names and then began hunting in his head for the requisite heavenly replacements.

"Poll, pol...pal? Why, yes, you can be 'Palmiro!' It has the dignity your single syllable was always wanting! And, Cal, how about...how about...Calliope? That seems to suggest itself?"

Cal gazed at him blankly, not fully understanding what he was saying.

"No, no, of course not. You're absolutely right, far too pedantic. Perhaps we should go the other way and stick with 'p's'. P, p... P-cale. Yes, I have it! Pas-cale! 'Pascale!' That is your new name!"

Smiling with satisfaction at his power of creativity Pandit turned and knocked at the great portico. There was silence, which went on for a few minutes until he tut-tutted and knocked again, more forcefully. Finally they heard noises and all at once the doors were flung wide. A half dozen of the assistants appeared dressed in fresh robes, their faces and limbs newly oiled and wearing a look that said, despite all the craziness, this was now the real thing. Cal and Poll's eyes were drawn to the interior, along the converging lines of glittering lamps, and they too felt that something enormous was about to take place.

Poll steeled himself for whatever was going to happen. He was led forward by the assistants and he felt their hands stripping him of his clumsy undergarments. Emmanuelle was pouring two drinks, one of which she took herself and the other she handed to him. He drained it in one go and felt the same voluptuous caress as when he had opened the big doors to the Baths near his room. This time he consciously surrendered his body to the sensation and the intimate shock it gave him.

Meanwhile Cal was led forward by Jonas. She had begun to enter a different mental space well before Jonas put the glass in her hand. After her experience in the desert she'd returned to her room and slept soundly. When she awoke it was dark and there was the sense of something else, both beautiful and disturbing. It was like having a mysterious, dangerous friend present with her in the room. There was no name she could give to the feeling, and quickly it was gone. The sensation seemed to fit with what had occurred in the desert. Something new was happening to her apart from any initiation. Then even as she was trying to come to grips with it she heard confused sounds coming from the hallway. She slipped off the couch and found her robe. Pulling it over her head she made her way to the door. She opened it to see Jonas holding a lamp and about to knock. Behind him there was the shadowy impression of a small crowd of people.

Jonas smiled and invited her into the hallway, leading her out before a group who were all dressed like him, and very beautiful. She saw how Jonas belonged to these people; he was beautiful just like them. Then Poll came out from his room and Liz was introduced, looking so very different from before. Cal was happy to see her but she had also felt the tension rise when the name of Poll was spoken. Poll himself seemed composed, even if he looked crazy in his underwear, and she was glad that he seemed to be settled in his mind. However, all during this time she was not paying complete attention herself.

Everything that was happening was not really happening to her. It was as if she was observing the event from outside her own body, from above the crowd. So when they had finally made their way to the baths and Pandit began to talk about their names she found it extremely difficult to focus on what he was saying. When she was handed the drink by Jonas she drank almost without noticing. Her mind and her soul were elsewhere, experiencing everything in her own private state.

She allowed herself to be disrobed and immersed in the pool. As she floated on its surface her last connection to her actual surroundings left her and she saw suddenly the roof ripped open and the brilliant sun burst through, shining down on her with all its force. She lay there in its dazzling glare, closing her eyes but with the light beating through her eyelids. It was like a bomb had gone off and it continued to explode slowly and silently above her. After a moment the fierce light seemed to shift a little and soften. She opened her eyes and the sun had become a beautiful white bird with its wings outstretched. One of the wings seemed broken and the great bird began to flutter helplessly down toward her. As it did it became smaller, and smaller, so by the time it landed in the space between her breasts it was a tiny white bird trailing a broken white wing. The bird nestled there and she sought to protect it by keeping herself as still and stable as possible. Yet she

197

could not continue for suddenly the assistants were submerging her and holding her under. She feared for the little bird, and she was right because it was flailing out of its depth and quickly becoming waterlogged. The little bird was drowning. She started to thrash furiously in the water, trying to get back to the surface to give it a place to stand and live. It was too late. She was falling helplessly backward down a deep well and the bird was stretched lifeless above her in the water. She felt a fathomless terror and anguish gripping her soul. Then all was black.

***

Jonas would have been dead on his feet if Emmanuelle had not given him a couple of the little pills she miraculously still had with her. Now, on top of this stimulus, the prospect of the powerful initiation drug, inducing a mystical near-death, did not seem very safe. At all events he needed to keep going to be sure the things that were still to be done were in fact done. So he faked drinking from his own glass when he handed one to Pascale. Thankfully she did not seem to pay attention and she drank the cup to its dregs. He was deeply distracted by her beauty, in fact he desired this young woman intensely, more than anyone he could remember. But he knew if he were to have any relationship with her she had first to become a fully accredited part of the Homeland of Heaven.

The ritual wasn't over yet, so he was forcing himself to concentrate on the remaining details. He knew Pandit and other assistants would head straight for their colonies once their responsibilities were concluded. They too were exhausted and wanted their beds and familiar comforts. Perhaps Emmanuelle would stay on, but he still needed Cyrus. Cyrus the famed historian was the man with all the necessary gravitas to persuade inductees to accept the doctrinal principles of the Heavenly Homeland. In the case of Pascale and Palmiro he was needed more than ever. Which meant that he would have to head off once more in the car to find him.

He was growing desperate, would this thing ever end? Then abruptly everything became dramatically worse. The ritual had reached the point where the initiate was being held beneath the surface. Up to this point Pascale had been so relaxed it seemed the drug had taken its effect almost at once. Now without warning she

198

began to move her arms and legs with a dream-like slowness, in a way that said she was trying desperately to wake up. Jonas was immediately concerned.

This was a point in which the body should not be experiencing any stress and it meant Pascale was not having the personal experience of release essential for the mind of an Immortal. But he was helpless. Pascale was beyond communication. Whatever was happening to her there was no way of making contact with it. He wanted to reach under the water to hold her hand but even that could perhaps be wrong, interfering with the solitary nature of the ritual moment. The assistants thought the same thing, for they were simply looking at her as if this was Pascale's problem and nothing to do with them.

Quickly Pascale's movements subsided and she became lifeless. In a sense this was what was meant to happen, but the way she looked suggested she had gone well beyond a mere slowdown in organic functions. She looked dead. Jonas signaled frantically to the assistants to get her out of the water. Together they pulled her to the end of the ceremonial pool and lifted her up the steps onto the marble floor. She lay there naked with the water gathered in little domes on her oiled body. Jonas waited desperately for a sign of life. Somewhere in the back of his mind he knew there was such a thing as cardiac resuscitation, but in a world of Immortals it had never been needed, and again he was fearful of doing anything that could be counted as interfering with the ritual. As far as he knew the drug had some kind of self-regulating ability so no harm could ever come. Yet Pascale had experienced an unheard of crisis, reacting frantically when the drug should have been producing maximum sedation. He had no idea what that could mean.

He told the assistants to carry her to her room, and to retrieve their robes. For now he grabbed a couple of large towels from the racks at the end of the pool, wrapping himself in one, and when he got to the room he used the other to cover her inert body. He stood bending over her, watching her. She looked terrible, waxy and pinched, and still she had not drawn breath. Suddenly he did something which surprised him, and entirely so. He lay his head on her breast and started to weep. He put his hands on her shoulders and he spoke, between sobs. "Pascale, Pascale, please

199

don't die. Please, please come back. It's alright, everything is alright. You must come back"

Still she did not move. After a moment he controlled himself and raised his head and looked at her. "What's more, you know, Pascale, I love you, I need to be with you. I have since I first saw you."

There was silence and then something seemed to alter. There was a slight tremor in Pascale's body, and she drew a small short breath.

"Yes, yes, I knew you could do it. Now take a real breath!" Jonas clenched his fists and held his own breath, willing her to breathe deeply. After a few more moments Pascale took a longer, quivering breath and the bridge seemed to have been crossed.

Jonas staggered and collapsed against the wall, completely amazed at everything that had happened, and most of all at himself. He sat there in a daze. He felt drunk with sensations that were utterly new for him, and with exhaustion, one effect piling on top of the other. He knew there was no way he could get back in the car to look for Cyrus. And he almost didn't care anymore. He hauled himself up to his feet and with one more look at Pascale, who was now breathing slowly but regularly, he stumbled out to the hall. He found a Louis XVI upholstered couch set against the long wall and he collapsed on it. Almost instantly he was asleep.

3. LOVERS AND MENTORS

Late the following morning Jonas was rudely awakened. A tall figure with robes wrapped awkwardly around his torso was shaking him and looking at him intensely. For a moment Jonas did not recognize Palmiro.

"Jonas, what's happening? Where's Cal?"

Jonas tried to gather his thoughts. He had gotten up once during the night to check on his neophyte and found her sleeping normally. Now it seemed the anxiety was to begin all over again, and it was the one who had provoked so many of the difficulties yesterday who was starting it.

"You mean Pascale, don't you? And what are you saying? I left her in her room."

"OK, Pascale, whatever, she's not there. I looked out in the courtyard too, she's nowhere. And what's supposed to be happening anyway? Where is everyone?"

Jonas sat bolt upright, fearful again for Pascale. "I don't know, there should be breakfast and a tour, I'm not sure. I have to find Pascale. You better wait here, in case someone shows up. I'll look. She can't be far."

The Northerner was not satisfied, but Jonas had no choice but to leave him there. Perhaps Pascale's distress during the ritual had returned when she awoke, which would mean her initiation to the Heavenly Homeland had been a failure. He had to find her at once to try and cope with the situation. He hurried down the hall, through the courtyard and out onto the road, looking in either direction. She was nowhere to be seen. He crossed to the road's far edge, venturing out on the semi-desert which marked the western boundary of the Homeland.

The sky was a deep blue circle around a diamond sun. Little patches of yellow daisies and mistflower shone mirror colors back from the ground. As the land stretched into the distance a slight shimmer twisted the frieze of creosote bushes and juniper, making it jump unexpectedly: it would be very easy to get lost out here. He walked a couple of dozen paces, shouting Pascale's name. It was possible she could have found her way to the Agora, but he could not imagine why. His instinct told him she had to be here, in the open country. He walked on, calling out anxiously.

201

"Pascale, Pascale, are you out here? Where are you?"

He turned around in a full circle, searching, and as he faced back toward the desert suddenly she was there, right in front of him. For an instant the cascading light seemed to come to a full stop. He was stunned by her beauty. It made the desert a place of perfection. At the same time he was overwhelmed by a look on her face, so different, so full of an emptiness and pain he could not have imagined yesterday. She came toward him, hesitantly at first, almost as if she was sleep-walking. He put his hands out to her and she fell on his chest and clung to him. The pleasure of her embrace took his breath away, but his stomach was knotted by the affliction in her eyes.

"What happened, Pascale? What's wrong?"

She did not reply but slowly her body was shaken with sobs. He held her as grief pulsed from her belly up into her throat. He did not know what to say or do, the experience was so foreign and new. People did not do this in Heaven, or if they did it was because they were the very small minority incapable of the life of immortality.

"Please, please, Pascale, be happy. You are in Heaven now. Whatever you have experienced cannot take that away. Everything here is perfect, can't you see?"

She turned her head to look at him. "Jonas, you're real, aren't you? You came for me?"

"Yes, of course I did. I am your sponsor, your friend."

He bent at once and kissed her on the lips, running his hands across her face and neck and down her back. She responded instinctively, pressing herself close to his body, kissing him hungrily, desperately.

Jonas' heart was pounding like a drum and his legs were buckling under him. He wanted to pull her down and make love with her there on the sand under the flawless sun. But despite the avalanche of desire falling on him there was a still greater urgency. He had to make sure she was going to be able to calm herself, to be in her right mind. Otherwise the rest of Heaven would never accept her as worthy of immortality.

"Stop, stop, Pascale, you have to stop. Listen to me, please, look at me. Speak to me. Say something!"

Slowly, unwillingly she stopped and pulled herself back

202

slightly. Her eyes had lost their lifeless look, recovering a little of their light, but there was still pain and fear in them.

"Jonas, don't leave me. I feel sunshine again when you're near. You must promise to stay close, here in Heaven. You promise me?"

"Of course, of course, Pascale, I promise, I will never leave you. But, tell me, what are you doing out here? What happened?"

She did not reply. She just shook her head, and put her arms round him once more, this time just standing there with her head resting on his shoulder. He held her while the moment of intense desire seemed to pass, wrapped as it was in her sorrow that did not have a name.

"Tell me, at least, are you able to come back with me? Palmiro is looking for you, and I think people from the colony are bound to be here soon. You must decide clearly, Pascale, are you ready to be one of our company of Immortals?"

She pulled back from him once more, looking at him. She seemed to weigh his words, trying to understand for herself what they could mean. She started to speak, stopped, and seemed almost to shiver. Finally she said. "I don't know, Jonas, but with you I can try."

Just then they heard a woman's distant voice calling their names. "Jonas, Pascale, where are you? Are you out here?"

It was Emmanuelle, and Jonas knew that the answer Pascale had given had to suffice.

He shouted, "Yes, yes, we're here. We're coming." He looked at Pascale questioningly and she nodded. They grasped hands and together threaded their way back through the scrub oak and juniper to the road and the Baths.

Emmanuelle was waiting for them at the edge of the road. She looked even more tousled and rumpled than yesterday but when she saw them her face lit up with a radiant smile and a wink. "Well, look at you! I thought Palmiro was the love interest, but it seems the two of you have hit it off!"

Jonas mumbled something, embarrassed. He couldn't begin to explain. But Emmanuelle was having none of it. "No, don't apologize, really, I have to thank both of you most heartily. I haven't had such fun since I don't know when. What a Doblepoble! All the drama of a late-night initiation, a little sip of

Pandit's sweet brew, and then waking up to one more kick-start so I could bring in the cavalry!"

"You brought Cyrus?"

"Oh that dreamer, no, he's lost to the world. I couldn't find him anywhere. So I took things into my own hands. I rounded up some fun people who would give a pretty good idea of who we are in the HH. You'll be amazed! And I brought breakfast. You guys must be starving!"

Jonas was impressed. She'd drunk the narcotic, which he had very deliberately avoided, and yet was still alert enough to organize everything. And as they approached the courtyard he could see she was as good as her word. There was quite a crowd of people gathered, all smiling as they surrounded Palmiro who was seated at a picnic table demolishing a hamper of food. The recent initiate did not look up at first, but when he did, and saw Jonas and Pascale hand-in-hand, he paused in mid-mouthful. He half stood up, looking hard at what seemed evidently a couple. Some in the crowd noticed and glanced from Palmiro to Jonas and Pascale. They were used to newcomers pairing up after initiation, but of course it didn't always work that way. It was often the role of the sponsor to carry through the sexual awakening. That seemed to have worked out for Pascale, but Palmiro was looking quite clearly unfulfilled. Emmanuelle, arriving at the side of the couple, took in the situation at a glance. She came to the rescue. Clapping her hands, she called for attention.

"I do confess, I have been neglecting my responsibilities to my neophyte. In yesterday's unusual circumstances I had to abandon him to go summon you all. But now I am here I will be a model of solicitude." And she went directly over to Palmiro, throwing her arms around him and kissing him enthusiastically. Palmiro was so surprised that he collapsed down on his bench. The experience of the baths flooded back over him and he remembered his decision to surrender to the ways of Heaven, whatever they were, so as to learn from them. Certainly it was not difficult to give in to the feeling, communicated so directly by this beautiful woman. The look in his eyes melted slightly and he even managed a sheepish smile. Everyone clapped.

Almost without taking a breath and with one arm still around her protégé Emmanuelle continued to speak.

"Come, Pascale, Jonas, have some breakfast. I am sure you are just as hungry as Palmiro here." And she gave him an extra cuddle as she mentioned his name. Jonas and Pascale made their way over to the table and took yogurt, plum cake and grape juice. They carried the food to another table and sat down. All the while Emmanuelle continued to smile like the sun itself. Everyone was looking to her for the next move and she was enjoying the situation immensely. The moment the two were settled she addressed the newcomers.

"And now of course introductions are in order. I have brought this group of people with me to help you grasp who we are here in the Homeland of Heaven. There will be further explanations in due course but I thought the best and quickest way to start would be to get you to meet a cross-section of Immortals, some of the coolest people on earth! You know, once the word went that there were two young people who had made their way unaided from the Northern Homeland, there were scores and scores of folk clamoring to meet you. So I had to choose, and I brought the ones I thought you'd find the most interesting."

Pascale and Palmiro were looking at her with different expressions. Poll, who was now deliberately thinking of himself as Palmiro, was all attention, concentrating on her words and already scanning the reception committee with interest. His one-time companion, in contrast, appeared strained and was blinking vaguely. Emmanuelle pressed on regardless.

"First of all you need to understand Immortals live in groups or colonies dedicated to different pursuits—arts, crafts, technology, etcetera, each according to the individual's yen and fancy. You yourselves will be free to live in any one of the colonies that takes your interest, and free to change to a new one tomorrow, or the year after, whenever you wish. This beautiful company which stands before you, all belong to various colonies or specialty groups, and I will say just a little about each one as I introduce them.

"To begin then, here is Shimin and Kanna from my own colony," and she gestured toward a woman with high Asian cheeks and angled eyes and a body like gently flowing water as she waved politely. Kanna was a tall dark-skinned man with a similarly graceful yet slightly mocking manner. Emmanuelle explained the key role of her colony in monitoring news reports of outstanding individuals in the Northern Sectors. She and others with her decided on the few fortunate ones to be chosen for immortality. Pascale and Palmiro of course had done something unheard of. One of them had not in fact been chosen and together they had more or less forced their way into to Heaven. Not surprisingly this had provoked some comment within the colony, but the presence of Shimin and Kanna showed there were no hard feelings!

Next there were Nicola and Carmina. These two came respectively from the Viniculture and Dress Fashion Colonies. Nicola was a warm, vivacious woman, with a generous body swathed in swirling multi-colored scarves. Carmina in contrast had the appearance of porcelain, delicate and refined; her back, exposed in a deep collar draped from her shoulders, looked as if it would shatter if any weight were placed on it. In contrast her fingers were alive and expressive, covered in jewels. Emmanuelle said these two illustrated the huge fun of the colonies, their exquisite products in things to taste, eat and wear.

"But there are other exquisite products, even closer to us than the things we eat. And for these I must introduce to you Sachs and Vitolo, our surgical specialists."

She explained that all the Immortals were known for their physical attractiveness, and they had had these qualities right from the beginning. But occasionally certain minor adjustments could be made, always in keeping with the style of the individual. So advanced were the techniques of both tissue removal and tissue printing and growth, they always achieved a totally natural look. The two men she pointed to were walking advertisements for their craft. Both fresh-faced, tight-bodied yet relaxed, they exuded charm and professional expertise. Palmiro's interest which had so far been unsatisfied was piqued at the mention of advanced techniques. He scrutinized the men closely, wondering if these were the ones with whom he could advance his own knowledge. Emmanuelle, however, was forging ahead.

"And this here is Vanzetti, a colleague of Jonas. Both of them belong to the History Colony, which is so important in the telling of our heavenly story. Jonas is—as you can see—a little tied up, so Vanzetti came to provide the narrative of our beginnings. It is the story which completes the Initiation. But before I turn things over I must introduce the others, the rest of our immortal band!"

There were four left. She pointed to Marius and Blair who belonged to the Anthropology group. She seemed a little vague about what this colony actually did, but she said they were akin to the Philosophy Colony and that is why they had come. It was in fact an essential part of the newcomers' program to spend time with people like the philosophers. "Only with them do you get a full picture of all the beautiful thought that has gone into the Heavenly Homeland." She smiled at the two men who were a little older and more serious than the others. Marius, gaunt and imposing, did not respond. Blair, dark-skinned, bald-headed, with bright engaging eyes, returned the smile.

Finally there were Hona and Adorno. They came from the Tech Colony, a large group with a number of subdivisions. One of these was care of the rocket transports. In fact directly after this encounter Hona would need to reprogram the shuttle to return to the Sector and pick up the stranded guides. Emmanuelle was sure she would also want to know exactly how Palmiro and Pascale had figured out to fly the thing. Hona had dark hair and eyes with smooth single lids, and she was decisive and precise in her actions. Of all the reception committee, she was the one most obviously frustrated with the newcomers. She could hardly stop herself scowling, especially at Palmiro. But Palmiro was paying no attention.

Emmanuelle had finally come to Adorno, saying it was exceptional that someone like him should attend an Initiation. He was one of the most brilliant people in the Homeland and normally did not leave the laboratory where he worked. Still on this occasion he had wanted to come, intrigued no doubt by the fascinating circumstances. What was totally special about him was he was the scientist who'd made the revolutionary breakthrough of immortality. They would have the unique privilege of hearing him speak about it during Vanzetti's presentation. Palmiro was now riveted. Here without a doubt was the person he should learn from. Yet it wasn't just Emmanuelle's remarks that impressed him; in equal measure Adorno's appearance rooted him to the spot.

The man had managed to hide behind the others during the introductions and when the way was cleared for him he was

207

patently the ugliest man in Heaven. He was uglier in fact than anyone Palmiro had known back in the Sector. He was less than medium height with an angular bony frame that seemed to lack any meat. His face had the same skeletal form, with a pronounced cranium and forehead, gaunt cheeks and a long jaw that looked as if it moved somehow independent of the rest of his face. Beneath the jutting brow his eyes were deep set and shadowed, like creatures in a cave. When he came forward it was at first hard to conceive this was a brilliant man, but once you managed to catch his eye there was something there that immediately inspired respect. It was glittering and obscure in the same moment, like starlight on a bottomless sea.

"This must be it!" Palmiro thought. "With all these beautiful people everywhere else someone who looks like that just has to have a brilliant mind." He wanted to go up to Adorno directly to start talking to him, but just then Emmanuelle turned proceedings over to Vanzetti. Now was the time for the story of the Heavenly Homeland, after which the newcomers' Initiation was essentially complete. Of course they would later have to take a tour, but this point was the crowning moment of the experience. The story behind their immortal existence would give shape to everything. She invited all present to take a seat and enjoy.

Vanzetti had a light tawny beard and fine, composed features. He lacked Cyrus' theatrical style, but he spoke with ease and authority. He began with the disaster of the storm world, the terrifying death toll, the threat to human civilization itself. The Global Weather Shield had provided a desperate solution and of course Palmiro was familiar with this. What he had not heard before was the meteorological synergy between the Northern and Southern Homelands. Vanzetti was saying that by means of the chaotic conditions and then the technology of the Weather Shield the scientists had created an artificial jet stream which kept the Homeland of Heaven permanently warm and sunny. To sustain their world without rain a water supply was channeled in from the mountains beyond. Along with mists created by cooler air coming from the sierra at night, it kept everything alive and green. Palmiro could not restrain himself; he shouted, "I knew it, I knew it. The heat had to go somewhere!"

Everyone turned to look at him, including Adorno. Palmiro

at once shut his mouth and shook his head. He mumbled he was sorry and asked Vanzetti to please continue. The historian looked at him slightly askance, then returned to his narrative. He described the criteria used for choosing the different populations: strong religiosity for the north, beauty and prowess for the south. The continued recruitment of exceptional individuals from the north, such as present inductees, maintained a connection between the two, demonstrating they were ultimately one human race. Moreover it should always be remembered the whole system was essential for the survival of humanity as such.

"But," he added, "the triumph of the Heavenly Homeland is not just survival, it is much more than that. Our Heavenly existence brings the human condition to an absolutely new level, to an entirely new meaning. Out of disaster triumph was fashioned. And to tell you about it here is the architect of the triumph himself, our very own genius of immortality, Adorno."

There was a fervent rattle of applause as all eyes turned to the strikingly ugly man with the fathomless eyes. Adorno may have been appalling to look at but he was calm and self-possessed and the moment he opened his mouth to speak it was impossible to think about his physical appearance. His eyes held you and the timbre of his voice was deep and sonorous. By listening to him he was changed instantly from something horrible to a figure of enormous authority and, yes, beauty and wonder. He did not say much, introducing the topic of artificial enzymes in a few words. He emphasized the step-by-step engineering, resulting in the final logical possibility: reversing the coding which produced age within the cell. He said that no one had taken the idea seriously but he had pushed on with design after design, inspired he said by a personal sense of the fluidity of all information structures.

The pathway had been extremely complex, but in the end, when he had found the vital enzyme structure to override the deep cell programming, everything had fallen into place with the simplicity of a lock's tumblers. He had been the first to drink the formula and then he had given it to his mother. After a year she had shown no progress in age, and if anything appeared younger. Knowing its enormous implications he had been unwilling to submit his work to peer review. After assembling an album of photos of his mother over six years he had finally got the attention ol the biggest pharmaceutical company of the time. The company had close links with the intelligence community, and he and his mother were taken into protective custody. The rest, as they say, is history.

These last words were uttered with the phantom of a smile and then he turned the proceedings back to Vanzetti. Palmiro was floored and, for once, speechless. Never in his wildest dreams had he imagined anything like this. Now he understood the uncanny sense he had first picked up opening the door to the Baths, the feeling of an abyss into which he was about to fall. And right at this moment Vanzetti was smiling at him and Pascale. He was telling them they had already been given the formula to drink and thus the process of aging had already come to a dead stop inside them. Palmiro knew he had crossed an ocean as deep as the universe itself.

He wanted more than ever to speak to Adorno. He wanted to work with him, to be in his company each waking moment, to learn everything this wizard had to teach. Aside from that nothing felt happy or safe to him. He was an Immortal, yet not like all these others who had been chosen for the part. He was in with them now and there was no turning back, but it was also a fact he had gatecrashed the party. He had not forgotten Gaius' reaction and his words, that he had stolen a ride on the shuttle. The truth was he was an interloper. At the same time the newly-named Pascale was behaving as if she had forgotten him completely. She had begun something with Jonas whom she had known for barely a day. He felt isolated and disconnected from everyone, a situation not unusual for him, but this time it went much deeper. Back in the Sector he always felt he'd be proven right and then everyone would love him. Now in Heaven, when the truth was totally in the open, he was even more the odd one out and he could see no way of things changing. It made him feel horrible and fearful. He looked around for Emmanuelle who had defended him and then shocked him with her kisses. She was seated right behind him and she smiled at once and reached out her hand. He took it hungrily and it felt alive and inviting.

Vanzetti was still speaking, explaining that there was obviously no need for reproduction of offspring in Heaven and thus all the chaos that went with children was avoided. Instead there was only a calm mutual enjoyment of Immortals. He moved on to talk about the architectural wonders of Heaven and the endless variety of its entertainments. Normally on this morning there would be a tour for inductees, but because of the circumstances the group presentation had been arranged. However, at some point in the near future they would need to tour the city: it was an incomparable experience. As he wrapped up his speech Emmanuelle stood up, still holding Palmiro's hand. She looked over at Jonas and Pascale who were also holding hands.

"Well," she announced, "I think this has all gone splendidly. Everyone has done a fantastic job and it seems to me that our new additions to Heaven are well and truly initiated."

She pulled Palmiro's hand into the air with her own, waving it back and forth and arching her eyes in a way that declared she would personally ensure the truth of her statement. Everybody burst into applause, smiling and laughing. She continued, "So I think we're done. Evidently Pascale is in the best of hands, and Palmiro is with me. Our new Immortals will continue their orientation in our colonies and everyone can go home. I know for one I am ready for serious sleep. Many thanks to you all, and oh yes, Adorno, do drop by any time. I was watching Palmiro during your remarks and I believe you have found a true disciple. Call round, I will not be at all jealous, I promise!"

Adorno's eyes flitted like bats in a cave. "I'll make a point of it," he said slowly in his resonant voice. "I too think it might be profitable for me and your protégé to meet."

He turned and walked away, his awkward gait entirely fitted for a mind which would never be constrained by physical laws.

4. DREAM TIME

In the Heavenly Homeland there were no seasons. At that point on the earth's latitude there was very little movement in the position of the rising and setting sun. In addition the control established over the weather reinforced the lack of natural variation. In stark contrast the Northern Homeland had always experienced evidence of a shift of season, from periods when the sun seemed to stay forever in the sky to days of long darkness. The change which Pascale and Palmiro therefore underwent from the constant sense of a circling earth to the bland sameness of Heaven produced a profound loss of time. And to confirm the feeling, the new world lacked the ten and one hundred day calendar of the Sectors. The only feature that marked any kind of time was the Doblepoble, and while that came roughly every thirty to sixty days it happened on a random basis. It was the job of the History colony to announce the next one and they did so according to their own whim. People preferred the sudden thrill of the announcement, while the historians kept count of the period since the last one and of noteworthy happenings in the interim. By and large, of course, nothing ever happened, beyond the endless fun of Heavenly existence.

Pascale had returned with Jonas to his house and that night he had invited her to his bed. She hesitated only a moment. Her experience of Heaven had gone from ecstasy to inconsolable sadness in the space of twelve hours. Behind it stood the dramatic events of her rescue of Poll and the shuttle flight that brought them to this place. Nothing made any sense and all she was left with was the power of the sensations which came to her. After awaking from the initiation she instinctively headed for the open space where she'd known the warmth and joy of the light. But although the sun sparkled on her skin the edge of horror continued to shadow her. She saw everything in a haze of fear, with nowhere to escape. It was only when Jonas arrived and she felt his care for her and kissed his mouth that the sunshine returned. He belonged to Heaven, to this untrustworthy but beautiful world, and he alone had come to her rescue. He was gentle and passionate and alive, the best thing, the sole thing, possible for her.

The days and nights following were lost in her own personal

summertime disconnected from everything else, a private season into which all other purpose collapsed. The timeless aura of Heaven played along, spreading out the infinite moment, telling her every dreaming day, every hour, would and did last forever. She developed the quickest feelings for her fellow Immortal. He was an angel who had come in a moment of terrifying grief and his touch had brought her back to life. She was thrilled with the shape and strength of his forearm, with the solidity of his torso. At the same time he was tender, and good, and she felt completely secure. The terror and emptiness ebbed away from her, piece by piece, and she did not wish to step outside of her little heaven lest they return.

Her new name, which Jonas always used, was of great assistance. It enabled her to think only of this present existence and it always made her happy. As for Poll, he was now Palmiro and he too was entirely new. If she thought about their adventure together, she told herself it was all over and done with. He was here now, in his own place, and he could be happy and safe just as she was. If she remembered Wes and Esh, and her declaration that everything would change, her soul told her they were thousands of miles away, and there was something huge lying across the path between them, something she did not want ever to go near. And when she thought any of these things she would turn to Jonas once more, embrace him and cover him with kisses.

As for her lover, he had never been so blissful. The thought did cross his mind that technically it was impossible for anyone in Heaven to be happier at one time more than another, but he was not about to let it ruin his enjoyment. He knew Pascale trusted him and loved him. There was no one else in Heaven like her. The whole thing about Immortals being a race of beautiful equals, endlessly interchangeable and available, began to strike him as a kind of dogma. Her glance enchanted him, the way it moved over his body and came to rest on his face. He wanted to keep that glance for himself and always. He was endlessly thrilled at the way her hair fell on her shoulder and fringed the line of her collar bone, and he could not see how anyone else but he could ever know its miracle. Through the timeless hours he did not think Heaven was or would be anything but this.

He forgot his tasks in the History Colony, things like

213

recording his observations of the recent Doblepoblo, and even of the emergency initiation of Pascale herself. Certainly this would not be counted as dereliction on his part: everybody in Heaven was far too relaxed for that. They would even expect that a sponsor devote quality time to a recent inductee. But for Jonas it was never a matter of giving his partner a quick, disposable honeymoon. It had become so much more real than that.

Cyrus had been introduced to Pascale the day after she arrived in the colony but his attitude was cold and aloof. He was very annoyed at the unscheduled Initiation, how irregular it all was, and especially the way the program had gone forward without him. He even muttered it would have been better to get Security involved right there, a thought which made Jonas shudder. At any rate, there was now no question whether Cyrus would do the formal tour for the inductees: as far as the great historian was concerned they were unworthy interlopers and he would have nothing to do with them.

Jonas decided to do the tour himself, and also not to invite Palmiro. The one individual who could justly be called an interloper would be looked after by Emmanuelle, while he would devote himself exclusively to Pascale. The idea of accompanying her around the splendor of the Forum seemed all together sublime. Everything he had ever experienced there, its smells, its play of light and sound, its thrills and mysteries, all this would be perfected with her: they would be a god and goddess, basking together in the timeless wonders of Heaven.

All the same Jonas delayed. It was as if he were in a dream, lying next to Pascale in his second floor room, getting up only to go downstairs to the kitchen to find items of food and drink and return quickly like a hunter with his prizes. He shared a multi-quarter house with other members of the colony. The wing he was in was also occupied by Vanzetti and Vanzetti's current partner, Masharu, a regal dark-skinned woman whose interests often took her to the downtown libraries. She and Vanzetti were indulgent to the two lovers and made sure there were plenty of supplies laid in, pastries, cold cuts, salads and fresh pressed juice.

Jonas' room had French windows with white silk curtains. It led out onto a veranda overlooking a hillside dotted with vineyards and scatterings of scrub oak and mesquite. In the evenings the sun would go down at the far end of the valley and Pascale would go out to look at the light withdrawing from the thickets and velvet night coming in. He would watch her from the doorway as the stages of nightfall became a foil for her own beauty. He'd gaze enchanted, until in the last twilight she would turn back to him and their embraces would renew their passion. For what motive would he possibly want to tear himself away from this idyllic place and its boundless delight?

In the end it was Emmanuelle who awoke him from his dream. Or, rather, she awoke Pascale. The party-loving blonde from the Sports Stars Monitoring Colony arrived one morning on a horse. She rode her chestnut mare wearing a short belted skirt and a loose silk vest, looking every inch a goddess of the hunt. She was beneath the veranda and its open windows, cantering up and down and shouting to the couple who were just finishing breakfast.

"Hey, you up there, are you in? Are you lovebirds receiving visitors?"

Jonas thought he recognized Emmanuelle's voice and he raised his eyebrows in question toward Pascale. She smiled and shrugged. He walked out onto the veranda and looked over the railing. Emmanuelle saw him, wheeled the horse about and came to a leaning stop just below him.

"Jonas! Such a pleasure to see you." Her face was raised confidently toward him and she spoke in her clear bell-like tones. "How are you coping with your sultry Northerner?"

"We're doing very well, thank you."

"It sure as heck looks like it! We've seen neither hide nor hair of you for the longest time."

"Well, the Initiation was a great success. Pascale's really very happy."

Emmanuelle gazed at him while she held in check the restive mount. "Great, yes, everyone did a great job. But that was a whiles back. I really felt this morning, you know, I should come over and bring everyone up to date..."

"Thanks so much, Emmanuelle, like I said everything's great. But time's such a tricky thing here in Heaven, it can just slip away from you." Jonas was surprised at his own words. Strictly speaking in Heaven time did not exist and people rarely spoke of

215

it like that.

Emmanuelle made a humorous, mystified face while the horse danced on the spot. Before she could reply Pascale came out of the room and crossed over to the railing. Her hair was mussed and she was looking at Emmanuelle as if she had just then remembered something.

"How's Palmiro?"

"There she is! The bright new Venus in our skies! How you have vanquished our prosaic Jonas!"

Pascale continued to look as if she were remembering something of her own, not paying attention to the words. Emmanuelle saw the continuing question on Pascale's face and followed through affably.

"Ah, yes, Palmiro, another rare bird. We had our little fling, but we weren't left undisturbed the way you sweethearts have been. There were visits from people asking questions, about the flight and other things, and then Adorno came and whisked him away like a hawk from the sky. I can't say I was upset. That boy's mind is always drifting off. Not really the romantic type." She released the mare's pent up energy, doing a circuit on the stretch of sage grass in front of the house.

When she came back again she said, "One thing we did do is the downtown tour. Palmiro was in the worst mood, but then we bumped into your brother, Pascale. Danny, he seems to hang out there a lot and he's such a nice guy. He's another reason why I came over. He really wants to see you."

Pascale remembered Danny with a shock. She had almost completely wiped him from her mind. Suddenly she missed him very much. She brushed her hair away from her face. "I would really like that. Why didn't he come over anyway?"

"Well, why do you think?" And she looked up at the couple provocatively. "Word went round you were having far too much of a good time. He said he was embarrassed!"

"Oh, I'm sorry, I didn't know...," Pascale trailed off, uncertain.

"Don't be silly, she's only kidding," put in Jonas. "Anyway I was thinking to go on the tour very soon. In fact we could do it today if you want. We will very likely find Danny, if that's where he's hanging out."

216

Emmanuelle cheered. "Huzzah! That's the spirit. Get back in the swim." And she took the chestnut in a tight circle below them with a couple of showy curvets thrown in. When she got the horse settled again she continued.

"Now there's one more thing, my pets. The philosophers, they're dying to host a big gig for all the newcomers, with Sarobindo present. Jonas, you know what that means! But they've been delaying and delaying, out of deference to you two. Apparently Hypatia and Friedrich absolutely would not hear of your little island being invaded."

She did a fake double-take. "Ooops, but I just invaded it, didn't I? Well, too late to worry! What I do want to say is if you show up downtown you'll also be getting a speedy invitation to their colony. Don't say you weren't warned!"

With that she reared the horse and plunged directly into a gallop, looping across the hillside in front of the house and yelling, "Such fun talking with you guys. Say hello to Danny for me!"

She disappeared down the slope between the trees, her body glued to the chestnut like an elegant craft on a fast-flowing river.

Pascale turned back toward the room, "I think she's right, we should get changed and go downtown."

217

5. VENICE

Under a sidewalk awning Danny lay on a recliner idly watching the people of Heaven from the corner of his eye. His chosen spot was a setting to the south of the Sacred Way, a vast esplanade dominated by a full-scale Venetian cathedral and lapped by a lake of turquoise water imitating the famous lagoon. This was his favorite place. On another lounger close to him lay another beauty, black-skinned with a cloudburst of dark ringlets framing a high forehead and lustrous eyes. It was Eboni, his companion from the last Doblepoble and inseparable ever since. After sunup at the Fairy House at the end of that wild night he'd said he wanted to get away from everyone and everything, just for a while, and she said she knew the perfect place.

She led him south from downtown by dirt paths through the parkland, onto a dusty rolling range dotted with sage, bunchgrass and live oak. At length, after almost two hours, they arrived at a large enclosure with nobody in attendance. Inside were more fences and behind them were mighty animals, which Danny had only seen before in holograms. Not a great number, essentially a few examples each of animals known from children's stories and which the Immortals could not bear to be without, elephants, tigers, lions, bison, zebra, camels, giraffes, monkeys, rhinoceroses, bears, leopards, pandas. They were fed synthetic food by automatic dispensers and they sat or stood around in a gentle tranquility suitable for beasts which had been granted immortality too.

Eboni told Danny this place was the specialization of her colony, it was called a zoo. There, on the spot, he fell in love both with these creatures and with her. His mood brightened considerably and when finally they arrived at Eboni's home in the early afternoon she gave him her bed. He collapsed at once into deep and grateful sleep.

After he'd surfaced late the next morning Eboni showed him round, explaining that members of the colony kept the zoo supplied and clean. Another thing they did was to rear dogs. She took him to large kennels down a track from the colony and there he met several dozen of the major breeds of man's best friend. She explained that dogs were the one animal the Immortals agreed to let procreate. This was because original pets brought by pioneers had sometimes run off and were either eaten by coyotes or had joined forces with them. In other cases owners had split up and neither party wanted to keep the animal, in which case unwanted dogs had to be put down.

The attrition in dog numbers meant there was a carefully controlled replacement program. This wasn't the case for cats because from the beginning some strays had headed downtown and the neutering program obviously had not been comprehensive, for they proceeded to infest the temples and palaces there. They and their offspring served to keep the rodents in check so, apart from occasional culls, people were prepared to put up with them. Cats were the one truly independent species in Heaven. When people wanted a feline companion they simply hunted out a recent litter and took the healthiest and prettiest kitten home.

Danny saw his first brood of puppies—a small family of Dalmatians about three weeks old—and he was totally smitten. This was all he wanted, to care for little creatures like these, and of course the marvelous beasts at the zoo. He moved in with Eboni who was also a fanatic for animals, and they were a happy couple from day one. It was shortly after that the news of Cal's unconventional arrival in the Heavenly Homeland reached him. He really wanted to see her but he also felt uncertain and embarrassed. He had found it very hard to come to grips with the whole experience of Doblepoble—the way he'd split up with Charlize that night without hardly knowing it. Then the vague, unsettling stories surrounding the Initiation of Cal and Poll, now Pascale and Palmiro, had further confused him. Cal had at once become the lover of the Immortal called Jonas, and a little later he heard she was with him all the time and was not meeting anyone else. He badly wanted to see her and speak to her. She had always been able to make sense of things for him, just because of who she was. But he was less sure now, so he hung back.

Eboni, hearing him talk wistfully about seeing Pascale, said she knew a great place to bump into people in a neutral setting, the Venice piazza. Sooner or later everyone seemed to show up there. They should get up early, put in a couple of hours at the kennels or the zoo, then trek downtown. Danny readily agreed and they fell into the routine. They would arrive about midday and head to the café next to the cathedral, order Amari and crackers and doze in the sunshine. It was always a pleasant and interesting place to be. Danny grew confident that one day soon Pascale would find her way there.

He lay on his back gazing through the awning at the brilliant sun, idly thinking. He knew with his mind that this was the same sun which shone on the icefields of the north but, lying under it now, he felt it was not the same at all. It wasn't just the warmth. Everything really had changed and he didn't properly understand how. For sure there was the whole Initiation thing, and immortality, and the wonderful sights all around him. But there was even more to it than that, something deeper, something he thought only Pascale could show him. His little sister, Sam, always said he would be chosen as an Immortal. Of course she'd no idea how real all that was, but it had always given him a vague sense of always being someone special. Then there was that guy Palmiro. He truly was special; he seemed to have stuff already figured out back in the TEPs and now it seemed he had found his way to Heaven too. It felt like there really was something going on.

His thoughts drifted here and there, uncertain where to turn. Suddenly there was a movement, a shape that broke the hazy surface of his vision. Was that her? The figure coming across the sun-strewn piazza? She was wearing a simple cotton robe belted at the middle and she was arm-in-arm with a man he vaguely remembered. Yes, for sure, it was her, but her face was quite different from how he'd remembered and for an instant he felt he wanted to hide. She looked so different and he could not put a name to it.

Eboni had followed his glance as he propped himself on an elbow. "Is that her?"

"Yes, and that guy, I kind of remember him, Jonas...."

"Of course it's Jonas. Give them a wave, don't just sit there."

Following her own advice Eboni leaped up, waving. Without waiting she started across the piazza, beckoning Danny to follow. He got up and began to jog after her, for the first time in his life feeling nervous about meeting his sister. Pascale pulled to a halt and then she freed herself from Jonas and started running too. She headed straight for Danny, throwing her arms out and flinging them around his neck.

"Danny, how wonderful to see you. I didn't know how much I was missing you until this morning and then I couldn't wait to come find you!" She hugged him and kissed him multiple times.

Eboni and Jonas stood there grinning, looking back and forth from each other to the brother and sister. Danny was overwhelmed, and when Pascale finally let him go all he could manage was, "It's great to see you too, Sis!"

Eboni said, "This has got to be the most anticipated Homelands reunion ever. Danny and I have been hanging here for days and days, waiting to see you, Pascale. Oh, and by the way, the name's Eboni."

"It's been far too long, and I really am sorry. But it's good finally to get to see you, Danny, and you too, Eboni!" Pascale smiled brightly at both of them.

Eboni again prompted the conversation. "So what sights has Jonas shown you? What's your favorite bit of Heaven so far?"

"Well, we took a ride to the top of a huge tower. That was amazing. What was the tower, Jonas?"

"The Khalifa."

"Yes, that was it. We went to the viewing deck and it seemed like we were looking down on the whole world. I felt...I don't know what I felt. Definitely scared!" Then, after casting around for a moment, "But you know this place right here is very beautiful, I can see why you and Danny decided to hang out here."

Jonas seized the opportunity. The experience of downtown had not gone quite as he had hoped. It had been too rushed and Pascale's mood seemed flat compared to what he'd envisioned. So he followed up at once on her reaction. There were gondolas drawn up along the lido on the other side of the piazza and he suggested they take one out to the island in the middle of the lake. "There's a replica of an old building out there with a mosaic masterpiece inside. It's really worth seeing. And it's such a relaxing trip; the color of the water is unbelievable."

The others agreed easily. They crossed the piazza to the lido wall and picked out one of the violin-neck boats moored along the edge. Jonas took the oar, stroking the craft out toward the open lake. Eboni sat in front trailing her hand in the frothy blue water while Pascale and Danny took the main seats across the middle. Danny had begun to relax and feel something of his old self around his sister. He asked how Palmiro had persuaded her into the whole crazy escapade, to steal the rocket and come uninvited to the Heavenly Homeland, even though, of course, she herself was really invited. How had he pulled it off? How had Palmiro done something no one else had even thought of?

"Palmiro was definitely the first to figure out this sunshine world. He kept talking to me and finally got me to see it too. But you know, getting here, on the shuttle, was just as much my doing as his." Pascale went on to tell the story of her rescue of Palmiro, and then setting out to find the rocket with the sure intention of using it. "Palmiro wasn't thinking of that at first. He just agreed to come along!"

Pascale was speaking to Danny in such a natural way they could have been back at the Training Center, but what she was actually telling him was astonishing. He began to understand at least a part of why she looked so different and the way he had almost felt shy of her.

"So you're saying you really came here on your own, without the guides inviting you, and it was you who invited Palmiro. It's really you who upset everything?"

"Yes, I suppose so."

"No one here thinks anything like that; they think it was all Palmiro."

"Well I told Jonas everything, but we have been kind of cut off, so, you're probably right, no one else would know."

"You're not kidding you've been cut off! You were lost to the world. What is that about, you and Jonas? What about Palmiro?"

Pascale stopped and shook her head. "I can't really explain it, Danny. Something happened and...and I needed someone...Jonas was there for me. Perhaps like you and Eboni. But before that...." She stopped and looked away, out across the shimmering lake, and Danny knew he'd come to whatever it was that had really changed his sister.

Jonas had been watching his lover attentively. He had never really gotten to the bottom of Pascale's behavior during Initiation. He sensed it was off-limits and keeping it off-limits was almost a condition of his incredible relationship with her. He guessed if this thing ever was going to come to the surface it would be now, talking to her brother. He dreaded the possibility. It could put her back in the fearful state of mind she'd shown in the pool and out in the desert. The moment he saw her look away in that abstract manner, out to the open water, he knew she'd hit that memory. He spoke up at once.

"Look, we're almost at the island! We'll pull in at the jetty and take a walk to the monument."

Pascale looked back toward the outcropping of rocks and its stone building partly hidden by trees. It was only a few boat lengths away and she'd hardly noticed it talking with Danny. Her attention was now taken, and Jonas felt perhaps the crisis was averted. He pushed the boat in beside the low pier, bringing it quite skillfully alongside the wooden decking. As they clambered ashore, holding up their robes to avoid tripping, he continued talking.

"This place is pretty interesting. It's actually an abbey from something like fifteen hundred years ago. Most of the stuff in Heaven is only a replica, because by the time our architects started construction the storms had already done their damage. Most of the world's great buildings were just too badly damaged to save. It was much easier to create reproductions and assemble them here. But Venice, you know, already had experience dealing with rising sea levels. So they were able to move very quickly to preserve their treasures, and many features of the cathedral back on the piazza, and some of this abbey here, are original. You'll see, it has a very special atmosphere."

They continued down a sandy path, bordered by walnut trees, vegetable gardens and outbuildings. The abbey church soon came into view, a simple rough stone and brick structure with a terracotta tiled roof. They went inside and stood on flagstones that looked as if they had been worn by the passage of a million feet. Light came from a course of clear windows just below the roof. On a high wall just to left of the entrance was a strange fresco with human figures spread about in a vertical scene. Jonas saw them looking at it and smiled.

"Yes, this is very curious. It comes from a primitive religion of those times which had a very naive view of their god. It's called 'Judgment' and it shows the deity coming to earth to judge all that

223

happened in human history. Very odd "

The group stood in front of the wall of faded images trying to figure out what was going on, but it was very hard to make sense of or relate to it. Jonas continued. "The whole wall is encased in a very thin but extremely tough sheet of transparent plastic. That's how it was preserved and brought here. But really don't waste time on this. The absolute jewel is at the far end, in the apse."

He turned away and they all followed him beneath the shadows of the pillars, down to the far end. Gazing up at the circular apse they were confronted by the enormous figure of a woman six or seven meters in height, made out of tens of thousands of pieces of glittering mosaic. She was wearing a cobalt blue robe that framed her hair and swept down to the ground. It was her face that held your attention, passionate, imperious, gentle, all at the same time. Her figure filled the building with an urgent energy which did not impose itself but just hung there in the air, waiting to be embraced. It was doubly unnerving that she was only an image, composed of so many individual pieces of stone without shape or personality.

"Wow," said Danny. "Who's this?"

"The subject is probably a Byzantine Princess, but in this setting, in the abbey, the image would be evoking a holy woman from that time, a kind of goddess."

"How could an artist capture so much power just by little stones laid next to each other?" Eboni also was impressed.

"The mystery of art! Mere line and color transcend themselves to become the ideal."

There before the mosaic Jonas' words sounded slightly pompous and at once he tried to distract from them with a joke. "Though, whoever the model was, she would fit right in here, in Heaven, don't you think?

Pascale was standing in front of the mosaic stirred to her soul. Her own eyes were held by the eyes of the icon and she felt that they were looking at her just as much as she was looking at them. She continued both transfixed and energized by the majestic portrait and something inside her shifted. She felt purified, stronger. It was as if a spring that for the longest time had been pulling against its catch suddenly broke free and opened a valve within. The others had chuckled politely at Jonas' joke but she turned to him. "No Jonas, what you just said, that's wrong. It's not a mystery. The artist experienced a power, a life, and he showed it real because it was real."

Eboni and Danny were taken aback and Jonas actually blushed. "Yes, yes, I dare say you're right. One person's mystery is another's reality, yes for sure."

They stayed there for a few more moments and then drifted away, starting to walk back out of the abbey. Shafts of liquid sunlight were falling through the high windows, casting up a sea of motes. Pascale came behind the others. She called out, "Look at the dust how it rises and falls in the sunshine."

Eboni returned a few paces. She replied, "Yes, it's really pretty."

They stood there watching until the others retraced their steps also

Pascale said, "Some of the dust may be very old, from these paving stones. It could be tiny bits from the people who walked on these stones more than a thousand years ago?"

Danny asked, "What are you saying?"

"Isn't dust mostly dead pieces from people's skin? It could have got lodged in the crevices of these flagstones and then kicked up when people walked here."

Jonas looked horrified. Where was Pascale getting this from? He tried to change the tone. "Hey, at least we don't have to worry about being trodden on a thousand years from now! Thankfully we're immortal!"

Pascale bounced his quip right back. "Yes but isn't it sad too, no one will ever see us like this, dancing like stars in the sunlight?"

A void opened up in Jonas. Pascale was focusing on obscure, dead things. He couldn't get off the island quick enough. Almost definitely he had been wrong to keep Pascale to himself, no matter her mood. She should have met all the other Immortals, and certainly the best minds of Heaven, the philosophers. They would have impressed her with the true, healthy thinking of immortality. Still perhaps it wasn't too late. Emmanelle had mentioned that the Philosophers' Colony urgently wanted to host a dinner. He hoped it would happen as soon as possible.

"You know what?" he announced. "I just thought of it, there's possibly someone from the Philosophers' Colony waiting for us back on the mainland. Emmanuelle remarked there might be. We have to get back."

They returned without discussion to the pier and climbed back into the gondola, pushing off across the water. This time Eboni took the oar and stroked the craft smoothly away from the landing. The sun had created a haze over the lake and for a moment or two the domes and pinnacles of the cathedral seemed to float in the filmy air. The creaking of the oar together with the color and warmth of the lagoon produced the most pleasant sleepy feeling. Pascale took Jonas' hand and squeezed it gently. She smiled at him and he suddenly felt much better. Probably he was worrying too much; things were bound to work out one way or another. He looked out on the water and said, "You know, one of the names of the Republic of Venice was *La Serenissima*, the most peaceful. And it's true, a city built over a calm sea really is heavenly!" This time his remark seemed apt and was happily received.

When they tied up at the lido Jonas' wild guess of someone waiting turned out to be true. Danny was the first to see them. He stepped up onto the embankment and his keen eyes caught the figure of Charlize at a considerable distance across the esplanade. She was with another woman and they were both casting around as if they were looking to see someone among the couples and groups wandering back and forth. He pointed them out to Jonas who squinted into the shimmering space. He recognized the second person with Charlize.

"That's Colette. She's come hotfoot with a message from the philosophers."

They began waving until the two women saw them. Colette and Charlize started walking toward them hand in hand and Jonas' party set out to meet them. When they all came together in the middle of the sun-dazzled flagstones everyone exchanged hugs.

Danny was slightly embarrassed to be around Charlize whom he hadn't seen since the Doblepoble, but she was totally relaxed. She introduced Colette, then turned to Pascale. "It's great to see you, Pascale. You look wonderful."

"So do you, and I'm glad to say hello properly, after that brief meeting at the Initiation."

"Oh right. What a night! I wasn't really at my best. But I'm happy it all turned out well."

Pascale nodded agreement, "Yes, it does seem to have all turned out for the best."

Charlize underlined, "For me too, I'm actually with Colette now."

Pascale looked at her blankly, and then she understood. "Oh, I see, I see. Heaven is so full of surprises!"

Colette laughed indulgently, hugged Pascale and smiled around at everyone. "It's quite the occasion, isn't it? We heard a rumor our dear Pascale was out of purdah. Sure enough, here you are, a goddess learning the ways of Heaven!"

She had captured everyone's attention and she continued to hold it. "Of course, we're missing your fascinating friend, Palmiro. We've been deprived of his company too. But all that's about to change. In two days' time our Philosophers' Colony is holding a grand banquet. Everyone will be there and it's a must for all you recent inductees." She included Danny and Charlize in her smile.

Danny said, "Yes, I remember, they said a very special guy was coming the next time, and we should go."

"Perfectly right, but you know what? You're certainly lucky because we're getting not just one special guest, but two. Sarobindo, the saint of Font Eterno, he'll be there, but the news is Adorno, our genius scientist, he'll be attending also. Someone visited his mansion to inform Palmiro, and Adorno volunteered to come too."

Jonas was impressed. "That's amazing. I can't remember the last time Adorno came to any kind of banquet. With both Sarobindo and Adorno there, the conversation should be brilliant."

"You see what I mean!" Colette nodded to Jonas, but as she continued she also arched her eyes in Pascale's direction. "And wouldn't you say it's an absolute must for your Aphrodite here. So far her scallop-shell has been riding exclusively on your private ocean, Jonas!" She gazed at Jonas and Pascale with more than a tinge of mockery.

Jonas felt the sexual barb but he took her comment in the most innocent sense. "Oh yes, it's high time for Pascale to get a wider knowledge of Heaven." Then he decided to add his partner's brush with death in extenuation. "But what with the trauma of her initiation she really did need time to recover and adjust."

It worked. Danny had picked up both the jibe and the hint of her ordeal and he came flying to their defense.

"Don't take any notice, Jonas. I'm glad you and Pascale were holed up. People may not know it but my sister has some very special talents: what goes by fast for the rest of us is slow for her. It can take her in strange directions. It's not surprising she needs extra time."

Jonas followed on Danny's statement.

"That reminds me, Danny, we haven't completed our sightseeing yet. We need to visit the lookout point so Pascale can see the sun go down over the Font Eterno. Especially now that she is going to meet Sarobindo!"

He grabbed Pascale's hand and they made their goodbyes in short order. Really they had only just enough time to get to the parking plaza and drive the car to the ridge before sundown. Jonas grinned and Pascale smiled and went along with him, and they both ducked away and were gone. Colette gazed after them. The shadow of the domes inched its way along the stone pavement catching the hem of their robes and ankles as they ran across the great square. "My, what a pair they are. And Danny, you have me intrigued. I'd love to hear more about what you call these special skills of Pascale's."

6. POISONED BANQUET

Palmiro accompanied Adorno in his car to the Philosophers' Colony. His state of mind was self-assured, even triumphant. What had happened to him over these past weeks was astonishing, and yet it was always meant to be. He had broken free from the world of ice and had come to another one beyond his imagining. This other world was not composed of fairy tales, of old stories, of religion, but was something created consciously, piece by piece, by human beings. He had not forgotten at what cost its beauty had come, both his own suffering and that of many others. The reckoning was never absent from his mind. But the fact was he had landed in this world and had discovered very quickly that he could learn from it: he could discover its secrets. Not only that, he had found the best teacher possible, Adorno, the genius of immortality.

The dramatically ugly, brilliant man had adopted him as a protégé. After only a few days spent with Emmanelle Adorno had appeared, abruptly summoning Palmiro to come live in his mansion. By that point Palmiro's honeymoon with Emmanuelle was already a shabby affair and had been interrupted more than once. Hona had followed them directly from the Agora and interviewed Palmiro irritably on how he had managed to fly the rocket. To her further chagrin he told her he and Pascale had done it purely by guesswork. A couple of days later Marius and Blair had come from the Anthropology Colony. They questioned him as to whether he belonged to any kind of wider group back in the Northern Homeland and whether anyone else had found out about the shuttle. Palmiro assured them that it was just him and Pascale. All they had to do was ask Charlize and Danny about how many personal friends he had. It was only Pascale with whom he'd had any contact. They seemed reasonably satisfied with his solitary obsessiveness and knowing they would soon get a full security report from Brutus and Fyodor, the stranded guides, they left. A couple of days after that Adorno appeared, and Palmiro's brief fling with the blonde goddess was over.

Palmiro was definitely not indifferent to Emmanelle's seductions; they had helped him feel welcome in quite an unmistakable way. But after the first few times his enthusiasm had waned. It seemed somehow absurd to keep having sex with this woman for no other reason than to pass the time. He remembered his vague feelings for Pascale and the embrace they had shared out on the icefield. It continued to bother him to think of how completely she had fallen for Jonas. The fact she had so quickly become intimate with a virtual stranger somehow had a reverse effect on him. It made him still less inclined to surrender to casual intimacy. So it was when Adorno arrived and explained that he was interested in Palmiro's education, and was prepared to take him as a private student, he had more or less rushed out the door. And Emmanuelle was perfectly happy to let him go.

Adorno was not a man for small talk, but what he said counted a lot. On that first drive to where he lived the master told his disciple they would engage in an extensive course of study, which he would lay out for him the next day. That was all he said, but spoken in his rich baritone it was as if Palmiro was reading from a long and classic book. The scientist did not belong to a colony, rather he had a mansion almost entirely to himself. A couple of quiet and dedicated assistants occupied the upper floors of one of the wings. Apart from that he was alone. Behind the main building was a huge rambling laboratory where he worked and whose purposes only he seemed to know. He showed Palmiro a comfortable annex to the side of the mansion and told him this would be his private accommodation. He should consider it his. He said there was a library just inside the grand portico entrance and Palmiro should meet him there first thing in the morning. With that introduction he was done.

The following day Palmiro began his private apprenticeship with the inventor of immortality. He was informed of the range of subjects they would cover, things like cell biology, evolution, inheritance, RNA, DNA, enzymes, information theory, fractals, signaling, neurons, thermodynamics, relativity, quantum mechanics, small particles, string theory, the four forces, dark matter, on and on so that he could not keep pace, only glance briefly at the papers and textbooks Adorno tossed at him.

"What I'm giving you here is fairly basic. When I was working before, before the construction of the Homeland, there was a tremendous amount of high-level research. But we knew we were all on borrowed time. The storms were horrendous, you can't imagine the chaos; laboratories, experiments which had taken years to set up, computers filled with data, everything destroyed. A lot of results were shared of course, but everybody knew scientists were also working secretly for their companies, striving for a breakthrough, just like I was. Then the Global Weather Shield was announced and what was left of the world economy simply collapsed. The lights went out everywhere and the only people with resources were the biggest companies, those with developed links to the intelligence services and international government. That's of course where I had ended up but it was a terrible pity, so much good work was lost. Either it was secret and not shared or simply wiped out, irretrievable. When we came here I was one of a few who wanted to continue working, pursuing the research we had recorded, yet over time the others too lost interest. They couldn't see the point. So, now you can understand, I've been waiting for someone like you. I needed someone I could train myself, who wanted to acquire knowledge and who would eventually be able to help me with my own long-term inquiries."

Palmiro was staggered. The idea that he, and he alone, was to follow in the footsteps of the most important scientist of human history and even help him in his work, this exceeded his most extreme expectations. It seemed to prove conclusively his own unique status, his role somehow as a chosen one. He accepted his situation and its tasks with all his soul; and so it was his life in Heaven unfolded. He would get up with the light and as he made coffee his head would already be in a book. After eating yogurt and fruit he would make his way to the library where Adorno kept the important papers and reference works he had preserved. He would continue reading there until Adorno arrived.

His teacher reviewed the material with him, pursuing a topic with intense interest, illustrating it with examples which would always lead on to other connected themes. Palmiro found it extremely hard to keep up but he scribbled notes furiously and when Adorno finally left he would begin to look up all the terms and references he had not understood. After a break for lunch he would go to a well-equipped laboratory that Adorno's assistants had set up for him on the ground floor, opposite Adorno's own study on the other side of the garden. There he would work on experiments demonstrating the concepts he had been learning.

Adorno would show him what to do and then leave him there among the microscopes, retorts, pipets, fume hoods, slides and specimens, the generators, X Rays, lasers and computers.

Throwing himself into the work he never noticed the time passing. As the sun went down Adorno would come to look at his results, make some remarks, then send him back to his apartment and close up. Later, on most nights, he would have Max, one of the assistants, bring a cooked meal and even a bottle of wine. Palmiro would shower, eat and read until he was too tired to hold the book any more. Crawling into bed he would think this was the best day of his life, and it wasn't because he was in Heaven. For the first time there was a meaning and purpose to his life. He was doing something real in order to do something important.

It was out of this amazing experience that he came with his mentor to the main gate of the Philosophers' Colony, garlanded with vines and lit by torches. As they drove in they could see a large marquee had been erected on the central compound between the dwellings. It was brilliantly illuminated with lamps hanging from its roof and suspended beyond the tissue cotton drapes flowing at either end. The whole expanse of the compound was framed by a circle of free-standing ornamental pillars wound with acanthus and poppy flowers. Inside the tent huge tables had been set out, richly spread with plates, silverware and glasses. It was already occupied by a dazzling throng of guests seated and standing about. As the two got out of the car Zeno and Xanthippe came across at once. They were wearing gold brocade pricked out with silver stars and they flung their arms high in the air.

"O thou gods and heavenly beings, such honor and blessing you bestow on us. You cast your light on our banquet, so feebly lit without you!"

"Palmiro, a true Prometheus who stole heaven's fire! Adorno, the father of all the gods, our Zeus if there ever was one!"

The two guests accepted the encomiums of their hosts and were led by the hand across to the grand marquee. As they went Adorno spoke, to no one in particular.

"I'm sure you know the father of the gods is Cronos, the ruler of the underworld, not Zeus."

Zeno replied, "Of course, Adorno, but we gods are allowed to re-write mythology a little, if simply for beauty's sake. Cronos has such an unpleasant ring to him, don't you think? It is but pure pleasure to see you."

As they arrived at the side of the marquee Zeno stepped inside and, again holding his hands aloft, waved them around, declaiming, "O divine philosophers, hear me, I have here with me our very, very special guests!"

Standing to the side he gestured the two men to step forward. "This is Palmiro, already a legend among us. He found a way from the cribbed, cabined existence of his Northern Homeland, stealing a ride on a rocket ship intended for someone else. We are absolutely longing to hear his story, to reflect with him on the pathway of thought that led him to us." He paused for dramatic effect, then announced, "And we have with him the man who has given him his blessing, who has now become his teacher, someone whose company we have not enjoyed for far too long, our very own diviner of immortality, Adorno!"

There was a sustained burst of applause, with people cheering and shouting and even banging spoons against dishes and on the table. It was as if the combination of Palmiro and Adorno together had thrown a switch, making everyone giddy. Later people would say they had been carried back to the very beginnings when they'd become gods for the first time. A time they hardly remembered, drowned in years of dream-like pleasure, it had now all come rushing back to them. Even the exuberant Zeno was astonished. He grinned inanely, looking around. Xanthippe came to his rescue, falling in beside him and tweaking his sleeve. Pascale and Jonas had arrived directly behind Palmiro and Adorno, their figures masked by the scientist and his student. Zeno looked round and saw them. He quickly regained his aplomb. Raising his hands once more he called for order.

"Yes, yes, what a splendid welcome, fitting indeed, but we must also save some of our devotion for the other neophyte and her companion. Let me introduce Pascale, who also flew the shuttle here, and Jonas the Historian, who has become her lover." He waved the pair forward between Palmiro and Adorno. The applause rattled again but this time with less fervor. Zeno invited the whole party of newcomers to come forward and take their seats. The tables had been laid out in parallel arms, one end of which was open and the other closed by a head table.

233

"Pascale and Jonas, you will be here, between Andre and Alex. And Danny and Eboni, with our beloved Bacchus and Hypatia, farther toward the top."

Turning to Adorno and Palmiro he led them to the head table. "Adorno, you will sit beside me and Xanthippe. Palmiro, you will be there to the right next to your teacher. On the other side will be guests from our sister colony, the anthropologists, and in the middle of course will be the master of our feast, Heaven's most dear and treasured Sarobindo."

At Zeno's mention of the honored guest Adorno visibly stiffened. "No one told me Sarobindo was coming."

Although it was common knowledge that Adorno nourished an acute dislike for the ascetic, no one had thought it necessary to ply him with details. Adorno had volunteered his presence simply hearing an invitation to the philosophers' banquet, and given the unique attraction of entertaining Heaven's heroes at the same table it had been left at that.

"Oh, yes, we have been expecting Sarobindo for months."

"Well, put me and my student as far away as possible. We will not sit up here next to that charlatan."

Zeno had not imagined Adorno would make a scene, despite his well-known aversion. He thought the evening was becoming more entertaining than he wanted. Still he replied without missing a beat.

"Certainly, as you wish. I am sure Pascale and Jonas won't mind sitting close to the seer, and you can change places with them down there."

By this point a lot of people had found their seats so the rearrangements were very obvious, involving scrapings of chairs, bumpings and excuse-me's. It did not dampen people's enthusiasm. On the contrary the getting up and moving, the curious glances and excited remarks only served to whet their appetites. Palmiro was now sitting between Danny and Adorno. Facing them, almost directly opposite at the parallel table, were Charlize and Colette, flanked by Friedrich, Hannah, Abelard and Heloise. Down at the ends were various nominated people invited for the occasion, including Shimin and Gaius from the Sports-Monitoring Colony, and Cyrus and Vanzetti from the Historians. Meanwhile, the other privileged guests, flanking the place where

Sarobindo was due to sit, were also seated. They were Marius and Blair, with their respective partners.

Marius was accompanied by a striking, statuesque woman with a shock of tawny hair. She seemed slightly older than the norm, although as always this impression did not arise from the condition of the skin or general body-tone. It was more the immense firmness of her glance and set of her jaw. Beyond these two there was Blair accompanied by a dusky, dark haired woman who held her head like a bird of prey, fine, aloof, unfathomable. All four were dressed in glittering golden gauze, which complimented Zeno and Xanthippe's robes. Jonas and Pascale stood out in contrast, wearing their normal loose white tunics. Pascale had not had time or concern to develop any kind of wardrobe. Jonas dressed in solidarity with her.

Pascale looked down the line of people seated at right angles to her. Palmiro had given his seat to her and she was struck by his calm, confident manner. It seemed as if being with Adorno had enabled him to find his footing; he was adjusting on his own terms to the Heavenly Homeland. She was glad and hoped there would be a chance to talk and catch up.

She looked at the other faces in the line and across at the table opposite. Everyone was animated, thrilled to be present at the feast. Jonas had not gone into detail, saying that it was important simply to experience the philosophers' banquet and the special privilege of having Sarobindo present. Now she couldn't help but share the sense of excitement. In the two days since her tour downtown she had undergone a progressive feeling of change. She thought she was more like her old self, the one who had stolen a tractor and taken an epic ride to rescue her friend, the one who had confidently told Palmiro to learn whatever the sunshine world had to offer.

At the same time it was not her old self at all. The experience of the Initiation remained within her, something terrible and immense. Yet since her visit to the abbey she had been able to face it more clearly. Perhaps she was seeing it with the strong eyes of the woman, those amazing eyes which had awoken her own eyes. Whatever the reason she was able to accept the experience had a meaning, even though she was not sure what it was. In any case she certainly felt a new freedom and it was wonderful. With Jonas at her side she was entirely happy to relax, to allow herself simply to be carried along by the current of electricity in the air. She decided that perhaps this evening would genuinely be important for her, just as Jonas promised, enabling her to find her way in Heaven.

Jonas observed all this from the outside and was very pleased. He was relieved that Pascale seemed so much more willing to face the public world of Heaven. And he was very much looking forward to the philosophers' evening, as something to round out her education. He looked up at the roof of the marquee and contemplated it with a vague satisfaction. It was a beautiful canopy decorated with the zodiac, the shapes picked out with silver against a glowing purple backing. He drew Pascale's attention, pointing up to it.

"Back in the old world they measured time by the sun and the moon. The period of the moon was called a month and there was a set of stars for each of the months. Each set was a shape found in the skies, a recognizable figure, a crab or a scorpion, or a bull, that kind of thing. Depending on your month of birth the figure attached to it became your sign. It was meant to have a huge influence on your character and destiny."

Pascale looked up at the canopy and at once was captivated. The various signs seemed so beautiful. It was magical the way the stars formed the shape of the sign and together created their own special meaning.

"Do you know what your sign is, Jonas?"

"I don't remember anymore. I suppose if I went to the trouble I could work it out, but all Immortals see themselves as truly immortal and basically forget all about time or destiny, that kind of thing. Nobody wants to think about their sign."

"So why have the philosophers put the canopy up here?

"Because they are philosophers. It's their chosen occupation to think about things, including the way people in the past thought about everything. They look at the zodiac as one of the ways human beings created meaning. They think of it abstractly."

Pascale continued to stare up at the tapestry of stars. Neither had the people of the Northern Homeland thought about their signs. Time was kept in divisions of one hundred days and although the sun changed its position dramatically no one reckoned by it. As for the stars people really never observed them. She was most unusual in having braved the terrible cold to gaze at them. Looking up now all her old fascination returned with added force.

She felt light-headed with their closeness, their warmth and meaning. From Jonas' balcony she had only vaguely noticed them, feeling they were part of a beautiful but alien world which had overpowered her. Here in the tent, under the canopy, she was connecting to a system of stargazing stored deep in the bones of humanity, and she felt a total kinship. She wanted to cry. She was seeing shapes which people had seen for thousands of years and, although she did not know what they meant, they filled her with love. It was like looking at the mosaic on the island, and she understood for the first time that shapes mattered just as much as numbers. The thought came that perhaps there was a shape to everything, a real true shape and she could be part of it. She wanted to stand up and shout but instead she threw her arms round Jonas and kissed him.

"Jonas, it's so beautiful, I love you very much!"

Her partner was acutely embarrassed. By that point Zeno had assumed his official place at the head table and already launched into a gushing introduction of the guest of honor, Sarobindo. Pascale had managed to tune the philosopher out completely and was now displaying public affection while interrupting a hymn of praise for Heaven's most revered member. There was a chorus of scowls and irritated shushes, and a really angry, mid-sentence glare from Zeno. Jonas pushed Pascale away, colored deeply and offered mouthed apologies. The only person who was not offended was Adorno who gave a loud "Ha!" looking fabulously amused. Zeno stared at him outraged but once more collected himself and resumed his stride.

"As I was saying! Sarobindo is a legend in our Heaven. He brings a depth to our collective experience which is irreplaceable. Through Sarobindo we experience a truly mystical dimension. Because of him not only do we live a life of perfect pleasure but we do so in harmony with the whole universe in all its abiding mystery."

There was a very audible snort of contempt from Adorno but Zeno kept going, regardless.

237

"For the sake of our gathering of neophytes my colleague Abelard will explain the divine teaching that Sarobindo has brought us, but first we need to welcome this man in person to our midst."

Zeno raised his arms once more, and gazing mystically into the outer darkness, he cupped his hands before his mouth and let out a long "Oooaaahhh" as if he were invoking an invisible spirit or deity. A thrill ran through the assembly and instinctively everyone followed the direction of his eyes. From a corner of the compound emerged four dancers clad in red-and-gold full bodysuits and bearing before them decorated urns giving off long shooting flames. As they sprang forward into the open they formed two wings of an honor guard and into the space between there slowly stepped a very tall, olive-skinned, muscular man clothed only in a loin cloth. He walked in a serene, majestic way, planting his feet as if the earth itself should bend before each step. There was an intake of breath from the company, a kind of gasp and sigh together. Only Adorno failed to share the general reverence, his eyes withdrawn and soulless as they followed the approaching figure.

Sarobindo came straight to the head table without looking around or down. He took his seat at the center as spontaneous applause burst from all sides peppered with cheers and shouts of his name. His head was shaven clean and his features, rugged and deeply incised, suggested a discipline of spirit impossible to most other human beings. As he sat down he radiated a benign, indifferent smile while continuing to gaze directly forward from dark eyes. Abelard was now on his feet, clearing his throat and attempting to speak above the general din.

"Welcome, O welcome. We welcome you, Sarobindo, to the Philosophers' Colony: too long have we missed you at our tables. Tonight, in this moment, you assuage the heartache we have suffered in your absence."

His flowery words were only half-heard, but they did have the effect of quieting people down and eventually everyone turned to hear Abelard's address.

"It is a most pleasant duty to remind everyone, and for the first time to inform our new initiates, of yogi Sarobindo's unique contribution to this our heavenly estate. I will not detain you much, I am sure your appetite for our Zeno's food and wines can only be put off so long! But it is fundamental to us as thinking creatures to recall the nature of our being and without Sarobindo and his teaching our universe would lose a priceless reservoir of truth. We here are Immortals and have overcome the doom of death, yet we also know that philosophy from its primal days begins with the transcendent fact of death. Plato said, in so many words, philosophy was the practice of death. He meant that by dismissing the narrow claims of the body—by being, in so many words, set free from the body—you could nourish the mind or soul on things immortal or eternal. However, we are in the strange situation of being immortal ourselves, yet still wishing to practice philosophy! How can we do that honorably, as part of the great tradition, when none of us dies? In a sense we have overcome the narrow world of the mortal body only to find the body pressing closer than ever. It could even deprive us of the mysterious impetus to thought which only death provides..."

All the philosophers and most of their guests were now listening respectfully, nodding and smiling at the familiar themes and thoughts. They were waiting happily for the big punchline they knew was coming. Danny and Charlize had heard this kind of talk before and were prepared for it to drift over their heads: except the extraordinary figure of Sarobindo now held center stage and they were keen to find out what was so special about him. Palmiro was thinking in the opposite direction. He felt his teacher's powerful contempt for the guest of honor and he wanted to understand the reason. He was listening to Abelard but his mind was waiting for Adorno's rebuttal which he was sure would come.

Pascale, in contrast, was following as closely as she could what Abelard was saying. The moment he mentioned death her attention was caught. She was carried back forcefully to her Initiation and her experience of death during the ritual. She had not spoken about the terror of that night, even with Jonas. Now somehow it seemed to be the central topic at a gathering of philosophers, people who thought about everything. It struck her that, really, this evening was turning out to be more crucial than she could have imagined. She sat up and focused intently on what was happening.

Abelard was describing Sarobindo's part in the actual

construction of Heaven. Sarobindo's group had originally been chosen as representatives of a great cultural tradition in which certain noteworthy techniques had been developed. One of these techniques was the practice of trance brought about by non-breathing, a kind of mini-death which could cause in the practitioner an elevated state of consciousness. The ritual of Initiation was in fact a version of this, only it was produced by a chemical rather than prolonged training.

Naturally, if the experience could be chemically induced people were not interested in the hard work of the old techniques. More critically the technique did not really fit with paradise: what was the point of rehearsing death when death was never going to happen? When Sarobindo understood this, however, he did not abandon his craft, rather he produced a stroke of genius. He devised a strictly limited situation where death could return to Immortals. If in such a situation there really was the possibility of death for himself and his followers then his powerful techniques would regain their noble purpose. At once the idea gained enormous support, to the point that the whole city, whose construction was already underway, suddenly found its true horizon and spiritual core. The bowl-shaped arena where Sarobindo and his disciples would be willing to gamble with death would become the crowning glory of the city's architecture. It would be called the Font Eterno.

"So it was that death was preserved in Heaven. The great semi-globe you see from downtown is a cross between the Coliseum, a temple and a small-particle accelerator. There is seating for thousands upon thousands in the three hundred tiers of circular galleries. Down in the center is a great crystal lake filled with a foaming sea. Words cannot do justice to the awe the place inspires. You can only appreciate it by being present yourself at one of the sacrificial immersions. Only then will any of you newcomers to Heaven be able to grasp what I am saying. Mahatma Sarobindo stops his own breathing and is thrown physically into the foaming waters. He would drown if he took a breath but he does not. He stays under the surface for twenty minutes until he emerges by his own power just a few seconds before the sea dissolves into a thousand billion random particles. Nothing retains its form in that chaos and a human body would instantly disintegrate, never to be gathered again. We know this from terrible experience, for none of the first practitioners have survived the sea, none except Sarobindo. It is a place where even gods go to die. But Sarobindo, he remains to this day, continuing to sail the vessel of his body to the edge of the abyss, for all our sakes."

There was a quiet "Hmmmm" from the assembly, like a sound after biting chocolate. The ascetic at the head of the table for the first time looked around, bestowing his detached beatific smile directly on the assembly. Two things then happened together. Adorno leaned back in his chair and clapped his hands slowly, sardonically. People turned horrified to stare at him, but almost simultaneously Pascale made eye contact with Sarobindo, shot her hand in the air and asked him a question. "Sarobindo, what do you see when you are so near to death?"

The holy man gazed distantly at the woman to his right. He had not met her before but because she was seated with him at the top table he assumed she had some kind of importance.

"I see the world as it is."

Zeno was now dealing with the two guests who seemed unable to keep the decorum essential to a philosophers' banquet, and in the presence of such a distinguished figure. His practiced calm was wearing thin and he was looking somehow to get a hold of an evening which threatened to be cheated of its grace. He stood up and gestured impatiently to Abelard that he should sit down.

"Ah, how perfect an answer, Sarobindo, and how accurate to what dear Abelard was describing as the reason for our devotion to you. But despite our desire to engage in just that kind of reflection, our evening has a couple of prior purposes to which we must attend!"

His insistent tone managed to gain the initiative once more, and he continued. "We have among us two new recruits to the Homeland of Heaven. We, as philosophers, have always brought newcomers to our table so they might savor the greatness of thought at the heart of Immortality."

He paused, clearing his throat to deepen his tone. "The two who come to us for the first time tonight are distinguished among all inductees to Heaven in that they came here, if not uninvited, then certainly unplanned. They are most unusual and it is part of

241

our many pleasures tonight to be able to hear from them first hand.
Palmiro over there is reputed to be the first to have broken free
from his conditioning, and reasoned the existence of our Heavenly
world from the scanty facts available to the Northern peoples. The
eminent character of his current patron, the wondrous Adorno, is
testimony of the esteem in which Heaven now holds him. Pascale
who was with him and helped him fly the rocket has just shown
us something of—what, should I say, the unorthodox approach?—
that enabled them to enter Heaven on their own. We will have a
chance to hear from them very soon before we turn to the
evening's main delectation, our revered Sarobindo. But enough
feeding on talk! Right now is the time for the food of the body, the
necessary step on the ladder of beauty and bliss: our evening's
feast!"

He looked around at everyone inviting them to join in the
pleasure of his words while clapping his hands sharply. Everyone
nodded happily and looked around expectantly. There was a short
pause, then from one of the houses next to the compound emerged
an explosion of dancers. They sprang forward carrying trestles and
boards between them which they hurried to set up in the space
between the tables. Quickly behind there came servers carrying
large, laden platters and big-bellied jugs filled with wine and
cordial. They brought caviar and French bread, foie gras and
California truffle, garlic-and-thyme confit duck, asparagus-stuffed
chicken and glazed pork, with onion, celery, spring potatoes,
carrots, celery, leeks and baby turnips, with red lentil, couscous,
eggplant curries and grilled cumin tofu, on and on, and all rounded
out with magnificent selections of cheeses and fruits, a feast which
outdid almost any other banquet which the philosophers could
remember. The dancers, who had been especially recruited from
the Classical and Free Dance Colony, had to work hard to get
everything set up and begin serving each of the guests as they
made their choices. There was quite a commotion as plates were
filled and glasses were charged, with everybody shouting out their
selections and making loud murmurs of satisfaction. Finally
everything was in place and the majority of the dancers retired
leaving a few to offer top-ups and further choices.

A period of hearty eating and drinking ensued in which there
was really no sound except the clatter of knives and forks, the

clink of glasses, and the ecstatic groans of the diners. But the moment of pure gastronomic pleasure did not last long. Almost at a signal people began to look up, sensing the need that the talking begin too. Zeno knew the moment well. In an instant he was on his feet and calling attention.

"Ahem! If our bodily food is anything to judge by, that of the mind will be nothing less than sublime! So let us begin. A few words from our two newest inductees are now in order. As you know, in a subtle way they have changed everything. They have brought into our midst an element of what we might call unpredictability, something we had almost forgotten in Heaven— except, of course, for the noble risk Sarobindo has always been willing to undertake. But I digress. Let me ask Palmiro here, to tell in his own words what it is that made him unique in a score of generations. How did he become the only one in the Northern Homeland to form a logical connection to the existence of Heaven? And even more, what drove him to risk his own and his companion's life, finding and taking off in a rocket to travel through the storms without preparation or permission? Palmiro, my friend, what have you to say?"

Palmiro had been expecting this but he also felt the shift in Zeno's tone. The master of ceremonies wasn't quite so effusive as he was before and his remarks seemed a little more pointed. Even though he could sense how Adorno did not respect these philosophers he could also feel quite distinctly the power of the group, and he needed to be careful. He glanced up at Pascale and saw how relaxed she looked. He recalled how good she was at handling these situations. Looking around he made up his mind. He would direct attention to his companion from the TEPs, and do so in the kind of matter-of-fact language he had learned from Adorno.

"In the Northern Homeland we did not have experimental methods by which to test our world. We were given general ideas and basic engineering principles. Nothing that would allow us truly to investigate our physical reality. Personally, I always felt there were major questions about the amount of energy expended to maintain the frozen conditions and about the overall dynamics of the stormworld. I felt there was something wrong with the picture: the heat had to go somewhere and have some effect. But my questions were really the full extent of my contribution. A great deal more was due to my companion, Pascale. Once I communicated to her my thinking it seemed she was able to grasp the overall picture better than me. She saw the pattern of everything, one that even included Heaven. Perhaps even more important, she was able to gain access to her father's computers. It was there we found trace evidence of the existence of Heaven. After that things took their own course. I was arrested for blasphemy and sent to the camps. But Pascale was able to find a job that gave her access to transport, including eventually an ice-tractor belonging to guides from Heaven. It was programmed for the Shuttle Port and she used it to come and rescue me. I would have died or been killed if she hadn't. It was then she told me of her idea to continue on and take the rocket. Her plan was of course the best plan, for what else were we going to do? And obviously, as you can see, it succeeded."

No one had heard the story told this way before, succinctly and at first hand. In particular no one had grasped Pascale's role in it all. A few mouths fell open slightly and all eyes turned together toward the young woman in the white shift seated at the head table.

"Ahh! That is most fascinating, Palmiro. We thank you for your account." Zeno understood that here was something different and new. A figure who had just disrupted proceedings, and irritated him considerably, but who had so far only been thought a little weird, now turned out to be critical. He sensed an opportunity. He would be able to turn the spotlight away from Adorno to shine it on an entirely new subject, one able to capture everyone's energy and reaction.

"But from what you say it seems we need to hear from Pascale herself. Pascale, please, tell us the story of your remarkable intuition. How did you manage to see a pattern that included our Heaven? This shows an astonishing perception on the part of someone without any kind of training. What kind of person are you, Pascale, and from where came this near mythical—I am tempted even to say militant—resolve to search your father's computers and to steal the rocket ship? It sounds truly fascinating."

The mention of her name and the questions directed at her

had a galvanizing effect on Pascale. It was as if she was waking up in the middle of a dream. She looked about, and then looked down, remembering. She was being asked who she was, and that was an enormously important question, one which she had been circling around ever since she came to Heaven. And now, just now, she was beginning to have a clarity about that. Her newborn sense of freedom rose up within her, finding and giving her voice. She lifted her head and spoke.

"I do not know many people here but the little I have discovered about philosophers tells me they like to find a pattern in things. I like patterns too, as Palmiro said, and I look for them all the time. But I must warn the philosophers that you will not like the pattern I see. It has some very big holes, holes so big that perhaps you may fall in them. Let me tell you about myself. I was born and brought up in the Northern Homeland, a child of the TEPs, and my life there was always a question to me. Palmiro showed me that questions could be real, with substance. I am always grateful to him for that. When I understood what he was saying I prayed one night to God and I believe I saw down, all the way down through the storm world. I saw that there really was a land beyond our own. It meant that almost everything about the Northern Homeland was one big lie and everyone there was living a lie. After that I could not rest until I found a way to rescue Palmiro. And, by searching for him, I discovered the rocket. Now the evidence of my ordinary eyes confirms what I saw before as a pattern. I see that if everything in the North was built on falsehood, then as sure as day follows night everything here is the same. I have enjoyed the life of Heaven, I will not deny it, but now, just now, as you talked of death, I saw the pattern of a lie. And as you question me, so must I answer: all this here, all this splendor of words and wealth and immortality, it is a lie!"

Her words had a shocking clarity and confidence. It felt as if all the air had suddenly been sucked out of the tent. The rich texture of the evening became a torn shard of metal twisting stupidly in the wind. People were struck dumb, outraged but not knowing what to say. For the first time Zeno himself was at a loss and the permanent bliss on Sarobindo's face ricked into a frown. Jonas wanted the ground to open up to swallow him and Pascale with him. Cyrus threw his hands in the air and intoned, "Gods in

Heaven, Lucifer has arisen". The only ones who were not fazed were the four to the other side of the head table, Marius, Blair and their companions. Blair smiled without blinking and Marius was expressionless. The woman beside Marius gazed at Pascale with frank hostility while the bird of prey next to Blair shifted her head slightly, dangerously. Marius scraped his chair and spoke softly between narrowed lips.

"I think there has been some failure here, of Initiation, of monitoring. The Anthropology Colony is itself at fault for not having debriefed this person, Pascale. We spoke only with Palmiro, and subsequently accepted that he was vouched for by Adorno. We assumed his companion had been selected and vetted in the normal way. Clearly we were not as careful as we might have been, given all the circumstances. I strongly suggest this recent inductee refrain from further remarks until we've had a chance properly to interview her."

It was a most unpleasant situation but people were relieved that a voice of authority had spoken. They nodded and a few managed to force a smile, hoping that someone could now get the conversation back on track. Zeno, however, remained inarticulate with failure; the evening had become a total embarrassment. The silence continued to thicken, like blood in a bruise. Then strangely it was Adorno who came to the rescue, though any help from this man was bound to be at a price.

"Now, now, Marius, no need to be so grim. This is a philosopher's banquet after all, not a courtroom. It seems to me this young woman is fully within bounds to question the value of our world. In fact, questioning our world is something I have been doing for years. Or should I say, forever? Actually, what I do want to say is my recent situation of having a student to instruct has served enormously to sharpen my own thinking, including for public consumption. So do I have your permission to proceed?"

Everyone was quickly as terrified of what Adorno would say as they had been horrified by Pascale. But they were helpless. Zeno was overcome with confusion; his plans had now completely misfired. No one else could stop the scientist from pressing on with his speech, his voice sounding like the creak of an expensive staircase as a cruel visitor ascended. The company round the tables were like condemned prisoners, waiting for the ax.

"Good, so I have your indulgence. Let me begin then with an obvious fact. We live within the universe, of course. Next, to this evident fact I would add it doesn't really matter why or how the universe got here. What matters is that it is here and that the modes and systems of its construction are unbelievably complex and layered. Each of you here believes because you are immortal you are the greatest thing there is. You sit crowned at the apex of existence, you are gods. But the universe itself is far, far greater. We are just flecks of dust blown mindlessly across its surface. We are ants crawling on a vast plain, which extends across galaxies and dark matter and has no end. Truly to be a god, therefore, would be to share existence with the universe itself. To be cognitively identified with it. But the way you live now, even if you seem able to live forever, you will always be a slave to a cosmos you have no knowledge of, no control over. This place you call Heaven could be hit by an asteroid tomorrow, or the planet itself could fly apart, and then where would all your precious immortality be?"

It was another direct challenge to the self-esteem of Heaven, but unlike Pascale's more spiritual attack it was made in hard rational terms. The philosophers were on more familiar ground.

Heloise found her voice. She spoke nervously, but with feeling.

"Adorno, you go too far. By going so far, so high, you exceed the possibility of rational discussion. At that point what you say is sheer hubris, and like Icarus you come crashing down. You become both exalted and pessimistic."

The scientist laughed easily. "Not at all, my esteemed colleague. I could just as easily argue the universe is doomed, and us with it—that the exhaustion of energy will produce a bottomless pit of dust in which all movement has died. That would be pessimistic. But in fact I believe the universe is predisposed to its own existence. In which case its life may be indefinite. What I'm suggesting is that we here, in comparison, are mere blips in its fourteen billion years explosion of light. We are playthings of a vast wanton child."

"Bravo," blurted Friedrich, suddenly finding himself in perfect agreement with Adorno. "Mein Herr Professor is following the only valid direction. How could the one who drove death from its hidden lair be called irrational? Rather, he is the one

247

who is really thinking. His thoughts are of the sublime, the impossible. But they make us taste the insipidity of our existence, so we regain its vibrant truth!"

Zeno finally recovered his tongue. "No, no, no! I cannot allow this to go unchallenged. It is very easy for Adorno to come in here and declare our world pointless, to set up his own cathedral in its place. What has he ever done to become our priest? Unlike Sarobindo here who has always risked death in order to bring us the presence of the measureless?"

But again Zeno had miscalculated. The mention of Sarobindo was the one thing guaranteed to provoke Adorno further and Zeno had made a direct challenge. Adorno's casual drawl took a steely edge.

"You think Sarobindo's Font Eterno somehow has meaning? It's nothing but a circus, a freak show! It degrades everything we came here to achieve. It has made me despair of what you call Heaven and everyone in it. Listen, I will try to explain in as simple terms possible the facts of the universe you inhabit. There are basically two principles at work, unity and separation. Two more or less identical elements A1 and A2 can combine on a random basis to form a new reality AA. But this can only happen if there is some kind of principle of combination, and at the same time one of continuing separation or difference. Absent either of them, you could not have the new phenomenon, the combination. To simplify enormously, you could choose the example of water: it contains two elements in combination, hydrogen and oxygen. They combine and yet remain different. And this peculiar combination creates the unique substance of water. These principles—of combination and difference—may themselves be a grand chance but you cannot have a universe without them, and if you beg them into existence each time you come across physical phenomena then in point of fact you proclaim them as law. No, they have to be stable and real and be the case for all imaginable universes. This of course does not imply the existence of a Supreme Being, but what it does do is force you to admit the universe was there before you, and is greater than you, for you did not create these principles, they created you. We did not will them into being, they willed us, and therefore they outrank us."

Abelard interrupted, "Where are you going with all this? I

don't see the point." But Adorno didn't seem to notice.

"At the same time—and this is what really fascinates me—there is also randomness, chance, a totally different principle in the midst of attraction and repulsion. There is spontaneity in the midst of order, or freedom together with pattern, whatever way you want to put it. How can that be? And how can I penetrate that secret? The whole thing seems very much like it is designed for life, or rather it is the design of life itself, neither more nor less. So then I say, if we were able somehow to connect ourselves to this overall life-design in the universe, to plug ourselves into its program, well then we would indeed be gods. But until then we are nothing but children imagining themselves to be fairies, and your honored Sarobindo is the biggest fairytale of all."

For the second time this evening there was a strangled silence but this time it lasted only an instant. Down at the end of the tables there was an eruption. Cyrus had cried out earlier but apart from that had not engaged in conversation. He had observed the proceedings tight-lipped but with ever increasing agitation. Now he stood up abruptly and began to clamber awkwardly up onto the table, not caring that he was kicking the person next to him or sending the table contents flying. Dishes of chicken, fish, bread and vegetables were sent toppling into people's laps. Glasses toppled and wine spilled and spread out in dark stains across the tablecloth. But Cyrus was oblivious. He was already shouting as he struggled unsteadily to his feet on the trestle.

"Enough, enough, I say! I have no idea what the honored scientist is talking about, I am an historian not a philosopher. But I will not tolerate disrespect for the mystery at the heart of our homeland. I see with absolute clarity it is these interlopers from the North who have brought this anarchy into our midst. We can allow Adorno the privilege of private research but when this Pascale comes uninvited, openly insults our Heaven and opens the door to chaos then I say she is undesirable. I demand here and as of this moment, she be taken into custody. I demand Magus be contacted and she be detained as an anti-social."

Cyrus had spoken in an oratorical manner, his voice rising and reaching a crescendo in the last phrases. Gaius and a couple of others were already clapping and shouting agreement. As he repeated his demand he pumped his fist in the air and the effect was one more time to shake the board on which he was standing. Already dislodged by his scrambling on top one of the corners slipped free and tipped down. Cyrus lost his balance and pitched forward. He fell headlong onto the ground between the tables, with a cascade of dishes, jugs, food and wine beside him. People screamed and cried out and there was a dull snapping sound as his extended arm took all his weight. Everyone was now on their feet and shouting. Many were calling out that Cyrus was right, that such a night had never been witnessed before and Pascale should be arrested at once. Danny and Palmiro were thoroughly frightened, casting around uncertainly. Jonas grabbed Pascale and whispered they had to leave. She saw everyone staring up at her, their faces twisted in horror and anger. She felt the danger and nodded: Jonas was right, they should go. The two of them backed out of the tent and ran toward their car. No one followed: the name of Magus had been invoked, that was enough. All the same Jonas swerved the car around hard, breaking and changing gear as fast as he could. The tires squealed as he launched forward, escaping the philosophers' courtyard on the darkened roads of Heaven.

7. THE CANYONS

The desert scrub at the western limit of Heaven—the place where Pascale had wandered off the morning after her Initiation—continued along its southern edge. Progressively the land changed, falling away from the plateau into a series of fractured mesas penetrated by narrow, forbidding canyons. Heading from the mesas farther south, the canyons collapsed into an arid rocky waste and finally a true desert, a lifeless expanse of scalding white sand. It was this natural geography which acted as the anchor for the climate of Heaven, a kind of heat trap protected and reinforced by the constant warm air which fell in a great loop from the Northern Homeland.

At the intersection of two canyons at the base of a mesa, about thirty miles to the south of the nearest Homeland habitation, lay a straggling assortment of adobe cabins and stock pens. A few individuals could be seen moving about in desultory fashion with buckets or tools. Others were not doing anything, just sitting or sleeping. The scene had none of the pride and vigor of Heaven, rather a profound sense of loss. People still held hints of great beauty, but they were dirty and unkempt. Some carried disfiguring scars and mutilations. All of them had the most awful look in their eyes, infinite boredom flecked with anger and fear. If Heaven was only a few miles away, up along a dirt track, here was its classic alternative, Hell.

The place went by the familiar name of "The Ranch." Most people in Heaven did not even know it existed. They had a vague idea that there had to be some such location, but they preferred not to think about it, drowning their minds in the constant stream of distractions and thrills Heaven provided. The figure of Magus was known and he was the connection to the possibility of such a place, but exactly who Magus was and what he did, again no one cared to think. And Magus liked it that way.

He'd had the job of warden to anti-socials since the first days of Heaven's story and in fact he was recruited precisely for such a purpose. He came from some shadowy intelligence agency specializing in black sites and disappearances. But his task in Heaven was quite different from the summary violence of the bad old days. He was a sensible man who appreciated that no one could or should be executed in Heaven. Everyone was a god and to eliminate one was to threaten the immortality of all. In consequence anyone who proved unable to maintain the values of divine existence had to be quarantined but never killed. In the event it proved remarkably efficient. Exactly because of the mental pathology of his charges Magus' work was very simple: there was nothing stopping them throwing themselves off the top of a mesa, an ultimate solution which residents now and then employed. If a god decided to terminate his or her existence that itself was a divine decision and no one had a problem with it. In Heaven undesirables were essentially self-regulating.

As far as Magus was concerned his work was indispensable to the meaning of Heaven itself. He took pride in keeping immortality free of all breakdown, and part of the job was allowing Immortals to be blissfully unaware he was doing just that. He ruled his fiefdom with a cold heart but great pleasure. If his charges caused trouble he generally allowed them to sort it out among themselves. Only occasionally would he beat them. For the rest he ensured they had food to eat and work to keep them busy if they wished it. His only real concern was that they did not escape and return to the city, and that was very unlikely. There were padlocked gates on the canyons, and only he had the keys, so it was impossible to ride out on a horse. Iron stakes and footholds were carved into the rock so a determined individual could climb to the top, but the road back to Heaven was treacherous, brutally hot, and impossible to cover in one day. At night it was hunted by packs of feral dogs and coyotes which ranged through the badlands and no one stood much chance out on the trail after dark. Thus, when an inmate was not present at evening roll-call he would simply wait until the next morning then set out with a couple of horses. Any missing individual who was still alive, and not hopelessly lost, invariably lay exhausted at the roadside. Magus simply loaded them on the horse and returned with them to the Ranch.

It was actually a lot of fun if someone tried to escape, but people rarely did. The state of mind of the prisoners was usually one of robot-like withdrawal while they went through the motions of an endless life. Anyone too angry never lasted. As a result Magus experienced a quiet and constant satisfaction preserving the purity of immortal existence.

The day Pascale arrived, accompanied by Marius and two bodyguards, Magus was seated in his usual spot, a large fan-backed wicker chair under the adobe arches of his cabin. The party had radioed ahead and let themselves in through the gate with their own security key. As they rode up the sun was receding across the canyon to the west and the shadows of the arches were cool and inviting to the trail-weary riders. They hitched their horses to a rail and Magus invited the men to come in. He gestured curtly to Pascale that she remain outside.

"Sorry you were obliged to leave the sweet airs of the city to make your way into my inferno. Please sit here and rest. Let me get you something."

He was a short heavy-set, dark-tanned man with buzz-cut hair, a straight-edged nose and narrow lips. He was dressed, unlike anyone else in Heaven, in desert fatigue pants and clean black tee. He beckoned with a wave behind him and a woman in a frayed denim dress emerged from the cabin door carrying a tray of glasses and a pitcher of lemonade. Marius and his agents came in and sat in the chairs offered them.

Marius replied, "Thank you, Magus. As always Heaven owes you an immense debt for providing this service. Here is another deviant for your charge, and I have to say one especially maladjusted."

He launched at once into the story of Pascale, her unconventional arrival, reclusive behavior and her outburst at the philosophers' table. The banquet had taken place just a couple of days before but the Anthropology Colony had needed to move quickly to prevent the rot spreading.

Meanwhile Pascale stood outside in the broiling light and without a drink for her thirst. She was dressed in her usual shift but had managed to tie a kerchief around her head, peasant-style, to protect herself from the sun.

Magus commented, "You know me, Marius, I'm always happy to deal with the psychos. Whatever her story is I am certain she will soon find her level here, one way or the other." Again he hardly looked in Pascale's direction but waved to the woman with the frayed dress, still standing in the doorway. "Koyo, get her to the Women's Building and find her a bunk."

253

Marius looked at him. "We go back a long ways, you and I, Magus. You remember when we started all this?"

Magus nodded but without expression.

"I quite often think about it. We invited you to be an Immortal, but on condition you did this isolated job. It probably seemed like a good deal, back then, and really it has worked out very well. But now, you know, an eternity later, I don't understand why you're so willing to keep doing it?"

This time Magus smiled. "You mean, why do I not want to come up to the city and live in a colony with everyone else and do Doblepoble?"

"Well, yes. That's right."

"I have everything here, Marius. More than you can appreciate. I am Zeus, a god who rules over other gods. The only alternative for the Immortals under my power is death. And even then I am happy. What does your guru, Sarobindo, say? That death gives meaning to life? Well, I believe that. Every time one of these failed Immortals throws herself off the mesa it purifies Heaven. And I feel it. I really do feel it. It seems to me I have helped make Heaven perfect for everyone." And he smiled again, with smug self-congratulation.

Marius grimaced despite himself. "Ah, thank you, Magus. We are so grateful, for all you do. Well, we must be going more or less immediately, I'm afraid. I and my companions do not want to be delayed on the road."

He stood up, glancing at the others and they at once followed him. No one extended his hand. The men just nodded at each other and Marius' party led their horses across the canyon to the water trough. They put a lead rope on Pascale's horse, then mounted and headed for the gate. Magus remained seated, watching the party of gods with ironic detachment as they exited his kingdom.

***

Koyo had come out of the house, her head down, without looking at Pascale. She was a short Asiatic woman, her black hair matted and her dress dirty. As she passed by she touched the new prisoner's arm with her hand. Pascale understood she was to follow.

She caught up and said, "Hi, my name is Pascale. Yours is

Koyo, no?"

The woman did not reply and did not look up. She continued walking in what seemed an awkward manner, as if she had a disability. Pascale slackened her pace and fell in behind. Magus' cabin was at a corner where the northern canyon made an oblique angle into a second ravine. The woman led her around the corner, along a razor edge of shadow. They passed a stockade in which a pair of horses stood in the gloom, wagging their heads at the flies. There was a tall wood-board building which looked as if it were some kind of store, then there was another adobe cabin with a long veranda bounded by a low wall.

Koyo went behind the low veranda wall and entered a front door. As they passed through the shadowed space Pascale could make out a woman and a man sitting on a bench and a younger woman in a rocking chair. They were dressed in the same dirty denim as Koyo. Only the woman on the bench looked up. She had a narrow, striking face, dark hair, matted like Koyo's, and haunting black eyes. Except, on closer inspection, one eye was missing and the expression in the other complimented the missing one with its total emptiness and indifference. She stared right through Pascale, as if she were a ghost.

Pascale passed through the screen door and then a main door, and they were in complete darkness. The immediate sensation was an intense choking stench. Pascale stood there fighting for breath and trying to get her eyes used to the blackness. She heard Koyo fumbling about, and suddenly a light flared as she lit an oil lamp. Pascale could see a big rough wooden table heaped up with odds and ends, cups, old food, clothes, shoes, scissors, sewing machine, tools, boxes and yellowed papers. Along the walls were bunk beds, similarly strewn with clothes and trash. Koyo scooped a space for the lamp on the table and then crossed over to a bunk, beckoning Pascale to follow. As Pascale stepped forward she saw the floor also covered in junk, including torn clothes and blankets in layers on top of other objects. She stumbled her way to where Koyo was standing while her guide climbed the steps to the upper bunk and proceeded to toss a heap of detritus onto the floor.

She climbed down and cast around for a moment. Presently she came up with a blanket, pulling it out from where it had gotten caught on a cage for birds or an animal. She threw the foul-smelling item toward Pascale. "Need this." Again she returned to floor and after more searching she came up with a denim dress, similarly filthy. "Need this."

Then she was gone, leaving the oil lamp still lit on the table. Pascale placed the blanket on her bunk, dumped the dress on the floor at the bottom, and went back to the table. She picked up the lamp and shone it around the room, counting sixteen beds. She took a mental snapshot of the route back to the door, set the lamp back on the table and blew it out. She traced her route to the door, found the handle and went out.

She sat on the veranda wholly ignored by the other three. This then was it, the sudden catastrophic end to her existence in Heaven. After the events of the philosophers' banquet it had all played out very quickly. There had been no time for Jonas and her to think of a plan, to try to put things right. If they had known of a place to escape they would have, but they were entirely at the mercy of public opinion which had swung so fully against them. Or, against her.

Blair had visited the next day, speaking with Jonas alone. He informed her lover that there was no intention to penalize him for Pascale's behavior. His record was far too good and his services too valuable to be categorized as an anti-social. Everything in his relationship with Pascale could be put down to the unusual responsibility he'd been forced to take organizing the Initiation, and the bewitching power she had established over him. All that was necessary, therefore, was that he agree not to make any difficulty when they rendered Pascale to the care of Magus. Jonas was horrified and had pleaded with Blair this was unnecessary, that Pascale would definitely learn to adjust. But Blair was unmoved. No one could remember anyone leading such a militant assault on the very meaning of Heaven. He bluntly warned Jonas that if he continued to stand in the way then suspicion would fall on him too.

Jonas reported all this to Pascale and they came to the unavoidable conclusion that he had to fake compliance. The memory of Palmiro's imprisonment was still very recent, as was the way she had been able to rescue him against all odds. In the same way Jonas would find a way to set her free, or get a pardon. In the meantime the mood was so hostile they just had to submit.

Thus it was that when Marius arrived the following day she surrendered without protest, while Jonas absented himself, watching the scene from the hillside. She had gotten on the horse and experienced her first horse-back ride, clinging to the neck of her mount for thirty excruciating miles. During the journey Marius had not exchanged more than two sentences with her, explaining that from now on she would live at the Ranch where she would be free within the canyons but could never return to the city.

Inside herself she braced against the fear, the pain and the total strangeness of everything, preparing to face whatever she must just as Palmiro had done. Now, sitting on the wall of the veranda, she suddenly became conscious of the fierce ache of her limbs and the horrible wrenching sensation in her throat. She was desperately thirsty. She got up and went over to the man and woman on the bench, asking where she could get some water. Neither replied. She turned to the young woman in the rocking chair, her voice cracking with dryness.

"Excuse me, I do not know your name, but could you please tell me where I can get a drink of water?"

The woman looked at her. "New here? Don't worry about water!" She laughed shrilly at her own crass joke.

She was an Immortal who had obviously been selected as little more than a teenager, having the unmistakable quality of youth in her face and body. However, she was much plumper than the usual goddess, and she had her knees up under her chin and was rocking herself back and forth on the chair.

"Please, I'm begging you, I just recently came to Heaven from the North, and now I've been sent here. I'm dying for a drink of water."

The girl looked at her, then stopped her rocking. She got up and went to the porch entrance, pointing back in the direction of Magus' cabin. Across from it, on the far wall, still in blinding sunlight, it was possible to make out a water-trough with a line and faucet above it. "There!" she said.

Pascale went up to her and hugged her, smiling. "Thank you, thank you! What's your name?"

The girl did not respond, standing immobile without expression, but then as Pascale ran down the steps and out toward the faucet she suddenly shouted after her.

257

"Name's Zena."

Pascale stopped, turned around and shouted back hoarsely. "Hello, Zena. I'm Pascale, and we're going to be friends!"

When she got to the faucet and turned it on a rope of hot brackish water fell into the trough. She waited for a few moments then cupped her hands and drank greedily. As she did she felt there were eyes on her back and she turned around. There was no one there, but she could see Magus' cabin sunk in the shadows behind her. She turned off the faucet and walked away, heading along the first canyon that ran in a north-westerly direction. The shadow here was almost up to the far wall and dusk already shrouded the buildings. The first one was long and low and had two or three stove pipes coming through its roof. To the side of the near end there was a big chicken coop encased in very heavy wire netting. At the far end, joined to it, was a foursquare structure which seemed to be the largest of all the Ranch buildings. She took it as the cantina, with the long building before it probably the kitchen and store. There were glimmering lights in the cracks between the shutters in both buildings and she thought an evening meal was probably being made ready.

Next in line she passed a cattle stockade, but there were no animals in it. Last of all, there was an adobe cabin that looked a lot like the cabin for women back around the corner. Her eyes were now getting used to the evening shadow and she could make out two men seated on the veranda. She walked over and went through the archway onto the porch. The men were dressed in the same regulation denim shirts and pants, and again they had no interest at all in meeting her. One of them was dark skinned, a very strong-looking man with a thick wooly beard which he fingered incessantly with one hand while tapping himself on the forearm with the other. The other man had crippled legs dangling uselessly beneath him and a hopeless empty glance.

Pascale was about to introduce herself when there was a loud halloo from farther up the canyon. She looked out and saw a rider emerging in the wedge of shadow. It was a woman leading a string of about twenty scrawny cattle returning from the day's pasture in the branch canyons. At the rear were two men, also on horseback. She watched as the line of animals passed her, coming to a halt at the stockade to the right. The woman leaned down and opened its gate and the cattle filed in quietly. The woman swung herself out of the saddle, and so did one of the men. The second man took the horses and trotted off with them. At once a triangle bell sounded from the big square cabin—as if it had been waiting for this moment—and the dismounted riders made their way directly toward it. The dark-skinned man got to his feet and scooped the crippled man up in his arms, like an armful of laundry. He marched off with him to the mess hall, the man's withered feet flopping under him.

A line formed at the entrance to the cantina, including the threesome from the women's cabin. Pascale followed along and found herself behind Zena, who went through the spring-hinged door but did not hold it open. Pascale caught it as it snapped back and kept it open until the person after her put out a hand. As she turned into the room she was greeted by the same odor of ageless squalor she had smelled before, but this time overlaid with a stench of decomposing food. There were flies everywhere, on the tables, in the air. Her stomach turned and she gagged uncontrollably. Zena saw her and smirked.

Pascale covered her mouth instinctively and struggled to calm her gut. Continuing to breathe through hand and mouth she saw there were already half-a-dozen people in the room seated at the tables, leaning on their elbows, or fast asleep, their torsos flat out on the table tops. It was clear that the cantina doubled as a lounging place for people who were not working: they simply waited there from one meal to the next. Many were enormously overweight, and it seemed obvious they hardly ever moved except to eat whatever was placed in front of them.

Pascale did as the others did, seating herself at one of the tables, while still fighting the impulse to retch. After a moment a door in the back of the room was flung open and three people came in carrying pots and a dish. They set them down on a table at the end and then one of them, an obese but energetic man, banged a ladle against one of the pots and shouted, "Eeeaatt!"

Most of the people got up from the tables and shuffled over to the serving counter. Pascale followed them, breathing hard through her teeth. The group picked up dishes and the servers ladled out corn soup and beef carnita as they swatted away the flies. One or two carried servings for others to the tables, including the dark-skinned man for the man with crippled legs. Pascale took up a tortilla and had a little of the meat and corn scooped onto it, then she went back to sit down, close to Zena. No one was speaking, except for an occasional grunt or incoherent remark. Pascale folded the tortilla over and tried to take a bite, but immediately she did she knew she was going to throw up. She stood up abruptly with both hands on her mouth, staggered to the door and crashed it open. She fell against the railing outside the door, vomiting over its edge.

No one followed her. After she had finished purging the little she had in her stomach, the silence of the canyon was complete. She straightened and looked around. A beaten strip of gold lined the top of the canyon wall opposite and there was the strangest feeling, one of total peace. She felt a little unsteady but she made her way in the near darkness over to the angle of the canyons and found the water line and trough. She turned the faucet on full and the water was cooler than before. She rinsed her mouth, splashed her face and drank a little until her throat felt normal. Then she traced her path back to the women's cabin. She came to the veranda wall and, pushing herself up on it, sat there in the silence.

The canyon now was in full darkness and looking above her she could see the glittering ranks of stars marching across the eastern cliff. They hung there, more intense and vital than she'd ever seen. She thought at once about her friendship with the stars and how that night back in the Northern Homeland they all seemed to abandon her. Now they were back again, more alive than ever, even though it was just a narrow crack in the sky where they were visible. How could that happen? Why should they feel so different? Maybe it was the canopy at the fateful philosophers' banquet, and the way Jonas had explained the ancient figures and how they shaped human lives. Maybe that had changed things, so now the stars were alive and good again, shaping her life for her. And yet here in this canyon she was among people for whom all shape and meaning were gone, and her world was locked in with theirs. How could the stars seem good in this place and, more to the point, how would she ever survive in it? She was relying on Jonas to rescue her, but was that possible? Or would she be stuck here forever, with the flies and the stench and the men and women without souls?

She remembered how she had prayed to God that night on the frozen tundra, that she had made some kind of a deal. Had God held up God's side? Well, yes, you'd have to say so. She had not lost her mind and she and Palmiro had been able to discover the whole truth about their world, and had actually come here to Heaven and got to enjoy the boundless pleasures of immortal life. So, definitely, yes, in a certain way you'd have to say everything had worked out.

On the other hand, she was now here, down in this canyon with people who were dead, though their bodies were breathing. Was this what being helped by God meant? Suddenly something made her shiver. Perhaps it was the thought of the Northern Homeland, or death, or perhaps just the canyon which was rapidly losing all its daytime warmth. She got down and went into the cabin, pausing at the door to orient herself. Somehow the stench did not hit her quite as badly. She found her way to the table in the middle, stepping carefully across the floor. Feeling around she found the gas lighter and after a moment split a flame. She lit the oil lamp and identified which was her bunk. She went over, retrieved her blanket, wrapping it around her shoulders despite its bitter smell. Then she went out and sat back up on the wall. She needed to think things through.

But she couldn't think. All she could do was look up at the stars. In the dry air they seemed somehow to counter the smell of the blanket, their glow giving off a scent, like incense. She found herself trying to discover a pattern but there was just a vast meandering river flowing above her. She was floating with them, lost in their glittering stream. Abruptly Zena was next to her, handing her something.

"Here. Missed juice." She held out a metal mug. Pascale was startled but she put out her hand and took the offered drink. Zena had already turned and was heading into the cabin before she could reply.

"Hey, thanks, Zena. What are you doing tomorrow?"

Zena paused and looked around. She replied in her standard monotone "Tomorrow never comes." There was the slightest catch before she did, a barely detectable break in the awful sameness of reaction that seemed to characterize all those doomed to the canyons. Pascale put down the drink and jumped down. She ran up to Zena, flinging her arms around her. Zena did not resist, but neither did she return the hug. She just stood there while Pascale pressed her close. After a moment Pascale let go but continued to hold one of her hands.

"You know, we could go for a walk in the morning. You could show me around."

"Nothing to see, but walk if you want."

"Yes, I do, I do want." And Pascale hugged her again. Once again Zena did not respond, but this time when Pascale let her go her body seemed involuntarily to rock back toward Pascale. Then she caught herself and turned away, opening the cabin door and disappearing inside.

Pascale retrieved the cup and walked out to the middle of the canyon where she could see the stars best. She drank the guava juice and felt she was tasting the same fragrance as the stars. She lay down on the ground wrapping the blanket close around her, gazing upward into space and its infinite canopy. As she looked she tried to remember some of the shapes she'd seen at the philosophers' banquet; perhaps she would pick out a couple from all the points of light. A fish, a bull, a crab? She could see nothing, but then in a moment right above her among the stars was the figure of a man stretched at an angle along the sky, his waist, his legs, even perhaps his face.

Yes, there was no doubt: how was it Jonas had not mentioned the man? She fixed her eyes on the figure and the more she looked the more she thought how wonderful he was. She felt she could hold onto him and love him there in the canyon. She reached her hands up and held his shoulders, his waist, and she brought him down to her. A feeling of enormous joy and love pulsed through her, a love that had no bounds nor end. She lay there united with the stars, with the shape of a man who had been there for all of time waiting for her. Or, at least, that is how it seemed, for time was all rolled up in a moment and the great universe of things bent down toward her and gave itself to her soul. In the form of a loving being, a being of love, it gave itself.

She lay there in absolute peace and silence. She did not know for how long. Eventually the ground grew cold and penetrated through her blanket, bringing her back to herself. And yet she lay there longer, filled with confidence and incredible strength. She did not need to fear Magus or the canyon, or any of the deadness in it. She had found a way, a friend and a feeling which could truly make heaven happen. Not the fake Heaven of the colonies and their festivals which were unable to prevent the sadness of Zena or the misery of the man with the crippled feet, and rather in fact caused their suffering. Instead, a real heaven filled with life, or, more exactly, an earth like that... She stopped. She did not need to think any more. She knew what it was she had to do.

8. STAR STUDENT

Palmiro adjusted the scanning electron microscope to a finer resolution, zooming in as close as he could on the strange structure in his view finder. He was looking at a tube with rounded ends like a pod. There was an inner membrane which was folded over and back, like a maze, and there was a nucleus at its core. It was something called a mitochondria and the material inside its inner membrane was a kind of factory in which essential reactions took place in the production of cell energy. Adorno had set him to study these reactions in painstaking detail, scanning all the way down to the molecular structure of the chemicals. One by one, stage by stage, he was to document them until he understood everything implicitly.

On the way home from the philosophers' banquet he had been in a state of shock. Pascale's stupid words and Adorno's attack on immortality had produced a scene of chaos, something that up to then seemed impossible in Heaven. The moment Marius opened his mouth Palmiro knew Pascale was in trouble, that she had awoken something powerful and dangerous. At the same time he could not understand what his mentor, Adorno, was doing. He had shown utter contempt for Sarobindo, in a way that was sure to upset everybody, but his argument did not seem to go anywhere. All it had done was stir everything up until there was bound to be a reaction and it was easy to see that it would not focus on him, but on Pascale. He wondered if the inventor of immortality had for some reason done it deliberately.

"I know what you're thinking." The scientist finally broke the silence after they'd traveled for almost ten minutes. "You're thinking I just made things very bad, possibly for yourself, but definitely for your fellow conspirator, the passionate Pascale. Well, don't be too quick to think that way, my friend. You still have a great deal to learn, and you will most certainly continue your studies with me. No one is going to interfere. And I wouldn't worry at all about your erstwhile companion. She has friends of her own. If anyone should appreciate her ability to find a way you should. Just concentrate on your studies, and remember the real loser here is Sarobindo."

And that was that. No more was said, and when they arrived

back at the mansion they went their separate ways. Next day Adorno returned to directing his studies as if nothing had happened. The only difference was he began to point him more urgently in the direction of biology and genetics, covering topics in physics only in summary fashion. Palmiro obeyed dutifully but while he researched structures and organelles, proteins and DNA, his mind returned like the swing of a pendulum to Adorno's words. What had he meant, "The real loser is Sarobindo"? And, behind his words, his intentions at the banquet still remained a mystery. What had he wanted to achieve? It was inconceivable he had done those things just out of spite, or a mere desire just to push his point of view. He was a scientist not a philosopher. What was he up to?

And, no matter how Adorno had played it down, there was the problem of Pascale, the person everyone had ended up blaming. He remained continuously anxious for her and always had his ears alert for news. It wasn't long before one of Adorno's assistants said something which realized his worst fears. She was a quiet bookish sort named Phillipa and she casually let drop that she had heard about the disruption at the banquet. It seemed the woman Pascale had quickly been deported as an anti-social. He questioned her at once as to what that meant but she only had the vaguest idea. She believed perhaps there was some kind of colony, perhaps to the south. Her puzzled irritation at his further questions showed more clearly than any words that for someone to be deported meant they were to be forgotten.

Palmiro was beside himself. That night he couldn't sleep. Everything he and Pascale had done together returned to him now, memory after memory, like waves beating on a shore. He felt he had thrown her to the wolves when it should have been him to speak the truth about Heaven. It had always been his job to denounce the falsehoods of the Homeland. But here instead it was Pascale, the one who had always had his back and been there for him. She had spoken and suffered the consequences, and he had let it happen.

The more he thought the more he couldn't bear it. He got up as soon as it was light and went to Adorno's study to wait for him. He drifted around among the books and articles on genomes and sequencing and mutation but couldn't settle to read. It was as if all his understanding and purpose were now wrapped up with

Adorno, and yet there was one other person who had been truly important to him and she was now in real trouble. It was essential that he speak to his patron and find a solution. Normally Adorno seemed to know when he was in the study, but this time when Palmiro wanted to see him urgently he delayed. By the time he finally arrived Palmiro felt exhausted. When the scientist came through the door his apprentice could hardly open his mouth and simply stared at him in a kind of anguish.

Adorno's shadowed glance darted back at him. "What's wrong with you? No, don't tell me! You've heard news of your friend, what's her name, Pascale?"

Palmiro nodded. "I...I needed to talk, sir. She's been sent to some kind of punishment camp. Do you know what and where that is?"

Adorno's glittering eyes held his apprentice in a prolonged look, something very unusual for him.

"I need to show you something, Palmiro. Once you have seen it and heard my explanation you will perhaps feel less inclined to worry about your friend. Or, at least, you may have some sense of a way out. Come with me."

He beckoned and brought Palmiro through a door he had never entered before. It led down a paneled corridor toward the back of the building, passing through the kitchen area and finally to a boot room. At the back of this Adorno opened another door and suddenly the old-world elegance of the mansion was changed into a bright hi-tech environment. A long featureless corridor built of white acrylic and permanently lit by recessed lighting stretched in front of them. Several doors led off it and Adorno explained their meaning as they went along.

"These are all workshops and labs on either side. They contain a lot of material and equipment, materials, bio-forms, machine tools, all that kind of thing. A great deal of it is needed for the work I am going to show you. The first place on the tour is just up here."

He continued along the corridor as it swung through a curve, then straightened and ran fifty meters further. Half way along on the right there was a large door with a security scanning device next to it. Adorno put his eye to it and after a moment a green light showed and there was a click as the door unlocked. He swung it open and he and Palmiro entered a cavernous room filled with large screen monitors, clustered cables, banks of computers and a huge free-standing transparent panel containing a holographic map. There was a dry warmth with the distinctive odor of electrical components, and a background buzz of cooling fans and hiss of radio static. The impression was that nothing in here was ever switched off.

"This is my observatory control, terminals from the radio telescopes and processing for their signals. The dishes are out on the hillside. I operate them from here and record their data." Then with a slowly deliberate release of breath he added, "And I have been observing and recording day after day for over four hundred years, according to the solar calendar."

"You're saying, sir, that for four hundred years you have been coming in here?"

"Yes."

"May I ask why?"

"Of course, Palmiro. I want you to know what I have been working on during all these extraordinary years the fates have allowed. I have been recording the radio wave frequencies of galaxies and their observable stars. I have been building a kind of inventory of the universe, a data-base of what might be called signature tunes of the cosmos. Let me show you."

He took him over to the holograph screen which was covered in globes, planes, axes, letters and numbers. "Before the storms destroyed our world, scientists had succeeded in creating an increasingly sophisticated three dimensional map of the known universe. See here..." And he twisted the space with his fingers, and it changed orientation. He made a flicking movement and it rushed sideways into an entirely different quadrant. He pushed it slightly and it plunged down into a vast abyss of new objects and surfaces.

"Each of the objects on this map is a source of radio signals and other wavelengths of the spectrum. Over these long years I have gone on great quests throughout the universe, researching and analyzing these signals."

Palmiro was astounded. "You have been assembling a record of signals from across the whole universe?"

"Yes, that is exactly right." Perhaps for the first time in their

267

acquaintance Adorno smiled. A kind of smile at least. "But it's what happens to the information, how it may be used, that's what's really important. For that reason I eventually narrowed my researches to one galaxy, Andromeda. I decided it was this spiral galaxy, a relatively close neighbor of a trillion stars, which exactly suited my purpose."

Adorno's eyes were no longer hooded. They had abandoned their hollows and were now poised and bending like hawks, directly and forcefully on Palmiro. Palmiro was unnerved and for the moment his concern for Pascale was driven from his head. He repeated Adorno's last statement hypnotically, as a question: "Andromeda suited your purpose?"

Adorno continued to fix him with his stare, a man savoring his secret before the moment when at last he must reveal it. He said, "There is one more thing to show you. Come with me."

He led his pupil out of the radio telescope room, with the security door clicking shut behind them. They continued along the glaring white corridor a dozen or so meters to where it suddenly came to an end at a further large door. The entrance was controlled by another retinal scanning device and also this time a fingerprint reader. Adorno followed the steps and finally pulled an electronic key from a lanyard round his neck and poked it in a slot under the scanner. The door made a number of heavy clicks and swung open revealing well-lit steps leading downward. Palmiro had never seen his teacher more eager, so unlike his usual acerbic self. The stairs descended through a left turn into a big vault which at once felt cool and dry.

As they turned into the room Adorno stopped abruptly, almost making Palmiro stumble. His hands were slightly spread from his sides and this gesture, together with what presented itself before them, made Palmiro's hair stand on end. There was a large upholstered chair, like a throne, in the middle of the room, with a harness hanging on the back. Above it, attached to a huge cantilevered frame, was a metal half-sphere about four feet in diameter with thousands of transparent fibers shooting from its gleaming surface and a padded helmet-shaped niche suspended on its underside.

The transparent cables were swept up on either hemisphere into huge bundles which went snaking off behind and the whole thing was ensconced in layered shields or baffles, like a distended artichoke surrounding a great freak-haired cranium. At once it was obvious that whoever sat in the chair would have this monstrous skull attached. Around the spacious walls were high metal stacks filled with what looked like computers and where all the cables were plugged in. There was almost no sound and only one or two flickering activity lights gave any sign there was power connected to the machines. After a moment Adorno turned back and faced Palmiro. He seemed to be trembling and was still holding up both hands.

"It is the Hyperbrain. I built it many, many years ago, and a day hasn't gone but I dream of putting it to use. It is what sustains me, what makes my life worthwhile. But the time has come to share it with someone else, and it is to you I am according that incredible privilege. This machine is the first step toward the next human revolution, so much bigger than immortality. But forgive me, of course, you are confused. I have to slow down and explain."

He stepped over toward the chair and its suspended metal crown and his gaunt body seemed to express a deep reverence, almost as if there was someone already sitting there and he was advancing toward a king or a deity.

"I created this computer-brain interface by bringing together electronic imaging and neural signals. Electron waves are able to produce very precise mapping of brain activity. They can also be made to detect extremely minute changes in brain electrical current. I simply took the next step and made those waves capable of recording information from specific neural pathways, and in turn uploading information to those same neurons. An extremely fast array of targeted electron waves is able both to receive and impart signals to hundreds of millions of neural clusters in the brain. By transmitting to and from these individual clusters the brain's activity can be downloaded on an external computer, or alternatively it can be reconfigured by the computer. In effect my device allows total access to the internal structure of the brain."

Never in his wildest imaginings had Palmiro thought of anything like this. He knew that Adorno had his secrets, but in his mind they had remained of a theoretical nature, exotic formulae of biology or physics, nothing remotely approaching the extraordinary technical construct he was showing him now. But what was its purpose? The astronomical observations from the previous room and the proximity of the two projects suggested some kind of link. An insane thought was struggling to form itself inside him but Adorno beat him to it, putting it directly in words.

"The human brain has billions of neurons and the signaling permutations between them are virtually infinite. Initially I was going to take all the recordings of the universe and upload them to the Hyperbrain, but then I realized I would have to factor in the enormous distances of time and those would exceed simultaneous consciousness. Much better to take one galaxy in its own space and upload that, and that's what I decided, settling on Andromeda. The radio signals of the daughter of Cassiopeia can be programmed into a human brain and then that brain can bounce them back with its own distinctive signature added. If a human brain can 'think' all the wavelengths of the galaxy simultaneously, and its synthetic thought be beamed back to the galaxy, then effectively the galaxy will take on that person's identity."

Adorno drew his breath and released his resounding climax. "That person's mind will become Andromeda!"

Palmiro was caught between believing with full faith what Adorno was saying, and thinking his teacher totally mad. What was certain was Adorno believed it, and that he, Palmiro, was now an essential part of his plan. Suddenly his mind flashed back, to another dominating figure, his jailer Guest, and how he had been employed by him to hack into the refrigeration control system. What was it with these powerful men always trying to make him part of their schemes? But Adorno was continuing to speak and he had to listen.

"I know there are all sorts of questions going on inside you, not least whether what I am saying is too farfetched, in fact impossible. Yet think about it: the most significant function of the human brain that distinguishes it from animals, is language, the way we put together a world of artificial signs detached from immediate needs. Creating a verbal system is *the* human practice bar none. All I am doing is making the signals of the stars into the language of the brain, into its set of words. I will download Andromeda to the Hyperbrain and its subject, so the galaxy will become its language. It will speak the stars. It will sing them, with a trillion combinations and sequences. In all the resulting slight deflections in voltage the subject brain itself is represented, so when I broadcast the whole thing back into space the signals of the galaxy will become tuned to the Hyperbrain. Effectively it will reproduce its language, its consciousness."

Palmiro felt the urgent need to know where this was going in real terms. "Do you mind if I ask, sir, have you been able to test this device in any way?"

"Excellent question, Palmiro. That is the experimental attitude I have taught you. Yes, I have used the helmet on myself to record the key configurations used for language, and my researches were extremely productive. I discovered the language pathways, and how delightfully complex, almost infinite they are. It is these actual pathways I will program with the star signals. But as for a direct download of the signals themselves, no, that has not been tried."

"Why not?"

"Because one by one, or even a few together, they would mean very little. They all have to be downloaded at once if they are to create a universal language. And in that scenario I am not sure whether the test subject would survive the exercise. You understand, it will involve the scrubbing of a great deal of present memory, the stuff we need to get by every day. But for the purpose of the Hyperbrain, all that is necessary is the subject survive long enough to download everything and then the new brain configuration be sent to the radio transmitters. I, of course, am planning to be that subject. I am perfectly ready for this useless flesh to die but my electrical brain activity to continue at a cosmic level."

Palmiro's breath was taken away. He now grasped the full dimension of Adorno's vision. His master was willing to die for it, in fact his death seemed necessary for him to reach his goal. Palmiro also understood Adorno's contempt for Sarobindo. The two men both sought the same thing, an encounter with the universe. But the yogi had created a theater of dying while the scientist planned the real thing. Yet the nagging issue of his own part was now more pressing than ever: it was obvious he, Palmiro, had an insider role in the whole thing and he did not know why, although he was getting an uneasy sense of that too.

271

"Why are you telling me all this, sir?"

Adorno was gazing at the chair and its enormous headpiece in a kind of trance. It took him a moment to return to himself. "Ah, yes, I must not forget that—the reason I am showing you all this in the first place." And his eyes snapped back to their hawk-like fix on Palmiro.

"Well, the fact is an evolutionary leap for humanity cannot happen unless all agree to it. Evolution is always at the level of the species, a solitary evolution is a failed evolution. Therefore, I need people to know about what I am doing, for them to be taught and accept ultimately to follow me. But that is not going to happen so long as they are obsessed with their version of immortality."

His eyes were a lightning strike. Palmiro almost ducked protectively but he held his glance. Then, all at once, the interview was over.

"That is all. Please return to your studies and consider carefully everything I have shown you. Do not forget that you came to me expressing concern for your friend, Pascale. And most of all, do not neglect my breakthrough in biology."

He gestured Palmiro to the door and turned back toward the Hyperbrain, beginning to fiddle as if he were making adjustments. Palmiro turned away himself, making his way back up the stairs and out to the corridor. He traced his steps back to his study, finding his desk and collapsing into his chair. He fumbled for his notebook while he stared out the window. He could not believe what he had just witnessed.

9. SIERRA RIDE

Like Palmiro, Danny returned from the philosophers' banquet in a state of shock. But he lacked the guiding force of a patron like Adorno and his feelings were angry and confused. Cal, or Pascale as she now was called, for the first time seemed to have done something foolish. He could not work out what had gotten into her. She had seemed a little strange on the island but nothing like this: the way she had come right out with that stuff in front of everybody, it was asking for trouble. And the chaos at the end of the banquet, that was something new and really frightening. The crazy scientist had just made things worse and everyone had come down on Pascale. What would it mean for her?

Eboni tried to reassure Danny, confident that Jonas would smooth things out and everything would be fine. Within a couple of days, however, they got the news about Pascale's arrest and Danny was thrown into despair. He'd heard the stories about Magus and it did not take a genius to understand now there would be no way back. He and Eboni could not talk. He had always loved Pascale, probably more than anyone else, he just had not been good at demonstrating it. How would he ever again get a chance to show her? Over and over he wondered where Magus' place was, where they had taken her. He asked Eboni but she shrugged helplessly, waving in a southerly direction and saying that was all anybody knew, or wanted to know.

Eboni felt Danny withdrawing into himself, into his grief and anger, and she looked for a way to help him, for something that would keep his soul alive. She decided to introduce him to the horses. There were a number of quite large herds ranging free in the north-east corner of the Homeland. They were the stock from which all the personal horses of Immortals were drawn, the big hunters, the ponies, the racing horses. When people no longer wanted to keep them they would return them to the sierra, and when they were looking for a mount they would ride up to the high grasslands and simply rope one out from the herd.

Eboni had her own horse, which she stabled at the villa, a smart, quick Appaloosa. She used it for the round-ups, and also loved just riding for pleasure. The colony had a couple of quarter horses for people going up to the herds and she invited Danny to

Pascale's Wager

take one out. She saddled a well tempered bay and after a just a couple of sessions he was sitting the horse like a natural. It seemed only a few weeks before he was able to vault into the saddle and accelerate smoothly up to a canter, as if he'd been doing it all his life.

"I've got to get me one of these! I could do this all the time!"

"Sure, I'm planning on it. We'll go up to the sierra. You'll snag a good one. You'll be spoiled for choice when we get up to the grasslands!"

The planned trip would last three days and they packed the necessary supplies. They trotted along the paths and side roads, dressed in thicker cotton tunics and breeches, ready for a long trail. Reaching the downtown area they continued past it, across the racetrack and under the shadow of the massive Font Eterno. From there they struck up into the hills and by nightfall pitched camp looking down on the glimmering lights of the city and the mystic glow of the great semi-globe marking its eastern limit.

"Have you ever been to one of those things of Sarobindo's? You know, where he almost dies?"

"Yes, a few. Don't tell anyone but I always found them a little boring, except for all the people there. That's what made them fun."

"The next one's pretty soon, isn't it? Are you going?"

"If you want to go, I'll go."

One of the horses whinnied softly behind them, and the moon was cresting over the southern horizon. "I can't imagine anything better than this, Eboni. But ever since that banquet I know it's all wrong too. I've got to find out really what I think, about everything. So, yes, I believe I will be going."

Eboni pulled him close to her and drew a blanket up over them. "Don't worry, I'll be there too."

The next day they headed to the high valleys and caught sight of their first herd. It was led by a black stallion, with a band of subordinate males tagging along. The black regarded them calmly as they rode up. Eboni laughed, "This herd is always a good place to start. It's as if the stallion is looking after them for us, keeping them in trim until we come for one. What do you think about these?"

Danny was delighted with the whole thing, the tribe of horses

274

and the way it worked, but he did not see one he wanted. They continued west along the grasslands, skirting a tree-lined spur. In the distance they saw another group but as they moved closer it turned tail and retreated. "See that huge roan, that's Roland. He was one of the greatest racehorses of all time, but only the best jockeys could ride him. He's the undisputed king up here and has gotten used to his freedom. He and his brood are practically wild."

They rode up onto the ridge, threading a path through tall conifers until they came out on the far side.

The view was enchanting, a vast natural arena surrounded by tree-covered slopes and rising up behind ranks of high, treeless peaks. Framing the furthest peaks a rack of gray cloud gave a telltale sign they were nearing the borders of the stormworld, but here everything was a green and vivid peace. At the bottom, only a few hundred yards from the edge of the trees, there was a small herd grazing. Eboni and Danny came down the hill slowly, taking the opportunity to check the group. There were about twenty horses. The leader was a splendid Arabian gray, and almost immediately they'd seen it Danny said, "That's the one, that's the horse I want."

"That's right, go for the hard one. Well, this will be fun."

She unhitched her lasso and led the way out on to the meadow. The Arab's head went up and it did a half turn, its rich mane bouncing on its neck. The heads of the mares followed in a circle and they shifted their feet and whinnied.

"Easy, there, easy..." Eboni walked her horse slowly out toward the group, Danny behind her. The Arab was looking warily at the approaching riders. Suddenly it tossed his head and trotted away. It was followed by some of the band but in ragged fashion. Others just glanced at the riders in an uninterested way and returned to grazing.

"Hey, I remember now. That's no stallion, it's an alpha female. You still want her, Danny?"

"Sure, I do. Male or female, it's the one I want."

Eboni nodded and held out her hand for him to keep still. Then she moved in among the herd and stood there. The horses relaxed and the Arab did so too, turning her back to the rider to show she didn't care. Eboni edged the Appaloosa closer until it was just a few paces behind her quarry. Eboni was speaking soothingly. The horse looked around and at first didn't seem to mind, but suddenly she changed her opinion, flung up her head and bolted skittishly away.

"Damn! Playing hard to get! Danny, you circle up to head her off. I'm going to have to make a run for her."

Danny set out in a big loop then moved in closer, close enough so the Arab noticed. He too started talking, telling her how beautiful she was, how already he loved her like crazy. She seemed interested, pricking up her ears and regarding Danny appreciatively. All at once Eboni booted the Appaloosa into a charge, whirling her lasso over her head. Too late the Arabian caught the motion. She sprang to the right but Danny urged his horse forward to head her off. She could probably have outrun him but as she saw his direction she twisted left and then Eboni was on her. The lasso fell plumb over her neck and she was caught. Eboni yanked the rope around the saddle horn and quickly pulled the mare to a halt. She called Danny to come up next to her as she fished a halter out of a saddle bag. "Here, you seemed to be making an impression. Put this on her."

Danny dismounted and walked up to the captive horse. "My, my, you're beautiful! But you be good now! Let me put this on you and we'll be friends for life."

She snorted indignantly but did not back away. Her legs and flank were quivering, somewhere between anger at loss of independence and remembered pleasure at human contact. Danny stroked her nose, "Why would anyone want to leave a jewel like you out here in the hills, unless of course they thought you wanted the freedom. I kind of agree with that, but still I think you'd be happier with me." He slipped the halter onto her head and pulled the buckles in place. "Not sure what I'm going to call you, but whatever your name you're all mine now!"

With Danny holding the halter rope the two Immortals cantered back across the meadow to the tree line. From there they hiked to the top of the ridge. The Arab was clearly accustomed to a bridle and she co-operated without resistance, leaping sure-footedly over the rocks and fallen pines. She seemed almost happy now to be one of them. They camped near the top, close to a small spring, tethering the horses in a group with the Arab in the middle.

Danny and Eboni gathered brushwood to build a fire. They

sat with their backs against a log watching the stars come out between a ragged frame of branches. The shapes of the high peaks were still visible under a twinkling violet backdrop. An aromatic smell rose from the heart of the fire. Danny said, "I'm going to call her Stardust, that's the name for her."

He turned to look at her. "You'll carry me clear to the other side of Heaven, won't you?"

The Arab regarded him calmly and Eboni said, "I'm sure she's up for it. But heaven knows what you'll find when you get there!" And they both smiled and laughed, glad to be together, and with the horses, there in the high sierra.

10. CUTTING-EDGE RESEARCH

Palmiro carefully squeezed the bulb of the pipette between his finger and thumb, releasing a tiny drop of chemical into a dish. The liquid was a complex organic compound and the dish contained tissue from the lung of a mouse. He was working at a relentless pace, obeying Adorno's command that he continue with his study in the area of immortality. Without explanation Adorno had connected the research to Pascale. He had directed him to focus on this work immediately after reminding him of his friend and her situation.

Palmiro took the hint entirely at face value: if he was to help Pascale, it was essential to pursue his master's biological breakthrough. Alongside of this, the whole experience of seeing Adorno's lair and learning its secret purpose added urgency to his efforts. His mentor wanted immortality in outer space, but that meant he was going to die in Heaven, and he, Palmiro, was part of the plan. He would be the link between the scientist's vision and the rest of the Immortals. It did not matter whether he understood why or how, or whether he doubted Adorno or thought he was crazy, he was the one Adorno had told his ideas to, and there was no way out.

He could not untangle everything in his head, but he felt he was now on a strict timetable, one he was obliged to keep to in every waking moment. No longer did endless days of study and research stretch out before him. Rather, every minute's work was urgent. It was of paramount importance that he penetrate the physics of immortality in order to fulfill Adorno's dream of re-educating the Immortals.

He was working feverishly to finish his experiment and go on to the next. From articles Adorno had given him he had learned about a built-in function of cells which caused the collapse or death of certain cell elements. His work with the mouse tissue had shown it was possible to slow down this process or stop it entirely. By administering the correct chemical signals through the cell walls it was more or less possible to switch off these functions. However, that did not in itself make for an end to death, in fact it could lead to a very unwanted outcome, the cancerous growth of cells. It seemed essential in fact that cells die off and be replaced in turn by new ones. What was needed was the ability to promote an indefinite healthy renewal of all organ cells, a kind of everlasting regeneration. The signaling device would have to be highly complex, a piece of bio-software which surpassed in sophistication everything he had come across so far.

He had always known of course that the enzyme, as it was called, was already in the water supply and consumed by everyone in Heaven. That was the reason the water always had a very slight texture to it. Adorno had warned him against trying to analyze this too soon, telling him that without the necessary preparation he would never be able to understand it. Now he decided to look anyway. He prepared a drop with a fixing agent for molecular structure and placed it in the microscope chamber, adjusting the magnification and resolution. After several tries he thought he had identified Adorno's masterpiece, a fuzzy complex architecture that did not look like anything that he had seen before. He pored over it intensely, viewing its separate parts and trying to recognize any possible sequence. But there was nothing he could grasp onto. It was like an unknown object from deep space.

He fell back wearily in his chair and tried to think. He remembered Adorno had described a very accurate technique of establishing the structure of materials. It was a method of using X Rays to bombard the object and observe the unique pattern then created. But again it took training to manage the process correctly and he knew a crystalline form was needed. At the same time he really did not know how to extract the enzyme from the water without destroying it. What he needed was a pure solution of the enzyme and then perhaps he could produce a crystal form. With that he would get an accurate analysis and compare it against the computer data base. Everything was getting more and more complicated and he wondered what Adorno could be thinking, setting him this impossible, frustrating task.

Suddenly, he sat bolt upright. What had Adorno said on his way down the corridor to the Hyperbrain? That the workshops and labs to the side contained equipment, including chemicals? Wasn't it possible, even likely, that they still held a lot of the reagents from his original experiments? And if Adorno had revealed to him his most secret research, what possible objection could he have to him seeing these other items, too? All he had to

279

do was gather anything that looked like an organic solution, come back and produce a crystalline form and he would be on track to the information he needed.

Palmiro jumped from his seat and ran to the window of the laboratory. He could see no movement in Adorno's study opposite. He raced across the garden with its flower urns and fountains, and knocked on the study door. No reply. He opened the door, the room was empty. In three bounds he was across the floor and through the doorway that led to Adorno's laboratories, running down the first corridor, through the boot room and into the passageway connecting to the other buildings.

The first side door he tried led to what seemed like an all-purpose warehouse. It contained crates stacked to the ceiling, overflowing with books and articles and various tools and pieces of electrical equipment, circuit boards, processors, spools of wire and cable, but no chemicals. The second door led into a hi-tech welding and casting shop, with a couple of electrical furnaces and what looked like an overhead transport rail. On his third try he knew he was home. It was not actually a room but another walkway that ran at an angle to the first and led to a further door. It was the smell that gave it away, a faint but distinct odor of acids and bases, similar to his own workplace but staler and heavier. He ran to the end and pushed it open. In front of him was a long interior lit by just a pair of security lights. He cast around for the main switches and turned them all on. He saw ranks of bright steel shelves and freezers on either side and steel lab tables along the middle.

Everything was filled with complex testing apparatuses, along with jars, vials, bottles and boxes. He pulled open three or four of the freezer doors creating immediate clouds of vapor. On most shelves were tubes, dishes and boxes, stored every which way, everything bearing labels with the formulas covered with frost or faded by time and unreadable. What he was looking for could have been here but there was no clue to be had.

He pulled open more freezers on both sides of the workspace. Halfway down there were two heavy chests which took a brute effort to open. Inside there was not the usual chaotic jumble but neatly stacked rows of liter-sized steel canisters all marked with the same heavy stamp. Rubbing off the accumulated frost from a couple of them he could make out "Prometheus Labs" and the image of a naked man pulling fire from the sky. He knew almost certainly he had found what he was looking for. He picked up a crate filled with boxed compounds and slid them onto the floor, then lifted in four of the flasks. He shut the open freezers and shivering from their cold made his way back along the corridor with his haul. He carefully cracked the door to Adorno's study, but it was deserted just as before. Exiting the room he crossed the garden and arrived back in his own lab undetected.

It did not take him long to compare a defrosted sample from the flasks with his picture from the microscope. Zooming in he thought he could see what looked much like the same structure, simply in much denser concentration. He stored the flasks in his own refrigerator and then turned to his next task, creating crystals from the liquid. He had only made the simplest crystals before and this was much more complex. He had to follow instructions carefully and over several failed attempts. He struggled for days with the repetitive tasks, trying to establish the correct conditions for crystallization. As he repeated the steps mechanically again and again his mind began to move freely on other tracks and little by little a picture of what he was really doing came to him. It was as if he was walking through a gradually dissipating mist. He saw that he did not really want to know how the enzyme worked. That did not interest him. Instead he was seeking some simple but crucial information, something that would give him the ability actually to control this thing.

As his mind wandered on this track another thought struck him, like a thunderbolt. Just as with his old master, Guest, he was looking for a switch. This time it was for Adorno, but he was still seeking the power to turn something off. He was researching a technique to stop the enzyme working and it was Adorno who had given him his orders. What was it he had said? "I need people to know what I'm doing and to follow me. But it is not going to happen so long as they are obsessed with immortality." Adorno had clearly suggested an end to immortality, planting the thought in his head as the final goal of his research.

At that moment the realization made him want to give up entirely. How was it Adorno had so entered into his thinking that he was able to direct him almost unconsciously? At least with

281

Guest everything had been out in the open. The scientist, instead, had infected his mind with his wishes so that he had been working toward his master's goal without even knowing it. As he mechanically placed another drop of the liquid on the crystallization tray he could see the strategy behind it all. By not simply giving him the data Adorno had sent him down the narrow pathway of his own brilliant research, getting him to think of himself as a second Adorno, pursuing the unknown. That way his student would work as hard as he could to get results and at the same time would come round to accepting their final objective.

Palmiro felt horror, but at the same time there was a huge and terrible thrill. He had been initiated into something fateful and enormous and it was exactly what he had imagined when he first accepted his situation in the Homeland of Heaven. He was a Tepper who would learn the secrets of Immortals and become a pioneer in a way no one else had ever been before. He was very near being able to do that, to bringing about a cataclysmic change in immortal existence. And undeniably it was Adorno, the greatest scientist the world had ever known, who had led him to it. In his subtle and devious way Adorno had wanted him, believed in him, and brought him to the threshold of this amazing achievement. Strangely, he had never felt closer or more bonded to his teacher than at this moment.

Palmiro redoubled his efforts, placing the drops from the flasks on the little platform, sealing the crystallization chamber, calibrating the temperature, hoping for the crystals to form. Slowly he began to get results, one or two crystal formations, which he then placed in the X ray device to produce a reading. He pored over the data on the computer. In a matter of an hour his long efforts paid off: he found some very close matches and the compound began to reveal the secret of its chemical composition. All that was missing was the overall formula, and its absence from the journals would make sense if Adorno alone had devised it.

He guessed that part of the final compound was a powerful signaling ability which made sure the enzyme communicated with every cell in the body without fail. This had to be Adorno's major contribution, a way to make the restorative enzyme a foolproof messenger to the whole organic system. Palmiro at once recognized that if so all that would be necessary would be to disrupt this signaling somehow and immortality would collapse like a house of cards.

He threw himself even more fiercely into the study of the enzyme. If he was able to splice to it other chemical sequences there would be the possibility of disrupting or blocking the signals. This then would be his path of work, introducing the new reagents and observing the results under the microscope.

He had not seen Adorno for over thirty days. His mentor had totally disappeared after revealing the Hyperbrain. But Palmiro didn't really care. He was consumed with the incredible challenge the teacher had set him. More than once he felt he was talking to Adorno in his head, or thinking his thoughts, even that he was Adorno himself. Of course he knew this was not true, but the feeling had somehow become part of him as he pursued the endless research. Now at last he was closing on his quarry and the immense excitement of the chase filled his every moment, driving everything else from his mind. He had taken to sleeping in the laboratory on a couch and having his food delivered by Max. He was glued to the electron microscope watching the communication of the super-enzyme with living cells.

It was a fascinating process taking place in several steps that were always the same. Every time the cell reacted with the enzyme molecule it would seem almost to quiver and vibrate with new energy and life. He added chemicals that bonded to the surface of the enzyme to see if they could prevent the process. However, the communication between the cell and the immortality agent always seemed to override them, somehow ignoring the shield. Again and again he tried new reagents, staying up past midnight to produce just one more bonding, or getting up before the dawn because he had thought of another possibility. Nothing seemed to work, but he did not give up.

One late afternoon he was sitting at the microscope keeping an eye on the latest combination. He was watching the slow tango of the enzyme and the cell, and as always he was hoping for it to trip on the alien factors he had put in there. Suddenly, a thrill ran through his body and his heart began to pound. Something absolutely amazing was happening. At first it seemed that the interaction of the cell and the molecule had succeeded as always, that the cell had absorbed the enzyme. But then there seemed to be something different. The cell did not seem to quiver with life but to droop and lose its shape. After a moment the whole cell broke apart and clearly died, and then the most astonishing thing appeared. As the cell broke up small pod-like pieces burst from it and proceeded quickly to enter new healthy cells and at once the same process was repeated. He was used to the formation of new cells through splitting but that normally took over an hour to happen. Now it was as if someone was taking a saw and cutting through the cell in seconds, releasing the attacking organisms.

It was a multiplying explosion, the creation of a whole new race of agents that moved directly to destroy other cells. He flinched and recoiled from the microscope, as if this thing was about to attack him physically. Gingerly he put his eyes back to the viewer and he could see everything continuing to happen, a terrible expanding army was on the move. He had no idea how it had happened or what the body would do to cope. It seemed clear that the process was so rapid it could easily overwhelm the immortality effect in an individual organism. He had created a catastrophe: instead of discovering a way to prevent the enzyme working, he had turned it into an agent of its own destruction.

He was in a state of shock, but he knew he had to treat this thing with the utmost respect, to contain it, but also to preserve it. After sitting there for a few moments he got up and prepared a culture dish with more of the original liquid. Putting on rubber gloves and opening the viewing chamber, he carefully tipped the sample into the dish and then sealed it airtight. He put the tray into his fridge, threw his gloves in the trash and left the building. It was almost dark.

He returned to his annex and immediately downed half a bottle of wine that was sitting there on the counter. He pulled off his cotton tunic and plunged in the shower, remaining under the warm downpour for thirty minutes. Already half asleep he stumbled to his bed and collapsed unconscious for several hours. In the middle of the night, in a single moment he was awake, staring blindly at the ceiling. The exploding army of cells marched across his vision, a terrifying monster that only he knew. He gazed at this thing that he had released into the world.

The true face of nature, he thought. It is the world of the storms, simply at the microscopic level, and what is the barrier that can be created against it? The refrigeration zone and the wretched life of the Teppers serve no purpose. Heaven itself is defenseless. The philosophers and Sarobindo, they have no idea. They think they have everything perfectly in order and can look at each other and hear their voices speaking stupidities forever. Adorno was right, they are children playing at immortality. He felt an overwhelming, astonishing sense of power. He held onto it and it held onto him. He was a creature transformed.

Right there and then he seemed to make up his mind. He did not know exactly what he would do, but he was certain he would do something. It was inevitable given everything that had happened to him, everything he knew. Yet there was one last task he had to complete before he threw the switch. He had to find Pascale and set her free. He sat up on his bed and realized abruptly he was suffering a splitting headache. He stumbled out to the kitchen and found pills Adorno had provided for just these occasions. Downing four he returned to bed. Very shortly after he fell asleep.

11. DETECTIVE WORK

Danny took to riding Stardust around Heaven. He would rise early, pack food and drink, saddle up and leave. He had no particular plan. He simply felt happier to be on the move with Stardust. And she loved it too. She got used to him arriving in the early morning for the daily outing, pricking her ears up and knocking the stable door with her hooves. He would bring her a treat, an apple or carrot, and she would munch away and look at him out of the corner of her eye as he cinched the saddle. Then they would head off, a pair of outlaws somehow within the law.

At first he had no direction to follow, simply wandering wherever fancy took him, or his horse. But little by little a pattern began to form, either in his mind or in Stardust's he could not be sure. He was beginning to get a clearer idea of the geography of Heaven, of how the land lay, from the scrub desert in the western corner, through the steady rise of the broad central plateau, up to the encircling hills in the north, and then back again to the southern edge where the hills broke away into a chaos of canyons. As he went on it was increasingly evident that he and his mount were mapping the territory, getting to know it, progressively moving through its divisions from east to west, north to south. He was getting to know where all the colonies were, area by area, and how the terrain folded and unfolded around them. He was becoming acquainted with the landscape of Heaven.

People did not take much notice of him, especially if he passed by only once, a lone rider drifting through the endless day of Heaven. At the Zoo Colony Eboni covered for him, delighted her idea of getting him a horse had worked and hoping this long soaking up of the sights of Heaven would bring him to a better place. Yet Danny was really nowhere near finding inner tranquility. Something continued to drive him forward, and when he had come close to knowing all the populated areas of Heaven, he turned in a different direction. He and Starlight began to wander south into the canyons, to the forbidding badlands below.

As they ventured down the corkscrew track from the plateau he rapidly discovered how alien this terrain was. Either the ravines were roasted by the sun and their heat unbearable, or the shadows filled them and they became cold and threatening. Once or twice he had mistaken the route and only found his way back because he gave Stardust her head and trusted her to get him home. One day on his second or third trip down he pulled Stardust up and stood there under the fortress walls with the desert juniper and cactus sprouting from cracks and tiny ledges. Every surface was baking and the light sliced the air like a hatchet. He shielded his eyes and admitted aloud to himself that he was looking for his sister here in this wilderness. "Cal, Pascale, whatever your name is, you're down here somewhere, I'm sure of it. What do you say, Stardust?"

The Arab responded to his voice and tossed her splendid white head in front of him.

"I take that as a yes. But how are we ever going to find her? Sure as heck, they left no signposts down here."

He looked up and down the broiling corridor with its maze-like breaks, angles and dead-ends: and he decided. "We need help, Stardust, we can't do this on our own. I think we have to go talk to someone and I think it has to be that guy, Jonas. He's definitely got my sister's back. And if anyone has a chance of knowing where this God-forsaken prison camp is, it's going to be someone in the History Colony like him."

He pulled the horse around and headed back along the harsh, steep track to the plateau. It always took hours to get back and horse and rider were as usual spent at the end of the climb. They both needed to rest. He decided they would ride out to see Jonas the next day.

When he got back to the colony Eboni had news which interrupted his plans.

"That guy you knew back in the North, the one with Adorno, he came over today. Palmiro, isn't it? He wants to talk. He said he'd be coming back tomorrow."

"Wow, that's a first! I can't imagine what he'd want with me. Did he say?"

"No, just that he needed to talk. He looked terrible. Like he hadn't slept or eaten properly for weeks."

"Well, something must be up. He's never wanted to talk to me before. I guess I better hang around for him then."

When Palmiro turned up the following day even Eboni's description wasn't enough to prepare Danny. He was used to

287

Palmiro having a strange look, but now it was as if he had become a different person. He had lost weight and his face was drawn and unshaven, but it wasn't just that. Unlike his previous impatient and distracted attitude he was now controlled and focused. Danny was actually impressed. He thought perhaps Adorno had really helped him. As they talked he felt Palmiro seemed to have moved beyond all of them. It was similar to the experience of talking with Pascale, but different again.

"It's good this activity of yours, Danny, horse-riding. It's a healthy way to spend time and will prove very useful. What I need to talk to you about is your sister, Pascale. I am sure you're just as unhappy about the decision of the authorities as I am. Perhaps you have actively considered doing something to help her. I would like to know what it is, and whether I can assist you in any way."

The matter-of-fact tone of the question—which just happened to be against the whole way of thinking in Heaven— astonished Danny. All he could do was agree, and say, just as matter-of-factly, that he had been spending time looking for Pascale down in the canyons.

"But they're impossible to penetrate if you don't know where you're going. They're hot and grueling and it's terribly easy to get lost. I was thinking actually of going to ask Jonas for help."

"Actually that's a good idea. Jonas loves her and will want to help. If he knows anything he will definitely tell us. But why do you believe the canyons are the place where the colony for anti-socials is?"

"Well, people generally point in that direction and anyway that's where we ended up, Stardust and me. We trekked all over Heaven and I never had the slightest feeling she was anywhere around. It's only when we went down to the canyons, I just got a really strong sense she was there."

"I would trust your judgment, Danny. But if she is down there I want to go with you to find her. I also will need to ride a horse. Do you think that's possible?"

"Sure it is. We have horses here for new riders. That's just how I started!"

Palmiro said he wanted to begin right away. Danny took him out to the stables and introduced him to the bay. He tied the saddle on and helped Palmiro mount up. He led him out behind Stardust so he could get used to the motion. Palmiro kept asking him questions, about the correct way to sit, where to put his knees, and what were the signals to give to the horse. Danny answered his questions and little by little Palmiro relaxed so he was able to take the reins and walk on his own. Danny told him to advance to a trot and he did so, bouncing around in an ungainly fashion but basically staying upright. After that Palmiro pulled up and said this was enough for the moment and they should take the car and go visit Jonas.

"You want to go now, with me?"

"Yes, if you don't mind. I would like to get Pascale's situation resolved as soon as possible."

They stabled the horses, cleaned up, and took refreshments of tea and bolillos. Then Palmiro drove his car to where Jonas lived. The journey took over two hours, winding along the foothills with their clustered oak and mesquite and the colonies in the watered folds surrounded by plantations and crops. On the way Palmiro asked Danny how he had adjusted to the experience of Heaven and immortality.

"What do you mean, adjusted?"

"You know, what are your feelings about being here in Heaven?"

"No one asked me that question before, not even Eboni. I suppose the idea is you have to love it. The truth is, I was loving it, before the thing with Pascale happened. Since then I've been in a kind of dream, waiting for something else to happen."

"What do you mean? What are you waiting for?"

"I don't know. It's just a feeling. It can't be right that Pascale is locked up forever. And for what? What did she do wrong? I suppose that's it really. I'm waiting for something to happen for Pascale. What about you? What do you feel about Heaven?"

"I don't think I've ever been in Heaven, if you see what I mean. This place has always been the same to me as the Northern Homeland. I see no real difference."

"You've got to be kidding. They're about as different as they could be. Don't you remember the vicious cold, and those miserable TEPs we lived in? And all the stupid religion?"

"I've not forgotten a thing. But you have forgotten who put all that together, who created it. The same people who live here, the pioneers, the Immortals."

"But they had to do it. There was no other way. You have to admit that."

"There's always another way."

Danny looked over at Palmiro. "Maybe. But you came here, didn't you? You got the one-way ticket to immortality."

"Did I? Perhaps it's not such a one-way ticket."

"Talking like that, you know, you're beginning to scare me."

Palmiro showed no reaction and he continued to stare ahead at the road. They were now very close to Jonas' colony and they dropped their conversation. As they drew into the compound at the back of the villa the place looked deserted. They got out of the car and knocked on the main door, but there was no reply. They went around the side of the house, hallooing to attract attention. At last Masharu appeared at French windows inside an arbor. She was annoyed and suspicious.

"What is it? Why are you shouting like this?"

"We're looking for Jonas," Danny replied.

"He's not here. He's gone for a walk. Who are you?"

"I am Pascale's brother, Danny. And this is Palmiro. Which way did Jonas go?"

"I hope you are not going to create any more trouble for him. He's had more than enough." All the same she pointed, "He might be out on the hill somewhere. He spends a lot of time out there."

She was gesturing to the front of the house to where the hill fell away among rows of vines surrounded by chamise and stands of oak. They made their way out onto the slope, over the ocher ground. Danny kept calling, "Hey, Jonas, are you out here?"

A white robed figure appeared a couple of hundred yards away close to a buttress of rock, looking up at them. They hurried down, leaping in their sandals across the hillside. The figure stood there waiting and as they got closer they could see it was certainly Jonas. If Palmiro had changed, the historian was a mere shadow of his former self. His face was storm-washed and his body lacked any vitality. He did not raise a hand in greeting and his expression did not alter to greet them. Danny was ahead but he waited for Palmiro to catch up. For a few seconds they all three stood there. Finally Palmiro spoke.

"Jonas, we've come to talk with you."

He did not reply. He continued looking at them, expressionless. Danny went up to him and put his hand on his arm. "Are you O.K., buddy?"

The touch seemed to revive Jonas, as if out of a dream. "Oh, yes, Danny, Palmiro, it's good to see you."

"How've you been?"

"Well, not quite myself. Which is really not the thing to say in Heaven, is it? I spend a lot of time out here, sitting under my rock, trying not to think at all." And he indicated a space around in front of the rock, a kind of natural seating overlooking the valley.

Palmiro stepped in, putting his face directly in front of Jonas.

"Well we need you to start thinking, and thinking for yourself. We want to rescue Pascale from wherever they've taken her and we're asking for your help."

Jonas' eyes twitched. He was shaken by Palmiro's challenge; but it made him focus. "Rescue Pascale, you said. Ah yes, that's right. That's what we'd hoped. But how, how? It's impossible. Even if we could get to her, then where would we hide her? No colony in Heaven would take an anti-social."

"Let us worry about all that. Just tell us how we can find her."

Jonas backed away from the two of them, throwing his hands down in a pathetic gesture.

"I don't understand what you're talking about. It's all too terrible, terrible. Pascale is gone and we can't get her back."

Again Danny stepped forward, this time placing himself between Palmiro and Jonas. "Listen, Jonas, I love Pascale just as much as you, and I know you love her a great deal. But I'm not sitting out here under a rock dreaming about her. I really intend to find her, come what may. What's more I know she's down in the canyons somewhere. I got that figured out on my own. But I could wander down there for years and never find her. I just need some kind of map or at least a key direction."

Jonas squinted at Danny and a light in him seemed to flicker. "Yes I think that's right. Everyone has always said that Magus' place was down there to the south... So you really do intend to find her? It's cruel to raise hopes that go nowhere, don't you think?"

"Come on Jonas, help us! Do you have any clue at all where she might be?"

291

Jonas shook his head, seeming to stall. "You are asking me to go against the whole code of Heaven, everything it was founded on. An Immortal does nothing to lessen the perfection in Heaven. To plan actively to help anti-socials is to place chaos inside bliss. If I help you now I am as good as an anti-social myself."

Once more Palmiro intervened. "Of course you are. Did you ever think there was any other way? Now are you going to help us or not?"

Jonas had really been making a speech, working his way through his deepest convictions. He was turning his thoughts, on the way to a final decision, but Palmiro's cutting across jump-started the engine. He flinched one more time and continued, "However, I find myself compelled to a feeling I do not recognize among Immortals. Therefore, actions that will not be understood by them may well be close behind. So, yes, I suppose I am an anti-social and, yes, I do wish to help you."

Danny grinned broadly, "Way to go, Jonas, I knew you'd come through. So what can you give us?"

Jonas bit his lip, staring at a point in the middle distance. Finally he looked up, "I do not know the whereabouts of the colony you seek but I can offer one clue. The residents there drink the same water as the rest of us, so there must be a water pipe or conduit to carry it. The water-treatment plant lies in the south-east of Heaven, not far from the Plaza of the Fountains. It should be possible to search for a line headed out into the badlands. It may well be buried some of the way, but if it crosses a canyon it will have to come down one wall and up the other side. If you look in the south-east quadrant and if you're attentive you should find it. Having found it there is then a direction to follow. There, I have told you!"

Danny cried, "Attaboy! Why didn't I think of that?"

Palmiro nodded approvingly, "A simple idea but effective." He at once wanted to move on. "Danny, I can take you back now. On the basis of Jonas' plan you can begin searching tomorrow. If you need my help I'll come with you, but I think I would slow you down. The moment you have a lead I will come with you then. It is absolutely imperative we get to Pascale and bring her out."

"Dead right, Palmiro. I'll be on Stardust first light tomorrow and I'll let you know directly I get anything. Jonas, we've got to go now. Thank you! You've given us the code to unlock this thing. When we find Pascale we'll have to hide her somewhere, and we'll let you know."

Jonas felt the ground shift violently under his feet. "That would be incredible. Yes, please let me know."

On the way home Danny told Palmiro that back in the North he would never have dreamed of being on the same team with him. Now he was and he felt it was working very well. Still there was something nagging at the back of his mind and he had to get it out. It seemed to him at the philosophers' banquet Palmiro had tried to push attention away from himself onto Pascale, and that had brought disaster on her. Didn't he feel sorry in any way?

Palmiro was caught off balance. He actually stammered replying. "I...I didn't know that was going to happen. That was a mistake on my part."

"But are you sorry?"

"I'm not sure what you mean. I regret that it happened that way. There hasn't been a day since but it's been somewhere in my mind, to reverse the events of that day. And it's exactly what I'm trying to do now. If that is being sorry, then yes."

"I was thinking of something else, a feeling about yourself, not just about the thing that happened. Do you know what I'm saying?'

"No, I don't, Danny, but I will tell you this. Nothing like that is going to happen to me again."

Danny changed the subject. "You know Sarobindo, that guy your boss attacked at the banquet, which was the real reason everyone got stirred up?"

"What about him?"

"Well, he's doing his thing at the Font Eterno pretty soon and Eboni and I are going. I thought I should see what all the fuss is about. You want to come with us?"

"I don't think so. The whole thing seems like a bad joke. But you never know. Thanks for asking me."

PART FOUR

1. PITCHING TENT

The morning light in the north canyon fell softly on the tops of the Ranch cookhouse and cantina next to it. In the shadow below nothing was moving except a small dog nosing around the edge of the chicken coop hunting for scraps. As the dark peeled away from the canyon walls it was possible to make out a change in the scenery. At about thirty feet from the steps of the mess hall something like an encampment could be seen, a haphazard collection of poles sunk in the ground with coverings stretched across the tops and some of the sides. In the middle was a table made up of planks and trestles and scattered around were boxes and stumps for seats. The colors of the cloths were faded but the effect was brightened with sprays of flowers tied to some of the poles, rock daisies, poppies, marigolds.

Opposite the desert tent about another thirty feet away, toward the junction of the canyons, there was a smaller more symmetrical structure, a kind of pavilion with white canvas and a single table and chair. Together these tents created a very different feel in the harsh setting of the canyon. They were almost festive and suggested a sense of movement, as if everyone was about to begin a journey, even if there was really nowhere to go.

Farther up the canyon the livestock were getting restive, awaiting their daily trip to pasture. The two cowboys appeared, ambling along from the men's cabin and plunking themselves down under the tent. A moment later the woman who drove the cattle arrived and joined the men. A door from the cookhouse opened and someone brought out a tray with a pot of coffee, cups, bread and eggs, placing it on the trestle. The little group of cowhands took their breakfast as the wall of beaten gold above their heads descended toward them.

***

The day after Pascale's arrival the first thing she did was go to the water trough and thoroughly wash and rinse the denim dress and blanket she had been given. Once she had hung them out to

294

dry she went to find Zena and tell her she was ready for the promised tour. Zena in her unemotional way seemed pleased and led her out along the canyons. She was right that there wasn't anything to see, as Pascale had already discovered almost all of it for herself, but there were a couple of things which she did not know about. Zena mentioned the canyons went on for quite a few miles before they got to the gates that kept everyone locked in. And she pointed out the steps cut into the north canyon wall a hundred yards down from the men's cabin. Pascale asked her if she had ever been up there and Zena said she hated heights but others had done it.

Pascale said she'd come back to climb it some other time but first of all she wanted Zena to introduce her to people, so she could say hello to them properly. Zena's face closed down and she walked away. Pascale ran after.

"I know this isn't the way things are done and I'm sorry. But at least tell me the names of the people I already met. How about that woman on the porch with you last night?"

Zena did not reply.

"Come on, what harm is there in telling me? If I say hello to her she might come for a walk, too!"

After a moment finally Zena said, "Katoucha."

"That's great! And the man who was there?"

Again after a moment, "Ravel."

"What about the guy with the crippled feet?

"Orwell."

"And the great big man who helps him?

"Zoltan."

"And the lady who runs the cattle?"

"Magada."

"Fantastic! I'm going to talk to all these people, even if they don't talk to me. And then we're going to do something. Not sure what but we'll do something to make everything better. "

Pascale spent the next days finding opportunities to introduce herself to the people whose names she had discovered. She followed the routine of canyon life, from coffee, eggs and rolls in the morning, through division of chores for those willing to work, to rest in the heat of the afternoon, and then the evening meal. She learned that as well as the cattle the colony produced food from fruit orchards and corn plots located in a branch canyon with its own water line. These places provided work, but it was mostly for just two people, a man and a woman named Louis and Joanne who seemed to treat the orchard and fields as their personal preserve. It was more or less that way too with the cattle drivers. So if you wanted something to do you were restricted to helping around the kitchens and cantina. However, the people she had met the first day never wanted to work in any of these places, so she was able to find them and talk to them easily.

She sat next to Zoltan and Orwell, greeting them by their names and just keeping them company. They ignored her completely but every now and again she would make a remark about the color of the canyon walls, a gecko that showed itself, or telling the time of the day from the line of the sun on the cliffs. She would offer to bring them drinks of water or tell them little stories about the Northern Homeland, about her favorite holograms or even little bits about her rescue of Palmiro. She would leave them then and go back to be with Katoucha, Ravel and Zena, doing the exact same thing. Zena would reply to her greeting but the others ignored her just as the two men before. She was undeterred and for days kept up the routine of communicating in any way she could.

One day she brought a bunch of wild flowers and placed them in a glass on the table on the men's porch. Zoltan stopped rubbing his beard and looked at the flowers. "Poppies," he said slowly.

"Yes, you're right, they're so pretty, don't you think?"

Zoltan said, once again, "Poppies..." and that was all.

But when Pascale finally got up to leave he said, "Where are you going?

She sat back down again and told him that she was going to the Women's cabin where she also sat and talked with people. Zoltan said, "You should stay."

"The women will be waiting for me and I have to go back. But I am happy for the invitation, Zoltan, and I will come back first thing tomorrow."

She said goodbye but he didn't respond and the rest of the day his remark lingered with her. That night as she lay in her bunk wearing her shift with her denim dress as a pillow she thought of a solution. She would make a common meeting place, a kind of marquee with poles and blankets, anything she could find. It would be a new space and she was sure people would be drawn to it. She would be able to keep company there with all those who wanted it and not go back and forth between the cabins. The thought of it gave her a happy feeling and she fell asleep thinking that her life in the canyons was perhaps even becoming something beautiful.

The next day when she went to Zoltan and Orwell's she announced her plan. She said she wanted them to help her set up the tent but first she would have to scavenge round for materials. Once she had enough assembled she would come back for them. She asked them to be her supporters in the scheme. For the first time Orwell's eyes flickered, and Zoltan nodded, "We'll help."

She found staves and poles behind the corral and digging around on the floor of the Women's cabin she gathered a half dozen unclaimed blankets. She asked Zena where there were tools and Zena pointed around behind the cabin. "Back there."

She discovered a sagging-roofed shed hidden under the canyon wall with a jumble of tools on the floor. She selected a pick, a bar and a club-hammer and dragged them back to the porch where Zena and the others were now watching her keenly. She explained her plan and told them that Zoltan and Orwell from the Men's cabin were going to help. She invited them to join in too. Zena grinned and got up. "Should be interesting."

Katoucha cast her one eye past Pascale's shoulder and didn't speak. Ravel said, "We'll visit when you're done."

With Zena's help she brought the blankets to the trough where they washed them, beating them energetically on a flat stone, then hanging them to dry. They went back and dragged the rest of the equipment to her chosen spot, in front of the cantina. Then they went to get the men. As always, Zoltan carried Orwell and between them Pascale and Zena carried a chair. When they got to the site Zoltan sat Orwell in the chair and then got to work digging holes and planting poles. It was about midday when they went to get the blankets and spread them across the top of the poles, establishing the first bit of shade in the middle of the canyon. They placed Orwell on his chair in the middle and stood around clapping and laughing.

Fifty yards up at the junction of the canyons the front door to the cabin flew open and Magus in his boots, pants and tee came striding down towards them. He was yelling, "What the hell do you think you're doing? Take this thing down immediately."

Pascale went out to meet him, placing herself between the Ranch governor and the tent. "Sir, there is no rule that says we cannot put up a tent."

"Don't quote rules to me. I am the rule!"

"In which case you can just as easily give permission for our tent as refuse it!"

"That's far too smart-mouth, lady, for your own good. Just shut up, and take the tent down. You there!" And he gestured to the others. "Take that contraption down at once!"

Pascale turned to them too and held a hand out at them, stopping them as they automatically began to obey. She turned back to Magus.

"Listen, sir, this place is intended for the health and pleasure of all. If you want we will build you a tent too, separate from this one. You can come out and sit here in comfort, observing us, taking your meals too, if you wish. Everyone will know that you are in charge."

Magus was attracted despite himself. The idea actually had appeal. He had never really been publicly on display before, like an emperor. And in regard to this upstart newcomer it would be a means to an end: all he had to do was appear, and watch and wait for an opportunity to humiliate her. Yet he could not give in too easily. "I'm not sure what your game is, lady. Perhaps you don't realize how bad I can make it for you down here. But, OK, first build my tent and then, if I like it, I'll think about yours."

"That's wonderful, sir! But if we are to do a good job for your tent we need the best materials. Will you give permission to look for things inside the Ranch store?"

Magus was caught. For his own status and prestige he had to agree. "OK, OK, just show me exactly what you're taking."

He stalked away not sure whether to be pleased or angry.

So it was that Pascale made her desert tent. She let herself into the store with Zena and Zoltan and they discovered pine poles and even a canvas tarpaulin. They were also able to find shears, thick needles and strong cotton thread. Pascale said it would be better to show Magus when they had made the best use of the materials, and so they set to work directly. At first they didn't know what they were doing, but Zena showed herself an intuitive seamstress and soon she was cutting and shaping and giving directions to everyone else. Attracted by the activity two or three people came out of the cantina to observe, standing around watching as poles were driven in place and the canvas covering took shape. After a day or so watching two of them joined in, Alaqua and Eliot, both grubby and overweight but excited now by an activity never witnessed before at the Ranch.

It wasn't long then before the private pavilion was complete and Pascale and Zena walked down to Magus' cabin to knock on his door and inform him. Koyo came to the door and said Magus was busy and would come and inspect the tent when he had time. But again Pascale did not wait. She returned directly to finishing the big communal tent. The activity was now more eager than ever, with more poles going up and the remainder of the canvas being used for the central portion. The continued work on the main tent brought Magus out within the hour, furious that his order had been ignored. Again he was shouting before he got there. And again Pascale was quick to intervene.

"I clearly told you I would look at my tent first and then decide about yours!"

"But, sir, we were sure you would approve once you saw it. Look how fine we have made it!"

There was already a chair inside, an antique dining room piece that someone had found in the store loft. Magus despite himself looked impressed but he was not appeased.

"You have gone against my orders and I want this thing taken down stat. Get it down, now!"

"But what if we did, what would you say about your own tent? You would judge it a fine thing and then have to give permission to put the communal tent right back up again!"

The confrontation between the Ranch boss and the engaging newcomer was rapidly drawing a crowd. People in the kitchen and mess hall who had observed the growing structure of the tents and the initial encounter with Magus were pushing out the door to witness this one. Magus normally never had to impose his will publicly. If he beat anyone it was unobserved, and for the rest he relied on the deep paralysis of soul that possessed all Immortals

299

living in the canyons. That is, until now.

He was raging inside, but he held himself in check. This young woman had been able not only to survive the shock of coming to the canyons but was even now attempting to change them. In an ugly way he was fascinated. He found himself wishing not to stop her outright, but to wait for an opportunity to crush her in as public and humiliating a fashion as possible—and then deal with her privately. So, yes, coming here to his private booth to observe the show would be entertaining, for, as sure as one day followed the other, the occasion for bringing her downfall would present itself. "I don't give a damn about any of your contraptions. Your logic is flawed but I agree to accept it. Your tent may stay in place for now, but"—and he placed himself within inches of Pascale's face—"I warn you, it will never be safe to turn your back anywhere in these canyons!"

He turned and swaggered away. For a moment Pascale stared after him. Then she faced around to her helpers and clapped her hands. "We have permission! Let's finish the tent!"

That day the communal tent was completed and a table brought out of the cantina to set near the middle. The crew of helpers found boxes and logs to use as seats and some of the remaining blankets were spread on the ground. At once they took ownership, sitting around, looking satisfied with their work, and making remarks about how this would be a good place to eat meals. They seemed surprised and embarrassed at the sound of their voices conversing, but also pleased and proud, like schoolchildren trying out a foreign language. As promised, Ravel came down with Katoucha and she took up pole position at the table her good eye leveled across it as if she were already the hostess of the party. No one minded, rather they were even more impressed with their own work, having enticed the queen of the Women's cabin to abandon her porch.

That evening Zena and Pascale brought their meal out to eat in the tent and Zoltan did the same for himself and Orwell. As the shadows covered the awning the blankets and the ground retained the heat for a while and the little group lingered in the half light. Finally Pascale picked up the plates and brushed the table down. She took the dishes into the cantina and then asked Zena to walk back with her to their cabin. As they passed Magus' cabin there was no light in the windows. Both women tensed and shivered, but they arrived at their own place safely. Pascale asked Zena whether she would get up with her at first light because she wanted to climb the cliff. Zena laughed, "I knew you'd not be able to resist that for long. Sure, we'll go tomorrow. But I'll stay below and watch!"

2. WILDERNESS CAMP

The water-treatment plant was not far from the Zoo Colony where Danny lived. It was further south and west in the low hills beyond the Font Eterno and it only took an hour on horseback to get there. Danny made a visit on Stardust the day after the meeting with Jonas. He found a mile-long sparkling oval reservoir fed by streams diverted from the sierra. He'd passed it once before, but without investigating. This time behind the eastern wall he found the chemical treatment plant which supplied the immortality enzyme to the water. Everything was fully automated, with long storage barns, stainless steel silos, tanks, processing units, pipes and mixing chambers. Circling to the westerly side he found what looked like a main supply flowing into an underground tunnel with a heading to the north-west, in the direction of the majority of the colonies. Continuing around farther he found a small surface pipe, this time running south. On Jonas' hypothesis, this had to be it.

He nosed Stardust along the side of the steel pipe as it crossed a dusty perimeter and cut through a ridge. At the top of the rise, Danny could see the land fall away in a long pleasing sweep past a cluster of villas surrounded by fields of alfalfa. He wasn't sure which colony this was but, more important, he could see the pipe head in that direction, disappearing into the ground. It was clear this was the water source for the colony and the question now was where it went after that. He took the road past the cluster of buildings, looping round to the other side to the point where the track ran out. Here the land fell away more rapidly, covered with sage and straggling bunch grass. The surface was bumpy and cracked, with dips and rises running across his path, with brush in the washes and creosote bushes on the slopes. He could see no sign of the pipe but he judged it must follow the same line as the reservoir to the colony. He pushed Stardust on in the general direction and as he crossed the low rises he could see smudges of brown and shadow beyond and a smoky yellow tinge to the air. In half an hour he ran out of land and the stony ground in front of him suddenly plunged into thin air. There before him stretching to the horizon were the canyons, the badlands at the edge of Heaven.

He scouted the edge of the canyon looking for a point where

the water pipe might be visible as it turned downward. There were any number of depressions along the edge where it could have been laid, but there was no sign of a pipe. It could just as easily have been placed in a gulley several feet deep and then covered over. The only sure place to look would be from below. There was no other option then, he would have to find this canyon, the most northerly one, and ride along the bottom to see if and where the pipe descended.

He climbed down from Stardust and found a palm-sized rock. Carefully he tied his red bandana round the rock and then flung it out into the canyon as far as he could. He thought he heard it hit, but could not be sure. He gazed out over the serried ridges, to where he could see no further. They ran in a jagged pattern, some following the angle of the one below, roughly south-west to north-east and others cutting across from the south-east. The effect was a jumbled maze with some canyons coming to a dead end and others opening into a transverse or forming an oblique angle. As he knew from his previous explorations, it was horribly easy to get lost. This time at least he had some points of reference, but he would have to be very systematic, or his efforts would be wasted.

He remounted and together he and Stardust took a route along the top of the canyon. They were heading southwest and he knew ultimately he had to hit the main track down. He was hoping he would connect directly with the descent along this present canyon, but his hopes were dashed when abruptly it came to an end and the land was a mesa stretching south to another separate canyon. He would have to follow that one, or even another one farther south, and so on until he finally got to the way down. At the bottom he would then be obliged to double back to the north until he found the original canyon or the water pipe, whichever came first.

He could not begin today: he needed supplies for a long, demanding trek. He headed home to the colony and when he found Eboni he asked her for a notebook, in which he could map his exact route with all its twists and turns. The previous day, after he had gotten back from the visit with Jonas, he had told her about his plan. At first she was totally opposed and tried to dissuade him, but when she saw the purpose it gave to him something in her own soul was stirred. She decided not to stand in his way. Today she was even excited about it all and wanted to help. She went at once to find the notebook and handed it to him.

"When you get Pascale out you'll have to hide her somewhere. I'll support you with supplies, that kind of thing."

Danny hugged and thanked her. "Looks like this could be the beginning of a movement! But probably we shouldn't tell anyone else until we're sure we can trust them."

The next day Danny began his systematic search. He set out early to the point where he had left the mesa, then followed the land until he came finally to the main way down, the track he had always descended on before. He had mapped the blocked canyons in his book as best he could, but he could not be certain that he had copied everything as he could rarely see clear to the bottom. When he finally got to the canyon floor he started to work his way back to the east and north, following the line as best he could. He got as far as he was able that day and then returned once more to the uplands. The following day he headed straight to the last point of his search and continued on from there. If there was a branch canyon going to the north he would take it. If this was a dead end, he would retrace his steps and continue heading east. Wherever the canyon angled east he would stay with it until he could go north again.

In this way he continued, tacking east and north. All the while he was scanning the walls for any possible water pipe and keeping a keen eye out for his bandana. Observing the walls made him attentive to the way the canyons were formed, how sometimes the sides were less steep and there might even be a possibility of climbing to the top with Stardust. Perhaps he could go over an intervening mesa and not have to backtrack along the bottoms. Still at this point he was too nervous about losing his way, so he kept down below.

Each day his search brought him farther away from the plateau and he was stretching the day to its last rays of light. After three days of his threading the canyons he seemed to reach a final dead end. He sensed he had gone well past the point of the water-treatment plant and there was no way further north. He got down off Stardust and gave her water from the canteen pouring it in a leather bowl.

"What do you think, Dusty? I suppose this means we

overshot the pipe. It has to be toward the western end of one of the canyons. Some place we didn't look?"

The horse pawed the ground. "Glad you agree, but I reckon you also want to get back home before sundown."

He packed the canteen and bowl, climbed back on the saddle and set off at a smart trot, following the turns in his book exactly in reverse. He traveled smoothly but it was almost dark when he finally made the ascent to the plateau, climbing with Stardust on a lead rope in order to spare her and avoid the danger of a slip. As he struggled to the top he thought how much less exhausting it would be if he could stay down in the canyons a few days at a time. Yes, there were the dogs and coyotes, but if he could find some high ground protected by rocks, and perhaps light a fire, then he should be alright. His days down in the badlands had given him confidence and he felt it was time he took control of his story.

He told Eboni, "I think I'm becoming a canyon rat. I feel O,K, down there and I know I'll be safe. I want to bring supplies for a few days and have more time to finish the search."

Eboni laughed. She said, "I always have a feeling you'll be O.K. and if it will speed things up then do it. I'd be down there with you myself except people here would notice and ask questions. Tomorrow we'll put things together for a longer stay and you can leave before sun up the day after."

Thus Danny's day trips grew into a full expedition. Before first light he and Eboni brought everything to the stable and saddled up. He led the horse out of the yard and a short distance from the colony he mounted and rode away as the dawn was flickering in the east. He arrived at the last point of his search in the early afternoon. He headed back west but the canyon was a box at the other end too, so he had to double back south again until he found a further passage west. Effectively he was heading the other way along canyons which he had pursued in an easterly direction. He felt certain he would have seen his bandana or the pipe if he had passed them, so this was the only logical thing.

As he continued searching, he was also constantly on the look-out for a safe spot up on the mesas, at least somewhere on higher ground. He was now in a deep canyon running west and it was not coming to an end. He'd already checked out two dead-end northern brunches and still it kept going. He was well beyond the point-of-no-return before nightfall. It felt both scary and exciting to be out in the wilderness, facing a night camp completely on his own. It was easily the most daring thing he'd ever done, so much more than back flips by the poolside in Tepland or taking the drugs at the Doblepoble. He scanned the cliffs for an ascent and he thought the whole thing was the best ever. He was so glad to be Pascale's brother and, yes, to be friends with Palmiro. Without them he might be in Heaven but he'd never be having so much fun.

To his right there was another branch and to his left, set high on the wall he spotted a craggy rock buttress with what looked like a fissure in its wall, perhaps large enough to pass through. There was also a possible ascent along a ridge starting five or six feet from the ground. Below that the bank was at a steep angle but the ground was hard and stony, scattered with cactus.

"This is what you're made for, Dusty. Let's see if we can rush the bank and reach that spine."

He pulled away and pointed Startdust at the canyon wall in the direction of the buttress. She seemed to understand and tossed her head a couple of times in excitement. He held her still and then dug his heels against her flanks, urging her on.

She plunged into a run and took the bank in two leaps, making the beginning of the ridge and continuing her impetus up the cliff, her ears pulled back with the thrill of the charge.

"Yeeehaah! That's my girl!" Danny yelled in excitement even as he slowed and steadied her on the narrow path. But she was sure-footed, continuing higher and higher until they got to the band of rock and the opening. It was a few feet wide and Danny was able to guide Stardust in over the rockfall. At once they were in a natural stronghold about the size of a wide sitting room with high walls behind and to the side and clear ground in the middle. Nothing could come at them except one at a time through the split, and anyway he could build a fire.

"Perfect, it's like it was made for us! We'll leave everything here and go look at that branch canyon we saw."

He unloaded the supplies, stashing them in a corner and covering them with rocks. He then led Stardust back out, remounting and carefully descending the ridge to the point where the narrow shoulder ended. He slipped out of the saddle and slid down the remainder of the bank, letting Stardust hop and skitter down alone. It was already early evening and there would not be a lot of time to explore the canyon opposite, but he made a start. As he headed down the burnished chasm, still giving off intense heat, he found it quickly broke into another canyon at a sharp angle. He turned into the switch and the feeling grew stronger and stronger that he was closing in on the point where he had thrown his rock. The canyon became a deep ravine and seemed it would probably go on some way but he still wanted to press on a little farther.

He almost passed the opening because it was only a few feet wide, but suddenly there was a branch to his right. He steered his horse through the defile, following it for thirty yards, then it abruptly widened out. From above it could easily have looked like a dead end and he thought it was possible this was the first blocked canyon he had seen from the plateau. But now there really was no longer time to explore. The shadows were thickening fast and he would have to return tomorrow.

As Danny retraced the way back to his camp, the final light of the sun made a frieze of brass along the length of the canyon. He stopped to gather brush for a fire, snapping dead stalks and picking up bone-dry branches. He made a bundle with his rope and slung it across his shoulder, then remounted Stardust. The Arab hardly needed to be told where to go or what to do. She passed the buttress, then faced around. Danny touched her and she made the run, leaping with circus-like precision. Within a minute and a half they were home, safe among the towering rocks.

3. STORY TELLING

In the tented meeting space twelve or more Ranch citizens were seated around the table. Across from them, half a dozen yards away, Magus was installed in his private booth observing. He was leaning his head on the braced fingers of one hand, like Caesar. To fit the role, his expression was at once bored, contemptuous and hostile. He now took it as his function to supervise what went on in the tent, but all along he was bitterly eager to find just one opportunity to crush Pascale and pull it all down. So far, however, he had not been able to break either her logic or her will.

People had gotten used to meeting in the tent every day and organizing certain simple chores. In the days after it had first been set up, Pascale had persuaded Zena to help her do something about the Women's cabin, clearing the floor, opening up the shutters and letting light and air in. The place was unspeakably filthy, with piles of old clothes where mice and rats had nested until someone had spread piles of poison around and their bodies had rotted on the spot and dried to dust. Cockroaches scuttled in every direction the moment anything was picked up and flies buzzed relentlessly against the window panes. Pascale and Zena began dragging everything out the door and tossing it on the porch.

Katoucha who was sitting there turned her head and looked as if she had never seen any of this stuff before. She uttered a stifled gasp of horror and stood up. She turned to Ravel beside her, pointing at the trash, clearly indicating he should do something about it. Ravel showed the whites of his eyes but his devotion to Katoucha was great and he began to help, pushing everything into a pile in the middle of the canyon. After saving some of the blankets and a couple of the more tolerable dresses, they heaped brush on the pile. Zena got some old oil from the kitchen and poured that on too. Pascale set it all alight.

When others smelled the pungent fire of the first cleaning, they wanted to join in. Alaqua and another woman from the cantina, Carly, came up and asked what they could do to help. Pascale set them to washing the saved articles. Katoucha marched Ravel and Zoltan down to the Men's cabin and got them to make a start there too. Thus the custom of house chores became established and, little by little, there was a regular detail of canyon

Immortals heading off with pails, brushes and rags, or carrying out blankets and clothes to wash and then dry them on the canyon walls. The cleaners' efforts extended to the cantina. Working their way around the recumbent figures who still spent the day there, they swept the floors, carefully washed tables and dishes, and threw away old food. They also repaired the bug screens and went on fly hunts, swatting them or driving them out the door.

On this particular day Zena and Katoucha were organizing the tasks. Pascale had not arrived yet. She had adoped the habit of climbing the clifftop in the early morning to watch the light filtering from the east and be quiet. She had gotten used to the ascent and was able to make it swiftly, almost without thinking. She was also much less troubled about Magus. She sensed, for the moment at least, he was looking for an opportunity to humiliate her, not physically attack her. Indeed, there at the top of the canyon a lot of things came into perspective.

Her experience of love looking up at the starman on her first night in the canyon had not been repeated but its effect had remained. She felt connected to everything around her and to a mystery of love within and below everything. Alone on top of the trackless wilderness she was able to renew this feeling, to let it seep through her bones and through the great panorama extending on every side. Sometimes it was almost like a physical weight bearing down on her, and at other times it made her as light as air. On these occasions she couldn't help but shout out random, happy things and give thanks with all the fiber of her soul.

She looked for a way to give her feeling a more permanent expression. Almost automatically as the days went by, she began to collect medium-sized rocks and place them in a circle, creating a space which was her own and which contained her story and experience. Each rock represented something which had happened to her and she scratched a mark on it to symbolize the event. Today on top of the canyon she had gone back to the edge and looked down. She could see the tent as the light uncurled across it and she knew the canyon felt enormously different because of it. She collected a white rock the size of her two hands and scored the outline of a tent on it, adding it to the circle. One day, she hoped, she would create some kind of final picture of the things she felt, and the tent would be a central part of it.

Pascale's Wager

As she climbed back down, Pascale understood the tent was important because it held the stories of everyone in the canyon. It was like her circle of stones but in this case the stones were the people in the tent. She thought that if people began telling some of their stories out loud they would know the meaning of the tent better and it would be harder still for Magus to take it down. When she got to the tent she told everyone.

"You know why this tent is special? It's because it holds all our stories in one place and doesn't let one disappear. We all have a story, or many little stories. Wouldn't it be something if we began to tell each other some of our stories? Little things, you know, they don't have to be anything really big."

People looked at her blankly, not knowing what she was talking about.

"Listen," she said, "I'll show you. I'll start."

She told them the story of Palmiro, of how she had met him at school, how he never accepted what his professors told him, and how he got arrested for blasphemy and sent to the camps. Eventually she had been able to rescue him and actually bring him with her, here to Heaven. But that was too big a story and she would keep it for another day. Right now she wanted to hear from someone else.

There was a prolonged silence. No one spoke. They just stared ahead with tunnel vision, waiting for Pascale, or someone else, to continue. Pascale said, "I know it must seem hard. But you have your stories. You must have. All you've got to do is reach down into your memory and find one!"

Suddenly something unimaginable took place: Orwell spoke. No one knew the last time the man with useless legs had uttered words and people were genuinely amazed. His voice was a whispered croak, but he used words. It was as if a deaf mute had spoken. Even Magus in his royal box sat up in astonishment. But what Orwell had to say was a crushing rejoinder to Pascale's encouragement.

"There are no stories when every day for hundreds of years is the same. Every story is gone."

Pascale reacted instinctively. She had heard his words because they were spoken directly to her and she repeated them so everyone else knew what he said. She replied in a clear voice, "No,

310

no, Orwell, you are wrong. Those words you just said have remained inside you, and if you have words, you have stories. You must only find the will to tell them."

Orwell looked away. When Pascale met the eyes of the others they looked away too. She could feel Magus' smirk burning the back of her neck. She heard him say, "My bet is you're the only story here! You brought the circus to town and it's got one act only, the clown!"

She looked around at him, struck by something. Turning back she said, "Maybe Magus is right. Perhaps I should tell you more about myself, about something I have never told anyone before, something I've covered over. If I can bring it out to make a story, perhaps you can bring out your own stories, the ones that have been covered up."

The group looked at her again, the connection renewed. She had promised them something, even as she challenged them and they again felt a stirring, as when they first built the tent. She told them of her initiation, of the experience of the sunlight exploding through the roof and the beautiful bird with the broken wing fluttering down upon her breast. She described how she had tried to guard the bird from drowning, but how it had become impossible because the assistants pushed her under. The bird drowned before her eyes and she had experienced a terror and pain beyond comprehension. She had died. No, she had not died, not in the usual sense, because eventually she had revived. But she had died in her soul, without a companion, without point or truth, in an infinite dead black space. That memory was always with her, but now, more and more, it pointed beyond itself. She had come back to life, and she had learned many things since to give her hope and courage. In fact, she believed death was a passage, as it actually had proven to be for her. She had experienced it in order to heal the broken wing of the beautiful bird and to save it from drowning. Being down here in the canyon with everyone did feel for her like just like giving wing to the beautiful bird, the bird born from the sun.

There was silence, a long silence, but not like before. Something was coming to life and people could feel it in each other.

Zena put her hand up with a hesitant movement. Pascale

311

nodded encouragingly. Zena cleared her throat, speaking awkwardly, almost unable to believe this was her own voice raised in public.

"My parents, they were professors...and like Palmiro I didn't accept what they said. They taught...they taught in a big university, and were invited to be some kind of advisers. They were always telling me to work, study harder, but I couldn't see why. The world was a complete mess, so many people were dying. Then, without warning, in the space of a few months all this happened. They brought me here. They said I was immortal. But it seemed like more of the same. I never had a choice. They didn't ask me whether I wanted to be a goddess. Really, I just wanted to be happy as a mortal, like humans used to be!"

She came to a halt, tired out by the effort and unsure of whether what she'd said was good or bad. But her words were revolutionary. No one ever mentioned the old time either in Heaven or the canyon, and now she had made it the main point of her story.

Pascale stood up and hugged her. "That was incredible, Zena. Your story goes back to the old time and to your feelings of not being free. Up in the North we had our old time too, but Palmiro knew, and I did too, there had to be more. The beginning of our freedom came when we discovered the whole story here in Heaven. And now you have helped set me free some more, because you have begun to tell your story. I hope it will help set you free too."

Zena did not respond. She just smiled in a dazed kind of way, as if something had happened which she did not quite grasp. Magus twisted in his chair in outrage, yet at the same time he was fascinated. The talk of freedom was definitely subversive. Again he told himself all he had to do was wait until it became specific, and then he would make his move. But also he could not believe what he was witnessing. These dull beings whom he had controlled without raising a finger were now coming alive before his eyes. He could hardly tear himself away.

Suddenly Orwell spoke again and everyone strained to hear him. His attitude had changed remarkably, in the space of minutes. He was still barely audible but he was no longer harsh. "I would like to be free too. What I said before was untrue. Not every day in a hundred years is the same. There was a day when I jumped, from the cliff, hoping to die, but I hit the edge and all I did was break my back. This is my story, and if my mind could forget it, my body could not."

Pascale went over to his chair by the table and took him gently by the hand. She looked at Zoltan who was sitting next to Orwell. "Your story is Zoltan's too. He is alive because you are. And I am, too."

Magus could restrain himself no longer. He spat on the ground and swore viciously. "Give me a fucking break! What are you going to do next, make love to both of them there on the table? And what's it all for anyway? You're still all here, stuck in the canyon. You're not going anywhere, ever! Believe me, after a few weeks of this tent and story crap you'll be back to the same old zombies you always were."

It was Katoucha who rose to the occasion. She directed her one lethal eye at him. A croak came out of her mouth, hard to understand but easy to comprehend. "You... a foul tongue... polite company... a barbarian. Moderate...language, or leave!"

At that point Magus knew his strategy had failed. He had delayed too long and things had spun out of his control. This bitch upstart from the North, this Pascale, far from being crushed in the belly of the canyon, was going from strength to strength. She was giving voice to everyone around her and soon he would wield very little authority at all. Yet still he felt obliged to wait. He had gotten used to his spiritual power over the canyon's citizens, his implacable destruction of their souls. If he could not bring Pascale down by humiliation then it would have to be by another spiritual power—the full fury of the law. He told himself he was sure if they went on this way, very soon something truly illegal would happen and he could move then with extreme prejudice. In the meantime he had to play the game. He returned Katoucha's stare as hard as she gave it to him. And then, again to his surprise, it was Pascale who stepped in.

"There is of course the other alternative, sir. You could tell us your own story!"

Magus was relieved at the chance to assert himself, with a sneering dismissal. "My stories are entirely my own affair. Still I will tell you this. *I* will always be part of *your* stories. You can

313

count on that!"

He stood up from his chair contemptuously and returned along the canyon, his hips swaying and his boots kicking up spurts of dust as he went.

This time, however, no one paid much attention. They were far too engrossed in their new-found freedom of story-telling.

4. BRIEF ENCOUNTER

Palmiro was waiting impatiently for Danny to return. He felt confident Danny's search would yield results, so it was just a matter of time. But time was not something he had much thought for. It was immortality that controlled the world, something which said time did not really exist, and he had immortality before him at every moment, night and day. For he carried around with him, in his thoughts, a weapon that could destroy it. The more he carried that weapon the more it made immortality the only thing he saw. He had not talked with Adorno; neither did he want to. Adorno had given him a task, but the task was no longer from his master, rather it came from his own deepest self. It was his destiny, his meaning, and he yearned to make it happen.

However, Pascale was also part of his destiny. He had to set her free and it was vital that he do that first. Adorno had connected the two things and he now understood how that had worked. One of the reasons he had done the research was because he thought it must be complete before Pascale could be rescued. But when he found what he was looking for it had become an end in itself, and he knew from now on everything would change. At the same time she was still wrapped up in it all and it was imperative she be brought to safety first, and by whatever means necessary.

He'd taken to driving over to the Zoo Colony almost every day. Eboni would help him saddle up the bay and then give him a half hour or so of lesson. Afterward, he would wander around the lanes on his own, occasionally spurring into a trot and trying to sit comfortably with the motion. He'd seen Danny a couple of times coming back from his initial searches for the water pipe and he'd gone over his notebook with him, creating his own mental picture of where his friend had been. Then Danny decided to make camp down in the canyons and Palmiro could hardly bear it when he drove over and Danny wasn't there to talk to. Today, however, was the third day and he knew Danny would have exhausted his supplies and should be returning before nightfall. He waited out on the trail but the sun went down and still Danny didn't arrive. He rode back, unsaddled his horse, rubbed it down and went to find Eboni.

They sat nervously together as the light vanished and still

Danny did not appear. They imagined how dangerous the trail was, how easy to mistake, how constantly under threat of wild dogs, and how fatal it was to slip in the final ascent in the dark. They wondered how they could possibly help. At the very most, they could venture out to search for Danny at first light and then, which way would they take? Palmiro might perhaps remember some of the route but after that Danny could have traveled miles in any direction. It was of course possible that everything was O.K. and Danny was safely camped somewhere but surely his water was used up, and to be down in the canyons even for a few hours without water was dangerous to both man and horse. They felt helpless. Eboni said she had never considered anything like this happening, she had such confidence in Danny. Palmiro nodded grimly. There was no back-up after Danny. If he failed then he had no idea of what came next.

They slept fitfully in armchairs wrapped in comforters. When the first rays of sun glanced off the wall, they both awoke with a start. They decided at once they would ride out to the trail head and down to the level of the first canyon. They quickly filled canteens with water and stumbled out to the stable to saddle the horses. At this point they were no longer bothered to disguise their actions from other colony members. They readied the horses and rode out with a clatter across the courtyard onto the road, heading southwest. By late morning they were at the top of the descent. They paused, gazing down the switchback fringed with cactus and scrub oak hugging the steep drop. Out before them stretched the endless rutted panorama of the mesas and canyons, already baking in the sun. Palmiro had never tried anything like this before but there was nothing else for it but to keep going. They pressed on at the slowest possible pace, Eboni telling him to follow her, keeping the bay close to the wall. When they finally made it to the bottom Palmiro was wholly wrung out from hanging on to his saddle and the neck of his mount. They dismounted for a rest. But they were also uncertain of what to do next.

The canyon stretched in either direction but Palmiro knew Danny had begun working his way to the east. Eboni suggested they ride in that direction and look out for signs, anything, that might show the direction he'd taken. There was no better idea so they remounted and began to move slowly along the canyon bottom. Suddenly, from a branch canyon up ahead, a figure emerged, coming at a steady canter.

"My God, it's Danny!" Eboni spurred her Appaloosa into a dash and Palmiro followed as fast as he could. Danny saw them and began waving and yelling.

"I found her, I found her!"

In a moment they came up on each other, pulling the horses to a stop.

"Are you alright? You spent the extra night. We were worried stiff!"

"I'm fine. Pascale brought water and some food. You'll never believe where I found her!"

"You found Pascale? You found the Ranch?"

They sat on their horses in the middle of the canyon as Danny recounted his story. He told them about the camp he had established under the rock tower and how he had spent the first night there, not far from a canyon reached by a narrow corridor It was along that canyon the very next day that he had at last found the water pipe and, not a hundred yards from it, the rock wrapped in his bandana. He had then begun the task of tracking the pipe across the mesas. He had quickly gotten a feel for it, doubling around the canyons, guessing pretty well where the pipe would come down, or sometimes, if the cliff was low and fallen, being able to climb up and over. He had begun to understand the lie of the land, sometimes being able to guess the route of the pipe without checking each canyon. The second day he covered a good distance and made it back to his camp before nightfall.

On the third day he had begun looking out for tracks and it was in the late afternoon he had seen unmistakable signs of horses close to a place where the pipe crossed. He had followed on, his heart beating with excitement. After turning into a canyon running south-east almost immediately he had come upon a large metal fence and locked gates. He knew for certain he'd found the colony. Although it was late, he at once began looking for a way up onto the mesa overlooking the canyon. Retracing his steps he eventually discovered a broken part of the cliff where he was able to urge Stardust over the scree and up. At last he was at the top. He could see the sun going down but he was so close he couldn't stop.

"But you actually saw Pascale?" Palmiro was impatient to know.

"Yes, yes. Let me tell you how. It was getting dark but I found this thing up there and I immediately knew it was from her. Don't ask me how. It was a circle of stones that had obviously been placed there. I stood in the middle of it and I could feel her there. So I knew she had to have some way of getting up from down below. I looked around and in the half-dark I found these steps and hand-holds cut into the rock. I knew then I'd be able to get water, and Stardust and I would be O.K."

"I waited until after midnight when everything was totally quiet, then I climbed down, carefully, with my canteen. It was pitch black. I followed the water pipe and found an outlet. I could vaguely see cabins on the other side but there were no lights. On the way back, a dog caught wind of me and started barking like crazy. But no one seemed to bother and I made it back to the top. I curled up in my bed roll and fell asleep. One moment I was sleeping and the next I was awake. She was right there, standing right there smiling, with the sun behind her like an apparition, but it wasn't."

"Wow," said Eboni. "Wow!"

"Can you believe it?"

"What did she say?"

"Well, there wasn't much time, but basically after I told her how I'd found her and that you guys were part of it, she said that she'd found something herself, down in the canyons, and it made her happy. She wanted to tell you all about it. I said it would take a couple of days to get back to her but probably we could be back there, at that spot, in two more mornings. So that's what we planned. We hugged each other and then we hugged again, and then I left."

"Fantastic, Danny. You did so well!" Palmiro was thrilled. The prospect of seeing Pascale touched a nerve inside him that had been forgotten. For the first time in the longest while he actually felt happy. They turned their horses back toward the ascent and the long trail somehow did not seem so challenging. Even Palmiro seemed to take it smoothly, sitting his horse more surely and not flinching as they zigzagged back and forth to the top. The animals were winded when they got there, so they dismounted and walked some of the way back to the colony. Danny needed to rest and Eboni had duties at the kennels; on the other hand Palmiro was too excited to stay in one place. When they got to the villa he washed up, got in the car and drove downtown.

He arrived at the parking plaza and wandered up the great central boulevard, the Avenue of the Monuments. The light was cascading off the buildings like atomic diamonds. As always, people were moving around among the palaces and temples with that air of blissful self-confidence which characterized Immortals and had provoked such resentment in him when he first encountered it. This time, however, it did not seem offensive. He merely thought the people he saw were in a play, acting a part. They believed in the part with their whole soul and would never dream of changing the theater or the script, but still it was not anything real. Moreover, because of him, the curtain was about to come down on a final act and they were completely unaware. He even felt vaguely sorry for them, strolling around in their foolish ignorance.

He stopped at a kiosk, ordering a drink of crushed fruit juice and ice cream and some almond pastries. He took a seat at a café table under a parasol, stretching his legs in contentment. On the wrought iron surface, next to the napkins, was a colored flier for a forthcoming event. He immediately recognized the splendid face of Sarobindo. The advertisement declared that over the next days the great yogi would be undertaking the spectacular "Voyage of Death at Font Eterno," something which had claimed the lives of so many, but never of Sarobindo. Palmiro asked the volunteer waiter when this flier had been distributed.

"Just yesterday. The first Immersion is the day after tomorrow. There'll be two more nights after that."

He remembered the description of the event at the banquet and Adorno's contempt. The scientist's words came back to him, tumbling into his head, "The real loser is Sarobindo." There arose in him an overpowering desire for Sarobindo's downfall and disgrace. All of Heaven was close to the moment for which Adorno longed but it was the mystical role of Sarobindo which seemed to represent the real enemy. His dicing with death and the way the philosophers swooned over it seemed to constitute the lie at the heart of everything. It was perfectly understandable that nobody wanted to die, and it was also understandable that people would devise an existence of endless pleasure. But to gild it all with phony mystical meaning, that was the truly contemptible thing. He decided that before anything happened he would make sure he attended one of the yogi's Immersions to witness the myth for himself and relish its imminent destruction.

"Well, look who it isn't, hanging out downtown. I'm surprised you have the nerve to show yourself after the fiasco at the philosophers' party!"

It was Gaius with Roland, taking a stroll along the Avenue of the Monuments and gliding in among the cafe tables.

"Come on Gaius, you can't blame this one. They got the real culprit and she's no longer with us happy Immortals, right?'

Palmiro was shocked abruptly from his thoughts. He half stood and then caught himself, sinking back to his seat. Only a few more days and their immortality would be history.

"Oh, hi Gaius, just taking a break, you know. Nothing like the Avenue of the Monuments, is there?"

"I don't think someone like you ever takes a break. And I wasn't fooled one moment at that pantomime. I saw how you shuffled things off onto Pascale, to keep your own nose clean. I'm glad she's gone, but in my book you're next!"

Roland took hold of Gaius by the arm and shoulder, "Hey, calm down, the guy's just chilling. Leave him alone!"

Palmiro tried distraction. "Actually, I was just thinking about this!" And he held up the flier of Sarobindo. "I want to go to it."

Gaius' attack was deflected, but he remained sarcastic. "How so? You surely don't want to fit in like the rest of us?"

"I'm interested in Sarobindo's technique. I think I could learn a lot from it."

"Yeah, why don't you try it for yourself? Why don't you do 'The Voyage of Death.' That would save us all the trouble of getting rid of you!"

Gaius clapped Roland on the back as he said this and pushed him past Palmiro, bringing the encounter to an end on the slap-down. Roland laughed and spoke over his shoulder as they walked off, "Take no notice, he's just a little wounded today. We'll see you at the Font Eterno!"

Palmiro continued to follow them with his eyes as they walked off under the onion domes of the Kremlin. A vague idea hovered in his thoughts.

5. A GOD IS DEAD

The following mid-afternoon Danny and Palmiro rode out to rescue Pascale. Danny had slept late while Palmiro spent the time assembling supplies for a well-stocked camp at Danny's fortress. They needed some place to hide Pascale at the beginning and from the sound of it the place seemed ideal. Eboni stayed behind and continued to fend off increasingly suspicious questions about the trips on horseback. She decided a partial truth would be the best deceit. She said Danny had discovered a passion for climbing the canyons, it was a kind of extreme sport for him. She and Palmiro were supporting him and helping him establish a cache of supplies at the bottom of the switchback. Colony members were horrified at the idea. Heaven was a mental state as much as a place, and their thoughts had never extended to the badlands. There was never an actual rule against going there, but it was decidedly odd, even perhaps anti-social. Eboni was a little worried by the reaction, but Danny—and definitely Palmiro—did not care.

Because of the added weight and bulk, they took the descent with even more caution than usual. Danny had volunteered Eboni's Appaloosa for Palmiro, because it was nimble and strong, and would give greater security on the long ride. Indeed, Palmiro felt much more confident riding her on the way down. When they got to the bottom they headed straight to Danny's camp. They would arrive after dark but these were nights of a full moon rising early, so they decided to risk it.

As they arrived at the rock tower, the canyon was bathed in a quiet, milky light and, although they could hear coyotes yipping, they did not feel afraid. Danny made the first jump with Stardust. He let down a rope and pulled up the extra supplies, and then Palmiro too at the lowest part of the ridge. Finally Danny took Stardust and tying a long lead rope to Eboni's horse headed some way back down the canyon, then turned and charged the cliff. The Appaloosa followed suit after Stardust and with a spring and a kick made the ridge behind her.

Once inside the enclosure of rocks they built a fire. The two companions stretched out on either side of the burning logs, gazing above at the stars. Palmiro knew that tomorrow he would be telling Pascale everything and Danny would surely be there.

After a few moments he let out a deep breath and turned his head toward him.

"You know that guy I've been studying with, the scientist, Adorno?"

Danny propped himself up on an elbow. "Go on."

"Well, he taught me a lot of things, and about immortality in particular. He showed me it was flawed as a concept, and then he pushed me to investigate its science."

Danny continued to stare at Palmiro. Somehow it was as if he knew what was coming.

"I worked hard and discovered what I think is some kind of antidote to the immortality enzyme. I'm not entirely sure how it functions but it seems to destroy the whole process, killing the cells. I'm pretty sure any Immortal who took a sip of that would, well...no longer be immortal."

"Let me get this straight, you've discovered a way to destroy immortality and you're thinking of using it?"

"Danny, you know it's a lousy fake, all of it. These people here were the most privileged in the world at the time of the storms and they found a way to preserve that privilege infinitely. Meanwhile the descendants of everyone else, the ordinary people, slave in the Northern Homeland without even knowing they are slaves. What they call immortality is not really immortality, anyway. It's just a way of putting off death that's going to come one way or another someday. I'm talking about returning things to their natural and true state, the one humans have always had. Death, the great leveler!"

"And exactly how do you plan to do it? Just walk up to people and say, here take a swig of my great leveler, this anti-immortality thing?"

"As yet I haven't planned it in detail. But one possibility is putting it in the water-supply. You know, up in the treatment place you found."

"Are you insane? You'd have people dying everywhere. It would be horrible. And what about us? What about you, me, Pascale, and people like Eboni and Jonas?"

"Well, all we'd have to do is stop drinking the treated water. If people directly from the North flush immortality out of their system over two or three days then the anti-enzyme will probably have little or no effect on us. We're young and healthy in the ordinary way and we'll stay that way. The deviant form of the enzyme depends, I think, on the programing already in the cell, to gain entry."

"You think! You're going to kill us all! And that doesn't help people like Eboni or Jonas, people who love us and who are not young in the ordinary way, as you put it!"

Palmiro fixed a cold hard look at the stars and then at his companion.

"Listen, I don't know what you expected in all this. We're rescuing Pascale from a black hole where people disappear without trace, and that's done to keep the rest of Heaven happy. If we get her out, the Immortals are just not going to accept her again, no matter what you or Jonas might hope. They would have to make adjustments and they simply can't do that here. So they'll be looking for blood, and they'll be coming for you and me too. We don't have a future in Heaven and you better get used to that. Besides, what about everyone back in the North? Have you thought about them? What hope is there for any of them the way things are?"

Danny looked back at Palmiro, not with hostility but because he felt the ground opening up beneath him. He had not thought this through like Palmiro and he had no answers to his questions, no alternatives to propose. The whole thing was suddenly way out of his depth.

"You're right in a lot of things, I can't argue with them. But I want to hear what Pascale has to say, especially about the anti-immortality potion."

They both lapsed into silence. Their eyes blinked up at the starlit night as their minds drifted toward sleep. Tomorrow they'd be leaving at sun-rise.

***

Pascale climbed the cliff steps with a mounting sense of happiness. Her complete amazement at meeting Danny two mornings ago was something she'd had to keep to herself. Magus was bound to pick up on the news if she'd mentioned anything to the others. Now finally she was able to give rein to the excitement of talking with her brother once again, and with Palmiro too. But just beneath the excitement there was also unease. She was going to tell them everything she was doing and what the canyons meant to her. Would they understand?

That other morning when she had got to the top and found Danny lying in the middle of her stone circle it had been such a joy: she was so thrilled to see him. Then he told her how he and Palmiro planned to return in two more days to take her out of the canyons. There had been no time to talk as he had to get back to Eboni and Palmiro. She tried to say something about the canyons, but there just wasn't the chance before he rushed off.

Now as she reached the top of the cliff and stepped onto the level, she knew for certain she could not return with them, and it would be very hard for them to grasp the reasons why. She sat down in the middle of her circle and prayed. She still was not sure who or what she was praying to. Was it the starman who had filled her with love? She wasn't sure. Despite the wonder of that experience, it seemed the pattern of stars really belonged to something that could not be seen. There was no name to give to it except perhaps the face of love, a face the more it was seen, the more it was invisible.

She prayed that Danny and Palmiro could feel some of what she felt. She did not know what their plans were or how her refusal would affect them. Almost certainly they would be upset. She asked for strength. She could not leave Zena, Orwell, Katoucha and all the others, not after everything she had started, not after the tent and the stories. What would happen to this, the latest and perhaps the best ever story, if it simply came to end with her riding off on Danny's horse into the sunset?

Pascale looked out over the canyons. Their striated pattern was already fracturing in the heat, twisting as if the canyons were no longer solid but supple, alive. She watched the shivering light but she was conscious also it was still dark in the canyons under the eastern walls. It felt like a law, that there was always darkness with the light, that the light was always held in a womb of darkness.

She heard a noise and looked around. There riding along the top of the mesa were Danny and Palmiro. She stood up, waving madly, and ran toward them, stifling her cry of happiness in case it might echo below. The two jumped off their horses to greet her, smiling broadly, then hesitated, perhaps because Danny and Palmiro did not know who should embrace her first. Or maybe it was she who held back from them.

"Danny, Palmiro! It's fantastic to see you. You tracked me down out here, I can't believe it!"

"No way could we leave you in this wilderness. You did the same for me in the ice camps and that's just the first reason!"

"Palmiro, it's so good to hear your voice! How are you anyway, it's been such a time since we had the chance to talk? Come over here. Look, this is my circle. I built it to remind me of everything important. It's my zodiac on the ground!"

Palmiro and Danny allowed themselves to be led to the group of stones. At this point there was no hurry and it seemed as good a place as anywhere. They tethered the horses and fetched out water and cups. Then they sat down with Pascale, like they were all at a picnic.

"When I first saw this I guessed it was you who made it. It seemed just the kind of thing you would do."

"Well, I should explain why I did it, Danny. We started something down in the canyons and it's there for everybody. But this is where I come for my own sake, to remember my own story, and to listen to the silence."

She began to tell them what had happened in the canyons from the day she had been brought there by Marius. It didn't take long to see Pascale had changed once again, but this time in a lighter, better way, one that made her happy.

"Some of these people have not spoken for so long their voices are barely a croak. You have to listen really hard to understand them. Katoucha, for example, has abandoned the use of her voice almost entirely. She wrote down her story. She told how she refused to become a lover, rejecting many people and on numerous occasions. One day she took a spoon and pushed her own eye out. Then they sent her to the Ranch. I cannot give her eye back, but I've helped give her story back to her."

She continued to tell other stories. Of Ravel, who had been a concert pianist and was promised immortality as a way of preserving his art, but he'd never played another note from the day he arrived. Of Zoltan, a first-class athlete who had continued training for Olympic competitions which would never take place, and had been sent to the canyons because in his mind he preferred the ways of the old world. And there was Magada who had been both a popular film-star and campaigner on social issues and had been chosen for her fame and prestige. She had been persuaded into thinking Heaven was for the benefit of everyone, then when she found out the truth she had slashed her wrists in public. Someone had staunched the bleeding and saved her life, but they sent her to the Ranch. There she took a liking to the cattle, and caring for them became her sole concern. One evening after returning from the drive she had ridden her horse to Pascale's tent and without dismounting she told her story.

Palmiro could contain himself no longer. "Pascale, I need to tell you another story, one that will put an end completely to stories like that. You know, more than anyone, I never went along with this whole Heaven thing. I wanted to tell you my ideas about changing everything that very first day we came here but we never got the chance. Now they are no longer ideas, I have found a way of bringing everything down."

Pascale was listening attentively. "What do you mean?"

"I mean I have discovered a way of countering the immortality enzyme so that it breaks down the cells instead of preserving them. It makes Immortals mortal again."

Danny screwed his lips shut and focused tautly on Pascale, waiting for what she might say.

"I am still confused. How does this thing work?"

"It's a fluid. If it were mixed with the water it would enter people's bodies when they drank and then do its work."

"You mean everyone would die?"

"Most Immortals would. I'm pretty sure people like us, who came here only recently, we would survive."

"Palmiro, you can't do that. You can't kill everyone off. They'd have no idea of what hit them! It would be horrible, horrific."

"It's not killing. It would simply be returning things to the way they always were. The normal state of organic life for millions of years."

"That's not the point, and you know it. These people are alive at the moment and free to choose. You have to respect their freedom, let them decide themselves."

"How would they ever freely choose to die? How could they? They are trapped by immortality. It's only death that makes people free to choose. That's why they're always play-acting at death, with that Sarobindo ritual."

"Which means they want to be free and their wanting is the first step to choosing to be free!"

"Pascale, I'm not splitting hairs with you. Danny and I are in this too. We've got a camp ready, where you can be safe for a long while, but they will start looking and they will come after us. We have to have a plan."

"Palmiro, please stop. You have to understand, I'm not coming with you. I never intended to. I'm staying in the canyon. This is where my life is."

Both Palmiro and Danny were taken aback. They were actually speechless, not knowing how to respond. Pascale seized the initiative.

"Listen, you know how I'm good at counting and I always liked to count and could count quicker than anyone?"

Danny nodded vaguely while Palmiro shook his head in a kind of spasm, querying what possible bearing this remark could have. Pascale pressed on.

"Well, when I first came here and saw the beautiful light out in the desert, I thought no one could count as fast as the particles of light. If they could, they wouldn't be able to see at all. All they would see would be flashes in the darkness, which is really what light is, except we join it all together. Do you believe in God?"

Again her words caught them off guard, and again her two companions were left floundering while she forged ahead.

"Well, I sit here and I imagine all the atoms and all the particles of light, and I think this universe of light and dust can only be God's own personal experience. What I mean is, all this chaos and order around us, it's God's skin, just like it's ours. But for God all of it is visible. Because if God is anything at all, it's love, and love also has its own way of seeing. It counts faster than light, much faster. Love can go back before the beginning of time and before the beginning of light, and turn round again, all quicker than you can think. Love sees everything without eyes, without the light...before the light!"

"And what *that* means is that when you are faced with a

choice to love you have to stop looking with these eyes"—and she pointed to both her eyes with her fingers—"and instead start counting with love."

She paused and Danny said, "Wow! Where on earth did you come up with all that?"

"A lot of things taught me, beginning with my Initiation. I stopped trusting my eyes. I started seeing with my skin. And the canyons helped me. I began to embrace this wilderness, the places barely alive and the dark in the sky between its stars. I cannot know what darkness is, because it's just darkness, but love can know it, and love always goes on regardless. Love is searching for endless love and it searches all the way across the empty universe until it meets itself coming back."

Palmiro shook his head, this time in surrender. He really did not understand what Pascale was saying, but he knew her well enough to know this came from deep inside her and was not going to change. It would be useless trying to convince her. From her point of view, what he was suggesting was the last thing she needed. She would stay in the canyons, and he would not be able to guarantee her safety if he went ahead with his plans. He had always wanted her with him in what he was doing. It had almost been the condition of everything. Now she was thinking something so totally different his motivation seemed to desert him.

He stood up. "We're done here. There's no more to discuss."

As he looked at Danny, waiting for him to agree, he suddenly saw his expression change, his eyes narrow in fear, concentrating on something over his shoulder. Palmiro swiveled in time to see Magus pull himself up at the top of the cliff steps with a leveled gun in his hand. He and Danny had never seen this man before and for an instant they were paralyzed. Pascale stood up and instinctively backed away, but there was nowhere to go. Magus did not hesitate. Clambering over the cliff edge he strode swiftly up to Pascale, grabbed her round the neck and pointed the gun at her head. Then he pointed it back at the others.

"All of you, you're under arrest for conspiracy. Get over there to the steps and climb down into the canyon. If you don't I'll shoot you or her"—and he waved the gun quickly back at Pascale—"not sure which. Now get your dumb asses over there and climb down."

329

Danny was nearer the steps than Palmiro. He felt he had no choice but to obey and he began to back slowly over to the cliff edge. Palmiro had his hands in the air but didn't move.

"You too, wise guy, get moving"

Palmiro began moving reluctantly toward the cliff. Danny had arrived at the top but was now hesitating and backing away.

"What the fuck are you doing? Climb down now!"

Danny pointed at the cliff edge and as he did a head and body emerged and a woman scrambled up onto the level.

She said breathlessly, "I saw him coming up and followed!"

Pascale cried "Zena!" and in the same instant Magus shot the woman point-blank. She staggered back and disappeared over the cliff. Pascale screamed in horror and half twisted free from Magus' grip. He doubled down to hold her again and, as his attention was distracted, Palmiro lurched toward him, grabbing for the gun hand. Magus saw him coming from the corner of his eye and flipped his hand away, upward into the air. Palmiro fumbled his grip but he managed to keep underneath the gun and get a hold on his forearm. Magus released Pascale and with his free hand brought a stunning blow down on Palmiro's temple. Palmiro collapsed and let go of the arm, but Danny was racing to help his friend and coming round from behind Pascale. At the last moment Magus tried to bring his gun down to shoot but Danny was ducking and charged him full force in the stomach. Magus keeled backward, badly winded. Danny continued to drive forward against the big man and, as he did, scooped up a hand-sized rock, slamming it up as hard as he could on the ridge of Magus' chin. The governor of the canyons went slack at the knees, swaying at the edge of the cliff, his eyes rolling in his head. The gun fell from his hand. He teetered, his foot slipping on the rim, and then he was gone.

All of this happened in a few seconds but it seemed to last for an eternity. Danny and Pascale looked at each other in shock and disbelief. Palmiro was on his knees, dazed and propping himself on one hand while holding his head with the other.

"Wha... what happened?"

Danny was breathing hard. He said, "I think, I think we just killed someone. That guy. He went over the cliff after I hit him. Who...who was he, Pascale?"

"That was Magus, our jailer. He's gone, and so is Zena. I have to go down, and tell people..."

Danny said, "Of course you have to. I'll come down too, to help explain." And he added, "Palmiro, are you alright?"

"I'm dizzy, but I'll be fine."

Danny said, "Listen, I'll find the key to the gates. If you feel you can do it, bring the horses round. If not, I'll come back up here to get you."

"Wait, wait. You're going down there? And that guy we think we killed, that was Magus?"

"Yes, and yes."

Palmiro struggled unsteadily to his feet "That means we've already changed everything. Look, try to keep it as normal as possible down there at the Ranch. I don't know what kind of contact they have with the plateau but the less everyone finds out for now the better. I'll wait a few more minutes here and then return to the colonies. I've got things to take care of."

Danny shot him a worried look but Pascale was already climbing over the edge and down the steps and he had to go with her. As she began to descend, she suddenly stopped and called out. "Palmiro, thanks for saving me. You are my dearest friend, and you must remember always, you're in my heart."

Then her head dipped below the level of the ground and Danny was following after her. "I'll keep things as calm as I can," he shouted as he turned. "But, Palmiro, please don't make things any worse!"

331

6. HEAVENLY RITE

A great crowd was streaming across the parkland and up the broad steps on either side of the long bank overlooking the racetrack. From there they funneled together onto two ceremonial causeways which crossed the reflecting lake beneath the Font Eterno. The marbled path glittered beneath them, a shifting kaleidoscope of designs, white, amethyst, amber and black. The giant globe loomed above, like a vast spaceship, the colors on its surface moving and morphing and reflecting continuously in the pool below. It was as if the massive sphere was communicating in code to another planet, bouncing its secret signals off the water.

Just to walk in a gathering crowd on this road was to experience a sense of the extraordinary, and the thousands of people arriving were all in a peculiarly heightened mood. It was not the same as Doblepoble with its reckless abandon to pleasure. Here instead there was a feeling of something sacred and pure, yet still with a strong hint of excitement. On the other side of the lake, the road divided into two arcs sweeping round left and right. From the circle, at intervals of a few dozen yards, paths extended inward connecting to large elevators with gleaming crystal forms. These carried the people up and around the curve of the globe to its different levels. They looked like pearls of water rising and falling upon its surface.

Palmiro had arrived after a long hard ride back from the canyons. He'd not had time to change so he was dirty and dust-streaked and the people near him looked at him disapprovingly. He felt bone-weary from the trail and his head still throbbed where he had been struck, but it was essential he witness this event so he could plan what he was going to do. He ignored both the sneering glances and his protesting body, and pushed on through the mob, trying to find the best spot to see the action.

He got to where the crowd was thinning a little and took one of the first elevators with free space. It ascended the globe as if floating in air, kept vertical inside an elegant gimbal mechanism attached to the track. He exited about half way up, where there were available places and you could most clearly take in the full dimensions of the arena.

Crossing the automated bridge to the globe he entered a

circular corridor, an endless crystalline tube with the colors from the globe's exterior glimmering softly through panels in the floor and wall. Windows on the inside surface gave a dim glowing impression of the enormous auditorium within. He was struck at once by a distinctive smell, an indescribable mixture of physical electricity running through everything and a trace of something else, fearfully dangerous and exciting at the same time. It was as if this really was a spacecraft from another planet, or a previous time, carrying in its hi-tech body the scent of a cosmic event. The shock was similar to the one he had experienced when he first entered the Initiation Baths. But this time it was not seduction, rather something much more elemental. It came to him that this was the scent of the stars remade on earth by Heaven.

People continued to move steadily, without rush, but with a sense of anticipation, which reminded Palmiro a little of the atmosphere at the Presentations back in the North. He passed through one of the golden glass doors nearest him and at once his breath was sucked away, partly by the scent, now even more marked, but mostly by the awe-inspiring architecture of the globe seen from the inside. Directly in front of him was a continuous cushioned bench which people stepped over to sit upon. It looked out across a red and ochre balustrade, which continued around in a massive sweep, so vast it was impossible clearly to distinguish figures or faces on the other side. Below them swept tier after tier of similar balconies, slowly extending downward like the pages of a gigantic book, their gilded edges pressed outward toward the bottom. Above, arcing up in a great overhanging cliff, was a mirror reflection of the levels below, glass-bottomed stalls and boxes, jutting out in the same sweeping circles, narrowing one-by-one as they climbed higher. Far above, at the top, a final circle held the night sky in its radius, like a huge inverted cup filled with indigo and the shimmer of stars still visible at its dark core.

Plunging from above, the eye dived to where the pool of the sky was mimicked below by a great circular sea, the true focus of the whole structure. The water was turquoise and sapphire. A small flux of waves ruffled its surface, displaying an infinite shading of colors. Whether because of the design of the building or the knowledge of what happened there, it was the sea which relentlessly drew the attention. Palmiro gazed around at the whole space, once again impressed despite himself at the uncompromising feel of everything, by its sense of inevitability.

He didn't have to see faces or hear conversation, the atmosphere everywhere and in everything spoke of something immeasurable. His eyes continued to turn downward, as if a weight were dragging them. He watched the shifting color tones spread across the water, heard the murmur of the vast crowd that had gathered, and began to feel a deep calm come over him. It was almost as if there was a voice inside him telling him to stop thinking and just surrender to the wonder of it all. Yet he was not about to do that. There was far too much at stake. He knew in fact that what he was observing was the full-face image of everything he intended to bring down.

Adorno was right. Immortals were hooked on their immortal life and they had no idea how desperately phony and unfair it all was. Whatever he felt right now, it was simply a strong dose of the brain-dead and pointless world they lived in. Anyway all this was Sarobindo's big show and he'd already decided it was Sarobindo he had to stop in order to bring Immortals to their senses. He cleared his mind and renewed his attention to each detail before him.

Soon a dramatic organ chord burst from an enormous sound system, so deep as to make the whole of the auditorium tremble. A god greater than any Immortal was about to enter and all you could do was give reverence. Palmiro felt his whole body vibrating and again he had to resist the desire to surrender. Many stood up to focus their attention on a spot to the side of the lake. He followed their example and strained to see what they were looking for. Down to his right, to the side of the great blue expanse, a narrow cantilevered bridge was being lowered slowly down across the water. It was cream in color and decorated with sprays of blossom like a bridal arch. As the bridge reached the horizontal it was about a quarter way across the surface, and then the ramp was stretched some more by auxiliary lines and boards until it was about a third of the way across.

The organ chord died away and a lighter flute and drum music took its place. There was a shiver of excitement in the crowd and out onto the bridge came an unmistakable figure dressed in an amber colored loin cloth. The regal stride and bearing declared at once this was Sarobindo, but two huge video screens flashed into life at either end of the amphitheater and confirmed the impression with dramatic close ups of the guru's face.

At first Sarobindo stood motionless at the end of the bridge. His eyes were unseeing, partly because the irises were rolled up under half-closed lids, and partly because his consciousness seemed to have detached completely from his body. The effect was powerful. The image of his face on screen was of exceptional discipline and will, of someone belonging to a higher, other-worldly dimension. Palmiro could not help being struck. This was not the arrogant, condescending Sarobindo of the banquet, but a person who had achieved results beyond anything the vast majority of people could imagine. He was in his way a worthy adversary to Adorno, and Palmiro could understand the grip he held on the Immortals. Here was a figure who could put you directly in contact with the whole cosmos because he had handed himself over to it. He was a walking mirror of the universe because, at least for the moment, he had left his ego at the door.

Yet Palmiro was not deterred. In the end this unique skill of Sarobindo's was simply part of one big game of fraud and falsehood. The sound of the flute died away and a voice was heard announcing what was about to happen. The voice was solemn and devout, and what it said had the feel of a ritual formula, something that had been repeated many times before.

"The great yogi Sarobindo carries our spirits and souls as he goes to the depths of Font Eterno. He journeys to a time and place where death was the common lot of all human beings. Death controlled our biology and all our human existence. By means of death we discovered who we were and death gave truth to life. Now, even now as Immortals, we cannot forget who and what we were. We travel with Sarobindo to the place of our ancient meaning. Once we were mortal and we are so no longer. But Immortals too may know the great truth of mortality, brought to us by Sarobindo."

There was a reverent wave of applause and the yogi began to move, almost automatically, one step exactly in front of the other. About six paces behind came an attendant dressed in an orange robe, with folded hands and head bowed. After two or three minutes of his ceremonial walk, Sarobindo arrived at the end of the bridge, which stood out over the surface of the abyss about six feet high. In one fluid motion he sank to his knees and and then slowly slipped onto his back. There he remained, supine, for about sixty seconds more, the video camera trained intently on his face. If before he had been detached, he was now in a state that could only be compared to what the announcer had described. The face of death, of the final absence of any life and soul, this was what appeared on the screen. It was utterly enthralling. Sarobindo's breathing had come to a stop and, as everyone watched, their breathing too seemed reduced to a vanishing point.

There was a total silence. At a certain moment, without breaking the attention of the crowd, the attendant moved forward and touched a switch, and the end section of the bridge dipped into the form of a slide. Sarobindo's prone form began to slip and gain speed and suddenly he was off the end. His feet hit the water and he disappeared.

Simultaneously the video switched to a new screen, a digital clock set at twenty minutes, immediately running down through its seconds and minutes. The crowd remained totally silent, fixated both on the video and the surface of the water, which had closed over the body and resumed its restless lapping. Here, then, was the great test which Abelard had spoken of at the banquet, the challenge to Sarobindo to remain beneath the surface until just before the Sea's switch to nuclear annihilation.

Palmiro was himself completely fascinated but he was also feverishly planning as he watched. Pascale had thrown a road block across his intention to introduce his antidote into the general water supply. He wasn't really sure why but her opinion mattered enormously to him: he had only discovered how much when she had been talking to him there back on the mesa. Her objections had in fact helped him, for almost at the same moment as she voiced them, another and better idea came to the fore of his mind.

The symbolic value of Sarobindo's sacrificial immersion was greater than any other event in Heaven. If it was possible to undo that it would achieve Adorno's goal of shifting the perspective of Immortals with one blow. To destroy the ritual of Sarobindo's plunge would overturn their world, and, just as Pascale had insisted, they would then be able to respond freely. He'd made up his mind back there on top of the canyon directly after Magus' fall, and it was unwavering from then on. Sitting now in the great arena, he was deciding the practical details to make his idea a reality.

The minutes slipped away and the tension in the crowd increased once again. It was different from the previous rapt devotion. Now there was excitement mixed with the awe. Palmiro registered the changed feeling and kept his eyes glued to the lake. He noticed that at intervals round its edge there were flights of steps leading up from the water and he assumed it would be on one of these that the yogi would ascend. He had no doubt that Sarobinbdo would make it out in time. Whatever Sarobindo was, he was totally in command of his craft. The only question was what the effect on the crowd would be.

There were less than two minutes to go. The digital seconds were peeling off and a hum of voices from around the balconies rose steadily in anticipation. The sound of organ chords softly progressing and increasing in volume fed the excitement. There were now less than thirty seconds to go and still there was no sign. Fifteen seconds, twelve, ten, and the unmistakable head and shoulders broke the surface and the unique stride ascending the steps declared unequivocally Sarobindo had triumphed. A massive cheer broke out from around the amphitheater, which was drowned immediately by a thunderous blast on the organ.

Sarobindo cleared the top of the pool and, almost at the same moment, its turquoise surface appeared to warp in on itself, imploding like a collapsed drum. It roared to life, a swirling gray and yellow chaos generated and held in place by the huge concentric rings of particle accelerators lodged behind the containing bowl. Its ferocious sound drowned out all other noise and its smell rose immediately to the balconies, electric and intoxicating, the distinctive, dangerous breath of the amphitheater refreshed at its core.

The video camera panned around the balconies showing images of people no longer cheering but watching the pool with the intense fascination they had previously given to Sarobindo. They almost all had the same expression, halfway between horror and profound satisfaction. They stared into the depths, carried there by the yogi's sacrificial immersion barely concluded, and the terrifying power of the atomic flux. What the moment before had been the drama of Sarobindo at the bottom was now a monster which would have destroyed him utterly if he had stayed there ten seconds longer. It could also destroy the whole building and everyone in it, were it not for the extraordinary technology which held it in place.

For perhaps the last time Palmiro wondered at the world the Immortals had created: how they had reached into the depths of human dreams to bring their creatures to the surface. But the end of that world had come and it was his personal destiny to reveal it. Gradually the chaos began to subside and patches of blue began to reappear like strips of torn cloth. Then the entire thing coalesced once, broke apart and formed again finally, back to its original state. The dimpled waters had returned and the show was over. Actually there was a second act to follow, a full symphony orchestra and concert, but Palmiro had seen all he needed. He knew what he had to do. He headed for the exits, back to Danny and Eboni's colony.

7. HELL'S FIRES

The shot that hit Zena had been heard in the canyon, and Katoucha who was sitting in the tent had seen with her one eye the falling body as it struck a shoulder of rock and plummeted down. She had been watching the area of the steps nervously ever since she and Zena had seen Magus march along the canyon and make the climb with a gun in his belt. He had come to the tent demanding to know where Pascale was. The women were too intimidated to lie and said Pascale had gone to the top. He noted it was much later in the morning than she usually stayed.

"Very out of the ordinary, isn't it? That's suspicious behavior."

The governor stalked back to his cabin and returned with the gun, which he very rarely wore. He totally ignored the women as he strode by the tent. They were beside themselves with worry and finally Zena could bear it no longer. She had to go up to be there with Pascale. Katoucha had seen her denim dress hitched above her knees as she climbed the face above a spur and mounted the crest. It was very soon after that Katoucha heard the shot and saw the body fall. She let out a strangled screech and began to thump the table furiously with one hand while pointing desperately with the other. Orwell began calling out for help as best he could. Zoltan came running with Alaqua and Elliot, and a few more rushed out from the cantina to see what was happening.

The ragged group made its way up the canyon toward the base of the steps. As they came around the small spur they found the body, with the head at a horribly twisted angle and blood pooling underneath. They stood there appalled at the abrupt and brutal death of the girl, but they hardly had time to take it in before another body came hurtling down, hitting the ground a few yards farther up. The group cowered in terror at what seemed like a rain of bodies coming from the clifftop. When someone then gave a hoarse cry, "It's Magus", they were even more terrified. The jailer's body was face up, motionless, but the head rolled a little to one side and Alaqua screamed. Everyone was paralyzed with fear, but after a little while, when nothing further happened, Katoucha went over, continuing to glance nervously above. She knelt beside the man's body and felt his neck for a pulse. After a moment she whispered, "He's dead."

"What happened up there?" "Who did this?" The questions were on everyone's lips but the group was so unused to voicing anything the words remained unspoken. And no one had any wish to go up the cliff to find answers. As they stood there helpless they heard a call above and recognized Pascale descending. Following behind her was a man they didn't know. By now the catastrophic scene had attracted the attention of almost everyone in the canyon. The cook and his assistants were coming and the shot had alerted the cattle drivers as it echoed and bounced along the canyon walls. Magada could be seen on horseback coming from the other direction, riding hard, followed by one of the cowboys.

Pascale got to the bottom and at once was confronted by the horror of Zena's broken body. She collapsed to her knees beside her, reaching out her hand to touch her friend. Horror and grief welled up within her and she began to sob, her body racked with the force of her emotion. Everyone watched hypnotized, beginning to experience feelings they had all but forgotten. After a couple of minutes, Pascale made an effort to control herself. She gently took Zena's head and pushed it to a more natural position. Then she bent her body down upon the corpse of the woman and hugged her. She was no longer crying.

She straightened and Danny took her by the hand and helped her up. He felt he needed to say something.

"My name is Danny. I am Pascale's brother. I came here with another friend to free Pascale and take her with us. But she refused to go. She prefers to stay with you down here. Magus came and ordered us to climb down into the canyon. He had a gun. This woman arrived at the top and he shot her. We fought with him and he fell. I think we need to talk together about what this means."

Magada, still on her horse, whistled. "I'd say. Looks like you started a revolution."

Pascale looked up at her and spoke in a strong voice. "A revolution? I'm not sure what that is, but if there is a revolution I think it started when we built the tent. Magus wanted to kill it all back then, and he couldn't do it. His wish to kill brought him to this, to his own death. We here, we wish no killing."

The sound of Pascale's voice brought calm and the shock of the situation began to ease. Magada gave the bridle of her horse to the other cattle driver and dismounted. She went across to the body of Magus and knelt on one knee looking at him.

"This was one evil bastard. I never thought to see him dead." She put her hand down the top of his shirt and ripped a pouch with a set of keys from a chain around his neck. She walked over to Pascale and held them up.

"You might want to check his cabin before you talk like that."

Pascale took the keys. "What do you mean?"

"Back in the early days quite a few people, they disappeared without trace. I never did figure it out. Well, we can now check on at least one possibility."

Pascale got a sudden sick feeling. She had always felt a chill passing his cabin. She said, "We should investigate. But first, listen, we have to do something with his body, and Zena's also?"

Magada spat, "Leave him for the dogs. As for Zena, it would take forever to dig a proper grave in the canyon. We will have to make a shallow pit and cover it with rocks."

Katoucha shook her head and whispered forcefully. "We should burn them both. We don't want to leave evidence."

It was the first time someone had raised the issue of how to present all this to outsiders.

Danny said, "We don't have anything to hide. We were attacked! All the same, I think you're right. It might feel better if the whole episode were to go up in smoke!"

Pascale was quickly in agreement. "Actually I think I'd like that, for Zena, and also for Magus. It's healthier, in many ways. I would suggest we build fires for them both. What do you all say?"

People nodded, preferring this option. Pascale proposed they go to Magus' cabin first to investigate and because they might also find bits and pieces in there to build the fires. She gave Danny the keys and asked him if he'd open up the building. She asked Zoltan and Ravel to start gathering any brushwood they could find. She said she would wait by Zena's body until the fire was built.

Danny set off to the cabin with everyone following behind him. This was the revolution and in the order of priorities nobody was going to miss the opening of the big adobe cabin with its back end under the overhang. They had lived with its crushing weight all these centuries but it was slipping away from them even as they marched to its place of command at the spot where the two canyons met. Danny in the lead passed through its arches and knocked on the big framed door. A voice inside answered, "Go away. Master is not here."

"It's Koyo. She doesn't know," whispered Katoucha.

"Listen, I am Pascale's brother. Your master has been killed in an accident. We're coming in."

Danny tried the door and it was locked. He fitted keys until he got the correct one and the lock turned quickly and smoothly. He pushed the door but it remained firmly shut.

"It's bolted," someone said. "You'll have to break it down."

Danny looked at Zoltan and he understood. The two stepped back and then ran at the door full tilt, their shoulders crashing solidly against it. Part of the door jamb split and came loose. They ran at the door one more time and it tore free, skewing down across the entrance. Koyo was inside screaming. The first one in after Danny and Zoltan tumbled through the opening was Magada. As others picked their way over the door she took Koyo by the shoulders and shouted, "Magus is dead, up there in the canyon. You need to go look."

Magus' servant was hysterical but everyone was in agreement and pointed toward the spot. They more or less ushered her out, and, torn between protecting the cabin and seeing what had happened to her master, she kept looking back as she hurried frantically up the canyon. The invaders cast about, taking in this space which they had never set eyes on before. There was a long unlit corridor, the only light coming from the doorway. On either side there were rooms, and everybody at once began trying and opening doors.

Immediately to the right was a kind of study, with a desk, some bookshelves, a couple of easy chairs, and a radio. Its shuttered window gave directly onto the angle between the canyons and the whole area in front of the canteen, including the tent. It was obvious that hardly any traffic in the canyons could escape the notice of an observer positioned here.

Opposite this room was a small kitchen and dining area. A quick scan of the cupboards revealed luxuries not seen anywhere else in the Ranch, preserves, chocolate, wines, tins of paté, even a few cigars. For citizens of the canyons these goods were now so remote they hardly knew what they were and anyway there was no time to spend on them. Others were already trying doors farther down and an irresistible instinct seemed to draw everyone with them.

The next rooms were bedrooms belonging, it appeared, to Magus and Koyo respectively, and after that there was a shower room and a store room. The latter contained tools, blankets, chairs, a generator and what looked like old radio and video equipment. After a few more paces the corridor came to an end in a facing door. Here it was very hard to see anything because the only light was filtered through from the entrance and the shuttered windows in the rooms. Someone broke open a window in the store room, letting in some extra light. Danny began looking for a key to the final door, and then all at once something made him gag uncontrollably.

An indescribably awful smell had reached his nose from somewhere. It shocked him to the core and he did not want to carry on. Magada was right beside him and she too caught the odor. Although she was used to the profound squalor of the canyons, there was a yet more terrible corruption here. She put her hand to her mouth and looked intensely at Danny.

"We have to go in."

Danny gritted his teeth, breathing through half-closed lips, looking for the key. He needed to get this over with. It seemed that after the front door this one should have the largest key, and he was right. The lock turned easily. The door was very heavy, tightly fitted, and opened outward. He grasped the handle but the whole crowd was now behind and pressing on him. He yelled at everyone to step back. They gave him room and he pulled the door. It yielded slowly, bringing with it the air behind. The gust of enclosed air carried a rottenness beyond human imagination and the whole group fell back, gagging and horror-struck. There was almost no light in the passage beyond and their only clue about what was down there was the stench.

People were covering their mouths and noses but the cry went up, "We need light. Is there a light?" Ravel darted into the store room and after a moment they heard the generator kick into life. Danny who had fallen back, paralyzed by the smell, was spurred again into action. He pushed back past people into the store room looking for light switches. Ravel was already on the hunt and

Pascale's Wager

simultaneously they found a main panel. They turned everything on.

A powerful electrical hum rose in pitch from the corridor and bright light flashed up and down, blinding people's eyes. The noise was from a large exhaust fan and they could feel the current of the air moving by them, lessening the intensity of the odor. As their eyes got used to the light they could see what looked like a large, low hall or den. To the right side there was an open area bounded by the same adobe walls as the rest of the building but this time, rather than their neutral brownish color, they were painted a strange mottled white.

There were chains dangling from the ceiling and from the walls, and the space was furnished with a couple of metal tables, one with a collection of surgical instruments and the longer one with what looked like straps attached. On the left hand side the wall continued straight down in line with the corridor and there were three wooden doors set in it, indicating there was a continuation of rooms there too. The putrid smell was lessening, but the overall effect was now even more disturbing, a sense that they were entering a secret chamber of true evil.

The group hesitated at the entrance, unnerved by the prospect of what they might find. Danny suddenly had the feeling that probably everyone there already knew about this place but had forgotten about it deliberately. That was the way everything had worked in the canyons and only now were they slowly waking up to their own world. He experienced a sudden overwhelming anger against the Ranch and this part of it in particular. Magus was no more, dead on the canyon floor, and it was high time for his secrets to be revealed.

Danny stepped forward into the room and tried a key to the first door. It didn't work and he tried another. It slipped smoothly in the lock and the door opened almost by itself to reveal a strange, jarring sight. Rather than any kind of horror, there was a woman reading at a table lit by a softly glowing lamp and decorated with desert cacti. The cell seemed to lack all the stink of the corridor and it even felt domestic, with an easy chair, a book case and a comfortable bed covered with a patchwork quilt and a flowered valance hanging below. The woman had a pleasant, clear and roundish face, framed with nut brown hair. She was dressed in a calf-length plaid skirt, belted high, topped by a crisp white blouse with a lace collar. She looked up and at first registered no surprise. Slowly, as the group edged into the room, she blinked and seemed confused.

"Who are these people?" She asked as if she were talking to the book or the room.

Danny went closer to her chair. "We are from outside, from the canyon. Magus is dead. You are free to go."

He held out his hand to her.

"Magus, my father, he is dead?"

"Yes, there was an accident. Please come. We are your friends."

"My father dead? Oh, how terrible, it cannot be true! Who will kiss me and wish me sweet dreams now?"

"I'm sorry, but it's true. Magus is dead, you must go and see. He was your father? What is your name?"

The woman put her book on the table. She took Danny's offered hand and stood up. "My name is Greta. And, yes, I must see this thing for myself."

Danny guided her to the doorway and gave her to Alaqua to accompany her up the canyon to where the bodies were. He told Alaqua to be sure to introduce her to Pascale when they got there. They watched as the two of them walked up the corridor toward the blinding light, Greta shading her eyes and clutching Alaqua's arm.

Ravel said, "Never knew Magus had a daughter."

Magada replied. "Seems it was a bit more than that he had!"

Danny quickly turned and, flipping through the keys, found one to open the second door. Immediately it fell ajar, the group was met by a distinct undertone of the general stench, a smell partly anesthetic but bitter and poisonous at the same time. A dark-skinned woman lay naked and unconscious on a bed under a large overhead light. There was some kind of drip stand by her bed with tubes hanging down. Again everyone struggled to cope with the fetid atmosphere. But Magada did not hesitate. She was first in the room and walked straight over to the bed and looked down at the body. It was covered in scars and there seemed to be some kind of surgical implant in one of the arms. She yelled, "Need to get her outside. Zoltan can you carry her?"

345

The big man came over and scooped up the prone body. Magada told the cowboy who had held her horse to follow with the mattress and sheets to cover the woman, and once outside to try to wake her and give her water. Everyone stood back as Zoltan edged his way out, followed by the cowboy. It was a sight, full of terror and compassion, stirring the deepest forgotten memories in the onlookers.

Danny was already at the third door and the first key he chose turned the lock. There was a muffled movement from inside the door, like rats scuttling for cover. This door was heavier than the other and it took a firm push to get it open. As it swung back it showed a space lit with a single electric bulb. The only furniture was a bed frame and a bucket toilet, and cowering in a space between the bed and the wall was a creature that may have been a man or perhaps some kind of animal. The stink was at its most intense, fecal and pungent, and once again everyone fell back, clutching their throats. Magada gave a hoarse cry and said something inaudible. Danny was again paralyzed, unable to say or do anything.

The face was obscured by filthy matted hair stretching to the lower back and by an equally encrusted bush around the mouth and the nose which was simply two holes on a planed surface. From the sides of the naked body protruded strange stumps which could have been twisted forearms. The only thing that gave a sign of humanity were the eyes, glazed and traumatized, yet with a hint of fathomless endurance, like a baited bear which in its pit of suffering carries still the breath of its freedom.

Slowly people entered the room, with their mouths and noses covered. After a moment, Magada once again took the initiative. She went over to the bed, dropped on her knees, and held out a hand. Danny summoned his will and followed her, dropping down beside her.

Magada said, "This is Danny. My name is Magada. He and his sister, Pascale, freed the Ranch from Magus. We want you to come with us into the open air and the sun."

The eyes of the figure looked blankly back and forth, from Magada to Danny.

Danny joined in. "Magus is dead. Whoever you are, you are free to leave."

The figure furrowed its brow as if the sounds of the words had woken some sort of meaning and it was trying to place what it was. It remained in the same position between the bed and the wall.

Magada said, "I think you are perhaps from the time before Immortality. I think perhaps I remember you. What is your name?"

A flicker of awareness went across the face. A voice issued from the mouth, a congealed gluey sound.

"Magus, dead?"

"Yes, that is right. He fell from the top of the canyon."

There was a pause and the figure crawled on misshapen limbs from behind the bed, like an insect attached to a monstrous head. The voice said, slowly and with immense labor, "I am Francisco. I represent the movement against Heaven, the Resistance."

Magada cried, "Francisco, I was sure it was you!" And turning to Danny she said, "He was the most famous activist of all. He tried to expose the plan for a privileged world for the few. He was called a crackpot and a terrorist, and then he disappeared."

"Well, now he's reappeared, but different, I think." Danny faced Francisco, raising his hand in an awkward impromptu salute. "We thank you, sir, for keeping true, whatever it cost, and what it cost you seems impossible to count."

The foul leonine head trembled. The bunkered eyes all at once relented and water welled up in them and a pair of tears rolled onto the filthy cheeks. "...never believed to see...this day. Take me out...of here!"

Danny rushed back up the corridor and fetched a chair from the study. Returning he saw there was one last door at the end of the corridor, directly opposite the entrance at the front. He tried it quickly and it opened. Glancing in, he could see it was simply another store room. He turned back into Francisco's cell and asked Magada to help him lift the crippled survivor onto the chair. Someone had wrapped the spidery body in a sheet and they were able to lift him with some kind of dignity. Once he was there they hoisted the chair between them. It had become now a throne and they carried it through the door and down the corridor with a feeling of triumph. Ravel held a cushion he'd found over Francisco's head to shade him from the sun and he emerged into the early afternoon light, an alien king welcomed with honor to earth.

They carried the chair to the tent where they found the second woman from the cabin still lying on her mattress, covered with a sheet, and apparently coming to her senses. She seemed restless and her eyes were wandering from side to side as if she were trying to figure out where she was and what was happening to her. The cowboy, whose name was Cormac, was squatting next to her holding a canteen of water. Orwell was at his usual position at the table; he had been there in the tent from the time Pascale first went up the cliff in the morning.

Danny and Magada placed Francisco down close to the mattress and told him the woman had been his neighbor in the cabin. Francisco nodded as if he already grasped this but he didn't say anything. He was opening his eyes for short intervals and the closing them again, trying to restrict what was for him an intense stimulus of light and activity around him. Magada took the canteen from Cormac and said she would stay with the two freed prisoners and he should help back at the cabin.

Danny was aware that his horse, Stardust, was still at the top of the cliff but he couldn't go get her yet. He had been thrown into the middle of something shocking and terrible and he had to see it through. By this time everybody in the cantina had come out to witness the world-ending events of the day, and there were now about twenty people around the tent, including Zoltan, Cormac, Ravel, Eliot, the cook and his assistants. Even Louis and Joanne had come down from the orchards to observe. Danny told everybody that they should go to Magus' cabin and empty it entirely of its contents, bringing everything into the open. He asked Zoltan to build a bonfire for Zena while he went to check on Pascale and the others. Ravel was to return to Magus' cabin and get a couple of sheets and then follow him to the steps. It seemed everybody was prepared at this point to take directions from him and they all went off as they were told.

Danny walked back up the canyon. As he rounded the spur by the cliff steps he could see Pascale no longer next to the body of Zena but sitting slightly apart with Alaqua and Greta. A little farther again, closer to the body of Magus, there was Koyo squatting on the ground her head covered in canyon dust. Every so often she would let out a parched cry and flick some more dust on her head. Flies had already begun to gather on both corpses but the horror of the scene did not seem to affect the group of three women. Danny walked up to them and asked what was happening. Greta looked up.

"My father is dead, just as you said. I have seen him. But I have found new friends, Alaqua who brought me here, and Pascale who has told me a story about a frozen land far away and another one close to here where everything is beautiful."

Pascale smiled sadly up at Danny. "This morning was terrible and all together tragic until Greta arrived. I am grieving inside, for Zena, but Greta is a new friend. She likes to talk of books and stories, so I told her some of ours. Unfortunately Koyo here will not talk at all."

Danny said, "Magus' place was a house of horrors. There are only evil stories out of there. I am not surprised she won't talk. But we have to dispose of the bodies. They are building a fire for Zena now, and we will place Magus in his cabin and burn it over him."

Koyo let out a penetrating scream. "No, no, no. You cannot burn, you cannot burn"

Danny glanced at her coldly. "If we don't the dogs will eat him. And the only thing fit for that cabin of yours is to burn it to the ground!"

They could see Ravel arriving with the sheets. Danny went to meet him. He took the cloths and gave one to Pascale. "Here, if you and Alaqua can carry Zena, Ravel and I will take Magus."

They rolled the bodies into the sheets and hoisted them as best they could. Greta stayed away from Magus and helped Pascale and Alaqua instead. The two groups of bearers made their way with difficulty down the canyon, stopping frequently to rest and regain their grip on the cloths. As they did Koyo followed behind, continuing to throw dust on herself and crying out, "You kill the master. You kill!"

When they got to the tent they set the corpses down and went under the awning to take a drink from the water bucket now kept permanently on the table. The dark-skinned woman on the mattress was conscious but behaving in an extremely distressed way, clutching herself and grinding her teeth. She was speaking but what she was saying was barely intelligible.

Magada said, "I think she wants some of that stuff Magus had her hooked up to. We could give her a reduced dose to wean her off."

Danny shrugged, "That sounds right. You should get the stand with the tubes by her bed. There was a bag on it with some liquid. Someone else will stay here."

"Sure," Magada said. But she did not move. She stood there gazing at the two bodies the group had brought with them. Koyo had resumed her position on the ground close to Magus, continuing with her public mourning. Magada turned to the maimed figure on the chair, gesturing at the corpse. "Here's the source of all your misery, Francisco, plus more of his handiwork. Don't you want to spit on him, curse him? You know, this time you send *him* to hell?"

Francisco looked at the corpse and its attendant mourner. His eyes spoke for him, gripped with helpless anguish and at the same time surrendered to another space where all destructive intention had been abandoned. He struggled to speak. "My soul owes nothing to Magus, not even revenge."

Magada stared at him but was not appeased. She walked over to Koyo. "You there! You can quit your moaning right now. That guy you're crying over, breaking his neck was far too good for him. If I had my way he'd be roasted over a slow fire. If you're not careful it'll happen to you instead. You knew everything going on in that cabin!"

She strode off on her errand. By this time a huge pile of the cabin's contents had been carried outside by a band of eager looters. In between the pile and the tent Zoltan had also built the base for a funeral pyre, using the booth for Magus that he had collapsed and dragged into position. The fuel was now up to chest height and Zoltan was extending it on either side to create a broad platform. The group that had carried the bodies watched as Magada disappeared past the bonfire and into the jumble of furniture and stores, looking for the drip stand. The only sound was the continual moaning of the the woman on the mattress. Pascale went over to Francisco.

"May I introduce myself, sir? My name is Pascale, Danny's sister. I liked what you said to Magada, that you harbor no revenge. "

The disfigured man, perched uncomfortably in the study

chair, opened his torn, half-closed lids. His voice was heavy but he spoke with a little more fluency. "My name is Francisco. You are Pascale. You are one who helped to set the Ranch free. I owe you thanks. "

He shut his eyes again. Pascale replied, "I am sorry we could not help before, Francisco. I did not know you were in the cabin. We started this tent we're in now, as a place to tell stories. It was the first step in changing things. Magus wanted to crush it but he couldn't. He thought he had his chance, when he arrested me at the top of the cliff. I'm sure he was planning to bring me to the cabin. But he shot Zena and then he fell to his death."

"You are fortunate. He would have been merciless once he had you. My memory is confused, but in the early days I know there were people he killed. He did not do it once he'd established control. Instead, he kept his normal entertainment."

Francisco's shoulders suddenly slumped and he began to tremble violently throughout his misshapen body. Pascale hesitated just a moment before the stinking, barely human form, and then she bent and wrapped her arms around him and held him to herself. Immediately the shaking got worse. It was as if the survivor of Magus' cabin was terrified and was trying to break free. Inarticulate cries came from his mouth. But Pascale did not relent, rather she placed a knee on the chair and folded her arms more securely round his shoulders, pressing him to her breast. She spoke into his ear through the matted hair.

"Francisco, you have been to a deep place of darkness. I also have touched the darkness. When I came here first I died, and all hope died with me. But afterward I remained alive. I found my way back to life and I began to see all the darkness around me become light. Because love is able to see in the dark. I believe love can see all the darkness you have known and turn it into light."

Francisco's deformed body gave a final great spasm, almost as if it was trying to leap off the chair and outside itself. Pascale was knocked back but she held on and more or less caught the pitching man with her weight, held him and lowered him again to the chair. All the tension within Francisco crumbled. He fell back unresisting and the shaking stopped. He let himself be embraced and dropped his squalid shaggy head down on Pascale's shoulder like a child's. Tears rolled on his ravaged cheeks.

351

After a minute Pascale gently detached herself and stood back. Her own dress was grimy now and her face smudged. She said, "Francisco, you are a great man!"

Danny had stood behind Pascale and witnessed everything. He could see Francisco's soul laid bare and how he had preserved its truth despite an endless age of suffering. "Yes, you are, Francisco. You held out against Magus during all his reign of terror and your heart was always free! You are king of the canyon!"

Orwell had been observing everything intently. He cleared his throat and joined in, "I did not think this canyon could hold more evil than I had already seen, and yet it did. But here is a man who was never destroyed by the evil. I honor this man!" And he too held his hand to his head in an awkward salute.

Francisco's near toothless mouth opened in a deprecating grin. His wounded eyes took on a clear expression for the first time. At that moment he looked fully human and a spontaneous cheer burst from the whole group. He said, "Being here with you, it's like I died and came to heaven!"

There was a clattering noise and they turned to see Magada arriving, dragging the stand behind her. She took it straight over to the woman who by this time had rolled off the mattress and was sitting on the ground, still moaning and hugging herself. When she saw the drip stand she cried out in expectation and held up her arm. Magada fiddled with a valve until she got the fluid in the bag flowing. Then she plugged the end into the implanted port in the woman's arm. The woman immediately relaxed and lay back on the mattress with a mindless look on her face. Magada fiddled a little more and got the drip down to its slowest rate.

As she did Francisco said, "Her name is Elise. She was Magus' plaything, worse than me. I have to confess, often I was glad to hear her screaming; it meant Magus was not coming for me."

Magada looked over. "I'm going to get my horse. The cabin is cleared out and ready."

Danny wasn't sure what she was suggesting and he and the others waited as she quickly crossed the canyon back to the cattle stockade where she had tethered her horse. She mounted up and came cantering back, loosening the rope on the saddle as she came. Before anyone had fully grasped what she intended, she had jumped off and whipped the lariat around Magus' feet and remounted. All in one move she wound the extended rope around the saddle horn and booted her pony into a run. The rope snapped taut and jerked Magus' prone form off the ground, catapulting him after the horse. Koyo, who had hardly been paying attention, had the body dragged instantly from in front of her and she let out a piercing yell. Both Danny and Pascale gasped but there was nothing anyone could do. Magus was skidding and bouncing along the canyon floor, returning one last time to his cabin.

Everyone who could started running after Magada. They saw her pass round the bonfire and head toward the adobe arches, stooping low and guiding her mount straight through the big front door. Magus' body bumped over the threshold and disappeared. A moment later the horse and rider emerged on their own. Danny and Pascale came up as Magada was dismounting, Koyo and Greta close behind. The people who had been engaged in emptying out the cabin were all standing about. They began to gather in closer. Magada flat palmed her horse on the rump, sending it running. She yelled out triumphantly, "Time to send this thing all to hell!"

Coming from behind Koyo charged at Magada screaming furiously. Magada saw her coming, neatly sidestepped and Koyo fell headlong. Magada swore, "So help me, you touch me and you're in there with him."

She called out to Cormac to bring a barrel of the vegetable oil used for the generator and to empty it on the cabin floors and surfaces. Pascale and Danny were down on either side of Koyo, holding her, uncertain of what she might do next. But it was all over in a moment. Cormac spread the oil and Magada got Katoucha to help her bring armfuls of brush and bits and pieces from Zoltan's bonfire. They went inside with it and in less than a minute there was the unmistakable crackle of fire. Magada and Katoucha ran out amid gathering smoke and suddenly it was if the whole place exploded. The cabin was engulfed in angry red flames shooting fifteen feet from the windows and roof.

Koyo kept whimpering, "My master good! My master good!" But no one cared. The sight, the sound and the smell of the inferno and what was inside it held everyone captive in its power. Even Koyo's fury seemed abated by the blaze and Pascale and Danny stopped holding onto her.

The fire's heat made everyone fall back to a wider circle and Pascale and Danny found themselves on their own for the first time.

Pascale said, "I haven't had the chance to thank you, Danny. You and Palmiro saved my life. Also for opening up the cabin. That was a hard, terrible thing to have to do."

"I'm glad it's burning to the ground. It's the worst thing I've ever seen."

"I know, Magada is very angry. There is a lot of anger in this fire."

They were both quiet for a while. Then Danny said, "Let's go and set the fire for Zena, and we'll make it a more peaceful one"

The sister and brother walked back to the tent. Francisco had seen the fire and he spoke, seeming at first to quote. "The smoke of the land went up like the smoke of a furnace.... May I have some water please? If you just fill a cup I believe I can manage."

They gave him water and he was able to grasp the beaker with the stumps of his arms. Greta and Alaqua had now arrived and Pascale asked them to help her and Danny carry Zena. The four together lifted the sheet with the body of the woman, the daughter of university lecturers and the first canyon resident to tell her story. They brought her to the bonfire and with a lot of clambering and shoving they got the body into place on the platform. Danny walked the fifty paces to the smoldering wreck of Magus' cabin and picked up a timber that had fallen from the roof. He went back to the pyre with the glowing brand aloft. Zoltan, Ravel and Katoucha saw what he was doing and came with him.

He thrust the torch into the base of the pile and stood back. A wisp of smoke rose from the dry sticks and slowly the pile caught fire. As the flames began to lick upward, the rest of the crowd that had been watching the destruction of the cabin turned and moved instinctively toward the other pyre. The mood was a peculiar mixture of horror and happiness. The world had come to an end with the death of Magus and yet everyone was still here and, it seemed, more fully and truly than before. Their rapt gaze and strange emotions shifted quite naturally to another violent death and its purifying fire. Zena was innocent and nothing like the monster that Magus was, in fact she was his victim. But somehow the deaths seemed wrapped up together. All the horror and disgust surrounding Magus had gone up in smoke, but now all that was made doubly pure by the fire and smoke engulfing Zena.

The community of the canyon gathered around the bonfire and as the flames rose higher, Pascale decided to speak. She raised her voice to a pitch where all could hear her.

"Zena did not like heights but this morning she climbed the cliff for the first time. Zena was a prisoner in the canyon but this morning she gained her freedom. She never had the life she wanted, she wanted to be a mortal. This morning she found the life she wanted."

"I came to the canyon, sent by forces which put a murderer and torturer in charge of people who would not fit in. Zena was my first friend here. The first to talk to me. The first to help build our tent. Today she was the best friend I ever had, when she overcame her great fears in order to protect me. Because of her Magus was distracted and was not able to capture me and Danny. Magus shot her and she fell. Her life was spent for me and truly for all of us."

"Magus' reign has come to an end. His violence rebounded on him. When he fired the gun at Zena he started a chain reaction that brought his own death. But his reign cannot truly be over if we carry his death inside us, if our anger lives on, if the fire that consumed him consumes us."

"That does not have to be, for here before us is a much different fire, one we can truly take to our hearts. It is not the fire itself that counts, but Zena's love that it represents. Zena willed herself to love even when it was most dangerous. She embraced a love which taught her to fly when she thought she never could. And it set her free from fear even as she fell. The fire of love gives wings to our hearts and lifts us even when we fall."

Pascale pointed upward to where the now raging flames disappeared in a rich plume of smoke. People followed her gesture and continued to gaze into the late afternoon sky where the light was already diffusing and the smoke rose in it like a single gray pillar on which the whole sky rested. No one spoke. They simply remained there, watching the smoke and hearing the echo of Pascale's words, whether they could grasp them or not. After a while some people moved back to the tent and sat down. A few went over to the cantina.

Danny thought the moment had come to rescue Stardust. He went back to the tent, found a water canteen and set out directly to the steps in the cliff. He made the climb, thinking that the last person to ascend them was Zena and so much had changed, and so dramatically, since. When he got to the top Stardust, who was tethered to a small tree, whinnied with relief. He went up to her, stroked her and gave her water, apologizing for being away so long. He untied her and climbed in the saddle. He still had Magus' keys and was sure one of them would open the gates to the canyon.

As he swung Stardust around he glanced out at the rugged wilderness to the south where the shadows were already etching the western walls of the mesas. He saw the spiral of smoke from the fire rising straight up, and realized that it was composed of two threads, one fainter than the other and leaning over and winding itself around the stronger one. He thought that the main plume had to be from the more recent fire, from Zena's, and the other must be the remains from Magus'. They had come together to form one solitary finger above the land. He wondered if anyone in Heaven would notice.

8. PLAGUE BRINGER

The morning after the Font Eterno Immersion Palmiro woke early. There were a couple of essential things he had to do. The previous night he had left a note for Eboni telling her he wanted to meet before breakfast, and she showed up promptly, anxious to find out everything that had happened. He told her about the journey to the canyon, about Pascale's decision to stay, and then the succession of events in which two people had been killed. Eboni was totally horrified and even more so when she heard the details of Danny's involvement.

It was no longer a matter of trying to hide Pascale from the authorities, something impossible in the long run. For the first time in Heaven's story one of the Immortals, and a key one at that, had been attacked, and was actually dead. It was unthinkable, impossible. She almost fainted, sinking unsteadily to the ground. Palmiro got down next to her and set out his argument.

"Listen, I know this is a bad shock, but we just can't sit back and wait for the other shoe to drop. We need to do something to distract people from news coming out of the canyons. Then perhaps they won't get so crazy and we'll have a chance."

"You're the crazy one," Eboni reacted." What could possibly stop people thinking about a shoot-out at the Ranch in which Magus was killed? It won't be long before inquiries are made, and they'll follow the trail right to here, to Danny and me."

"Danny acted in self-defense. Magus had already shot and killed someone he was supposed to be looking after. Pascale was in danger too. Look, there's nothing we can do to change the facts, but I want to propose an idea. If you and I show ourselves to be devotees of the Font Eterno, opinion could easily swing round to our side."

Palmiro did not feel bad about duping Eboni. The whole thing was much bigger than a minor rebellion in the canyons and eventually she would come round to seeing that too.

"What are you talking about now?"

"Well, I was thinking. What if I was to volunteer to enter the Sea of Chaos along with Sarobindo and last as long as I could before the nuclear storm. It would look like I was giving respect to the greatest institution in the Heavenly Homeland."

Eboni gaped at him in disbelief. "First you persuade Danny to search for the Ranch, going against the whole of Heaven, and now you want to fake being a yogi, the most respected figure in Heaven?"

"Great isn't it? There couldn't be a better plan. People will find it very hard to think of us as subversives if I'm a trainee yogi!"

At this point, with the charge of being terrorists hanging over them, Eboni really couldn't think of anything better. She let out a despairing sigh, but willing to grasp at straws.

"And just how are you planning to do this: I'm sure you have something in mind? It's not going to work but I suppose it's better than sitting around waiting for a knock at the door."

"Exactly. I want to go to the Font Eterno today and tell them I'd like to do an Immersion. If you have some friends you can get to come along and vouch for me then it will be harder for the organizers to refuse. Can you get a few people to come and meet me there early this evening?"

She threw her hands up in exasperation. "Yeah, I'm sure I can persuade Cyrus to speak for you. Or, how about your precious Adorno?"

"Please don't be difficult, you know what I mean."

"OK, OK, I guess I can round up a few. There's Chen Jin. And you never know, Omar might come along, just for the heck of it."

"Good. I'll meet you and whoever you bring at the service entrance early this evening."

Eboni was not convinced but she went along with it. She had a growing feeling she was now part of something with a life of its own; no one could stop it. Danny was in it up to his neck, and she had already decided that whatever his fate it would he hers too. She took her horse and rode directly to the Silk-Making Colony where Chen Jin lived. It did not take much to persuade him—a new volunteer for Font Eterno sounded pretty cool—and he agreed also to recruit Artemis and Omar at the Fabric Colony nearby.

In the meantime Palmiro took the car. He planned to drive all the way to the Agora of the Baths and get back in time to meet Eboni and the others. He remembered from the dramatic night of his Initiation that no one had been carrying anything when the assistants first gathered in the end hall of the Baths. He'd decided the elements necessary for the ritual had to be all stored somewhere in the building. He intended to search the storerooms until he found the drug they administered to inductees. If he took just the right amount, he could perhaps drop his breathing rate and stay conscious long enough to do what he had to do. It would be a big risk, but he remembered he had not gone unconscious straight away. He had remained underwater and felt no strain. What he had to do would need very little time and the extra moments given him by the drug would provide all the window he required.

He drove along the Appian Way with the morning sun behind him. The gentle lick of the tires on the highway contrasted with the bumping gait of the horse which over so many days had been all he'd known; he'd never really gotten the hang of it. For the first time as long as he could remember, he began to relax. He watched the tall trees drifting by, the occasional car or tram with their blandly smiling occupants, the glimpses of the pleasant colonies between the trees and across the hills. He thought, really, how beautiful it all was, how serene and uncomplicated. Why, after all, should not this be the end goal of human existence? If at least some were happy, why not let that be enough, and forget the rest? Why tip over the universe? He knew his answer at once. The reason was people like him, or Adorno, or even Danny. People who would not let things be. Simply that! People who were prepared to put everything at risk rather than accept something unfair, false, or pointless. Then there were other people who seemed to go even further, people who imagined a completely different way of being. People like Pascale.

Ah yes, Pascale. He'd realized just yesterday that her opinion meant a lot to him. Maybe the reason was that he loved her! But what kind of love was it that did not wish to be with the beloved at every moment? Even he knew this was what love meant, and it was not what he wanted. At least he didn't think so. All he had desired, it seemed, was to learn from Adorno, and to use the knowledge he had gained to bring an end to immortality. But when he thought about it, he saw every step had been marked out for him by Pascale. It was Pascale who had brought him here to Heaven. It was her arrest and detention that had sent him to talk with Adorno, who had then pointed him toward research in the area of his own momentous discovery. True, he had wanted to become a second Adorno and was well on his way to fulfilling that dream, but had not Adorno somehow infected him with this? Had not his mentor gotten him to take the bait of scientific genius when really all he wanted was to save Pascale? Even now the plan he had made, was it not in order to cause an upheaval so wide-reaching that the inhabitants of the Ranch could be set free?

He arrived at a junction and almost unconsciously he took the turn off the Sacred Way, leaving the route that led to the Baths. His thoughts of Pascale had brought Jonas to mind and he happened to be close to the road which led to the Colony of Historians.

He followed the winding single track along the ridge, into the valley dotted with vineyards and up across the shrubland where the villa was situated. He had very little time but he thought he had a duty to Pascale's former lover, to let him know what had happened. He found him almost immediately, in the courtyard as he nosed the car through the gates. He was wearing a broad-brimmed floppy hat and seemed to be pruning the Manzanita trees. It was almost as if he were there waiting for him.

Palmiro invited him to walk with him, saying he had to be quick. He gave a brief outline of Pascale's rescue, not leaving out the violence. He described her bizarre decision to remain in the canyons and how Danny had chosen to stay there with her. He said Eboni had the directions and if he, Jonas, could ride a horse he'd be able to get there easily. He told him that he was very hopeful about the situation overall and he was going to do some things he thought would make everything work out for the best.

Jonas staggered and almost keeled over when Palmiro mentioned the fight with Magus and its fatal consequence. Palmiro had to reach out to steady him. When he had finished, Jonas shook his head and spoke in a hopeless voice. "Ever since I saw you last I knew it would only lead to trouble. And I doubt what you are planning, whatever it is, can make things better. You have no idea how determined the Immortals are when they make a decision. But, please tell me, did Pascale mention me at all?"

"I'm afraid not. As I said there was very little time, and then Magus came."

Jonas seemed to be struggling with violent emotion. "Pascale was always a bird flying off to some strange place. Now the canyons have claimed her. Am I even a memory for her?"

Despite himself Palmiro reached out his hand once more, placing it on the Immortal's shoulder. "Jonas, all I can tell you is you should go see her. You don't know what you are to her until you see her. Anyway, it may be safer there until the storm blows over."

"What storm'? What is it you are going to do?

"Listen I've said too much. I've got to go. Get a horse and go see Pascale."

Palmiro walked directly to the car and drove away without looking back. He did not understand why he'd been letting himself get close to the Immortal; he didn't even like him and it was dangerous anyway. The man had to make his own choices, while he, Palmiro, had to complete the task before him. He got back on to the Sacred Way, and in little more than an hour and a half he arrived at the Agora of the Baths.

As the honeyed stone of the walls and the encircling green of the cypress trees came into view, he was flooded by the most vivid sensations. Here was the setting in which he had first met Heaven. Here was where he had experienced his first reaction of anger and resentment, and where Pascale had argued that he could learn a lot from these people. And it was true. He had penetrated to the heart of their secrets and was returning to the Baths as a conqueror. Meanwhile, Pascale had willingly surrendered to one of the most depressing places he could imagine.

He found the gate that led to the sandy courtyard at the end of the building, swinging the car in and shutting off the engine. The silence was immense. He felt like just sitting there and thinking, trying get to the bottom of all he was feeling. But there was no time. He had to keep moving.

He tried the handle of the apse door leading into the end hall: it was open—nothing was ever locked in Heaven. He made his way at once into the room where he had spent his first hours after arrival. He did not remember seeing cupboards in this room but he had to check; he needed a flashlight or flare of some sort to see his way into the main chamber. There was nothing there. After drawing a blank also in the room where Pascale had stayed, he continued down the hall, but again found nothing. He went back and grabbed the antique couch halfway down the hall, the one on which Jonas had slept, and dragged it up to the big ceremonial doors at the end, hauling them open and kicking the couch into the gap to prop them wide. The heady scent that had impressed him so much when he first pulled open the big doors returned once again, but it seemed less dominant. He felt he was able to detect the presence of drugs in it and he was no longer amazed. In fact, it told him he was close to his goal.

The serene light of the hallway struck a path across the marble surface inside the door. Palmiro stepped in and waited until his eyes got used to the gloom. Although he wasn't intimidated any more, he still felt the awe of this place, the way it had shaped and made a universe. He could see the racks of veils and towels, and farther down he could see shelves filled with oil lamps and flasks. He made his way in the semi-darkness and picked out a lamp with a straight handle and plenty of oil. He fumbled along the shelves looking for some way to light it. He could find nothing, but then in almost pitch blackness he stumbled upon a low cupboard and, feeling inside, he found a flint lighter. After a couple of tries he got it to produce a flame which he then transferred to the lamp.

He held his lamp aloft, glimpsing the lustrous pools of water behind him. They were like a dangerous black and golden animal slipping between the walls of onyx. A shiver of power flooded through the building, but he resisted the feeling. He walked further on and could see a row of doors along the far side of the hall beyond the pool. What he was looking for had to be inside one of them. He tried the first and found a room with a tiny window, a small table, a couch and several large cushions scattered on the floor. Throwing open two more doors he found the same thing, and then on his fourth try he found what he was looking for. He saw a long wall-shelf stacked with the flasks of liquid and the beakers used in the Initiation. Almost at once, a moment after he opened the door, there was an echoing shriek and a groan and long narrow shaft of daylight pierced across the pools and fell directly on him.

He gave a start and instinctively let go of the door. At the same time he heard a voice. It made him jump once more, but the moment he heard it he recognized whose it was.

"There you are, the plague-bringer! I knew it was you in here, Enemy of Heaven!"

One of the main front doors had been opened and framed in its angle of light was the woman without a name, the first person he and Pascale had met in Heaven. Palmiro swore fiercely to himself and re-opened the door he had just let shut, entering the room. He could hear the woman's voice resounding through the building.

"Don't be angry, Adorno's boy! Yes, I know about you. Adorno was my best, but now you are! I never wanted Heaven anyway, and when you have brought its end I will be content."

Palmiro put his lamp down on one of the shelves and grabbed a flask, pulling off the big cork in the top. He held out his hand and dribbled a little into his cupped palm. It had a slightly syrupy texture. When he sniffed it and touched it with the tip of his tongue, he recognized at once the sweet pungent taste of the Initiation drug. Even as he tested the liquid he could hear the sound of the woman's feet scuffling on the marble and her continued flood of words.

"Adorno brought me here and I said I never wanted it. He just put me on the plane and I came. But see, now he has given all his secrets to you. You are the new Adorno. And you will fly me home!"

If the baths had given him an uncanny sensation, what the woman was saying sent a chill through him. What did she mean? And if she meant what her words seemed to mean, how could she possibly know these things? Had Adorno talked to her, and, if so, what was she to Adorno? He stepped outside the room and she was right there in front of him. He noticed her hair was gray and unbrushed and she had teeth missing. He was obliged to confront her.

"Who are you? And don't give me that stupid "no name" routine. How do you know Adorno?"

Before he could stop her she had flung her arms around him and was hugging him close. "My dear child, don't you know? Didn't he tell you? I am his mother! And since he has adopted you, you are my son, too! And a better one than he ever was!"

"You are insane, get away from me!" For a moment he was trapped, with the flask in one hand and the lamp in the other. He threw the lamp over the low wall into the pool where it quickly sunk to the bottom and extinguished. He used his free hand to unclamp her arms and twist away. He dodged from her flailing grasp and walked as quickly as he could in the murky light back to the door to the hallway. He passed through and almost ran the length of the hall, down past the sleeping rooms and out to the car. As he did he could hear her voice following him.

"My son, do not worry, do not worry. Your secret is safe with me. You are Heaven's doom. Heaven's doom!"

***

As he drove back along the Appian Way Palmiro's mood was in stark contrast to the one he had set out with that morning. He reasoned that the woman calling herself Adorno's mother was regarded universally as crazy, so there was very little danger anyone would listen to anything she said. At the same time, it was deeply unnerving that she seemed to understand so much about his plans. Even assuming that what she had said about her relationship to Adorno was true, it was inconceivable he would jeopardize everything he so greatly desired by telling her, or indeed anybody, about conversations he and his student may have had. So the question was, how did she get her information?

He was forced to conclude that somehow her mind had leaped from one tenuous detail to another and in a kind of huge lucky guess, she had come up with a picture resembling the truth. He thought with a hint of irony that what she had done was not all that essentially different from the genius of her son coming up with the immortality enzyme. Like mother, like son! Combining random facts in an entirely new formula could indeed produce a miracle of truth. The idea gave him a strange, paradoxical comfort and served to calm him as he continued his journey toward downtown. If this woman's deranged mind could guess the strict truth in a relatively narrow field, would it not be possible for unfettered minds to come up with hitherto unknown truths and on a large scale?

He thought again of Adorno, of his theory about the human mind, computers and the stars. He also thought of Pascale, and her strange words on the clifftop. Perhaps there really was a way of counting in the dark, faster than light, the way that Pascale called "love"? But then if this was the case immortality really should be considered the enemy of love, because it would allow no darkness inside itself. It simply flirted at the edge of darkness, at a great pantomime called Font Eterno. There everyone enjoyed seeing someone go to the edge just for the chance they might not come back. Soon, however, all that would end.

Pascale's Wager

9. VOLUNTEERING

The authorities in charge of the Font Eterno were a group of Sarobindo's disciples with Sarobindo presiding over them. Given the whole thing was his idea, and how triumphantly he always carried it off, it was impossible that anybody else would govern the institution. However, procedures were lax to the point of non-existent. Sarobindo would turn up, enter his personal meditation area and prepare himself. His assistants were already there before him, checking the sound, lighting and projection systems, testing the bridge and powering up the particle accelerator. A couple of them functioned as the regular announcers for the ceremony and one of them would take up position in the commentary box and wait for Sarobindo to show himself. Apart from some other people from the Tech Colony, who provided support for the engineering, that really was it.

When Palmiro crossed over the ceremonial causeway in front of the great globe it was already dark and the crowd was beginning to gather for the second of the three days of Immersions. He pushed his way quickly to the arched tunnel at the front of the building which provided a service entrance and access for officials. Against the shimmering crystal of the sphere he could see Eboni waiting together with three people he didn't know. He walked toward them and Eboni turned and saw him.

"There he is, I told you he'd come." She sounded relieved, and when he got near she at once introduced to him to Chen Jin, Artemis and Omar. He remembered hearing a little about them from Danny, but he had no wish for small talk. He thanked them for coming and asked them if they had any questions.

Omar said, "So you're really going to risk going under? No one but Sarobindo has done that as long as anyone can remember. What's your game Palmiro? You think you can do this and survive?"

"No game, Omar. I can't stay down as long as Sarobindo, but at least I'll manage a few minutes. That way I will honor him and the Font Eterno."

Artemis gave him the thumbs up. "Charlize said you were quite the rare bird. I'm always ready for the unexpected, so you

366

have my vote!"

"Well, I thank you for that. So let's just go and find someone and if you're all agreed you can tell them you're sponsoring me."

Without waiting for further discussion Palmiro headed for the tunnel. The others followed, infected by Palmiro's uncompromising approach. They entered the deep heart of the building, walking the length of a tunnel lit by recessed lighting, with walls covered in glittering mosaics of dragons, centaurs, griffins and other mythical beasts. At the end there was an ornamental stone stairway leading to a grand, four-sided landing like the mezzanine of an opera house. The group mounted the stairs and at the top found a marble screen and set back against it a long dais.

Seated on the dais, framed by lambent candles, were two women dressed in the orange ceremonial color of the Immersion. They were cross-legged and meditating, facing at an angle toward each other, like book ends. They did not open their eyes when Palmiro coughed "Hello". The sight of them was imposing against the carved frieze and flickering lights and the newcomers remained silent, waiting for the attendants to respond. But they stayed wholly unresponsive, until finally Palmiro lost patience and interrupted the reverie.

"Excuse me, I am here to volunteer for the Immersion."

The guardians of the threshold opened their eyes in surprise. Their normal job was simply to mark the holiness of the place, signaling the sacred precincts and deterring people from wandering further toward the preparation rooms. So much time had passed since there had been any other candidate for Immersion that the thought of someone volunteering for the Sea of Chaos was almost totally foreign.

"I am sorry, what are you volunteering for?" It was the woman on the right. She had long auburn hair, high cheekbones and expressive lips.

"My name is Palmiro and I wish to join the Master in the ceremony of Immersion, as homage to him and to honor the tradition he represents. My companions are here to vouch for me."

"I'm afraid I still don't understand. Are you a disciple of the Master? I have not met you before. People cannot just come here and join the ceremony on a whim, they must be prepared, surely?"

Pascale's Wager

"I am prepared. I have prepared privately. And my companions here will testify that I am capable. I believe I am correct that there is no closed membership to this club?"

The woman's confidence was undermined by Palmiro's direct approach. She turned to her companion, an Asian woman with long black hair and a gentle, composed face.

"This is most irregular. What do you think, Padma?"

"I'm not sure. Normally we refer any request to the Mahatma. Of course in the days surrounding the Immersion he speaks with no one. I suggest you wait for another time?"

"I have prepared intensely and I have come to point where I will never be better prepared. It must be tomorrow or I will lose the power of this moment."

Padma regarded this strange man with his lean face and fixed eyes. Perhaps he really had arrived at a critical spiritual moment.

"We should hear what his companions have to say. Please tell us who you are and why you think your friend should take part in the Immersion?"

Omar stepped forward without hesitation. He introduced himself and the other two and then declared, "Absolutely. I can say this man is physically and mentally prepared. Exactly as he said, there is no private club here. We are all Immortals and all its rites and rituals belong to us as birthright. There can be no hierarchy in Heaven."

The others had been nodding their agreement while Omar spoke, and his words made the guardians even more unsure. It was so long since anyone had volunteered they had no recall of guidelines, and they certainly did not want to argue with the equality of Immortals. The auburn-haired guardian sought to recover the high ground.

"In principle I suppose it should be possible. If someone like you, Palmiro, is spiritually ready for the challenge then, after all, that is what the whole ritual is about, and there is no more to be said. What do you feel, Padma?"

"I agree, Alceste. And our Mahatma has kept the Passage of the Sea alive for so long not for his own sake but for the sake of Heaven. I am sure he will be thrilled to find someone else joining him again in the Waters of Chaos."

Alceste was reconciled. "Well then, it seems to be acceptable.

I'm sure you have also taken the risks into account, and really that is all part of it. What a surprise for us! We will have to let the announcer know, and we must also find you a suitable robe. But, really, it cannot be tonight. It has to be tomorrow, the final night of the Immersions. Can you come tomorrow a little earlier than this? We will provide you with a room and show you the approach to the bridge. We will also give you an attendant to cue you. Really, how exciting this all is!"

Omar pumped his fist in the air, "Yes!" Artemis clapped and danced around in a little circle. The guardians were shocked by their response, and Palmiro's reaction did not seem totally right either, although from another point of view. He had blanched and seemed dazed, as if the reality of what he'd entered into was just dawning on him. Eboni reached out to him silently.

Padma looked at him, tilting her head to one side. "Are you sure you want to do this, sir? There is no urgency. Perhaps you should wait to consult with the Mahatma first."

Palmiro stared at her, then he shook his head like a man shaking loose something inside his skull. "Oh, no, no, Padma, no need for that. I have reflected on this long and deeply. It is time."

***

Jonas was walking round in his bedroom, the one with the big veranda, holding on to furniture as he went from side to side. If he was no longer trembling externally he was shaking inside himself. As an historian he knew the die was cast. An Immortal had been killed in what could only be construed as an act of rebellion. Whether they initially intended to, there was no doubt that both Palmiro and Danny had now made a choice against the established order in Heaven. They were not giving themselves up, they were not begging for mercy, and there would be no mercy shown them. Palmiro even seemed to be pushing things toward some kind of showdown. He dreaded what this would be, both for its own sake and because of what it would mean for Pascale. She was already deeply implicated and would be seen as a co-conspirator. Any hope that she might be pardoned on the basis that it was all a mistake, that was over.

He blamed himself for his earlier passivity, dreaming away his time and allowing Palmiro and Danny to search for Pascale

369

when it should have been him. He went over and over this in his mind. He sensed that his whole attitude was mistaken, a desperate clarity dawning on him. He had spent his time in a fantasy, drinking from the well of memories, content that somewhere she was still alive and dreaming ultimately they would be reunited. Instead, matters had taken their own course. Oh yes, he should have done something. If he really loved Pascale he should have acted. He sank to his knees, clenching his fists and banging them up against his temples. How pathetic he was! Now it was too late to do anything.

He remained there on the floor, curled over on his knees, going round and round the same track in his head. But could that really be the case? Was there really nothing that could be done? Perhaps he should try and follow Palmiro, to find out what he was doing and possibly stop him. But he had no idea where he had gone, so he couldn't follow him. Anyway, if what Palmiro was going to do, no matter how dire, could help Pascale, well, he didn't want to stop him. Even as the thought crossed his mind, he was shocked at himself. Had it gone this far that he'd become what they falsely accused Pascale of? Had he in fact become a subversive, an anti-social?

The question echoed inside his head like a big clamorous bell, yet even as it continued to clang inside him, it did not seem quite so impressive or imposing. It even felt tinny and false, while another part of his mind felt at peace. He thought to himself he was changing, and possibly had been for some time. It was becoming clear right there as he knelt on the floor, and in a way he'd never dreamed possible. He was caring less and less about the whole set-up in Heaven and shifting willingly to something new. What that new thing actually was he could hardly say. It didn't seem concrete and clear, like Heaven, but he definitely felt it inside himself.

It made him want to stand up and take action although, once again, he didn't know what to do. He stood up anyway, and he threw off his robe. He walked naked downstairs to the central wing of the house and the big marble inlaid bathroom shared by the community. He entered the shower room and turned on all the jets, full. After he had buffeted his body, and his skin was blotchy and throbbing, he pulled a towel from the rack and wrapped it around his waist. He walked back down the long corridor to the stairwell leading back to his floor. He started to climb the stairs and then a door he had passed swung open. Cyrus stood in the entrance. His arm was still in a sling.

"Jonas, what are you doing? I saw that man with you earlier, the troublemaker friend of your anti-social lover. Your body looks roasted. Why were you were in the shower all that time? What's going on?"

"Pascale is not anti-social, and it's no business of yours to whom I speak or how I take my showers."

Cyrus sputtered and called out, "How dare you talk to me like that! Masharu, Vanzetti, Bernice, come out and observe the behavior of this man!"

Various members of the History Colony emerged from their rooms or the house library, drawn by Cyrus' complaint. They looked toward the stairs where he was pointing. Jonas didn't wait but continued steadily upstairs and back to his suite. He entered his bedroom, crossed to his closet and flung open the door. He ransacked the drawers and rails, throwing down robes and hauling things out he had never used and flinging them on the floor. Eventually he found some leggings for horse-riding and a short tunic of tougher cloth that pleased him. He had decided to do what Palmiro had said. It was the only thing that made sense. There were no horses at the History Colony, so he would go directly to Eboni's place and get a horse there. He left the room without shutting the door and walked back down the stairs and along the hallway to the front entrance. Then he doubled round the side of the house to the compound, hoping to avoid people. However, Masharu was there by the back door, leaning on the wall.

"Cyrus thinks you're bewitched. Where are you going?"

"I'm not sure where I'm going, Masharu. As for Cyrus, I believe he's obsessive. He provoked the arrest of Pascale unnecessarily."

"Cyrus spends a lot of time obsessing, over paintings especially."

"You're right, one in particular. He was always talking about it, a kind of medieval Doblepoble he said."

"I know the one, it's weird, with fruit and people and animals all mixed up in what looks like sexual positions. It's by

371

Hieronymus Bosch."

"I don't know it."

"You should check it out sometime, but not right now. It looks like you're heading for a hard road. Perhaps I should say farewell."

She looked at him directly and without judgment. Impulsively and to his own surprise Jonas embraced her, feeling a deep affection for his colleague.

"Farewell, Masharu."

He turned and walked over to the big open-sided garage where the colony's cars were kept. He got into one, backed out and drove away along the single track, down the sun-burnt hillside to the highway.

10. BROTHERS IN ARMS

When the guardians of the inner sanctum of the Font Eterno had given him permission to take part in the Immersion Palmiro experienced a moment of terrible clarity. Up to that point access to Sarobindo had been a mathematical problem, like moves in a long game of chess: he had never dwelt on the outcome. But the moment the way was opened for him, he had seen with startling precision what was going to happen. He would take some of the breathing suppressant, enter the waters, move as rapidly as he could to the yogi, administer the anti-enzyme and then sink for a few moments to the bottom before escaping from the Sea. He had known with certainty that he would do this, and in the same moment, there in the bowels of the Font Eterno, he had understood the full significance of his action. He would be killing the king and with him, his kingdom.

For sure, this was the thing Adorno desired and Palmiro finally accepted as his destiny, but it had been thought in the abstract. He had never felt the enormity of what that meant and the intense reaction it would draw. The whole of Heaven pivoted around Sarobindo and his ceremony of dying. When he, Palmiro, had brought the ceremony to a shocking end, he would be administering a death blow to the soul of Heaven. The fury of Immortals would descend on him. He was gripped by terror, as if he was already surrounded by uncontrollable rage and would never get out alive. It was only the gentle voice of Padma that returned him to the present and helped him get control of himself. The fury of the Immortals would be real, he thought, so he would simply have to take steps to escape it.

He was driving into the northern foothills of the sierra, again toward the western end of Heaven, to the place where Adorno had his mansion. The previous night he'd returned directly from the Font Eterno without attending the ritual, and found Jonas waiting for him. Pascale's lover was looking for a horse and directions to the Ranch. Palmiro sat down and drew a map to Danny's camp and from there to the Ranch. He told Jonas that to meet Pascale at the cliff top he would have to spend the night at Danny's camp and then leave early in the morning to find her. He could leave for the camp tomorrow but it was hard to get up there without the right

Pascale's Wager

horse, so he should build a fire at the base and wait. He himself would be arriving quite a bit later that night and his horse would be able to make the jump. Night rides in the canyons were very risky but desperate times called for desperate measures. Jonas asked him what he meant and why he too was heading for the canyons.

"Listen, you have made a choice for Pascale. I have too. Let's stick with that and don't ask me questions."

It sounded right to Jonas and he just shrugged. Eboni came in and Palmiro told her what Jonas was planning and asked her if there was a bed for him and a horse to use. She raised her eyebrows a little, but agreed once more to help. She took Jonas off to find him a room. When she returned, Palmiro asked her if she would also get a horse for himself and to have it ready and waiting directly after the ceremony tomorrow. She should also make sure there were a month's supplies in the saddle packs. Finally, he asked if possible the horse could be her Appaloosa, as it knew how to make the jump to Danny's camp.

"O.K. O.K., you've now officially gone too far. It looks as if you're planning a quick getaway, without me, while you're also taking my horse. Don't you understand, whatever you're up to people will know you were staying right here and they'll come straight for me. Anyway, I thought the plan was to convince people of your good intentions?"

Palmiro saw her point. "You know what, Eboni, you're right. I really can't tell you anything right now but it's best you come too. You should ride your own horse and bring another one, to the Font Eterno, and pack enough supplies for both of us. Wait for me at the entrance to the tunnel just after the ceremony gets started. I won't be long."

Eboni shook her head. "Why do I get the feeling you've done nothing but lie to me all the way along?"

Palmiro opened his mouth but only a helpless "I...I..." came out.

Eboni stopped him. "Please don't bother. You're something else, you really are. But I reckon I'm in deep now and can't get out. At least I'll see Danny. So, OK, you get your way. I'll be there with the horses. And I'll stash the supplies along the trail somewhere so people won't see the saddlebags and get suspicious."

374

"Thanks, Eboni. And you'll see, it'll all be for the best!"

"I don't know about that, I really don't."

After that Palmiro had one essential thing left to do. He had to experiment with the drug from the Initiation ritual, to find the right dosage. He secluded himself in his room, pushing a chair under the handle, and began with a small amount, the size of a bead on his finger. The effect after four or five minutes was to suppress his breathing a little, like the rhythm of someone asleep. He waited for the sensation to disappear, then he gave himself a considerably larger dose, a tablespoon-full, and started timing himself carefully with a watch. After about five minutes he felt almost the full effect of the initiation ritual. His breathing stopped and his heart rate slowed dramatically. He fought to stay conscious and to walk across the room. He felt a strong pain in his chest but he managed it, collapsing into a chair.

Judging from his watch it seemed he then passed out for just under twenty minutes. When he came to he'd had a sharp moment of clarity and taken his first breath. Like a train, a thundering headache hit him and he realized he could not risk doing this anymore. The physical stress was too great and he needed all his remaining forces for the actual event tomorrow. He would just have to make a guess at the correct amount for his Immersion. He decided he could perhaps manage what he had to do with about half of the dose he'd just taken. Once he'd come to his decision he threw himself on his bed and tried to sleep.

But his headache stayed with him and he only slept fitfully. Now, as he drove higher into the hills, past the Plastic Surgery and Agriculture Colonies, he felt as if there was a stone in his chest. Despite this, his mind was strong. Almost all the pieces were in place for what he had to do. He had committed himself to this path and he knew it was necessary, if only for Pascale. But it was not just for her. It was for the Northern Homeland too, and it was also for the Immortals. Just as Adorno had argued, they were living a phony, futile life, which had to change. All that remained to do was to get the anti-enzyme.

He arrived at the mansion and drove directly to the drive at the front of the house. He got out and entered the door to the east wing, the one leading to his laboratory. He expected to go straight to his fridge to retrieve the culture dish with its lethal liquid, but was shocked to see Adorno sitting in an easy chair with a journal on his lap. The scientist looked up and smiled.

"I've been expecting you. I've come here every day waiting for you to appear. It is a delight to see you, Palmiro. How are you?"

"Hello, sir. It's been a while. A lot has happened."

"I think so. How is your friend, the captive Pascale?"

Palmiro thought there was no good reason not to tell his teacher of the rescue mission to the canyons and its fatal outcome. In a few sentences he sketched the story.

Adorno whistled softly. "Well, certainly, change is in the air. That psychopath Magus fully deserved his fate. But I don't think you have told me everything, Palmiro, have you?"

Palmiro hesitated, both embarrassed and irritated at this point to explain to Adorno, who had instigated everything, exactly what he was planning to do. Adorno smiled and saved his awkwardness.

"Don't worry. I believe I have a pretty good idea of what you intend. Look, I have something for you."

He reached into a small satchel he had slung under his shoulder and took out a hand-sized device. "I found the product of your research in the fridge there. Well done, indeed, a work worthy of my greatest student. I took the liberty of placing your invention in a pressurized capsule here. It comes with an applicator. You unscrew the top one-and-a-half turns and a nozzle pops out. All you need then is to hold two fingers round the top and squeeze from the bottom, and a continuous dose will be administered. Here, take it, you will find it expeditious to your purpose."

Palmiro was staggered and all his previous ambiguity about Adorno flooded through him again. By dint of hard effort and willpower he was going to do something to change the world, and he had not felt Adorno's help in that for quite a long time. Yet here he was, inserting himself at the last moment, still claiming a role. Even so, he could not help but feel the old thrill that he and Adorno were brothers-in-arms, that history's greatest scientist was treating him as a colleague and even an equal. At that moment it felt only right and made him incredibly proud to be taking the instrument for Heaven's demise from Adorno's own hand.

"Thank you. I think that will be useful."

"No, thank you! The credit is all yours. I analyzed your work and I have to say the pathogen you created is so aggressive that any contact with mucosa will have catastrophic consequences."

Palmiro opened his mouth to say something but he stopped.

"What? What were you going to say?"

"I, I can't really go into details, sir, but I was thinking, should I be exposed to this, this liquid, could it be dangerous for me? I'm pretty sure, since I am still young in actual body years, it should not affect me in the same way as a long-time Immortal."

"An important question, of course. In whatever way you plan to use this, I imagine you feel at risk. But, yes, your instinct is entirely correct. Being exposed to this organism might cause an allergic reaction, lightheadedness or feeling sick, something like that, but your normal cell reproduction has not been suppressed. In fact, in studies I conducted, I found the immortality enzyme to be largely redundant for someone with your chronological age, all the way up to about thirty years. It is only absorbed by the cells as the chemical signals of aging begin to really kick in. So, no, you will have minimal symptoms. And, by the way, this discovery of yours does best at normal room temperature! The reactivity slows down considerably in the fridge."

At that moment Palmiro felt hardly a separate person from his teacher. They were acting as one, thinking as one, and there was nothing he could do about it. He knew he should be going soon, to be back at the Font Eterno in time, and yet he could not leave just like that. He had at least one more question to ask.

"Sir, if you will forgive me, there is another question I have. A woman, at the Agora of the Baths, she lives there. She claims to be your mother. Is that true?"

"Ah, you met her, my mother. Did she harass you, make prophecies? She must have seen something if she told you about me. To cut a long story short, I brought her here right back at the beginning. She didn't want to come and she caused a lot of trouble. Under normal circumstances it would have earned her a one-way trip to the Ranch, but I protected her. She took to hanging out at the Agora, threatening doom on all. Most people have learned to shut her up but I can imagine her homing in on someone like you."

"She said I was her son, also."

Adorno gave a crooked, almost gentle smile. "That would make us brothers, eh? My mother was a very smart woman in her own way, but Heaven drove her crazy. That is another reason I am glad you're doing what you're doing. You'll bring that sick immortality of hers to an end."

Palmiro was taken aback to hear Adorno suggest what he was planning would bring about his mother's death. In all probability he foresaw him putting the organism in the general water-supply, just as he'd originally intended. But it was too late at this point to explain his thinking, setting out Pascale's position. It didn't matter anyway. Adorno would definitely hear about the death of Sarobindo and the spiritual upheaval it would cause. The heart would go out of Heaven and Adrono would have an audience of Immortals ready and primed for his new vision.

The scientist was getting up from his chair and Palmiro did too. The same cracked smile was on his face, making it appear happy, and, for the very first time, attractive. He crossed the space between them and to Palmiro's total shock he hugged him.

"I want to thank you, Palmiro. You are the best friend I ever had. You have set me free."

He released him abruptly. "Go now. You must do what you have to do. And so must I."

11. SACRIFICING THE IDOL

When it all finally happened, it was like a walking dream. He returned to downtown just as it was getting dark. He knew he was late and started toward the Font Eterno at a half run. His headache and the weight in his chest had almost disappeared but he found the effort exhausting. His heart was pounding and his breath labored as he lumbered through the service tunnel and climbed the opera house stairs. Alceste was waiting impatiently at the top.

"Sir, you have left very little time to prepare. The great Sarobindo himself has already been here two hours. Don't you need to do your exercises and meditation?"

"Of course, I do. I was detained at Professor Adorno's. I will go directly to my room and start the process at once."

She was prepared to be mollified and asked him to follow her. She led him round the loggia lined with marble capitals and crimson damask walls. It connected on the far side to a long, green marble, vaulted hall, with a row of elegant doors situated on either side and small incense braziers set on pillars in the middle. She led him to one of the doors and opened it.

"This is your room." She pointed back to the hall. "Over there on the back wall is an elevator that will take you to the ceremonial area. You have just over an hour to prepare. An attendant will come and knock for you."

She left without raising her eyes to him—very likely she considered he should already be withdrawing from external contact. He went inside, closing the door behind him. Opposite him, set in the floor, was a tiled bath with a burning oil lamp at either end. The surface was gently flowing and a cluster of live lotus blossom bobbed softly against one of the walls. On the far side of the bath was a cushioned pallet spread with an orange robe and seated facing it was a meditating stone figure with eyes blank, and blissful lips. A muted organic fragrance filled the space.

Palmiro leaned his back against the door and struggled to calm his breath. He cast his eyes around the room and drank in its serene atmosphere. It was as if a switch had been thrown, shutting off the stress and tension of all the recent days and hours. The effect was so strong it surprised him and he was more than willing to surrender. He went over to the pool, took off his sandals and dangled his legs over the side. The water caressed his ankles and feet and he suddenly had an immense desire to lie down and go to sleep. He reached inside his tunic to a small belt and pouch, taking out Adorno's applicator and a vial with the Initiation drug.

There was a table against a wall with a pitcher and a glass. He got up and went over, laying down the applicator, and pouring water from the pitcher into the glass. He tasted a mouthful; it was cool and refreshing. He poured out a little more and drank it. Then he set down the glass and emptied out the measured dose from the vial, mixing it with just a little water. Then he went back to the pallet, shrugged off his tunic and put on the orange robe, wrapping it around his waist roughly the way he'd seen Sarobindo do. Then he lay down, covered himself with his tunic and very quickly he was asleep.

The sound of insistent knocking woke him. He felt rested and calm. He waited a little as the knocking continued and then called out, "It's O.K. I'm coming."

He got up, crossed to the table and picked up the glass. He tilted his head and poured the liquid into his mouth and held it there. He took up the applicator, unscrewed the top one and a half turns and concealed the device in the palm of his hand. Then he went to the door and exited. The assistant was already walking to the end of the hall to the elevator. When he got to it he pressed a button and its door rolled open. Palmiro followed across the marble floor and into the elevator, without looking at the attendant. The man pressed another button and the elevator closed and descended smoothly to the lower level. At the bottom the door pulled back onto a lobby area which communicated directly with an arched tunnel sloping gently downward. The entire surface of the lobby and tunnel was covered with a million points of diamond light. The effect was at once brilliant and calming, like diving in a sun-dimpled lagoon. The attendant pointed ahead down the tunnel and Palmiro could see the unmistakable silhouette of Sarobindo framed against its opening.

"We wait here until the Master is announced and begins his walk to the bridge, then we follow."

Palmiro continued to hold the liquid in his mouth, its delicate pungency now filling his palate and nasal passages. He thought he could already feel a slight slowing of breath. He had calculated that he should swallow his mouthful at the moment he stepped on the bridge and he would rely on the assistant to send him off the end at the point when his breathing had stopped. It was a gamble, but everything was, and something inside him assured him it would work. He could hear the sweet sound of the flute dying away, as the announcer's voice broke in and began the prologue to Sarobindo's immersion.

"The great yogi Sarobindo carries our spirits and souls as he goes now to the depths of the Sea of Chaos..."

The announcer's speech came to an end and he watched as Sarobindo stepped out from the tunnel and a long wave of applause burst from around the stadium. The attendant motioned to Palmiro: it was time for him to set out too. He walked the length of the tunnel trying to duplicate Sarobindo's pace and attitude as closely as he could. When he arrived at the bottom of the tunnel, he paused instinctively. He heard the announcer begin again.

"And, now, we have the most unusual pleasure of introducing a new candidate for the Immersion, someone who came forward at the last minute, but accompanied by the highest recommendations. Here is another citizen of Heaven, ready and willing to risk the depths for our sake. Remember, fellow Immortals, that if he stay too long, he will instantly be annihilated. I am proud now to introduce to you, Palmiro, from Adorno's Science Colony. Please welcome him to the passage of the Sea!"

When he heard his name he started walking again, conscious that the camera would be trained on his face just as it had been on Sarobindo's. Another wave of applause broke from the stadium and Palmiro sensed with astonishment the eager welcome he was being given. He was conscious also of the intense light around him and the deep darkness in the circular dome above. He walked as deliberately and calmly as he could in the direction he saw Sarobindo taking. The applause died down and a charged silence took its place. He saw the famous guru reach the beginning of the bridge, pause and then start to walk. He too continued to walk and as soon he reached the edge of the bridge he waited.

The glittering sea stretched out in front of him, far bigger than he had imagined it, more full of motion, and its scent now close and sharp with danger. He stood and watched as Sarobindo came to the end of the bridge and sank to knees, then onto his back. He heard the voice of his attendant telling him to go ahead, but he paused one moment longer to swallow what was in his mouth. The sense of it had been increasingly potent, and as the drug cleared his throat almost at once he could feel it begin its work in earnest.

He started walking, timing himself internally and hoping he would get it right. The end of the bridge seemed distant but he was not hurrying to get there. He could see the great expanse of blue around him and it was pulling him down into itself. He walked further and then, suddenly, the bridge quivered and he could no longer see Sarobindo. He felt his breathing slowing and his movement more labored. He increased his pace by the slightest degree and it was like he was walking in his sleep, with stones attached to his feet. He pushed forward, and in a few more paces he was at the end of the bridge, grateful to sink to his knees and sit there on his haunches. He remained motionless and his breathing became almost imperceptible. He gave his head the faintest forward tilt, willing the attendant to release the slide. There was a long moment when nothing happened and then the end of the bridge pitched away from under him and he was falling headlong toward the water.

Palmiro had his eyes closed but the moment he went below the surface, he opened them and with a great effort brought his arms forward and propelled himself downward. His chest began to hurt severely but he was conscious and alert. His eyes searched the cyan blue as he forced his arms in front once more, pulled them back and kicked his legs. He was about four or five meters down and the pain quadrupled in intensity. The light was now muted and he cast around beneath him looking for the bottom. Once more he kicked and it was like a blunt spear thrust to his chest, but he saw what looked like a human form, over to his right. Straining to get a closer look he realized it was Sarobindo, resting on a raised platform. Absolutely inert, like an effigy on an ancient tomb, his eyes were closed but the lips of the mouth had fallen slightly open, adding to the impression of death. Palmiro turned and, with a last crucifying effort, he kicked toward him. The pain was unbearable but he held the applicator out, pointed like a gun. As he came up over the body he used his last reserves to push down on the base of the device, shooting its pressurized liquid toward the yogi's nose and mouth. A murky cloud fell upon Sarobindo's face, its weight carrying it downward until it surrounded its surface like a mask, almost as if the anti-enzyme was seeking its target. The Northerner's momentum carried him forward but he kept his hand in place, continuing to eject the last of the contents. As he did his torso made a slow-motion arc, flipping him over on his back. The diffused light of the stadium above hit him squarely in the eyes. At the same moment the pain in his chest exploded beyond its walls and he blacked out. The applicator fell from his fingers.

He floated in suspended animation just a few feet away from Sarobindo. Very gradually his body began to rise. He lacked the yogi's habitual mastery of the watery environment, second nature to his body. Instead, the remaining air in his lungs carried him slowly to the surface. Centimeter by centimeter his spread-eagled form ascended. The minutes and seconds trickled away and the crowd scanned the surface for signs of the new yogi. He arrived about ten centimeters from the top and suddenly someone shouted, "There he is!" In a moment everyone was pointing at a place not far from where he had entered the waters at the end of the bridge.

"There, there, it's Palmiro, on his back. Has he drowned? Is he dead? He will never get out!"

A thrill of horror gripped the stadium. It was a long time since anyone had perished in the Sea and the Immortals had gotten used to Sarobindo's miraculous escapes. Now, it seemed, the night could end in genuine catastrophe. Just under the surface Palmiro's eyes opened and his lungs jolted back to life, at once taking in water. He choked violently and, with sheer animal instinct, he lifted his head above the surface, coughing harshly and gasping at the same time. He could not remember exactly where he was or what was happening but something inside him told him he was in immense danger. He tried to strike out for dry land but his limbs were as heavy as lead and he was barely able move. His chest felt like it had been crushed and he could only breathe with great difficulty; he knew he had to will himself to swim. With horrible labor he began a breast stroke toward the rim of the Sea, hardly seeming to make progress. He could hear a thunderous progression of organ chords and the distant shouting of voices and in an instant remembered clearly he was in the Font Eterno.

He felt the clock running out above him and the crowd watching and doubting he would make it. He was kicking out of sequence and breathing in short gasps, taking in water and choking and coughing as he did. But like a three-legged dog he made some headway, pushing slowly and desperately toward the shore.

There was less than two minutes to go and he still had ten meters to cover. Some in the crowd were now counting down and he himself began to think he really could not do it. His lungs were screaming, his limbs felt they had chains attached and his heart was pumping so furiously it made his whole torso tremble. He heard a roar of voices and his eyes, straining at the edge of the Sea, caught a glimpse of a head and body breaking the surface and grasping one of the set of steps. It was the magnificent Sarobindo striding from the lake and the sight of him inspired in him one more desperate surge of willpower.

His assistant was waving at him directing him to a set of steps. He saw the gestures and swung drunkenly in that direction. Five seconds, four seconds and his hand lunged for a rail. The assistant descended on the steps and grabbed down for his arm, hauling him vertically with manic strength. There was a deep growl and the water sank away, coiling into a poisonous gray snake, just as Palmiro's feet cleared its surface, flailing onto the steps. The whole stadium erupted in a wild roar. He collapsed forward onto the decking, while Chaos roared below.

Lucid memory of everything returned to him immediately he hit the ground. He knew he had to get out, as quickly as possible. The stone was back on his chest, but this time fifty times heavier, and he could only breathe in small tight gasps. He struggled to his feet, leaning on the assistant.

"Take me...to my room...."

The assistant complied, pulling Palmiro's arm across his shoulder and half-carrying him from the stadium. The organ music was blaring triumphantly while a peculiar concentration seemed to have fallen on the crowd. They were staring at a split video screen as it tracked both Sarobindo and Palmiro. The former was standing waving, greeting his public, but he did not have his usual ramrod posture and was in fact a little hunched and unsteady. Palmiro of course could hardly stand. They looked like two fighters who had just gotten out of fifteen rounds together.

Padma had come to the entrance of the tunnel and she took Palmiro's other arm. She and the assistant dragged Palmiro up to the elevator, supporting him as it ascended, and then helped him to his room. He asked them to wait for him outside as he changed. He went inside, took off the sopping loin cloth and pulled on his tunic and sandals, breathing from his stomach in short gulps that each felt like a knife point. He found the emptied vial and dropped it in the pool, then went back, opened the door and asked the two assistants to take him to the exit tunnel.

Padma protested politely. "You are not staying for the celebration? We always have one at the end. You can rest, and you will have a chance to meet Sarobindo and the others from the Meditation Colony. They will be most interested in your technique."

"I can't. I need to...recover. I have a friend waiting...outside."

They could not stop him and felt bound to help, so they supported him again, turning to walk out into the loggia. At the same moment the elevator arrived and Sarobindo emerged, accompanied by two disciples. As the door drew back the first thing the yogi saw was Palmiro and he stared at him as if he was trying to remember something. He had lost his normal lofty calm and seemed, for the first time, uncertain. Palmiro glanced back toward him, then looked away.

"Come on...let's go."

Leaning on his helpers he walked out toward to the stairs. As the party was leaving they heard Sarobindo suddenly give a convulsive cough and sneeze. Padma looked round with concern, but Palmiro pressed onward along the balcony. When they got to the stairs he thanked them and said he would take it from there. He stumbled off down the stairs holding the rail and, along the access tunnel, leaning on the walls. Eboni was waiting with the horses half way down. She helped him mount and turn back toward the exit, to the darkness outside. They were facing a long, terrible ride to the trailhead, then a perilous descent in the starlight. But whatever the risk the night was their friend. It would cloak their disappearance and once down in the canyons they would ride without stopping to the camp. He was fearful his lungs would never return to normal or he might collapse entirely. But he knew if he could hold out as far as Danny's camp then he had a chance. In any event, Heaven was no longer the same place, he felt most certain of that.

12. CHANGING PLACES

In the few days since the dramatic events surrounding the death of Zena and Magus a remarkable change had come over the canyons. Physically they had altered. There was the dark scar where Magus' cabin used to be and the silent pile of ash where Zena had been cremated. The sensations the two places provoked were far more powerful than mere scenery: one horror and anger, the other respect and something else, something profound, hard to put in words. These reactions were definitely part of the change that had taken place, but they were not all.

Where before there was endless oppression, a form of living death, now there was almost total freedom, together with a constant feeling of peace and joy. Everybody felt it, and there was no one who did not come visibly to life in its atmosphere. The residents who had spent almost their whole time—if it could be called time—in the cantina, slumped on the tables, now sat out on the steps, or in the tent, looking around as if they'd found themselves miraculously transported to a beautiful resort. They smiled and greeted each other continually by name, confirming again and again this was what they were doing, and who in fact they all were.

Everybody's speech improved and they began to talk among themselves more naturally and spontaneously. They talked about the colors of the canyons, the wild flowers among the rocks and the birds that made their home there. They talked about their clothes, how to clean and repair them and even make new ones, using the good cotton sheets found in Magus' store. They talked about each other, about how well a certain person was looking, or the talents that others had. Some of them started making things to give as gifts. It was Zoltan who began it.

He found a twisted stump and whittled it away until it looked like the head and wing of an eagle. He gave it to Francisco. Then Greta found some wool and bits of felt and made a small, knitted doll which she presented to Pascale. Everyone wanted one, so she unpicked a sweater and soon was turning out a stream of pleasant faced woolen figures. Best of all, a Spanish guitar had been discovered in Magus' store and someone passed it to Ravel. He took it in his hands and gently plucked its strings. After that he did not put it down and in the next days he began to produce from it an increasingly beautiful, haunting sound. Any time of the day if you visited the tent you would hear passages of classical music being teased from its strings. People sat around mesmerized. Only the need for sleep could bring the concert to an end.

The only person who did not quite react with joy was the cook. His name was Pepin and when Magus' cabin was raided and set on fire he could not believe it, declaring it an outrage and there would be hell to pay. No one was listening, not even his assistants, and all he could do was watch it happen and run up and down stamping out cinders falling next to his store. Later that evening after the sparks had died out he wandered sullenly over to the trove of items taken from the cabin and found the food and liquor. He couldn't believe his luck; it was like the heavens had opened and rained their blessings on him. He downed a whole pound of chocolate, unscrewed a bottle of straight Bourbon and within half an hour was stone drunk on the canyon floor. Magada found him in the morning and threw a bucket of water over him.

He came around suffering from a blinding headache and terrible stomach cramps. He cursed her and swore solemnly that from now on everyone could cook for themselves: he would never go near the kitchen again. Katoucha straightaway seized the opportunity, asserting she'd always thought the food disgusting and she could do a much better job. She said there were edible herbs, roots and berries in the canyon, and the original native peoples had eaten the beans of the mesquite bushes. She promised if they foraged for items like these they could make the diet much more interesting. She began directly, making sure not to overcook the vegetables and mixing in a bunch of wild onions which she dug up. She also took into the cantina all the food and liquor left out in the canyon, lest anyone else be tempted again.

Still, when people saw that Pepin was now on his own, sulking and separated from the general happiness, they persuaded Katoucha to find a way to get him back to the kitchen. She sighed and rolled her one eye, but gave in. In fact, she had just the idea to make it happen. She went to Pepin and suggested they might take turns cooking, but even before that they should plan a massive feast using the delicacies from Magus' cabin. There was no point hanging on to them, for what better occasion could there

387

be to celebrate than the present?

At the prospect of another gaudy night with chocolate and liquor Pepin was quickly reconciled. He abandoned his boycott and agreed to share the cooking. They set the date of the banquet for two days' time. As for the menu they would slaughter one of the cattle and roast it outside on a barbecue spit. Plus Katoucha would flavor squash and corn with wild peppers and scented grasses she said she could find in the canyon. They would open the bottles of wine and share toasts for the whole company. Afterward, they would eat canned oranges and peaches from Magus' store and finish with chocolate, cigars, whiskey and brandy. It would be the first feast for residents celebrated in the canyon, a first in their collective story, and an experience no one would ever forget. The mouths of the two cooks were already watering with the flavors to come.

In the days following the fires, Pascale continued her normal routine, rising early and going to the cliff top, then coming back down to hang out in the communal tent. Things felt very different for her in each place. In the tent it was no longer necessary to get the conversation rolling: it sprung naturally to life. While Ravel played his continuous concerto in the background people began spontaneously to recall details of their past. So many of these had disappeared from their minds and from existence itself. Now they came welling up from oblivion.

Orwell remembered growing up as a child on a farm, the cattle coming in a line for milking and the warm sweet smell of the dairy in the morning. The farm was flooded by the rains and they had to abandon the land. At school he had excelled at engineering and had risen to become part of the team planning the Global Weather Shield. He had been one of those chosen for immortality, and he accepted because he was sure that after a time attempts would be made to recover the lost spaces of the earth. When it became obvious there was no policy in Heaven for recovery, Orwell started a street-campaign downtown, speaking and handing out leaflets. And that very quickly got him sent to the Ranch. Now, he said, for the first time since he was a boy he was beginning to feel close to the land again.

Alaqua agreed. She told how she came from one of the aboriginal races and had worked for an environmental campaign protesting the Global Shield. The protest claimed the Shield would leave indigenous peoples totally exposed and without any help. The authorities replied there was no other way, and then they told her she had been chosen for immortality. They said that individuals like her had been selected in order that native peoples would be represented. She had agreed, but without fully understanding what was intended. Once she got to Heaven she was unable to fit in, retreating into herself, preferring only to sleep, or wander in the semi-desert. Very soon she was sent to the Ranch. Now, for the first time, she had begun to feel a contact with those tribes of the earth left behind. She thought the residents in the canyon were like one of those tribes.

These stories did nothing to lessen the jubilant feeling among the residents. Rather, they helped give it fuel, always ending up with a statement of how the present situation in the canyon had changed everything and how the speaker felt so incredibly happy. The tent had become a place of transformation, gathering a kind of aura around it, bigger than any one individual or all the individuals put together. Unless people had work chores to do, everybody was certain to be found there. Almost automatically its space had been converted into a care center or field hospital, where Orwell, Francisco and Elise could be looked after. As a result Zoltan and Eliot soon set about driving in more tent poles and stringing lines for blankets to extend it. Pascale felt enormously at home in the tent, able to relax and listen to what people were sharing and to the music in the background. Like everyone else she had never felt happier or more at peace. In contrast, it was up on the cliff top that she was obliged to confront her deeper questions.

The first morning after the fatal events she could not make the climb. The experience below in the canyon was so positive and she feared what the cliff top would say in contrast if she went up there. On the second morning, however, she did go up. She looked around quickly and everything was peaceful, just as it had always been; but she didn't stay. On the third morning she stayed, sitting down in her circle of stones. She could not meditate as before, on the big dreamy questions like the composition of matter and love. Her mind returned like the recoil of a spring to what had happened in that place, and especially to Zena and how she had saved her.

Zena had become Pascale's friend, with total sincerity, like a child, and she had not hesitated to climb the cliff for her sake. The whole episode reminded Pascale of her Initiation vision, of the white dove that had settled on her chest and then almost as quickly had drowned. It was different though, because this time Zena had been the one to protect Pascale, saving her from death, or even worse.

Because of this, her life was not her own any more, or not completely. Through Zena, and Palmiro and Jonas, she was spread out, beyond herself. Other people held part of her life in their bodies, their hearts. The fact that Zena was dead made the thought even more difficult and disturbing. How could a dead person hold a part of you? She remembered the fire and the plume of smoke which had carried Zena's remains away to the sky. The memory gave a very different meaning to particles of dust and light, and to the possibility of love being able to count them.

Her thoughts and questions stopped there. She did not want to follow their path any further. Instead she let her mind go blank, looking out over the shattered earth with the sun glinting yellow along its edges. She remembered the sun back in the Northern Homeland, how distant and cold it seemed. Here the sun was always such a passionate thing, always bright and hot on your face. She turned toward it, shielding her eyes, and suddenly she felt much older.

At that sudden feeling all that had happened before seemed to be the experience of a naive girl, who had not understood anything. It was as if she was looking at herself from a great height, and horribly annoyed and angry at her former self. She had been so locked inside her own feelings, so quick to choose the road for herself and others. She stood up and paced restlessly around her retreat. The events of that fateful morning flooded back on her, and she was there again, with Magus, Palmiro, Danny, Zena. Would any of this have happened if it had not been for her? No! Zena would not have been at the cliff top that morning and she would be alive now. As for Palmiro he would not be in Heaven at all.

With a sudden aching free-fall inside her she recalled her conversation with him. It had been relegated to the back of her mind by all the intense drama, but now she remembered clearly he had been planning a terrible catastrophe, and even at this moment could be putting it in effect. She had pleaded with him, but again was she not directly responsible for bringing this situation about. Who had appointed her the decider of other people's fates? What made her so special? Sure, she saw things, counted things, found meaning in sunlight, stars and shapes. But who was to say she was right? And even if she was right, by what right did she drag other people into her schemes? She looked around at her circle of stones and they filled her with disgust. The scratched designs on some of them and the shapes of others recalled major events in her personal story, but they seemed infantile, self-obsessed. Infuriated she bent down and began hurling the stones outward, anywhere, just to break up the circle.

She picked up the stone with the tent scratched on it and was just about to fling it to oblivion when she saw somebody on the skyline, a horse and rider. It was as if Danny and Palmiro were arriving all over again, as if the universe was repeating itself and mocking her. Was it, in fact, Palmiro? Had he thought better about his revolution or had he carried it through and come here to find refuge? She hesitated, between hope and dread, but then for the second time that morning the world flipped inside her. With an inner leap of joy that even surprised herself she recognized who was on the horse. It was not Palmiro but Jonas, her gentle-mannered historian and lover.

She watched him nudge the horse through the stand of bushes and into the clearing. He saw her and dismounted slowly, his face a mixture of happiness and apprehension. She wondered how she looked to him, with her frayed denim dress, her pulled-back hair and her face she knew was so much older. The two former lovers approached each other like swimmers in a murky pool, seeking each other out in the dreck and half-light of everything that had happened since they were first in each other's arms.

"Jonas, you came..."

"Yes, Palmiro showed me the route. I am sorry I did not come before."

"No, no, how could you? I made things impossible for you."

They looked at each other, so different from their time together at the Historians Colony: she with a line of steel etched on her cheek, and he with smudges of pain beside his eyes. She was holding a rock and as he approached she dropped it, almost

391

guiltily. She held out her hands to welcome him but stiff armed, to keep him at a distance. He held her hands briefly, but feeling the barrier they made, he let them go.

"Every day was made only of your absence, and each night I dreamed of you...."

"Jonas, I am thrilled to see you, but terrible things have happened..."

"Yes, Palmiro told me some of it, and now he has added to them. He is hiding at Danny's camp."

"Oh my God! What has he done? "

"I'm not certain. He could speak only in gasps. I was waiting at the camp and Eboni helped him and me to the top. He was flat out and only woke up once. Eboni said something about him taking part in the Font Eterno Immersion. I believe he has done something irrevocable. But his actions helped me find you, and for that I can only be grateful."

"Palmiro is bringing the world to an end, and we are all caught up in the consequence. Yet it was I who started him on that road, and I have led you down it too."

"The day you and Palmiro showed up in Heaven, it was the best day of my life."

She took both his hands and pulled him to her, hugging him, but releasing him at once. "And your coming today, Jonas, is the best thing that happened to me for the longest time. But I am not what I was, and we cannot be that way again. It's not fair to you, or anyone..."

"Pascale, I don't care about that. Really, I mean it. All the time we were apart I just wanted to be in the same room as you, the same house. Everything else I would give up gladly for that."

"Jonas, you say that and I know you mean it, but I have to tell you something plainly, so you understand it. It will hurt you, but you have to know. After the Initiation and then at your colony, I was using you. You were there for me and I made full use of it. At the time I loved it all, I loved you, and I still love you, but I am different now, and so sorry I did that."

Jonas was not hurt. He felt the weight of what she was saying, but it did not matter. Immortals all made use of each other, all the time. So, as far as that was concerned, he had made use of Pascale. But now he had made a choice for something else, more profound, and the past did not count. He was not offended by it, he just wanted to move beyond it, and it was important that Pascale understood this. The essential thing was that because of her people had made choices for something new and different. He saw this very clearly and began to understand what his role might be in his relationship with her.

"Pascale, it doesn't matter. I'm glad you did what you did. Everything has changed now, because of you, but it all started back then. I'm glad I was able to be there for you, with you."

A kind of dam broke inside of Pascale. She began to sob, tears welling from her eyes, her frame hunched and rocking. Jonas put out his hands and instinctively she reached out her own, this time pressing herself to him and allowing herself to be enfolded in his embrace. She sank her head on his shoulder, letting all the tension, the fear, the struggle and the grief of the canyon pour itself out onto him. He let it happen, overwhelmed that once more they were together and it was good and wonderful to him to feel her closeness and the wetness of her tears.

"Thank you, Jonas," she said at last. She was drained of her anger, but still she was older, different. "You have given me more than I can say or even know. Will you come down to the canyon with me? I want to show you everything, and the people there will be so happy to see you. You can tether your horse here, it will be safe during daylight and Danny will ride up to get it."

Jonas went to secure the horse. He would follow Pascale willingly. He was ready to climb down to the canyon, ready to go with her anywhere.

PART FIVE

1. THE PLAGUE

Once it began it happened with devastating speed. Sarobindo became sick directly following the Immersion and within twenty hours he was dead. He sneezed and coughed and he couldn't stop. His temperature spiked, then he fainted, lapsing into fever and delirium. Those around him were terrified and totally at a loss. There were no illnesses in Heaven. The impact of harmful bacteria had been eliminated as a side-effect of the immortality enzyme, overwhelming any pathology. As for viruses, the population had been screened and inoculated for all known illnesses. Should a fresh virus have somehow crept into Heaven, the Immortals' immune systems were so strong it was swept away without anyone even noticing. The only thing left was an occasional allergy for which there were dozens of treatments. And an allergy is what his disciples initially suspected. There must have been something in the environment to which he was reacting. The thought did obviously occur that the new element in the ceremony was Palmiro, so perhaps the reaction was linked to him, but simply as an allergy.

When Sarobindo fainted they realized he had something worse. They didn't know where to turn. The Plastic Surgery Colony doubled as a First Aid center for cuts and broken bones, and it was the only thing anyone could think of as a possible medical resource. Alceste and another disciple called Jamal were dispatched to inform them and get advice. As the two of them hurried through the horde of stragglers still exiting from the Font Eterno, Alceste herself began to sneeze. Then she started to cough, and after a couple of minutes fighting the sting in her nose and the rough edge in her throat, she knew that what Sarobindo had was beginning now in her.

So many long years had passed since anyone had experienced it that the concept of droplet-borne infection had more or less been forgotten. Yet now the evidence of some connection between Sarobinbdo and Alceste was begging to be recognized in each explosive sneeze. She stopped and told Jamal he had to go on alone. She was beginning to feel weak and dizzy and might not make it. The symptoms could well start with him too, and he had to get the information to the experts before he was struck down. By this time, however, she had sneezed and coughed in close proximity to numerous individuals in the crowd and two or three of them had contracted the infection. She struggled to the bleachers overlooking the racetrack and sat down, coughing violently. She felt dreadful, a sense of sickness deepening inside her, as if her vital organs were collapsing until there was nothing left. She had a sudden horrible realization that she was, in fact, dying. She experienced a vacuous fear and a gripping sense of loss. Nothing had prepared or warned her of this. Death had descended out of the night sky like an invisible bird of prey, carrying her off in the blink of an eye and without appeal. The endless satisfactions of Heaven were disappearing in an instant. She tried to scream but she could only gasp and cough, again uncontrollably. She slumped over unconscious, rolling from the seat and falling between the bleachers out of sight.

Jamal had made it across the park to the terminus and the continuous circuit of trams that ran from there along the Avenue of Monuments. He took the next one in line and began sneezing almost at once. By the time he got to the parking lot he was coughing and feeling dizzy. He knew he wouldn't make it. It was over an hour's drive to the colony and he would not keep going that long. If this was the way for Sarobindo, him and Alceste he had to believe the remaining disciples back at the Font Eterno would be falling too. He had to warn somebody.

There was a public phone line to the fire brigade outside the first monument, a replica of the Taj Mahal. He limped, coughing and wheezing, back through the huge Babylonian-style gate leading to the Avenue. A couple of hundred paces past the reflecting pool he found the booth with the phone. The blood was pounding in his head and the reflecting pool and the brilliant white domes and minarets were swimming around his head. He could not remember the last time he had used a phone and did not know what to do. He picked up the headset and heard a voice telling him to wait and his call would be answered very shortly. After about ten seconds, a live voice came on the line and asked him where the fire was. Jamal tried to say there was no fire rather an impossible sickness mowing people down, but all that came out was a ferocious bout of coughing punctuated by unintelligible words. He could hear the operator asking him to please repeat what he had said but he could hardly breathe. He felt his legs buckle under him and he saw the night sky above twisting into a vortex and the empty universe spiraling through it.

Back at the Font Eterno, Padma was sneezing into the folds of her orange robe. She had left Sarobindo's room when the announcer and another assistant had started coughing furiously. Sarobindo lay semi-conscious on his bed. His breathing was harsh and every now and again he would thrash frantically from side to side. She had understood with sudden clarity he was dying. When the other two showed symptoms she knew with the same clarity they would die as well. Now she too had joined their ranks. Nothing like this had ever been seen in Heaven and it was happening faster than anyone had time to think or plan. All of Sarobindo's constant meditation on death, which before was a limitless mystical game, had become in the space of minutes, a brute reality. Death moved among the disciples, instantly and totally recognizable, a guest constantly invited but never expected. She felt there was an animal inside her chest, tearing at her lungs. She coughed harshly and remembered Palmiro. She recalled his unorthodox request to take part in the Immersion and how sick he too had been at the end. His participation had to be the cause of what was happening. But how, and why? Why would he do something like this, so necessarily premeditated and ruthless?

She crossed the great hall with its braziers of burning incense, the effort and the smoke both intensifying her coughing. Gasping she entered the room where Palmiro had been and cast around. Nothing seemed out of the ordinary. She went to the small table and opened its drawer. Inside there was a notepad and pen. She took it out and wrote a note between spasms of coughing. "We are dying, all of us, those with the Mahatma. Something to do with the man, Palmiro. He was in this room. Search it, and you must find his friends too. One of them was Omar."

She tore off the sheet and laid it on the table. The jug of water was in front of her and overpowered by another bout of coughing she poured some into the glass and took a drink. As she swallowed she caught the sweet pungent taste and a slight syrupy texture. "Oh my God, it's a drug, a drug. That's how he did the Immersion!"

The idea of anyone using a drug to fake an Immersion was almost inconceivable, it was so alien to the devotion in which the Font Eterno was held. The fact served to deepen the horrible cynicism she felt arising from the whole thing, but she had no further chance to reflect for she coughed again and this time began to heave uncontrollably. She dropped the glass, staggering instinctively toward the pool. Hunched over at its edge, she spewed the contents of her stomach, her head spinning. Her sight blurred and her limbs went slack. Helplessly she pitched forward, falling face down in the contaminated water. Within minutes she had drowned.

The infection could perhaps have been contained if not for another circumstance. The rapid onset and term of the disease might well have slowed its spread, and provided more general warning, if it were not for a woman who had been on the bus with Jamal. Her name was Ivana. She lived in the Farming Colony providing overall care of the collective vegetable plots and greenhouses worked by Immortals. She took great pride in ensuring the freshness and flavor of the vegetables grown for the Heavenly tables and she regularly accompanied deliveries to the daily market located at the heart of the Heavenly Homeland. She had arrived in Heaven about twenty five years before, recruited in the usual fashion as an outstanding athlete of great physical beauty. That meant that she was still relatively young from a chronological point of view and her body had only just begun to make use of the immortality enzyme, while retaining some capacity for normal regeneration. So when Jamal began a wild bout of sneezing in the seat behind her, she caught the germ but she did not become acutely ill. She showed symptoms but once again people around her thought it must be an allergy, something to be sorted out by an herbal remedy or acupuncture.

She spent an uncomfortable night but got up early the next morning and accompanied the trays of tomatoes, lettuce, onions and leeks to the market. Everything was misted down with fine spray before being placed in the delivery vehicle and her bursts of sneezing simply mixed with the droplets on the food. She continued to sneeze during the whole of the morning as she served the busy throng of patrons around the stalls. Later that evening much of the produce was eaten fresh and the microbe proved extraordinarily resilient, staying alive all the way to ingestion by hundreds and hundreds of Immortals. By the following day, Heaven was in the grip of a full-scale epidemic, with many thousands of people infected, and going on to infect others exponentially. At this point it was impossible to stop the spread of the disease.

Jamal's telephone call to the fire brigade had worried the dispatch operator, one of a large and fairly random group who found satisfaction in providing this public service. The unintelligible voice at the end of the line was so unusual that it stuck in her head. She knew about the emergency number if there was some kind of social crisis. She'd never had reason to call it and very few people had. The understanding in the general population was that it went to the head of security known as Magus, but the operators knew it to belong in fact to the Anthropology Colony. How things were handled from there they had no idea. The woman finished her duty hours, but told the next shift about the strange call and her concern that perhaps she should have phoned the crisis number. Early the following morning, there was another contact from the public stating there was an unconscious individual right there on the Sacred Way. This time the dispatch did not hesitate but picked up the phone and called Anthropology. It was Blair who answered.

Once he got the report of an unconscious man outside the Taj Mahal, Blair could only deduce a crime had been committed. It was unheard of, completely outlandish, and he struggled to organize logically what he should do. The Anthropology Colony consisted of a select body of power-brokers from the old world, people like Blair, Marius, Michelle and Benazir. They had stayed together over the years as a largely unofficial body of guardians with ultimate sanction over what went on in Heaven. Fittingly, their colony also included a loyal band of elite secret service who had organized security for the original migration to Heaven.

Blair wrote a message for his colleagues and then called on two of the most trusted agents, Truman and Szabo. He told them to get the large utility car from the garage and drive with him downtown to the scene of the presumed attack. The colony was not far from the eastern end of Heaven and it did not take long to arrive at the gate to the Way of the Monuments. As they passed through they found a small crowd of horrified onlookers. Jamal lay there motionless, barely breathing. But even more shocking was his appearance. It was as if he was being eaten away from the inside; his skin was shriveled, the normal robust muscles were wasted to thin cords, and his bones stuck out like slats. This was no external attack; it was some terrible illness.

The victim was still wearing his orange ceremonial robe and Blair concluded whatever this was, it had begun at the Font Eterno: he had obviously come straight from there when he telephoned. He told his assistants to pick him up and put him in the back of the car. They would drive to the stadium and get answers there. As they caught hold of Jamal's arms and legs the skin on his wrists and ankles broke away causing him to slip from their grasp and begin to bleed softly. People screamed and they dropped the body, recoiling in disgust. Blair kept his nerve, ordering them to be more careful, to scoop up the prone figure. Once they got him inside they drove to the Font Eterno, arriving at the service tunnel and continuing with the car to a point just before the ornamental stairway. The three climbed the stairs up to the loggia and followed it round to the imposing hallway with its private rooms. In Sarobindo's quarters they found a scene of inconceivable horror, with several individuals in a state similar to Jamal's, but Sarobindo far the worst, a shriveled husk, like an Egyptian mummy, still breathing in brief anguished bursts. The air was fetid, thick with the vapor of the sick and the scent of death.

They staggered from the room gagging and coughing and utterly horror-struck. This was a disaster beyond reckoning. What did it mean? Where had it come from? Across the hallway an open doorway beckoned and there they found further catastrophe, but also their first clue in answer to their questions. They discovered Alceste's drowned body in the pool and her note on the table.

Blair's voice rasped, "My God, it's that anti-social Palmiro, he's behind all this. We should have sent him to the Ranch with his girlfriend. Do either of you know the other one?"

Both Truman and Szabo were sneezing explosively but they replied they knew Omar, they'd partied with him on several occasions. Blair felt the scratch in his own throat, and then suddenly a warning light went on in his brain, blinking open an

ancient response from a past, dangerous world. He ordered them
to search the room as the note had said. He himself had to make a
telephone call. He made his way to the announcer's booth where
he knew there was a connection. He called his Colony, insisting
he speak to Marius.

He was now sneezing and coughing himself but he made
himself understood. "This is some kind of deliberate mass
infection, the action of a terrorist, probably Palmiro. I am as good
as dead, I'm sure, as are the two with me. So far the infection
seems confined to the Font Eterno and Avenue of the Monuments.
You must quarantine them, and also find Palmiro immediately and
a friend called Omar—he's from the Fabric Colony. Interrogate
them and you will get to the bottom of this thing."

Marius acted at once on his colleague's suggestion, sending
out his security men and women to cordon off the Font Eterno and
detain Palmiro and Omar. Palmiro could not be found, and
inquiries among the few individuals still hanging around the Font
Eterno established that he had left the area with Eboni. Further
investigation at the Zoo Colony suggested that the two of them,
plus possibly also Pascale's brother, Danny, had fled to the
canyons. If it was true it represented another first. Nobody had
ever gone to the canyons voluntarily. There was also the obvious
question, how could anyone hope to survive there more than a
couple of days? These thoughts prompted a connection to the
Ranch and Pascale's presence there, and the outrageous possibility
that she might be the ringleader of the whole thing.

A radio call was made to Magus and the worst suspicions
were more or less confirmed when there was no answering signal.
Marius dispatched six of his personnel to investigate. He provided
them with sidearms, from a cache that had been untouched since
the founding days of Heaven. As for Omar, he was picked up and
brought to the Anthropology Colony, wholly bewildered. Under
questioning he told the story of how he had acted as a sponsor for
Palmiro's Immersion. Little by little he got a sense that something
terrible had happened but he was completely in the dark as to what
it was. His interrogators had nothing to go on except his
connection to Palmiro and they kept asking him where Palmiro
was and what the two of them had planned. Omar said that Palmiro
was a friend of Eboni and Danny and that was all he knew. He had

agreed to sponsor him purely for the fun of it and after the ceremony was over Palmiro had left without farewells and he had not seen him again. Apart from that he could only add that Palmiro had almost been killed in the Immersion and the whole thing had been pretty wild. One of the interrogators had been Szabo's lover and when he heard she was very likely going to die he was in no mood for kindness. He beat Omar savagely until he screamed for mercy, and still of course he was unable to provide answers. Finally Marius intervened and ordered the interrogation to stop.

"This man knows nothing. Palmiro drugged himself to carry through the Immersion—Truman managed to phone saying they found evidence—and that suggests to me a real fanatic. Our friend here is not the type. He was just a patsy, although a criminal one. The urgent thing now is to go and check with Adorno to see what his favored student was working on."

But it was too late. Almost all the apartments in the colony were now eating their evening meal, including produce brought directly that day from the clearing market, fresh salad, tomatoes and basil, raw baby asparagus, raw snow peas. It was all infected. The agents who were detailed to visit Adorno had grabbed a bite before they left, and within half an hour they, like almost everyone in the colony, were sneezing and coughing. Marius had taken some of the fresh salad and he too was infected. The investigation ground to a halt.

Omar had been told that he would be held on charges of conspiracy. His case would be decided later. He was brought to a room with a bed and left there with the door locked. He was in too much pain to think about moving anyway, and when food and water were brought he could only take a sip from the glass. He lay there listening to the snatches of conversation from the corridor outside, trying to figure out what exactly had caused this. It was clear that because of Palmiro something awful had occurred and it involved the Immersion. He remembered both Palmiro and Sarobindo's unsteady reactions afterward and he guessed that Sarobindo had been the target of an attack. The crazy way the interrogator had gone after him suggested the result had been extremely serious, perhaps even fatal. If he ever got out of here he would make that bastard Palmiro paid for how he'd been beaten just now. He heard someone coughing and then snatches of abrupt conversation.

"...infected...fatalities...quarantine...warn the colonies"

A dawning awareness came over him. The attack consisted of an infection, and, at least in some cases, a lethal one. Sarobindo was probably dead and his assistants too. It seemed Palmiro had evaded the sickness he had introduced, or at least escaped, but now something else was happening. He heard more coughing and sneezing, and in a flash he realized that the members of the Anthropology Colony were also sick. The symptoms he was hearing were symptoms of the infection which killed Immortals. The attempt to confine the spread of the infection had failed. He jumped from his bed, all his bruises and pains forgotten in a terror-struck pulse of adrenalin. He had to get out of here. He had to find a place where he would be safe.

There was one window in the room, a single pane set high in the wall close to the ceiling, with a ledge about six inches deep. He pulled the bed across the room and was able to reach the edge of the sill. He cast around desperately for something with which to break the thick glass. The only furniture in the room was the bed itself. It was made of wood. With a strength born of desperation, Omar was able to smash the bottom board free.

Standing on the other end propped against the wall he propelled the frame at the window and continued thrusting frantically until it cracked across. A few more blows and he was able to dislodge most of the glass, freeing the space. He grabbed the ledge and hauled and jerked himself up through the opening. It was a first-floor room and there were dogwood bushes to break his hands-out fall on the other side. He picked himself up, beaten, cut and bruised, yet feeling very little pain, so thrilled he was to be out of the plague house.

As he limped away in the darkness he knew what he had to do. It was essential to stay out of contact with infected groups, and at this point he had to assume all colonies were in that condition. Alternatively, they could treat him like a criminal, just like the Anthropologists had. He would travel cross country, avoiding the main roads, and return to his own villa and group of friends, hoping some of them at least had not been infected. He had thirty or forty miles to walk. Setting out along the dusty track he could see the night sky littered with stars. They seemed hard, bitter points of light, no longer the friendly faces that had previously shone on Immortals. He pulled his cotton robe tighter around him and quickened his pace, cursing the man who had brought all this on Heaven.

2. WEDDING DAY

After Jonas descended the cliff with Pascale, she gave him the tour of the Ranch. The residents were amazed to find a fully certified Immortal, one who was not a relative of Pascale's, coming voluntarily to stay with them. He smiled vaguely at their curious, semi-hostile glances, saying that Pascale was very important to him and he wanted to stay as close to her as he could. When Katoucha asked them if they had been sweethearts, Jonas colored slightly. After that the word went round that Pascale and Jonas were in love. This turned the residents in his favor and became yet another motive for the general euphoria.

Pascale showed him the tent, telling the story of how and why it had been built, and of its more recent role as a care center. He was deeply shocked hearing the account of Magus' secret prisoners and learning the age-long torture they'd suffered. Yet it was hard to remain with that sense of horror given that the victims now appeared at the center of the community and seemed to transmit a kind of joy to everyone.

Then Pascale brought him to the gutted remains of Magus' cabin and he saw at once the huge upheaval that had taken place in Heaven. He had a memory of Magus, from the few times he'd met him as an Immortal. He also recalled him from before Heaven, when he had been a ruthless security contractor, providing services for governments and companies alike. To be confronted now with his continued atrocities and then his sudden end, it was as if the whole of the past had been brought to account. He'd thought of it all as done with, that the only important thing was the endless repetition of the Heavenly present. But history had been kicked into life again, totally new things were happening, and it was both unnerving and incredibly thrilling. He gave Pascale a hug.

"Something really astonishing is happening. And you're at the center of it. I feel so lucky to be a Historian with you around. I have something actually new to write about."

She laughed. "I can't believe it's you saying that. You never wanted to think anything new or different. Remember how horrified you were at the abbey on the island, when I started talking about bits of dead people dancing like the stars?"

"Well, certainly, you now have the best of the argument. You seem to have wakened the dead, here in this canyon. So I suppose I should keep an open mind about the dust particles!"

The couple continued their stroll around the canyons, arm in arm, chatting and laughing. She showed him the women's cabin and described her first night and how the stars had come to her aid. She thanked him for pointing out the Zodiac back at the philosopher's banquet. It had started her looking for star shapes up there between the canyon rims, and she had found one, of a man, and it was really wonderful. It had felt like she could reach out and touch him and that somebody bigger than her was with her, looking out for her.

"It must have been Orion, the constellation. It was known to many ancient cultures: it can be seen from just about anywhere on earth. But you did well to spot it here in this narrow canyon."

"There you go again, professor, talking down, taking all the fun out of things."

"Oh, I'm sorry, Pascale, I definitely don't want to do that. It's a rotten habit. But if I hadn't lectured you about the Zodiac, you wouldn't have discovered Orion, would you?"

Magada saw them returning toward the kitchen and came out to meet them. "You two seem so happy together. So happy but with no place to hide!"

"What do you mean?"

"What do you think I mean? Our little paradise is not going to last forever, is it? Don't you think the rest of the gods up there on the plateau are going to get suspicious, sooner or later? And then they'll come to take back their kingdom?"

Pascale and Jonas were brought back to reality. The situation was likely worse than Magada might imagine. They had no idea of the results of Palmiro's action. It could come to nothing, but it could also prove devastating for the gods up there, as Magada termed them. Right now they had no information and they hesitated. Magada mistook their hesitation as a desire to maintain their happy mood. She changed her tone abruptly.

"But of course you're right, let's not worry about that just yet. Our big feast is being prepared and we must embrace the moment. You two love birds will be guests of honor. We could even make it as a kind of betrothal for you. Yes, why don't we do just that?

405

We'll celebrate it as our first and only betrothal banquet in the canyon!"

Before they could say anything, she had turned back up toward the tent to make arrangements. Katoucha would manage the seating and other people would make table decorations. She went off to find Danny and persuade him to prepare a speech.

Jonas was laughing. Pascale's mouth was open, half astounded, half laughing. "This is so stupid. We're not getting married. Anyway, nobody gets betrothed and married in Heaven."

"Well, that seems to have changed for Magada. And I think it's because everything's different, like I said, because of you."

"That still doesn't mean we're getting married!"

"No, of course not. But you belong to everyone here. So it's a betrothal to everyone, for everyone, including me! I think that's what she means. And as Historian I think we should definitely go along with that. It's a great story, and you're up for a story, aren't you?"

"You're crazy, Jonas. I would never have imagined you talking this way." She was silent for a while, then she added. "But I suppose I can see your point. It would be a way of showing love to everyone. Things could get very bad round here very quickly, so perhaps we really should give this story one last chapter, a happy, beautiful one."

They carried on talking and remarking back and forth as they walked to the tent. They traced a path around and around it, like they were a young couple without any cares in the world, taking a stroll in some fine park in some old-time elegant city, before the storms changed everything.

Tables were set up and enough seats found for everyone. Orwell and Francisco had developed a kind of bond, with Orwell solicitous for each of Francisco's needs and calling out for help if he couldn't supply them himself. They were placed to one side of the central table and on the other side there was a large high-backed easy chair where Elise was ensconced, propped up on cushions. She was already much brighter and aware of her surroundings, looking at people and prepared to say hello and grin back at whoever smiled at her. Greta hovered over her. She had appointed herself Elise's guardian, taking her instructions from Magada and monitoring the dosage of the intravenous drip plugged twice a day into Elise's arm. Whatever her life in Magus' cabin had been, she had been able to create a rich fantasy existence for herself and now she had the chance to play out one of its roles, the attentive nurse. Dressed in a variety of neat, crisp clothes she provided a sharp contrast from everyone else in their beat-up denim, but the little bit of theater seemed entirely fitting and it contributed to everybody's upbeat spirits. It seemed to promise a clean bill of health to the woman she attended whose body and soul were so ravaged

Alaqua and a couple of others brought out the plates and glasses. Ravel had found yellow and crimson cactus flowers and dug them up entire, placing them in pots on the table. He then returned to playing his infinite guitar concerto from the back of the tent. Koyo was seated next to him. She had emerged one day from her angry isolation and with hardly anyone noticing had sidled in beside Ravel as he played. He had not driven her away and now she was always sheltering beside him, making sure it was the side farthest from Magada.

Zoltan had taken possession of a number of good quality sheets from Magus' trove and used them to replace some of the older and shabbier blankets used as tent cloths. As a result the tent took on both a more permanent and more beautiful look. It really did seem a wholly different architecture from the old atmosphere of the Ranch. It communicated its breath and spirit to everything, so the whole canyon was a new and different place.

Danny came up from the corral after retrieving Jonas' mount from the clifftop. He'd met Magada on the way and was smiling as he called out.

"You guys are a sight for sore eyes. You look so happy, this really could be your wedding day!"

Greta heard him and came out of the tent. "What's that? A wedding, today? I hadn't heard. How wonderful!"

Pascale protested. "No, no, Greta, it's just a silly game Magada's playing. She's imagining the feast as a betrothal banquet. But really it's for everyone. We're all betrothing each other!"

"Well, whatever you call it, you absolutely have to be the bride, Pascale. And my personal contribution is that we find you something suitable to wear, something better than that drab you've

Pascale's Wager

always got on. Isn't it fortunate we're just about the same size, I think I have just the thing! So, please, do come with me, and try it."

"Greta, I've gotten used to denim. I like it. And anyway, like I said, there's no wedding."

"Don't be a spoilsport! You don't know how many times I dreamed of going to a wedding and I've never been to one, ever! Now I have the chance at least to imagine. All you have to do is wear my dress!"

Pascale rolled her eyes, but she was smiling too, shrugging and surrendering. "OK, I suppose it's a party game, I'll do it for you guys. You're right Greta, it will be something to remember."

Greta led her off in triumph. She had gotten Zoltan and Elliot to carry her armoire to the women's cabin, setting it up on the veranda. She told everyone they could have any of her clothes except for two dresses she wanted to keep for herself. One of these was now the one she picked out for Pascale, an elegant sheer silk evening dress, trimmed in silver-dust brocade and topped with an organdie bodice and collar. Tiny diamonds had been stitched along narrow seams of silk splayed across the shoulders and around the collar. While Pascale was struggling into the sheath, Greta fussed with her hair and finally got it into a bun like hers. From an inlaid jewelry box she took a fabulous silver hairpin, a long heavy clasp with a deep patina of age and the shaft blossoming at the end into a filigree of jasper and diamond flowers. It looked storied and priceless, as if Magus had looted it from a palace somewhere after the assassination of its royal household. Greta pushed it through Pascale's bun to hold it in place and set off her hair and dress. The effect was stunning.

Pepin was now banging the triangle impatiently, letting everyone know the food was ready. The meal was beginning in the mid-afternoon directly the first shadows hit the canyon tops, so there would still be plenty of warmth. The remainder of the residents came hurrying, and Katoucha directed them to their seats at the table, reserving the middle two for the wedding couple. Jonas was already in place, awaiting the arrival of Pascale. He had nothing to change into, but the tunic he wore was good quality and still not too dirty, and he had washed his face and slicked his hair. Pepin said they could wait no longer and he and his helpers began

408

serving the first course, an amazing pozole made with chicken and wild tomatillos, hominy from the store, and chili peppers and garlic found in Magus' kitchen. Just as the last bowl was being filled Pascale and Greta could be seen rounding the junction of the canyons, walking toward the tent. They were moving slowly as Pascale was barefoot and holding up the hem of her dress in order not to trip on it. As they drew closer almost everyone rose from their seats at the table, awed by the sight before them. Pascale was transformed, her natural grace and beauty now something ethereal, made of light itself. She had always shunned the sophisticated or revealing robes of Heaven but now her dress and jewelry had the effect that every Immortal always aspired to. It drew out an inner electricity and made it crackle in the sun-stretched air.

She took her place and the meal begun in a mood of intoxication without a drop of alcohol yet consumed. The idea of the wedding had been a kind of game but now there was a side to it which was totally real and no one could quite say why. At the same time the food was better than they had ever expected. They finished the soup with multiple satisfied sighs, and Carly and Elliot cleared away the bowls. Katoucha and Pepin, glowing both with pride and the heat of the kitchen, brought out the main course. It was barbecued beef in a sauce of tinned mango with wild onions and bird peppers. The sides were helpings of thyme-seasoned sweet corn, black beans with herbs and chili, and a handful of baked Indian potatoes from one of the box canyons, a find made this time by Magada.

Directly after the food was served Carly and Elliot hurried out with a crate of Burgundy, of impossibly fine vintage, uncorking and pouring the wine into each outstretched cup. Once everyone was served the absence of conversation testified to the meal's own, mighty eloquence. Danny was eating like everyone else but he also looked around with contentment. He knew that a visit from the authorities was bound to come and it would not be friendly. He'd reinforced the gates on the northern canyon, adding a couple more chains and padlocks, although he realized this would not provide any barrier to a determined assault. But now he felt it did not matter. What they had here was all that counted, and it could never be taken away. He hoped the Immortals could come to see it and accept it, but whatever happened it would never be lost. After waiting a few more minutes, allowing time for people to take the edge off their appetite, he got to his feet holding his cup in hand.

"I have been asked to offer a toast to this occasion. There is nobody here who knows Pascale better than me. I have been her brother all her life. I was with her in our family TEP back in the North and then as a companion in the experiences of Heaven, and now finally in these prison canyons. We all have seen how beautiful she is, but what has happened here among you all is still more beautiful. I do not understand it properly, but Pascale has been able to make something come alive here. For that there are no words adequate. Jonas and she are getting betrothed, or we all are, it's kind of confusing. But anyway it's a beautiful thing, and it seems like the only thing that measures up to what has happened here. It makes everything perfect. So, please, a toast! To Pascale and Jonas, the couple of the canyons! And to the rest of us who all love Pascale too!"

Everyone raised their glasses and echoed, "To Pascale and Jonas!" Then they drank, put down their cups and applauded. Someone said, "Jonas, Pascale, please reply, say something!"

"No, no, first let's finish the main course, then hear from the couple when dessert is served." Magada insisted that everything be spaced out as in a proper banquet, making it more enjoyable. So the company continued to feast on the main course, including more *grand cru* from the bottles. Everyone was becoming splendidly relaxed and mellow as the meal proceeded. Everything felt right in every respect and all at the table felt the same. At last the dishes and plates were removed and a large bowl was carried out containing an astonishing fruit salad of oranges, peaches, grapes and papaya, all taken from Magus' store of canned fruit. While this was being served Magada signaled to Jonas that this could be the moment to say something.

Jonas got to his feet, clearing his throat. "It seems I must play a part, but to be honest it's not hard for me. If even in make-believe I am Pascale's promised one then this is the happiest day of my life. When I first set eyes on her, back there at the Shuttle Port when she arrived with Palmiro, she captured my soul before I even knew it. That was not something that was supposed to happen in

Heaven. We Immortals are meant to be beyond crazy love, aren't we? We're supposed to effect pleasant liaisons, or even dangerous ones, but not to fall in love. Well, I am hereby a deviant. I have fallen in love with this woman."

"But I know also this feast is not just about me. It's about all of us, and all of you here have given your heart to Pascale, just as she gave hers to you. And there's nothing better to express this betrothal thing than the place where we're sitting, this tent. So now I want to show you something special. When I first saw Pascale this morning up on the mesa she was holding a rock. It sounds strange, but it's a fact. She dropped the rock when she saw me coming but just now, when she was getting ready, I went back up there and looked around for it. And I think I found it!"

He bent down under the table and triumphantly retrieved a piece of yellow sandstone about the size of four fists. "Here, look!" And he pointed to a scratched design on one side, a rough but clear image of the tent they were in. "You see, Pascale believes the tent is important. Important enough to draw it in stone. So, for a betrothal gift from all of us I want to give you back, Pascale, your own tent. Everything that it has meant for you it has meant for us and more, much more. To you, then, with all our love!" And he handed her the stone with both his hands.

Pascale grimaced to herself remembering her intention to throw the rock as far away as she could. However, now that it had been returned to her with love it was impossible to treat it in that way. Indeed, as she held out her hands to take it, she felt a sudden upwelling of emotion. All that she had set out to do had really happened and it was coming back to her as love. She could not help it, but tears filled her eyes and came rolling down her cheeks. She held the stone in her hands on the table, and she felt its weight, heavy and light at the same time. It was like holding something to eat, but inside her, filling her with contentment and life. Her spirit jumped beyond the stars and descended deeper than the seas, and the people round her all seemed to belong to the same sensation, to be in the same beautiful space with her.

She got to her feet smiling and blinking through her tears. She could hardly see and right there in front of her were points of light like the shape of the starman. For a moment she just stood, holding her hands out to her beloved. But quickly too she turned and hugged Jonas next to her, whispering in his ear, and then, one by one, she went round everyone at the table and those serving, including Katoucha and Pepin. She embraced and whispered something to each one, telling them she loved them, how beautiful they were, that they truly were gods. It was a long moment but everyone followed her with their eyes, watching the expression change on the face of the person she was hugging, from general happiness to deep feeling. She was communicating to each person her own intensity of life, and each person seemed in their reaction to find the same boundless feeling in her embrace.

All the same Pepin could hardly bear the length of time she took. He was dying for a real drink. He crept away after Pascale had hugged him, back to the cantina store. He knew there were only one or two people left before Pascale had hugged everyone so he waited for what he thought was a suitable interval, then staggered out carrying a large tray. On it were balanced bottles of cognac, tequila and rum, bars of chocolate and boxes of cigars. He timed it just right and arrived at the tent as Pascale was returning to her seat. He set the tray down announcing joyfully and banging on the table, "Good liquor and smokes for all who want 'em! Come and get yours!"

At exactly that moment, at first confused with the banging on the table but then fearfully distinct, there was the sound of gunshots echoing down the canyon, coming from the west in the direction of the gate. Everyone froze, rooted to the spot. To one side of the assembly, the shadows had crept out from the southern wall to bisect the tent. Where Pascale stood she was in the semi-gloom and Jonas could not see her clearly as he looked toward her with sudden trepidation. Magada cried, "Here they come, sooner than anyone wanted!" and she dashed out from the tent. Danny looked for a moment as if he was going to follow her but he checked himself and stayed put. Everyone else seemed to shrink physically, as if what they'd been doing just a moment ago had rendered them exposed, in danger, and they needed to hide away if at all possible. Everyone, that is, but Pepin.

He used the moment to snap open a bottle of cognac and pour two generous cupsful. One he handed to Cormac and the other he drank quickly himself, pouring another at once. The soft thunder of galloping horses could be heard, gathering steadily in power.

All eyes were turned in the direction of the sound, hypnotized by its quiet fury. No one said a word and then round the bend of the northern canyon came the stretching legs and heads of a body of horses ridden hard. They tore past the men's cabin and the cattle pen and came plunging to a stop as they drew level with the tent. The riders slowly circled round to the front and drew up, sitting the horses while they gazed incredulously at the scene before them. One of the men spoke.

"What in hell is going on here? Where is Magus?"

Out of nowhere Magada appeared. She placed herself between the tent and the riders, her hands squarely on her hips. "Magus is dead. He fell to his death from the top of the canyon. It was his own fault. He was attacking unarmed civilians and fell."

The news and the tone in which it was delivered clearly surprised the riders. They looked at each other with quick eyes. The man who had spoken stared at Magada. "That is a lie. We are holding you and everyone else responsible for the murder of an appointed official until we get the precise facts on what took place. In the meantime we are looking for a man named Palmiro and wish to question his companion, Pascale. Where is she?"

Magada's hand darted behind her back and from her belt under her shirt she whipped out Magus' pistol. She pointed it straight at the man doing the talking and swiveled it quickly back and forth across the faces of the others as she saw their hands go to their own belts.

"None of you motherfuckers move. So help me the first one to go for his gun I'll blow you away and be glad to do it. Now get going, all of you. Get out of our canyon, now!"

Nobody moved. The men were clearly taken aback but long memories of other days served them instinctively. The woman was outnumbered and they knew it. The situation was extremely dangerous and it needed only one false step to become fatal. Pascale stepped out from the shadows of the tent and walked swiftly to stand next to Magada. If the riders had been surprised by Magada they were left open-mouthed by Pascale. All of them were aware of the general conditions of the Ranch and were used to viewing its residents as dirty, deviant, less than human. The only reason they were not all dead was death did not happen in Heaven. Yet here, emerging from the rags and shadows of the tent, was a vision of beauty which would have flattered any soiree in Heaven and indeed anywhere in history. The elegance of the robe and the classic signature of the hairpin were impeccable marks of power, but what really took the breath away was the simplicity and grace with which the woman wore them. It was she who gave these things their splendor, not the other way round. The moment before they had been rigid in confrontation with Magada. Now they were visibly distracted, their horses tossing their heads, dancing on the spot and a couple of them turning in tight circles. She put her hand on Magada's shoulder and spoke in a clear, commanding voice.

"Don't worry. We want no trouble. I am Pascale. My friend Palmiro is not here, I assure you, but I am more than willing to put myself at your disposal. This in fact is a wedding celebration, my own, and I invite you to join us. Drinks and cigars have just arrived and there is food for all. The only thing I ask is you do not disturb our company. They are guiltless in every way."

Magada looked disgusted and shook her head, but she was out-maneuvered. She deferred reluctantly to Pascale, lowering the gun and retreating back toward the tent without taking her eyes from the horsemen. She didn't have to worry. Their attention was now fully on Pascale. The rider who had spoken couldn't quite understand what he was seeing and he glanced uncertainly at his companions. Finally he recovered his voice.

"Am I to understand you are surrendering to our custody?"

"Yes, certainly. And may I ask with whom I am speaking?"

"Ahh, yes... The name is Stavros. But you, you are actually getting married? Here?

"Yes, please forgive me, I did not introduce my groom, Jonas. You may know him." And she turned and beckoned to the tent. Jonas came out and stood beside Pascale and once more the riders were floored. They were well acquainted with the mild-mannered Historian.

"Hello, gentlemen, I'm sure you recognize me. This is a very happy day, so, please, do come join us, share in this wonderful feast!"

Stavros and the rest of the agents were quite seriously disorientated. They had no clear idea of how to proceed. A full-scale rebellion seemed to have occurred at the Ranch, and they were somehow watching its aftermath, but the most urgent task was to catch up with Palmiro. He was implicated in the worst outrage Heaven had ever known, the deadly infection of some of its citizens, and there was a good possibility he was also implicated with what was happening here. At the same time there were two obviously A-list Immortals in front of them, Jonas and Pascale herself. Seeing her this way it was impossible to deny it. They needed to question her but all the customs of Heaven pushed against any brutal treatment of a goddess. Perhaps the best path would be to accept the invitation and continue seeking information as they could. After all she had surrendered to their custody and she was the best link to Palmiro. Stavros turned to his men and offered this as a plan. They nodded ready agreement, muttering that the refreshments would be welcome; but they should just watch their backs for the gun-toting Magada. Stavros turned to Pascale and Jonas. "We accept your invitation. We will also look around."

He and another rider dismounted, handing their reins to the others who took the horses and wheeled about, setting off to scout the area. The afternoon shadow had now engulfed most of the canyon floor, reaching almost to the opposite wall. It was possible to see well enough but the contrast between the muted interior and the bright canyon face made it hard to focus. Magada had moved in behind Danny and as Stavros and his companion dismounted she whispered fiercely. "You gotta get out of here now. If they find out who you are they'll take you too."

Danny agreed. He slipped down from his chair and ducked out the back of the tent while Magada too disappeared The outside washing station consisted of a large table with two big fifty gallon drums filled with water. He dived under the table, behind the drums. He heard the sound of horses going by and then in the gap between the drums he saw the other man who had entered with Stavros come out of the tent to check around. He gave only a quick glance and vanished back inside again.

Danny edged his way to the corner of the tent and looked up and down the canyon. He could see two of the riders with the horses over at the cantina and kitchen. The others had cantered down to the junction of the canyons where the dark scar left by Magus' cabin could be seen. He waited until the riders at the kitchen had gone, heading up toward the men's cabin, and the

415

other two had disappeared beyond the corner of the canyons, and then he shot across to the cantina. He ran through it, out a back door and got in between the kitchen building and the canyon wall. He stayed crouched in the narrow space waiting for the coming darkness. It didn't look like the agents were doing a thorough search. They were too fascinated with Pascale and the offered refreshments.

Stavros and the other rider, who had introduced himself as Ryker, were sitting opposite Pascale and Jonas. They were firing questions, having downed two straight shots of Magus' best. What did she know about Palmiro? Where was he? Pascale answered she thought he was possibly hiding in the badlands but she didn't know where. Why did she think that? Because the canyons were the best place to hide. Why would he want to hide? Well, they would know the answer to that, they were the ones looking for him.

They turned to Jonas and asked when he had arrived at the Ranch. He told them this morning. Why did he come here? Because he loved Pascale and wanted to be with her. How had he found the way? He was an Historian. He'd researched and found a map. Where? In some neglected archives. How long had it taken to get here? A couple of days. Had he stayed in the canyons overnight? Yes. What about the dogs? He hadn't been troubled: lovers' luck. Still suspicious but back now to Pascale. Had Palmiro been here? Yes. When? About four or five days ago. How had he found the place? He said hed followed the waterline. What? He'd figured out that if the Ranch had the same water supply as Heaven there had to be a line. Stavros wanted to pursue this but at that point Ryker could not contain himself. Did Palmiro tell you what he was going to do? Pascale replied he had a plan to infect the water supply but she'd argued to dissuade him.

Stavros and Ryker looked at each other with undisguised alarm. Was that what Palmiro was doing? Pascale didn't know but thought it unlikely to have happened, because they were still drinking the water here and no one was ill. OK, that makes sense. But, regardless, why had she not informed the authorities? Because that was the day Magus had shot Zena and had himself fallen from the cliff top. The residents had then burned his cabin and there was no way of contacting anyone. OK, what about that day. What exactly happened?

Pascale had been waiting for the opportunity. She glanced around and saw that Danny was no longer in the tent and was likely hiding. She did not want to implicate him, especially as Jonas had left him out of his story. So she began to give her account omitting mention of her brother. As she was starting, the riders who had searched the men's cabin returned to the tent saying they had found nothing. She invited them to sit while Jonas filled their glasses, and replenished Stavros' and Ryker's. Then she told them about her lookout spot, and how that had been the point where Palmiro had discovered her, when the gates were locked below. The two of them had talked and she had tried to dissuade him from his plans. Later, Magus had arrived with a gun, grabbing and threatening her, and ordering them both to descend to the canyon. Totally unexpectedly Zena had climbed to the clifftop and Magus shot her point blank. Palmiro then made a lunge for Magus' gun and while they were struggling Magus had staggered back and fallen from the edge. She had then returned to the canyon while Palmiro escaped. Directly after the whole drama of Magus' cabin had unfolded. A search was made inside and its torture chamber and victims had been found.

She introduced the agents to Greta, Francisco and Elise and spoke of their existence at Magus' whim during the endless years of immortality. The agents looked blankly at the three survivors, and saw, as if for the first time, the infinitely abused bodies of Francisco and Elise, and the weird, doll-like preciousness of Greta. There began to dawn on them a sense of the horror that had been going on in the canyons south of Heaven. Whatever suspicion they had of Pascale's story, it was pushed to the back of their minds by the account of atrocities and the revolution that had exposed them.

They began to lose the thread of their investigation. It had been such a long time since the agents had known a world with any sense of struggle or protest at injustice, it was like an earthquake under them to feel there was something radically wrong with the whole set up in Heaven. The dark in the canyon was thickening rapidly and Zoltan was lighting flares of oil-soaked rags tied against stakes in front of the tent. The writhing flames in the belly of the canyon increased the sense of being out of their depth.

The other two riders had returned saying there were six horses in the corral but they'd found nothing else of note. They all felt there was more going on here than they knew, but in these circumstances it seemed impossible to get to the bottom of it. They could wait until tomorrow to do a thorough search, but no one wanted to spend the day at the Ranch, especially now they had heard its story. Above all they were also anxious to return to Heaven to find out what was happening there. Their one clear achievement was to have Pascale in custody. They had their prisoner. If they could return with her at first light to the Anthropology Colony there would be the chance of a proper interrogation and a hope of finding Palmiro.

Once again Jonas filled the glasses and asked Katoucha and Elliott to bring out any left-over food. Ravel had started up his incomparable guitar solo and Greta had turned Elise's chair away from the company and was making her comfortable for sleep. Pascale asked Stavros what was it actually that Palmiro had done. What was his crime? At this point Stavros was only too willing to let her know. He described the report from Blair telling of the physical condition of Sarobindo and some of his disciples in the aftermath of the Font Eterno. Blair had said it was as if something was eating them away from inside, and it was happening in a matter of hours. The Anthropologist believed the outcome would certainly be fatal and that he and the two agents were also infected. He had said the only way to contain it was to quarantine the whole Font Eterno area, including himself and the two agents inside the cordon.

It was unthinkable. Heaven had never experienced anything like this in the hundreds of years of its existence: a disease of Immortals, ruthless, swift, and deadly. The only new factor was Palmiro. He had entered the Sea of Chaos along with Sarobindo, and before that he had studied with Adorno, giving him privileged knowledge of Immortals' biology. He had the opportunity, the likely means, and as for motive, well, the whole scandal of the philosophers' banquet showed clearly where he stood. It was not he who had spoken, but it was his point of view that had been expressed.

By now Stavros was too drunk and confused to notice he was

talking to the very person who had voiced the subversive opinions at the banquet. Although he and his fellow agents were happy to have Pascale as their trophy from the canyons, they were also seeing at her as their peer, and even more than that. They had begun to feel she was a noble prisoner able to protect them from the horrors around them, even somehow the ones they were recounting.

Their ambiguous attitude was not a comfort to Pascale and Jonas. They were both appalled to hear what Palmiro had caused, for they had no doubt it was him. Earlier Jonas had said he supported whatever Palmiro was planning, but now he heard the actual details he was repulsed. Even worse than this was the fact that the agents clearly saw Pascale as implicated, despite showing her so much respect. They were bringing her in as a stepping-stone to Palmiro, someone connected to him and his atrocity. Both Pascale and Jonas remembered the way the philosophers' banquet had turned so quickly to hatred against her and they were terrified.

Jonas told Stavros he and Pascale were going to bid goodnight to Elise and Greta and would come back directly. Once they got to the other side of the chair he whispered to her fiercely. "You cannot let them take you. If they sent you here for disrupting the philosophers' banquet, what will they do if they see you as party to murder?"

"I know, I know, Jonas. I am so scared of what might happen, but I don't have a choice, do I? My promise is the only thing that kept the peace here. But, you, you have to escape. They have not yet linked you to Danny and Palmiro, and they're *this* close to doing so. You have to get to Danny's camp so you can be safe, and Danny and you can look after everyone here."

"But, wait a moment. What about you? It sounds like you're just giving up. You escaped before from the north. You can get out of this!"

Stavros was standing up looking for them and motioning to Ryker. Pascale spoke in a hiss. "Jonas, this is it. Everything has led up to this. I've got to get the agents away from the canyons before they decide on another Magus. They don't understand anything at the moment but when they do... Please, you've got to go. And you must remember, I love you!"

Stavros and Ryker stumbled round to where Pascale and

Jonas were crouching, leaning over Eline's sleeping form. "Listen, we don't want you wandering off like this. We're leaving before first light, so you stay close."

Jonas' mouth was open. The day that had begun so blissfully was crashing into a bottomless pit. Reinforcing the feeling the once festive tent had become a house of ghosts. A few residents had disappeared, drifting off when no one was looking. Others, including Pepin and Cormac, were crashed out on the tables in the old cantina fashion. Francisco had his eyes firmly closed and had been like that ever since the agents arrived. As for the latter they were slumped apart at a table on their own while one of them stood guard, watching blearily for Magada who was nowhere to be seen.

Jonas followed Pascale back to the table and observed her sit down. She was still radiant, seeming to give off light even as Zoltan's flares were sputtering their last. She was also a million miles away, suddenly and permanently removed from him by her own decision. His heart crumbled inside him, like land sinking into the sea. He could hardly bear to look at her but neither could he tear himself away. It had all happened so fast that he was unable to be angry with her, just infinitely shocked and undone. As he stood there he was conscious he was drawing attention to himself, and to her. At any moment Stavros would begin to get suspicious and ask what was wrong. He had to make a decision and do so now.

With a gigantic effort he turned his face away, as in a dream, one of those dreams in which a farewell is made, the kind that goes with a death. Then you wake up and the death did not happen. But right now, here, it was happening. He moved directly out of the tent and kept walking, or stumbling, into the night. He thought he would in fact die, the giant sucking void was so much an agony inside him, a weight and physical drag on his heart. He continued to go forward, gulping for air, falling on his hands and picking himself up, until at last he got to the cliff wall and collapsed behind a boulder. He lay there in near paralysis, unconscious of everything except the wound his soul had undergone.

At last—he wasn't sure how long—his head cleared a little and he felt the ache of his body, the numbness and stiffness of the side on the ground. He pulled himself up painfully and sat back against the cliff. All the flares were out and the tent was in total darkness except for what looked like a single flashlight inside. Up above, a few stars were twinkling in a dirty sea of ink. There was no Orion, no constellation. The emptiness inside him was bigger than the dark reaches of space, but strangely he knew he also would live.

Suddenly there was movement and from the bend of the canyon came two riders leading a band of horses from the corral. They brought them up to the tent and a flurry of activity followed as people mounted up. After a moment round the side of the tent nearest him burst the company of riders stretching at once to a gallop. Six men and a woman. He clearly saw her as she went by, hanging on tightly, her wedding dress cut in rags up one side to enable her to sit astride the horse. Nobody looked over as they went by but just as they got past she turned her face and she saw him. The antique silver pin was clinging to her hair and there was fear on her face. But strength, too. She smiled at him, with love, and she was gone.

Not quite. Almost as soon as the riders had passed four single pistol shots rang out followed by wild cries and a tremendous volley of other shots. There were three more shots, then one. A period of near silence followed and then once more the sound of horses' hooves, this time drumming away to nothing. Jonas stood up and ran up the canyon to the small spur where the steps to Pascale's lookout were. Lying at its base, the spot where all in the canyon came to die, was Magada's bullet-ridden body. He knelt beside her and held her hand. She was not breathing. Looking away, out into the middle of the canyon, he saw something glinting. He stood and walked the twenty or so paces to where the object was. It was Pascale's hairpin, the jewels catching starlight even on the canyon floor. He picked it up and returning to Magada he took the pistol from her hand. He placed the priceless trophy on her breast and folded her hand on top of it.

3. GATHERING CHAOS

Omar traveled through Heaven's night in a state of horrid frustration. He could not believe this was happening. Ever since he arrived here about twenty or so years ago—he had not kept careful count—his life had been an unbroken stream of purest pleasure. He had been a sports star in a Sector which specialized in gymnastics, excelling on the parallel bars and the rings. When he had been inducted to Heaven, it had, of course, been a surprise, but it also made perfect sense. It only seemed right there should be a place where his magnificent physical skills, which had always been part of him, should be celebrated and preserved. Of course they would want to keep him around forever! If anyone should possibly hint that he was lucky or privileged compared to other people, he simply did not understand what they were saying.

Now, literally in an instant, everything had changed. He had been brutally beaten and accused of a hateful crime. The only reason he had escaped was due to the effect of that crime, a deadly illness that was sweeping all before it. It was a nightmare and as he ran and stopped and started to run again he repeated over and over, "I can't believe this, I cannot believe this!"

He was moving along a track between hills covered in low pine and oak. He had already passed a colony, dedicated, he thought, to some kind of technology, judging by the large buildings that looked like machine shops. He thought it was probably vehicle maintenance because of the number of well-kept cars scattered around on the drives of the mansions, and on parking lots around the buildings. There were a few lights on in one or two of the villas but he didn't hear or see anyone. Neither did he want to. He just kept running. This was the higher and more central part of the plateau, suited to colonies that distributed frequent goods and services to the rest. And sure enough, as the track looped over the next hill, he entered a long high valley, an agricultural area planted with sunflower and wheat, and with greenhouses end to end along the low ridges on either side.

As he got to toward the center of the valley, the road passed by a series of big villas approached by drives, and he could see a couple of them were completely lit up, as if for a festivity of some sort. Despite the alarm bells going off inside his head, the brilliant light drew him to take a look. He turned off, jogging up one of the half-circle drives. Immediately and to his intense horror, he found two bodies sprawled in front of the house's open front door. They were breathing in short agonized spasms and their body mass had somehow shrunk dramatically. They looked hardly human, more like animated stick figures. He recoiled as if bitten by a snake, and dashed frantically back the way he'd come.

The sight of the bodies renewed his initial terror. He had no clear idea of how the disease was transmitted. It could be that the air he was now breathing was full of the sickness. He continued running and walking, waiting anxiously for symptoms to show themselves, but nothing happened. Perhaps he was safe, but it was also possible the infection did not always reveal itself at once. He struggled on, torn by fear, following the track toward the main west-east highway. He knew now he didn't have the strength to go all the way cross-country: he had to head for the quickest route. After another hour, forcing himself to maintain his bursts of running, there was a glimmer of light on the skyline and he knew the new day was about to begin.

The sun came up quickly and he could feel its warmth on his face and neck. It should have given him comfort but his lungs were tortured and he felt totally exhausted. Rather than a good feeling, the daylight brought him only fury. This was not a night of Doblepoble where there were designer drugs and fun to keep you going, and sunup brought its unparalleled sense of magic. Instead, it was a hell and a horror brought about by the sheer malice of one person. He could only imagine the vengeance he would wreak if he ever got near him. It was only the fierce promise of such revenge that kept him going.

All at once going round a bend there were three persons approaching him. Two men and a woman. He didn't know what to do. He could head off into the brush, but then they could well have information and it might be possible to talk to them without getting too close. He came to a stop and held up his hand in a halt sign, yelling, "Stay where you are."

They seemed not to understand but kept coming. He screamed at them, "I'm totally serious. Don't come any nearer. Are you infected?"

They came to an ambling stop, about ten meters away. They

423

were smiling and looking bemused.

"What did you say?

"I said, are you infected? Do you have the disease?"

They looked at each other and shrugged. "We don't know what you're talking about?"

He could see they were not sneezing, and they looked genuinely puzzled. The two men were dressed in fine woolen cloaks and the woman in a deep blue cloth swathed around her shoulders, waist and hips. The men were pleasant faced, both with long wavy hair, and one with a closely trimmed beard and mustache. He recognized the woman. Her name was Clare.

"Where are you going? It's very early to be taking a walk."

"We could say the same of you. But if it helps we've been out all night. We were discussing who should live with whom. We thought we should dedicate a whole night to it and still we have not reached a conclusion!" It was Clare who was speaking.

"Where is your colony?

"You really are jumpy, aren't you? Rupert is from the Produce Farm." She was looking at the clean-shaven man and she gestured in the direction from which Omar had come. "But he was staying with Mark and me in the Poetry Colony and we walked over here during the night. What on earth is wrong with you?"

"There are people dying or dead at the farm. You cannot go back there. It's possible you may be one of the few remaining Immortals uninfected."

By this point they were only twenty feet from each other and the threesome could see the unmistakable fear and confusion on Omar's face. They asked him to explain from the beginning what he was talking about. When he had finished they were speechless. There could be no arguing with what Omar had said. It seemed totally genuine, and even if Omar were deranged, they could not take the chance.

"Where are you going now? Where can we go to be safe?"

"I have no idea. I'm just heading to my own colony to see if any of my friends have survived."

Omar walked on, taking a wide circle round the three others. They consulted together, thinking about returning to the Poetry Colony: there had been no sneezing by anyone at the time they left. Still, they were so terrorized by the picture Omar had painted, and impressed by the measures he took to survive they instinctively decided to stay with him. The terrified party continued heading south and east, like a tattered skein of geese, Omar running and keeping his distance, the others struggling to keep up. They were all very tired, especially Omar, and he was still aching from the beating. Yet it was unthinkable he should stop: they had to find some safety, their very immortality depended on it.

It was about ten o'clock when they got to the highway, and as they turned due east they at once came upon five more people. This time it was the other party which stopped, shouting out questions, asking whether Omar's group was infected. Omar yelled back he was fairly sure he wasn't, and probably the people behind him weren't either. The two groups drew a little closer and Omar asked how they knew about infection. How had they found out?

They shouted back, telling the story of how they belonged to a Carpentry and Construction Colony and had been out on a building job. Last night they finished late and when they returned there was one of their members at the gate. He was doubled over and at the same time waving his hands like a madman. When they approached he ran away and coughed and waved even more insanely. Eventually they understood that everyone at the colony was sick and they'd sent him out to warn the latecomers to stay away. After that they spent the night in a shed together and in the morning had taken a back way into the colony and carefully approached one of the windows. Peering in they'd seen people collapsed on the floor barely breathing and in a horribly shrunken condition. Terrified, they'd made their way to the highway, hoping to find any advice and help they could get from people passing by.

Omar was encouraged to encounter people who'd had more or less the same experience as him and he moved still closer to them. Once again he told his tale of what had happened, of the source of the infection at the Font Eterno and its likely deliberate cause by a man named Palmiro. The Construction group was incensed. How could anyone possibly do that? And where was this man? Omar said he was hiding somewhere, but he couldn't hide forever. In the meantime, the important thing was to survive. They all agreed. The three behind had caught up, hanging back a little.

Pascale's Wager

Omar turned and asked how they were feeling. They answered they were feeling fine, apart from being exhausted. He began to relax, sensing that very likely none of them was infected either. He turned again to the Construction group and inquired, did they use a pickup when they went on jobs? They said they did and it wasn't far: their colony was back along the highway, just before the turn. He suggested they go back for it. It was important that non-infected people stick together and help each other if they were ever to get back to the way things were. Everyone agreed wholeheartedly. What else were they to do? He asked them also to bring food and water, but from the stores, not from kitchens where anyone infected had been. Two of them went off to collect the utility car and the supplies, while the rest continued walking with Omar and the others.

The road ran along the edge of the plateau, at the point where the terrain began to change from the low pine woods and upland valleys, falling away to hot rolling hillsides covered with scrub oak and sage. After walking a mile or so, Clare called out, "There are two more people up there, on the side of the road!"

Everyone strained to see, and, sure enough, there was a man and a woman sitting on a large boulder looking out over the southern landscape. As they drew closer, Omar was able to recognize them. They were from one of the Fruit Growing colonies. At about a dozen paces away he stopped and shouted.

"Kurt, Sonya, what are you doing here?"

The two showed no fear. In fact, they showed no reaction at all.

"Are you infected? Do you know about the infection?"

They looked at him with expressionless faces. He repeated his question, drawing a little closer. They replied in a small voice which he had to strain to hear. "You mean the sickness? Yes, we know."

"What happened to you?"

"Everyone became sick. They were coughing and fainting in front of us, crying for help. There was nothing we could do. It was horrible. We went to another colony, Sports Monitoring, and it was the same thing there. We came up here to get away."

Omar said, "Are you saying that you were near these sick people and you didn't get sick? How long ago? Did they sneeze

426

near you?"

"They were sneezing and coughing terribly. We left last night."

"You're not infected, after all that time! Does that mean you can't be infected, that you're, what? Immune?"

"We don't know. We felt a little dizzy, but it didn't make us unwell."

A flash of blinding insight struck Omar. He was rooted to the spot. After a moment he pivoted toward the others and the words came tumbling out of his mouth. "Those two came to Heaven not long after I did, about ten years ago. They were ice-skaters, and were selected for immortality. I remember clearly because I was still a newcomer myself. That has to be the reason why the disease does not affect them. It's why they've survived. Because in old world terms they're still actually young. They've still got ordinary cells. The infection only hits old Immortals, who need the enzyme. That would explain why Palmiro was willing to risk his life, because, in fact, it wasn't a risk. And it means that I'm immune too. Because I'm still young!"

And he danced around triumphantly pumping his fist in the air.

Clare said coolly, "It also means you lose immortality just like the rest of us."

A frown creased Omar's face. "Of course that's true. But at least I'll live long enough to get my revenge, and many times over if I can."

They heard the sound of a motor and turned to see the pickup arriving. It had been supplied with boxes of dried fruit, nuts and biscuits, and a big twenty-gallon water drum. Omar at once slaked his thirst, cocking his head under the dispenser. Then he climbed in the front. Others took a drink and it was agreed that Clare and her two friends could ride in the back. A small caravan was formed with the utility car moving at walking pace, leading a straggle of followers. It continued down the road while the sun moved upward to its zenith. It became uncomfortably hot, providing another unprecedented experience for Immortals who rarely ventured out in the midday. At the same time, a peculiar faint haze seemed to hang in what had always been a pure blue sky. Nobody remarked on it but it seemed to fit the catastrophic experience

427

while creating its own ominous feeling, as if a battle had been fought just over the horizon. As they crested a rise, suddenly, again, there was another group: this time four persons. They drew a little nearer and pulled the pickup to a halt.

Again the same questions were asked and a similar story emerged. They had returned late from a visit but this time someone had pinned a large note to the front gate. It advised them that the colony had been struck by an illness that spread visibly from one to another, that the situation was serious and they should not enter. The word "serious" was heavily underlined. They also had looked through windows and seen prostrate bodies. After that they had come to the highway, looking for help just like the others. They stood there looking lost and frightened but they were suffering no symptoms. Hearing and observing this a consensus began to emerge: the illness seemed to communicate very fast, so if people had been in proximity to people sneezing and were showing no signs themselves, it was almost certain they were not infected. So the four were also allowed to join the train. The party was now fifteen strong and there was a feeling of growing strength and confidence in this band of healthy individuals steadily gathering more recruits. Along with that went an increasingly defensive, protective attitude.

They had reached one of the turns to the south which would lead in the direction of Omar's colony. Mark said it would be better to stay on the road as the highway seemed to draw people who were healthy, looking for others like themselves. They could all turn south later on. Others agreed and they started to move forward past the junction. Just as they did, there was the rattling sound of hoof beats and they stopped and turned to look in its direction. There below, on the long dusty track winding up from the hills to the south, came a band of horses and riders. The utility car stopped and waited, and the walkers instinctively grouped on the far side of the hood. If they'd had weapons they would have trained them. The horsemen urged their mounts up the end of the track and onto the level of the road. They turned toward the pickup and came to a stop. One of the riders kneed his horse forward. "Who are you? What's happening here?"

Omar rolled down his window a crack. "First, I'm asking you. Are any of you infected?"

The rider stared and stared, and flashing lights went off inside his head.

"The infection, it's spread. Everywhere?"

"You got it, genius."

"But you're healthy?"

"Same as above. Now how about you? What do you know about the infection?"

The man didn't answer but addressed the whole group around the utility car. "Is this true? Is there infection in your colonies?"

He could see them all nodding. He wheeled his horse around and shouted to his companions. "The infection's out of control. These people say it's everywhere! But they don't have it."

The agents were aghast. Almost instinctively they moved their horses closer to the group, as if they too were seeking a common protection. As they did, a rider at the back, who was not seen clearly before, came into view. It was a woman in a ridiculously out-of-place white evening dress, her hair loose and dusty from the trail. Yet her appearance was striking, her face filled with tension and, at the same time, gentle and composed. The man turned his horse back to face Omar.

"My name is Stavros. We're from Anthropology. We're looking for a suspect, the person responsible for the outbreak. And like I said, who are you?"

Omar opened the utility car door. "We're a bunch of survivors. We found each other, on this road. We'd like to help you. Do you have any leads?"

All the time he was talking he was looking directly at Pascale, and he couldn't help but add, "Is the woman with you a suspect, too?"

Stavros was fully demoralized by the spread of the infection. His investigation was in fact too late, and he had a terrible sense he and his agents had been fooled. At this point he did not see any point in security secrets. "She's Pascale, a connection to the man named Palmiro, the suspect in question. We are taking her to our colony for questioning."

The news struck Omar like a sheet of flame. There was something about Pascale that filled him with dumb loathing. He'd felt it even before Stavros had said anything, but when he learned who she was and the connection to Palmiro, it blossomed into a life all its own. Like everyone else he'd heard the original story of her and Palmiro's arrival in Heaven, and thought very little of it. Now she had appeared in flesh and blood, and in the middle of this disaster, he felt immediately she was behind it all. To hurt her would be better than any revenge on Palmiro. It might very possibly inflict a deeper wound on that fanatic than whatever he could do directly. But much, much more than that, she was right here, right now, and he could think of nothing more urgent and satisfying than to cut her down physically. Suddenly, out of nowhere, an idea came to him. Without hesitation he rolled the dice.

"You cannot go back to Anthropology. My name is Omar and I escaped from there last night, when they all got sick with the infection. Some of your fellow goons had taken me in for questioning, and they beat the crap out of me. Yes, it's true I met Palmiro and I sponsored him for the Font Eterno, but it was all just for fun and I had zero idea what he was going to do. What I want to do now is find the son-of-a-bitch so there can be some justice! And I believe I can offer some help for your interrogation!"

Stavros and the other riders were listening to him intently. They knew that agents had gone to arrest this man before they had been sent to the canyons for Pascale. Clearly he had escaped and was now leading a party of survivors. It didn't seem like the action of a conspirator and they had no reason to disbelieve him. Moreover he was offering a way to find Palmiro and they were out of fresh ideas themselves.

Stavros said, "Go on."

"Let me talk to your prisoner."

Stavros gestured ironically to him to continue. Omar walked down between the horses to face Pascale. He took in her slashed dress and exposed thigh, looking up at her mockingly.

"Well, aren't you the wild one, riding your horse in a punked up gown! Tell me, how come you didn't make any of my parties? You would have been queen of the ball. What, no reply? Cat got your tongue?"

There was a slightly embarrassed snigger from a couple of the men and one or two around the pickup who heard him. The atmosphere began to change from the more or less professional attitude of the agents to something looser, much more dangerous.

"Well let me ask you one simple question then. Where is the terrorist Palmiro? He's your bosom buddy. Where is he?"

Pascale continued in silence, looking ahead at the skyline with quiet, unblinking eyes.

"OK, so you're not talking, but I think maybe you will. Let's see. It's midday now. It will take us about three hours to arrive downtown, at the Font Eterno. If you haven't told us by then you're going to take that famous journey of Sarobindo's yourself, you know the same one your friend took to start all this genocide. Except this time there'll be no last second escape. You'll be vaporized in an instant, including your punk robe. Think about that!"

And he turned and walked back to the car. This time instead of sniggers there were gasps. Stavros jumped down from his horse, with Ryker following him. They came behind Omar, calling to him. "What the hell are you talking about? We can't do that, the place is quarantined. We'll all get the disease."

Omar faced them. He was now in full flood. "Well, you go ahead and un-quarantine it. Who's the authority now but you? Listen, you can monkey around, following protocol, while Heaven rots! If you want results, if you want to find Palmiro and some kind of cure for Immortals that are left, we need action. And you'll see, this will get you your information!"

"But how can we enter downtown if there are infected people there? And who's going to go inside the Font Eterno?"

"If infected people come too close you shoot them, simple as that. You've got guns. As for the Font Eterno, if you're scared, I'll go in there, with Kurt and Sonya. We're immune because we're still young. We can't get sick."

This was another surprise for the agents and everyone around saw it. Momentum and power shifted visibly from the riders to Omar. They had no response and the fact that the infection was still a risk to them but not, apparently, to this man only confirmed his superiority. Suddenly they were mortal and he was the god. They clamped their jaws and nodded helplessly. What he was suggesting, that would be the plan.

The procession got moving, heading down the Sacred Way toward the Avenue of Monuments and the Font Eterno. Omar had Pascale's horse brought up on a lead rope, directly beside the car

431

window on the passenger side where he was now permanently ensconced. After that came the walkers holding onto the side of the vehicle, and behind them the cavalcade of riders. Omar spent the whole time gazing at Pascale with a fixed, gloating stare. It would be true to say he was in a state of acute pleasure, overseeing his victim. Every now and again he would say something like, "How are you feeling now, your highness, great queen of the canyons! Can't you feel that nuclear bomb going off all over your precious skin? I think I can feel it myself, I really can!"

As they moved forward they encountered more and more individuals and groups who had been led to the road as if by instinct, fleeing the infection. Stavros and a couple of other riders would go ahead, guns drawn, and ask if they had any symptoms. They would warn them they would be shot at once if they joined the procession and started sneezing. They all declared themselves without symptoms and in every instance that proved to be the case. They were then allowed to join the convoy. The crowd grew to over a hundred strong, stretched out behind the truck, and despite the length of the walk they did not feel weary, carried along by a militant feeling of doing the one thing necessary. The mob was still gathering members and building in fervor as it drew close to downtown.

Omar's constant harassment of Pascale still had not brought a response. She continued to look straight ahead with a tense but steady gaze. Omar continued to enjoy himself famously, but Stavros was increasingly uneasy when she showed no sign of giving in. He rode up beside her and said that this didn't have to happen. All she had to do was give some indication of how to find Palmiro, or of someone else who might know…something, anything. She remained steadfastly silent. He insisted the whole thing was way out of hand, that he didn't think Pascale should have been sentenced to the canyons, it was just a mistake. Definitely the whole idea itself of the canyon needed reform. Immortals were not meant to attack Immortals and the sooner that was established the sooner they could all get back to enjoying Heaven the way it was intended. She did not respond. Omar laughed and leered.

"No luck, eh, Stavros? Don't worry, once she smells the Font Eterno, she'll break. She won't want to become just a hint in the overall bouquet. Will she, O Queen of Heaven?"

They had made their way past the museums and libraries and were now in sight of the Babylonian gate. The crowd let out a cheer and the atmosphere became actually festive, as if they were going directly to find a solution to the epidemic. They passed inside and straightaway they saw nobody alive but bodies scattered around in the courts of the Taj Mahal and on the roadside. A few raised their sleeves to cover their mouths and many ripped strips from their robes to make masks, but no one lost their nerve. They were all in a strange exalted state, as if having Pascale in their power and bringing her steadily toward the Font Eterno granted a magical barrier against infection. Even Stavros was emboldened to ride in front without shrinking from the scenes of death all around.

They passed the giant pagoda with its magnificent blood-red roof and were now under the Khalifa. As always, the crowd threw their heads back to view the summit of the tower soaring up in the blue abyss. This time, however, they could not clearly see the top. The thin brown haze had thickened and they could only see through it dimly, uncertainly. It suggested the terrible threat that Heaven was under but it did not dint the crowd's spirits. It served only to stoke their fury, increasing their desire to carry this thing through to its end.

Omar kept up his taunts. "You don't think you're going to escape, do you? That somehow at the last minute we'll all stop, or some superhero will come rescue you? Don't kid yourself. These people here, they want your blood, and they'll get it too. So, surely now lover-girl, you have something to say?"

Still she said nothing.

The procession was passing between the Eiffel Tower on one side and the Sagrada Familia on the other and suddenly Pascale did speak. She said, "Omar, you have no idea what you are doing. Whatever happens to me, the sun will still rise, and, yes, the wind will blow, and love will never have an end."

Omar momentarily lost his spiteful confidence. "What? What are you saying? Are you for real?"

Pascale said nothing more. After blustering a bit Omar got his edge back. "You know, I thought perhaps we could have some fun together, before the night was over. But now you're just disgusting to me. I'm going to put you straight in the cooker."

They'd arrived at the park and the race course bordered by its grassy bank. Up beyond loomed the Font Eterno perched on its reflecting lake. Its luminous skin had been shut down and the afternoon sun glittered harshly across its huge dead bulk. Notices had been placed all over the grassy expanse, warning people to keep out by strict order of the authorities. Omar jumped from the utility car and shouted to the agents, "Get her off the horse and tie her hands." Then he swung himself up on the roof of the cabin and yelled to the crowd.

"This is her last chance. She can tell us where to find the mastermind behind the infection, or she can die as its provocateur!"

The crowd already in its heightened state roared in answer to his words. A shout went out, "The Sea of Chaos!" and it was taken up by everyone, "Sea of Chaos. Sea of Chaos!" Stavros came forward and ordered Pascale to dismount. She leaned out of the saddle and dropped to the ground. Ryker brought some rope and Stavros held her hands behind her back while he bound them. Stavros then faced her and without realizing the irony of his words he said, "For heaven's sake give us information, and all this will finish at once."

Pascale did not reply, but looking at no one she raised her voice for all to hear. "I am innocent of anyone's death, but if I must die you should know, I believe it is right that Heaven falls and by its own design, so that love may arise!"

There was a moment of silence and then Omar seized on her words. "What more do we need to hear? She is behind this, she has willed Heaven's fate. The Sea of Chaos for her, the Sea of Chaos!"

The crowd bellowed back the chant. "Sea of Chaos, Sea of Chaos!"

Omar jumped down and shoved Pascale forward. "Walk," he commanded, pushing her up the bank toward the Font Eterno. The crowd surged after them. Two people grabbed her arms on either side and surrounded by the press of bodies she was half carried, half propelled toward the huge belly of the globe. Omar turned and shouted to Ryker. "Ride ahead, to the control room. Get that particle machine powered up. Go!"

434

4. CANYON THUNDER

"They said 'infection,' there was an infection?"

"Yes, you could see they were blown away by it. They really didn't want to handle things at the Ranch, even though Magus was dead. They were so obsessed with what was happening back in Heaven. They couldn't even think straight about finding you."

"But who was infected? And what was it, did they describe it?"

Jonas and Danny were in the fortress camp relating the events of the previous day. They had arrived late in the afternoon and scaled the hogback to find Eboni keeping watch and Palmiro sleeping, rolled up in a blanket. Eboni and Danny were overjoyed seeing each other and hugged and kissed happily. Palmiro woke with the clatter of the horses entering the enclosure. He sat up slowly, saying he felt a little better. He asked what had happened. Had there been a visit from the authorities to the canyon? They told him the agents had come, but because of the infection, not because of Magus. At first he didn't understand what they were saying but when they repeated themselves he cast around desperately and began to fire questions at them. They said that Sarobindo and his disciples and some people from Anthropology had got this thing and, according to the report to Anthropology, the master and disciples had looked little better than corpses.

Whatever color there'd been in Palmiro's face was now gone. Jonas saw his expression and said, "This was not your plan, then? Your bright idea to bring Heaven down?"

"No, no, nothing like it. Originally I was going to put it in the water-supply, for direct ingestion, but Pascale, she was against it. And I decided myself not to do it. At the Font Eterno I thought only Sarobindo would be affected. And that would be enough!"

His studies in biology were passing like frames from a film before his mind's eye, the intense absorbing journey he had made through cellular research to the sudden devastating discovery of the anti-enzyme. Everything had been science, with the single goal of a chemical signal to turn off the effect of the enzyme. Never had he thought of a communicable sickness. But it was obvious: the moment he'd seen the anti-enzyme at work, he should have known he was witnessing the most virulent of organisms,

435

intensely communicable. How stupid he'd been! Thinking of it now he also realized the casualties would not be limited to the ones reported. It was highly probable the organism had got beyond the Font Eterno the very first night.

Danny broke in and even as he did Palmiro was also anticipating the next thing he was going to hear, his greatest fear about to be confirmed. "You've not heard the worst. They have taken Pascale for questioning. They think she'll lead them to you."

He had completely miscalculated. He'd believed the single death of Sarobindo would provoke a widespread re-examination of the whole idea of Heaven, along the lines Adorno wanted. Now instead there were multiple deaths, and of course the people from Anthropology were looking for answers and had made the standard connection from him to Pascale. Once more she was going to take the blame for him, and this time much, much worse.

"We have to rescue her. We have to get her back."

Danny looked at him glumly. "They were carrying guns and were in no mood to argue. I had to hide, or they would have taken me too. Magada opened fire on them when they were leaving and they killed her. I think we'd have very little chance of carrying out any kind of rescue in Heaven."

Eboni broke in, "Well, at last you've gotten some sense, Danny. Between you all you've brought the world crashing down. Don't think you're going to put it back together anytime soon!"

"That's about right," Jonas said. "If you didn't plan it, Palmiro, it doesn't matter. It's happened, and they'll be out for blood. Even if you were to give yourself up, there'd be no mood for mercy. And there's something else you should know. I don't understand it but Pascale actually wanted to go with them. She said her agreement to go had kept the peace, and it did, more or less. After that she wanted to get the agents away from the Ranch, to protect it from another Magus. You know we had just been betrothed in a beautiful ceremony, and she was wearing the most beautiful wedding dress. But despite all that she seemed ready and willing to go." He added ruefully, but without bitterness, "There always was a part of her that could never belong to me."

Palmiro stood up and paced around between the horses and the rocks, with his friends looking on. His lungs had suffered strain; he could only take shallow breaths; and he was still very tired.

"Regardless of whether they have mercy or not, I've got to go. I've got to find where she is, to talk to her. I've got to let her know all this was not my plan. But I also really need rest. I have to wait one more day."

He turned to Jonas. "It may be true, a part of her will never belong to you. But you still owe it to her to find her. You have the advantage of being able to move around freely. You will have to be very careful of the infection, but that could also help. People will not be out in crowds."

Jonas didn't say anything, staring at the ground. At length he nodded, "It's true, Palmiro. I owe Pascale. But I must do it also for my own sake."

Palmiro explained as best he could about the anti-enzyme, the way it destroyed cells programed by the original enzyme but did not affect chronologically young people. He had experienced no ill effects from the exposure, only the strain of exerting himself under water. That meant Danny couldn't get it. And it turned out that Eboni too had arrived fairly recently. She had been a gymnastics star, she said, along with Omar in Sector Eight, and had been inducted something like fifteen years ago. Palmiro said certainly she too would be immune. As for Jonas, well, he had to be very careful. In fact he should wear a mask at all times. Right there they made him a good one, a square of cloth torn from his undershirt, running from the bridge of his nose and under his chin and double tied at the back of his head.

Jonas said he would waste no time but head off at once. He packed supplies and some of the water they had brought from the Ranch, and arranged a meeting place with Palmiro, at the last turn in the track before the plateau. He would be there tomorrow in the afternoon and would bring him any news he had gathered. Everyone inside the rock fortress was so concentrated on their talk that they had not noticed the skies darkening overhead. Just as Jonas was about to mount up, they heard a terrifying noise which Palmiro, Danny and Eboni had never heard before and Jonas only a long time ago. It reminded the northerners of some of the sounds in the Presentations back in the Sectors, but they had never once heard it in the open. They all gave a start and the horses shied instinctively. Jonas went running through the gap in the rocks out to the ridge to stare across the canyons. They followed him and he pointed.

"There, look, look!" And for the first time they saw a bundle of clouds like a big ugly mountain above the northern tableland and surrounded by the normally blue sky of Heaven tinged in a yellow haze."

"It's thunder, and rain clouds. That's impossible!"

Palmiro said, "The Weather Shield, something's happened! My God!"

"Holy shit!" gasped Danny.

Eboni said, "For sure, the world is crashing down."

There was a flash and another boom and rumble came rolling down from the plateau, falling and bouncing in the canyons. The younger people had never witnessed anything like this and Jonas himself had forgotten the brute strength of a thunderstorm. They could see the sheet of rain emptying from the dark cloud across the territory of Heaven. They watched it tracking toward the east and could almost feel the shocking impact as it hit the stone and marble of downtown.

"Who would have believed this, at the same time as the infection? It's like it was planned."

"You're not saying Palmiro made this happen too, are you?"

Eboni was joking with Danny, but before he could reply, Palmiro said matter-of-factly, "Actually it could have been me, at least in part..." And he told them briefly about Guest and how he had gotten him access to the live monitoring of the refrigeration system.

"He only had to experiment a few times and he could have figured it out. He said he could use it, too. Perhaps the Global Weather Shield is down."

The three others looked at him with a mixture of horror and amazement. Had this man single-handedly changed everything, providing the germs of destruction for all the systems devised by human beings? If so, had anything really been by chance? Indeed, what part had Pascale played in it all?

Another peal of thunder crashed across the canyons, hitting against the bluffs and tumbling into the ravines. Jonas said, "This is the end of the world. And, Palmiro, you are Vishnu, the one who brings it to an end."

Palmiro regarded him irritably and shrugged. "I don't know what that is. I'm not anything special, if that is what you're saying. I just did some things with more consequences than I planned." "I am not so certain about that," said Eboni. "It seems all too much of a coincidence to me."

The sky with its brown tinge now looked almost green and suddenly Jonas tensed and almost doubled over, turning to grab the rock next to him. Danny asked, "What is it, Jonas? Are you OK?"

He said nothing and shook his head. Then he straightened up. "I had the most terrible sensation, like everything was falling inside me. I'm alright now. Look, I've got to go." Facing Palmiro he added, "I'll see you tomorrow, at the final turn before the plateau."

He went back inside the rock fortress and took his horse, leading it out and down the ridge. When he got to the bottom he mounted and, looking round, he waved, shouting something. But his words were drowned by another burst of thunder.

Danny and Eboni decided they would let Palmiro rest and both return to the Ranch at once. Danny felt much more part of the community of the canyon than any colony of Heaven, and it was important to get back quickly to support it. Earlier that morning Jonas had organized a funeral pyre for Magada, getting help to drag charred timbers from Magus' cabin up to where she lay. The cremation was carried out at the spot to try to preserve the feeling around the tent, but the mood in the canyon had shifted anyway. The euphoria had disappeared and in its place there were sadness, fear, anxiety. Danny and Eboni made their farewells, telling Palmiro they would be thinking of him and Pascale every day until they were all reunited in the canyon. Nevertheless, as they rode down the ridge to the bottom and saw him standing there at the crack between the rocks, with the thunder still booming around him, something made them doubt they would ever see him again. He was a strange man who did not fit into any world, and continually brought worlds to an end. If he had not loved Pascale and she him, they did not know they could ever have been his friends.

5. ROCK BOTTOM

Palmiro went back inside the natural fortress and lay down. The ground was covered with fine white sand, and when he wrapped himself in his blanket, it made a reasonable surface. The thunder was drifting away to the east and no rain had reached the canyons. He felt safe, even protected, but he could not sleep. His mind returned over and over to the whole course of events like an animal chewing on a trapped limb. Where was it he had made the mistake? Where was it that everything could have been different if he'd only seen it? The thing he had missed was so elementary. Of course an organism as aggressive as the anti-enzyme could leap from person to person. All it would take was a sneeze or micro droplets in the air and it would wreak its havoc with the next body in line. What was it that Adorno said, that it did best at room temperature? How could he have missed that?

He had studied pure biology in a world without illnesses. Viruses or bacteria did not exist in Heaven and even back in the Sector they had been practically eliminated. He had never reviewed them. Instead it was all the amazing, complex chemistry of the cell and the wonder of the Immortality enzyme as his guiding star. He had ended by devising its antidote, but again he told himself he had never anticipated anything else but the symbolic death of one man.

Like a hammer-blow it struck him. Adorno had known this would happen. He had examined the solution and knew the power of the organism, he knew it would be highly infectious. For one final time Palmiro felt used by his master, exploited like a pawn on a chess board. Just as Adorno had directed him like a puppet to look for the anti-enzyme he had also hypnotized him into releasing a pathogen into Heaven. Yet, in almost the same moment, Palmiro doubted himself. He had allowed himself before to be used by Adorno, even after he had become aware of the game he was playing. Was it not possible, even likely, he'd also known how this would create a plague?

He gripped himself around his stomach and groaned and cried out. He had made happen the very thing that Pascale had pleaded with him not to, and he had done so as the most pathetic slave of Adorno. He had simply blinded himself to what he was doing. Because of his terrible self-deception his thoughts had not been concerned with getting Pascale out of the canyon, rather his actions had set a trap for her. A trap which had now sprung. He had never felt so disgusted and repelled by himself. How had he become such a tool, and an arrogant and hateful one at that? How had he betrayed the best friend he ever had? He felt like going out on the ledge and throwing himself from it, in order just to end it. He got up from his bed-roll and paced around thinking that, yes, he should do this. The only thing that stopped him was the slim chance he might yet rescue Pascale, and destroying that final chance would make him even more contemptible than he already was. Finally, he threw himself back on his blanket and curled up. He let his mind go blank, which it did more or less on its own, because every thought was too painful and impossible. He became as close as materially possible to the rock and broken land beneath him. At last he slept.

He dreamed he was in a dark underground space. There was a procession, white robed figures emerging from a long gloomy corridor. Suddenly he could see Pascale. She was being brought for trial. Gaius was there, he was screaming at her, "You destroyed the Weather Shield, you brought the plague. You are a demon from hell!" Palmiro was trying to speak, trying to say it was not her who had done these things, it was him! But nothing came from his mouth.

He woke up sweating and his heart aching with a bottomless ache. He thought the walls of his chest would cave in, so emptied out and hopeless he felt. It was night but unlike always before he could not see the stars. The haze in the sky during the day seemed to have continued and was now obscuring the starlight. He shut his eyes and sobbed quietly to himself. "I am sorry, so sorry...so sorry." He did not think it was possible to feel more wretched, despairing and alone. He continued to repeat these words to himself, over and over, until once again he slept, from sheer grief. And once more he dreamed.

He was in the Northern Homeland and Finn was walking toward him across the ice. Suddenly it cracked, and Finn fell and disappeared. Then just as suddenly there was Pascale. She came across the icefield with calm confidence, leaning down into the crack. With two hands she pulled the boy free. Finn came up out

441

of the crevasse smiling and laughing as if it were all a game. Palmiro felt a tremendous love welling up inside him, a thing so physical it shocked him, even in his dream, and brought him to semi-consciousness. He never wanted the feeling to go, so he just lay there between sleeping and waking, not thinking, not trying to reason, just holding onto the sensation in his heart. Finally, as he lay there, the feeling was so sure and solid he simply opened his eyes. Pascale was standing right there in front of him, beautiful and smiling. His first thought was "How did she escape and get here?" She said, "It's all going to be alright, Palmiro. Don't worry. Everything was for the best. Go and rescue Finn!"

She was so calm, like in the dream, and her words so strange that the next moment he could not believe his senses. He blinked to see if he really had opened his eyes, and in the instant he opened them again, all he could see was the faint glow of the sky above him as the sun came up.

Yet there was no doubting the sense of a presence among the rock walls of the enclosure, as if a beloved friend had just left the room. He could almost smell her. He was startled and jumped up directly, looking round him to see where the figure had gone. There was nothing, just the quiet space and his horse observing him in the gray and pinkish light. The feeling of love was still with him.

He went to look outside on the ridge. He saw nothing, but the sky was on fire in the east. From end to end the horizon was a quivering red curtain that expanded even as he watched. It was a dawn like he had never seen before and he was mesmerized. Inch by inch the sky turned crimson and amber with long smoking tendrils of flame reaching across to where he stood. It seemed the two events were connected, seeing Pascale and the radiant sky. The sky, he was sure, was exceptional because of atmospheric changes, but it was also true something huge was happening to him. He had never really seen anything before. He had always been thinking about his world, seeing it because he was thinking about it, never just seeing it. Now in the space of a few moments his vision was transformed, both blinded and made to see all over again, and all he could ever do was see. At the same time, with that, there was a pleasure and happiness he had never tasted before. He did not know himself and he stood there soaking up the electric newness all around him.

The morning tasted fresh, like freedom, like those memories of childhood when you see your first clouds, first flowers, first bees, first grass, except he'd never really seen any of those things. All things had always been the same and never new, even when he first saw them in the holograms. He realized that nothing had ever been new until now, and the newness was astonishing and dizzying. He could smell it and breathe it and he was light-headed with the unforeseen youth of everything.

What had he seen when he saw Pascale? How had he heard those words? The questions crossed his mind, but he did not wish to pursue them. With the humility of his total failure he did not know the answers anymore and he was ready not to demand them. Everything had changed, from despair to light, from sour darkness to...what? To life! How could he go back on that?

He remembered how beautiful she was, in a white dress and diamonds in her hair. Of course he was in love with her! More than ever, more than he understood. To be in love was unlike anything else. He did not want Pascale in the usual romantic way, he thought. She had not come to him like that. He could not really give it words but her love had changed everything for him. He allowed himself to wonder what had come first, his love or the vision. He didn't know and he knew he would never know. In any case, was there a real difference? Whether there was or not he knew that from now on his own life would be different. He would live for this love, not for any intellectual or selfish pursuit. He would go now directly to meet Jonas and tell him about his changed world. If anyone would understand it would be Jonas. Jonas had always loved Pascale.

He saddled his horse, gathered a few supplies and set off down the ridge. It would take him until the afternoon to get to the ascent but he could not remain in one place anyway. He was bursting with life and he had to be on the move. As he got to the bottom of the ridge and skittered down onto the level, he realized that the ill effects of the immersion seemed to have disappeared. His lungs felt back to normal and the dull ache in his head had gone. He gripped his horse with his knees and threw his hands wide in the air, yelling to the echo. And then he was laughing to himself, for doing something he had never dreamed possible.

443

Down in the canyon he was not able to get a wide view, so he could not be sure of the progress of the weather. Still, the sky was now more of its normal color, with only some patches of the haze remaining. He thought of the storm the previous night and its implications for both Heaven and the Northern Homeland, but he refused to dwell on them. There was a time for all that and it was not now.

Right now for the first time in his life he was free to see what was around him and he was not about to miss it for the sake of anything in the abstract. He saw the colors of the canyon, from salt white, to tan to bronze. He felt the age of the rocks and the labor of the earth in bringing forth this rugged landscape. He saw the yucca and the bunchgrass, the desert flowers and the birds, finches, hummingbirds…a hawk. All the while it was as if everything was bright inside him and he couldn't stop being happy.

It was the mid-afternoon when he climbed the switchback track up to the plateau for his appointment with Jonas. He'd almost forgotten the purpose of their meeting and it was only as he made the twisting climb to the mesa that he remembered, almost with a shock, that he was returning to Heaven in order to find and rescue Pascale. He had seen her that very morning and she had remained in his mind's eye ever since, so why would he be looking for her up here? As he rounded the last-but-one bend, walking ahead of his mount up the gradient, he could see a figure at the next and final turn. It was Jonas but he was not looking out for him. Rather he was sitting on a rock with his elbows on his knees and his head bowed almost to the same level. It was a picture of exhaustion and despair. When Palmiro drew closer he did not look up, and, eventually, when Palmiro was right next to him, he had to call out to him.

"Jonas, what on earth's the matter? What has happened?"

Slowly Jonas looked up but he didn't speak. His face was pinched and haggard, almost as if he were dying. For a moment Palmiro thought he had caught the infection, but then he understood that Jonas' pain was something else, something within him. Instantly all his frame of thought shifted, like a wall in reality collapsing to reveal another one utterly different. He understood. Pascale was dead. There could be no doubt of it.

"Oh my God, what did they do?"

His day of delight came crashing up against another day. How had it been possible that he had not thought of what had actually happened to Pascale? All the terrible possibilities had been blocked from his mind by the experience of the vision. Now he was meeting the other half of the truth head on, here at the head of the trail.

"Tell me, Jonas. Speak, tell me!"

Jonas at last found his voice. It was just a whisper and Palmiro had to bend to listen to him. "What did you do, what did you do? You and your plans, you brought everything down on her."

"Please, Jonas, tell me. What happened?

"They took her to the Font Eterno and they threw her in, that's what happened. They turned on the Sea of Chaos and put her in."

It was Palmiro's turn to be speechless. Somewhere in the back of his mind he'd thought surely she was dead, but he'd never pursued the thought. The joy of his encounter with her had been far too vibrant and real. But this! He gave a harsh cry. They had done the very thing to her which he had risked three days ago in his plan to bring down Sarobindo.

"They stripped her of her wedding dress and threw her in naked. It was a man named Omar who led them."

Of course, Omar. Very likely he'd been questioned and was furious at being tricked and blamed. So it was just as Jonas said: his actions had unleashed a terrible assault on her, one that should have been his own fate. Yet Pascale herself had come to him this morning and told him everything was for the best, and would not that include even this? He was struggling to assert the earlier revolution that had taken place inside him.

"When did this happen?"

"Yesterday, in the afternoon, just as the storm hit."

"It's OK Jonas. She is alive. Don't ask me how. I saw her and it has changed everything."

Jonas gazed at him bleakly. His pallid face flickered. "What? Is this some other crazy idea of yours? Not only have you got her murdered, you are mocking her suffering too."

"No, no, Jonas. I'm absolutely serious. I know she's alive. And even the Particle Accelerator, it fits with her whole way. What was it she said, "Love counts faster than light?" That means her

445

love was faster than the machine, she counted quicker than it, and she, her body, her love, is pure information which is still alive. It is nowhere and everywhere, and it can reshape everything."

Palmiro spoke of the night he had endured and his vision in the morning and the way it had made him feel. A feeling he never wanted to lose. He was astonished at his own words, uncertain of where they came from. Yet he truly did believe them. Jonas was still regarding him blankly, hardly hearing what he was saying and not following any of it. His words did have the effect, however, of getting him to voice his own story. He cut across Palmiro and began to speak, mechanically, in a monotone.

"I came up here yesterday, and rode to the Avenue of the Monuments. There were lots of bodies. It was dark and everything was still wet. I went into the Capitol to spend the night and I met Stavros there. He had been sheltering since the afternoon. The others had gone with Omar to his colony. Stavros told me everything, the abomination that took place. He was a broken man. The night I spent with him was the worst of my life, worse than the one in the canyon after Pascale's arrest. Now what is this latest folly you are telling me?"

"This thing that happened to me, Jonas, is the biggest thing in my life. Bigger than coming here to Heaven, bigger than my studies, bigger even than this terrible disease I unleashed. If not, I would be in despair myself and would probably end my own life."

This time Jonas understood Palmiro meant what he was saying and he felt, yet again, Palmiro was pushing him toward something new, but so farfetched he couldn't begin to consider it. At the same time Palmiro's shockingly positive attitude in face of the horror shifted him, whether he liked it or not. The morning after the night with Stavros he had dragged himself to the head of the trail out of loyalty to Pascale's friends, without any sense of a future. Now Palmiro was once more opening a door in front of him, and although he could see nothing on the other side it did mean, at least for Palmiro, the story of Pascale was not over.

Palmiro questioned him about Stavros. "That man, the agent, what happened to him? Why did he feel bad?"

"He never wanted Pascale to die. He said Omar tricked him. Omar claimed she would break and give information about you."

"I think you need to go find him again. He needs to know

what Pascale told me, that it was for the best. Tell him about Danny. He could join him out in the canyons."

"You're saying I should tell him I'm in contact with you? He'll think I was part of the conspiracy and arrest me on the spot."

"No, he won't. The whole thing has changed, and he will change too. Something different has to happen now in Heaven and he needs to be part of it. In the meantime I have business to attend to, at Adorno's. After you speak with Stavros you could come and meet me there."

Jonas continued to observe him with a mixture of incredulity and pain, saying nothing.

"Look, I know all this is very difficult for you to take in, but I'm asking you to believe what I told you, what she told me…everything was for the best!"

He did not wait for an answer but turned and mounted his horse, pointing it up the trail to the plateau. Jonas said, "Wait! Tell me, please, what did she look like?"

Palmiro stopped. He got down one more time and faced him. "I was asleep, then I was awake. I opened my eyes and she was right there. She was in the dress you described, but her smile and her eyes were the most beautiful. They saw everything but they also made my soul feel light, as if it had its own light inside, and they still do. "

He remounted his horse and started up the trail. Looking over his shoulder he shouted, "Don't worry, Jonas, you will see her too."

447

Pascale's Wager

6. RIDING ALONE

The late afternoon was brassy yellow as Palmiro trotted along the single-track road, heading north and west toward the Appian Way. He saw very few living people. One lone man standing on the side of the road stared at him as he went by. He did not stop to talk, especially when the man called out, "Hey, hey, you!" He was sure by now that whoever had survived had heard his name and description, and knew he was on the run. At the same time, he felt reasonably safe, so long as he kept on the move. From Jonas' descriptions the hunt for him lacked any organization. Still, he could never be sure, and he was constantly on the lookout for any body of people on horseback. If he were to meet a group of vigilantes he would be in desperate trouble.

Everywhere there was the scent of death. It was not so much physical as a palpable sensation that behind every hill, every wall, every line of trees there were dead and dying people. Indeed, in the fields and vineyards he saw glimpses of bodies and when he passed the driveways and workshops of the colonies there were corpses scattered by the entrances and doorways. Once he stopped to look and was able to observe the remarkable loss of mass, as if the person was immensely old and had shrunk to little more than skin on a stick frame. He reflected the anti-enzyme was so aggressive most of the cytoplasm was lost within the first twelve to fifteen hours and the organs all but destroyed. It meant, in fact, there was little odor, little more than that of a dry, faintly rank cloth. But the sense of death and its power was immense.

The day was still hot, but as he left the shrub land behind and gained the main highway the tops of the spruce and pine on the northern hills were beginning to shake in a way unprecedented for Heaven. Directly to his front the red ball of the sun was going down framed in a thick misty halo, again something he'd never seen before. It was as if the skies were announcing themselves all over again and the endless present of immortality was being swallowed up again by change and time. People dying was part of that. Every individual who died signified something come to an end but also something begun. Perhaps this was another reason Immortals had been so fascinated with Sarobindo's play-acting: it

448

meant they were escaping the tyranny of sameness, always on the brink of something new. Yet not quite. It was never truly new. That, he said to himself, is why something like he had done had to be done, in order to bring about something honestly and truly new.

He wasn't making excuses for himself. He wasn't justifying what he had done. He knew where his guilt lay. He did not think it was in the deaths, despite the horror all around. The shriveled corpses seemed to proclaim the natural life-span of these people was well and truly complete. Rather, it was in the power he had assumed to make choices for them. That is exactly what the Immortals had always done, assuming power over countless generations of Teppers. They had even assumed power over life itself. It was in order to undo that power he had taken action, but in the process he'd repeated exactly their way of doing things.

Pascale, on the other hand, had never wanted power. She had never been touched by it. She had gone to the canyons, a place where people were abandoned, and she had not resented her situation, but instead made something new happen from it. She had gone to the Font Eterno and she had triumphed there too and in a totally astonishing way. And this new thing now was the greatest of all. Because of the Font Eterno, even all these deaths around him were not the end. The future was not cut off even for these people.

The last glow of sunset along the western skyline was propping up a band of ragged cloud tumbling in from the north. Over to his right, intermittent flashes along the hills and a distant rumble announced the coming storm. Soon there would be rain. Palmiro wanted to give up his power. Or, rather, he wanted what Pascale had done for him to be his power, the strange kind of power that came with loving. Yes, that is what he wanted more than anything, to become the new thing she had shown him. The horizon ahead was now a long purplish bruise and the rain started falling, in great sheets blowing down from the hills one after the other. Palmiro felt intensely alive and he urged his bewildered horse faster down the darkened highway. If he'd known any songs he would have sung them.

Adorno's was still three hours away and the rain which had been warm at first was turning colder. There was, of course, no cape in his saddle pack, so he had to make do with his bed-roll as

449

u cover. It was fairly thick but after half an hour it was soaked and clinging to his back and shoulders, absorbing all the warmth from his limbs. He threw it onto the ground, and continued cantering into the blowing rain, his teeth chattering and body shivering convulsively. It was too dangerous to stop, so once more he was obliged to push himself to the limits, willing himself to make it to the safety and warmth of Adorno's mansion.

As he urged his horse forward he remembered the last time he was so cold, back in the Northern Homeland. The whole story of the Ice Camps came to his thoughts, for the first time for a very long time. It seemed he had been journeying against the elements all his life, against ice and water, against wind and time, and, most of all, against other humans who wished to destroy him. He held his head down against the storm and thought once again he could not do this except for Pascale. So much in the past was bitter to him and it was only her love that had kept and could keep him going, and make his journeys worthwhile. He wanted to believe her love could still bring him friendship, that he could still have sisters and brothers in this world. Despite the soaking cold he could feel the warmth of tears running down his face. Their touch shocked him. As the feelings inside him gave him pain they seemed to promise the very thing they wept for. He stopped shivering, finding strength from a circle of mercy. Once again he found the will to reach his goal. He reached down and patted his horse, "Not far now!"

7. STAVROS

Stavros had gone to the Capitol knowing that few people would seek it out. It was set apart on a low hill behind the Piazza of the Fountains, some distance from the Way of the Monuments. Climbing the hill and then the steps always seemed too laborious, so hardly anybody went up there. It was a good place to get away from the crowd, and he needed it desperately as a refuge from the mob urged on to its fatal term by Omar. He had been swept up in it all, helpless to stop the humiliation and destruction of the woman called Pascale.

From the first time he had encountered her at that so-strange ceremony in the canyons, he had been struck by her quality as an Immortal. He himself had come to Heaven in the very first migration, part of the security set-up ensuring everything went smoothly, without information leaks or terrorist sabotage. He'd helped in the recruitment of the large labor force from the poorest nations, brought in for the construction of downtown and the colonies. Later on, he'd overseen the same workers' return to their wretched countries of origin. With the help of mercenaries, hired on temporary contracts, then paid off and abandoned at airports across the globe, the men and women around him had succeeded brilliantly, without a hitch of any kind. And that applied also to the enormous project of the Weather Shield. The construction was carried out by engineers who were in the know, but the media disinformation needed to disguise it, and the selection and training of the Northern Homeland's first citizens, this was all the responsibility of the intelligence community. In sum, the whole thing ranked as the most difficult and complex security undertaking of human history, but it had been carried off with absolute efficiency. The chaos of the storms had provided the best possible cover, disrupting communications, isolating groups and often simply wiping out traditional centers that could have provided opposition.

It was a dream operation and any of its darker aspects were far outweighed by its stunning success. The abandonment of whole communities by withdrawal of support, all this was a rational decision. The pursuit and assassination of anyone who created a public risk for the project, that too was inevitable. He

451

and his colleagues had been convinced by the urgency of what they had been doing. It was only later, in the endless summer afternoons of Heaven that stray, unwanted thoughts had come to him. Was it true that there was no other way? Would it not have been better for all humans to die together, rather than abandon the unlucky ones to oblivion while slaughtering those who protested?

He did not know whether anyone else had these thoughts. He knew it was totally against the way of life in Heaven even to hint at them, and anyone who did naturally ended up at the Ranch: that was what it was there for. So, he swept them from his mind, filling it instead with the perfection of the thing he had helped create. The constant beauty of everything around him was justification, more than enough, for all he had done. He had in fact become a total devotee of beauty, and all that was beautiful gave him contentment. When he had gone to the Ranch searching for Palmiro, and encountered the supernatural beauty of this woman he'd concluded there must have been some mistake. Nothing this beautiful could or should be at the Ranch. Here was an Immortal the way an Immortal was meant to be. The fact she had been a companion of Palmiro did not change that. Moreover, it only seemed natural in that setting she should not betray him: all he'd expected was the opportunity to question her in the conditions of Heaven where she would surely see reason. He had never anticipated what in fact happened.

He lay on the couch on the upper floor of the ancient Roman palace drowning in shame and hopelessness. He had not moved from the spot since he arrived here over twelve hours ago. There was nowhere to go to that did not have the threat of infection and anyway he had no desire to see anyone or do anything. His own colony was infected but it was also repulsive to him. After his fellow agents had joined so easily in the death of Pascale he could not be around them. At the last moment when he realized it was really going to happen he could not watch. The other agents along with all the crowd had been baying for blood, chanting out rhythmically, "Sea of Chaos, light her up, light her up!"

He had left at once and gone to the Capitol. Surrounded by busts of antique Romans, of Caesars and orators and writers, he had sunk into despair. Beauty had been destroyed and the world of beauty, all produced at such a cost, had come to an end. To underscore the point that same hour the perfect weather of Heaven turned, giving way shockingly to thunder and rain. He lay there as the day darkened and the great room was bombarded by deafening noise, by rain blown through the windowless casements and by flashes that made everything ghoulish and distorted. Demons danced around the walls in sickening malice, mocking every work of man. Indeed it was as if the whole cosmos agreed that beauty was destroyed and Heaven should come crashing down. Finally the storm passed but he may as well have been already dead for all the feeling left in him. Evening turned to night and the hours crept by and he kept no track of time. It must have been in the small hours of the morning when something broke in on his semi-conscious state. There was a light from a torch coming up the stairs and someone entering the room. He didn't move but simply watched from the corner of his eye. Whoever it was spoke and he heard a muffled, "Is there anyone here?"

He felt he recognized the voice but he did not reply. The figure sighed and sat down on a couch at the far end. It was Jonas, the gentle historian and partner to Pascale in the ceremony back at the canyon. He could hardly believe it and the shock actually made him sit up. Jonas saw the movement and also sprang up, holding his flare above his head and edging slowly toward him across the room.

"Who's there? Is that someone?"

"Jonas, it's Stavros. I can't believe it, you came here..."

Jonas relaxed and pulled down his mask. "I always reckoned this as a good place to sleep, you know, during Doblepoble. I'm glad it's you, Stavros. I'm looking for news. A man back on the highway said he'd seen you all heading downtown..."

Something about the situation and Stavros' face in the guttering light made Jonas stop. "Wait, why are you here? Alone? You're not infected, are you?"

Stavros could not help himself. He saw Jonas standing there, the man who only a little time ago had sat next to Pascale in the strange and beautiful ceremony of the canyons, and it turned a key inside of him. The story came pouring out. He did not know he had it in him, so much emotion, so much remorse and grief.

His words now plunged Jonas into horror, but he himself felt a bit better. For the Historian the group murder of Pascale was a shook beyond thought itself. Both the fact and manner of it broke his heart and crushed his soul. He withdrew to the couch at the other end of the room without saying a word, lowering himself down in a catatonic state. As Stavros observed him sink the security agent himself finally surrendered to exhaustion and fell asleep. Jonas endured the total emptiness and darkness alone, the hours leaking into each other like congealed blood. At first light he forced himself to his feet. He exited the building to retrieve his horse at the public stables. He had to go to inform Palmiro.

Stavros awoke much later. He felt stronger, encouraged to remember there was someone who had shared his sorrow and disgust at what had happened. He got up and looked around for his friend but found no trace. He felt hungry and went outside to search for food and something to drink. It was not hard to find one of the specialty carts abandoned on the sidewalk. Rooting in its containers, he got dried fruit and nuts and some cake, and he drank from one of the fountains in the piazza. The rain on the ground was beginning to dry and there was a vaguely rotten smell in the air. He still had his mask and he held it closer to his face.

He returned to the Capitol in order to think things through. Almost to his own surprise he wanted to live. Yet the way it stood now in the Heavenly Homeland you did not know whom to trust. People could be infected or they could form a deadly mob. Jonas was somebody he could trust. He would guess in all likelihood he had returned to the canyons to tell people there the awful news. The point was Jonas would have friends in the canyons, people he would be able to trust, and at this point it was definitely one of the places safest from infection. Again to his own surprise he decided firmly he would head back to the canyons. He even suddenly felt happy with his decision.

He had to find a horse. He did not know what had happened to the horse he'd brought from Anthropology. Everyone had been so carried away they simply abandoned their mounts. He went to the public stable close to the Piazza of the Fountains but there were no horses there. He remembered there were stables attached to the racecourse, somewhere to its south end. He set out walking, recognizing the buildings in the distance across the grassland. The sun was warm and bright and the air was still. A slight mist hung above the ground. As he got closer to the barns and paddocks a man came staggering out toward him. He was coughing and sweating and shouting in a way Stavros could not understand. He pulled his mask up tight and yelled that the man should keep away. The man continued to get closer. He looked angry and desperate and Stavros began to panic He drew his gun, and aimed about ten feet above the man's head and shot in the air. The man threw his arms up and actually fell down as if he had been shot, lying there with his hands over his head. Stavros skirted around him and passed on toward the stables. He kept his gun drawn as he entered one of the biggest barns, but he saw no one else. There were about a dozen horses inside and they all looked well cared for. He wondered if horses could get the infection and felt pretty certain they could. Would they have been infected by the man? He held back, terrified lest any of them start sneezing and he be covered in the droplets. All was quiet, however, except for an occasional whinny. He plucked up courage and grabbing a saddle he returned to one of the first horses in the row which looked calm and even-tempered. He saddled it as quickly as he could, clambered aboard and trotted out smartly from the barn.

As he rode back across the parkland he could no longer see the man, but then in the distance he saw three people heading toward the stables with determined steps. He stopped his horse and watched them. When they drew closer he could see they were three women and had evidently come with the same intention as himself, looking for horses. That meant they were probably trying to escape the city and were healthy.

He decided to take the chance and ask them whether they wanted to join forces with him. He cantered up, stopping about a dozen paces away, shouting out he was not infected. They did not respond, observing him suspiciously. He moved closer and could see they were in good health. He recognized a woman from the Philosophers' Colony but the other two he didn't know. He pulled away his mask, stating he was from Anthropology and was about to leave the city. What were they planning?

The philosopher replied, "My God, has it come to this? Troy is fallen and the guard is fleeing! But, yes, we too are looking for horses to escape."

"I recognize you, you're Colette."

"Yes, and you're Stavros, I remember. This is Saoirse and

Charlize."

Stavros said that as far as he could see most people in the city were dead but his information was the infection could still spread through the air. They should certainly get horses, but they should also be careful to avoid any horse that seemed sick. The women were shocked to hear animals might have this thing too. He said he was not certain and had seen no signs of sickness himself. He offered to help them if they wanted. The women agreed and together they continued to the barn. Stavros went to collect saddles while the women chose out two horses, one for Colette and the other for Saoirse, with Charlize riding behind. They saddled the animals but before mounting they held a council of war.

Colette asked, "So what plans does Anthropology have? We were thinking of searching for some uninfected colony."

"That's not an option. The Anthropology Colony is gone, infected from day two, and probably most colonies with it. This thing is everywhere."

Charlize said, "I think that too. Both Sports Monitoring and the Philosophers were fully infected. Everybody was dying."

"Charlize is right. Look, I'm heading to the canyons. The Ranch is the only safe place. Do you want to come along?"

Colette gasped, "Are you out of your mind?"

"Not at all. I have thought this thing through. No one is infected down in the canyons. I have just come from there, and I should tell you, the place was—what should I say?—under new management."

Colette still looked horrified.

The woman named Saoirse interjected, "Colette, do we really have an option? The longer we spend around the colonies the more likely we are to catch this plague. I can see Stavros' logic entirely. If the canyons are the only safe place, the canyons it really should be."

It turned out later that Saoirse was a singer at the Fairy House and had become Colette's partner. They'd been blissfully unaware of the catastrophe on their doorstep until Charlize turned up just a day ago with the horrifying news. They didn't want to believe her but, venturing out, they caught sight of the bodies. At first they were paralyzed but little by little they began to respond, seeking a way to escape. Now, at this point, Stavros' suggestion had the virtue of a radical solution in the midst of extreme crisis.

The group decided to gather as many supplies as possible and Stavros explained they would sleep at the head of the trail before descending to the badlands. The women made masks from the hems of their robes and finally they all mounted, setting off toward Avenue of the Monuments. They picked up non-perishable items from the food carts and venturing into a couple of the less-frequented temples they found a store of unused blankets to use for bedrolls. They found dead bodies spread-eagled in the entrances of many of the main buildings and at the intersections. Apart from that they met no one and it became increasingly obvious that the disease had swept with devastating speed through the whole area and probably the whole territory of Heaven. Perhaps a few colonies or individuals were spared, but it seemed plain no one at this point was willing or able to contact others or bring them together.

As they set out on their journey, Stavros recounted to them the whole series of events from the first news of Sarobindo's collapse, to the experiences at the Ranch, Pascale's execution and the night meeting with Jonas. He told the story as the women rode beside him, unable to keep it in. It was impossible not to hear in his words his own reactions to everything that had happened and the sense of a profound shift in his awareness and feeling. Everyone was deeply shocked at the story of Pascale. Charlize gave a gasping scream and Colette was stunned.

"All this in the space of a few days! Is the veneer of divinity so thin, we turn to barbarism so soon? "

They were now out on the Sacred Way, leaving behind the city and its monuments, the elegant memorials of collected human culture. Saoirse asked Stavros whether, after the things he had experienced, he still thought the Homeland of Heaven was a good idea. "I'm beginning to doubt it," he said. "Really, I don't know, perhaps some good might yet come out of it, if we can survive and learn from it all."

Colette commented sourly, "If we do not learn from the experience of divinity, what can we possibly learn from disaster?"

Stavros found out that Charlize had come to Heaven in the rendition which eventually brought with it Pascale and Palmiro. He was curious about her own reactions and asked her what she had witnessed. Charlize nodded and rubbed away her tears with her hand. She was glad to have a chance to tell her tale, to relieve the horror of events which had so completely destroyed her world. She called out her story above the tattoo of hoof-beats, bumping along behind Saoirse. She explained how she had recently begun a relationship with Dante, so she had been in residence at the Sports Monitoring Colony.

"It was only two days ago but it seems an eternity. Everyone got sick, right after the evening meal. The whole thing was terrible, all in the space of ten minutes, twenty minutes at most. Almost everyone was there, all the people who keep a track on the Sectors: Milton, Gaius, Emmanuelle, Brutus, Shimin, Amala, Kanna, and Dante, of course. They began sneezing and coughing and falling down, it was horrible, unbelievable."

"For some reason it didn't happen to me. I felt nauseous but that was all. I tried to help, but I had no idea what to do. I stayed with Dante, and the others, too. Gaius at first kept calling out this could not be an accident, someone should get hold of Anthropology, but very soon no one could talk, or do anything, because of their coughing. People began to faint and then go unconscious. One of the last things that anybody said, it was Emmanuelle. I remember because she walked up to me like she was going to hug me. She said, 'Charlize, all good things come to an end.' Then all the color went from her and she dropped like a stone. I think I was screaming, but it didn't matter because there was no one to hear me."

"I stayed for a while but it was unbearable. Eventually I went to my room, just lay on my bed. I tried to think what to do. I thought about Colette in Philosophy and decided I would go see her. In the morning I took a car, drove to the villa. I was surprised there were so few people on the road, but at the colony I understood why. The sickness was everywhere. I found the philosophers all unconscious or raving, although Lara was able to tell me where Colette was. It seemed like they were doing philosophy even as they were dying. Cyrus was muttering something, over and over."

"What was it, what was he saying?"

"He said it so often it imprinted on my mind, 'Mortals are immortals and immortals are mortals....' "

"Of course," Colette said, "His beloved Heraclitus. And the rest of the fragment is: 'The one living the other's death and dying the other's life.' "

"What does that even mean?" demanded Saoirse.

"Not sure, but it seems Cyrus finally may have understood!"

The others laughed despite themselves. They were now well along the Appian Way, not far from the turn-off across the rolling scrubland down to the canyons. They no longer felt threatened by infection and there was even perhaps the stirring of a hope they could still make a life for themselves in the aftermath of Heaven.

8. CROSSROADS

Jonas was camped under an overhang a little way along the cliff from the final turn on the trail. He had felt totally drained when Palmiro left him. He'd tethered his horse, rolled himself in his blanket and fallen asleep almost immediately. When he woke up it was getting dark. He decided it was too late for him to travel. Once again he had accepted Palmiro's suggestion for his next move, this time because he really could not think of anything else. Still he had no desire to rush ahead to find Stavros. He needed and relished this time on his own. He needed to come to terms with the contradictory emotions inside him: despair at Pascale's death and the strange, perverse hope Palmiro had awakened. He busied himself collecting a large pile of brush and branches, and started a fire. He gave his horse water and feed, took some bread and dried meat from his saddlebag and sat down beside the small blaze to eat. He was idly prodding the glowing wood when he heard the sound of horses coming directly toward him on the trail. He wondered why anyone should be going down to the canyons, especially this at this hour. It was too late for him to hide and so he simply sat there as the riders approached. They could just make out the hunched figure behind the flames and it made a striking impression, arousing ancient images of a medicine man or prophet at the roadside.

Stavros shouted out, "Who's there? Show yourself!"

Jonas stood up and faced the group of riders. They looked anxious and disoriented, like refugees from a war zone. "It's Jonas. Is that you Stavros?"

"Jonas? I can't believe it. You've been sitting here waiting for us?"

"Of course not. It's just coincidence."

It was more of a coincidence than Stavros could know, as Jonas' plan had been to go and find him and tell him about Palmiro. Faced now with the foursome of Immortals, he retreated mentally from the possibility. Palmiro was everyone's public enemy. How could he possibly expect them to embrace his story of a miraculous conversion.

"Well, we were planning on making camp ourselves then we saw your fire. Can we join you?"

"Yes. Come and sit. You can tie up the horses over there." He pointed to where his own horse was tethered, a stunted oak gripping the edge of a small patch of level ground. Stavros and the women dismounted, saddle sore and uneasy, but glad to find a camp ready-made. Jonas recognized all three of the women as they came up; he said "hello" in a featureless voice.

Colette did not wait for small talk. "Jonas, please forgive me, but I am overwhelmed at meeting you, of all people. Stavros told us everything, and I cannot express enough my condemnation of what happened. It was and is unforgivable."

Charlize joined in. "I can only imagine how you feel, Jonas..." And she trailed off.

Jonas didn't reply but nodded indifferently, "Thanks."

There was an awkward moment's silence. Stavros changed the topic to something more immediate. "If you were not waiting for us here, what exactly are you doing, Jonas? Were you waiting for someone else?"

"Oh, I guess I needed time on my own. I wasn't waiting for anyone"

His words had a hollow ring, given the fact that he was camped at a crossroads. Stavros looked hard and a memory came to him. "We never really got to the bottom of you being at the Ranch so shortly after Palmiro was there. Everything got so confused in the canyons. I really did not carry out a proper investigation. If I had questioned you more closely some of this perhaps could have been avoided. Are you sure you were never in contact with him? Did he help you to get out there?"

Jonas had not been asked this before directly and there was a clear hint in Stavros' words that if the investigation had focused on him, rather than Pascale, she might not have died. The thought had not crossed his mind and he was devastated.

"You're not saying if I had information I would have saved her life?"

"I'm saying she did not lead us to Palmiro. Perhaps, instead we should have concentrated on you."

Jonas was trembling. Saoirse said, "Are you OK? What's wrong?"

Jonas shook his head. Saoirse turned to Stavros, "Your question seems to have touched a nerve, Mr. Security!"

461

Pascale's Wager

"So, Jonas, you did have information?"

Jonas could not bear it. "I simply could not stop her. I wanted her to escape but she refused. She told me I had to escape instead. And, yes, the reason is I knew about Palmiro, I knew where he was but I protected him. I protected him for her sake and everything she meant."

"My God, Jonas, you were involved in all this, and your precious Pascale, she was too?"

Jonas looked almost frantic, faced now by a reckoning from Immortals. He was trying to make them understand.

"It's much more complicated than that, Colette. In the end no one knew what Palmiro was planning. Pascale argued against his first doomsday plot. Because of that Palmiro himself did not want it and he changed his plan. He thought only Sarobindo would die, and he told nobody what he was doing. Then, once the infection had started, it's almost as if Pascale decided to take the blame. She must have known from the philosophers' banquet how quickly things could go bad. It's almost as if she walked straight into it."

"How do you know about Palmiro and Sarobindo? You met with Palmiro?"

"Yes, I've just seen him. And he knows about Pascale."

Everyone was silent, trying to process these words, trying to imagine what they meant if they were true. The fact of Pascale's horrible death weighed heavily. What would it mean if Pascale had both tried to prevent the catastrophe and then accepted the blame for it?

Stavros, however, was still following the trail. "You were a small player in all this, Jonas. The key agent remains Palmiro and you shielded him. Will you now tell us where he is?"

The recall of Palmiro reminded Jonas of the dramatic claim he'd made, that everything had changed, and Stavros would too. He thought of how Palmiro always responded to things so positively; it helped him recover a little of his own composure. He replied, "I knew you would ask that, Stavros. Before I answer I have to ask what you yourself were planning. It seems plain you were all heading down to the Ranch as a safe place. I think that's because you have seen something of what Pascale made down there. I believe that puts you pretty directly in her debt."

"What's any of that got to do with it? You can't possibly be saying I should just ignore that Palmiro committed murder and single-handedly destroyed the Homeland of Heaven?"

"I'm suggesting that everything has changed. Nothing, whatever you do, can restore the past, and meanwhile something new may have begun. What do you want? Revenge or a future?"

Colette broke in. "It would seem a big dose of revenge has already been taken. More to the point is whether the inventor of the disease can provide an antidote, what did they use to call it, a vaccine? If he can, that would give us all a future."

"Very little chance, Colette," Jonas replied. "From what Palmiro was saying the immortality enzyme is itself the basis for how the cells are destroyed. It's reprogrammed so it becomes its own destroyer. I don't think there's a cure, unless it was an entirely different code for creating immortality."

"That lad has settled our fate. I would certainly like to have fifteen minutes one-on-one with him. But I want to say something else here. From your description, Jonas, it seems Pascale was shielding him for reasons of her own. You said she wanted to take the blame. I feel it was deeper. I remember at the banquet how she said some things about patterns and the pattern she was seeing then, that this Heaven of ours was based on a lie. In which case she must at least have believed in the possibility of another pattern. And when the deaths started happening did she see a pattern in the deaths, including the possibility of her own? Once the wheels were rolling did she just let them roll?"

"I don't follow at all. What do you mean?"

"I mean Pascale was just not a shoulder-the-blame type, you know, a martyr. She was much more than that. She was a visionary, fulfilling a vision. She was Sarobindo, but more besides. Remember her question to him at the banquet: 'What do you see when you are so near to death?' "

The others were astonished. Even for Jonas, the possibility of thinking about Pascale's death as deep purpose had not entered his thoughts. Willingness to take the blame, that was one thing, but a deeper pattern, it was simply incredible to consider. Once Colette had said it, however, he knew it fitted with all the strange things Pascale had ever said and done. At the same time, it seemed to fit the amazing things Palmiro had been saying.

For a minute there was silence. Saoirse got up and put some

463

more wood on the fire. She went over to the horses, retrieved a water canteen and passed it around. Jonas spoke. "I have to tell you, Palmiro believes something like what Colette was saying. He also seems to have gone through a change himself."

"Whatever he's gone through, he's still a murderer, and you have not told me yet where I can find him." Stavros was still on point.

"I will tell you, Stavros. In fact I'll take you to him personally. Then you'll have to exercise frontier justice. You'll have to shoot him yourself, because who's going to try him? But first I want to ask you this. Is he really a murderer? Did he really kill anyone? Or did he simply allow nature to take its course, by removing an artificial barrier? In fact didn't he allow Sarobindo to complete the journey he always was starting?"

"Ah, the question of nature and finality!" Colette put on her philosopher's hat. "A time to live and a time to die. We discussed that quite frequently in the Colony. We generally held that human beings are able to change nature if they wish, including whether to die or not. To be able to change themselves is in fact their nature!"

Saoirse pushed the issue. "So, let me see if I've got this straight: Palmiro is a murderer, but only in terms of a human redefinition of human life?"

Despite himself Stavros was drawn into argument. "That is way too abstract, Saoirse. The Heavenly Homeland was established by a historical decision of the human community. By what right did Palmiro set himself up to overturn that democratic decision?"

"It wasn't democratic for Northerners!" Charlize interrupted with surprising feeling.

Jonas was emboldened to keep going in Saoirse's direction. "Colette said Pascale was seeing some kind of different pattern, and I think Palmiro is part of that. If Pascale and he really have found a new pattern, even a new way of being human, then they're no different from the group that discovered Immortality. If the first group could say the whole picture was changed because of their discovery, then why not Pascale and Palmiro? Immortals are already a revolutionary group, so why not another revolution? And if the new nature Pascale and Palmliro discovered seems good to us, by what logic will you then condemn him?"

The sky had become dark and heavy as they were talking. Drops of rain were falling, making the fire hiss and plunging through their cotton tunics onto their skin. The sudden sensation was so fresh and invigorating it felt like the earth was introducing itself, as if for the first time. It seemed to be saying, yes, it was possible for everything to be new. They looked up and saw the clouds rolling past at hardly more than tree-top level. It began to rain harder and they all had to stoop and retreat back under the overhang to avoid the downpour.

As they huddled against the sandstone wall watching the water splash and course by their feet Colette said "Well, what do you say, Stavros? That seems a pretty reasonable wager. If we feel there really is something new and good going on, then Palmiro is in the clear! If not, he is your prisoner!"

Stavros didn't reply at first. He had his hand out, catching drops in the cup he made with his palm. Then he said, "I would be happy if Pascale's death in the Sea of Chaos had some final beauty in it."

Jonas looked across at him with a big smile. "Palmiro told me to meet him at Adorno's. I'll take you to him tomorrow."

465

9. HEAVEN'S END

Palmiro arrived at Adorno's mansion soaked through and shivering violently. He managed to stable and rub down the horse before finding his annex, strip his clothes and plunge into the shower, turning the water on hot and at full blast. On his way in he had seen no lights. The whole place seemed deserted and he had no desire to look around at night. Once he left the shower he threw himself in his bed and instantly was asleep. He slept for a long time, catching up on the rest he'd been deprived of for weeks. Basically he felt safe in this place. It was a long way from downtown and it still had the prestige of Adorno protecting it. Omar's gang would not have the nerve to come blasting in here looking for him, if in fact they were bothered to come this far at all.

The sun was shining through the slats of the blinds when he finally awoke round midday. He remembered his experience of awakening the previous day. It was still vivid in his head, in a way sealed off from everything else but also giving life and energy to everything. He got some coffee started and looked in the fridge, finding stale cake and watermelon. He brought the food to the table and began to eat and reflect for the first time about his reason for being here, at the home of his former master. He'd always known that he had to return but the amazing cascade of events had prevented him from thinking clearly about the reason. Now he endeavored to put his thoughts in order.

Adorno had called him his brother and best friend, and Palmiro wondered what that meant. He believed Adorno had known the virulence of the anti-enzyme and that he'd been set up by him, just like at every other point along the road. And yet again he questioned how much he himself had been willing to let this happen. Had he not at some level in fact agreed with his mentor? This was an especially bitter taste in his soul, that he had allowed himself to be Adorno's cats-paw, his plaything, and to a horrifying degree. He very much needed to get all of it in the open, to reject his passive relationship with Adorno and so finally free himself.

The image of the Hyperbrain came to his mind and with a dull start he remembered Adorno's plan to upload his own brain to its computers. He had been so focused on bringing down

466

Sarobindo he'd actually given very little thought to the scientist's own endgame. Now he recalled with sudden intensity the fantastic theory Adorno had proposed and the technical means he had devised to carry it through. Except it would be an experiment with only one trial and an almost certain failure, killing the test pilot and producing unverifiable results. It might already be too late to talk with him.

He got up from the table and went directly out the door into the bright sunlight. He walked along the gravel paths between the trailing bougainvillea which had been battered by the rain, their petals bruised and scattered across the ground. Circling around to the front of the building, he did not enter the east wing laboratory where he'd done his work and where he'd last seen Adorno, but walked up through the garden, turning left to the west wing and the scientist's study. He knocked briefly on the door then opened it, stepping into the room. Sitting on a chair to his left with a gun held in two hands and pointed straight at him was a woman he barely recognized.

"The gun is loaded and I will use it. Walk over here slowly and sit." She gestured with the gun to a chair in between herself and the door.

Palmiro had not been expecting this and the sudden appearance of the armed woman froze him with fear. He half put his hands in the air and stood rooted to the spot.

"I said come over here and sit."

The woman was Asian in appearance, with a smooth, limpid face, and dark, fierce eyes. He vaguely remembered that he had spoken to her at Emmanuelle's after he first arrived in Heaven. Palmiro moved unsteadily to the chair, his heart clattering and his hands still half raised.

"That's it, now sit down. I knew you'd come back eventually. All I had to do was camp out and wait. I frightened you, didn't I? Yes, you should be afraid, for I intend to kill you. But first I need some answers."

Palmiro stammered, "Why...why do you want to kill me?"

The woman laughed derisively. "Well, let me think! Let's look around this Heaven of ours! Most of the gods are dead, their bodies litter the roads, rotting before our eyes. The colonies have stopped producing food. Those of us who are left hardly know

467

how to survive, and anyway we know no decent reason to do so. And why, why has this happened? How did this happen? You tell me, sir! Only you can tell me!"

Palmiro was still floundering. He had felt safe in the mansion and all his thoughts had been about Adorno and the complicity between himself and his master. Now this person was looking for answers from him. Of course this was everyone's attitude. He had begun the infection in the Font Eterno and they had sent the agents to the canyons to arrest him. The gods had just caught up with him in a place and manner he had not expected.

"Please forgive me, I can't remember your name. Were you sent here by Anthropology?"

"My partner was from Anthropology. I found him dead on the road. This is his gun. They are probably all dead anyway. I am from Technology. Except not with your genius scientist. We look after real machines, like the rocket you hijacked to come here."

"Oh, I remember you now. You're Hona. You were there after the Initiation and then you came to see me."

"Yes I was. I couldn't believe, even back then, that you were accepted, a criminal and infiltrator! When all this happened I knew at once it had to be you. Four hundred and fifty years and everything perfect. The only new thing? A couple of kids who thought they could change the rules. It had to be you. So, tell me how did you do it? And why did you do it? If you don't talk to me, I'll shoot you here and now and be done with it."

"My laboratory is across the garden. I will show you if you want. In there I developed an organic process that destroys the immortality enzyme, but I didn't think it would be infectious."

"You didn't think it would be infectious? What are you, a liar? Or stupid? Anything that disturbs the function of that enzyme could cause all sorts of unintended consequences, including mutations. You didn't think about that?"

Almost for the first time in his life Palmiro felt actually stupid. He did not know what training Hona had received but what she just stated seemed like plain common sense. He felt forced to offer a lame defense.

"I was working under Adorno. He approved my research, and its results."

"In which case he was part of the conspiracy too. I never

468

ruled it out as you were his student. That's why I came to his study. I was sure either you or him would eventually show up. If I'd found him, I would have questioned him, too. But now, tell me, exactly how did you introduce the organism?"

Palmiro was obliged to rehearse the drama at the Font Eterno, all the steps in the introduction of the anti-enzyme into Sarobindo's body and its catastrophic consequences.

"Adorno, he knew this, what you were going to do?"

"He did not know it in detail, but he obviously knew the organism would prove infectious. So the details of where I would introduce it did not matter, the outcome would be the same."

"But you say you did not think it would be infectious, so are you claiming your teacher misled you?"

Here was the point at which he himself was stuck in his own conscience. Should he admit he had tacitly accepted all along Adorno's intentions and had simply not admitted them to himself? Or was this taking on too much blame?

"I'm not sure, Hona. Like you say, I'm either a liar or stupid. I can't make up my mind which."

"Well that's refreshing to hear. Maybe you will have learned humility before I shoot you. But first you will clarify things. Tell me why you did it and then say why Adorno did it."

Palmiro said, "Hona, I want to answer your questions, I do. But I can't if you've got that thing pointed at my chest. I hardly know the answers. Being threatened doesn't help."

Hona's dark eyes burned, but after a pause she relented, lowering the gun onto a table and pointing it away from him, while still keeping it in her hand. "OK, if it helps you be truthful. But don't think I am going soft on you. I still intend to kill you. My partner died because of what you did. You have destroyed the fabric of Heaven and its technology is useless. You deserve to die."

"But not before I tell my story, right?"

"Right. So tell it!"

Palmiro tried to be brief yet faithful to all the reasons he'd had to develop the anti-enzyme. He told of his quest for truth in the Northern Homeland and how after he'd arrived in Heaven he'd felt its enormous injustice. When Adorno had chosen him as his student, it was a dream come true. But then Pascale had been

469

arrested and Adorno began to direct his studies into the area of biology and his own famous discovery. By half-hints he'd indicated that it was the necessary pathway to getting Pascale released. He'd also introduced him to his own secret project and involved him in it. He had shown him something called the Hyperbrain and said it would bring a better immortality. This had flipped his research into finding a way to turn off the immortality enzyme, which is what eventually happened. At a certain point he had no longer been able to distinguish clearly between himself and his master's efforts. He had become a second Adorno, achieving something as great as his master, and perhaps even greater. He did it for all these reasons, all together, and he could not isolate one element from another, or after another.

Hona, despite herself, was caught up in the story. Her hand relaxed on the gun and left it there on the table.

"So what is this secret project? Show it me, it has got to be something dramatic."

"You are right, it is dramatic, but before I show you I have to tell you something dramatic of my own. Without it my story is not complete and you still will not understand."

"I'm all ears. Tell me!"

"I'm not sure how much you have heard, but Pascale was killed by a mob. She was thrown into the Particle Accelerator at the Font Eterno."

"Yes, I did hear that. I thought it unfair she should be killed and you survive!"

"I felt like that, too. At one point after she was captured I thought I should take my own life. Then something happened. Yesterday morning Pascale came to me. I saw her."

"What do you mean, you saw her?"

"I don't know how else to say it. It happened before I knew she was dead, but I was in the canyons and she was a prisoner, so obviously there was no way she could have gotten there."

"You were dreaming. Hallucinating!"

"Yes, I thought that, but it was so real, and it left me with a feeling I'd never known before. Everything was new, and I was in love, with her, and with everything else, too. Afterward, when I found out she had been killed, it still didn't change. It was like she really wasn't dead."

"That makes no sense at all. Are you saying she was thrown in the Particle Accelerator and then somehow she came out to the canyons and presented herself to you? She was reduced to electrons but then she wasn't dead?

"I know it sounds ridiculous and I don't really expect you to believe me, but yes, that's about it. That was my experience. Because of that, everything that happened before cannot be the same. Because of Pascale, everything has shifted. I allowed myself to be controlled by Adorno, I did, but that would not happen now. I am a different person. You might shoot me, but you would be shooting a different person from the one you hate."

Hona's hand went back to the gun, almost absent-mindedly. She picked it up. "You said you would show me Adorno's secret project. Shall we?" She got up from her chair but with the gun held down at her side.

Palmiro stood up too. He asked, "Have you looked around? Do you know anything of the laboratories?" And he gestured over his shoulder.

"I was back there a long time ago when Shuttle Maintenance needed some special work."

"There are a couple of big rooms which house the project. They have biometric locks. We might need your gun to blast a way in."

He led her through the corner door along the paneled corridor to the boot room. Opening the connecting door he took her along the white passageway with its storerooms and labs, continuing past them to the curve and the remaining distance to the observatory and its security entrance. As he walked in front of Hona he felt his heart beginning to race wildly, but this time for a different reason from the threat of being killed. How was it going to be with Adorno? How would he feel? Could he, in fact, make a clean break from him? Would the genius scientist even be here? Or was the irrevocable step already taken?

The questions ran through his head and he couldn't be sure which one was disturbing him the most. They got to the observatory control room and could hear its low incessant hum. Palmiro placed his hand on the door; it yielded to his touch and somehow he was not surprised. They stepped inside and the hangar-like space with its monitors, cables, computers and huge

471

central holograph screen spread out before them.

"What in hell is this?" Hona cried.

Palmiro told her about Adorno's four-hundred-year quest to map the stars of the universe and their patterns of radio frequency.

"He was gathering a kind of symphony of the universe. He narrowed it down to just one galaxy, because he also had another, more specific purpose in mind."

"I'm sure you're going to tell me what that is."

"Yes. The information in this room has been relayed to computers in the next room, and I will take you to it. In there is a device which Adorno believes is able to download very large amounts of radio data to the human brain and then upload it back to the computers with the signature activity of the brain added."

He described the construction of the Hyperbrain and Adorno's intention to make himself its first test-pilot, with the goal of his personal frequency broadcast to harmonize forever with the stars.

"Adorno is not happy with immortality? He wants a life among the stars?"

"That's one way of saying it. But he also wants other Immortals to follow his lead."

"Ahh! So he sets you off to produce an infection to destroy the old kind of immortality, so those of us who are left will be convinced to use the new kind?"

Palmiro could only nod in hapless agreement, "Yes, that was it. It's possible he's already experienced the new kind for himself."

He returned to the corridor with Hona following. The passage descended slightly as they continued to the next security door with its triple locking device. Once again it was open, giving to the pressure of Palmiro's hand. It was obvious Adorno now wanted his secret research facility available to the public.

As the door swung wide a wash of heat and a powerful electrical hum came up the stairs to meet them. Palmiro was reminded of the compressor halls of the Ice Camp and their constant blast of heated air, but here there was something else. There was the smell of hot electrical components and then another faintly sweet and sickly mixed in with it. They descended cautiously, taking the right-angled turn and continuing a dozen more steps until they stood on the floor of the underground room.

The heat was oppressive and there was a dull quality to the air, a filmy miasma that at first made it hard to see precisely. Amid the general fug their peripheral attention was caught by the glimmering and flickering of hundreds of lights on the computers stacked along the walls, together with several screens showing green oscillations continuously bunching and stretching like centipedes. At the same moment their eyes were drawn relentlessly to the huge structure facing them from the middle of the room, the throne of an Aztec god with its glittering carapace above it. Palmiro's focus went directly to the chair and he recoiled immediately.

His Heavenly mentor was fixed on the seat by straps, contorted and discolored like the victim of an execution. He would hardly have been recognized except the cadaverous frame and gaunt head could only belong to one man. Now under the white chiton the skin was purple and black and the limbs looked as if they been pulled into spasm and been unable to release. The head was pushed up under the helmet all the way to the bridge of the nose, hiding the hooded eyes. Threads of dried blood could be seen running down on the cheeks and also on the side of the neck from the ears. The lantern jaw was thrust out in rictus and the lips splayed back from the teeth, making his deformed appearance more hideous than ever. Above the face, in the dense spray of optic tubes shooting from the helmet, occasional lights and flashes were still occurring. The overall effect of the body, the helmet, the illuminated headdress and its monstrous crown of baffles was grotesque and terrifying beyond words. Palmiro gasped in fright as Hona let out an uncontrollable scream.

"That, that...what is that?"

Palmiro could hardly speak. What he was seeing did not look like the transport of a mind to the stars, rather an experience of extreme torture and cruelty. Now there would never be the chance to talk, only this ghastly image of death before his eyes. He felt an angry revulsion. Who was this wreck of a man with his pitiful body reduced now to an even more terrible parody? How had he so totally fascinated and dominated him, leading him down the road to become an agent of catastrophe? Yet, at exactly the same time, he felt a peculiar upwelling of compassion.

Adorno had gambled everything for his vision, but his

brilliance of mind had fooled him and brought him to a shocking and shameful end. And still, in the next instant, the other, obvious possibility struck him: perhaps this was not the end, perhaps what he was seeing was simply something that had happened to Adorno's body, something he had anticipated and risked for the greater victory. Perhaps, indeed, the gamble had paid off and Adorno's brain was even now uploaded to the computers and being broadcast to the stars!

"That is...that is the Hyperbrain, and Adorno has put himself under it. He has done the Andromeda upload. Perhaps it worked. Perhaps those computers there are his new self and the information is right now being transmitted to the heavens..."

"You mean you think all those flickering lights and screens, they're Adorno, and that body there, it's just dead meat?"

"I don't know, Hona, I don't know. There's no way of telling."

"Well, I do know, and I can tell for certain. It's horrible, disgusting and wrong." She was extremely agitated. She kept turning her back to the chair, not wanting to look at it, then looking at the computers around the room, gesturing at them.

"What was this man doing, what was he thinking? I find you personally stupid and blameworthy, Palmiro. You were a willing dupe. But this, this here, this is evil. My life once was immortal, I was a goddess. I never thought I was greater than the space I occupied. I loved my partners, and I enjoyed the Doblepobles. But I was always happy to feel there was something bigger than me. I was happy I was part of it, and I never needed Sarobindo to show me. I always knew the stars above never belonged to us and never will. This man led you on and destroyed Heaven for the sake of a selfish, swollen dream. He has turned it all to hell because he wanted to be lord of the universe!"

Palmiro was stung into defending himself. "Hona, I agree with you one hundred percent but you have to understand Adorno was a scientist and had already been responsible for the discovery of immortality. This, for him, was the next big step."

His defense only infuriated Hona. "In Heaven we'd done away with science. That was the whole point. We'd achieved Heaven, you understand, Heaven! All the science was in the past and it was Heaven from here on! He and you changed all that, giving us genocide instead, and for what? For this?"

She pointed with repugnance at the chair with its twisted cadaver, then adding, "And this?" as she gestured with her gun hand at the computers. "Are we supposed to bow down in front of these computers from now on?" She cocked the gun and aimed it at one of the wall stacks.

"Hona, stop! What are you doing?"

"I came here to shoot you, but this is better. This is the true source of our suffering." Immediately she began to fire into the computers and their screens, aiming at the ones with the most flickering lights and working her way round the room until the magazine was empty. The noise of the gun was deafening in the confined space and the bullets smashed into the computer stacks causing sparks to fly, knocking out display lights and starting small fires. Palmiro could do nothing but cower from the sparks and the two or three ricochets which whined around the room.

The effect on the fiber optic headdress was terrifying, making brilliant blue, pink and red flashes shoot through most of them, like the physical display of a huge, angry demon. Adorno's body, apparently so dead, suddenly twitched in several of its limbs, making it change position in the chair. Palmiro cried out in terror but Hona was too enraged to be moved. The already heavy air of the bunker was now thick with the acrid smoke from the gun and the fires, a couple of which were gaining strength.

Hona shouted at Palmiro, "I've done what I came to do. Time to leave. You can stay if you wish."

She headed back up the steps leaving Palmiro to gaze at the tormented body of his master slowly wreathed in coils of smoke. There was nothing he could do. There were no sprinklers, he could see no fire-extinguishers, and anyway it did not matter. Adorno was dead and if the computers linked to the radio had time to transmit his personal star symphony, then Adorno had part of what he wanted, at least. If not, Palmiro had no wish to restore the experiment. He was no longer Adorno's disciple. Something else had come to shape his life, something much more vital to him than the scientist's far-fetched enterprise. For Hona he was a stupid man, and it was true, that was what he had been. But that was in the past, and now he needed Hona's help. He said a mental goodbye to his one-time master, and turned and ran up the stairs. Before he exited the door he found the control panel for the security locks and switched them all back to active. He pulled it tight shut and heard the bolts clunk into place. Then he raced up the corridor after the vengeful goddess.

10. FIRE IN THE HOLE

Palmiro caught up with Hona as she entered the boot room. He had to walk quickly to match her stride. "I guess you used all the bullets back there, so there can't be one left for me!"

She was still carrying the gun, but at the mention of it she threw it away from her.

"Thank you for that, Hona. You're right, and you and all the others were right to condemn me, but I've got some others things to do and I need to be alive to do them!"

They were entering Adorno's study and she stopped abruptly to face him. "OK, so now you're really pushing it. Haven't you done enough damage? Shouldn't you just go crawl into a hole somewhere?"

As Adorno's mad experiment erupted in fire and all the high science of Heaven was shattered to pieces Palmiro had understood with lucid clarity what he should do. Pascale had told him to go and rescue Finn, and he felt from the depths of his soul this would be his redemption. It would be his life, to bring love in place of all the havoc he had created. Hona's work had been with the shuttles that connected the two Homelands. She was the one who could and should help him return to the world of the TEPs.

"Please, just listen a moment, Hona. What about the solar panels out there on the hills, the rocket shuttles, the power stations in the north? Do you care about them?"

"Of course I do. Everything was working just fine before you came along, and I enjoyed keeping it that way."

"Hona. I'm guessing you're a fairly recent recruit to Heaven and that explains why you're healthy. The anti-enzyme doesn't affect people who are chronologically young."

"You're saying I can't get your killer virus because I'm young?"

"That's correct, and in that case you're going to be very important round here. You'll be one of the few with any expertise, and the rest of us are going to need you a lot."

She glared suspiciously. "So now you're suddenly become our leader, guiding us all to a brave new world?"

"No, no, Hona, it's not like that. How many times do I have to say it, things have changed with me! You might think I'm starting another ego trip but I really want a completely different life. Far from leading the people here, I want to go back to the North, to the people of the TEPs."

This time Hona truly was surprised. The life of the Northern Homeland was canceled from the thoughts of Immortals. It was practically another planet and even now, after Heaven had collapsed on every side, it was still a million miles away. To want to go back there for the sake of its people suggested Palmiro actually was different.

"You're kidding me, aren't you?"

"I'm perfectly serious. Everything started there for me, all my questions, and I feel a responsibility. What's more I think they're in some kind of trouble. It's possible some of the power stations or turbines are offline and that explains the rainstorms here."

"Yes, that's possible, even probable. Did you have something to do with that too?"

"No, no, but there was this guy in the Ice Camp, Guest, the chief guard...it's a long story."

"Oh brother, I really was just joking! So you've got another criminal psychopath involving you in his plans?"

"Something like that: I was his prisoner. But look, the Northern Power Stations were always monitored from here, right? In the normal course of events someone from here would have to go and take a look, wouldn't they?"

"What's normal anymore? But, yes, that's the case."

"Well, I want to be that person. I need you to give me as much information as you can on the power stations and turbines, and also on the shuttles. Then I need you to let me take a shuttle back north."

Hona had no clear idea of what Palmiro intended. She found it extremely hard to forgive or trust him. In the circumstances what he was proposing sounded like some sort of plan and better than nothing. Yet still she was not convinced. "Give me one good reason why I should help you."

"Because the business of your colony was to keep things working, wasn't it? And that's why you were angry enough to kill me, because the whole of Heaven stopped working. All I'm asking is to allow me to get some things working again, so I can make it up to you in some way and we can all have a future?"

As they talked they were standing next to one of the tall manor-house windows looking out onto the garden. Palmiro saw the movement first and Hona followed his distracted glance: a troop of horses and riders were trotting in from the drive, turning onto the central track between the flower beds and coming up toward the pillared entrance.

Hona said, "What now? Some more people looking to kill you?"

At first Palmiro had thought the same thing and he was about to make a run for it. Then he saw Jonas at the head of the riders.

"No, I don't think so. The one at the front, it's Jonas. He's no vigilante. He was Pascale's lover and knows the whole story."

Palmiro and Hona moved together out the door, into the afternoon sun. They waved at the riders who turned and picked their way across the garden toward them. Jonas led the way and dismounted when he got up close. "Good to see you, Palmiro. I've brought some friends to meet you."

"I'm glad. I was scared you were all here to lynch me!"

There was a nervous laugh and Palmiro recognized Charlize. "Oh hi, Charlize. Good that you're here. Seems things are always pretty dramatic when we meet!"

Charlize gave a non-committal shrug and Jonas said, "Let me introduce the others."

Palmiro nodded to each of them with his usual direct glance, but without hostility; then he introduced Hona. "She came here to question me and I'm pretty sure you have questions too. I suggest we all have dinner together and we can talk properly. You can stay here, there are plenty of guest rooms."

"That sounds a very welcome proposition after days on the trail. It's also a first for me, to be a guest at Adorno's mansion!"

It was Colette speaking and she was already dismounting, but Stavros was looking upward, over the west wing. "Is that smoke up there?"

Palmiro glanced backward awkwardly. "Probably. We just had a fire in the laboratories."

"Well, it's not out. It could burn this whole place down!"

"Uh... it's at the end of a passageway and I didn't think it could spread this far."

"It looks like it's generating a lot of heat. You need to check

479

it."

Saiorse agreed and asked where the stables were. She said she'd stable the horses with Colette's help, while the rest looked to the fire. In a moment Palmiro was showing Stavros and the others back through the study along to the boot room and the door connecting with the walkway. Starvros pulled it open and directly they felt the wave of heat and saw a thickening pall of smoke clinging along the roof of the passageway, almost all the way up from the turn.

Stavros asked, "How far from the end is the fire?"

Palmiro told him and Stavros said they needed sledgehammers, axes, that kind of thing. Palmiro recalled the warehouse down the corridor on the left and Stavros set off at once. Amid the toolboxes and piles of electrical hardware they turned up a sledgehammer, an electrically operated chain-saw, and a crowbar.

"We have to smash the corridor open to stop the heat and fire reaching the house. We'll start as far down to the turn as we can, to save the workshops."

Palmiro, Hona, Jonas and Charlize all fell in easily with Stavros' urgent directions. It seemed natural to follow his lead, saving the fabric of the Heavenly Homeland, despite—or even because of—the total disaster that had been wreaked on the life of Immortals. Neither did Palmiro's joining in seem out of place. Within minutes Stavros was smashing a hole in the laminated facing on either side. Palmiro and Jonas began levering and twisting the aluminum studs, forcing the gaps wider, while Hona and Charlize used the saw to slice open the boarding of ply.

It did not take them long to get to the roof, standing on stepladders from the warehouse and breaking through the board at the top. The smoke and heat drifted into the sky, but they could also feel and see the flames reaching the mid-section of the covered way as the fire pulled in oxygen. Stavros yelled out they should douse their side of the broken passage with water. Filled with the energy of their battle they dashed back together to the boot-room and located the kitchen. They quickly gathered pots and buckets, running the faucets to fill them and establishing a chain back out to the corridor.

By now Colette and Saoirse had rejoined them and within

half an hour they had fully soaked the smashed portion of the passage. The flames continued to lick around the broken section on the far side and it was clear that the laboratories at the end were now swallowed by the fire. They kept up the supply of water, dousing the other side of the break. After a while they saw the flames along the walkway falter and lose intensity. They continued to keep watch until they were certain the last flames had died and they had beaten the fire. They were soaked, grimy, and tired, but they joked and laughed with each other as they walked back to the house.

11. MASTERPIECE

Later that evening they gathered in the magnificent formal dining room of Adorno's mansion. They seated themselves around a long, glowing walnut table, while on the paneled walls to the sides were enormous portraits of royal families, kings and potentates. Directly facing at one end was a famous fresco of a supper table with all the diners side-by-side in a row, the original surface set entire in the wall. At the opposite end there was a carefully lit, half-length portrait of a woman with a subtle, faintly mocking smile. The meal consisted of grilled fish they had netted from a kitchen pond behind the east wing, together with some vegetables from the kitchen garden and savory biscuits from a tin. They had also investigated the wine cellar and brought up an amazing original Chateau Lafitte. Meanwhile Palmiro's explorations established that the house had not been spared the plague. He went searching for Max in his apartment at the far end of the west wing and discovered his almost unrecognizable body in his sitting room. Colette and Saorsie reported seeing another corpse out by the stables and on checking Palmiro confirmed it was Phillipa's.

The visitors had sought out the guest rooms on the second floor, showered, found fresh tunics, then returned to the kitchen to help prepare the meal. While they were cleaning and cutting the vegetables Hona started to explain the background to the fire. By the time they sat down to eat people had a fairly good idea of the confrontation between herself and Palmiro, including the revelation of Adorno's Hyperbrain and the gruesome discovery of his body. Hona presented Palmiro as naive and used by Adorno, but when asked why Adorno had revealed his project to Palmiro, the explanation still made it sound like a conspiracy. The infection was crucial to Adorno's plan to introduce the Hyperbrain, and Palmiro had fulfilled the plan to the letter. The thought was no longer of Palmiro as the single agent of catastrophe, but definitely a key member of the plot.

When they took their seats Stavros did not wait but at once set out the charges. "You and Adorno cooked this whole infection up to force Immortals into a new way of thinking. You decided to kill just about everyone to make the rest of us prefer being part of the stars."

"Yes, but I never intended to kill everyone, just Sarobindo, and because he himself was always anticipating death..."

The group dove hungrily into the food and when the wine was poured they took time to savor it, relishing its splendid body and bouquet. After a moment Colette gave a sigh of satisfaction, then she spoke bluntly. "So, yes, you are a self-confessed killer. On what grounds would you expect mercy from this court? "

Palmiro put his own glass back on the table. He felt all the portraits of the powerful and mighty looking down on him, asking the same loaded question and not expecting there to be mercy. "I accept my responsibility for Sarobindo, and for all the deaths, although I did not will the others consciously. My hope for mercy, therefore, is not from the facts, it must always be from the future. I believe something different and wonderful is now possible, arising from what happened."

Stavros almost spat out his wine. "Ha! The end justifies the means, exactly what Adorno believed. How are you any different?"

"I did not say what happened was a means to an end. I said something arose from it, even if I'm to blame for what happened. It came by itself, out of the disaster, and changed the meaning of everything."

"But are you sorry for everything?" Saoirse interjected. "Would you undo it if you could?"

Palmiro was stuck here. He was forced to play his last, best card. "I can only answer by telling you about Pascale. I do not know how to explain it but I saw her, the morning after she was killed. I did not expect it, but it was wonderful. She was right there, alive and beautiful. She filled me with a completely different feeling. I know people will say 'hallucination,' that kind of thing. But I think you'd agree I'm not the hallucinating kind of guy. And the way it made me feel did not go away: it wasn't a freak mental event. It's still with me. I cannot be sorry for that."

There was a long silence. The smile on the woman in the portrait at the end of the room twinkled ironically.

Saoirse spoke first. "I don't think anybody quite knows what to say about your experience. But if, as you say, it gave you a different feeling, I can ask my question again. Are you sorry for what you did? Would you undo it?"

483

Again Palmiro paused. He was pushed to the sticking point. "I am sorry for causing the deaths, but not that they happened. I am not sorry about the end of immortality. I am sorry for the killing of Sarobindo and for my part in the infection, but I cannot will to undo it. I am very happy that, from it all, Pascale found another way. I am caught between the two things and I have no other answer."

Colette spoke carefully, "You are suggesting Pascale found another kind of immortality? And that must change everything, including your guilt."

"Yes, that's exactly what I'm saying."

Colette continued to speak quite deliberately, in a way that sounded unusual for her. "I think we need to think hard here. Palmiro is claiming the issue is not what he did, but what has become possible. For some philosophers what is possible overrules what is necessary. We cannot ignore that Heaven was born out of violence and death that were considered necessary. First the storms we ourselves caused, and then the Northern Homeland. The frozen north was the dumping ground for all the bad weather and misery needed to make Heaven perfect. We never gave it another thought because we believed there was no human alternative. But now something different and new seems to have happened, at least to this man, and perhaps even to Pascale. So maybe we should allow the possibility of a new way, and a more decent one at that."

Saiorse prompted, "We should forgive the past for the sake of a different possible future?"

"I believe so."

"I happen to agree!" Saiorse suddenly gave her vote. "I've been thinking about this place, this mansion. Can't you just see Adorno here, in this villa, with all its noble art, and his arrogant experiments just a score of paces away! Can't you feel him? Heaven was never enough for him, right from the beginning. He brought Heaven into being and he brought it to an end. We were always at his mercy. So how can we blame Palmiro when Adorno was the spiritual architect of it all, and the rest of us, we just followed him along?"

Suddenly Charlize got to her feet. She was a little flushed and nervous, as if she was taking a difficult step. "I, I want to say something..."

All eyes turned toward her. "I knew Pascale back in the North and I liked her. I knew you, Palmiro, and I have to say I never liked you. I considered you a trouble-maker, and really that is what you proved to be. I should feel angry with you for what you did, and I do. I was going to live and have fun forever! But I can also see you have changed, and in a good way, so whatever it is that's happened to you, I'm in the best position to see it. Because you say it comes from Pascale I feel I want to hold on to it. And I want to know more about it. So, I agree with Colette and Saoirse, we have to forget the past, and look to the future."

She sat back down and Colette and Saoirse both gave her warm smiles. Jonas looked at them, then he sprang to his feet holding a glass of wine. "A toast," he cried. "A toast! To the future which Pascale showed Palmiro and Palmiro has brought to us!" He focused directly on Stavros. "Stavros, what do you say? Can you agree?"

The women, including Hona, responded, raising their glasses. Stavros was staring moodily at the paintings on the wall. After a moment he pulled his gaze away, back to the company. He nodded slowly, not looking especially at anyone.

"You all have me disarmed. I, too, was captivated by Pascale. If honoring her memory requires forgiving the past and hoping for the future, then I am bound to do it. Anyway, I don't have the heart for any more killing."

They could not help themselves. Everybody let out a cheer, as if for the first time since all the terrible events had begun they'd heard some genuinely good news. Jonas who was sat next to Palmiro leaned over and hugged him. Palmiro put his elbows on the table and his head in his hands and began to weep, at first trying to suppress the sobs, and then more and more uncontrollably. His shoulders shook and his sobs became harsher, rising up from some hard hidden place. It actually hurt him physically, but much more emotionally as he came to terms with his whole life. So many things had happened, and he had done so much without ever stopping to think what he was doing.

He'd been brilliant at finding the way everything worked, but he'd never thought seriously about himself, the way he worked. It was intensely painful now, suddenly, to enter that place, to consider himself at this other level where he could see the pettiness and spite behind so much of the glory. How stupid and arrogant he'd always been! How predictable and mean and pathetic! Yet, at the same time, the feeling of finally being accepted by the people around him had brought him to this place. He knew and felt everything really had been forgiven and it was this that forced him so abruptly to come face-to-face with his true self. He continued sobbing while Jonah kept his hand on his shoulder. The others could not help but be moved by his reaction and instinctively waited.

Finally his sobs subsided and, embarrassed, he raised his head, displaying a stained face and reddened eyes. Jonas, who was wearing a toga from his room, offered him a corner to wipe his tears. He said, "I knew one day I'd discover the purpose of this useless bit of drapery!"

People laughed gratefully and the mood lightened. Palmiro wiped his face on Jonas' sleeve and there was more laughter. He cleared his throat and said "I also want to offer a toast. I want to toast you all, for what you just did for me." And he raised his glass, "To you, the future of the Homelands!"

Everyone echoed "The future of the Homelands," and once more they tasted the exquisite wine. The mood now was euphoric. The catastrophic circumstance of the infection had destroyed the world for this remnant of Immortals, but the empty space it made had let something new enter, a complete surprise. They were bathed in the experience of forgiveness. Palmiro, the great destroyer, had been forgiven, and in same moment they experienced their own forgiveness, from the age-long cruelty and selfishness of Heaven, from their inhuman way of being human. On one side of the table Colette hugged Saiorse and then she hugged Charlize. Saiorse went round the table and hugged Jonas and then Stavros and Hona. Charlize followed her round and touched Palmiro on the shoulder. "I never thought I'd say anything like this, but you've changed me, Palmiro. Right now, I feel it, I feel different and without you it wouldn't have happened."

Palmiro stood up awkwardly and she hugged him. All at once he was back in the Homeland, in the Training Center, the dining hall, with Danny and his gang, and once more his whole journey from the narrow world of the TEPs to the apocalypse of Heaven sped before his eyes. He already knew he had to return to the North but the drama of his personal story and its destiny had not hit him before like this. He remembered his mother, and, before that, his father. He remembered the men of the camps. He remembered Finn, and once again he remembered Pascale's words to him. He pulled back from Charlize, looked at her and kissed her softly on the cheek. Then he turned and said, "I have something important to say to everyone. If you would, please, can you sit down?"

The others found their seats again and he began to explain what he thought was the background to the recent bad weather Heaven was experiencing. Something had gone wrong with the Weather Shield and he had a good idea of what had happened. He told the story of Guest and his intense desire to find the switches to the refrigeration system. It was essential now to return to the Northern Homeland to try and stabilize things. The Heavenly Homeland would probably survive in the interim, but if the situation in the north continued to run out of control, a second catastrophe would take place, this time overwhelming the other known community of humans on earth. They had already suffered so much, and continuing chaos in their Homeland would inevitably spill over here into Heaven. He turned to Hona who had been a silent observer during the whole meal. He recalled that because of the arrival of Jonas and the others, she had not had a chance to reply to the final question he had asked her, about preparing a shuttle to return to the North. He needed to know, would she be willing to do that? If so, he would be able to present his vision fully to the others.

Hona had not intervened in the argument, letting Palmiro's confrontation with the Immortals take its own course. But she too had been impressed by the feeling of forgiveness and the decision of the group to seek a future. The mood of hope made it impossible to stand in the way. "Yes, you are right, something must be done. If we are the only ones who are left to do it, then it must be we who do it."

"Thank you so much, Hona. I appreciate your help. In that case, here's the plan. I need at least one other person to come north with me, to vouch for what I say. Best of all it would be someone who was an Immortal from the beginning, who could describe everything first hand. We could bring a supply of the immortality enzyme and that way there'd be no risk to that individual's survival."

Suddenly again there was silence around the table, so deep each one could hear the other's breathing. The thought of a return to the North had been, up to this point, literally unthinkable. Now it burst like a bomb into the range of possibility. Forgiving the past had been liberating, joyful, but this was fierce and real and beyond anything they had foreseen. They imagined the bitter cold and the hardship and their spirits buckled before the thought.

Again the portrait at the end of the room smirked knowingly.

At last it was Colette who answered, and in an entirely unexpected way. "You ask the impossible, Palmiro, but, you know what? It's perhaps time for that. I've got a sneaking feeling even the possible is no longer enough. How long before this disease catches up with all us oldies anyway? At some point it could get into the water, and what will that do, eh, Mr. Adorno's Apprentice?"

Palmiro nodded with a rueful expression. "You could be right, Colette. It's possible the organism would survive if it gets into the water supply. Younger people, like me, or Charlize, or Hona, don't have anything to worry about, but..." and he trailed off.

Colette nodded, grimly mirroring Palmiro. "So, yes, there it is. Unless we are chronologically young, our days are numbered anyway. So here's what I'm thinking. I and all the philosophers, we flirted with freedom for hundreds of years, but always up in our heads. We used to talk about the timelessness of our existence allowing us an infinity of choice. Yet there was really never anything to choose, just more of the same. That is why we idolized Sarobindo because he gave us the semblance of true choice. Now the choice you set me is real. I have to choose, and everything has become possible because of that, even the impossible. Palmiro, you have given me the greatest gift, one I do not want to lose. If I decide to stay here then I must continue in a life that provides everything and promises nothing, or more likely I will die like Zeno blathering clichés. If I choose to come with you then everything is...real again. And so I do chose. I will be your witness, Palmiro."

Everyone was dumbstruck, but Jonas especially. He had

some idea of what she was saying and it amounted to a philosophical rejection of Heaven. Instead she was opting for the Northern Homeland as the place of meaning. He gazed around at the paintings on the walls, locked in Adorno's dead world and even they seemed to receive a shock of life from Colette's decision. The fresco at the end particularly seemed to glow, its image of a shared meal almost leaning out and joining the company at the table below.

Saiorse leaned over and took Colette's hand. "After a speech like that how could anyone not love you madly? I for one couldn't! And I could not bear to be separated from you for one instant. I want to come too, Palmiro."

Charlize blinked incredulously. People were lining up to go to the most wretched place on earth. But she also understood why. Everything had changed. And the truth was she had too. She hardly believed her own voice as she spoke, "I can't believe I'm saying this but I don't think I can be left out. They'll be just as surprised to see me as you guys. I am a key witness in the chain because I left the TEPs just before Palmiro and they all know me."

Jonas cried in amazement. "Looks like you've got your ship's complement, Palmiro. I'm afraid I'm going to have to resist the urge to join you all. I've realized I have some real history to write for a change and I need to put pen to paper. Also I need to keep Danny and Eboni up to date on what's happened."

Stavros concurred, a little sheepishly. "Yes, I think I should go check on them, too. I don't think the North is for me, I can do much more good here. Anyway, there's no more room in the shuttle!"

Palmiro looked over at Hona. "How long to get the rocket prepared?"

"Oh, I don't know. A few days. It's been some time since I went to the port and the hangers. I'll start tomorrow and you should come with me. We'll have to load the fuel pods, and boot up the link to the landing station at the other end, and check the computer guidance."

"For sure. Sounds like fun! Meanwhile everyone can live here at the mansion until we're ready. Jonas, I look forward to your book, but I have no idea how you'll publish it!"

They all laughed and looked around at each other as they did.

Colette said, "I want to remember this, this very moment. It will never happen again, just like this. I want it to stay with us always. She raised her glass but there was nothing in it. Stavros grasped the one bottle left and emptied the last of the wine in splashes to everyone's cup. "To now and the future!" he offered.

For the last time they echoed, "To now and the future!"

12. END OF TIME

Four days later the shuttle's incandescent flare streaked north-eastward over the Homeland of Heaven, carrying Colette, Saiorse, Charlize and Palmiro to an unknown future. Together with Hona, the group of witnesses had spent the time getting the craft and themselves ready for the journey. They had to find therm-suits to fit them, along with thermal underwear, boots and gloves. They were told to select the few personal items it would be possible to carry in the shuttle, mementos, books, cosmetics, a bottle of wine. The Shuttle Port was a vast rambling facility just to the north and west of the Baths and Agora. As well as command and control centers, with satellite links and computer monitoring, there were miles of equipment sheds, electrical and engineering installations, and sophisticated assembly and machine shops. Towering over everything were several hangers containing at least a dozen shuttles or rocket vehicles. Close by were giant tractors to transport them to launch aprons or onto an enormous take-off ramp lunging at a vertiginous angle into the sky. It was from this ramp that their shuttle would depart. Under Hona's direction they moved the craft slowly into place at its base. Once they had it raised in position they began the fueling. The process required filling the required number of fuel pods and inserting them carefully in the shuttle while keeping them cooled with refrigeration lines.

The fuel was produced as needed from an array of storage tanks and mixers, then condensed and pumped at high pressure into the pods. While they were filling and loading the pods, Hona booted up the satellite link to the Northern Shuttle Port. She tested its remote guidance, reviewed it visually on the monitors, and ran through a virtual re-entry and landing. She did the checks on the shuttle they would use, carefully testing all the systems that Pascale and Palmiro had breezed through simply by clicking "O.K." This time everything was done with scientific precision.

Palmiro found a couple of old laptop computers with images of Heaven in its heyday. He felt they would be important as added evidence and managed to find space for them on board. As the take-off drew closer the memory of the Northern Homeland forcibly returned to him and also to Charlize. Images of the

Training Centers, Worship Centers, TEPs and Bubbles came flooding back and the claustrophobic feeling of their little existence pressed in on them. They had to remind themselves continually of the dramatic new horizon they would bring with them, and only then were they able to renew their sense of purpose and commitment. For Charlize it was the thought of seeing Esh again which especially consoled her.

Colette was also experiencing an attack of second thoughts. Was she out of her mind? How could she possibly survive the conditions of the North for which she had zero preparation? Still, she could not let them get the better of her: she had spent hundreds of years play-acting as philosopher and now for the first time everything was real. To her own surprise she encouraged herself with the thought of Pascale and the unbelievable courage she had shown. At least the frozen north did not threaten to vaporize her in an instant. As for Saoirse, wherever Colette went she would go too. She also told herself they would be part of a new history and Jonas would be writing it. Epic tales enchanted her; to be part of one in the making fulfilled her dearest wish. Finally, all four found strength and encouragement from the fact they were doing this together.

Meanwhile, Jonas was preoccupied in a very different way. He had felt no inclination to join Palmiro on the mission to the North, partly because Colette had volunteered and he was sure she had as much authority to tell the story of Heaven as he did. But it was deeper than that. All during the meal at Adorno's mansion there had been something nagging at him, something personal which had very little to do with the question of Palmiro and the future. Earlier, on the journey with Stavros, just before they had all turned north off the Appian Way, he had felt a powerful urge to keep going to where the highway terminated at the ancient Baths and the Shuttle Port. He remembered with vivid clarity his first encounter there with Pascale, how it had set in motion the whole sequence of events leading to this very point. He felt so strongly that he wanted to go back, to recapture that first moment and think about everything that had followed. It was a need to touch all the memories one by one, to pay attention to them like living things, and then perhaps to understand.

Afterward, when the meal had begun, he had been seriously

distracted by the presence of the paintings around the table. They simply exacerbated the desire to return to the Baths and the feeling only got stronger as the evening wore on. Perhaps because the images represented the old world and its history and they were calling out and insisting he look to his own history. By the end of the evening it was almost as if the paintings were ordering him to return to the Baths.

The next morning he excused himself, saying he was going out riding. Without explaining further, he saddled up and headed west toward the Agora. The weather had returned to its normal Heavenly state and he traveled under a perfect sky and a high, dazzling sun. It was toward midday when he entered the lush precincts fronting the ancient building. As he led his horse forward he saw the rain from the previous days had stripped much of the flower blossom and all along the central pergola there were pools and puddles on the ground. On every side the silk cushions which had never known rain or damp were sodden and stained and the drapes were fallen or hanging limp.

It was a strange, disquieting experience to view what was clearly the end of Heaven. He saw no corpses but there was the constant hint of their presence, and at one point he was certain he heard the scuffling and snarling of dogs behind the arbors. It gripped him with fear and he quickened his pace. The whole thing gave off a feeling of complete devastation, like the sack of an ancient city and the slaughter of its citizens. But the sensation did not change his wish to be there. The tugging inside him continued and pulled him forward.

He passed through the Agora and came to the Baths with their glistening portico. He tied his horse to the final gate and crossed the small plaza, ascending the steps to the great entrance. He pulled back one of the doors and peered in. He could see the beginning of the baths across the threshold and got a vague sense of the walls and shape of the interior. He needed more light so he released the door and returned to the Agora. In the first courtyard garden he cast around for suitable stones to wedge beneath the doors to hold them ajar. After he gathered a handful he went back and hauled back the doors one by one, banging stones under their bases to hold them open. The light poured in across the marble floor and down through the recesses of the building.

493

He moved inside, cautiously skirting the pools, looking around at a building that before he had always experienced shrouded in the flames and shadows of an intense ritual. As he moved toward the back and his eyes got used to the dim light something caught his eye in the upper space of the building, something he'd never seen before in all the centuries of coming there. It was a small gallery running round the sides close to the level of the roof. Perhaps it was some kind of viewing platform that had been forgotten about soon after construction. He was certain there was no access inside the building. If the access were somewhere unnoticed on the outside that would explain why it had been overlooked.

He went back outside to his horse and rode it out of the Agora onto the track which led down the southern side of the Baths, all the while looking for an external door that might lead to the gallery. He saw nothing. When he got to the enclosed courtyard at the end, he dismounted, opened the gate and went in. The tables and chairs were still in the same places they'd been when Emmanuelle led the final part of the Initiation ceremony, when he'd taken the role of Pascale's sponsor.

He sat down and closed his eyes, recreating the scene in his mind's eye. He saw Emmanuelle in full sail addressing the newcomers, working the crowd. He saw Palmiro with Adorno and he understood that a decision had already been made in Adorno's soul and probably in Palmiro's too. He reflected how all that had now run its course and Palmiro had changed dramatically. He claimed to have seen Pascale, and it had affected him deeply. Did that mean, in fact, he had become Pascale's partner in some kind of way? Jonas felt a pang of grief so sharp it made him open his eyes. Even as he opened them he remembered Palmiro also said that he, Jonas, would see her too. Almost immediately the jealousy left him and he was half expecting to see her there in that sandy courtyard. All was still the same, the stone walls and the tamarix tree and his horse waiting patiently by the gate. Yet the tugging in his heart was greater than ever, almost to the point of being painful itself.

He got up and remounted his horse, taking it through the gate and nosing it round to the north of the building. Here there was a forgotten cluster of cypress and pinyon pines for shade and it was hard to make a way through. Clearly no one bothered to prune the trees, and it had become a dense stand sheltering the ancient building. But he persevered and forcing his way through he was rewarded. There in front of him was a steep wooden staircase, almost a ladder, leading up the side of the building to a platform and a door. Staring up at it the thought came to him of what he should do and at once he felt much better. He turned the horse around, heading out of the wood and back to the mansion.

***

The following day the weather was still fine and Jonas had a gentle, pleasant ride back to the Baths. He was in good spirits and was now equipped with food, and tools taken from Adorno's warehouse. He rode directly to the back courtyard, tied up the horse and went out, pulling the gate shut behind him. He threaded his way through the trees behind the building, carrying a stepladder and a sledgehammer. He got to the stairs and carefully ascended, bringing the tools up with him. When he got to the top he was directly under the great eaves. He tried the door and it opened outward, showing a small threshold and two steps down onto a landing. He climbed in and found himself on the gallery he had seen the day before from below.

The huge doors of the Baths were still propped open, letting in a stream of light. From up at this level and in the light of day, the Baths looked less imposing and even contrived. He peered down at them and tried to imagine what it was that had happened to Pascale to cause her to be so distressed during the Initiation. She had never explained it and now, in hindsight, he was certain that whatever it was it had provoked all her unorthodox behavior, the behavior that got her sent to the canyons and made her an easy target for arrest and blame once the infection hit. At the same time, he had to admit it was also responsible for driving her into his arms when she awoke after the Initation. The whole thing was a mystery and the only thing that he could do in response to it was what he had in mind.

He was going to demolish as much of the roof of the Baths as he could. That way he would try to undo the catastrophe that had its origins in this building. He went back out, brought up the ladder and set it in place. Climbing up he swung the hammer as hard as he could between the joists and hit the heavy clay tile lying across the battens. There was a dull crash and bits of tile broke away and fell to the gallery floor. He hit it again just as hard and more pieces smashed and showered down, bouncing off the gallery and fifty feet down to the marble floor below.

He could see the light showing through as he dodged the chunks flying past him. It was intensely exhilarating. He felt more invigorated than he'd ever known and he continued propelling the ten pound hammer up through the roof with all the force he could muster. The hole was jagged and the size of a human head and he worked at it, lengthening it and moving up and down along the rigid cross ties. After about ten minutes he began to tire. His muscles were not used to this kind of exertion and he felt the strain on his back and his forearms. He was sweating and had cuts on his hands and another on his forehead. He decided to give the labor a rest and tend to his wounds, but he felt enormously satisfied.

He left the ladder and hammer where they were and descended the stairs. Back in the courtyard he stripped and showered. He washed out his tunic and riding shorts and lay there in the sun, letting his clothes dry. Again he closed his eyes and his thoughts flew to the canyons. Pascale had said to him they could never be together again as they once were and he had agreed, and of course that was anyway impossible. But the tugging inside seemed to witness to a desire at another level altogether and he found it very difficult to understand.

It had become a painful tightness in his throat, and almost a physical tang in his mouth. He put his clothes back on and mounted his horse. He rode it out the gate and across the road to the scrub desert on the other side, heading out into the endless expanse of ginger-spice earth dotted with outcroppings of rock and spread with cacti, creosote bushes and juniper. Unlike the last time, he was not afraid of getting lost. His journey in the canyons had given him a much more confident sense of orientation and he knew this time he could find his way back.

He rode for a couple of miles until there was nothing on any side except the desert stretching away to the shimmering horizon in the south. He saw a tumble of rocks with a gnarled and ancient juniper spreading out from it, an inexplicable life where nothing that old should survive. He dismounted his horse and tied it to one of the snaking branches. He clambered up and sat in the fork of the tree and yelled with all his strength, without words, just an inarticulate shout of longing welling from his soul. The sound of his voice rolled and crashed in the wilderness, the howl of a lost child of man. Even as it boomed it was absorbed at once by an immemorial silence. The air stole it and the vast spaces ignored it, and after a few moments he fell silent, crushed by the desert. His head sank and he stared at the ocher rocks under his feet, thinking nothing. He did not know quite how long he stayed like that, but suddenly he heard his horse whinny nervously and he looked up.

About twenty paces from him just this side of a thicket was a wild dog looking at him. It had the color and cut of a coyote but with a heavier head and shoulders. He kept absolutely still and stared straight back at it. After what seemed an eternity, the beast got up and wagging its head a little trotted back into the bushes. Jonas waited a moment longer, then carefully descended from the tree back to the horse. He mounted it and rode in the opposite direction from where the creature had gone, circling as quickly as he could back in the direction of the Baths.

He was not really afraid, just taking the necessary precautions. His strongest feeling was still by far the hunger and the want. As he rode he decided what he would do. He would bid farewell to the others that night and prepare for a longer stay at the Baths, making his home in the courtyard and sleeping in one of the rooms for the Initiates. He would continue his work of demolishing the roof, as that absorbed his energy and seemed in some degree to soften his hunger. He came to the road outside the Baths and followed it around to the west and north where it ran a mile or so to the Shuttle Port. When he got there he rode across the great concrete landing strip toward the complex of buildings and installations behind it.

It was many years since he'd been here but he knew the shuttle would be launched from the fixed take-off ramp which wouldn't be hard to spot. Sure enough he quickly made out the elevated steel structure like some enormous funfair contraption rearing into the sky. It was preferred to vertical launch as the shuttle's engine was able to develop critical thrust without the need for rocket boosters. As he got nearer he could see there was a shuttle already in place, a thin curl of vapor venting from the

497

refrigeration system showing fueling had already begun. He knew it could not be much more than twenty four hours to launch and it struck him forcibly that here was a parting of the ways. The group traveling to the North were all to one degree or another inspired to do so by Pascale. He realized that when they were gone he would lose a community of shared feeling that he had only just discovered. He spurred his horse and returned quickly to the track that led back to the mansion.

When he arrived he joined the others for an evening meal. Hona was saying the shuttle would be ready in two days or less. Someone said these were their last days in Heaven and asked if that made them falling angels? Saoirse replied she always saw herself more as a fairy and was bringing her wings with her. Jonas broke in, announcing his decision to move to the Baths and at once the mood was serious. No one could feel confident that this company, which had so recently formed such a deep bond, would all be together at the same table again. It really was the parting of the ways. They made their farewells in a subdued mood, each one thinking of his or her own separate destiny and how it had played out so much in fellowship with these others. Jonas particularly thought of Palmiro, the only other one to share such an intense relationship with Pascale. He had sometimes been jealous of it, and yet again and again it had served to spur on his own relationship. When the meal ended he went up to him.

"Palmiro, I want to thank you especially. Pascale I loved. But because of you I learned to love her all over again, and perhaps better. I considered myself an intellectual, someone who could think for myself. But you have taught me more than I could ever have known on my own. I believe you are the greatest teacher I've ever had."

Palmiro gave a deprecating grin. "Not sure about that, Jonas. But I must say I am grateful to you too. You gave Pascale something I could not, and I was always, well, more than a bit jealous of you. Still I'm glad you did. Without that she would not have become who she was, and what she is. You were very important both to her and to me."

They hugged and said goodbye, and Jonas did not see him again. The next morning he got up early. He packed an extra tunic and as much nonperishable food as he could scrounge together,

498

along with feed for his horse, and rode out to the Baths. He had decided on his program of work and was looking forward to it. Once more the sun was shining in its classic Heavenly way. The rainstorms seemed to be a thing of the past, but their effect on the landscape was dramatic. Everywhere seeds and flowers that had lacked the necessary moisture were now producing shoots and breaking into blossom. As he rode down from the upper hills onto the scrubland it became more and more a riot of color, with daisies, phlox, snapdragon, gorse and manzanita, in pink, yellow, white, blue and amber. It was a dazzling display and the perfume of the flowers added to the intoxicating effect.

He was caressed in a bath of color and scent, and the yearning hunger inside him was at one moment brought to peace and at the next it was made sharper. When he got to the Baths he went to check the immediate results of his handiwork, directing his horse to the grand entrance, up to the steps, across the portico and in through the doors. He could see the ground scattered with shards but what really got his attention was the gap in the roof that he had made and the strange shape it produced when seen from below. It looked like a big bird made out of light, crashing through the roof. He stared up at it for a few moment, captivated by its force. He almost wanted to leave it there just as it was, but he remembered his project, and decided to take it as encouragement to carry it through.

He rode his horse back out and down the steps and continued round the building to the courtyard, letting himself in the gate and dismounting. He gave his horse a feedbag and provided it with water, turning on the valve of a small fountain basin in the corner. He took off the saddlebags with the food and brought them inside the building. Then he exited the courtyard and went round the north side of the building, through the stand of trees to the stairway. He climbed up and passed through the door which he'd left open. He retrieved the sledgehammer, mounted the stepladder, balanced his body with the hammer and hit the first blow. His plan was to work steadily an hour or so at a time, rest, begin again, and continue that way throughout the day.

His first hits were experimental, testing the right amount of force to use. After that he settled into a rhythm, striking the tiles at the distance he knew would break them off, pausing and then hitting them again. He watched the shadows to estimate the amount of time he should work and continued very deliberately breaking his way along. After an hour his arms and shoulders were very tired but he had not cut himself again and he was not exhausted. He took a rest, returning to the courtyard for a drink of water and a snack of raisins and nuts, then lying in the sun for ten minutes. After that he went back to work for another hour.

He spent the day in this fashion and made continuous progress opening the roof. By midday he had demolished all of the northern side and was beginning on the west, opposite the doors. He took a longer break at lunch and lay in the sun for an hour, feeling the soreness in his arms and back but happy that he had done something, at least symbolically, to neutralize his pain. Whatever it was that caused this terrible thirst inside him, it was more tolerable if he was working. But it was especially soothing to be doing something against the scene of Initiation that had so hurt Pascale and eventually taken her from him.

By the time the sun was striking directly through the gap in the western roof, turning the stone at the opposite end to gold, he was half way along the southern side. Now he really was exhausted and as the shadow pushed the gold up the eastern wall he knew he could do no more. He came to a halt and, descending the ladder, made his way around the gallery to the stairs. The roof was now in a generally dangerous condition and it would have been inadvisable to walk below. He was satisfied at this, satisfied that he'd carried out this gesture of revenge against an institution that had first violated and eventually murdered his beloved.

He let himself painfully down the stairs and stumbled through the wood back to the courtyard. He dragged off his clothes and fell into the shower, turning on the jets. The water coursed down his body, washing off the dust and sweat and easing his limbs. When eventually he got out he wrapped a towel around himself and went into the building. His thought of getting something to eat was interrupted by a desire simply to rest. He found a bed in one of the Initiates' rooms, the one that had been used by Pascale, and collapsed onto it. Within seconds he was unconscious.

When he came round again, it was dark. His body was so stiff he was hardly able to move but he lit a candle and limped out to the saddlebags on the floor by the door, pulling out some smoked sausage, apples and a bottle of fruit cordial. He sat there next to his candle on the ground and ate his supper. He was too physically drained to think. He went back to bed, falling once more into heavy sleep. The last thing he did was to speak into the dark room, "Pascale, this was your room once, be with me here tonight."

He was awakened by the violent trembling of his bed and the room around him. An oblique orange light struck through the open window spaces of the room and he immediately understood what was happening. He leaped off the couch and dashed from the room and out of the building into the courtyard. Scanning the sky to the north he saw it at once. The dazzling white balloon behind glinting metal and a noise like the fabric of the heavens being torn apart: it could only be the shuttle with Colette, Charlize, Saoirse and Palmiro on board.

Its low trajectory was quickly disappearing behind the wall, so he dashed out the gate and across the road to keep a clear view of it. The sky above was purple-blue and in the east the sun was a molten crescent on the horizon. He gazed at the craft plowing ever farther away and imagined his friends strapped in, with the weight of the acceleration crushing them to their seats. He felt the weight of separation and a sudden loneliness, both of the shuttle in the vast violet sky and of himself in the desert below. He kept his eyes fastened to the white plume as long as he could. His eyes were glued to the coruscating speck and at first he hardly noticed as the heavens began slowly to revolve around it. He felt suddenly dizzy and averted his gaze, but it did not help. Now the whole vault above him was turning around an axis point right above his head and he could not stop it.

Slowly the disc of the sky accelerated and the bluish light began to dissolve into the concentric bands of the spectrum, from indigo to yellow to blue to black and back to violet. He sank to the ground and buried his eyes in his hands. But now the universe was a rotating spiral inside his head and he could not stop it. He opened his eyes once more and instead of a whirlpool of colors the sky was raining fire and ice together. Huge drops of liquid flame came down on him, again red, green, purple and black. At the same time, sheets of ice were falling, mountains of ice plunging from the sky and embedding in the ground. He felt horribly sick and shut his eyes instinctively once more, but again the same scene continued inside his head, the same as outside it. In panic, he opened his eyes yet again and this time the fire had turned to machines, to rockets crashing down, to enormous memory and circuit boards exploding, to particle accelerators like the Sea of Chaos swirling above him, to images of Adorno's Hyperbrain with its terrifying helmet and Adorno's own face sitting beneath it in the midst of the chaos. He could not possibly stand it, he would go crazy if it continued. He began to run blindly, out into the desert, screaming and screaming, opening and shutting his eyes at random, punching his forehead and temples, scratching himself on bushes and trees, tripping on roots, stumbling and recovering once more. Running, running to get away, running as hard and fast and far as he could: and the next moment he tripped headlong and helplessly, crashing against a pile of rocks, hitting his head, and he was unconscious.

When he awoke there was someone standing over him, looking down and smiling. The sky above was calm and clear. For a moment he had the crazy thought one of the surviving Immortals had tracked him down out here in the desert.

"Jonas, you gave yourself a nasty bump there. Though I'm sure you'll live."

The moment he heard her voice he knew it was Pascale.

He blinked his eyes, shut and open again. She was still there, everything was still calm and even though he remembered a stunning blow his head did not hurt. He struggled to sit up.

"Pascale, are you dead? Am I dead?"

"No, not dead, not at all, neither you, nor I."

He looked around and could see he had fallen against the tumble of rocks crowned with the juniper tree where he'd sat before. He realized with a start that the wild dog he'd fled from was also there standing right next to Pascale.

"Oh, don't worry about him, he's very friendly. Let me help you up!"

She reached over to him, held his hand and pulled. He was astonished at the warmth and goodness of her hand and the easy, strong yet gentle grasp. A thrill coursed through his whole body, an electricity which made him feel immensely alive and young. The hunger inside him evaporated and he did not notice its going.

She was dressed differently, not in her usual, belted tunic, nor in the elegant wedding dress he'd last seen her wearing. She was covered by a robe but it was unlike those of the Immortals, not sculpting the body for seduction, but more flowing and at the same time fully a part of her body and expressive. If it were possible he'd say she was more beautiful than ever.

She gestured with her head. "Come, will you walk with me? We'll go back to the courtyard."

They began to walk, with the dog trotting between the two of them.

"So, will you tell me, Pascale, how did all this possibly happen? How is it you're alive?"

"My beloved Jonas, you should ask Danny. Back before, in the canyons, I talked to him, about love and counting. In its way it might help, but nothing I said would ever be enough."

There was silence as they walked on. The desert was alive with flowers and they seemed to imitate Pascale's way of saying something by not saying anything.

"Well, perhaps you can answer me this. Was it all meant to happen? I mean it could not be an accident, if you're alive now. So, who planned it? Or is it really an incredible accident, an incredibly beautiful one?"

"That's easy, Jonas. You planned it, Palmiro planned it, I planned it, the Immortals planned it. And, yes, I will say something you could call 'Accident' planned it! For the source of all accidents is incredibly beautiful, and loving, more than I can possibly tell you."

Jonas seemed to hear a capital A given to the word, and he felt perhaps she'd answered him, or at least the answer allowed for no more questions. They walked on in silence for another while, then she said, "Palmiro and his friends are seeing the whole planet from the outer atmosphere. The storms are beginning to break up. The North is changing too. Palmiro and the others must tell the Teppers everything. You too, Jonas, you must write the story, and send it all to them."

They arrived at the courtyard, and sat down under the tamarix. At the table a meal had been prepared, of fish and rice and Jonas recognized the bottle of wine he had brought with him from Adorno's. He was reminded of the first meal he had shared with her in this place and of the feast they had celebrated at their betrothal in the canyon. Now she served the food and poured the wine and the place was filled with light and warmth.

She said, "Also, you must go back and tell Danny and Eboni everything, and Omar too."

"Danny and Eboni, yes, I can do that. But Omar, he won't believe it."

"It doesn't matter. Tell him anyway."

They continued eating together and he felt such peace and happiness it was as if time had ceased passing, and really he did not know how long they were there together.

"Will you stay with me?"

"Yes, of course, Jonas. But you know I also have to leave you. You will not see me again."

Jonas knew at once this was true. He said, "Before you go, will you kiss me?"

She said nothing but leaned in close and kissed him on the mouth. It was only the most fleeting touch and she was gone. But he kept his eyes shut in the ecstasy of time. He was completely motionless and did not feel his body. Rather, the whole earth around him was his body, and it was on fire with love. As he continued without moving he knew she was no longer there and when the intensity lessened and he opened his eyes, he would be alone.

At last he did so. The courtyard was the same, with the horse standing in the corner and the tamarix tree in the middle and him at the table. The kiss with which she left him still burned on his lips. He looked down and the dog was there right by his foot, observing him and waiting. After a moment he leaned over and patted the animal. It lifted its head and licked his hand.

Almost at the same time there was a movement at the gate. Jonas looked up and saw it was Stavros dismounting from his horse. The man from Anthropology lifted the latch and came through. He looked around curiously, narrowing his eyes at the dog, but he could see it was peaceful. "I came to check how you were. Was there someone here with you? I could have sworn I heard voices."

Jonas smiled brilliantly at him. "It was Pascale, Stavros. Pascale!"

ABOUT THE AUTHOR

Anthony Bartlett emigrated with his family to the U.S. in 1994. He gained a Ph.D. in Syracuse University's Department of Religion in 1999, and went on to teach theology in seminaries and local church programs. Born in 1946 he was ordained a Roman Catholic priest in his mid-twenties, resigning the clerical ministry in 1984. Currently residing in Syracuse N.Y., he and his wife lead a small study and prayer fellowship, *Wood Hath Hope*. He is the author of *Cross Purposes, The Violent Grammar of Christian Atonement*, and of *Virtually Christian*. He blogs at http://hopeintime.com/

Made in the USA
San Bernardino, CA
02 May 2014